ASHES OF HONOR

A STATE OF THE UNION NOVEL

BOOK THREE

ASHES OF HONOR

A STATE OF THE UNION NOVEL

BOOK THREE

NELLE NIKOLE

MONTEREY BAY
THE PIT
NORTH GATE
SCHOLAR BUILDING
INFIRMARY
BARRACKS
PRESCOTT & COUNCIL QUARTERS
THE KITCHENS
THE GARDENS
COMPOUND HALL
WEST GATE
THE ARENA
ENTERTAINMENT SQUARE
SOUTH GATE
THE MONTEREY COMPOUND

THE DOCKS
FISHING & NAVAL QUARTERS
EAST GATE
THE GARDENS
THE STABLES
LIVESTOCK
N
W

CANADA
SALEM TERRITORY
THE PACIFIC OCEAN
MEXICO

STATE OF THE UNION
THE EXPANSE
THE COVERT PROVINCE
TRANSIENT NATION
THE ATLANTIC OCEAN

CONTENT WARNING

PRONUNCIATION GUIDE

- **Amaia** — ah-MY-ah
- **Alexiares** — ah-LEK-see-ah-rees
- **Abel** — AY-bel
- **Caleb** — KAY-leb
- **Elie** — EL-lee
- **Finley** — FIN-lee
- **Jax** — JAKS
- **Lola** — LOH-lah
- **Luna** — LOO-nah
- **Malachai** — ma-LA-kai
- **Millie** — MIL-lee
- **Prescott** — PRES-kut
- **Reina** — RAY-nah
- **Riley** — RY-lee
- **Ronan** — ROH-nan
- **Serenity** — seh-REH-nih-tee
- **Seth** — SETH
- **Sloan** — slown
- **Tomoe** — toh-MOH-eh
- **Yasmin** — YAHZ-meen

MAGIC INDEX

ELEMENTALS

- **Fire** (*Ignis*) masters of flames, wield the power of fire
- **Water** (*Aqua*) manipulators of water in all forms
- **Earth** (*Terra*) controllers of the earth
- **Air** (*Aer*) commanders of the air

SKILLS

- ***Umbra Mortis*** ability to make anything and everything a weapon with unparalleled precision
- ***Scholar*** knowledge is power
- ***Tinkerer*** (*Physiscus*) possess a knack for all things science and technology

THE OTHERS

- ***Supra*** heightened physical abilities–faster, stronger, taller
- ***Pansie*** zombie mutation
- ***Brujas*** wielders of the dark arts

WORLD OF RISING

You've come to the right place if you're a reader who craves vivid imagery and immersive worlds. Scan the QR codes below to discover the World of Rising and its characters.

Pinterest Board

Ashes of Honor Playlist

The real life 'Harley'
To my Mistey, see you on the other side of the rainbow bridge.
2008-2024

This is a story about hope and destruction.

The cost of love is grief.

CHAPTER ONE

AMAIA

I was tired of saying, *"When this is over."* Alexiares was right. It never would be.

Humanity had many chances to get things right. To act like we had some damn sense. Three hundred thousand years on this planet and counting, and barely a lesson learned to show for it. We are what we always have been.

Savages.

Seth had always held the belief that this earth was riddled with godless savages. On that topic, we were aligned.

So why I continued to root for something better—to try after so many greats known and unknown had failed before me … who fucking knew. Perhaps habit? That idea that evolution worked both ways. Yes, the strong survived, but the lessons were learned from the weak.

They taught it in schools—never outright, yet the lesson remained. What else was the phrase *history is told by the victors* supposed to mean? The strong survived, yes, but the weak weren't forgotten. Their stories were still told—just from a different angle. A carefully crafted one. Educational. Meant to enlighten. To indoctrinate.

That was the other thing about humans. We were creatures of habit. There were three things that decided what we did every day: eat, shit, and sleep. One break in that routine, and it affected the others. The cost of one without the other two?

A hell in which only savages could prevail.

The Pansie population was out of fucking control. Our border patrol had been massacred in the attack on Salem Territory over a month ago, and what was left of our troops were too busy with more pressing matters. Which, if I was being honest, was fine by me—another excuse for me and the girls to have a day out.

Morning fog swept around my knees, making whatever went crunch under my thick combat boots a mystery. Based on the ooey gooey slush under my feet, I'd guess it was a head flung my way from the ruthless strike of Tomoe's katana. A loud click to my right had me turning on my heels. A small Pansie, around my height, stared back at me.

"We got a conscious one over here," I called out to my friends.

"Aw," Tomoe bantered back through the chaos. "We should tell it to say goodbye to its little friends."

Killing them had become … easier, to say the least.

For me, there had always been a person behind the empty, decayed gaze of a Pansie. But for everyone else, that realization was still somewhat new since our discovery up in Duluth. I'd expected at least Reina to hesitate, but ever since she'd come back from her mission in Montana and Wyoming with Tomoe and Abel, she hadn't been the same. She hadn't even asked where her brother's remains were. Didn't so much as flinch when Moe argued that

Seth deserved to be buried with the rest of our fallen. Ultimately, I'd left it up to Reina. And Reina … well, she'd settled on the fact that no traitor had ever been buried at The Graves and that we weren't about to start now.

"What should we name it?" I teased, toying with it by offering up a finger before pulling away the moment it snapped for a bite.

"Seth," Reina said, not breaking in her stride toward her next victim.

My knife got caught in the skull of Reina's so-called undead version of her recently dead brother. I let it fall with the now inanimate corpse and pulled Jax's twin swords from the holster on my back. With another spin to the side, I sliced through two Pansies without much effort, my focus still stuck on Reina's words.

"Been there," Moe cooed, though the life slipping from her eyes told me she was anything but okay with what Reina had said. "Done that."

Where Reina's successful attempts to avoid all things depression, Moe had spent weeks wandering around—lost in her mind. She was neither present nor distant. Always where she needed to be, when we needed her to be there, but she was … not the same Tomoe Sato I'd come to know.

How could she be when she had killed the love of her life with the very katana that she'd sworn to use to protect those she adored? Wrath. And she had plenty to spread.

"Yeah, okay. No more naming things. Fun's over," I said, placing the swords back where they belonged at the sight of the last Pansie splattering against the pavement.

"We should get back," Moe said, glancing at the position of the sun. Monterey Compound would be alive with construction and activity by now. It was almost time for me to report for duty.

Duties. Plural—since they expected me to do it all. After Prescott's death, his responsibilities had been dumped on me, stacking on top of my already endless list. General of Salem Territory—and, apparently, the rest of the continental United States. An exaggeration, sure, but with the fallen compounds Ronan left in his destructive wake now leaning on me, Duluth's mess of a settlement, and Covert Province always lurking in the background, my hands were full. Too full. Which made chasing down Pansies at the asscrack of dawn about as close to peace as I got.

I pulled Prescott's favorite compass from my pocket. I didn't need it. I knew exactly where we were and a million ways to get us back. But I wanted it. I'd kept it by my side since I'd gone through his belongings.

No one talks about that part much.

What it's like to go through the life of someone who left you behind. How deciding who gets what and what goes where forces you to confront a lot of shit about both yourself and them. Jax's stuff, omitting his swords, still remained untouched in our quarters. *My* quarters—the correction still not coming naturally. Somehow, invading Prescott's life had been easier, a less daunting task. There were memories in his room, good ones, bad ones, but mostly the comfort of all things familiar.

"What a beautiful day for more bullshit," I said, leading us back to our home that had not felt as such in a very long time.

CHAPTER
TWO

AMAIA

Today was about confronting all the shit I'd been putting off for as long as possible. Jax used to say that I could only outrun my problems for as long as I could steady my breath. I ran half-marathons every day. Steadying with every inhale and exhale was kind of my thing. Right now, there was no more air for me to gulp down. My world suffocated me. I was deprived of all oxygen and the only way to keep moving forward was to claw my way out, one problem at a time.

I stared up at the ceiling. With the glow coming in from the window but the lack of sun streams, it was around 5 a.m. The day wasn't going to face itself. I sighed, moving Alexiares's heavy arm off my waist to free myself from his bed. It was nice to sleep on a mattress for once. I hadn't slept on my own since we'd gotten back.

It'd either been the couch in my study or here, sprawled in his bed, or the couch in his and Riley's living room.

We, as a unit, were collectively out of space. Abel and Alexiares rotated between the couch and what used to be Abel's room—now used by Alexiares. Moe avoided her space after Seth's betrayal. Which was fine, given that Hal, Emma, and her siblings were holed up there—remnants of her time before The Compound she was more than happy to run from. It *wasn't* always fine for Reina who struggled most, craving privacy with Jessa but unwilling to stay at her place after learning about her ties to Ronan. Jessa hadn't asked, and Reina hadn't offered.

Elie had made things difficult enough for us all. Her brother, Rex, had finally returned, making it feel somewhat safe to go back to her home. But that didn't mean that was where she'd end up. She was mad—at everyone, herself, the world. Between Prescott and her parents, death was hitting her hard. Elie went where Elie pleased and that was that. We were lucky that at the end of the night, she *always* came to stay with someone in our little band of misfits. And we always made space.

I crept out of Alexiares's room, letting his soft snores fill the room as he grasped a pillow and snuggled deeper into the sheets. He deserved the rest. He'd barely shut his eyes since Reina gave him the all clear from the recovering—after knocking at death's door—on the condition of intensive physical therapy. Which was why I needed to get moving on my long list of shit to do.

We couldn't keep going this way. The amount of free space we had was limited. There had been an influx of scattered residents from fallen settlements arriving at our gates and nearby groups deciding to seek shelter inside our walls. Even if my family had the space, no one would use it. I don't think any of us had spent a single night alone since our world crashed in around us, *again*.

There was a solution to our problem and I couldn't tell if I hated it or not. Sleeping in my bed was fine if I was alone. But

I didn't want to be alone. I despised the idea of sleeping without Alexiares wrapped around me. Still, bringing another man into the bed—the room that Jax and I had shared—felt … wrong. Like it would be an insult to his name. To our memory.

Prescott's place made sense. It was as fresh of a start that I could get, and given my recent, extremely reluctant promotion, it was close to all the politics and paperwork I now had to immerse myself in.

The warm, fresh air blowing against my cheeks as I made my way over to my quarters was welcomed. The wind swept down a tear that threatened to fall from the corner of my eye.

"You're doing the right thing. I love you, kid." Prescott's last words to me before I'd taken off on our cross-country journey had haunted me since I'd learned of his fate.

Did I? Do the right thing?

It didn't feel like it. He was dead now. As was Seth. Would confronting Seth here have made a difference? Maybe. Yes. No. *Fuck.* Who knows?

Ramona, a woman he had trusted, dare I say, respected, enough to appoint Stable Master after his promotion to Lieutenant, had thought otherwise. It was to no surprise that half of the cavalry had split once they'd learned of Seth's death. They wanted to fight for him, and his honor wasn't on our side. That had been the danger I had feared.

The risk of blind faith behind a figure they were never meant to idealize, only respect enough to follow. Seth was complicated. Too many sides to him, too many ways he could be seen. If he'd been given the chance to defend himself, his actions, his ideology … how many would have turned to Covert's side?

And he did have honor. Just not the kind I'd hoped for.

The more time went on, the more I wanted to hate him. But the truth was, I hated what he did to our family—for betraying us, abandoning us—not him as a person. Seth had his beliefs. I'd always known that. It had been real work trying to deprogram the mess his father had molded. But he hadn't resisted, he had tried. I could acknowledge it had been hard on him, but he. Had. Tried.

Seeing the good in him had damned us, so why couldn't I hate him for it? In truth, the answer was blatant. It was hard to think ill of a dead person when you loved them for longer than you hated them. The good memories constantly battled to keep the bad ones away. There had been more smiles than tears, more jokes than threats. Seth had been a partner far longer than an enemy. Forcing myself to see him as anything more than a boy lost inside his mind hurt my heart now that it was absent of rage.

I slid my key into the metal latch and listened for the click. Coming into my study was not the problem, it was walking through the door to the back that had my heart beat thundering in my ears. I clenched my fist, patting it against my thigh as I took slow, deep breaths.

The door opened behind me, but I didn't bother turning around. I knew who it was. I could always sense him. Alexiares came up behind me, his hands intertwining with mine, and he kissed the top of my head. No words left his mouth. There was nothing for him to say; he knew why I was here.

"I … I haven't …" My voice trailed off.

"I know," he answered softly against my curls. "I can handle the paperwork. Say no to everything and yes once. Right, that's how politics work? I can help organize the back too, while I'm here. You don't have to do it all."

It was an out. One I would not take. I didn't have to do it all, but *this*, this I did have to do on my own.

"No. I need to do this on my alone. I owe it to him to have this last moment. Just us."

Alexiares nodded, the scruff along his jaw from a few days away from a razor scraped against my temple. I loved that about him. His ability to understand and read in between the lines. The privacy he provided while making me feel safe. Supported beyond reason.

His hand fell to my waist as he pulled me close. "Whatever you need. I'll be out here going through your dust piles."

I waited for him to slide into the seat at my desk before taking a step into the past. One last goodbye before I set my sights solely on the future.

CHAPTER
THREE

REINA

Everyone called me crazy.

Personally? Quiet looked better on them and taking a gander in the mirror to grow the heck up wouldn't hurt. So my best friend beheaded my brother and my dad—the infamous Ronan Moore—I couldn't care less. Oh well. Boo freaking hoo. There were more important things to waste brain power on— whether that was the long-legged blonde who spent months lying and spying for him, or the communication patterns of the Pansies he'd created. Or how could I forget—practically living in my lab, trying to figure out this whole bionic arm thing and get it to con- nect with Abel's nerves without putting him in more danger.

You know, things that mattered. Made a difference.

"So," Abel drawled. "I know I can't feel anything right now, but if I could, you'd be hurting me."

"Shut up," I mumbled, fumbling with the clunk of metal. "I need to focus."

"Or you could pay attention to the hundreds of fires The Compound needs you to put out."

"I can multitask," I huffed, blowing a stray strand of my choppy hair out of my face. A quick but mighty spark had me jumping back in my chair. "Dang it!"

The sleek titanium and carbon-fiber arm seized at the elbow, and Abel's fingers went limp. Rubber padded against the hard wood paneling as the stress ball he'd been holding fell. At this point, any attempt at gripping things or a bit too much strain had the arm breaking in one way or another. Abel couldn't just have *any* arm, he needed something that did the impossible.

If I could get it to respond directly to his neural signals, it'd be like he never lost 60 percent of the use of his arm at all. Henry had done his best after Malachai sliced through it, but in the mix of all the drama and the time it'd taken to get it back from Riley … this was as best as best could get. Only a miracle could give him full function back without a little innovation. Granted, it had only been a few days of work and the help of Moe's limited yet helpful visions. I took a few centering breaths. *Meditation won't help ya now, girl.* Sighing, I rubbed my temples as though circulating the blood in my brain would produce a quality idea.

Abel's warm right hand fell atop mine. His thumb rubbed a calming pattern over my clammy skin. "It's cool. As thrilled as I am that you care enough to do all this … You've been at it for weeks. I'll still be broken tomorrow."

I pulled away, yanking my elastic band out of my hair and frantically trying to get it back up and out of my face. *I really should have thought about this before cutting it all off.* "Yeah, well, Abel darling. Tomorrow is never guaranteed. Not in this family. And you're not broken."

"Then stop trying to fix me like I am." There was a strain in his voice as he freed himself from the bionic arm. Cerulean streams of electricity danced in the air, flickering ghostly veins that were eager to find a body to connect with.

"I want to make sure you have every advantage possible out there. Is it a crime to not want to mourn the loss of another member of my diminishing family?"

Abel exhaled sharply, a flicker of something unreadable crossing his face before it settled into open disgust. "Okay. I'm out. Enough with the pity party." He shoved away from the table and rose, towering over me. "It's unbecoming. And frankly, it ruins your charm." He bent to plant a quick kiss on my forehead before striding off, his left arm hanging at his side.

Abel was a jokester. No matter the circumstances, he could always find something to say that lightened the gravity of whatever crazy situation we were in. It was why I loved having him around. Even though he had been the one to lose a part of himself, he'd been the calming force against all our friends' anger. But right now, he wasn't joking. And I wasn't sure if that should humble me or not.

I groaned, sliding everything that cluttered the table onto the ground.

The hair on the back of my neck trickled in warning and I stiffened my posture. "Forget something?" I asked Abel, not wanting to see the stare of disappointment on his face at my loss of control. The disgust seeping off him when he looked at me on the way out was more than enough for today.

"Uh, no." A penetrating voice pierced the air. It was deep. One of those voices that vibrated against your ribs when they spoke. "I was actually searching for Alexiares."

"Why would Amaia's lap dog be in my lab?" I slammed, turning around to see who could have been so completely lost they'd winded up here. Alexiares hadn't been allowed back in here since he stole my good surgical tools to torture some poor soul. My eyes went wide. "Oh, wow. You're—"

"Tiago's brother, Tomás. Yep."

Sadness hit me. Some from him, an overwhelming wave of loss and heartache coming straight from his soul, but mostly, my own. Alexiares had mentioned Tomás was a spitting image of his late friend. His only friend before he showed up, quite honestly— tough guy to love until you dug *really* deep.

Twins were such a funny force of nature. The way they challenged our core understanding of basic human things, like individuality or connection. Whether they were identical or fraternal, there was that telepathic bond that existed, no matter the distance between them.

"Uh, you okay?" Tomás asked. He tilted his head, his honey-hued skin a greenish hue under the candles lighting my lab. It was raining today. Any light that may have filtered in through the windows was absorbed by the darkness of the heavy clouds.

"Yeah. Sorry, I was … thinking of my brother," I said, the words mute as I thought not of Seth, but Hunter. What could have been if only he'd survived.

"Seth … right." He whistled, shoving his hands into the pockets of his tan chinos. "I should go. Sorry for bothering. We were supposed to meet out in the courtyard, but he never showed. Some guy named Henry said you might know where he is."

"Yes, because I keep a tracker on all my hounds." The sass found its way back to my voice.

Tomás released another long, drawn out whistle. "Anyway. Nice meeting you, I guess. Kinda. Not really."

He made it to the door before I noticed his slightly uneven gait. I sucked in a gasp at the sliver of metal shining right at the base of his ankle.

"Hey, wait." I called out, striding over to him. "Did you make that yourself?"

"My leg?" he questioned, arching a brow that had a long healed cut down the center. "No. I grew it in The Gardens."

Curiosity overpowered the rationalization of acting like I had some home training. I crouched, tugging up the hem of his pants without thinking—a sleek, beautifully crafted piece of machinery stared back at me. Its design both intricate and practical. I chuckled, "You're pretty funny."

"Thanks? I didn't say much." Tomás and I were nearly eye to eye as I rose back upright in my platform combat boots. He peered behind my shoulder through narrowed slits, then stared back at me in recognition. "That for Abel?"

I nodded. "You've met him?"

"Briefly, he saved my ass out there right before it all happened," he said with a motion to his arm.

"You fought?" I couldn't hide my shock in the sputter of my question, nor could Tomás hide his followed up look at the unintentional insult.

"Was my leg supposed to keep me from doing my part same as every other individual was doing to protect this place?" Tomás crossed his arms over his chest, the veins in his toned arms creating a surprisingly pleasant distraction from the conversation.

"Well, no, I just thought—"

"Whatever you're about to say can't possibly be politically correct." An arrogant smile pulled at the hard, stoic lines of his face. My eyes fell to the ground as I bit down a grin. He seemed to be my kind of person. *I think.*

"... is that like, safe though? What if it came off, or it broke or something?"

"It's an apocalypse, Reina. Everyone here is a survivor of some sort," he said, brushing past me and over to the arm that was now a shattered mess across the floor. "Every day is an opportunity to become a little more badass, wouldn't you agree?"

"Yeah actually, I would." I smiled as I trailed him around the room. He stopped at the mock up I'd sketched out on the wall next to a clay replica of Abel's upper body Riley's girlfriend Yasmin had sculpted for me. "Want to help since Alexi bailed on you?"

Tomás stiffened, his head craned slightly as though he was asking the Lord for some patience. "How do you know——"

"It's the hour before dinner," I said. This routine was one I never expected Amaia to fall out of. "He's with Amaia. It's kind of a whole thing. He must've forgotten to let you know."

"Since my calendar unexpectedly cleared, show me what you're working with."

CHAPTER FOUR

AMAIA

The least Prescott could have done was get his affairs in order before he up and died. Everything was a damn mess. To be honest, I wasn't quite sure what the hell I was looking at. A bunch of numbers and political jargon that wouldn't make any sense to me even if I had it explained as if I were six years old.

When I'd told Alexiares that our economy did some cyclical economic shit that I didn't understand, I'd been dead fucking serious. *Aren't I supposed to have an advisor or something? Who set this all up?* Right, *we did*.

"You haven't touched your pie," a raspy voice whispered in my ear.

The tips of them turned red as Alexiares's hands fell to my shoulders and offered a gentle massage. "Neither have you," I said, meeting his eyes and catching the shadows carved under them. I'd been scouring over the same documents for the last few days, still not coming to a final conclusion on how to move forward.

"Dessert before dinner is still weird for me," he teased, taking half the stack of papers from the desk.

Life at Monterey Compound didn't just come to a halt, even though we'd lost 10 percent of our population and 40 percent of our infrastructure during the attack. In fact, life here seemed to be speeding up with the influx of newcomers, quickly replacing the numbers we'd lost but with half the space. Which meant more paperwork and shit to figure out with an imminent due date. People needed jobs, things to do to keep them busy and us safe.

A message from Elliot had arrived in the night: Outside of what they could grow with their hands and the natural cycle of their garden harvest, they were low on food. Duluth had gone months locked in their bunker. Ronan had been relentless in his attempts to destroy them, so they could only come out when necessary. Under normal circumstances, Monterey would help—try to establish a new trade deal until they were able to adjust, but we were hurting too.

With Covert's 'emissaries' sitting in on every council meeting and morning debriefs with our soldiers, I had little say in operating as business as usual. We didn't have a choice. No matter the sick, sweet revenge I was still intent on bringing to Ronan's front door.

"I'm in way over my head here," I groaned, slouching down in the heavy leather chair.

It still had the imprint of Prescott's ass on it. A joke popped into my mind, wanting to endlessly tease him that the evidence of his 'laziness,' was here all along. Except the thing was, Prescott wasn't lazy. In fact, he did it all. He was a good leader. A sound one. Both in judgment and in practice. I couldn't top that. The only one who could had been Jax._

Scattered papers fluttered to the floor. A few landed on his black boots as I pushed The Compound ledger and register toward the middle of the desk. The perfect amount of room to slam my head against it in shame stared back at me as a shiny wooden surface. I smirked.

"Is there a reason you're refusing to ask for help?" Alexiares asked, swiping a stray strand back into his carefully slicked back hair.

"Huh?" I questioned, turning my body completely toward him. "What are you talking about?"

He offered a nonchalant shrug. "Do you need me to say it in Spanish? Is there a specific reason why you won't ask Luna or anyone else on The Council for help?"

I thought it over. The answer was yes, but it was also no. So maybe, I don't know? But what was I supposed to say? I was now the face of certainty and I had to remain that way for everyone, him included. "Trust isn't a factor here, so not particularly, no."

"Then why are you stressing yourself out for no reason?" There was a glint in his eye, a slight narrowing of them at my lie. He wanted to call bullshit, but wouldn't. It would all come out in the end. It always did with him.

"Because this is what was expected of me," I replied, motioning to the rustic-looking room adorned with wooden planked walls and ceilings and trinkets from God knows where. "This is what Prescott wanted. He didn't have help, he simply *did*."

"How do you know this is what Prescott wanted? All he said was to take care of the place. And he did have help—he had the two of you."

My eyes glazed over as the memory tugged at the corner of my mouth, a small smile beginning to form. "A few years ago, Monterey Day. He made Jax and I give the closing speech."

"A speech …"

"Not just any speech." I glared at him. I needed to get this story out, to reflect. It helped me process things, thinking back on all the little moments where he'd shown me he believed in me.

Thought the world of me. "He said that the day would come, that he wouldn't be here and—"

"You'd be there to pick up the pieces?"

"Essentially," I said.

Alexiares sighed, his head tilting slightly as his gaze dragged over me. I hated it—those moments when I became the prey and he, the predator, already closing in. Usually a direct read came to follow. The only thing that pissed me off more was that he was usually right. "For as long as you've been a pain in my ass, you've been a rule follower, Princess—despite my best efforts."

"I am not," I scoffed at the thought.

"I mean, *you* think you're not. It may not be the rules everyone else adheres to, but you have another set of rules. Ones you don't hold anyone else accountable for when shit hits the fan. All you've ever cared about is what was expected of you. Maybe it's time you set your own expectations of yourself *for yourself*."

The idea was ridiculous. I had to hold myself to a different standard. That's what a leader did, lead by example, exemplified strength. "Yeah, I don't appreciate where this is going."

I turned my back to him at the same time Elie's bedroom door cracked open. She strolled out, Harley and Suckerpunch in tow. Her cinnamon-colored curls were tied up into a bun. The knife I'd left as a parting gift last year was holstered into the side of some cross body bag Reina had crocheted, which didn't match the burgundy work out set she had on. Those items were for two different events.

I stood up, pushing the chair away from the desk. "Where are you going?" I asked.

"And what's in the bag?" Alexiares followed up, noting the same oddities that I had.

"Out." Elie didn't break her stride as she passed by us, the scent of coffee and eucalyptus from her morning shift at The Kitchens following her on the way out. "You gonna stop me?"

"Behave yourself," Alexiares warned, his voice more relaxed than I cared for.

"Always do." She tossed up a peace sign behind her and slammed the door on her way out. Suckerpunch and Harley let out clipped howls that faded quickly into the distance as they ran off. *Traitors*.

I looked at Alexiares at a loss, then groaned again, this time making sure to effectively slam my head against the hardwood. Alexiares chuckled. "Hear me out, we can control The Compound or we can control Elie, but even together, we don't possess the skills to do both."

"And yet she still needs stability," I muttered, rubbing my forehead. "With Rex leaving with the navy again, making her my official ward was the best option."

Alexiares hummed in agreement, stretching out on the couch. Elie's brother wasn't either of our biggest fans—there were … disagreements when it came to her care. "We gave her space when she needed it. Now we remind her she has a home."

"Yeah. If she actually stays in it." I flipped back through the ledger, biting down the chirped laugh he was aiming to get. He grabbed the stack from me. "Hey!"

"We're asking Luna for help."

"*No,*" I insisted. "She's working on an updated trade agreement for Ronan to sign off on. Luna has enough to worry about."

She'd been head of emissaries before she and Prescott had ever become a couple. It was her idealism that had brought them together in the first place. He respected her, trusted her innately.

"And you don't?" His forehead pinched, another arrogant smirk forming from his perfect lips.

"If we ask Luna to step in," I relented, the rest of my statement coming out as a whisper. "… everything can fall apart."

"That's not on you."

"Compound first. One unit, one compound." The voice of a general found me again. In this, I would hold steady.

Alexiares's light brown eyes widened in mock horror. "That will never not sound dystopian."

"That's how things work here." I snatched the hours and hours of work back from him. "I thought you were on board."

The ledger plopped against the desk with a soft thud, knocking over some weird wooden carving filled with Prescott's coin collection. I picked up the spilled coins, switching them between my palms. He'd collected them over the years as we sifted through houses within our territory. Another oddity to his collection of gadgets and gizmos. *I suppose they're yours now.*

"I am on board, just not at the detriment of your health."

I shifted in my seat, tilting my head in annoyance. Having this conversation over and over again was tiresome. Everyone had an opinion these days. "It doesn't matter what happens to me. What matters is that this place keeps standing. I can't set a precedent of selfishness. Not in this role. I can only imagine what would come of that. I have faith in our people, but not that much."

"A fight is going to come to our gates again," he reasoned. His accent grew from slight to heavy as his agitation grew. "Which is exactly why you need to check your ego at the door and get your head on straight. So Prescott did it all. Who cares if Luna does *some* of the shit that you can't. Your only responsibility to these people is to keep this place going. That includes allocating responsibilities to someone else."

"He's right you know," Tomoe strolled in, her long, dark hair following like a ghost as the door thudded closed behind her. I watched her curl into the couch across the room, entering the conversation as if she'd been here the whole time. Her eyes said she'd seen this all unfold before—and she was here to make sure I didn't screw it up again. "Don't be an idiot. No one here expects you to know it all, no matter how much you think you do. All that matters is that you care enough to find the right person to get the job done right."

"Someone close," Alexiares alluded. "Who you don't have to question interfering with the real shit we have to take care of behind the scenes."

"And you both think that person's Luna?" I asked, glancing between the two of them. A knock sounded at the door and Moe smirked. I wanted to punch it off her face.

"Let me guess, Luna?" I glared at Alexiares, who didn't appear to be the slightest bit surprised.

"Who the hell else?" Moe stood from the couch, passing by Alexiares to get the door, who only slipped her a soft high five.

RAMONA CAME TO PRESCOTT'S QUARTERS—*MY* QUARTERS—TWENTY minutes after Luna showed up. Half of the Cavalry that remained had officially dissented, broken off during their training exercise about twenty-miles out. Planned, of course. I did not want to scold Ramona on her first failure. They should not have been permitted to leave these walls—not with the information they possessed. You were either with us, or you were the enemy.

There was no more *in the middle*. I'm not sure there ever was. I supposed the time for peace was over, and with it, the time for acceptance. We had everything to lose at this point.

Compound, or death. With Salem Territory, or death. Dealer's choice.

I'd half expected them to leave at the news of Seth's death. They were loyal to him. All of them. Seth had betrayed them too when he left, but they respected his decision because most had the same values. Understood the lengths one would go through if it meant getting their family back. I think everyone had that dirty thought at some point in time. Still, they'd fought for us, on our side—until he'd died. Until Reina had decided we'd burn his body instead of burying it. Last straws and all.

Even if we had the resources, I couldn't send anyone after them. They were trained as efficiently as my soldiers, quite frankly, a bit better. They were multifaceted in a way I couldn't always guarantee with a foot soldier. The bloodshed that would come from chasing them down, hunting them one by one or in a group wouldn't be worth it. They knew that, which is why they'd made the choice to flee when they did.

Their brothers and sisters in arms wouldn't kill them, not without pause first. The problem and the blessing with the cavalry was that they were a small, tight-knit unit. They would die for each other. Killing their comrades would be worse than driving a knife through their own heart.

The decision and timing to bring Luna here was … sound. I'd have a new set of advisors for the areas I didn't have the expertise. Subjects in which I didn't have the time to get up to speed. Despite her oversight, Ramona would remain Stable Master, helping keep up with livestock, breeding, and such. Until and if I found an apt replacement for Seth, she'd also be temporary captain of the cavalry.

While I could no doubt lean on Reina for anything that had to do with our infirmary, working with her mentor Henry made more sense. He'd been here since the beginning and Reina herself still needed to catch up. Henry was already aware of The Infirmary's needs to keep up with the ever-growing population. A population which inevitably showed up in worse condition every day. That left other more mundane matters to Luna.

Even with her help, there were an impossible amount of decisions left to make. Neither of us had a clue all the shit Prescott had taken care of. All the things that went on behind the scenes to keep this place up and running. And the problems and questions were nonstop. Everyone needed help with something.

There was the bigger picture stuff; the resource management, external relations, and long-term planning to the more granular decisions like what kids learned in school. Pythagorean theorem sounded like a silly thing to dwell on now but what would happen to all the knowledge humanity gained over the thousands and thousands of years of civilization? Suddenly, the small world we were left in felt large.

I had to consider the 'what if no one else is doing the thing?' at all times. Now, it might be on me—whether humanity started from scratch or making sure none of the knowledge we'd gained was lost through time and devastation.

Who was I to decide what was worth keeping around and what we didn't have enough time to cover? At what point do I determine survival tactics outweigh classic literature? If I toss one thing, then I inevitably toss something else out too, and if not the citizens of Monterey's responsibility to maintain, then who?

At the end of an exhausting conversation, Luna and I'd agreed that a *partnership* made more sense. An arrangement until—or as I tried to explain to her—*if* I was ready to take over on my own. No one outside our inner circle would know. It went against everything I believed in.

The core value of transparency that we'd built this place on. Only reason I'd be able to sleep at night was because it was safer for everyone not to know. Though that belief had already failed me once. But with Ronan watching, I refused to risk him suspecting anything off even though this had nothing to do with our plan. *Our plan.* A wry laugh threatened to escape me as I laid in bed staring up at the ceiling. Alexiares stirred at the muffled sound, mumbling in his sleep before turning away from me.

What plan? Right now, all we had was hatred in our heart and vengeance on our mind, but not one of us had asked what was next yet. I had my ideas. I knew they all had theirs. Perhaps, that is why none of us had spoken up.

CHAPTER
FIVE

RILEY

"You want each of your movements to be quick," I said, listening for the slightest shift in the air, the scrape of a boot against the floor—anything to track Abel inside The Ring. "A surprise. Then, retreat."

His voice came from the left corner, but I knew better than to trust it—Abel was sneaky and used to being underestimated. It was his greatest strength, the time to lean into it, was now. By the time he finished speaking, he'd already moved. "Hit and run."

"Exactly, brother." I laughed, unable to see anything through the black cloth tied around my eyes. "Exactly."

"Make sure you clock him in the jaw," Elie called to Abel.

Honestly, I was just glad she'd forgiven me enough to keep showing up. Amaia hadn't been thrilled about the position Elie'd put herself in during the battle—trying to fix the trip wires had nearly taken her, Emma, and Alexiares out when Soulfire erupted. Even so, it had been enough of a wake-up call for Amaia to approve her official training. Every morning, Elie was here with Abel, sparring with the soldiers before debrief.

This training was for me as much as it was them. Although Henry had done his best work, I was still not back at 100 percent. A blade through the gut would do that to a guy. Reina insisted on using her gifts to speed up the process but I needed this. Needed to experience what it was like to be at a disadvantage, considering what lay ahead.

With me not at full speed, working with Abel put me at about the same level. He'd done well to keep up with his training up in Duluth, but now, without the complete use of both arms, he was vulnerable. It was nothing training couldn't accommodate for.

Stealth and shadows on his side were more important now than ever. He needed to remain light on his feet. The general essence of him as a human being needed to dim. No one should sense his presence until it was too late. Hence, me training blindfolded.

"Eleanor, go take a lap," I called out for her snide remark.

She groaned, "I'm not going anywhere until you call me Elie, *Ryland.*"

"That's two laps, fifteen burpees, and fifty push-ups."

Elie mumbled something about me being unreasonable considering the heat when a sharp pain snapped my jaw. The impact of Abel's punch sent me to the floor of The Ring. He straddled my lap, pinning my back to the ground, unable to move. Elie cheered off to the side as a thanks. The sound of her running off on the gravel followed.

A few jokes at my expense circled The Ring at the sight of their Lieutenant downed. If I was still just *Riley,* I'd laugh with them, but I couldn't do that. Instead, I kept the scowl on my face that let them know this was no time to laugh. As quickly as they had stopped, their sparring commenced once more.

"That's not his name, ya know!" Abel called after Elie.

"I know," she replied, the smile evident in her voice. "Just don't care."

I flipped Abel onto his back, blindfold or not—it took little effort given he couldn't put his full strength into the move. "Dead."

"I had you. That's not fair!" He grumbled. His left hand rested on my wrist, unable to put the amount of pressure required to shove me off.

"Which part? You getting distracted by Elie's nonsense or using a move that requires the use of both arms to make the kill?"

We'd been working on his options, what would give him the greatest chance of making a kill with limited hand-to-hand combat. Instead of remembering his training, he'd let Elie distract him. It was interesting, watching him interact with Elie and Reina. The contrast in his behavior with both. Reina was comfortable around Abel for the same reasons Abel felt at home around Elie. One reminded the other of the youth they were forced to forgo in order to survive. That angst they'd forced themselves to bury deep to do what it took to make it to Monterey's gates.

"Uh, both?"

"Both will get you killed," I surmised, pulling off the blindfold and extending a hand up. "Then again, there's always what Reina's been working on."

Abel dusted off his all black training clothes, shifting his arm into a more comfortable position. "She thinks I'm broken."

I tossed him his water, making sure he kept his wits about him. "She said that?"

"It was implied." A tense chuckle erupted in between sips from his canteen. "Every day, she's asking me to stick my arm in some mold, poking and prodding. Testing and, sometimes, pretending it doesn't hurt, that the pain would be worth the result. At first I was thankful for the help—wanted it honestly. But now …"

"Reina is doing what she thinks is best," I said. It was instinctive to stand up for her. Reina's heart was in the right place—she didn't want to lose anyone else. "I am teaching you what *I* think is best, but only you know what's best for *you*, Abel."

He paused, glancing down at his arm. His fingers twitched. The deep wrinkling around his eyes made it obvious it took effort to do so. Abel would never hold a weapon in that hand again. Not without Reina's help. He was lucky to be alive, as was I.

Sometimes, the small blessings were the only win we could hold on to. The rest was another twist in the game called life. How we dealt with it, how we responded, that's where the difference was made. That was what determined the lens in which we saw the world through.

Jaded and frail, or a warrior. A soldier. A survivor.

Abel's response started off as a stutter before it firmed up, becoming the voice of a man ready to take on the world.

"I think I need to know how to live my life without it. It's a kind offer, and I love Reina for working hard on it. And maybe I'll want it in the future. But for now, I want to explore the person this war has made me. The Abel I was meant to become. I'm *Umbra Mortis* and it's 'bout damn time I acted like it."

"Oh." I smirked. "I've created a monster."

CHAPTER
SIX

AMAIA

Two best friends. Two fiancés. Two fathers.

One mother. One "brother".

They're all dead, yet I'm expected to keep going.

I slid Sloan's journal into the drawer of my desk, fingers trembling as they laced through my curls. The seat across from me creaked under Abel's weight, the legs loose after I'd lost myself in a moment of weakness.

I hadn't meant to scare him. He'd been through enough. His reasoning had been sound. I could not blame him for this. I could only blame Sloan, and that bitch was dead.

Now I finally knew what she'd been scribbling in her stupid little notebook day in and day out. Something of a memoir with a sprinkle of journaling, finishing off with a goodbye note addressed to yours truly. It also explained why she'd warned me all further communications would come from Elliot, as he would be 'stepping into a new role.'

She knew. She knew for more than half our stay, and Abel did too.

"She … she wouldn't let me say anything."

"Is that where your loyalties are, Abel? Duluth? To … her?" Sloan's name refused to pass through my lips. Weeks. I had gone weeks—months—without knowing that she was dead. Had been dead not too long after I left, thanks to Covert fucking Province.

Her small notebook was sewn into the bottom of my pack. It wasn't until I unpacked that last thing from our journey that I'd discovered it. Between the move to Prescott's space and everything else going on, making this place home and putting things away wasn't a priority.

By the time you finish reading this, I'll be dead. This is goodbye, Mai. Forever this time. Take care of them. I love you.

Damning words. *I love you.* I mocked as I reread the final sentences on the last page.

"No. I'm loyal to you. To Monterey. After all these years, I never forgot this place. The home you and Riley offered. The love …" Abel sighed, the guilt lining the youth of his face unnatural. A small part of me almost pitied him. "It's why I made the call to follow one final order from her. If you knew she was going to die, you would have never left. Then all the work we'd done up there would've been for nothing. And Salem would've been gone. You're the glue, Amaia. We need you, so I made a tough call. The same call you probably woulda made had you been removed from the center of the situation. I'm not sorry about it."

I'm not sorry. I chirped a laugh. At times, it was hard to tell the influence Riley had on him. Where Riley was serious and dry in his humor, Abel was consistently playful—his energy just *fun*. But he had this switch that, if turned on, activated a soldier.

He had done his duty. I could not blame him for that. His ability to *see* was a gift for a reason. He'd used his power of discernment and Sloan had given her life to secure the safety of her people for another day. They were still standing because of her sacrifice.

Abel was right. Sloan had done what I would have done if placed in her position. What any true leader would do.

That meant my time in Duluth was effective, a mission completed. But did that make any of it worth it? First Prescott, then her. If I let my thoughts wander too far at night, I thought about how it cost me Seth, too.

Worth it? Maybe. Sure. But would I let it play out the same way all over again knowing the outcome? I wasn't quite sure about that.

Sometimes all I wanted to wish for was a chance to be selfish.

"With Elliot in charge, things should be okay for a while. Until we get a chance—"

"A chance?" I cackled, "A chance for what?"

"For whatever you're planning. For it to work."

I scoffed. Abel didn't flinch.

Don't blame Abel. Please understand that this choice that I made wasn't an easy one, but I couldn't let ya choose. You would have chosen me, and that, my darling friend, would have changed history. We needed you to get back in time to defend Monterey. To make that deal with my uncle. I know you're tired of losin' people and I'm sorry.

I tore the page out of the book and crumbled it. A flame summoned in my hand as I engulfed the paper in fire and tossed it into the metal trash bin. My mind shifted back to the story Sloan had told her daughter Violet. The one she'd written down for me to share with her one day. As if she thought it was guaranteed.

The story of the warrior queen who saved the princess. Who offered the princess a kingdom to grow, to be free. To call home. The queen made sure no other damsel would ever be in distress because the queen did not want anyone to ever experience an ounce of the pain that she had. Who wanted better for others and dreamed too much.

It wasn't a fairytale. It was the Grimm Brothers. A story much like the fat tome we pulled out every spooky season, promising to share with our future children.

"Want to hear something funny?" I asked absentmindedly, staring off out the window as workers passed by preparing for the afternoon shift. Abel said nothing, only tilted his head in curiosity. "I have no plan, Abel."

It wasn't true. I had one plan. A last ditch effort if all else failed. A plan 'z' that had no 'a' to start with. But that plan didn't involve him or any of the rest of them. It only involved me.

"See, that's not …" He hesitated, searching my face. "I know you're not used to it, but jokes are supposed to be funny."

"You don't see me laughing?"

I held his gaze, unblinking. He was the first to look away. Pushing away from the desk, I took a deep inhale, an effort to stabilize myself before losing control. The door splintered as I threw it open, the crack of wood ringing behind me as I made my way toward The Pit.

"My turn." I hopped into The Ring, Alexiares and Riley already drenched in sweat. I scanned Riley over. Everything about him said he'd been here all day. "Move."

He stumbled back a few steps at my push, then stopped, taking me in and moved his gaze toward Abel. Abel frowned, his eyes on the ground as Riley shifted his attention to Alexiares, who only shrugged. The two of them peered between Abel and I.

Riley sighed. "What did you do?"

Abel's dark brown eyes kept steady on the ground. Meek in appearance, but the lack of softness behind his gaze reflected zero regrets. I groaned, unsheathing the small blade at my side.

"Out of The Ring, Riley," I grumbled, wanting a real fight and not the exhausted one he'd be able to provide.

He didn't budge. Instead Alexiares stepped between us. Messy brown hair fell over his narrow eyes. "What's the problem?" Alexiares asked.

"Fine." I huffed, raising my knife in his face. "Then don't."

The lean on my right leg gave me away. Alexiares was quick. His arm latched on to my shoulder out of reflex. I looped my free arm around at the cusp of his elbow and put all my weight into my left leg. Leaning back, I kicked out, meeting Riley quickly in the chest and then under his chin. The movements weren't full force, but enough to let them know I wasn't fucking around. I needed to exert this energy and if they couldn't handle that, then they needed to step out. Now.

Riley fell back at the impact. The point of our spars was to simulate. Getting rid of frustration or not, they were always a lesson. You fell as the opponent would fall and you figured out what *they* would do to get out of it. Alexiares went for the knockdown, but I turned it on him, using his own move as leverage. With Riley down, I put all my strength into putting Alexiares on his ass. After a punch to his temple, he tapped my wrist in mercy.

I let them up to catch their breath, circling them like a shark in murky waters. "Sloan's dead."

"The fuck …" Alexiares said, a hint of sadness in his tone. They'd never truly warmed up to each other, but he respected her—who she was when we left.

"Abel," Riley growled, his hand resting on his lower back as he feigned injury. I knew Riley. He had no tells but pretending to have one. It was how he blended in. The more programmed, disciplined side of him would never let him show weakness.

"He saw it," I said, deciding to take Alexiares head-on instead. He was watching me watch Riley, unsuspectingly. It was a ploy. Alexiares was always ready. Always on guard. *My Bloodhound*. I walked toward him with a smirk, watching his arm steady on my shoulder again. "Months ago."

Alexiares whistled, a dare in his brown eyes as I tossed an elbow, freeing myself from his grasp. It was back up in the blink of an eye, aiming for his nose. He dodged it with a cackle. "That's a tough hole to dig yourself out of, Abel. She is 100 percent pretending this is you right now."

I turned on my heels, tossing out a kick to the torso. He caught it, throwing me against the ground in rag doll fashion. Mental gymnastics whirred in my mind, a tangled equation, as I debated dropping the knife. I reached above me for something to grasp onto. I found his ankles, but not before Riley pounced.

Sliding across the floor, the boys gave it their best shot. But they were no match for an *Umbra Mortis*. I kicked out to escape Riley's hold, using the momentum to twist toward Alexiares's thighs. He released me and I set myself on Riley, wrapping myself around his neck with my legs.

Abel kept to the corner of The Ring, his head now held high. I could hear his gulp from here. "No hole to dig. I had no choice, man."

I scrambled for my knife off to the side, keeping my eyes on Alexiares, who had decided to circle *me* as his prey.

"I'm sure you acted within reason," Riley gasped out definitively, struggling from the force of my locked legs.

I found the knife, throwing it toward Alexiares, who was attempting to approach from the side. It grazed his ear, drawing the thinnest line of red. A drop of blood pooled, glistening in the hot sun of the approaching Monterey summer.

"In front of everyone?" he asked with an arrogant, lustful smirk. Alexiares was taunting me, letting me get this anger out. This insane amount of rage that continued to simmer within a never-ending well of pain. Of sorrow.

"You know this to be fact?" Riley asked, tapping out gently against my thigh.

Alexiares stopped his stalking approach at the sight of something behind me. I let Riley find oxygen and pushed myself off the ground to see what gave him pause. Moe strode toward us, her long raven hair tied into a loose braid. There was color in her tawny skin, though the dark circles under her eyes were a dead giveaway to her current mental state.

She slid her hands into the pockets of her jeans and took in the scene. "Oh. She knows?"

I held in a calming sip of air. She was about to be the next person down in this ring if I couldn't channel any more patience. I was sucked dry of it from these past weeks.

"You too?" I questioned in disbelief.

"I told you to take your time with your goodbyes," she answered dryly. "That's all I was at liberty to say."

She didn't need to defend herself and, honestly, neither did Abel. Anger was pointless when we had rules in place for a reason. I'd been gung ho on following them up till now. With everything else spiraling out of control, an emotional response to Sloan's death was the only thing I was capable of. One moment to react, to *feel,* before I had to put my responsibilities and priorities first again. I sighed. "What do you need, Tomoe?"

"I think Seth was the leak for the bunker—how Ronan knew you tortured the guy. Probably for other things, too. I've been searching my memories like you asked. It's the only thing that makes sense."

CHAPTER

SEVEN

ALEXIARES

Amaia was gone by the time I woke up. She hadn't been anywhere in our quarters, at Riley's or The Kitchens. Given the time, that only left one place. A groan sounded as Amaia rounded the corner and spotted me perched in a tree. Getting rid of the maze Riley crafted for battle was pointless. Still shielding us from any incoming Pansies and soldiers alike, we'd only sought to enhance it, changing up the patterns of trees every few days. Amaia had taken to running a half marathon each morning, scouting the areas that had succumbed to bloodshed. I'd been there each night as she silently cried. The only indication of grief being the soft shaking of wherever we'd laid our heads that night.

When she did sleep, she tossed and turned, the whispers in her sleep betraying the words she wouldn't ever 'burden' the rest of us with during the light of day. Monterey had been a place of peace for her. She'd created the world she had always wanted to see, brick by brick. Cobblestone by cobblestone. No part of her self-proclaimed haven remained.

So instead, she tortured herself. Forced herself to retrace the steps of her fallen soldiers every day as a reminder to stay focused on what she was fighting for—why she kept going. Security to prevent her from reaching for the bottle now that times had gotten hard. Harder than they were before, that is.

I leaped from the tree and landed in a crouch. She crossed her arms as I straightened up, towering over her with a smirk. "Ready, Princess?"

Her doe brown eyes traced over me with annoyance. Without saying a word, she turned and took off in the direction she'd come from. Evidently, she was going for the 26.2 today. I kept her pace, not saying a word. One mile after the next, her speed increased.

"Stop staring at me." She huffed out, the sound of violent waves crashed against the rocks along the coast.

It was safe to say I hadn't taken my eyes off her since Tomoe revealed that Seth and Ronan had a front row seat to my fun with their soldier. Seth's betrayal had already scarred deep, but this, *spying* on them in such an intrusive way, they'd thought it beneath him. I found it to be no surprise. Without the same memories, my sentiments were closer to 'scum of the fucking Earth' and less 'the brother who drank the Kool-Aid.'

"Are you going to keep playing dumb, or can we talk about it?"

There was a slight fumble in her steps. Nearly indistinguishable if I hadn't memorized her gait for every pace. "There's nothing to talk about."

"Seth mind-fucking that guy's head while I tortured him isn't what I'd call 'nothing'." A sharp scoff caught in my throat. "But all right, if you say so."

Amaia relented in her pace, coming to a steady jog. "I do say so. I wanted an answer to what Ronan alluded to taking place. There isn't anything we can do about the past."

"Amaia … it's more than that. You can't think it's that simple. Come on now. Think about it, Ronan knew what happened in that cell sure. But there's more than one link. Gotta be."

In sync, we scanned our surroundings, then came to a complete stop. It was flat in a total 360° for the next mile each way. If something was headed for us, we'd see them long before they posed a threat to our safety. Pros and cons to the position. As easy as it let us see someone, they could see us, too.

For years, I had no fear of exploring the world without walls. But now, with the enemy closing in from every direction, that sense of invulnerability was fading fast. Hell, there wasn't even safety within the walls of Monterey anymore. Not with the 'emissaries' crawling around.

Amaia's dark curls sprang free from her bun, a byproduct of the salty coastal breeze. She glanced down, her lips pursing to the side, skin pinched between her brows. "There's nothing that indicates that. Reina is confident that Jessa was the other link. Jessa said Ronan would send more, but Riley locked The Compound down immediately. Can't be anyone else."

I didn't want her to think I doubted her or questioned her judgment. That wasn't the case by any means. But in a world that survival requires trusting your gut, I'd be doing her a disservice by shutting up. "And you had Moe take a look at her?"

"Checked all our bases. Nothing she can see at the moment. Jessa's solid."

I ground my jaw. A shadow fell over Amaia's face as I shifted my stance, now blocking out the harsh sun. She kept her patience for approximately half a second.

"What? Say it already."

"You gonna tell me to bark next?" I arched a brow, laughing to the wind at my girl. Always straight to the point. "No judgment, got it? My past *Bloodhound* shit is out there in the open at this point."

I didn't expect her to judge me for it. If anything, it was my own shame. Pointless shame at that. Amaia understood—the world either changes you or you change the world. There is no in between. No teetering over that thin, nonexistent line to your morality.

Lion or sheep. Killers and those that are killed. Predators or prey. Everyone fell into a category, especially in the middle of a fucking apocalypse. She nodded, inching closer to place her hand within mine.

"How does one say this tactfully …" I said, rubbing my thumb against the outside of her hand. "Bad people … Men with Ronan's mindset don't waste opportunity and they damn sure don't waste effort. Using Seth to communicate with some random ass guy being tortured is more or less pointless—"

Amaia dropped my hand as she finally processed what had been damn near obvious this entire time. A fact that we all blissfully ignored out of the pure exhaustion that came from losing everything. The fucking desperation and dread of losing that one last part of you that had the desire to continue on. "A test run. Making sure we didn't have anything in place to prevent him from jumping in. Like the shit he has set up over Covert. He has eyes on us and it may not be anyone inside—not willingly, at least."

"Right. Seth didn't know anything new about Monterey. He only had info from when he was last here. But Ronan … He's never doubted you. He knew things had changed around here. If Seth got into his head, there was only one shot. And that shot had to count. He wasn't going to waste it on just anyone—there had to be information to gain."

"Information on how we operate." Amaia hissed a curse. A vein pulsed against her temple as I reached out to push a curl back behind her ear. There was this desperation to always touch these days. "To see how far we're willing to go in the name of war."

We'd have to be careful with our thoughts, our plans, until we were ready to strike. It wasn't possible to keep him out forever, not without wards that rivaled Coverts.

Amaia paced with her hand on her forehead. I kept my position though every part of me wanted to close the gap between us. Right now, I wasn't here as a boyfriend, I was here as her … whatever the fuck I was. Soldier, I guess—in the way that Riley was a soldier before the promotion to lieutenant. The color drained from her sienna cheeks. I clenched my fists, nails digging into my palms to substitute for the urge to reach for her. To comfort her. The silence was deafening.

"That means they know about Operation Midnight Veil and …" she finally spoke.

"Yeah," I said, nodding my head in agreement. "Soulfire, and everything else we thought was a surprise."

"We have no more advantages. Secrets." Amaia nibbled on her bottom lip, shaking her head in resistance. I could only imagine where her mind was going. How it didn't make sense but made all the pieces fall into place all the same.

I couldn't find the words—hell, I wasn't even sure there were any that would help. All I knew was watching things crumble around her *again* was tearing me apart. Despite wanting to help, there was nothing I could do to take away her pain. Only avenge it.

Finding out *who else* would be the easy part once we all workshopped it. It had to be someone he connected with mentally before, which meant it had to be someone he'd established trust with.

"Fuck. Fuck. Fuck. I should've—"

"What are you talking about?" I questioned, her dilated pupils and wide eyes raising my level of concern. The situation was bad, but finding one person was no cause for panic.

"The cavalry … those motherfuckers. I need a meeting." She took off ahead of me, kicking up dust.

I caught up, wrapping a firm grip around her wrist and pulling her to a stop. We needed to keep a level head. Irrationality would be damning. "With who?"

"Ronan."

"What good is that gonna do?" I scoffed. There wasn't much we didn't agree on these days. She took a step back at my hesitancy, hurt crossing over her exhausted features. "He's not going to tell you shit."

"This … this is *exactly* what I was afraid of," she cursed herself. "Why I wanted to keep Seth's betrayal a secret. The reason I didn't give him the opportunity to cause chaos here."

I let her speak. Let her voice her frustrations for a brief moment before I put them to rest. Seth was the only one to blame for his actions. Everyone else was collateral damage in the fallout of his shit. They could only respond to his fuckery, not prevent it.

"I didn't think … I forgot he could—"

"This isn't on you." I interrupted, unable to stop myself.

"No. But his reaction to the accusation will clue me in on enough. I need to know what we're working with, and he needs to believe that he's knocked me down to the point I can't get back up."

I sighed, knowing there was no stopping her. My only option was to follow her to hell and back. "Whatever you're thinking about doing is a bad idea."

"Yeah." She shrugged, used to running with her bad ideas and coming out victorious. "But if we don't know how many eyes are on us, then anything we do from here on out is subject to getting us killed."

CHAPTER
EIGHT

ALEXIARES

"Γ αμώ."

Amaia slowed in her steps and narrowed her eyes in the direction that had me cursing. "What? That means fuck, right? Who is that?"

We were back to the area I'd met her in earlier. A dark, hooded figure leaned against a tree with their back turned toward us. The hair on my neck raised at the sight of danger. A Covert soldier would be a welcome surprise at this point. At least then I could get some of this frustration out.

"Lola," I said, coming to a walk a few steps ahead of Amaia.

She caught up, curiosity written all over her face. "So what's the problem?"

"If she's here, it means she wants something."

The relationship I had with Lola was … peculiar. She scratched my back, I scratched hers. Sure, there were moments where things seemed familiar to say the least, but I never lost sight of what the base of it all: reciprocity. I gave Lola what she wanted.

"It's not like we have anything to give her," she mumbled with a shrug devoid of all hope. "First my home, then my family and my people. Next up, my sanity."

"Not sure you ever had that one, Princess." I smirked.

"How can you be sure that's why she's here?" She kicked a rock up the path as we got closer, her hand falling to a place of comfort at my waist. I leaned into her and wrapped an arm around her shoulders, appreciating the warmth radiating off her even though it was hotter than hell out. "Maybe it's just to help."

"We don't help people for free. No one does."

"We?" She grinned, nudging into me. "Go on. Enjoy a few minutes before we have to do business. If I had the chance to see Prescott again, I'd do the same."

Lola tilted her head and studied Amaia a few feet from our approach. Amaia's face lit up despite what she knew was coming her way. They had gotten along relatively well. Lola wasn't exactly the warmest person in the world, let alone to newcomers. My woman pushed to the tips of her toes and I leaned down, letting her kiss that spot on my cheek that made me want to kick my fucking feet like a school girl. She brushed past Lola, greeting her in passing, then made her way back toward North Gate.

Silence passed between us. The only sounds being the insects that decided to repopulate the earth thanks to Riley's gifts. Gifts that weren't particularly a favorite of mine. I swatted away a mosquito as Lola strolled toward me with open arms. Admittedly, the sight of her made me a little happy. I'd genuinely thought I'd never see her again after leaving St. Paul. Even if I didn't die in this war, it was rare to see someone you crossed paths with in another area unless it was intentional.

"Mi chiquito, Sabueso." The nurturing she was capable of came out full force with a kiss to both my cheeks.

"Claro." I rolled my eyes, still keeping up the 'I don't give a shit' act on the off chance anyone was out here lingering. "That's enough."

"Imagine if I had welcomed you with the same disdain," she said, stepping away and taking me in.

"Imagine," I jested as she looped arms with me, guiding us for a walk around the outside of The Compound.

I wasn't sure how Amaia would feel about that. If she would assume ill-intent on Lola's behalf, or if she simply trusted my judgment. That and the simple fact that stepping outside these walls had no guarantee on your return now. Especially for an extended period.

We weren't sure if it was Pansies or general dissent, but people who checked out had about a 1 in 10 chance of returning. With the influx of people, it was probably for the better, as much as everyone refused to think such a morbid thought. But I couldn't see how we could keep up with demand at the pace we were growing. Lola had no fear, though. A flaw by design, but it worked out for her so far.

"¿Cómo van las cosas?"

"Lola," I tsked. "Skip the small talk. I know you better than that."

"Sí, sí. What is the plan here, Sabueso?"

I glanced down at her. "Plan for what? War's over. Done with."

While Amaia was definitely up to something, she'd stuck to her usual MO. If there was a plan, no one knew of it other than to keep our heads down and act normal. Thing was, there was nothing to act *abnormal* about.

"¿Te parezco una tonta?" Lola scolded. The Lola I was used to showing her horns. "That girl will never lay down like a trained dog. She is a fighter. I expected her to give us a good show."

The eagerness in her tone. The smug grin on her face. It all rubbed me the wrong way. This was something we would have humored over in the past, but now, the thought of Amaia fighting front and center made me sick. Crazed. All the shit we'd gone through during that battle was enough for a lifetime. I *wished* it were all over. For good. But Lola was right. Amaia wasn't the type to roll over and play dead.

"There's nothing left to do. Ronan gave us his terms. She chose the safety of her people. As you would, need I remind you." I side-eyed her, not so subtly defending the woman I'd grown to respect. To love.

Lola removed the hood of her long linen hoodie. A bead of sweat against her ivory skin. Dark coal lined her unsettling black eyes. She kept her gaze forward, her grin unfading. Unbothered. "Tell me I didn't waste my time coming here just for you to have no plan."

"No one asked you to come, Lola. You're welcome to stay, but there's nothing going on here but rebuilding."

Her arm fell away from me along with her body. "Nonsense, I was guided down this path for a reason." With a step back, her temper flared at my secrecy—she'd always known when I'd put on a front. Dark smoke the color of night hovered in her hands as she murmured. Raw magic shot toward the well-kept path ahead of us. Hard work from the earth elementals gone to waste with the rot of Lola's magic. What was once green and brown earth was now a pit of tar and black mold. Decay slapped me in the face, the smell strongly unbearable. I bit down the urge to gag at the sight of amusement in her eyes.

"You invite me to stay as though you determine who comes and who goes," Lola chided, smug ass grin still present as she approached me and motioned me closer with two fingers.

Signaling for gossip, as Reina explained when I asked her why she was giving me that look in the middle of a crowded room of council members and leaders of The Compound. We fell back into step, her playful tone not overlooked.

"Guess I kind of do," I said, wondering when the hell that had happened.

So much had happened in such little time. I didn't know where I stood here. When Amaia or Riley disappeared, the questions ended up at my feet. Now Amaia and I were playing house with no real conversation about that either—

"Ah, you popped the question already?" Lola interrupted my spiraling thoughts with a knowing pinch of her brows.

I choked on air. The very thing responsible for keeping me alive, damn near took me out. "I'm going to pretend I didn't hear that."

"Oh sure. You mean to tell me there isn't a coffin-shaped ring you've kept—"

"Lola," I snapped, glaring at her as I yanked us to a stop. "Do I need to remind you of the sentiments I hold toward being watched?"

The mock forest around us fell silent at the power radiating from Lola. Her gaze turned stone-cold at my grip but she kept her darkness to herself. "It would be dumb to offer favors to someone who won't live to repay me."

"Estás mal de la cabeza," I muttered, continuing on and ignoring her silent warning. I trusted Lola, I did. But the way she was talking—her track record—trusting her with my life was entirely different from trusting her with Amaia's. Her being here meant something.

She wouldn't waste the trip unless she had seen an outcome that played to her benefit. Her people were already here, doing what she had promised and using their dark magic to enhance ours. Lola, while having taken many trips throughout The Expanse, had not crossed the line to any other territory since the war.

"I'll stay," she said as I attempted to hide the regret of my offer. "But only because you and I both know that girl understands how dangerous it is not to have a plan. Dare I say, more dangerous than compliance with a man who only speaks the language of violence."

CHAPTER

NINE

TOMOE

Dust filtered through the air in front of the windows of Reina's lab. The scent of chemicals stung my nose as I leaned across the thin wooden counter to crack the window open.

"At least they thought to capture the important shit," I mumbled as I sat back on the wobbly bar stool.

"Consider me ecstatic that it's helpful to your research. Tell me more."

Reina ran her fingers through her hair and out her face. She sat staring at some sketch with a blank expression. It'd been marked up in handwriting I didn't recognize, notes of recommended changes scribbled off on the sides.

"You're the one on some war path to help Abel." I slammed closed the tome in front of me and coughed up the dust. Ever since Reina moved out of her quarters, she'd stopped cleaning as much. I understood no one lived in the back anymore, in her old room, but I thought she'd at least keep up the shared space. It was unusual of her. If I had the energy, I'd bring it up, but I didn't. "And this is for you. Understanding the Pansie situation is every bit as important now as it was a few months ago."

"What do you think I've been keeping extensive data of, Moe? Injuries."

She slid the next set of records across the table and I narrowed my eyes in annoyance. "That's your job, isn't it?"

"You know what I mean."

A knock on the door startled us both. Reina gasped at the sudden brisk sound against the thick, glass door. "Need some company?"

Deep, Moore blue eyes lit up at the sight of the man leaning against the door frame. Bronze arms crossed over a simple dark gray t-shirt. I followed the sharp, bulging veins up the slender muscle in his arms up to the cocky smile and hazel eyes of someone I swore I recognized yet, failed to place. My cheeks burned under the scrutiny of his gaze. A more intense, observant leer I wasn't quite used to outside of Riley or Alexi. Memory teased me. Tomás. The brother of Alexiares's fallen friend.

"Hi!" Reina said, scooting her rolling chair away from the table and rushing toward him with a hug. "How are you? Never mind, you're good. I can feel it."

He offered her an awkward one-armed hug, not expecting the embrace. A reluctant pang slammed through my heart. Since when had Reina decided to be so open about her gifts outside of our group? Everything about our powers was out in the open now, including Riley. Consequences of war. But still, it wasn't as though we all walked around, advertising.

"You the *Seer*?" Tomás asked, eyes not falling off me.

"Sure," I said, glancing back down at what I'd been researching. "You the twin?"

"Sure." A smug crackle of a laugh escaped him and I shot him a glare.

"Alexi ditch you again?" Reina asked as though they were familiars. Confusion continued to linger as my scrutiny shifted back toward her.

Tomás shoved his hands in his pockets, crossing the room and leaned against a metal counter stacked with vials. "Nah. Figured I'd check back in on your progress with the arm and see if I could be of value in my down time."

"Let me guess, you're no good with idle hands?" I mumbled sarcastically.

"Oh no, I'm great with my hands—idle or not." He winked, eyes wandering over my body for far too long. "But it's kind of shitty to not offer help these days when everyone could use some. Wouldn't you agree?"

My stool nearly toppled over at the pace in which I strode across the floor and shoved two heavy tomes into his chest. "You take last names H and I from The Expanse arrivals."

He propped his elbows against the counter and tilted his head down to meet Reina's eye for a clue in. Tomás only stood a few inches taller, but his presence consumed the entire room. Reina's smile made me want to slap her. She was up to something, and I knew whatever it was, I would absolutely hate that shit.

"Hm. Yeah, what to address first?" A pale finger tapped against her pink lips. "No progress on the arm. Abel wants to see how things go without it so my tests have halted. Just doing some drafts on improvements for when he's ready. Moe's going through our archives for Pansie data. Trying to figure out when communication patterns were established with the Pansies and how they evolved. A general timeline on their evolution can help us break down what means what. Got it? You can ask Moe if you need any help, she's a *fantastic* teacher. Very eager."

Tomás shook his head slowly, clearly amused by the situation. "Guess I'll ask a question when I have one."

"Cool," I said, finding my way back to my seat. "I prefer working in silence so if you don't mind."

Tomás sat down in Reina's chair at an extremely forward distance, edging closer to the splintered counter. "Trying to get some better light." He excused himself and ignored my persistent challenge of a stare down.

The kind that said move the fuck back or else. My boots slammed into the ground as I scratched the floor with the movement of my stool. I stopped once my back hit the corner wall. Even an inch between us would be better than sitting arm to arm.

The proximity of a man … someone outside my family … unsettled me. A sin. Like the universe was punishing me with the false sense of closeness. Taunting me with the possibility of what else was out there though there would never be another Seth. And Seth was all I wanted. The old Seth. The one that loved me as much as I loved him. The sweet Seth who spent years keeping his distance until I was ready for our story to unfold.

Seth Moore, the man who held me at night when the visions of Jax's death haunted me in both my dreams and my waking moments. Seth Moore, the man who was responsible for killing my hope for the future.

Memories. It was all just fucking memories and visions on what almost was. I killed him. I did that. Boldly. Fiercely. Our story ended because I chose myself. My family. There were consequences to the choices we made. Spending forever alone was mine. Tomás and his flirting may be harmless, but I didn't want any part of it. I didn't deserve the flushing of my cheeks or the pitter-patter of my heart under the attention of a man who is just my type. Confident. A little arrogant. Strong. Charming in an unsettling way. All the ingredients for a catastrophe, waiting to ignite. Misery was due to me and I would happily welcome it with open arms.

The room fell to blissful silence as our attention rested upon our individual archives. It wasn't as though I ever doubted Amaia and Prescott's insistence on keeping historical records of each of our residents. In fact, I'd always respected it. I'd maintained much of my own family history in The Before and had carried it with me to The After. What wasn't remembered, was lost and when lore and legends were no longer enough for humans, we'd resort to was written.

Though the fascinating aspect of it all being—if you weren't interesting enough to be worthy of a memory that outlasted time, then you were forgotten. And now, we had to search through it ourselves. Remember the finer details no one had ever thought to flag, to note.

There may not have been Pansies in the past, but our research regarding how they communicated now was dependent upon the data. There were the usual entry questions, the core three that Amaia asked everyone that arrived at our gates. Then there were those who'd arrived inconsolable, leading us to ask more. Questions that helped Prescott and the others understand the mental state of each victim of the outside world.

What happened out there? What did you see? Why can't you speak?

The answers to those were what we'd find inside. So not everyone at Monterey Compound but nevertheless, a great deal. Everyone had trauma. Nothing new about that.

"Reina, you said it was something about acoustic signals and dolphins?" I pivoted around in my seat.

Reina sat cross-legged on the counter, a notepad in her lap as she ran through the profiles I'd pulled for her review. People she may want to talk to in person. Shit in their files that made me arch a brow and could be *something*, anything we could grasp onto.

"I say a lot of things, but yes, go on." Her long legs dangled over the side and she hopped down. Reina hovered over me upon approach, the silver chained cross around her neck that once belonged to Seth cool against the back of my head. "Find something juicy?"

Tomás's attention piqued, and he glanced over. His attention lingered on me as he waited for me to speak. "Could be nothing. But we had an arrival a couple of months ago specifically stating that the further they got from Covert, the Pansies clicks and groans became less rhythmic and more chaotic."

"Interesting," Reina said, tearing the page from the tome and parsed through it, jotting down some notes.

"Does it say where they came from?" Tomás asked, his hand fell over his buzzed, dark hair, his presence looming now that Reina had paced back across the room.

"Yeah." My voice came out as a whisper, and I cleared it. "These are from the Transient Nation arrival stack. So everywhere. Why?"

"Okay, a few months ago, the closer they got to Salem the fewer originals they saw in the area. That's a direct correlation to whatever Ronan had going on, yeah?"

"We already know that another species of Pansie was born about a year ago," I said. "That's what kicked this whole thing off—when Michael and Logan got bit."

Something danced in his light brown eyes as he spoke. I hated it. "Have you considered migration patterns? Pansies are people. People are animals. So are dolphins. There's less now than last week. It's getting hotter. Bodies decay in heat."

"Duh," Reina chimed in with an exaggerated nod, jerking forward at the statement. "The decay is still slower than what you'd expect from you and me on the way to the afterlife, since they aren't, like, actually dead, though."

"Following. But, hear me out Ms. Scientist and *Seer*, what's the typical behavior of a pod of dolphins?"

"Um, they're smart as heck. Complex communication patterns, coordinated group movements in both hunting and migration …" Reina's voice trailed off and her eyes glistened in distant thought.

Tomás sighed impatiently, sliding across the room on the wheeled chair and reached for the report. "And the Pansies are doing what …"

"Well hot damn." Reina muttered. "They're following the food source."

"Who's name is on that report?"

I shrugged and met his stare. It was unsettling, as though he was seeing through you but not in the creepy, cloudy way those around me described my gaze. Tomás watched people, as though their secrets were an open book to him, and he found humor in that. "Everything's blending together at this point. I'm not even checking unless I see something significant enough to set aside."

"That doesn't seem helpful." He teased.

I scoffed, tossing my hair over my shoulder. "And what do you do around here again?"

"What I do here is irrelevant to my po—"

"Oh brother." I groaned and rolled my eyes. "Reina, whoever it is, we need to go talk to them. Now."

Mischief decorated Reina's sharp features as she ruffled through the stack of interview papers in front of me. Her cheerful tone was a sickening giveaway that she was about to put me through hell and enjoy every second of it. "Sure, you lead though, since there's a good chance they'll tell you everything and then some."

I glanced down at the page she set before me. Tomás inched forward, his eyes narrowing. "You know him or something?"

It was Hal's interview. And we didn't have to go far to get more information. Down the hall and around the corner in fact. My old quarters. I'd avoided him as much as possible. If it weren't for Emma, we'd be no contact for sure. His wife, my fallen friend, Laurel dying hadn't made us like each other all the same. Instead, we operated in a sense of understanding and respect for all the shit we'd been through since we last resided in the same space. Sometimes trauma bonds you. Other times, you couldn't help but have a desperate urge to get further apart.

We both grieved too much. If we were left alone together, I feared we'd stay in a pit of each other's sorrow and depression forever. Ergo the kids and my family. If we drowned ourselves in other things, then we could both pretend this was how life was meant to be. There was no alternative to this. Shit happened, and you dealt with the hand you were given. The universe worked however the fuck it wanted to, and we were all victims of the whims and wind in which it took us.

For those reasons alone I was glad to have left them my quarters. I didn't want to go back. Riley's old place with Abel felt good … it felt better. A place to start over. Again. Or deal with the time I had left.

If I wanted to talk to Hal though, there was only one place we could find him at this time of day. And it was the last place I wanted to be.

CHAPTER
TEN

ALEXIARES

I took a deep breath before turning the knob of my home. *Home.* How fucking bizarre coming from my mouth. Over my nearly thirty years on this earth, there weren't many places I'd refer to as *'home.'* Matter of fact, there was no place I considered home. No place but here. With her.

But instead of being happy about the change in my life, I found myself consumed by the sorrow of how we'd come to be here. Evander and Tiago's belongings now lined the shelves next to Prescott's clutter of trinkets and other shit he'd collected over the years.

"Drakos." Bietoletti, one of Ronan's 'emissaries', brushed past me with a stiff shoulder.

Stopping a step out of the door frame, I glanced over my shoulder, watching him take the two steps down and out into The

Compound. I gathered myself, clenching my fingers to keep from drawing my knife and flinging it at him.

"Gonna tell me what that was about?"

"I threw a tantrum," she said casually, tossing a hand in front of her face. "He didn't understand that my request to meet with Ronan was nonnegotiable."

The fireplace was on despite the heat of the day. Heat radiated off it, smoldering the room to a damn near suffocating temperature. It gave her comfort. I knew that. The familiarity of it all with her slice of berry pie and cup of coffee seated on the wooden coffee table. A mancala board sat at the center in between the brown leather couches. All of it untouched. As it had been every night since we moved in.

"So?" Amaia questioned from the corner of the room she used as a study.

I closed the door, locking it behind me. "What?"

"Are you going to tell me why Lola is here or should I beg?"

"Begging works." I strode over to her, taking my time to observe her and pressed a gentle kiss to her forehead. The softness of Amaia's skin under my lips and her offer to beg made me want more, but I pulled back. Spreading my legs, I leaned back into the chair across from her. There was a hunger in my gaze and from the flushing of her face and the nibble on her lip, she couldn't hide her own. "I *always* enjoy seeing you beg."

Amaia's foot climbed up my leg from under the desk. My dick went hard at the sensation. Her heavy ass Doc Marten stopped directly over it, pushing slightly on my balls. It hurt like shit and not in the way that turned me on. "Talk, *Bloodhound*."

"As you wish, Princess," I said as I adjusted myself in my seat. "I don't know."

"You don't know …" Amaia arched a brow of disbelief accompanied with a slow nod.

She was no fool. Maybe she overestimated the weight I held with Lola, with our relationship. Or she read it right. I could press the issue, though something told me I shouldn't. At least not yet.

"Correct. Those were the words that came out of my mouth."

"Alexiares," she asserted, wiping the smirk right off my face.

"As much as I wish I had a better answer for you, I got nothing. She only asked what your plan was now that Ronan's running shit."

"He is not." Amaia grumbled, turning her attention back to the paperwork at her desk. "And you told her what?"

"The conversation was mostly compliments on your adeptness, her refusal to believe you'd roll over and play nice, coupled with a not-so-subtle inference for an invitation. Other than that, I told her nothing."

"You told her nothing?" Amaia's head shot back up. She inhaled and held it in, eyes narrowing.

"There's nothing to tell as far as I'm aware. You dropped a bomb a month ago about some plan to find Ronan's most wanted and then continued on business as usual. I feel like I can't take my eye off you for more than a few minutes without worrying if you've taken off. What happened? What made you change your mind?"

"Grief." Her raspy voice was a muted whisper. "If you sit with it long enough, it makes you reflect on what's important."

"And what conclusion did you come to?"

"That keeping this place running the way Prescott and Jax envisioned it is going to take a lot more than anger. I need to bide my time, calculate my next move and that's not going to happen overnight. I want revenge more than anything Alexiares." Her soft, doe eyes lined with tears. Amaia shook her head, tucking a wild curl behind her ear. "The timing has to be right, and it's not now."

"Then cancel the meeting with Ronan." There was no good that would come of it. I'd seen plenty of Ronan's in my day. Playing nice, playing *the part*, was exactly what they wanted you to do.

You needed to strike fast and hard. But it wasn't my call to make. I respected Amaia, worshipped her as a goddess, and whatever she desired, *I* desired. But that didn't mean I wouldn't voice my opinion. I would never stop that.

"No."

"Of course not," I said, the words leaving my mouth before she'd finished speaking.

Amaia sat up straight, her head held high and the tears receding. "Waiting for the timing to be right doesn't mean I want Ronan to think we are completely complacent."

"Art of War." I grinned, licking my lips in admiration.

"Timing, perception, and decisive action are fundamentals I expect each of my soldiers to understand."

I arched a brow. "Is that what I am? Your soldier?"

Amaia studied me for a moment. My vicious little General of Monterey Compound stared back at me. "How much do you still trust her?"

I paused. Careful consideration of my words was important here. I trusted Lola to an extent. Amaia's trust, similar to Lola's, was hard-earned and easy to lose these days. "Fuck, I don't know. As long as I'm around, nothing will happen to you. I know that much, she'd never risk the consequences of my wrath."

"Great for me, bad for The Compound, is literally the only thing I gathered from that response. I'm putting Riley on it."

Coming to Lola's defense served me no purpose. I didn't want to vouch for her, talk out my ass, only to be wrong. Better to lean on the side of caution, especially knowing the gift Riley possessed. It would be too easy for him. But if Lola ever found out …

"What bullshit are you working through now?" I asked, changing the subject.

Amaia slid over a canteen and the metal cup in front of her. She'd been using water to fight her demons. Going through the motions of drinking without giving in to her desires. I wasn't sure if there was any real science to it but it seemed to do the job. She hadn't had a drink since we'd gotten back.

I took a moment to appreciate that. Getting through Prescott's death sober was no small feat. And though she would rather fucking die than confess the dirty truth, Seth's death was taking a toll as well.

"Let's play 'would you rather'."

A wry smile teased my lips as I poured myself a glass. "Okay then."

"Would you rather go down to one meal a day or have one meal spread across three meal times?"

"Uh, neither." I took a shot then fought off a gag. "That's not water."

"No, it's kava. Lucky us, they were finally ready to harvest right as the food's running out, huh?" Amaia's gaze remained down at the paper in front of her face. She pursed her lips side to side, not paying me any mind.

"The fuck is—"

She let out a heavy sigh as her eyes rolled up toward the wooden paneled ceiling. The movement was slow and exaggerated. Her patience nonexistent today more so than any other. "Plant native to the Pacific islands. It has medicinal purposes among other effects."

"Effects such as feeling off your shit?" I rolled my tongue around in my mouth. The tingling sensation was rather unpleasant. Admittedly, the edges of my anxiety waned and euphoria took over.

"On this episode of 'at least it's not tequila' …" Amaia grumbled and we met eyes. Humor glistened back, dancing wild and matching the reflection of the fire catching them at the right angle. It mimicked her power. Her beauty.

Stiffing a laugh I pushed the canteen back over to her. "Want to tell me why we're reducing food intake? Are we working earth elementals in The Gardens for fun?"

"We aren't *working* them, they're doing their jobs, watch it. Since Ronan denied our most recent proposed trade agreement, we're no longer receiving resources we relied on before."

"If you're going to push back on something, it should be this. The initial agreement was our sovereignty in the exchange of resources. Resources he explicitly stated were human to help with whatever shit he has going on behind his borders—minus the experimenting."

"Yeah, unfortunately that wasn't the same deal he struck with others. Their material resources are his material resources, which affects us too. Yet another way to weaken us all. Plus I've had to divert resources with rebuilding and operations, but I didn't think …" Amaia gathered her composure and reached for the kava. She downed a mouthful, then two. "I didn't think pulling fifty workers from The Gardens to work on natural security barriers around our borders would have such a big impact, especially with the five hundred refugees we accepted this week alone—"

"And the thousand troops from Elko and Sacramento."

She glared at me. "*And* the thousand troops from Elko and Sacramento. How could I forget? Thanks. We're also supporting the soldiers we have deployed for border patrol. That combined with everything else going on … we're already reaching into our stored rations. The food situation is *tense* for now but not dire. I'm thinking of what will happen if we continue on this way before we're able to recoup what was lost in the first place. The Garden workers may be back but there isn't a great ratio of earth elementals among the refugees … yet another problem to exhaust myself trying to solve."

Covert Province had damaged far more than we initially assessed. They'd been strategic in their pillaging. The Gardens had been burned, The Docks exploded, and The Stables slaughtered. At least the slaughtering of The Stables had been thwarted by the breeders and stable hands that had refused to leave on the off chance of the worst happening. The fuckers had thought of everything down to poisoning the soil. We hadn't figured it out until too many important days of some shit had passed. Reina had explained it in great detail but all I'd gotten from the conversation was that we were fucked. I hadn't realized *how* fucked we were until now.

Amaia nibbled on her bottom lip, her stare distant, no longer here. I knew where her mind was going. To Prescott. To Jax. How she needed them.

She may have wanted them but she didn't *need* them. I only wished she could see that blatant fact. Everyone saw her as strong but that only mattered if she believed it herself.

Our minds had become one throughout our trials and tribulations. A fact proven once again as she read my thoughts. "Before you say I don't need them to keep this place going, don't. My entire life I've been a sheep and my entire life, people have followed me like a leader instead. Nothing I do is groundbreaking, I find someone that inspires me and aim to be like them, to do *good* the way they would. Now that's all gone and I have no idea what that leaves me with."

"It leaves you with you." Amaia's gaze snapped to mine at the words. Angry at first, then something of acceptance entered them.

Her gaze was fierce. It always was. But those rich brown eyes … They were the kind that weathered storms and still came out warm. Earthy. Mimicking the dirt I'd buried my hands in when the world fell apart. When I fell apart. Grounding. Real. Solid. I could get lost in them but always find my way back. And sometimes I swore there was a fire flickering beneath the surface, mirroring her magic. Eyes that had seen far too much but refused to surrender the soul behind them. Amaia's eyes weren't just brown—they were the color of home. And I'd defend that always, even if it meant saving her from herself.

I reached my hand across from the desk and she glanced down warily before taking it. "Come on. Let's take a break. I've been *dying* to fuck with that machine since we got back."

"Can we not say dying, please?" Amaia's laugh was clipped and morbid.

She rose to her feet, and I gave my girl a pat on the ass on the way out the door. "Anything for you, Princess."

CHAPTER
ELEVEN

AMAIA

Considering the amount of people that came through the Elemental Room the last few weeks, it was a shock to see it in such great condition. They'd only had to replace the sensory film on the wall fourteen times. Entrance interviews may be on a backlog, but our record keeping couldn't slow now. Now was when it was most important. Words could be manipulated, science could not.

The blank white room was illuminated by fire magic. No matter the conditions of the room or if someone lost control, the flames would forever burn, protected glass designed not to break in nuclear blast zones. This bunker was our last resort should the worst ever happen again and everything within it was built for survival.

I watched him as he entered and stopped in the center. He leaned over the machine with both arms, the muscle in them bulged against his black t-shirt. *Good on me for going with this uniform choice.*

Alexiares turned around and caught my stare. I tilted my head with a small smile as I watched with need. "Well, you know what to do."

"Maybe I want some assistance." Alexiares licked his lips with a heavy, weighing stare. "You are the blood queen, after all."

Bloodreina this, Bloodreina that. I fucking loathed the name, and he knew it.

I strolled over to him, shoving him out of the way. "Cute."

The motions were muscle memory as I pricked his finger and dropped his blood onto the dial. He kissed my forehead, smearing the blood across my lips as he pulled back. I pushed to my toes, kissing him and giving him a taste of his own medicine.

The computer chimed. "Ready?" I asked.

"Always. Fire first?"

"Probably safer that way," I chuckled. "But since I'm curious, let's try earth."

Vines and thick moss covered the main wall. The lush green appeared impenetrable as he toyed with his magic. A pattern evolved in a brighter green than the rest. The shape of a heart appeared before my eyes. My hand flew to my heart as I mocked him in flattery before he drew the outline of a dick in roses. I cackled. Amused didn't even begin to capture the feelings seeing a more juvenile, playful side of him stirred in me. It saddened me the more I learned about his childhood. He'd never had the freedom to express anything other than stoic anger. I couldn't imagine growing up in a world that was only colored gray.

The screen began loading data and caught my attention. Alexiares stole it away moments later as he shifted to fire. The air around him seemed to hum, a low vibration I couldn't ignore.

It crackled beneath his skin—lightning coiled right beneath the surface, waiting to be unleashed. The gravity of it was jarring. It stirred something inside me. Awe almost, but more primal.

My *Bloodhound*'s power was vast. It pulled at me in a way I could never have expected.

My breath turned shallow and my pulse quickened. A shiver snaked down my spine. I wanted to laugh and moan all the same. The ecstasy of it all. His power was beautiful. It called to me. Whispered the things it could do. The world it could bend … I wanted it.

My jaw damn near hit the ground before I remembered to fix my face. Alexiares glanced back at me, water dripping down the wall as he doused the flames. His gaze fell down to meet my stare, awaiting the results.

"Shit," I mumbled. "You broke the scale."

"I'm riding high right now." Alexiares studied his hands, then cast me a glance.

"I think that officially makes you the most powerful person I know."

"And how do you feel about that?" His large hand fell over his chest for a brief moment. Alexiares stared back at me for … approval? No. Fear. Acceptance.

"Like I want to fuck your brains out," I cooed, inching closer to him.

"Oh?"

"Oh," I mocked, tilting my head just enough to make it clear I wasn't letting it go. I caught his hand, threading our fingers together, daring him to pull away. He didn't. Instead, with infuriating ease, he dragged his finger along my bottom lip, like he had all the time in the world.

"Which part did me in, you think?" The sweet scent of fire and rain invaded my space. I welcomed it as he loomed over me, the harsh features of his face giving me a flutter in the pits of my stomach. "Moe's woo-woo antics or Reina's experiment?"

"You want the truth?"

His hands found my waist. "I'd expect nothing less from you."

"You were already incredibly powerful, but you were scared, so you held back. *This* was there all along, but you're in control now."

Alexiares scoffed. The distance he placed between us was un-intentional. I inched past him and back to the computer. With the prick up my finger, the screen offered me two options. An upgrade from before our time in Duluth. A new limitation of two allowed it to read both of our DNA at once. His jaw tightened as he watched me make my way back toward him.

"I mean it," I said, rejoining our hands. "I mean yeah, the earth magic is new but the rest. That was untouched and unaffected until we do *this*."

"You don't want to test your air first?" he asked, and a line appeared between his brows. His tan skin pinched out of concern.

"If I'm honest, I don't think I want to know. What I did scared me, controlling the life of that many people at once. I want to control it and I know doing that means I have to face the cold, hard facts. That's what a general would do. A responsible leader should want as much information as possible regarding a danger-ous weapon. Because that's what we are, you know? Weapons. But the *person* in me, *Amaia*, I don't think knowing how lethal she is will do her any good. No offense."

"None taken though, duly noted." His chin rested atop my head, and his posture relaxed as he pulled me close.

I pressed my head to his chest, trying to find some peace. There it was. All out there for the world to know that I was afraid of my power. Me. The general. *Again.* Prescott would be so damn disappointed. "I know how to maintain control, knowing the num-ber isn't going to help me at this point. Just remind me how much damage I can cause."

"Do you feel guilt?" he asked, pulling back and his hands crawled up my sides, landing on my shoulders. The intensity of his narrowed eyes was uncomfortable. "For killing all those people?"

"No." The word slipped out on reflex. It was the truth, however. "But I can't say I enjoyed the experience."

Commanding armies didn't make me immune to the weight of war. Sure, when my anger took over, it was easier to make a kill. But at night when I laid in bed listening to Alexiares's soft snores … all I could think about was how they were someone's family. Someone's husband, their father or their son or their brother. Maybe all the above. They had people who cared for them and would never see them again.

Jax had been a casualty of war. So had Prescott. We mourned them. Felt the stomach clenching, heart hurting, headache bringing pain of never getting to say that final goodbye. To know the last words we spoke to each other would be the end. In a different chapter of this story, those men that died in the field for Covert, they were the hero of their family. As Jax and Prescott were mine.

"While I can't relate to your … level of empathy, it makes sense. And I'm sure the people around here would prefer that you have those emotions. I'd imagine they sleep more peacefully because of it."

I took a moment to center myself, locking away the emotions. "All right, show me how much you got, *Bloodhound.*"

A tingling sensation crawled to the tips of my fingers as our magic teased each other. Threatening to join in a force meant to destroy the world. I turned to face the wall and held out my free hand. Alexiares mirrored my motions, dark gray. Our magic joining was orgasmic.

An ethereal hue of blue danced against our skin, flickering as ghostly shadows in the dim light. The mist-fueled flames of our *Steamfire* roared to life and slammed against the wall. The heat of it in this room was lethal to anyone but the wielders. It was thick and heavy. A second skin. Each wave of warmth left the wall glowing, yet not a single ember burned us. Only we could command it, and only we could endure its lethal embrace.

Tomoe was a damn genius. She had allowed us to harness power that no one else could rival, and in our hands, it made us unstoppable.

"That can't be good." Alexiares's laugh was one of pure chaos.

The white film coating the Elemental Room's wall had completely melted away. Raw, reinforced concrete was exposed from beneath. It glared back at us. Jagged and scorched, it posed a surreal reminder that *Steamfire's* heat index far exceeded anything we had anticipated. The wall wasn't damaged—it was obliterated. Charred beyond recognition.

Steamfire had turned it to ash.

"Eh, it's replaceable … I think."

That wasn't going to spare me from Reina's rage. Alexiares followed me over to the computer. I wasn't sure if I expected the data to populate or not after the destruction we caused.

> **Warning: Unregistered magical entity detected. Unable to process magic signatures. No prior records found in database. Error code 404: Magic Not Found. Please contact system administrator or initiate manual override for further diagnostics.**

"Dammit."

He stayed silent as I typed into the computer. I couldn't remember the last time I had to reboot this thing, and I knew nothing about coding it, but Reina had the same password for literally all of her shit so it had to work. I tried a few times, but no dice. Made sense, considering it was Seth's birthday.

I glanced up at Alexiares and found him watching me. His gaze lingered, unwavering, even as the data on the screen flashed with errors. *"Unregistered,"* the computer droned, but his eyes stayed locked on mine, more focused on me than our problems. It made me want to fucking melt into his arms. Forget all the shit we were dealing with and spend the day together—nothing else. We'd never had that luxury. I mean, we had but never a peaceful one.

Our 'dates,' besides what he'd planned for my birthday, had consisted of hiding out in an abandoned house during our travels. If we found one with a mattress, we could cuddle up on, it was damn near a vacation. Those little moments that most couples got to have never happened for us. Instead, we stole them in moments like this.

"What?" I asked after a few seconds passed, my voice steady despite the way my pulse pounded.

Strong hands gripped my arms—not rough, not demanding, just *there*, and I didn't fight them off. I barely had time to react before he pushed me back against the wall near the door. His body hovered close, heat radiating off him, an arm pressing against the wall above my head, the other tilting my chin up. A soft grip. Too soft for the way his eyes burned into mine. "Can't keep looking at me like that if you expect me to keep my hands to myself."

"We're on duty," I said, my hands trailing up his torso and stopped on his solid chest.

I swallowed hard, my hands dragging up the solid plane of his torso, fingertips trailing over muscle before stopping at his chest. I gave him a slow, deliberate push. He didn't budge. If anyone walked in here right now, it could be a problem. I mean, I kind of owned the whole damn place, technically, but still, it didn't feel right. Not when there was shit to do. In the same breath, I found myself not caring. I deserved a pocket of peace in my days. How else was I supposed to do my job without going completely fucking nuts?

Alexiares's eyes locked on my lips, his head tilting in that way that always pulled me in and refused to let go. His tongue traced over my ear. "I think it's time for a break."

That voice—low, with an edge that sent heat pooling between my thighs—stripped away any lingering hesitation. "Word on the street is you can make me do whatever you want. Especially with all that power."

Alexiares's lips hovered a whisper over mine, the warmth of him sending a shiver through me. His presence alone stole the air from my lungs, the space between us vanishing as his hands found my hips. "Seems to me we're at our most powerful when we're together."

He kissed my neck, the heat of his lips a slow burn as he nibbled and bit. Each touch was an agonizing taunt until he found his way to that spot behind my ear he knew made me squirm. The way he knew exactly where to touch, where to devour, was its own kind of magic. A soft moan escaped my lips—brief, before he swallowed it with his mouth. Gentle until he wasn't. Until he couldn't be. Our tongues danced. My back arching against the cold, hard wall as his teeth nibbled at my lip. I ground against him in need.

Alexiares tilted his head back with a groan as I pressed against him, feeling the hardness of his dick trapped between us. A wicked smirk played on my lips. I knew exactly what I wanted.

I dropped to my knees.

Alexiares sucked in a gasp for air, sharp and ragged, as I worked at his belt. My hands were desperate. Searching. I licked my lips, mouthwatering at the sight of him, the idea of him filling my mouth—thick, heavy, flushed with need.

"Fuck," he groaned, his voice low and ragged as my hands moved over him, teasing the length of him with slow, deliberate strokes.

I didn't rush. I wanted him starving for me—desperate, undone, begging.

Using both hands, I tickled the base of his balls as my tongue followed my hands. My tongue flicked out, teasing the tip, savoring the taste of salt and heat. I licked along the length of him, slow, torturous, my hand working in tandem. He tensed, fingers digging into my scalp, tightening in my hair as his hips snapped forward.

Hard, dark eyes stared down at me. Lust simmering in them as he whispered a command. "Open up."

Outside of these four walls, I was in charge. In the bedroom with Alexiares—I obeyed, parting my lips as he thrust deep into my mouth. His grip on my hair tightened, his hips snapping forward, pushing deeper, filling my throat. There was no such thing as air, as oxygen, as he pumped his way in and out of my mouth. Using me to feed an insatiable hunger that I understood all too well. Being with him was a different adventure every time. To say we fucked like jackrabbits at every opportunity would be an understatement. An air shield surrounding our room with Elie and the dogs on the other side of the house.

Each thrust sent a pulse of arousal straight to my core, a wicked kind of power coiling between my thighs. I moaned around him, the vibration making him hiss through his teeth.

His control snapped.

With a swift motion, he yanked me upright, crashing his mouth to mine in a kiss that was all teeth and hunger. I smiled a mocking grin, daring him to do his worst. Alexiares took it as a challenge. My cargo pants and briefs were burned off my body in his impatience.

It was his turn to kneel. He kissed the scar along my waist that spelled out his name. His hands moved to replace where his lips left, rough and urgent as he spun me around. A slap, sharp and stinging, landed on my ass. Large hands gripping my hips and pushing me forward. His lips followed, trailing fire along my hips. The wet stroke of his tongue found my pussy as he dragged it up, stopping at my lower back. He kissed it, then worked his way back down. I trembled beneath him, pleasure encased me at the sensation of his hand tightening its grip as he stroked himself to the sound of my muffled moans.

"Alex—"

He knew what I needed. But he made me wait.

I clenched my thighs around his shoulders, desperate, the edge of release so close, so maddening. I wanted us to come together or not at all. The tease was as much fun as that final release.

I turned around. A struggle given how anxious he was to finish me. He peered up at me with a grin, lifting me easily and pressing my back against the wall. I wrapped my legs around him. We paused, our eyes locking in that familiar way when words were a barrier, too dangerous to speak aloud. Those three words lingered on my lips, but fear held them back, locking them inside me where they'd stayed for so long. That didn't mean I didn't feel them. And he knew that.

"I love you," he said as he thrust deep inside me. The sensation made my head spin, but it wasn't just physical. Those words. They pulled at something raw and hidden inside me.

I held on to the space behind his neck and pressed my forehead against his. Our breath mingled as I whispered, "Inevitable."

A vow. A claim.

My own little way of saying that I intended for us to be forever. Whatever that looked like, it began and ended with him.

CHAPTER
TWELVE

AMAIA

"Ya know, I can practically feel the lust rolling off you two," Reina said the second we sat down at the long wooden table our group had claimed years ago.

I couldn't lie—being here was one of the last *normal* things in my life. An old reliable. Covert hadn't touched The Kitchens's interior. They hadn't had the chance. The low lanterns hanging from the herb and greenery-covered ceiling embraced us with a scent of home. Thankfully, Reina's commentary couldn't be heard by any PG-13 rated ears.

Elie sat off the side with her brother Rex, back home from his forty-eight hour deployment. They ate together whenever he was docked for the night. With everything going on, our navy spent more time out monitoring the water and coast line than ever before. She laughed at some joke he presumably told and his green eyes danced with joy. They shared the same caramel skin and pointed nose, but the similarities ended there. Where Elie's hair was thick with golden curls, his dark, wavy hair had been buzzed short when he enlisted.

His jaw ticked as he took me in and tossed me a nod. Tense words had been exchanged over the weeks regarding Elie's behavior. At the end of the day, he wasn't here to watch over her himself, and I had an obligation to more than one person's safety.

Harley and Suckerpunch bounded over, tongues dripping from water at the bowl at Emma's feet. She released them from the round table behind Elie's. Her father, Hal, pointed toward their scattered approach with a laugh. Emma's little brother, Luke, clapped his hands with a slobbered grin. Their sister Olivia ruffled his fine blond hair.

It was nice to see a smile on their faces. Tomoe had mentioned they were struggling when Emma asked for the dogs to come home with her a couple of days a week. It was odd sharing our babies with Elie and Emma, but it all served a larger purpose. If the girls were going to ignore the adults of The Compound and sneak around, then they might as well have some bodyguards. That was Harley and Suckerpunch's job during the day, to protect the girls at all costs, and they loved every second of it. More times than not, they came home exhausted, ready to sprawl out for hours in front of the fireplace. We knew they were sneaking outside the walls doing who knows what—they were going to do that whether we tried to stop them or not.

I kicked Reina under the table with a smile and her steaming liquid fell out of her bowl like a tidal wave. Bone broth and bread for dinner. Again. How joyous.

"Where's your girlfriend, Reina?" Alexiares tossed back at her in jest. "Shouldn't you be keeping an eye on her?"

Reina's smile faded, and she blushed. "Sorry, I'm too busy minding your business to worry about my own right now. Hope you at least washed your hands."

"Want to smell them to make sure?" Alexiares teased.

Tomoe choked on her bread, her scoff of a laugh music to my ears. She didn't do it often these days, but if she did, Alexiares tended to be the one to bring it out of her.

"Gross," Abel grumbled, his hand falling over his face.

"So," I said, my spoon clinking against the bowl of flavorless, murky water. "Everyone looks like they shat a brick. What morbid topic must I make my priority tomorrow?"

"Prisoners of war," Moe said, downing her broth as if it were tea from a cup.

The weight of the room shifted, no longer resembling a safe space. I hadn't given them much thought. It wasn't top of mind with everything else going on. I knew we had them and they were being taken care of within the Geneva Conventions. That wasn't an official rule or anything, but it seemed necessary to have some guiding principle for how to engage with them. A decision had to be made, eventually. God forbid I eat my dinner before doing so.

Riley draped his arm over the empty chair on his left. By the stacked dishes in front of him, he'd had dinner with Yasmin before the rest of us had arrived. "Any thoughts regarding how to move forward?"

I pursed my lips to the side and considered my options. We hadn't taken prisoners from Covert during the battle, but there were a few injured that had refused to die over the three days we left their bodies out to rot. Their suffering was scaring the citizens. We had to do something. Shooting them after the fact crossed a moral line I wasn't quite ready to hop over, so into the 'dungeon' they went.

"Well, don't give them to Alexi." Tomoe laughed darkly, her inked arms folding across her chest.

Abel exhaled sharply. "Is it too late to say thank you for not including me in that endeavor?"

Something about his tone made me glance up. His usual juvenile smirk wasn't there—just an edge of unease, the ghost of something heavier in his expression.

"You didn't want a personal Covert plaything?" Tomoe's words were playful, but her eyes held an edge. This wasn't mere jest.

Abel reached for his mug of hot lemon water, fingers flexing around the handle, before he sighed and leaned back instead. "Nah." His voice was lighter than it should've been, like he wanted to brush past it. "Spent long enough pretending to sympathize with them when they came to Duluth's gates. I don't need the reminder."

I frowned, curious to hear more about his time there. He hadn't spoken of it much … at least not with me.

He rolled his shoulders, shaking off an old memory. "People don't turn on you because they hate you. They turn because it's easy. Because it's practical. And once they do … I don't see torture as the end all be all method, is what I'm saying."

Silence fell over the table, the quiet more suffocating than any argument could've been.

I stared at him, trying to imagine it. Abel—loud, carefree Abel—living in enemy territory, smiling at people he knew would sell him out the second it benefited them.

Rex and Elie stood up in my peripheral before she slid into her usual seat next to Riley. She waved bye to her brother. Riley shifted his chair, scooting a bit to give her some space, but she had already leaned away into Tomoe's shoulder. The table grew some more as Emma followed in Elie's steps like clockwork.

Long, sandy hair hung down her back, her posture a mirror image of the woman she sat by. Emma had quickly become part of the family, glued to Tomoe's side if not Elie's. Tomoe had even had her a small katana made and trained her at dawn with Hal's permission. Emma was a little … rough around the edges for the other kids, even in the middle of an apocalypse. She needed more intensity. The life she had led before she got here required so.

Elie lifted her head toward Tomoe, admiration softening her features—until Alexiares's scowl pulled her attention away. I rolled my eyes. We'd become used to speaking freely in front of the two troublemakers ever since we realized if we didn't incorporate them into the plan, they'd find a way, anyway. Except without us being aware, their plans were significantly more dangerous. Reckless wasn't a strong enough word.

"Well." Alexiares's scowl fell into a self-satisfied smile, breaking the awkward tension among the group. "They don't call me *Bloodhound* for nothing."

"We see that now, lap dog." Reina chuckled, reaching across the table to grab his bowl of soup. They fought over it briefly until Alexiares burst into an uncharacteristic bout of laughter. A sound I'd never heard, let alone expected from him. The table stared at him with lost eyes until realization struck. Reina finished the portion she intended to steal, then slid it back to him, releasing him from her power. He snatched his spoon from her with a glare.

"You were worried about resources and what we have left," Alexiares continued in a more serious tone. "Is this really what we want to waste them on?"

I glanced at Elie. She had insisted on helping in some capacity and, with her refusal to quit at The Kitchens, I'd tasked her with working with the head of The Kitchens and Gardens. Instead of manning the coffee counter most days, she was part consultant.

Elie's shoulders raised to her ears, then dropped. "I mean, it's not like we have *no* food. We can give them scraps."

"Or you can just let the earth elementals restock," Abel countered. Oh Abel, and his *opinions* lately.

"No," I said firmly. "They have to pace themselves. Anyone running too low on magic right now is a bad thing."

The table remained quiet. They couldn't argue with that. Everyone had been on pins and needles, waiting for the other shoe to drop or another attack to happen. It wasn't as though Ronan posed a direct threat to us anymore, but one could never trust his true intentions.

Abel's eyes trailed around the table, his mouth parting to share more of his thoughts. "Since no one else is going to ask. Bad thing for what? Aren't we living life, going back to normal?"

"Oh, Abel." Reina rested her head against his exposed brown shoulders. The sleeves of his shirt cut off and showed off his lean muscle. "Haven't you learned a thing since we re-adopted you?"

"We're biding our time," Riley answered, having my back and making me grin smugly. After a second, I processed what he said. Everyone nodded in agreement, all but Abel and Emma.

"For what?" Abel's questions continued.

Tomoe's eyes widened in annoyance. As if it were obvious, but I was as confused as him. "Amaia's plan."

"Plan for …" Emma said, peering through narrowed eyes of admiration at Tomoe.

"My father's, uh." Reina shifted uncomfortably in her seat, tugging at the fold of her pleated black trousers. *Request.*

"There is no plan."

The scrape of chairs and shifting bodies made it painfully clear the entire table had turned my way—even over the hum of the dining room. The glow of the lanterns on their faces perfectly highlighted their complete disbelief. I couldn't lie to them if I tried my damnedest. Not over something this important.

I always had a plan. Not having a plan even in the best of times was to set yourself up for failure. I'd said it before and I'd say it again—a good soldier possessed a plan A, B, and C. But a soldier that *survived*—they possessed an artillery of blueprints, knowledge and a solid team at their back. I lived and would die by those words, and they knew it.

Still, if shit hit the fan, I didn't want to be responsible for them dying. They needed plausible deniability with Ronan. And if he was looking into their futures, I didn't want one of them to accidentally give anything away.

I stared them down. "Whatever."

"The plan to find whoever the fuck Ronan wants her to kill," Alexiares explained to Abel and Emma, not paying me any mind.

Reina damn near leaped out of her seat in excitement. "Ooo! Don't forget the other one. Ya know, about taking all this back. No more Bietoletti and his mean little friends disrupting council meetings." She tossed her pale, sunburned arms in the air.

"So many outcomes." Tomoe's all-knowing smirk made me want to pounce. "An abundance of possibilities."

I groaned, taking a calming inhale of herbs hanging from the ceiling and broth scented air. Dragging my hands down my face, I relented, telling them everything I'd been thinking since the day I left Ronan's war tent. This, they could know, this Ronan would assume was working in his best interest. "All right, here's what I got."

We needed to lure this mystery figure out. Bait them in a way that didn't come across as an obvious trap or a betrayal to Ronan. A waltz of war. Graceful and balanced in our every move if we wanted to pull any plan off.

After much thought, I realized contacting the person Ronan wanted dead shouldn't be a hard endeavor at all. They were already watching us. We just had to give them the opportunity to reach out.

"How do you know … about lingering eyes?" Elie whispered the latter. If she leaned any farther down the table, her neck might snap.

Abel's eyes became shifty, watching the only entrance to the room, scanning the people seated around us. "And why is no one else freaked out by it?"

This was a private dining area. It was reserved for any high-ranking officials in my troops, members of The Council, and any of our families. The decision to cut off access to the public hadn't been a slight or a way to distinguish power levels. Instead, it was to be a place of comfort. Where we could relax from our days with our comrades and loved ones and not worry about what was overheard. Business and family mixed more times than not at The Compound. The people around me evidence of it all. If anyone in this room were to betray us, it would be yet another blow to Monterey Compound, and I wasn't sure we could withstand it.

"Ronan hates them," I continued on, knowing I held their attention in the palm of my hands. "So much so, that he'd rather work with *me* than *them*. Which, if I was the dumbass his little misogynistic brain believed me to be, I'd think it was that simple."

"It's never that simple," Alexiares agreed, his grip firm on my thigh. His eyes locked on mine, steady and warm.

"He could get anyone to kill them—"

"But he didn't. He asked Amaia," Reina interrupted Abel and tapped the side of his skull as though she was disappointed he hadn't *seen* any further. Her smile slipped into something more sinister. "Daddy ain't as wise as he pretends to be. So easy to see through him once you figure out who he is."

"If I kill them, I make them a martyr. Covert thinks I'm a symbol. Peace, love, all that bullshit."

"St. Cloud thinks that too, by the way." My *Bloodhound's* laugh was silenced by my glare. The mockery in his eyes made me want to promise to punish him later. He used to have the same sentiments. I wanted to have my own laugh. If only the people of St. Cloud saw who he fell to his knees for now.

"Duluth too," Abel added.

"Actually." Riley's arm fell behind Elie and rested along the back of her chair. He quickly removed it as he caught her inching away once again. It wasn't a movement of fear, but rather disgust.

The way her small lips curled when she spoke to him. The daggers in her eyes. "Every place outside of Salem thinks that. Some more disdainfully than others."

I considered that for a moment. The impact my involvement would have on the others. Everyone had bowed to Ronan. Some because they trusted my judgment, others because they considered themselves cornered and without options, either way, I'd owe them answers by the end of this. "Whatever. If I take them out, it turns their entire cause against Monterey and Salem. More specifically, me as a leader."

"Still not seeing how that relates to them watching you," Elie said, her voice tinged with teenage defiance.

I clenched my jaw, weighing the best way to explain this. "Their cause *is* our cause." For a moment, I doubted myself. Doubted this was the right decision, to include them all. Alexiares caught my eye, tilting his head in encouragement to keep going. "They're already on our side. They're a threat because once our forces unite, that's a wrap. Covert's fucked. But if I take them out—he won't have to worry about killing me, the rebels will do it for him."

The room fell to a tense silence as people filtered out. Dinner time now moving into the time night shift filtered in to fuel up before their day began.

"So what's taking them thirty days and thirty nights to show themselves?" Reina whispered as low as she was capable of going, combing through the short ends of her hair.

"I'm not sure, but that's what we need to find out," I replied, doing my best to sound confident in what needed to be done. "Whatever the case, it's why we can't afford to do anything about any prisoners yet."

Alexiares squeezed my thigh, his hand stopping the constant bouncing of my leg. "If we torture them, and they're part of some secret militia then *we* become the fucked. And frankly, I prefer to do the fucking."

I jabbed him in the stomach as he sipped from his water. He spit it out and grimaced in pain. Elie's nose scrunched as Emma scanned the table in confusion. The others fought off their humored reactions for the sake of the youngest around. Emma's mouth was already filthy, no need to make things worse with Alexiares's vocabulary.

"Scraps it is, Els," I surmised as I maneuvered to peer past Riley and hold her gaze. "Can I trust you to take care of that?"

"Yes, ma'am." Elie smirked, a mischievous glint in her eyes.

Abel cleared his throat, his voice steady. "I'll help."

"We've got this," I muttered low and resolute. The weight of their stares didn't crush me—it fueled me. "Hell won't know what hit them."

CHAPTER THIRTEEN

TOMOE

The dark circles under her eyes. Her dark, curly hair a complete juxtaposition to the dull complexion of her sepia skin. Amaia was the poster child for dark thoughts embodied.

We left the others behind at The Kitchens. I'd offered to walk her over to the school houses to share what my conversation with Hal had uncovered. She glanced to our left, the edge of The Garden's a sad sight. We'd be okay—for now. I understood it was hard to believe when you couldn't *see* the options of the future yourself, but there was still hope.

"Okay, hit me with it." Amaia commanded as she kept her eyes focused on the world around us, her head held high.

"We finally found something from the archives," I said, tossing my braid back over my shoulder. "Lucky me, Hal was the source."

Her eyes widened slightly, brows lifting as her lips pressed into a tight line. "Yikes. How did that go?"

"Exactly as you think it would. Short and to the point. He gave me permission to look into his past so I took the faster option."

I could do whatever I wanted. I didn't need his permission. But after Alexiares had confronted me about how violated he felt about me 'watching' his past when we had an established friendship, I suppose at least a heads-up was due. After Seth, it would be dumb to say I would never cross that line. There wasn't a reason to not trust the people around me after all that we'd been through together. Unless they gave me a reason, I'd respect boundaries.

She choked on a laugh. "Would expect nothing more from you. So, the outcome?"

The stone gray stairs leading to the entrance of GLQ was a tight squeeze. I fucking hated it. When we'd been a proper compound, people kept their distance. Now it was impossible to pass through without brushing shoulders with the person next to you. The communal bathrooms had also become an issue. No one wanted to wait for over an hour to take a five-minute bath in dirty water. We couldn't build out fast enough.

It was almost as if our walls crumbling had been a gift from the universe. An opportunity to rebuild stronger than before. We held our silence until the crowd thinned out. Amaia ran her fingers against the tan bricks under an arch connecting some of the old dorms. They were temporary housing. What Prescott, Jax, and Amaia had lived in when the place first started.

"Before I say what I'm about to say, you should know this is only the word of one source."

"I'm aware of how ethnographic documentation works." She kept her voice low but her impatience was clear. Every day, all day, she was on a schedule. If there was even a second she could spare to chat with one of us outside of work, she wanted to take it.

"A simple reminder not to get ahead of yourself."

"Heard." She gritted her teeth and kicked a pebble down a side street in between a few of the Tuscan-style homes. "So out with the words or let me have five minutes of peace before I have to move on to my next task."

Wet concrete mingled with the pungent scent of dusty earth. The construction of the area moved as quickly as it could. We'd decided to build up in this section. The infrastructure supported it and it wouldn't be an eye-sore in the future given the architecture. At some point, people would care about that shit again and there was no need to do the work twice. Inefficiencies had been a pet peeve of the big three from the beginning. That hadn't changed now that it was just Amaia left.

"Hal came straight from Texas after Laurel got my note. When she died, he didn't hesitate—just headed west. That means he has no clue what's happening near Covert's border. Only thing he could do is speculate from his time on the road."

A breathy sound of amusement escaped her. "Naturally."

"Pansies were heading the same direction as them the entire time," I continued and we stopped in front of Compound Hall. The Victorian building loomed over us, casting a shadow over her face. "They moved in large herds. Typical behavior at first. That was until he realized the *pattern* of their movements weren't right. Organized. When one stopped, they all stopped. If one found food that couldn't feed the masses, they continued on. Not bothering to stop and prioritize themselves is weird as hell but it lines up with Reina's theory of migration."

"What the fuck …"

I couldn't help the way my lips curled, the expression on my face doing more talking than words could. "Said the same thing. They were everywhere. Thousands at once. More than you would think sustainable. And they ate everything. The OGs, we know they eat animals if they have no other option, but the priority was always human flesh. These guys, they took out entire fields. Cattle. Horses. Sheep. Cities filled with Transient travelers."

"They blocked off the entire city of Albuquerque. Hal and the kids barely made through with a few other survivors. Thing is, the further away from Covert they got, the more they saw. Then, they came across one of the camps."

"He's *seen* them? Firsthand? Where are they?" Amaia took a step closer to me, her rapid-fire questions said with a faux smile as citizens passed by us. She offered them a pleasant nod before turning her attention back to me.

"Middle of nowhere," I said, shoving my hands into the back of my jeans with the shrug of my shoulders. "In between major cities. He said it was about a week's walk in between."

The sun crested behind the steep, gabled peaks and ornate spires of Compound Hall. I swallowed down the lump in my throat. I didn't come here much. Even before Jax died but *especially* since he had. This was his pride and joy. All the original buildings were. Compound Hall. The Kitchens. The Arena. The places decorated with culture, thought, and care.

I was grateful those places had been spared amid destruction. My two red-haired, freckled boys were gone forever, and I hated one for taking out the other.

"With Luke and Olivia slowing his pace, that's about what? Two hundred miles?"

I dipped my head in agreement. "Give or take."

"Did he say the last time he saw one before he arrived?"

"Gallup." The fact that I had to watch Hal and the kids travel through New Mexico had been a sick joke from the universe. Talk about fucking déjà vu. "I know it's not what you're looking for—"

Amaia reached forward, gripping my hands firmly, a penetrating stare. "No. It's not, but it's a good start and I trust that you can help us figure out the rest."

"Let me guess. You want me to try to get in?"

"Mentally yes, not physically. Ronan knows what all of us look like. My guess is, so do all of his soldiers. If they 'capture' anyone on his radar, he'll know we're onto something." Amaia paused, her eyes narrowing in thought. "Scope out their security set up. Ronan's little toy can't block out any visions beyond his borders. Team up with someone in our network if you need to. Riley can handle the rest."

A mischievous smile teased my lips. "I love it when you give me orders. Don't forget the 'good girl' next time."

She gave me that deadpan stare she'd perfected—equal parts judgment and boredom. The slight glimmer in her eyes betrayed her serious demeanor. She turned, walking away without another word.

CHAPTER FOURTEEN

AMAIA

I did everything in my power to lock my emotions down before I made my way over to the schoolhouse at the edge of General Living Quarters. It was one of a few but this one in particular called to me. At Riley's persistence and my family's backing, this was my best bet on getting advice about moving forward with the children of Monterey Compound.

Three doors down, painted red. The late-spring sun warmed the wood of the door as my hand lay against it to knock. I stepped in uninvited, the knock a simple courtesy. A few dozen teenagers stared back at me in curiosity. Some of their muscles visibly tensed, their jaws clamped tight at their general standing at the door.

"General Bennett." Yasmin offered a faux smile. "What a lovely surprise."

I had no qualms with Yasmin. She didn't care for me and that alone made her irrelevant outside of her being Riley's girlfriend and a citizen of The Compound. Being general wasn't a popularity contest, and I'd forgone the idea of winning over the hearts of my soldiers' loved ones years ago.

What the fuck are you doing here, is more like the hidden daggers in her eyes. I didn't want to be here anymore than she wanted me lingering in her doorway. Duties were duties however, and I had obligations from a leadership perspective as much as I did on the battlefield.

Unfortunately for me, my friends had been correct. Delegating and consulting was my best path forward. There was no better way to decide than by gathering facts from the source. I didn't need to make every decision on my own, not when there were people who understood better than me.

Boots on the ground. That's what we called the intel soldiers we sent ahead of the masses.

"Ms. Iqbal," I greeted and closed the door behind me. "Just observing. Please, pretend I'm not here."

I offered a slight wave toward the kids grinning wide at me as I walked past them toward one of the few empty seats. The classroom was littered with art from what appeared to be different age groups. Remnants from the schools and daycare in the area had been scavenged through and brought here to decorate our schoolhouses. Maps of the world, former presidents, and all the other scholastic bullshit I'd grown up with hung in their respective corners.

Yasmin had a book down on her lap, her eyes trailing me with disdain. "Actually General Bennett, I hear this is your favorite book. Perhaps you could help the class dissect?"

Lord of the Flies waved at me in her hand. There were only a few copies, but now, with the recent influx, there were roughly 15,000 kids. That was the number of Monterey Compound residents under sixteen who attended school. There would never be enough books for them all, even if our population hadn't grown to roughly 48,000 since shit hit the fan. Taking that into account, the kids shared resources, often working in groups since we didn't bother with nonsense like homework.

I cleared my throat, the butterflies from my school days fluttered around my stomach. "Sure. In what regard? I've always found that there's something new to take away with each reread."

A boy around fourteen answered me, his coal-colored eyes boring into mine with a hint of confidence, "How the island is a direct parallel to the world that's at war."

"Yeah," the girl to his left chimed in, catching his attention and blushing under his stare. "How easily the group slides into violence comes from the science of us all."

Yasmin smiled gently. "Kathryn, I think I'm rather intrigued by that perspective. Tell us more."

"I … um, never mind." Kathryn's hair fell forward, hiding her crystal-blue eyes. A group of girls whispered behind her, snickering quietly as the kid's chin dipped, avoiding their glances.

Yasmin gave me a quick look, her eyebrow barely raised, but I understood. The kid never spoke up. I took the hint and stepped in, filling the silence before it dragged on too long. "I read it that way too—at first. Golding seems to suggest that humans at our core are savages."

"You don't believe that anymore, though?" She tucked her thick strands behind her ear with the bouncing of her leg.

"Oh, if anything, I believe it now more than ever," I said, leaning in as close as I could. "But I also think the message here is that even in our savagery, we yearn for some sort of human connection. With human connection, comes societal structure, so even the wildest of us all will still conform."

"Like Covert Province." This time, a different kid spoke up from across the room.

I couldn't see his face. With so many kids and such little space, each classroom had a minimum of a hundred students in it. More of a lecture hall than a place for quality learning, but we did what we could.

"Why do you think that is, Ryan?" Yasmin's, shiny hair was pulled into a low bun. Her sharp yet graceful features tightened out of eager encouragement.

"Survival," presumably Ryan, answered.

"I like the way you think," Yasmin winked, her dark, almond eyes captivating the surrounding students. She was good at this, the right person had found the right job, that had always been the goal here. I watched in silent awe as she turned back to face the rest of the class, her hands wild and free as she spoke. "Survival is a basic instinct for all living things, but *especially* us humans. The brain is a powerful tool. It wants to survive. Which leads us to another point: morality."

"You don't have to compromise your morals to survive," a kid, with a hint of defiance in his voice said, his posture straight despite his small frame.

"Oh?" Yasmin arched a thick brow. "That's quite a definitive answer, Raaj. General Bennett, any thoughts?"

I sat quietly for a moment, my fingers tracing around the edges of the magic-carved desk. So many thoughts circled around my mind. Weighing my words carefully, I gave the answer that any general would.

"It's easy to hold on to morals when survival is a given, when everyone's working together," I said, my eyes flickered around the class. Every single student I could see was focused on the words flowing freely from my mouth. "But that's not really survival, is it? That's just living. Ralph and the others stay grounded in civilization because nothing's truly threatened yet. That changes when the beast appears, when survival is on the line, everything changes.

It's only natural for Jack's psyche to shift—he's preparing for a fight, not just to live, but to survive."

Raaj was ready to hammer back my way. I think I had a soft spot for this kid. I hoped he never met Elie or Emma. Two were more than enough empowered children for me to stress about, I didn't need a third. "And that makes it okay for him to cast his morals aside? What he did to Piggy—"

"She didn't say that, dipshit."

"Chris!" Yasmin snapped, her glare lethal.

"The beast wasn't real though," Raaj continued, completely unfazed by the outburst. "Not really."

The class watched us debate. Their heads audibly turned as we went back and forth about the book. God, how I'd wished to be filled in a class with kids who truly gave a damn. Kids on base never cared enough, and I didn't count college since we were all paying to be there.

"Wasn't it?" I challenged. "Ralph recognized the validity of this 'beast,' but he still kept his morals intact. The beast is as real as they make it. In the end, it didn't matter though. Everyone lost."

The timer on Yasmin's desk went off. Students gathered their belongings and shuffled out, the buzz of conversation fading as the door swung shut behind the last student. I rose from the desk at the back of the room slowly, aware of Yasmin lingering up front, her eyes cool and unreadable. The silence stretched between us, thick and uncomfortable.

"You do rather well with children," Yasmin finally said, but there was no warmth in her voice, only obligation.

I glanced up, forcing a tight smile. "Thanks. I do my best not to be a raging bitch when there are kids around."

Neither of us moved. The air between us crackled with an unspoken tension. Yasmin crossed her arms, her posture a bit too rigid.

CHAPTER
FIFTEEN

AMAIA

"So," I said, hating that I was the first to speak. "I guess we're keeping literature."

"Excuse me?" Yasmin muttered, her tone flat, but her eyes sharp.

Sighing, I shook my head. "Nothing. Um, I stopped by to chat education."

"Ah," Yasmin mused, a smug smile tugging at her lips. "Riley mentioned you might, though he thought you would've done it weeks ago. I told him you wouldn't."

I watched as she made her way between the rows of desks, collecting the books left behind. *Tell me how you really feel.* Promising Riley I would try with her was one thing, dealing with her in practice was different. Even if I'd come to know her outside of

Mohammed or Riley, we'd still never be best friends. We were too … different. And I rarely enjoyed her self-satisfied attitude.

"Why would you think that?" I questioned, genuinely curious for why she thought she could read me. She didn't know anything about me outside of her partners.

"Pride." She answered as though it were obvious. "Such as in our book, Amaia, pride is a funny, dangerous thing. He kept faith in you though, and here you are."

"I'm going to go. This was a mistake—"

"No, I'm sorry. Wait." Yasmin dropped the stack of books on her desk and strode toward me. In her long stride she reached me within a few steps, latching onto my wrist. "We should try to at least be able to work together for the sake of Riley."

"Sure." I yanked my arm free, my patience wearing thin.

"So?"

"So what, Yasmin?" I snapped, the edge in my voice sharper than I intended.

"The reason you came here."

"Right," I muttered, already regretting this.

"Actually, before you say anything, there's something I want to show you." Yasmin gestured toward a set of paintings toward the far wall. Paintings hung like a silent gallery. She walked over and motioned for me to follow. "Beautiful, aren't they?"

I forced a nod, my gaze sliding over the brushstrokes. "Uh, yeah. A lot of talent around The Compound, I see." They were beautiful, but they weren't exactly Picasso. I played along, humoring her, unable to shake the sense that something wasn't right.

Yasmin nodded proudly before moving to a nearby closet. She pulled out a few more canvases, laying them carefully across the desks. I watched, my confusion growing as I scanned the paintings.

I moved closer. My stomach turned as I stared at one in particular—a chaotic swirl of jagged lines and smudges, the image so twisted it was hard to tell what it even was. Until you did. Then it was clear as the sky on a perfectly sunny day.

"What's this?" I asked, my voice barely above a whisper. The horror was unmistakable in my tone.

Yasmin leaned in, her eyes glinting with something I couldn't place. No. I could. *Concern.* "That one's from one of my evening students. She's ten."

"Is she a new arrival?"

"No." Yasmin lowered her voice, hesitation at words she itched to release from the tip of her tongue. "She's a *Seer.*"

"What?" I ground out.

Yasmin bowed her head, kicking her sneakers one foot over the other. "Her parents asked me not to disclose."

"You've got to be fucking kidding me. You're not that damn stupid, Yasmin."

She reached across the little space there was between us and covered my mouth. "Shh. Lower your voice."

I almost punched her. "Aren't you a mandatory reporter or something?" I asked, smacking her hand away.

"This isn't The Before. My only obligation is to keep the trust of these kids."

Various insults formed on my lips but I thought better of it. *For Riley. For Riley. For Riley.* I reminded myself. I pinched my hands in front of my face, forcing myself to center. "I understand that and commend you for it, truly. But there's a reason why we document magic, Yasmin. That's a hell of a gift with no guidance."

"And who's going to help her?" Yasmin, however, chose not to hide the disdain in her voice. "Tomoe?"

"Yes. Or literally anyone on The Council. This is a big thing, she needs mentorship."

She brushed me off. Dismissing me as though she had the authority to do so. "We can talk about this later, that's not what I'm trying to show you."

"Then spit it out or keep your secrets to yourself." This conversation wasn't finished. Not by a long shot.

"This is hard for you, isn't it?" Yasmin whirled on me, arms crossed over her chest. "Having Riley show someone else an ounce of affection."

And this was officially going about as well as I'd expected. I despised the way she said it. As if I owned Riley and his life wasn't his own. If that was what she thought then she didn't deserve him at all. "Given the gravity of our problems right now, Yasmin, that is the very least of my worries. Riley can do whatever he wants."

"Oh, he will. That doesn't change, no matter the issues I have with you."

"Good." I shrugged.

"Good?" Her eyes narrowed, disbelief etched across her features. "That's it?" The frustration in her tone simmered beneath the surface.

"What is it you want from me, Yasmin? To give Riley my blessing? He doesn't need that." I meant it. It was me and Riley against the world. He'd said the words himself. Even if Yasmin was Riley's forever, there was no threat to *our* relationship. He was my brother, my closest friend, that would never change.

"He wants it!"

That was fucking news to me. I winced at the words. The room plunged into a tense, suffocating silence. Neither of us moved, the air thick with unsaid things, the kind of stillness where even a breath might shatter it all.

"He has it …" I cleared my throat and shifted my weight from the built up tension in my knees. "I have no problem with you, Yasmin. If you think Riley is holding back for some reason, then that's not on me."

"Bullshit," she challenged.

There was so much bite in her. I knew she wasn't my biggest fan after Mohammed, but this, this vitriol, it was new. She wasn't usually this emotional—not to this extent.

"Look, I'm not exactly the warmest person in the room. I don't know what you want me to say—"

"Forget it," Yasmin cut in, her voice sharp with finality. "That one"—she gestured toward the piece by the door—"that's from a year ago. But this, this is now. All of it."

"I don't understand," I muttered, studying the gore art she shook in front of my face.

"You came here to ask which subjects to cut and which to keep now that things are shifting, right? Here's your answer." She tossed the drawing aside, her voice edged with frustration. "Nothing. You can't change a damn thing because what these kids need right now is stability. They don't feel safe. If anything, they need more. More survival lessons, more combat training—especially the basics. We're not sliding back into illiteracy on my watch."

"I don't know how to do any of that without working these kids to the ground. Between their work assignments and school, when are they supposed to be kids?"

"Amaia." Yasmin's tone softened for a brief second. "There's a time and place for everything. And trust me, 'being kids' is the last thing on their minds. What they need is confidence—in every aspect—to survive. You know it, every adult here knows it, and those kids need to know it too. This art? It's dark because they're terrified. Literature like *Lord of the Flies* helps them process that fear. They see themselves in it and learn to think critically, to prepare for the worst. Take away their literature and art, and you take away the only outlets they have for coping while we prep them for what's out there."

"How can they know what's beyond the wall?"

"The *Seer*, she shares some things." Yasmin paused and bit down on her lip. Her head swayed side to side, considering if she should keep going. "New arrival kids do too. Never in my classroom, but I see the kids rush around them for stories when they're done for a day and heading home. It's not just that, Amaia, they don't feel safe here—as in, Monterey Compound. Not since the walls were breached. To tell the truth, no one does."

I blinked, caught off guard. "That's news to me … Thank you, for sharing that. Can I ask why this is the first I'm hearing of it?"

"If you want a list of reasons, we'll be here all day. The main one? People respect you. They love you. Monterey Compound wants you as their leader—that's never changed. The effort you put into keeping us safe hasn't gone unnoticed."

"But?"

"*But,*" Yasmin said. "The effort of keeping us safe does not equate to the feeling of safety once it's been compromised. That takes time."

It was a fair assessment—one I couldn't deny. To be completely fucking honest, I possessed similar sentiments. *I* didn't have the luxury of expressing that, however. Alexiares was the only one who understood half of what I was going through, and even then, he didn't know it all. I didn't want my family to worry. If I showed any sign of fear, of doubt, then that was it. The rest would all fall apart. Everyone in The Compound was barely holding it together, if I broke, they all would. Last time was lesson enough. Jax had died, and Mohammed… he'd paid the price for my grief.

"And"—I hesitated—"how do you feel? Do you feel safe?"

"No." Yasmin paused, then sighed. "Actually … that's a lie. I do, when I'm asleep next to Riley. But I know it can be ripped away in a second. I try not to get used to it."

"I'm not apologizing for grieving," I said. My chest tightened as the fire beneath my skin clawed for release, pulling me back into that pit of grief, the unbearable tearing at my heart. "But Mohammed was special, and I should've kept it together. I should've been there for the soldiers, made sure we stayed protected. That's on me."

"Keep your apologies. The only thing I want is a promise that you won't let yourself fall apart again. That you won't make me lose another love."

I scoffed, a bitter laugh escaping. "Do I need to remind you the reason I fell apart? I'm only human Yasmin, and sometimes humans need to hit rock bottom before they surface again."

"As much as I wish that could be true Amaia, it is not." Her stone-cold gaze hardened. "You don't get to hold yourself to the same standards as everyone else because you are not *everyone else.* You are a leader. I had faith in you once, and I'd like to again."

"I hope that someday you can." I swallowed hard. "As you are acutely aware, healing and grief aren't linear. You can't control them. And I'm regretfully sorry to be the reason you understand that."

I turned to leave, but Yasmin's voice stopped me at the door. "You're going to get him killed, you know. Whatever you're planning … even if it's you, he'll die too."

My chest tightened, fire searing my skin. The candles around the room flickered out all at once.

I stood still for a moment, then faced her, my voice measured. "Thank you, Yasmin, for your advice. I'll be sending someone to work with the kids after their final activities starting Monday. Her name is Lola. She'll be at your disposal for as long as she's here. There's a lot to learn. As for the *Seer,* Tomoe is officially her mentor, effective immediately. I trust you'll find the right words to not cause an uproar with the parents."

I didn't break eye contact, my voice dropping enough to make sure the message landed. "And, Yasmin? Don't you ever say something like that to me again. If I even catch a whisper of you bringing it up around Riley—hinting toward my death or his on my account—we'll have a real problem. He doesn't need those seeds of doubt planted in his head. Don't let your relationship make you careless. I am still the general, and I *do* have final say on who stays and who goes."

CHAPTER SIXTEEN

RILEY

I didn't sob for Jax. There was no wail that burst free from my throat at Mohammed's death. I allowed only a few tears to fall in the wake of Prescott. My grief was a quiet, unrelenting ache. A slow leaking wound that was impossible to stitch.

It controlled my life. Haunted me, a ghost lingering in a graveyard. Grief seeped into my everything—my thoughts, my breaths, the damned spaces between my words. No one noticed it. I couldn't let them. They had their own shit to deal with. Amaia was focused on keeping this place going.

If I brought up Prescott or Jax, her focus could shift. She would lose everything they fought for. I refused to be the reason she let them down. Yasmin only wanted to move forward. To focus on the future. And maybe that's what made it worse. The fact that it lingered. Simmered. Waited and lurked until I was so beat down, I couldn't hide it anymore.

"Strike." I commanded over the chaos of The Pit.

Elie grunted. Her kick headed straight for my kneecap. I allowed it to happen, going with the flow of her training. It wasn't a full spar. Just going through routine, a mindless activity for the tension of our relationship and the lack of focus on both ends. I didn't want to be here anymore than she did, but I had responsibilities. Duties and oaths I'd sworn. Promises to keep to my family.

"Strike." I caught this one. The full force of her kick powered directly to my kidney.

Training her had become draining. The mental warfare of her anger beat me down in ways I refused to admit, let alone show. I knew there was more to it. Her anger toward me was justified on several accounts. That didn't mean each blow of her words or occasional strike with the intent to hurt didn't pierce my heart.

Elie tossed her body forward. Her curly brown hair fell free as her hair tie loosened at the movement. She hooked her arm around my knee and the consequence of such a fatal mistake hit me the moment it happened. Too eager. She always had been when it came to hand to hand. Elie threw her weight back too soon. Her grip loosened, making the momentum to knock me off balance impossible. I held onto her by the ankle.

"Urgh." Elie kicked out, not pleased to be left dangling in the air, curls skimming the ground. A sharp scowl twisted her face. I sighed, dropping her with less compassion than I could be proud of. "I'm too small. It doesn't matter what I do!"

"What do you think I'm trying to teach you, Eleanor? You aren't smaller than Amaia. You think she'd fare any better against someone my size without proper training?" My voice came out more clipped than intended.

Elie scrambled to her feet, brushing off the dust of The Pit with quick, jerky movements. "She's *Umbra Mortis*. It doesn't matter what she *would* be able to do." Her eyes flashed. That familiar stubbornness set in like stone.

"You think she hasn't met her match before? You don't become general by accident," I hissed. She'd damn near died gaining her position and I hadn't been there to save her.

"No," she muttered, the impending insult soft but sharp enough to cut deep. "But in your case, there's always nepotism."

I stepped closer, looming over her. "Stop." The command was simple, but my voice was low.

As far back as my memory went, I don't recall being angry—fueled by hurt from someone I never expected. I didn't want to add insult to injury and lose my temper. It would get us nowhere.

"What?" She shrugged, her arms folded tightly across her chest. "I don't know what you're talking about."

The way she looked at me, that smug grin powered by so much hatred—it made my blood simmer. I closed my eyes. *One Mississippi. Two Mississippi. Three Mississippi. Four Mississippi. Five Mississippi. Six Mississippi. Seven Mississippi. Eight Mississippi. Nine Mississippi. Ten Mississippi.*

Counting helped. Numbers helped. Gave me somewhere else to focus. I exhaled slowly. It was an effort to keep my voice steady. "Are we going to move past this one day, or should I call it quits and ask Moe to train you instead? We can't keep doing this. This is important for your survival. You will gain nothing from me as a teacher if you doubt every instruction I give."

I gestured vaguely between us, begging, pleading with her to stop. She was tearing my heart apart with the guilt of grief. A soldier cannot let it simmer, or it will destroy us.

"Move past? Move—" A clipped, erratic laugh bellowed from her. She shoved a harsh, pointed, intentional finger into my chest. Her light brown eyes danced in anger. In rage. In blame. "You killed him!" The words were a knife. "It is your fault he's dead. You are the only one to blame for him being *tortured.* You know you stole peace from him? Right?" Her voice cracked, but her fury didn't waver.

Eleanor. Elie. *Elie.* God, she was so similar to London. London, my little sister. A name long buried in the recesses of my mind. A fissure in my memory in an attempt to block out the pain. Yet here it was. Threatening to break through. I had to keep moving forward. I had to.

But everything about Amaia—it reminded me of her.

The fire in her eyes. The way she carried the weight of the world on her shoulders. Elie resembled them both. It was all a vicious cycle of reincarnation before I had time to grieve the pain I'd caused the last.

Why does everything in my life have to be so … so … so *this?*

Responsibilities on top of pain and sorrow and my God, endless amount of disappointment. To me. To others. Me to others. I was suffocating. *Why can't I just have a win? Why can't I do anything right? Why does everything have to end in failure?*

Why am I a failure?

I swallowed down an agonizing lump full of dishonor. Regret. I couldn't remember the last time I regretted anything. I'd built my life around the belief that everything happened for a reason. Every action had a purpose, every decision a consequence. Everything in life appeared to have an answer. Things made sense. Even in the landscape of a world filled with uncertainty and despair, there were answers. There was science. Things would happen that made you glad someone you knew didn't live to see it.

Prescott's death was none of those things. The more I looked back, the more I played the scene over and over and over again in my head, the ever burning flame of doubt simmered in my heart. It wasn't some unfortunate inevitability I could rationalize.

Emma walked up to us, tying a flannel around her waist and whistling an upbeat tune. She clocked the tension between us and took a giant step back. I watched her out of the corner of my eyes as she found something to pretend to be busy with.

"I did what I was told. What my responsibilities required of me. I have an obligation to put the people here first, even if it means screwing myself in the end. That's what being a soldier means. What being a leader is. You bear the burden and take the fall so your people never feel the consequence of your misjudgments."

"Bullshit." Elie's cackle pierced my ears. "You would have never done that if it were Amaia."

If she had stabbed me, it would have hurt less. For a moment, I stood there, still and quiet, the question ricocheting around my head. Could I honestly say I would've made the same call? I was a lot of things, but I was not a liar.

"We could have saved him," Elie whispered.

What I hated the most about her statement was the truth of it. Prescott had survived their torture, after all. But out there, in the chaos, with the fire of unknown weapons, magic, and death all around, it hadn't seemed as though there was much of a choice. Prescott had made that final call. Ordered us away. He had known the risk—we all did every time we left the relative safety of our gates. But that was a cop out. A way for me to avoid responsibility.

"Out in the field, there is always a chance you'll make a decision you'll live to regret one day. It's part of the job."

"So that's it?" Her hazel eyes ebbed closer to green as they blazed with fury. "I should just get used to it? Prescott was like a father to you. How dare you chalk him up to some dumb statistic! He was a *person*—*our* person."

I wanted to kick myself. She wasn't just talking about Prescott anymore. This was about her parents. About the loss she'd barely processed. With everything going on, I'd forgotten that Elie hadn't experienced death like the rest of us. Not in the same way. It wasn't a battle of losses, but rather the perspective I needed to know how to handle Elie going forward.

Elie was from a small town down the coast. Her family had remained intact as they sheltered, surviving on her father's boat, tucked away from the worst of the chaos. It wasn't until they ran out of supplies that they'd come ashore. It was there that they were picked up by one of the recruitment teams. She hadn't lived through the brutality the rest of us had. Elie had never watched her world crumble piece by piece until now.

"You never get used to it, Elie." My voice softened, but I didn't let the edge leave. She needed to hear the truth. "But this won't be the last time you lose someone. You need to find a way to deal with it, to process it, or it'll kill you. You'll end up dying chasing after ghosts."

There was a brief glimpse of acceptance behind her now blank stare. "What do you want me to say? Thank you? Thank you." Her tired voice dripped with sarcasm. "There. Happy? Does that make your heart all warm and fuzzy? Will it help you sleep better at night?"

Her words stung, but I didn't flinch. I wasn't groveling for her gratitude. I simply wanted her to understand—to survive. Everything else was outside my control.

My chest tightened as the memory of it all came back full force. "I had orders. Orders Prescott demanded I upheld in his last moments. Don't disrespect his death by questioning the outcome. He was a soldier before all else. Prescott went out the way he'd expected to twenty times over, protecting those he cared about."

The words didn't register with her. Instead, she stared back at me, jaw slack, eyes blinking back with disbelief. How could I expect her to understand my perspective, after all? With over a decade of life experience on her and navigating the onset of the apocalypse on my own, we would never see things the same way. The only one of us that had a chance of relating slightly was Abel, and he had the heart of a soldier. He would always put The Compound first. It was all he had tethering him to reality during his time in Duluth.

"Following orders? Sounds like a lame excuse to not have to do the hard thing. To make tough choices as unscathed as possible. I don't know, *empathize* a bit. Everything is so black and white with you, Riley, and honestly, it makes me feel bad for you. It's sad," Elie said, her entire demeanor laced with venom as she twisted, diving the knife through my heart deeper, doing irreparable damage.

I clenched my fists, nails digging into my calloused palms as I fought to maintain my composure, but she wasn't done. Another wisp of blonde hair came into view in my peripheral vision. Elie's eyes scanned behind my shoulder, taking them in before she continued.

"You lost three people close to you in less than a year and you haven't even shed a tear. Three people are dead and each one of them died mindlessly following protocol. Following *'orders.'* There are times to be a soldier, Riley, and then there're times to put your family first."

Heat surged through my chest, rage building with every word she spoke. Elie stepped closer, her eyes locked on mine, unflinching.

"I hope I never lose my humanity," she said, her voice quieter now but no less piercing. "I would hate to end up like you."

I swallowed hard, forcing down the lump of anger burning in my throat. Keeping my voice even took everything I had, but I couldn't let myself snap. She wasn't just talking about Prescott. She was talking about her mother. About how I'd told her to wait. How I'd convinced her mom to hold off on searching for her father until I could gather a team.

And maybe—just maybe—if I hadn't done that, if I'd let her go when she wanted to, things would be different. Maybe Elie's mom wouldn't have jumped. It was the maybes in life that weighed on us all the most.

"I answer to my general and only my general. If you want to be a soldier, Eleanor, then I expect you to do the same."

Her eyes flared with a heat that burned right through me, and before I could get another word in, she turned on her heels, storming off toward North Gate. Not once did she look back. For a brief second, I felt that familiar urge rise in my chest, the one that told me to go after her, to stop her from making whatever reckless choice was about to follow. I always tried to stop it. Always thought I could fix things if I acted fast enough.

But I didn't move.

Because I knew better by now. Chasing after her wouldn't change a damn thing.

I'd been down this road before. With Abel. I could still picture his face, the way his eyes pleaded with me that day. I tried with everything I had to keep him safe. To fix everything before it could break. I followed every protocol. Every rule. And none of it saved him. He still left in the end.

And now I was standing here again, watching someone else I cared about walk away, knowing there was nothing I could do to shield them from their choices. The weight of that knowledge, of failure … As hard as it was, I had to let her make her own choices. No matter how much it tore me apart inside. No matter how much it went against every instinct I had to protect her, to stop her from crashing.

Emma stared between us, trying to decide what to do, who to stay with. She shifted her stance, pacing side to side. Inevitably, she chose Elie. As she should. The two of them could protect each other if they wouldn't accept help from anyone else.

I released the tension building inside me, though it came out uneven and strained. Elie had to figure out her own path. This wasn't the time to coddle her or hold her hand through the pain. If I'd learned anything, it was that trying to shield people only delayed the inevitable.

I thought of my sister. Thought of how I hovered over her, watching every step she took, and how none of that stopped her from meeting death at its door.

No matter how much I wanted to believe I could, I couldn't save everyone. God knows I would try. But somehow all that trying had done nothing but carve out this empty, hollow space inside me, and now I was too damn tired to pretend it didn't hurt.

"Riley," Jessa's southern twang was the last thing I wanted to hear in this moment. "We need to talk."

CHAPTER
SEVENTEEN

RILEY

"We aren't familiars," I grumbled, finally turning away from the empty spot where the girls had stood to meet Reina's girlfriend, Jessa, face to face. "It's Lieutenant Sullivan."

She tucked her blonde strands behind her ear and tossed her hair over her shoulder. Coal was smeared around her icy eyes. Darker, more pronounced than Reina ever did. She smiled at me, "We're family adjacent. No bonus points for that?"

"Family adjacent, for now."

"Here I was thinking it was Reina that would take the longest to forgive," her smile didn't drop, though to my pleasure, it wavered slightly.

"Reina loves love, regardless of how dirty you did her by spying for Ronan," I dismissed their relationship. Not because I didn't have faith in Reina, but because I knew that in her heart, she would hold on to whatever she could from her life before she'd left our gates. Change was hard for her, so me, the others, we would step in where we could. "She doesn't see through you like the rest of us."

Her tan hand fell over her heart and she took an inch closer to me than appreciated. "Ouch. And she said you were the nicest."

"Imagine how the others express their fondness for you."

"I'm here to help," she said. "Doesn't that make a difference?"

"No. I'm not in the mood for this. What is it that you want to share?"

"Can we go to your office for this?" she whispered. It was unnecessary given the metal clinking and groans of pain around us in The Pit. "It's … confidential."

"You're a spy. I'd expect nothing less," I said as I brushed past her.

She followed close behind. Her presence sent a crawling feeling up my spine. I refused to trust her. I didn't care what Reina said. It was my responsibility to take care of The Compound and Reina was included in that responsibility. We'd become closer since her return. I wouldn't fail her either.

"*Was* a spy," Jessa clarified. "Now I work for The Compound … in any capacity."

I knew what she was hinting at. She was a fool if she thought me to be a fool. We weren't about to trade secrets with a former spy. There were no double agents within my ranks. I appreciated loyalty on top of everything, no matter the cost, no matter the emotions one may acquire while doing their job. A spy that flipped wasn't worth much more than the information they were able to provide.

"Once a spy, always a spy."

"You're a lieutenant. Abel's just a soldier now."

"Once a spy, always a spy," I repeated as I unlocked the heavy wooden door to what was now my quarters. She stepped in after me, and I motioned for her to take a seat. I hadn't changed any of the furniture out here. The memories that had been made … I didn't want to wipe them away. Fear of erasure. I supposed Reina wasn't the only one with a fear of change. "Can I get you anything? Water? Bourbon?"

"I'm more of a moonshine gal."

"Figures," I mumbled, taking a seat in the leather chair behind the desk I'd spent days making sure suited all Amaia's needs. Wood carving was fun when you had the magic to make it as elaborate as one could want in half the time. "Well."

"What if I were to tell you there's another *Seer* here?" Jessa's smile finally fell. Reina's girlfriend was no longer here, a spy falling into a debriefing routine now present before me.

That caught my attention. I leaned forward slightly, not wanting to appear too eager. "Go on."

"There's a little girl, around ten. Her family would have arrived around the time of Jax's passing."

"We would have known if another *Seer* entered The Compound," I said dismissively. "Gifts are recorded upon entry, as you know."

Jessa pushed to her feet with excitement in her tone. Her long legs crossed the room and stopped directly in front of me. "Not this one. She's young. Her parents would have claimed her as a simple Scholar to avoid detection."

"Do you have a name?" I asked, dragging my gaze from her dirty sneakers up to her eyes.

She didn't budge. "No."

"What do you mean, no?"

"I have a face." She grimaced. "Vaguely. It's been tugging on my memory."

"Ronan?"

Jessa offered two sure nods. "Reina mentioned Moe saw the VeilSight Disruptor from a vision. Has she told you the details?"

"This family has no more secrets."

She paced over to Amaia's bookshelves. Thumbing through the books she'd left behind, she pulled one loose and inspected it. Jessa flipped it over and glanced over the back before slipping it back where it belonged. "Right," she whistled. "Anyway, the Veil-Sight Disruptor has kept my mind fuzzy. Tugging on the tendrils of my memory before I was debriefed. The more time I've spent away, the more I remember."

I trailed her around the room, marking exactly what she had touched. I could never be too sure with this one. *No*, I certainly could not. "You want us to believe that Ronan enlisted a child as a spy?"

"What? Like it's beneath Monterey to do so?" She arched a sun blonde brow. "She's not a spy. But she was one of their best-kept secrets and her power extends beyond normal *Sight*. Ronan doesn't know where she is. He's been trying to find her."

"She's powerful?"

Jessa found her way back to the leather couch and lounged across it. "Extremely."

"We just have to figure out who she is," I muttered, more to myself than the woman before me.

"Exactly."

"I'm assuming that's no easy task?" There had to be some catch.

She shakes her head, "No. Her family fled to protect her."

"And they chose the place he hated the most?"

More questions surged through my mind. Why could Jessa remember some things and not others? What would happen if we found this girl? Why … why … did they seek refuge in Monterey, of all places?

That answer was easy to assume. We were the safest place they could be. With our walls and our military, for a long time, we had seemed impenetrable. And we would have been, had we not fallen from the inside out.

"Who better to protect her than Ronan's biggest fear," Jessa confirmed without me having to voice the question aloud.

"This is great information, Jessa." Jessa smiled though it fell at my next words, "How does this better serve The Compound? We have three *Seers*, and several more in our network. All who are powerful—"

"He designed the VeilSight Disruptor *and* the wards around her magic. If Ronan has it on, she has the potential to bypass them both."

Shit. We needed her. Unfortunately, to get to her, it appeared I may need to rely on Jessa.

"So, how do we find her? Take you around the classrooms, pile all the kids out in front of Compound Hall?"

"No." Her answer came fast and sure. She sat up straight, eyes boring into mine. "That will scare her family away. You need an in. Someone to gain their trust."

"Excuse me if I'm being presumptuous, but I don't think that's you."

Jessa's laugh was carefree, as though she had known that was never a solution. "Oh, it's definitely not me. Like I said, I'm only here to help."

"How thoughtful," I said. Picking up the stack of security enhancements to review for the gates, I shuffled them around with dismissal, not bothering to glance back up. "Thank you for the information. I'll take this to the general."

"That's it?" Jessa asked as she rose back to her feet. She tucked her hands into the back pockets of her trousers. They were stained with dirt from The Gardens. The only place she was currently trusted. Amaia needed the extra hands, anyway.

"Did you expect more?"

"No, I just thought—"

"What? That you could help us?" I chuckled. Rude as it may be, I didn't have any patience left in me today to care. "A spy is a spy, Jessa. We appreciate all the ways you have helped, but there is no room for anyone on our team who isn't Compound first. *You* are Reina first. Here or not, you will never be Compound first. My general allows for second chances, I do not."

Jessa may have told Reina she had spied for Ronan out of necessity, but we would never be able to prove that as fact. Facts were what I lived by. Facts were what I could trust. And the fact was, Jessa had only decided to do the right thing out of her love for Reina. That made her a liability. In love was desperation. She would do anything for the relationship, even if that meant spying for Ronan when she claimed she no longer did.

"But Alexiares—"

"Is not part of this conversation. A conversation that is now very much over."

The room fell to near silence. The only sound was the critters I now called on to help clear the room. Jessa stood still as a statue, her face hard, taking me in. Another moment passed, and she nodded once in acceptance. "If you need me, you know where she keeps me."

"Better than where Amaia would." With that, the door latched shut.

CHAPTER
EIGHTEEN

AMAIA

I didn't want to get comfortable. Something about being with Alexiares made me religious. I found myself praying every night and rising sun to be lucky enough to spend what time I had left in this life with him by my side.

There were times when I worried about what little humanity I had left. Around him, I didn't feel any of that. I felt normal, okay, *safe*. I didn't have to project false confidence or apologize for making the tough choices and tucking my empathy to the side. With him, there was security that I would never become the villain in at least one set of eyes.

Fire crackled against the wood inside the fireplace. The room was warm in both the sweet, subtle scent of ashen wood and heat that radiated from within. I teased the flames with my magic and they pulsated to my will. Alexiares trailed his fingers along the side of my arm as I leaned into him.

Suckerpunch slept lazily underneath the couch, ignoring the sensation of my combat boots stuck under his wide body. His soft snores deepened the comfort I had finally settled into, in what was once Prescott's. I reached down, rubbing Harley's long snout as she whined for the nonexistent leftovers inside our bowls. We'd ditched The Kitchens for our favorite little spot in Entertainment Square. Chili and smoothies weren't exactly on the menu, but the owner had been working her ass off to grow what she could. Small portions of creative delicacies were now the staple of her spot. She offered them at a fair cost a few times a week and had sent a message earlier demanding I stop through. She'd saved some for us, insisting that I deserved a decent meal too.

This was the quiet before the storm.

Tomorrow I'd meet with Ronan. I wasn't quite sure what I hoped to accomplish anymore. Ronan, if nothing else, was predictably unpredictable. What was the difference between his emissaries stationing their ass at every council meeting, reporting back on the details of The Compound and a spy? Nothing. Everything. *Fuck.*

The door opened behind us and I turned my head. Elie and Emma I expected. Two bloodied up small children accompanying them, I did not. The four of them stood there staring at us, not saying a word. I couldn't even make out their age or gender beneath all their grime and gore.

"Hi?" I greeted them in confusion.

The dogs were on her within seconds. Their interest shifted to our surprise guests, who stood frozen with unease.

"What's up?" Elie said. Snapping her fingers, she called Harley and Suckerpunch off. They sat instantly, watching as she grabbed the kids' hands and made a beeline toward the bathroom.

"These miniature people don't look like ours, Elie." Alexiares stood from the couch and watched on. He made no move to cut them off yet they stopped in their tracks at his words, regardless. His ink coated arms crossed over his broad chest, dark brows arching in expectation.

"They are now," Elie said slowly, fixing her tone. "Casey and Hayley."

Emma's messy blonde hair was stuck against her sweat beaded face. Her smile was bright and encouraging. "We found them."

"The weird thing about kids that don't belong here is that it's impossible to stumble across them." I grumbled and paced across the room.

The oldest winced as I dropped to my knees before them. I kept my distance. His eyes held no fear—only a menacing threat. Protective instinct.

"That's cuz we went outside the walls," Emma added, doubling over in pain from Elie's elbow jab to the stomach. "Why'd you do *that*? You know, you're so annoying. I literally helped you after my dad told me I'd be grounded forever if I left again. Gigs up. They aren't stupid."

"What?" The words were a near silent growl off my lips. Alexiares closed in behind me, his hand falling on my shoulder in an attempt to calm. I glanced over in warning and it fell.

Elie shrugged, either not reading or caring enough to read the room. "Too many people here. I needed some air."

"There's perfectly good air inside The Compound." Alexiares retorted, his hand running across the top of his recently shaved head.

With the cut low against his scalp, the detailing on the inked lines running around the side of his head were visible. I knew all of his tattoos held a story, but this one screamed nothing but pain. Wanting that pain to be known. To be visible. It was beautiful— and this cut did nothing but distract me.

"Yeah," Elie surmised, releasing her light brown curls from her bun. "Well, it's a bit stuffy with all the new additions."

"You came back with two feral children. Find a different excuse."

"And quickly." I added to Alexiares's statement, trying not to laugh. Right now I had to be serious. Firm. Elie and a gentle hand didn't work.

I hated it. I missed just being her friend. The flames went out in the quiet of the room. Elie's harsh stare didn't flicker. It was Emma who broke the silence. "I went so she wouldn't die alone. Can we call my snitching even and you not tell my dad?"

The sudden, sharp sneeze from the younger one made me jump. I'd forgotten they were even in the room. I blinked and bent to their level. My eyes flickered between them. The oldest, a boy, was no older than six which made the state of the smaller one, likely his sister, an even more jarring sight. They looked like hell. I softened a bit. Motioning for them to follow me, I placed them into the bay window, allowing them to watch the citizens of The Compound. A happy distraction for the conversation we were about to have around them. With a simple hand motion, the dogs understood what to do. Harley licked my exposed ankle as she passed by.

Alexiares stood hovering over the girls. Their eyes remained fixed on the floor, their shoulders hunched in the quiet tension of the room. I straightened up and rubbed my temples. My thoughts were soaring, racing through my mind so fast I couldn't focus on a single one. *How the fuck did I end up here?* The weight of this past year pressed on my chest at the most inconvenient of times. I couldn't keep wasting my energy focusing on this shit.

Life had flipped on its head in the blink of an eye. Here I was, playing house, lecturing someone who had been a sister to me, acting as if I were a mother hen. It seemed as if only yesterday Jax and I had our damning conversation about his ideal version of the future. It had shattered my illusions on what we were meant to be. Now, I was here. Living his dream. Playing house. Except in this reality, with a Bloodhound. I'd spent the morning leading. Tomorrow, I'd be back running shit as a general.

Leader today, protector tonight, warrior tomorrow. The constant shifting of roles nearly sent me reeling. A whirlwind of responsibility, decisions, and emotional fucking landmines.

I made my way back over to them. "Explain yourself."

"There were Pansies. There was a baby crying and a little boy doing his best to draw attention away from the house in a tree," Elie side stepped my question. "Would you have preferred we left them to die? Seems like that's a trend around here."

I fought to keep my cool. Her accusation hung in the air. The challenging gaze directed at me from someone I was accustomed to having nothing my carefree laughs with was heartbreaking. Elie was having a hard time. I knew that. But she refused to talk about what happened every time I tried. Without a way to understand what she was thinking or how she was coping, I found myself lost on how to support her. So I did the only way I knew how, the same way I would one of my soldiers.

"I know it's easy to relax now that things appear to have calmed down but that would be a mistake. Going outside the wall, doing something this reckless, it could get you killed. Both of you."

"Something reckless?" Elie snickered at me. "Didn't know reckless and helping were synonyms."

"Oh please. Preach to another choir because this one sings the same tune," I said, tossing a hand in dismissal.

Alexiares let out a low, amused sound, his arms folding casually across his chest as a hint of a smirk plays at the corner of his mouth.

"They were OGs," Elie added in juvenile confidence. "I think we can handle ourselves."

Technically, by today's standards, Elie was an adult. She was closer to seventeen than sixteen and here, that was The Before's eighteen. Still, I couldn't help but see her as someone I needed to protect. An extension of me. And some part of me knew she felt the same way. Otherwise she wouldn't be here. She'd be out on her own, doing as she pleased, instead, she chose to call my home hers—listening to lectures and guidance. Elie did not have to be here. The fact that she was told me enough.

"There were only a few. It's okay, I promise I won't let her hurt herself," Emma said, the reassurance in her eyes admirable. She genuinely thought she could protect them both.

I could see the worry etched into Emma's tan face. Subtle, but there. Unmistakable. Since the Soulfire explosion, Emma's confidence had shifted. There was always this hint of trauma in her eyes. Like she had seen death, stared it in the eyes several times and told it to go fuck itself but not walked away without the memory. Emma had a shadow over her that had never quite lifted though she'd been in good hands. Hal had done all that he could to shelter the girls from his grief at the expense of quietly unraveling himself. We all were in our own ways, I supposed. The only option we had however, was to keep pushing forward.

"Wait, all OGs?" I asked. "You're sure?"

"Yeah," Elie said slowly, her narrow eyes squinted back at me.

"Supports our reports," Alexiares leaned in and muttered in my ear. "One week without Ronan's sack of corpses."

I mulled it over. We'd try to decode this later. Another topic for another time. Whatever was going on, it wasn't an act of kindness. With Ronan, nothing ever was. Nothing ever would be. Gifts of sincerity that were meant to maintain the peace weren't his style of leadership.

"You can't ever be too cautious. Don't forget that," I warned.

Elie's hands fell to her hips, her face stuck in mockery. *"I'm proud of you, Elie. Keep watching out for the small guy, Elie. Don't forget your humanity, Elie. It's all we have left, Elie.* It's like I live with a totally different person!"

"You're mad at me because I want to keep you alive?" I asked, mouth hanging in shock if only for a moment. "I expect *everyone* to keep their wits about them at all times, but especially you. No matter where you are, home or not—with one of us or the dogs or not—no matter the circumstance, you must remain vigilant. The proof of the consequences if you don't are all around us."

The room sank into another heavy silence. Stilted, thick air filled with unspoken tension added to the weight of shared despair. No one dared break it this time. Not for a few minutes.

Elie's brows furrowed against her light brown skin. Irritation flashed across her face, but then, she softened. The tension in her eased as realization dawned in her eyes. "They're kids, Amaia. One's pretty much a baby. I don't care what happens to me. I refuse to walk away. We don't have to hide to be safe. You gave us the tools. All we need to do is use them. Trust our training. The best use of our skills will always be to help others. *You* taught me that."

Emma cut in abruptly, trying to reason in their defense. "Casey said their mom and dad were like, killed by some monster or something. Pretty sure that means they got eaten by a Pansie. They don't have nowhere else to go. Ya know, not everyone has an aunt to grant them access beyond the magical gates."

It dawned on me then, that they weren't escorted here by one of the guards. "How'd you get them in here?"

Elie scratched her head. "The slide."

A soft, incredulous sound escaped Alexiares, somewhere between a laugh and a sigh. "Real reckless of you, Elie. It could be a trap."

"Paranoid much? He's six."

"I forgot, in your sheltering, you never learned the lesson about live bait." It wasn't sarcasm. In fact, he was so serious that I fought to maintain my composure. The horror on Emma and

Elie's face as he explained his suspicions might have been more effective than any lecture I could have offered. "Leaving behind the innocent. Humans and empathy are so predictable that any-one with a sense of safety is bound to offer help. You follow them back to the source and then boom, take 'em down. Nothing too complicated of an effort. If their defenses are shitty enough, you usually hit before they even know you're there."

Red crept up Alexiares's neck and warmed his cheeks. He glanced down, having said far more than intended. I knew this. He had spoken about his work many times. Some stories more shame-ful than others, nevertheless, important lessons toward maintain-ing our defenses. The girls however, had their jaws on the floor.

"They can stay here one night," I said, clearing the air. "In the morning they're off to Ms. Schuller's to await placement. Com-pound Hall is backed up. It'll take a few days. She's sweet, they'll be fine there. Abel checks on her Thursday's anyway, she was his foster placement before Riley. I'll send a message to take them with him in the morning. In the meantime, they look tired and cold. Maybe get them cleaned up?"

Elie's attention fell behind me. She nodded slowly then made her way over to them. Casey responded to her touch with a slight wince. They'd need to stop by The Infirmary in the morning first and foremost. The slosh of water came from the bathing chamber in the center of our quarters. Elie glanced back at Alexiares in silent thanks for the magical assist before ushering the kids inside, the door closing behind her.

"I'm not so sure putting them with some random person just to pass 'em to the next is the best idea," Emma said with utmost confidence. We both turned, surprised she hadn't disappeared the moment Elie did.

"Uh—"

"I watched my mom die," she continued. "Right in front of me, same as these kids. Do you know what that's like?" Those sad, lost eyes brimmed with tears before she blinked them away. Emma never cried. Ever. Not even when her father did.

"Yeah," Alexiares replied with a hint of sympathy. "Actually, I do, kid."

"If I didn't have my dad or Aunt Moe, I'd probably be a feral child too. Those kids need a person to be their person. Can't they stay here?"

"Emma," I sighed. I didn't say fuck the kids, they weren't my problem. I certainly could have, but I didn't. I'd offered the best alternative I'd had in my pocket. "I don't think that's the best option for them either. This isn't what I'd call a stable household."

"Elie lives here. Doesn't that make you her parents?"

I locked eyes with Alexiares. A thousand unspoken thoughts passed between us—uncertainty. A shit ton of doubt. The question we hadn't dared ask out loud. *What did that mean for us? What did it make us? Me and him?* Our silence hung heavy. Simply put, the answer was far too complex.

My Bloodhound broke the tension, his voice as gentle as I'd ever heard it be. Resigned. "No, it doesn't. And even if it did, I think it's clear we're not doing a great job."

"Well, don't you know someone that can do a good job?" she asked, hopeful of a different outcome that I could not provide. Not under the current Compound circumstances. "Someone you can ask that you trust?"

I shook my head, uncertainty once again knocking me off-kilter. With the influx of people and parentless children, Ms. Schuller *was* calling in a favor. "I'll see what I can do."

"If we didn't save em, someone else could have and it would really suck if that someone was Covert. Right? Even I know that's worser. You leave them out there like that—if Alexi is right—that there's people out there to get us, then one day, they might grow up to become the next bad guy."

And with that, Emma was out the door.

I groaned, turning to Alexiares and leaned into him, "We aren't dead."

He kissed the top of my head. "No, we are not, Princess." His voice was steady. Reassuring.

"Rebuilding this place, it's not impossible. If I can get Ronan out the way, I still see that little glimmer at the end of the tunnel."

"Should I even ask how long this tunnel is?" Alexiares grinned, his teasing lightening the air from the shitshow this night had turned into.

"Long as shit but the lights still there." I laughed, a manic edge creeping into my voice as the sound erupted from my chest. Elie and Emma, as determined as they were, made their point. "Sometimes it's hard to remember that but damn is it fueling."

CHAPTER
NINETEEN

AMAIA

"What's up loser," I said as I pressed the door open to Riley's new humble abode.

He peered up at me with a grin as I let my air magic close the door behind me. "Paperwork before we go."

"Aw, poor baby. Maybe your girlfriend can wrap it up since she has so much to say about how I run things."

"Amaia," he warned, peering back down and signing the last of the documents before shoving them in the drawer. "I wish the two of you would stop."

"And I wish I had a million dollars before the world fell apart, but none of that matters in hindsight, right?"

He cracked a smile then hid it away. Pushing his chair tight behind the desk, Riley grabbed his go bag off the floor and tossed it over his shoulder. "Let's just go."

I walked to the storage closet next to my old bedroom door and grabbed my sack. We were only to meet Ronan along the coast a few miles away, but you never knew when you'd need shit to survive. "Want to take a shot first?"

He glared at me and I tossed my hands in the air. "I'm joking. God, you're grumpy today."

Riley smacked my hand away as I pushed to my toes and pinched his cheeks. "And you're in an oddly good mood." He held the door open for me and I ducked under his arm, before making our way into The Pit and straight for North Gate.

"I decided to fake a positive attitude this morning as practice for being fake as hell with Ronan."

"Great plan. Is that why you asked me to come with you instead of Alexi?"

I grimaced. "Yeah," I said slowly. "He's not exactly a ray of sunshine and I need Ronan as pliable as possible. He thinks I'm *just a girl* with a side of brains. If I bring Alexiares, then he'll be on edge. He doesn't know much about you other than what Seth told him."

"Okay," he confirmed with a grin. "I can do that."

"And on the off chance that he gets a little handsy," I said, giving him a well-practiced side-eye. "I need you to let him. I may be going in with a positive outlook, but this is the perfect opportunity to taunt him a bit, see where he bends. Play stupid a little."

"Excuse me?" He came to an abrupt stop.

"Like I said." I tugged him forward with his wrist. "I only care about him slipping up."

"Maybe you should bring someone else," he said, his discomfort evident.

"I brought you because you follow orders." I slapped his shoulder with a smile. "The others don't owe me that, they aren't soldiers, and Alexiares does as he pleases when it comes to me. Can't have that. Not today."

Riley grumbled at my back and I hid my laugh. It would be good to spend this alone time with him. We did not get it often these days between our responsibilities and relationships. Even if it was only a short hike away, I'd relish this time to catch up.

The gates opened after the guards passed off different call signs, communicating that we had the all clear to do so both here and along the wall. There would be no surprises at Monterey Compound. Not on my watch.

I stopped a few feet ahead as Riley stopped to chat with the guards for a moment. His touch on gate duty was light these days. He had trusted men in place for that with his new role to take on, but he was as hands on as I was. Never would we ever really let things slide. We were hands on with every role we had. It was simply how we operated.

His approach was announced by two bees buzzing around my face. I hated bees. Would run in front of a moving bus to escape one. Swatting them away, I yelped and froze as they landed on my forehead.

"Riley," I mumbled, too afraid to speak though I knew he had total control.

"Missed you, ya know?" he bellowed and walked on to the trail through our makeshift woods. "You have your time to torture me later, let me have this now."

"Fair enough," I said, not moving a muscle until the bees were far out of sight.

We trekked for five miles or so. Not too rushed in our steps, enjoying the conversation and slowness that being outside the walls gave us. I missed these simple moments. The ones I'd taken for granted many times before.

Our steps slowed in pace as we approached a collection of large tents off in the distance. We stopped for a moment, scanning the horizon and taking in our surroundings. Cliff on one side, Ronan on the other. I could see the soldiers stationed at various entry points of the camp. Somehow, they'd closed in behind us without our awareness. Riley's head had been on a constant swivel despite our conversation. My attention was a laser even in the worst weather conditions in the dark. They hadn't moved into position naturally—magic was at play.

Ronan had made it explicitly clear he had no intention of respecting our land. Hadn't done anything but provided a time to meet. The *where*, however, was relayed by my units patrolling our territory. Ronan had set up camp where he pleased, walked where he pleased, arrived when he pleased, and let my soldiers relay the rest. A show of power. Measuring his dick on my land.

As we stepped closer to the camp, the oddest thing caught my eye. A vine. Thick and dark green. It twined around a nearby tree, slithering up inch by inch, its movements slow but attention grabbing. Unnatural. Its leaves were jagged, unlike anything native to Monterey, and a soft shimmer danced across its surface.

"Did you just—"

"Nope."

"Right."

Riley shifted closer and thumbed a leaf. His eyes closed, he took his time. Processing as though he were downloading information he didn't already possess. He was feeling his magic, using it to identify what he already knew.

"Garnet ivy," he said as though I'd understand what that meant. "Grows down south."

Invasive. His lips tightened in a knowing way. *We are not alone. They're here, watching us.* Close by if I had to guess. Riley was powerful and even his magic had limitations. So where were they? *Who* were they?

I could take a daring guess.

The rebels were present, hidden among Ronan's soldiers. The garnet ivy was their mark, a way to silently communicate that they had infiltrated Ronan's camp without him ever realizing. To the untrained eye, it was a foreign plant creeping along the edges of his tents. To us, it was a symbol of defiance.

"Plan?"

"No plan. Plans can be watched. Just follow my lead," I said, head high, confidence even higher as I made my way to Ronan's front door.

CHAPTER

TWENTY

AMAIA

"*Y*ou do not, under any circumstances, summon me."

I rolled my eyes. What a greeting. His soldiers had done everything but buy me dinner first in their search of both our bodies and our bags. It'd be less irritating of an experience if they had bothered to take our weapons but they hadn't. No. That was just another display of Ronan taking autonomy from us any way he could without going back on our deal.

Riley was locked in a pissing match with Malachai. The two of them stared at each other, faces full of snarls of different meaning. Where Riley promised Malachai death, Malachai promised him more pain. I hated myself for bringing him here, taunting someone he wanted to destroy in front of him like a worm on a fishing hook. Nevertheless, he was the one I trusted the most to behave. So behave he would.

"What are you rambling about, Ronan?" I said lackadaisically. Crossing my arms, I scanned the room for any sign of the presence of rebels. None stared back at me.

Nope, only Bietoletti and Hollis—an emissary I rarely saw unless it was him going out his way to piss me off. They stared through me in the same way they usually did, as if I were unimportant enough to look at with unglazed eyes.

Ronan was on me within a few steps. His hand snapped across my face, the pain of this minute compared to the rage coursing through me at the action. "Respect, woman."

I kept my movements measured. Controlled. Meeting those eyes I had memories of love and hate in, I remained level-headed. Riley twitched at my back. One hand out to make him hold, I raised my head. He would not break me.

Violence was the easiest way to maintain power. But if I told myself his violence meant nothing, that it was no more than a training exercise for the fight I would bring to his side of the world, it was too easy to pass off. Physical pain meant nothing to me. That I could endure. Losing my home—my family—I could not.

"I want to make it abundantly clear to you who reports to who around here," he said, turning his back to me.

I scoffed, "You're the one that came running like a dog to a whistle."

He glared at me over his shoulder, pouring tea into two cups that appeared entirely out of place. "I've come to discuss business—other aspects of our deal. You demanding Bietoletti to organize a meeting was a behavior I'm lucky enough to correct in person. Let me be explicitly clear regarding my emissaries. They are guests in your home. Bietoletti, Hollis, and Tyler do not fall under your command. Any attempt to do so will be seen as an act of aggression, which I'm afraid leads you and me one step closer to talks of war. Is that clear?"

I clenched my fists, needing to feel my nails dig into my skin. *Deep breaths*. The smirk peaking above the cup of tea he held in the air triggered me. It was at that moment I decided to start digging into the well of my magic I'd never touched. I wasn't ready yet, but I would be. Ronan's time was coming.

My own grin in place, I pulled a chair from the long table in the center of the room. "I love it when you come to visit." I plopped down beside him. The simmering anger at my lack of respect practically had him vibrating next to me. He jerked his chair back. I fought back a laugh. "By the way, since I'm here and speaking with the source. I'm going to need you to sign off on the whole trade agreement thing before people starve."

"It almost makes you wonder if starving your prisoners would help your rations go further." Hollis smirked. It was more of an animalistic snarl. Bietoletti chuckled, only silenced by the harsh stare of Malachai.

Ronan raised a finger. "Ah, yes. Perhaps that. Now, I'm going to offer some leniency here and ignore whatever it is you thought you held over me. Kill them, release them—it is of no concern to me. I have little use for soldiers weak enough to have been captured."

"The trade agreement," I said through gritted teeth. "Ronan."

He cleared his throat, forcing his emotions back in check and meeting me with the same stone-hard gaze Seth had rewarded me with many times. "On the topic of trade, you and I have come to understand people to be a resource."

"Yes," I agreed. "Except I believe them to be invaluable."

"Same as I."

I snorted, taking a small spoonful of sugar and dumped it into the tea. Stirring, I peered at him from the side of my eye, answering as politely as I could feign. "Mm, not in the same capacity."

"No," he said with a laugh full of humor I could not relate to. "Perhaps not. How's my daughter doing, anyway? That girl can be a handful."

"Prosperous," Riley answered. I'd never seen him so cold.

Ronan's eyes moved over him, a pause stretching between them as he took him in. Dismissively, he waved his hand, no longer caring to discuss the topic. Odd for a man who claimed to focus on God, country, and family. Which is exactly why I would never bite his bullshit. This was about power. It always would be for him.

"She's dating. I'd say you'd get along great with her girlfriend but, you already know her." I shrugged. "And I heard you didn't get along too well."

Ronan's posture tightened. I was fishing. Did he know Jessa was there? For Reina's sake, I prayed she wasn't the leak we thought her to be. That she'd been honest in her confession to Reina. The blank stare behind his sea storm eyes was not fake. Ronan was the type to brag about his deceit—which, in theory, should have made it easier to trace leaks. But instead, it meant untangling truth from his web of half-truths and exaggerations, making the job of determining who among us was sharing information even harder. *If* there was anyone at all.

Again, Ronan changed the subject. Controlling what we did and did not discuss. I had my work cut out for me. Bringing him down would take patience. Time. There was no 'politicking' our way out of this. I could see that now. No. We'd have to hit him with brutal force and he wouldn't stand a chance if he saw it coming.

"The resources," his voice boomed, pulling me from my thoughts. "I'll need to call in for them now."

I smirked. "Resources? That's what we're calling people now? You're getting creative with your euphemisms."

He ignored me. "You've had a new influx of people. Quite the growing military you're building—of course, I assume there's no correlation between that and the lack of residents in Duluth."

Naturally, any soldiers that had arrived from surrounding territories had become part of mine. Technically, under the new treaty for the war we *thought* was going to happen, they were already my soldiers. But with an increase of population, an increase in military personnel followed.

I preferred to keep my ratios within the historical realm of victory. One soldier per every forty citizens. Like America in Germany during World War II. Of course, my ratio had always been a bit more than that. Now, however, we were looking at about two soldiers per every thirty people. And I wanted more. I wasn't done recruiting. I'd expected this to come up.

"No relation, pure coincidence." I crossed my arms, not bothering to hide my irritation. It was. Duluth's residents weren't here—it wasn't my fault he hadn't thought to check the bunker. "What else am I supposed to do with soldiers, turn them into gardeners?"

His eyes narrowed. "No. I'm requesting two hundred."

My mouth dropped open, then I laughed, a sharp, biting sound. "Two hundred? Two hundred of my soldiers? You're joking."

"I don't joke."

"That is what he said, yes." Malachai chimed in, standing off to the side, nothing more than a smug mouthpiece.

I held up a hand to stop Riley before he could instigate a fight we could not win today.

"No way," I said flatly, turning back to Ronan. "Over my dead body."

He watched me, waiting. I knew his game. I wouldn't give him that satisfaction. "Fifty."

"Fifty?" His lip curled. "Now what am I supposed to do with fifty soldiers? Do I appear to be the type of individual that bargains with *lesser* settlements."

"That's not my problem. Figure it out. What are you planning to do with them, anyway?" I asked, cocking an eyebrow.

"Nothing that concerns you," he said smoothly.

"My monkeys, my circus."

Riley, predictably, couldn't hold back. "So you want a battalion and we don't even get to know what for? You—"

I cut him off, my tone firm. "Riley, let it go."

He clenched his jaw, glaring daggers at Malachai. But he stayed quiet.

I turned back in my seat, eyeing Ronan over with a sweet, saccharine smile. "I want the trade agreement signed off right here, right now. You'll get seventy-five. Don't worry—they'll be there before you even know it."

I slipped my hand into my bag. The room tensed, everyone reacted, jumpy hands flew to their weapons—all but one. I took out the agreement and slammed it onto the table. Ronan didn't flinch. He simply licked the tip of his pen and signed it, his gaze never leaving me. He didn't read it. The issue had never been our requests—it was about making us suffer.

"It was a pleasure meeting with you. We'll be in touch soon." He dismissed me, but I wasn't ready to leave.

"Actually," I leaned forward, taking another sip of the now cold tea and entered his personal space. "I have a request of my own."

My head felt light. A bit fuzzy. My thoughts scrambled a bit as I forgot what I'd come here to discover.

Ronan smiled back at me. One that made my skin crawl. It wasn't pleasant but had hints of his own humor in there. He raised his head and tilted it, examining me out the side of his eye. "What would that be?"

It came back to me, just barely. I knew. I didn't need to ask. His smile. The way I felt after the tea. There was no need to question him because I no longer cared. It didn't matter. *Nothing* mattered.

The how long, the why, the who. I didn't need any other powering force to want to kill this motherfucker than his current actions. For once, the history, the root unrest and claim for power didn't mean shit to me. The present was fueling enough.

"Tea for the road?" My voice dripped with innocence. I waved my empty canteen in the air. Malachai reached for it and poured the tea to the rim with an out of place desire to fulfill my request. Too eager.

"Careful now," I said, smiling as I took it back from him, "wouldn't want to spill."

Malachai snatched me up from the chair, one hand on the back of my neck, the other slamming into Riley's stomach. He shoved us outside the tent and blocked the entrance with his body.

"Safe travels," I called out to Ronan now out of view as I brushed the dirt from my army green cargos.

Reinforcements swooped in and we took the hint. They escorted us to the edge of their encampment. Malachai's eyes followed us until we were out of view and I offered him a mock salute.

"Why did you agree to that?" Riley walked as close to my side as he could, his voice low. I formed my own bout of wind, the opposite of the natural breeze, not wanting our whispers to be captured and delivered right out of earshot.

"Seth gave him everything."

"What?" Riley whisper-yelled.

"The tea," I said, motioning my hand down to lower his voice. "It's poison. I took two sips and felt like I lost my shit. Reina and Moe said Seth was rambling nonsense before he … the last time they saw him."

Riley teetered on the edge of turning around. It scared me, the thought of Riley and Ronan alone. Head-to-head. I doubted he'd fight fair, Malachai was all too eager to do his dirty work. I grabbed his hand and gave it a squeeze.

He peered down at me. *Together*. That was our promise to each other. And I was right here with him, we were together, I was not harmed. I was okay. He exhaled slowly and gave a single nod. "You think he drugged his own son?" Riley asked.

"I think Ronan will do whatever he has to do to get what he wants. Including drug the person who loved him the most." I tossed him the canteen as we crossed where the tree had previously been swarmed in vines. The bark lay bare before us. "Reina can test it but I'm sure of it. Who knows about the cavalry?"

Riley blinked twice in quick repetition. He'd made notes too. Contact had been made, initiated, we could go from there. "No one, just the others and Ramona."

"Kill them."

"General," Riley said. It was a warning on the line I was crossing and confirmation that he would do as ordered. He only wanted to know why.

"Send your guys and kill them. That's twenty right there that died along the way, for all he knows. Make it happen in another territory, preferably one he can't retaliate against. Some place already in turmoil. It'll buy us some time." The words tumbled out of my mouth as the plan pieced itself together in my head.

Brutal, but necessary. I couldn't save everyone, but I could stall. The ones loyal to us wouldn't be the ones to suffer—that was all I could promise with the power I had left. "Then listen to the ground for anyone who remotely seems to sympathize with Seth. They're to be questioned and shipped within the week."

"Amaia," Riley said, his voice cautious, prepared to talk me off a ledge.

"Yeah, Riley. I know." I stopped pacing and met his gaze. "What choice do we have?"

He didn't respond. His silence was answer enough. We both knew there weren't any good options left. I hated this as much as he did, but our choice right now was morality versus mortality. One could be revived and the other could not.

"At least if he upholds our deal, the others won't be experimented on. They won't lose their lives, not like that."

"And if he doesn't?" Riley asked quietly, his eyes searching mine, searching for some sliver of hope.

I swallowed hard, the weight of it all sinking into my chest, as heavy as lead. "Better traitors than those 100 percent loyal."

His jaw clenched, and for a moment, the air between us grew tense, a thread on the verge of snapping. But then he nodded, a slow, solemn acceptance. "Right." His voice was steady, but I could hear the grief in it. He'd follow me through hell if I asked. I just wished I didn't have to.

CHAPTER
TWENTY-ONE

ALEXIARES

I think I was starting to hate this room. There wasn't a single conversation that went on here that wasn't based on fixing the problems of The Compound. The room was meant specifically for this, but that didn't make me hate it any fucking less. I was never part of the whole politics thing over at St. Cloud. That kind of shit was left to Finley and Cael. Me? I was just the dog.

Here, at Monterey Compound though, I was more than that. Happy to be if it helped ease Amaia's mind. But damn, were these long conversations draining. Empathy hit these people harder than crack on the streets in the eighties. My father had claimed it was a weakness. Finley ate away at whatever drop of it Tiago had managed to pass my way.

I cared about my family and keeping these people safe. So having *feelings* about what it took to get there was nonsensical. Two plus two would always equal four, no matter which way you went about it.

Sacrificing a few for the greater made sense. Especially traitors.

"The hero in our story is a villain in the next," Amaia mumbled.

She was out of energy. She and Riley called a meeting the second they'd gotten back this evening. Reina, Abel, and Luna had their own opinions on fulfilling Ronan's request. Riley and I would do whatever Amaia wanted to. Leaving Tomoe the tie-breaking vote on moving it forward with the rest of The Council. In the end, Amaia could do whatever the hell she pleased, but she wouldn't. She wanted their support. Craved it.

"What?" Reina asked.

Her dark brown hair had grown past her chin. Random strands hung in front of her pale olive skin, falling from the small ponytail at the base of her neck. Of all things this girl could have worn, she'd chosen a long, pink dress. At least she hadn't lost all her spunk.

"Prescott said it once," Amaia answered. "It means—"

"Just because we're a hero today doesn't mean we won't be the villain tomorrow," Riley finished for her.

We'd been going back and forth for hours—outlasting even the patience of Bietoletti and Tyler, who lurked in the back of every 'official' meeting. It didn't matter anyway, not when our options were limited and any conversation we'd had in front of them had been a folly. Now that they'd left with grumbling irritation, the others were starting to be swayed while Tomoe hadn't contributed to the conversation at all. Instead, she sat there silently watching us, a distant stare in her inky eyes. Which meant she knew something. And she wasn't interested in sharing yet.

"Pretty sure you're the villain in more stories than you are the hero," she said, finally breaking her silence.

"And fifty years from now, you might be the next Mussolini," I teased back. "Hopefully, your Sight will help you rebrand with something better than pasta."

Amaia and her humor were clearly wearing off on me. I tossed an arm over the back of her chair at the thought. She was fascinated by just about every historical period and was prone to ramble off facts no one should know off the top of their head any chance she got.

"Nothing's better than pasta. God, I miss a good baked ziti," Reina said, her head dropping back as she leaned back in her chair.

"So," Abel led, his eyes locked on Amaia. His hands made the motion of interlocking his fingers before realizing he didn't have the motion in one to follow through. He played it off, resting one atop the other as he leaned forward. "We're basically using these… traitors"—he chose the word carefully, reluctantly—"as pawns until we figure out who these people are that we're supposedly not *not* looking for?"

"We don't need to look for people when they've already found us, but yeah. Pretty much," Amaia said. I watched her in admiration. I knew this was hard for her. Her people were her people, no matter their loyalty. The faith she'd had in Seth to do the right thing up until Duluth was proof.

Luna sat quietly at the other head of the table. I knew she was here merely to offer support—so Amaia could believe Prescott was still with her. She trusted Luna's judgment to see things from all perspectives. There was wisdom with age. Even I could agree with that. Her hesitancy had not come from a place of right versus wrong like the others, but rather from the impact it would have on The Compound.

Compound first for her, for Riley, for Amaia. I got it. They had to hold on to that. If they didn't, this place could crumble. They had to set the example for when others got weak.

The lines of Luna's forehead creased with concern. Her dark eyes stared with warning, "If you do this, word will spread of a witch hunt. You'll need to ensure that the public is made aware right after. You'll move in the night, quietly, then make the announcement in the morning. *Before* word has had time to spread. It's the only chance to control the narrative. I must warn you, sweet girl, there is no coming back from this. You are a hero to these people. The problem with being the hero is that it usually costs you your life."

She didn't mean it would bring Amaia to her death. It damn sure could. The warning Luna relayed, however, was the situation Amaia would put herself in from making this choice. She would have to defend her position here going forward, and that would be draining as hell. The laughs she shared with the residents of The Compound, the trust she'd worked tirelessly to build, would be gone. They would always side eye her from this day forward. Wondering what decision she may make next. Forever worried if it would be them in the future that would be sacrificed in order for the rest of The Compound could survive.

"I understand. We move tonight. Riley, gather those you trust, brief them, start at midnight. Take Alexiares with you—start with those deemed highest risk, keep any mistakes to the minimum. Luna and Reina, prepare The Kitchens in the morning. I'll make my speech at the first shift of breakfast. From there, let word spread. Abel, I need my bags packed. I leave at dawn in two days to find out find whoever's got Ronan this rattled."

"Alone?" Riley was on his feet in an instant, his concern radiating in every rigid line of his posture.

He looked at me and I tensed. He knew I wouldn't like it; hell, *she* knew I wouldn't like it. But if a group of us left, it would raise suspicions with Ronan's bitch boys. We'd already had to sneak in one by one to avoid the eye of those who watched whenever we wanted to discuss things privately. Taking different entrances, arriving at different times. The planning, the notes, the damned blueprints—none of that was possible in any of their cramped little studies. We'd no choice.

"No." His voice was steel, sharper than I'd ever heard him. Riley—the same soft-hearted one who'd lay down his life for her without hesitation—stood there. An immovable wall. He'd block her path, strap her down if it came to that. I couldn't say I'd stop him.

Her eyes flashed, jaw ticking with that stubborn edge I knew all too well, but Riley didn't flinch. "Yes," she insisted.

A heavy silence settled over the room. The dust settled air thick with the challenge between them. No one moved. We waited, seeing who would give in first. I leaned in, my hand settling firmly on her thigh—a silent warning, *Stand down. Support's not coming from me either.* If she thought for even a second she'd be leaving this compound alone, she was dead fucking wrong. Her simmering rage beneath my palm was palpable. She was shaking, but I didn't budge.

"Clear the room," she directed, not sparing me a glance, her voice firm and resolute. "Riley, *stay.*"

CHAPTER
TWENTY-TWO

RILEY

"You have to stop doing this alone." I didn't wait for the door to shut behind the others. "Taking on the weight that you have for years, it's not sustainable."

"It's necessary." Eyes dark as coal pierced mine. We didn't talk to each other this way.

It was a first for our relationship and it was long overdue. There had been far too much I'd sat by for. Doing what she needed me to do. Playing whatever role she required. This would not be one of those things. I knew deep in my heart that if I let my sister go out there alone, without someone to protect her, I would never see her again. Felt it in my bones.

"It's not," I said, the words coming out rougher than I meant them to. "Let someone else solve a problem for once. It doesn't always have to be you."

Laying it all out there, I studied her face, hoping—praying—she'd hear me this time. I never argued. Never begged. I was now. "Please, don't go."

Her face softened for a fraction of a second. The familiar determination hardened her face to stone. "You'll have to forgive me at my funeral. I won't live forever, Riley."

"Trust me." I grabbed her hands and shook them. "Trust that I can do this with you. Trust that the others can, too."

Amaia hesitated briefly, then offered a slow nod. "Okay."

"I can come?" Relief flooded through me. Then hope abandoned me all the same.

"No," she said, her curls bouncing as she shook her head. "Alexiares, Abel, and Reina will. I have something I need you to focus on here." The corner of her mouth quirked into a sinister smile.

Of course. I exhaled and braced myself for whatever chaotic thing was about to pass through her lips. Without question, she was about to throw me headfirst in some challenge she only thought me capable of. Out of everyone here, through all that had changed, I still fit that spot in her life. It was an honor. "All ears."

"We need to mix things up, security wise. With what I'm about to do, the people I have to hand over … We need a distraction as much as we need people to feel safe inside their homes."

Her shoulders tensed and I reached forward to touch her shoulder in reassurance. She met my stare, her hand falling over mine as a sad, regretful curve of her lips formed. As Amaia spoke earlier, uncertainty clawed at me. *Where was the line drawn anymore? It's necessary.* I told myself, repeating it as a mantra until it was true.

The line was clear, and we were crossing it. Amaia hated that we were with every cell in her body. This was not easy for her. But she was strong. She would shoulder it for us all. Ronan did not possess that moral compass. If what Reina said about her childhood was true, I wasn't sure he ever did.

"Go on," I encouraged.

"One, we need patrols. Visible ones. Not just outside our walls, but inside, too. I don't want people to think I'm watching them or anything, but—"

"We are watching them. You need them to feel like others are being watched for their safety, but not necessarily themselves?"

"I knew you'd get me." Her smile was a gentle touch, soothing my soul. "With that, I think we need to bring back town hall. We're busy, but we aren't too busy to show face, answer questions, and make people under the impression that they have a say."

"Because they do."

"Always will," Amaia reassured. This was temporary—doing what we needed to survive. Nothing new. "All of this needs to come out as a leak."

I chuckled. It felt silly to use my network that way. Juvenile. It reminded me a bit of the joke of society we used to call the United States of America. "Why?"

"Because I want the people to feel like they've infiltrated us. That they haven't been left out of things. They're still top of mind. They found out first. Get where I'm going with this?"

"At some point, our minds will sync up, and we won't have to talk."

"I love you, Ril. Think you can get this rolling by the time I'm back?" I nodded, and she grabbed my arm with a tired smile full of misery. The bags under her eyes had deepened even from this morning. Restless and stressed. Things I couldn't help her with. Not if she wouldn't let me. She gathered the remainder of her belongings that Alexiares had left behind and made her way to the door.

But I couldn't let her go without addressing what was eating away in the back of my mind. "We need to talk about Elie."

Amaia stiffened, not turning back around. "That can wait until I get back."

"It really can't."

"I'm sure there will be a lot more to discuss with her by the time this is all said and done," Amaia said, her tone firm as she pulled all her curls to one side. "You'll tell her what you'll tell Bietoletti, Tyler, Hollis, and the rest of The Compound while you cover for me. We're meeting at the border of Monterey and San Jose to re-establish our trade lines now that an agreement has been signed. We'll be back in two days' time. The last thing I need right now is Elie and Emma trying to tag along. Make it sound boring."

I frowned, pulling my locs into a hair tie as I leaned against the table behind us. "Boring? Easier said than done. You know they'll want to be involved."

"Exactly. That's why I need you to make it sound like the dullest mission ever," she replied. As she finally turned back to face me, I could hear the underlying tension. "Just emphasize how tedious the whole process can be. Trust me, it'll keep them from getting any bright ideas about following us. Elie doesn't do boring."

"Her behavior is concerning, Amaia. It's dangerous," I replied, my voice low.

"It is," she agreed. "You don't live with her, Riley. Grief hits us all differently. You have to know when to approach and right now, is not that time. At least we can say she isn't reaching for a bottle of liquor. Now *that* would be a real uphill battle I'm not sure I'm strong enough to help her fight, so, yeah."

"Are you sure this is you looking out for her and not yourself?" I asked, needing to clarify my doubts. The last thing I wanted was for her to bear the burden of her decisions alone.

Amaia's expression shifted, and I could see the hurt in her eyes. *How dare you?* they said. Instantly, I regretted the words. Maybe she was right; I didn't live with Elie. If she said it wasn't the right time, then it wasn't. "I don't think I should train her anymore."

Amaia's nose scrunched, a mix of surprise and disbelief flashing across her face. I was no quitter. I didn't give up on my commitments once I made them. "Why not?"

"She despises me. It's not productive."

"Is she showing up every day on time?" she pressed, her tone insistent.

"Yes," I replied, each word laced with the tension of someone with nowhere left to turn.

"Does she at least attempt to follow your instructions?"

"Yes, but she's too distracted that it's *me* teaching to heed any of my advice."

Amaia tilted her head, her expression shifting to one of understanding. "But she is trying to follow said advice?"

"Yeah," I conceded, my shoulders slumping.

"Then it doesn't seem unproductive to me," she said with a shrug. "Remember who the authority figure is here, Riley, and who's the future soldier. You are a lieutenant—act like it."

Her words, though firm, were a lifeline, pulling me back from the edge of my doubts. I smiled, the tension easing as I pulled her in for a hug. "Be safe." I held it longer than necessary. She didn't push away.

"Wouldn't dream of doing anything but," she replied, as I released her, winking at me before stepping back.

CHAPTER

TWENTY-THREE

TOMOE

The announcement went the better of the two ways I'd envisioned. That was the good news and about as far as I was able to see on my own. Issue was, with an uncanny amount of people nervous and a healthy mix of those at ease, the rest of the future was a fucking toss-up. Too many possibilities, far too many shifting minds, thoughts, and opinions.

That was the problem. Thought wasn't linear, wasn't predictable—not when tangled with fear, pride, desperation. I could calculate odds, chart patterns, map outcomes, but the sheer weight of so many conflicting mental pathways made prediction impossible. It wasn't chaos, not exactly. More like static. Deafening, useless noise, drowning out what should've been clear signals.

The human mind was not as complex as one would think. Within a singular community, groupthink was far more common than theorized. No such thing as an original thought or experience when surrounded by like-minded people. The Compound, as most settlements Before and After, was just that—filled with individuals who shared common morals, values, and expectations. Predictable. Manageable. Until civil unrest cracked through the foundation. Then things got complicated. Less straightforward.

Which meant I needed help. Something I had a sour taste in my mouth asking for.

There were only three of us in Salem Territory that had the ability to *see*. I'd already had Riley send word to call them back to The Compound and with one residing right outside our walls and the other within, they'd be here within the hour. With little time to prep, I set up my space, laying out my Labradorite, Amethyst, Tourmaline, and Selenite around me. The devil was in the details. Every advantage we could get right now, I would take.

At the moment, finding out our exact number would help us determine how great our odds were. That's what our chances were—odds. Slim. Pretty much nonexistent. Doom and gloom were a far cry from glory.

What we needed was to see inside Covert Province. Problem was, to *see* the way we needed to, the amount of power required to get the job done was more than any of us possessed. I had a plan, and it was a fool's one. Walk among them. Take in every security measure, every magical enhancement, every creation they had. Use it to destroy them.

For Seth. For us.

A knock on the door startled me.

"Come in," I said, expecting Aileen or Guy to wander in.

Guy resided within The Compound and stumbled in and out of my study as he pleased. Usually to gather records or check in to cross-check any ominous visions. He never knocked, though. Aileen was more likely.

Instead, a small, frail child stood in the doorway, and I groaned. "Are you lost?"

Yasmin appeared behind her, with Lola in tow. They flanked the girl, the picture of reluctant bodyguards. A flicker of a vision passed through my mind, filling in the gaps as quickly as they formed—a fractured image of shadows and cages, an aura of fear. Hidden secrets. All of it connected to the child in front of me. Fascination had me leaning forward without thinking, eyes narrowed on the girl. She reeled back instinctively, her shoulders stiff with fear, only to be soothed by the gentle touch of Yasmin.

"It's okay, Lilia," Yasmin murmured softly, never breaking eye contact with me. Daring me to scare her further as she ignored my scoff. "This is Tomoe. The *Seer* we talked about."

Frankly, 'Lilia' looked like she'd been through some shit. Her hair was tangled, skin pale, eyes seeing yet unseeing all the same. All symptoms of a powerful *Seer* who saw far beyond anything they'd ever hoped. There was trauma in knowing the future, present, and past. To see the hope from here and now and watch it all fall away in the future.

"What is this?" I inquired, directing a meaningful glance at Yasmin.

"Lilia is from Covert Province," Yasmin replied. She stepped slightly to the side at Lola's advance. "She's here to help."

Lola's sharp gaze flicked to me, dark, shadow-like magic swirling around her before retreating at Lilia's hunching of her shoulders. "I am here to help the child ease into her gifts. Our expectations are that you will provide the guidance that only a *Seer* can offer."

"Yeah, I don't fulfill many expectations, much less on demand." I waved a dismissive hand. "This isn't a school. I have business to tend to."

Lola's expression hardened, her voice slipped into a tone more solid than steel. "Amaia extended help on your behalf. You will do as told by your general."

"She's not my general," I replied flatly.

Yasmin chuckled sarcastically. "Whether you're up for the task or not, her power reaches far beyond that title. And as her *sister*, I'm hoping your support can be offered as a willing favor."

"Favors have expected payments."

Attention from Lola sent a chill down my spine that could not come from anything other than the threat of unfriendly fire. "And yet, a favor is already owed. Allow me to call it in." She gritted through her teeth.

"Mind if I keep a record of that?" I muttered.

Yasmin's mouth twisted slightly. "That's not … that's not how this works, Tomoe. Be that as it may, Lilia here has seen a glimpse of something in the present that future-her deemed should have been shared with you. Did I get that right?" she asked, glancing over at Lilia, who only shrugged with uncertainty. Yasmin nodded as if that was answer enough. "Anyway, here we are. Well, here she is. You won't be able to see this information any other way. Not with the security Ronan has in place. We're here for moral support."

I sighed, running a hand over my face. "Fine. Take a seat, Lilia." I glanced over at the others, crossing my arms. "The two of you—there's only enough room in here for one to stay. I vote Yasmin, since I don't appreciate your attitude," I said, staring pointedly at Lola. "You, out."

Lola's gaze turned to ice as did the room around us. Her stare locked onto mine in a silent but potent challenge. Energy crackled between us—lightning before a storm. We weren't a coven, and we had no expectation of getting along. Sure, she had helped Alexi and Amaia, thus, me by proxy. I couldn't give less than a shit or two. I worked best alone. Her expression was unreadable. Without a word, she silently turned on her heel and left, the door snapping shut behind her.

Turning my attention back to Lilia, I softened my voice. "My colleagues will be here soon. If you don't want an audience, we need to do this now. Give me your hand. We aren't bonded, so this won't work the same, but we can channel each other enough to get the gist."

Lilia hesitated, glancing nervously at Yasmin, who gave her a small nod of encouragement. Tentatively, she reached out, placing her small hand in mine. Her touch was cold, charged with a latent power coiled tight and barely contained.

The vision came in fragments, fuzzy and unclear—*a dark corridor, rows of huddled figures, the pervasive feeling of dread.* I caught a flash of a small figure moving through what appeared to be rows of cages. I struggled to hold on to the image, but it slipped away, leaving only the faintest echoes of despair and something hopelessly insidious.

Lilia pulled her hand back, visibly shaken, and I steadied her with a strong gaze.

"You're sure?" I asked, my voice serious.

Lilia nodded slowly, and for the first time, her voice was barely a whisper. "Yes."

"What's wrong?" Yasmin asked, and eyed me with concern.

"I need the others," I muttered, already moving to make room, my hands quickly gathering various ritual items from nearby shelves and spreading them out on the table.

"Wait, what are you doing?" Yasmin demanded, sounding a little frantic.

"We need a tie," I replied, laying out the items with practiced efficiency. I'd only had to do this a million times since Duluth.

Her face twisted with alarm. "Wait, like … like that bonding ritual Lola sent those witches down here to do? No, not without her parents' permission."

I ignored the fact that the word *witch* left her mouth more bitter than a curse word. "I don't give a shit about permission—"

"I do." Yasmin's jaw set in defiance. "I'm her teacher. There's trust here. Trust that I already broke by involving Amaia in the first place. This is too fast for her—"

"Yeah, I don't have time for that," I snapped. "I'm sure her parents will get over it when they realize people stuffed in cages aren't just being worked to death. They're being experimented on, tortured, and turned into Pansies. I need a clear vision of this, and I need it now."

Yasmin's mouth fell open, her brown eyes wide with shock. She swallowed. "I'll, um … I'll go get her parents."

My gaze had already drifted back to Lilia. "Yeah. You do that."

I sighed at the nearly vacant room, eyeing Lilia's small, trembling form. "Listen, kid," I began, not sugarcoating shit. "This ritual we're doing—it's a tether. It links us, bonds us, allows us to share visions, sometimes a lifeline, whatever might help in the end. Normally, it's stronger between people with a deeper bond or blood connection. It should help make this vision a bit clearer."

Lilia's ghostly fingers twisted nervously in her lap, eyes darting to the Tourmaline in my hand.

"Our bond won't be that strong," I continued, placing the stone gently in her palm. "I don't know you and you don't know me. That said, I promise we can trust each other. The connection might be a bit loose, but it'll do for what we need here." I watched her fingers tighten around the gemstone, her grip surprisingly firm.

"Stay calm, and if anything feels off, let me know. After we're … connected, you'll be a bit tired, kind of weak. That's normal. No worries, I'll lend some of my magic once my colleagues show up. When we trigger this vision again, it will be intense. You'll feel like you're there in the flesh. It's important to remember that you are *not*. Whatever you do, don't let go of my hand."

Guy shuffled in, and I gave him the bare minimum rundown on what had just happened with Lilia—no frills, all facts. Aileen appeared right on his heels, catching enough to fall in line without questions. We joined hands, forming a circle as the room's energy shifted, our focus tightening. Channeling like this wasn't new, but if Lilia's vision had any use, I wanted every detail sharp. Unmistakable.

Our hands connected, and despite being only about ten, Lilia took control. She was powerful—more powerful than I'd ever had the grace of connecting with. I wasn't sure how we missed this during intake. The idea of hidden magic existing within The Compound was terrifying. For a long time, we'd assumed the technology we possessed to be infallible. Impervious. The consequences of such a possibility escaped me as the vision encapsulated us.

Hand in hand, we walked through a barren camp as one. As Lilia— she'd been present. Imprisoned. Dry, gold and green overgrown grass tickled my exposed ankles. The surrounding air was filled with smoke and the undeniable scent of sickness. Chaos ensued around us as people were shoved, pushed through what I could only presume was a workers' camp. There were no soldiers, only guards.

Crack.

The sound of a whip blistered my ears. A screeching, inhuman scream followed. I turned my head. A man covered the battered, beaten body of a teenager. His hands were covered in soot and ash as he coughed up blood. He pleaded with the guard, voice hoarse, desperate. Begging for more time. Swearing they could continue. That they just needed a moment.

His pleads went unanswered as the boy was pulled to his feet and dragged away. As Lilia's eyes, as our heads turned, we took in more of the camp. The edges of it were lined with metal cages as far as the eye could see. Behind them, sloppily constructed buildings made of earth, the only light filtering through from small windows no longer than a foot, one on each side.

The man clambered and stumbled after the guards only to be met with a sharp jab to the jaw. He fell, hands clutching at the side of his face. The lower portion of his jaw hung, unattached from the upper portion.

The scene changed. We passed through a side alleyway of tents in pristine condition. The flaps lay open on a few and here was where the horrors unfolded. Women and children alike were strapped to metal chairs, the leather bounding their arms in place containing them from fighting back against the injections placed intravenously into their wrists. Vials of blue and green bubbled in the background.

Suddenly, we were on our ass. A snapping, fresh Pansie was led out of one of the tents. The teenager from the previous vision. His skin was chapped and gray, his dark hair patchy, revealing the pointed tips of his ears that were hidden before. He yanked, tugged as the guards fought to guide him through the tight alleyway, but his newfound strength was unmatched. We watched in horror as he tore free.

His movements were a blur—fast, animalistic. An alarm sounded and the vision flickered, shifting from night to day before finally going out.

My study surrounded us once more. Lilia's grip on my hand had the blood rushing to other parts of our body. The cold touch and tingling sensation of our hands asleep from however long we were stuck in Lilia's head jarring. I was drained, my eyes closing as I sat up straight. One glance at the others and I knew they were near their limit but our work was not done. They wouldn't stop until it was.

Lilia's dark hair clung to her sweat-slicked face, strands plastered to the curve of her cheek. Her chest rose and fell rapidly, her pupils dilated, her entire frame shaking with tension as if on the brink of collapse. Guy sat rigid, his unshakable composure fractured. His jaw was clenched tight enough that the muscles twitched, hands trembling against his knees. A deep crease carved between his brows, and though he swallowed hard, he said nothing. Aileen was frozen, lips parted slightly, as if caught mid-gasp.

Her eyes jumped between us, rapid and unsettled, working to grasp the meaning of what we'd witnessed—what it meant

My own hands curled into fists, nails pressing into my palms to keep me grounded. My throat was dry.

But we weren't done. We wouldn't be until we had answers.

"Are you okay to continue?" I asked, Lilia's dark hair plastered in sweat against her face. "I saw a flicker briefly. I believe that you have more to share."

Lilia drew herself together, wiping a trembling hand across her forehead. "I'm okay." Her next pause came with a bit more strength. "This is for our people, right? Good people."

"Yes, honey," Aileen answered though her hazel eyes wandered to me. The nonverbal questioning if *she* was truly in the shape to continue with our efforts.

"But we want to make sure that you are okay too," Guy added, the sincerity behind his words not matching the hesitation in his eyes. "This is a lot for any mind, let alone a young one."

We all wanted to go on. Were desperate to. This was the most information we'd been presented since we started digging months ago. Things that could only be told through the eyes of someone who had experienced it firsthand thanks to Ronan's tech.

"I've lived through worse," Lilia said, ominously. Haze took over my clouding eyes, her vision sucking us back in.

We walked the cold, misted streets of a pristine city. This was the present or the future. I wasn't quite sure. The only thing damning my assumption that it was The Before was Covert's propaganda, plastered across the brick and stone facades of the buildings lining the street. A green-and-white sign hung from a fully functioning streetlight, swaying slightly in the breeze. Bank Street.

People stood on both sides, black sedans passing through the nearly silent streets. Though the area was full of people, no one spoke. Dark, heavy bags were apparent underneath their eyes. Exhaustion could not fully encapsulate the state they were in. Some sported suits, while others wore dilapidated clothing. Clean, but clearly worn past the point of acceptable in The Before. The streetlights were on. The hum of HVAC units filled the air, an invisible current wrapping around us.

Electricity. The coal stained hands. It all made sense now. Ronan was mining. Though he may have aimed for a sense of new-normalcy in his territory, the defeated faces of his citizens warned he faced the danger of rebellion, if only given the chance.

The vision flickered again, and then, I saw Alexiares and Riley. Arguing in the streets in front of the capitol building, but their words were unintelligible from the distance I stood. Wild, curly hair sneaked into the building behind them. They were distracted, no longer paying attention to her with their focus on whatever they were discussing. She glanced back at them, sorrow and regret displayed across her soft features. With a deep breath, she stepped inside and went fully out of view.

I glanced down, trying to figure out who I was watching this through. I saw a teenager reflected there—long, dark hair falling in unkempt strands, a gaunt face framed by hollow, haunted eyes. The ragged boots I 'wore' took one step, then two steps forward, following close behind her.

Another flicker and we were inside. I peered around the corner of a dimly lit long, narrow hallway. Amaia and Ronan's voices could be heard arguing from the other side of a door. A ripple of energy passed through the hallway—a shield settling into place. Not the kind we used in battle, but one of air, subtle and almost imperceptible, yet unmistakable in its intent.

Flicker.

Chaos. Running. Screaming. My heart-rate picked up, this time, I felt it as my own. Terrified of what I was about to watch unfold.

Flicker.

Amaia and I were face-to-face. Hopelessness soured her expression as her fire raged around her.

"Stay close to me," a voice said. The voice of the girl, whoever we were lurking through the eyes of.

The world around us erupted, and then went black.

I gasped for air, my hands flying to my chest. *No. It can't be.* My vision from only a few months ago was back, this time solid.

Decided. Coughs emulated around me as Lilia fell to the floor, choking on the oxygen of the room. Guy and Aileen surrounded her, comforting her though they were in no condition to do so. Aileen's gaze settled on mine, her face washed with pity. Whoever we were watching through, had died, and Amaia had been in the same room.

CHAPTER
TWENTY-FOUR

AMAIA

I made the decision a long time ago to keep who I was Before out of my mind. The girl I once was, carefree and optimistic … she had turned into a monster somehow, somewhere along the way. All in the name of preservation of others. My morality for theirs. The Compound represented everything and more to me but I think what I clung to the most was how much it encapsulated who I once was.

That person was never coming back. It was painful. But now, it was time for me to turn my pain into power. Fuck Ronan and fuck everything he stood for. I would destroy him for trying to take away my home. As the days went on, my path forward became clear. A plan was already in motion and if I played my cards right in this meeting, nothing would stop me from succeeding.

Sunday. A day I used to rest once upon a time. I couldn't remember the last time I had an entire day to just be still. It'd been months, actually, it was almost May. A few weeks shy of a year.

We crossed by the cliffside where it had all begun. Reina came to me in a hurry, telling me the worst had happened. She wrapped her arm around my shoulder and gave me a squeeze as she herself remembered that horrible fucking day.

"Can we jog?" I asked. Our packs weren't too heavy.

Alexiares reached for my pack, wanting to give me the freedom to slip away—barely beyond the others' reach for a few moments. Reina glanced toward Abel who nodded in agreement. They hosted a silent, quick conversation with their eyes, communicating about me I was sure. I needed a distraction.

The urge to spiral and thirst for a drink was strong. Physical challenges, exercise, those things helped. It was at Reina's recommendation after all. She'd studied up on ways to help me, determined to keep me away from the bottle. I was grateful for her yet concerned. All of her focus lately had been others and none on her own grief.

This was a good group to send outside the walls. We could all use the time away. Truthfully, Abel was best suited expanding his knowledge with Riley at The Compound but I knew he needed this. A low stakes mission to help rebuild his confidence outside the gates. He put on a good show but it was my duty to see through the bullshit, and see through it I did.

He took charge against the few Pansies we came across. I remained quiet. Coaching him could come later. I wanted to see how he would react, what strategies he would utilize while he was in a safe environment. With us here around him, no harm could come to him, at least from Pansies. I'd expected to come across a few the closer we got to where Ronan's camp had been only two days before. A parting gift from a man I'd marked for death.

It wasn't a guarantee he'd be gone when we got there but my gut said he would be. Ronan did not want to give me the opportunity to plot against him. Not from such a close distance. His intention on coming here was merely to show me that he could and that there was nothing I could do about it. Make it clear I possessed no control over the situation, our dealings—not to set up permanent housing.

We arrived at the thick stump that had been covered in vines that now lay bare. I brought my hand to it, resting it and searching for any unnatural ridges and edges to the bark. A hidden marking or note, some sort of evidence of invasive greenery, anything that let on that Riley and I hadn't been hallucinating. There were none.

"You sure this is it?" Reina asked with curiosity.

She sported her old attire. Posing as an emissary the way she had been years ago when Salem was getting settled. Her pleated navy trousers were tucked into the black laced up boots that stopped right above the ankle. The white of her short-sleeved dress-shirt was coated in light dust, kicked up from our run. With the frills and fluffs of it and the soft pink of her lips, it was all too easy to forget the trauma of what she'd been through, *almost*. The sad blue eyes that matched her pants served a reminder that much had changed though she was the same loving Reina she'd always been at heart.

An uncomfortable chuckle escaped Abel's lips. "Yeah, maybe she mixed it up with one of the many other trees around here," he teased.

There were no other trees around us. His humor was forced, a thin veil over something else. His chocolate-brown eyes darted nervously, scanning the horizon as he and Alexiares fell into position, back to back, bracing for what was coming.

"We never actually went over a plan or anything and um, you know how much I enjoy being prepared," Reina rambled on. "So maybe we can do that now?"

"If I say my only plan was to show up and hope they were waiting to make their move would that freak you out a bit?"

"Uh yeah," Reina said. "It would freak me out a lot, actually."

"Chill out. Take a breather. *We* are the danger, remember that," Alexiares attempted to soothe her worry.

Something was off. I sensed eyes on us but saw no one but us around. Alexiares's hand fell to my wrist, and he pulled me and Reina between the two of them. We fell into formation instinctively. No words needed to be exchanged. Seasoned in blitz attacks and bullshit, it would take a lot to catch us unaware at this point. Abel passed Reina his spare Smith & Wesson M&P. She was the only one who'd come unarmed.

The bow and arrow at her back made for a strange introduction to someone we were calling a harmless emissary. A person in between to help us and whoever the hell we were meeting see eye to eye. Even with no weapons, Reina's power was fierce, but there was no need to show our hand with her gifts before we were ready. Gifts like hers, like Riley's, that was the kind of shit you left classified for a rainy day.

"Oh crap," Abel muttered. "Someone cover me, I'm going down."

It was the only warning we had to step in around him as he fell victim to a vision. Like Moe, some were more powerful than others. The closer they were to coming to fruition, the larger the impact they would have on your life, the *more information* the vision contained, the more likely it was to take them out. Birds fluttered a football field away from the empty pasture. Empty as far as we could tell that is.

"That's convenient," Alexiares said.

Reina tsked, bending over to remove his finger off the trigger of his gun, eyes still focused ahead. "Stop, he can't help it."

"Brother? Brother. Brother."

We exchanged uneasy glances at Abel's mumbling. It could mean everything—or nothing—at all.

He gasped, suddenly sitting up, his hands flying to his chest as he struggled for air. Abel was a Seer, but his ability didn't compare to Tomoe's. His visions didn't come easily; he had to force them, whereas Tomoe's arrived willingly, without effort. It was one of his many gifts, but far from his strongest.

"You okay, kid?" Alexiares asked him, offering him a hand up. Abel took it, grasping back onto his weapon with one hand.

"As good as one gets when your mind takes over to do its own thing. Yeah." He turned to Reina with an intense questioning gaze. "You have a brother?"

"How hard did ya hit your head Abey-Abe?" She gave up her position and turned, checking him over. The palm of her hand reached up to rest against his cheek. She squinted when no diagnosis came immediately to her. "Seth? Remember him? Crazy cowboy that tried to kidnap me and Moe to take us to live with my even crazier father less than two months ago? Deader than dead in the soil?"

"Reina!" I gasped. We shifted instinctively, reforming our circle, each of us now facing inward. The world around us quieted, but an uneasy stillness filled the air. *Yeah, we're all going to need a shit ton of therapy soon. Elie, Reina, Riley, Abel. Who the hell knew what was going on in Tomoe's head.*

"I fell but not that hard. Two of you are nearly identical. About the same height as Alexi, same *I'll kill you* stare, but his hair is as dark as yours. Looks like he's never seen daylight. Like you," he grinned and slapped her shoulder at the taunt.

She replaced her gentle touch against his cheek with a hard pinch. Her face faded from a concerned scowl to the amused scrunching of her nose right before it fell to one of shock. "What?" Her cheerful voice wavered with a shaky laugh. "That's ... but that's Hunter. Why are you getting visions about my past? Dreaming of me day and night, ya Abe?"

He shook his head. His face was grave, not playing around anymore. "No. I, um, I don't think this has happened yet. You had your hair like this—like now. And, yeah, this is about right. You were talking on the coast line, right there."

Our eyes followed his pointed finger, and we crept closer to the cliffside. We peered over then up at each other. A cold, sharp sensation rippled down my spine. The prickle along my spine tightened, sharper than frostbitten breath in the dark. I reached for my gun. It flew from my hand before I could react, my throwing knives around my holster pulling free in the same motion, sending me stumbling back a step. The others yelped around me, and I knew then that we fucked up.

CHAPTER
TWENTY-FIVE

AMAIA

"Hey there, Sister. Did you miss me as much as I missed you?" The voice was familiar yet I knew I'd never heard it in my life. It felt like I should know it. Should recognize it. I was good with that kind of thing. If I heard it once, I knew it for life.

I glanced toward the others. Alexiares stared back at me. *Ready to jump?* And he claimed me to be the crazy one. My shoulders rose in a halfhearted shrug, mouth curving downward as I considered it. I was the only one with air magic. Reina and Alexiares could channel some of the water from below but from this height, it would be equivalent jumping feet first into freshly laid concrete. Leaving me and the magic I had no interest in mastering as our only easy escape.

Reina's eyes were wide, as though she had seen a ghost.

She collapsed.

Our weapons fell to the ground beside us then disappeared into what I could only refer to as the void. Hands were on Reina, dragging her away from the cliffside she had barely missed going over.

Time moved slowly as I turned around. I didn't know where to look first; at Caleb, the man I had banished from Monterey Compound eleven months ago, or at Hunter Moore cupping the shock ridden face of his little sister.

A woman stood with her hands directed at our reappearing weapons, surrendering them on the ground. Her hair hung in curls down her back. Bigger than mine and a shade lighter but the complexion of our skin was the same. She was laser focused on Hunter though it was obvious her attention spanned to the rest of us.

No one saw them coming. Caleb wielded fire, not air—but the air had gone unnaturally still, as if something were holding it in place. We'd taught him control, but this wasn't his doing. Which meant either the mystery girl or Hunter was behind it.

Telekinesis. Couldn't say I'd seen that one yet. But ya know what? Why the fuck not in this world. It had likely played a part in keeping their approach concealed, manipulating the surrounding space, altering perception.

"Ca-Caleb?" I stuttered for the first time in my life.

Reina's scream pierced the air. Her eyes blinked in quick succession, tears flowing from them. Hunter crouched over her. I wasn't sure if it was a flare in her magic or the emotions of reuniting with his sibling, but he cried with her.

Abel and Alexiares shifted closer to me. Neither of them appeared to trust their eyes. Hunter was dead. Had been for about a few years. At least that was the story Reina and Seth had told. The one I knew Reina believed.

Her brothers meant the world to her. She had done everything she could to protect Seth from the horrible fate she'd thought Hunter to have suffered. And Seth … *fuck*, Seth had never believed Hunter to be gone. It was why he'd fought desperately hard to get back to his father … he'd had hope. Hope he wasn't wrong for having.

"Shh, it's okay. It's okay," Hunter cooed, and he scooped her into his lap, gently brushing her hair out of her face. "Hey, Sis."

"Hunter? Is this really happening?" She pushed herself free of his grasp and turned toward us. The people she trusted. "Did I hit my head like Abel?"

Alexiares instinctively shifted in front of me. "What the fuck is going on?"

"Relax," the woman said, her voice dry and monotonous.

"Someone explain and do it quickly or I'm going to lose my shit first and ask questions second." I growled, the whiplash of the situation fading. "Now, what the hell is going on?"

"I told you she could be … *violent*." Caleb's face still made me want to punch him.

"Me?" I chirped a laugh and edged away from the drop side of the cliff. "Caleb, you haven't begun to see how violent I can get."

"This is a waste of time. Just like *I* said," the woman hissed and I couldn't figure out if I wanted to attack her or Caleb first.

"Waste of time but you sat around waiting for my general to show face." Abel bit back, taking the bait and pushing forward. He adjusted his stance carefully, his strong arm taking the lead in defense, while the other remained slightly behind.

Our backs to the cliff put us at a tactical disadvantage. Hunter may be Reina's brother, but we'd learned the hard way how little that could mean to some Moores. They'd disarmed us at first approach. While it was smart on their end, it wasn't a great sign of being on equal grounding—which is what most would want when approaching a potential ally.

The woman stepped forward over the weapons, her eyes glimmering with challenge. I studied her, from her tattered loose jeans hanging off her hips to the oversize t-shirt. She looked a mess. Like they'd been on the run and not stopped until they arrived in Monterey territory. "Were we supposed to walk through the front door?"

"Hey!" Hunter boomed. He stood now, compelling me to lift my eyes to meet his stare. "Everyone take a beat, dammit."

I studied him. He was identical to Reina—the same sharp angles in his jaw, mousy brown waves tousled around his head, thick dark brows stark against porcelain skin. And his eyes… fierce, piercing. Just like Seth's.

There was no denying he was a Moore. The question was how.

"How are you here?" I asked. Then, locking eyes with Caleb, "Why are you here?"

Hunter exhaled, glancing toward Reina. "If you don't mind, I think I owe it to my sister to tell her first." His voice was measured, but there was an edge to it. "The 'how' is a long story—one that's better told once we're out of the open. That part can wait. But the 'why' … I'm guessing that's the part you care to hear about now."

Caleb drew nearer, his strawberry blond hair ruffled with dirt and who knew what else. "You helped me. When everything pointed to me, you chose to spare me instead. Seth forced my hand. Threatened my family if I snitched. But you, you listened to your gut. I should have been executed for treason, and yet you sent me to defy the odds."

I took an automatic step back as he inched closer. His turquoise eyes met mine as he motioned for me to remain calm. I paused, accepting his approach. Caleb reached forward and pressed cold metal into my palm before pivoting back to his accomplices. Tears pooled, threatening to release themselves into the world and betray the tough exterior I was required to maintain in this role. I didn't need to check what he'd placed inside my hand to know what it was. Prescott's compass. The one I'd offered Caleb at his departure.

"I am sorry to hear about his fate," he said, voice earnest. "He was a good man. The world needs more people like you in charge, and we have every desire to make that happen."

"Why?" Was the only word I could force out. A whisper of a word, so fragile it might splinter and vanish behind the knot tightening in my throat if I didn't speak now.

Reina swayed on her feet, looming closer in the silence passing between our groups. I couldn't imagine what she was going through at the moment. Between battling her emotions and what was sure to be flying off us all from the tension and the questions, I wasn't sure how she was standing up right. Nevertheless, she remained at our side. Her stance defensive in the most subtle of ways. She would have our back because despite the pretty words flowing from Caleb and her brother, this was, on all accounts, an *us versus them* situation for the time being. Until all our questions had answers and then some.

"I killed your boyfriend—"

"Fiancé," I corrected on impulse.

It didn't matter now, anyway. It wasn't as though the world knew but it felt owed. I *owed* it to Jax to never let that bond we shared die or go misrepresented. I was only lucky enough to have a partner who understood, who didn't take it as a challenge to replace him. He respected Jax and his memory.

"Fiancé," he nodded with the slight raise of an apologetic wave. "I'm alive because, deep down, you knew killing me wasn't the answer. Some part of you saw past the revenge and trusted your gut. And that's the kind of instinct that keeps people alive. The kind that wins wars. The rebellion doesn't just need a fighter—they need a leader. Someone who knows when to strike, when to hold back, when to think ahead. That's why we want you to help lead the charge."

"War?" Alexiares's pupils dilated at the implication.

Hunter placed his hands behind his back, a line between his thick brows pinched. "The one against my father."

"You expect us to believe that?" Alexiares scoffed.

"Believe what you want. It doesn't change the fact that I'm the one leading the fight against him. I'm not my brother," His features shifted, the warmth from when he looked at Reina drained from his expression as his jaw tightened, every muscle in his face sharp. "It's in your best interest to keep that simple fact front of mind."

"He's … he's right." Reina chimed in, assessing her brother from the side of her eyes while turning toward us. "Hunter and Seth never agreed much when it came to our dad."

"A little hard to believe, isn't it? One son dies, and Ronan isn't interested in replacing him with another." Alexiares muttered, his eyes flickered with skepticism.

Abel swept his gaze over the group. Unease twisted his usual soft expression, "Not loving how this looks, Reina."

Hunter's voice cut through the tension, low and sharp. "Why do you think he's scared of me?" His mouth curled into a humorless smile. "He raised me to be like him. To think like him. *Breathe* like him."

"All things that can be used to hit him where it hurts," the girl beside him tilted her head. There was a fox-like glint in her eyes that made me uncomfortable.

Alexiares's gaze narrowed as he took them in. "And Caleb and this … one—how do they fit into all of this?"

"Serenity," the woman corrected, her tone cool and unbothered.

"Fitting," Alexiares growled.

"Truth? Shit just kind of fell in place." The sun peeked through a patch of clouds behind Hunter's head. "Abridged version ain't gonna hold your interest the same but here I go. We come from a group of travelers out in Transient Nation. A few months ago we received a warning from a passerby and her family, said trouble was coming and to pick a side. Not too long after, my father pushed into the city we were staying in. He was unaware of … my presence. They wanted us bad. Did anything they could to capture us."

"*Chased*," Serenity interjected, adding to Hunter's story. A gust of salt-tinged wind blew her curls in front of her face.

"Hunted," Caleb corrected, casting her a hard look.

Hunter nodded, a shadow passing over his expression. "Our community's a bit different from most, but we are, in fact, someone you want on your side."

I raised a brow and bowed my head slightly. "You've got our attention. Take your time getting it out."

Hunter's expression darkened, his glare cutting over to Caleb, a silent message passing between them that said, *she's going to be difficult.* He turned back to me, voice rough with warning. "There's a tremendous amount of power among us. Now, I'm not gonna go into the specifics with you—not yet. Not without grounds to trust you. All you need to know is we possess the amount of power Ronan wants. Since he can't get it, he wants us gone. Without control over us, we are a threat, and son or not, my father doesn't *do* threats."

"Does he know it's you he's after? Because he told me to kill you." I paused, letting the weight of the words settle. "Had your brother suggest it first, actually."

I zeroed in on Hunter. An unflinching stare did wonders on men. It made them squirm, stirred their nerves until they gave themselves away. A fidget. A hand to the neck. The swipe of an imaginary strand of hair. I waited. Watching.

"There's no way Seth would've made that offer if he knew," Reina said. Pleading his case, though it seemed to burned her tongue. To see the best in him, defend him, once more. "They may not have seen eye to eye all the time but Hunter was every-thing to him."

Hunter's head snapped up, his eyes clouded with something raw, almost wounded, as they fixed on her. "What offer?" he asked, his voice barely a whisper in the wind, a glint of sorrow darkening his sea storm gaze.

"The one to keep our autonomy if we take you out instead?" I regarded him carefully, taking my time before stepping forward. Alexiares trailed at my heels, not eager to put distance between us when the hair on the back of our necks still warned of potential danger. "You don't know?"

All three of them shook their heads. Either they'd solidified their stories before ambushing us or they were telling the truth.

"Then why the hell are you here?" Abel bit out.

"The camps?" Caleb said, his voice laced with confusion. "We have power but not enough people to dismantle it all. That's why we need your military."

I narrowed my eyes, taken aback. The soft, humid breeze blew my curls wild around my face. "We know about the camps but how is that a priority and why does Ronan care?"

"It's not a priority to you that people are locked in cages and worked until they collapse?" Hunter's eyes became an angry storm.

"It's not *not* a priority," Abel reasoned, but the lack of conviction in his tone gave us away. "There's a lot going on man. One thing at a time."

"We have a lot to tackle and it's hard when you're being baby-sat in every meeting," I added. My gaze flicked to Abel. We already knew about the camps—Tomoe made sure of that when she ran her mouth about Lilia's vision before we left. But knowing and acting weren't the same. Not when we had fires everywhere and only so much water to put them out.

"Let me guess? Emissaries?" Serenity questioned with a sarcastic scoff. I peered around Hunter to stare her down. She met me with a startling smile, pointing toward herself. "One of Ronan's best and brightest."

"You're a woman," Alexiares deadpanned, as though Jessa didn't exist. Which to all but Reina, she didn't.

"Scientist works nice." She winked. "Former. I made serums in his labs until I realized what he was using them for."

"You're a *Tinkerer*?" Reina put two and two together from Tomoe's original vision. The woman working with the test tubes and Ronan hovering in the background. They'd been faceless.

"The conscious mind makes up only about 5 percent of our brain activity at any given time," Serenity explained. "Ever wonder what would happen if that number hit fifty?"

We watched in awe as she lifted our weapons from the green and brown grass beneath our feet. No gust of wind, no shift in the earth—just pure force, bending metal and machinery to her will. I'd never seen anything like it. Elemental wielders shaped the world around them, but this? This was different. No air, no earth—just power, raw and unseen … until now.

"Cool," Reina muttered in fascination.

"Those camps are full of magic. Low levels for the mundane energy efforts he needs to keep the lights on in Covert's cities. People like Serenity and some of the others we travel with, that's the kind he wants to either militarize and experiment on. I can't let that happen, so yes, camps are a priority."

"It's inhumane what happens there." Caleb shuddered at Hunter's words. "No one should go through that."

I tilted my head, the outcome of us working together making me excited in a morbidly sick way. "What if we didn't stop there though? What if we destroyed everything he's ever touched?"

"Then I would say I'm interested in hearing what else you got to say." Hunter's face lit up.

There was a warm familiarity to Hunter. The making of him essentially the best parts of Seth and all of Reina. It made me miss Seth. The brother I'd come to know and love. Then the anger of his betrayal took over. What if they were the same in that aspect too?

"Before he attacked Monterey," I said slowly and cautiously, "before we were forced to surrender, I was gathering troops. Troops that now belong to me with others waiting for me to say the word. There's power and then there's *power*. We have both. I'm somewhat intrigued in exploring that with the forces you claim to have."

"I only have the power to speak for us at the moment. That can be revoked at any time. Don't want you getting the wrong idea."

"Wrong idea?" Reina asked her brother. His gaze settled over her. A look of longing passed over before the reserved version of the man she once knew took back over.

"The values we held out in Transient still apply. Our territory being temporarily inhabited doesn't mean our beliefs have changed. Our community is built on the foundations of rebellion against a centralized government. I can't make any promises that the others will be on their best behavior."

"Radicals," Alexiares muttered, his hand falling to the small of my back. "Fantastic."

I glanced at Caleb. His shifty demeanor held my interest. My curiosity. He'd been tested at Monterey Compound as everyone else had. He wasn't powerful. If he was, we'd have known. You couldn't bypass our systems.

Caleb read the questions right off my face. "Don't look at me. I found them by accident. Not everyone's supercharged, just most of them."

"Yet you advocated for me?" I refused to break his gaze.

He shrugged me off, "Hunter was going to come for Reina once I let it slip she was alive, anyway. I only offered him another reason to stick around longer than to retrieve her."

"No one's retrieving anyone," I said then sent a challenging glare Hunter's way. "Are you in charge, or not?"

"He is," Serenity answered for him, but she was not the person I asked, the one I needed to read answers from.

She had been trained and lived with Ronan, and for that, it would take more than words of confidence to buy her bullshit. Hunter and Caleb on the other hand, they were easier to read. Hunter had his sister here and, tentatively, that meant he had shit at stake, someone to fight for on our side. Caleb did too. His family still lived within our walls and apparently me vouching for him meant something.

"They're not bad people by any means," Hunter said, measuring but firm, "Most of 'em will follow my lead. Overplay your hand though, and they'll scatter."

"Well then, I trust we'll all get along just fine." I grinned wide.

Perfect. Everything was coming together better than I could have hoped. Maybe I wouldn't have to do this all alone after all.

Alexiares froze at my back. He couldn't see my face, the smugness mixed with mischief in my grin, but he knew me, "What?"

"Oh nothing," I said. "I love when all the pieces fall into place."

Hunter met my grin. Silent words passed between us. We were on the same page. Ronan Moore would die before the year was up.

I whistled, moving around Hunter and brushing past Serenity. Snatching my pistol and knives out the air, I paid her no mind as I strode further along the cliffside. "You aren't welcome in our gates and I'm not dumb enough to stay the night in your camp. We have twenty-four hours to chat before they expect us back," I called over my shoulder and I felt Abel and Alexiares at my back. Exactly where I knew they'd be no matter what. "I say we keep walking and set up camp out the way. See what kind of arrangement we can settle on."

CHAPTER

TWENTY-SIX

REINA

What the heck was freaking happening? I knew Moe was lying about that mushroom tea. That's right, yeah, you're hallucinating

I walked with 'my brother' less than two feet away from me. If I stuck a finger out to poke him and touched his flesh, I was pretty sure I'd vomit. Nothing that had happened in my life in the last few years made an ounce of sense.

Apparently, I was freaking blind.

At first I thought my daddy died. Then Hunter. God knows I never saw Seth's betrayal coming—though Amaia and Riley apparently had from a mile away. All that panic for nothing.

My heart beat out of my chest, sweat dribbled at the tip of my nose and at my temples. Our group was quiet as we strode along the overgrown coast, but my thoughts were migraine loud.

It had all been for no reason at all.

If I had listened to Seth and waited … better yet, had I gone north like he told us to, then maybe a bunch of people wouldn't be about to lose their lives. All Seth had wanted was his brother and his father; and I—silly girl he'd always claimed me to be— had made sure he never kept hope. Had it been selfish intentions? Maybe.

To be frank, I couldn't understand any of my decisions these days. Deep down, I knew this could be a fresh start for me. But at the same time, Seth had come first when I'd made the call to keep secrets from him. Even if my choice was wrong, even if he couldn't see the innocence in the choice I'd made, it had all been for him. At first, at least. Then I'd seen Monterey Compound and it had become about me.

Shame on me.

Side-eyeing Hunter, I took him in. His mouth was set in a permanent, tight-lipped smile. The same one he put on for me as a kid after scolding Seth for being mean, or when one of dad's passive aggressive comments silenced me at the dinner table. His gaze was set forward but his fingers spread outward as though he wanted to reach for me too and he was telling himself not to. There was no reading on him. For the first time since I figured this gift out, I couldn't sense what someone else was feeling.

"Why didn't you try and find me?" I blurted out. "Come for me when you realized I was alive?"

The others showed no indication of hearing, though they were within earshot. Hunter slowed his steps and created some distance. Unease seeped from Serenity, her body tensing, and I glanced between them briefly, eyes narrowed.

Hunter inhaled and held it for a few seconds. He shrugged with a sorrow filled sigh, "You left me. You both did. I called for you—searched for you both for days. I was in the area for months, hoping, praying, but you left."

"I … I don't understand. I saw you, saw it all happen. Uncle Harris shot you—five times. Twice in the chest, once in the stomach, the graze on your neck, and then …" My breath faltered. The last one—had it really been the head? I could still see it, clear as day. The way his body crumpled. The blood. But now, doubt curled around the memory wispier than smoke.

"You fell," I whispered, my voice raw. "And you didn't get back up."

Tears threatened to stain my face, but I held them back for everyone else's sake. If I let myself go right now, I knew I wouldn't be able to control my magic. The irritating, grating sound of chattering teeth assaulted my ears. It took long, silent seconds to realize they were my own. I clamped my mouth shut, fighting to maintain an ounce of dignity.

The soft, warm embrace of my brother soothed a part of my soul I hadn't expected to heal. A forgotten wound to my heart I ignored the pain of every day. Losing someone so close to you goes far beyond the gripping reality of tragedy. When they hold so much space in your heart that their absence becomes a physical pain, there's no choice but to push their memory away. It's the only way to survive it.

"Remember that week before it all happened?" he asked quietly, his voice almost swallowed by the sound of the sea.

We walked side by side, boots crunching against gravel-strewn paths that skirted the edge of a windswept cliff. The Pacific churned against the jagged shoreline, angry and frothing at the white capped mouth of each wave. I nodded, silent, giving his words room to linger.

Hunter had become withdrawn, leaving not just me to my lonesome, but Seth too. It was a rare thing for him. Usually, if he wasn't off riding or hunting with Seth, he was nestled up in the corner of the living room with me, listening to me ramble or reading as I crafted away with my hands. We were always busy, always productive; idle hands weren't tolerated on our ranch. And when the world had gone to hell, nothing much changed—at least, not at first. A ranch was a ranch. The only new thing about our circumstances was magic that could help.

His teeth clenched together, Hunter continued, "Well, I was up in the attic, going through the mess. Ma said she had some old books stored up there. Said if I could find 'em, they were mine." His light pink lips twisted into a knot as his memories flooded back.

A memory tugged me too. *Yes*, he'd finished everything we had downstairs twice over and was on the hunt for something new.

"Well, I fucked around and found more than I was looking for. Harris killed people. Lots of 'em. About twenty, from what I could tell. Dad, uh … he kept the newspaper clippings. Crossed state lines to keep people from connecting them all. I think Dad was the only one who did. Got him on the straight and narrow. It was before Sloan was born, before he met Auntie. Pretty sure he made him join the military and called it a day. Kept the clippings for whatever reason. "

I exhaled sharply, understanding settling over me like a weight. Our father had always known. He hadn't stopped Harris—he'd simply redirected him, found a way to make him useful. To control him.

Now he was doing the same thing. Treating people as weapons to be wielded, threats to be neutralized. The camps. The executions. The fear he spread was more destructive than a plague.

"Just like now," I murmured. "He doesn't fix problems. He repurposes them."

"Exactly."

A knot formed deep in my belly, slow and sickening as the horror set in. "So you confronted him?"

Hunter's gaze remained straight ahead. Most would say our eyes were the same from first glance, but Hunter's were slightly different. A dash of extra ice that differed from the rest of ours that made him appear colder than Seth, even if it had always been the other way around.

His words still carried the same bashful but fearless energy he'd always had, though the added confidence was something I'd have to get used to. "No. I mean, not by choice. I'd asked Seth if he wanted to go for a hunt. Was gonna ask him what to do. I didn't want him on the ranch, not around you and Ma. But he was due back to Minnesota soon. If it wasn't worth the fight, then there was no point. Harris noticed the distance I set between us, though. Cornered me when he overheard Seth and me on the walkie. Asked if he could come. I supposed I was a bit jumpy, but the immediate no set him off. He asked me flat out and at that point I couldn't deny. There was only one way out of that conversation. I knew it but stupidly I turned my back thinking we were family. There was no way he'd take out one of his own. Damn, was I wrong."

Hunter glanced at me. He laughed bitterly, and the sound cut through me like glass. "I was so wrong. I heard your scream, but I couldn't move. I thought you were comin' for me at first. Then I heard him take off after you. It broke my heart I couldn't save you. The terror in your voice. The shots fired not too long after and I thought that was it. This was how the Moore family ends, the smoke from the house made me give up. I closed my eyes, praying to the Lord he would take me soon and fast. I couldn't move anything but my arms, yet it all hurt so bad. I woke to Daisy nudging me with her nose to get up, to fight."

I froze, his words unraveling the past in sharp, broken pieces. "How did you even survive?" My voice came out as barely more than a whisper.

"There's another blessing that comes with water sometimes. Did you know that?" The pain in his eyes was naked as he glanced over at me. Hunter leaned close, his voice barely audible over the wind. "Only a few of us out there. Or that's what we thought at first. Turns out father has plenty locked away behind his border and he's doing his best to *breed* more."

The word 'breed' made my stomach churn. I could hear the disgust in his voice, the snarl apparent in his tone without needing to steal a glance at his face. Without the ability to sense exactly how he was feeling, I took a risk. I cut the side of my hand with my nails, then waved two fingers over it. The power of my magic offered a warm hug over my skin as I watched the wound close almost instantly. "Hunter … you mean like this?" I asked softly.

"Yeah," he said with a small smile, "something like that." Hunter's eyes went wide, breath shallow as he fixated on my hand, a flicker of fascination there.

His fingers moved with a phantom ache, the memory of pain etched into every tendon. "First one hit my stomach—knocked the wind right out of me. Next two tore through my chest. By the time the fourth hit my neck, I was already going down." His throat bobbed, eyes distant. "I saw the last shot coming. Right between the eyes. But I hit the ground first. Either he thought I was dead, or the angle was off. It never landed."

He was quiet and still, every part of him moving like he was walking through a dream. "When Daisy found me, I could barely move—just my hands, my right arm. I was pissed. Slammed my fist against my core over and over, furious my body wouldn't listen. Then … the warmth came. At first, I didn't notice that with every hit, sensation came back to my body. Once the nerves had healed enough for the pain to seep in, my brain went on autopilot to stop the bleeding. Plugged my finger in each bullet hole and healed right over it. Nasty shit, let me tell ya, Reina. Zombies coming down from the house covered in flames was enough pressure to get things moving and quick."

I wanted to ask many things, questions tangled up in my mind. There was only so much we could get into at the moment. I stuck with the heavy hitters. "How did you get here? Your people—Serenity—all that jazz?"

He chuckled, his gaze turning warmer, softer. "So many questions, yet I haven't had the chance to ask about you."

I laughed and waved him off. Part of me didn't want to repeat it because saying it aloud sucked harder every time. The other half wanted to keep it short because I was far more interested in what he had to say. I talked too much, but sometimes it was all too obvious when it was best to shut up and listen. "My story isn't as interesting. Seth chose Dad over us, or rather, over the family we could have had. A rumor of a rumor got him to do it. Screwed us all after Amaia and her people took us in. Then … the dad I wish I had from the beginning died. And here I am—farm girl turned faux emissary, helping fuel a rebellion. Can you believe it?"

Hunter laughed, and for a moment that flared and vanished like a spark, I thought I imagined it. His eyes lit with the warmth I remembered. "I believe it. There's gotta be one hell of a story in there. Serenity and I found each other not long after I left the state. It was an accident—a lot of spiteful tension too. One day I'll tell you. She was already with a group, and I fit in well enough." He paused, glancing away as if lost in thought. "And then our daughter…"

My heart skipped. "I have a nieceypoo?" I blurted out, barely containing the rush of excitement.

Amaia stumbled in her step, and Serenity paused at the words. Her head ticked to the side twice as if she were trying to stop herself from causing a scene. She turned back and bore eyes filled with rage at Hunter. Words unspoken passed between the two of them.

Hunter stilled, a faint sadness in his smile as his eyes met mine. "Her name's Adelaide. She's just shy of three now. Looks just like you did at that age. Big front teeth, always turning red from laughter."

I couldn't smile wider if the sides of my mouth were split. My name. Hunter named her after my middle name. Hushing to a whisper, I asked what I was afraid to hear the answer to. "Do I … will I get the honor of meeting her?"

He stopped, turning fully toward me, hesitation written in his eyes. "I would love that, but it's not up to me. I made Serenity a promise long ago that Adie's safety would always come first to me in this world. She'll need to agree. But if she does … Adie would be over the moon to meet the auntie she's heard about in bedtime stories."

Happiness, pure and unfiltered, filled me. "So you and Serenity are together then? She's your wife?"

"Don't let her hear you say that." He stared at her, the yearning clear in his eyes. "I tried for a long time, but no, Serenity's my best friend. She calls it a drunken accident, though either of us had barely had a sip that night. Adelaide is our world, Reina. She's the family we never had. And I'm grateful for that, for this family we're building, even if it's not exactly what I expected—it's better than what we ever had."

I watched him. Hunter was still the boy I'd known, but he'd grown into a man shaped by stories and scars I couldn't even fathom. He and Seth would have been thirty this year—older than James had ever lived to be. James, our oldest brother, the one we lost first, before the world had ended. Now there were only two—Hunter and me.

He and Amaia may not have come to an agreement yet, but this was the start of a new beginning. I knew it deep in my heart and from the peace that had settled over her at hearing the joyful bits of the conversation the two of us shared. She would find a way to work with him, with all of this, if for no other reason than for me.

"Never again," I reassured him, interlocking our fingers and giving them a squeeze. "I will never leave you again."

"Hey, we're Moores. The two of us. You and I." Hunter said firmly, with pride. "This ends with us, got it? I'll be damned if my daughter grows up in a world our father envisioned."

CHAPTER

TWENTY-SEVEN

AMAIA

"Here is fine," I said as I turned my back to the rocks. The dampness of the cold, slick moss kissed the skin around the straps of the black tank top tucked into my cargos.

The ocean churned under the setting sun. This corner of Moss Landing State Beach created a natural border of protection from the scariest thing out there; people. With the curve of the beach playing to our favor, anyone coming toward us would have no cover.

"Right, and let you set us up?" Serenity scoffed and turned toward Hunter. "No way. We'll stop when Hunter says we stop."

Rubbing my temples, I closed my eyes in irritation. I wasn't sure the relation between them. If he was *her* Riley or something more, either way, she was a nuisance. "I'm not going to like you at all, am I?"

Ignoring her protest, I gave her my back and dropped my bag onto the sand. I ruffled through it as I listened for hidden context. Waiting to see how the power dynamics of their group played out. Did Serenity have any *real* sway or was she all whimper no bite?

Would Caleb speak up, or would he sit back and let the two of them figure things out? I never pegged him as an alpha, but I would be a fool to assume the Caleb that lived at Monterey was the same one standing before me.

"Hunter," Reina's voice was small against the salty wind. "Please."

That was all it took. The plea of his baby sister. Hunter sighed, the sound drowned out by Serenity's groan of disbelief.

"I'll scope out the perimeter," Caleb said without pressing further.

The warmth of a palm settled on my shoulder, pressing down with a slight squeeze. "I'll watch him scope out the perimeter." Abel proclaimed, earning him a soft but clear snort from the former.

Two tents were erected in half an hour. One for them and one for us. Without ever saying the words, it was clear that one person from each camp would keep watch at the same time throughout the night. Dusk was fast upon us as we settled around the sand in a circle. No fire unless the situation was dire. That was the rule.

Hunter's crew watched on hungrily as we tore into our dried meats and mixed nuts. Reina offered some to Hunter from her go bag. He stared at the bags for a moment before falling victim to the weakness of starvation, offering some to Serenity. They were a lean bunch, that was for certain.

I tossed over three nutrient bars to Serenity with the smallest of grins. They were for emergencies. Shit out of luck scenarios. The average daily caloric intake was jam-packed into a 2 x 4 bar crammed with proteins, iron, and who knows what the hell else. Obviously, they needed it more than I did.

"Tossing us scraps like a dog," Serenity snapped. "Should I bark too?"

"Nah, that's my job," Alexiares said, voice flat. His stare followed with the clear message that lacked jest. I was under no obligation to divvy out rations we may need in the future, but I did anyway out of goodwill.

Serenity offered a curt nod as she met my eye. Hunter cleared his throat, switching the conversation into small talk with expert ease. Controlling the crowd just as all Moores had been gifted—from nature or nurture, I wasn't quite sure. Reina's head fell to her brother's shoulder as he talked, not stopping to catch a breath. Her vacant stare not matching her appropriately timed chimes of laughter.

If someone had asked me ten months ago who was the strongest emotional tether of my family, the answer would have wholeheartedly been Reina. She was the glue. Our tether to our morals. Evidence of the good that existed in this world. I'd always seen her as an unbreakable spirit. But now, the glass-eyed stare consuming her, I feared the dam was about to break at the thoughts of how much the assumption of Hunter's death had cost her.

Are you all right? I mouthed, making note of Abel and Caleb's approach.

She nodded, bit her lip, then shook her head no.

"Hunter," I called, my voice cutting through the low murmur of the group. His gaze lifted to meet mine, steady but unreadable. Blank in a different way than Reina's. I held it for a moment, forcing myself to see only him—not Seth. Just Hunter. "Our watch. Let's chat."

We walked in silence as darkness took over the beach. The great thing about minimal light pollution was that we were used to it by this point. Our eyes had adjusted, evolved to a more primitive state. The waves calmed as Hunter passed by. A quiet display of the mighty power he evidently possessed. I watched him out the side of my eye, his towering figure lethal yet off-kilter in his gait.

My fingers slipped into the pockets of my pants and curled around my little pot of gold. I brought the tip of my pointer to the end and sucked in the smooth, earthly sweet smoke.

"You smoke?" I asked, extending it out to Hunter with a coughed exhale.

"Can't say that I ever have."

I snickered at that. Reina always did claim him the golden boy. "Nothing like the present."

He took it with awkward fingers, falling victim to a first-timer's pull. I bit back a childish laugh as I watched him fight for a good pull of fresh, clean air. One and done, Hunter jammed it back in front of my face.

"So your compound is about to fall apart. My guess is y'all are near starving, but you got the time to grow marijuana in your backyard?"

"Always time for a bit of debauchery," I said. The cloudless sky offered a decent view of the empty beach. The perimeter was too quiet—the kind of silence that prickled under the skin and refused to sit still. "Soothes my mind, helps fight off the worser demon."

I glanced at him, a teasing edge in my voice. But the look didn't last. My tone dipped. "It's from a stash from before we left for Duluth. Shared it with your brother."

Hunter's head moved with disbelief in an extended shadow. "With Seth? Doesn't sound like him."

"Yeah, he did a lot of shit that didn't sound like him in the end. But you never really know someone, do you?"

"I knew my brother," he said, the words clipped but steady. "Knew him inside out. Can't say I'm shocked about how things ended. He's no better than my father when it comes to restraint. When life gets too peaceful, he finds a reason to make a mess and then clean it up. Reina said it was all for family, but … don't tell her I'm saying this."

I held his eye for a beat, then raised my hand and passed the blunt back. "I don't keep secrets. I secure future collateral to hurt you with."

He snorted, shaking his head. "I don't buy his bullshit. Seth has always tended to act first, then patch together a justification later. Sure, maybe he wanted to find me at the start, but somewhere along the way, it stopped being about reuniting our family."

I found his ability to rationalize the situation fascinating. How someone processed grief—what they chose to hold on to, what they let go of—was a complicated mess.

But Hunter's resolve felt layered, to say the least.

"You say that as if you knew what he was thinking," I said.

Hunter's gaze swept the area as he pulled a small toke, then pushed the rolled herb back my way. "Don't need to read his mind to know what was in it." The words passed through gritted teeth.

I cocked my head, skepticism creeping into my expression. "Except your brother *could* read minds."

"Since when?"

"Since day one," I shot back without missing a beat, eyes narrowing at the smallness of his voice. The remnants of curiosity in Hunter's tone.

"I didn't know." His presence shifted, the air around us thickening. The waves crashed harder against the shore. Seth had kept him in the dark about something.

I wasn't interested in comforting him. I was testing him. Reina had mentioned years ago that Seth hadn't even realized his gift until after they'd left the ranch. The waves slammed louder, the ocean rising with anger. I took a step closer, my voice colder as I stomped out the butt of the blunt. "So tell me something you *do* know. Something about your father that makes not killing you worth whatever retaliation follows."

"What if I told you I had people placed everywhere that matters?"

I stared ahead, the dark horizon in my sights, without acknowledging him. The salty sea air cut through the night, his emotions rocking with the tide. "What if I told you if any of them are behind my walls without my permission, they're dead?"

"Relax. I was speaking within my father's ranks."

I finally glanced at him, an eyebrow arched. "Consider me curious."

He gave a quick, almost bitter chuckle. "In the camps. In his ranks. At his table. Sympathizers are everywhere."

The faintest hint of a smirk tugged at my lips. "I'm high, Hunter, but I'm not fucking stupid. Your father runs a tight ship."

Hunter's boots tossed sand as his voice grew colder, sharper. "Not if you know how to sink it. Where to poke a hole."

Hunter was saying it as though it were a simple choice, a guilt-free initiative—take his father down. As if there was any easy way to do that. I had a good idea of what it took to pull something like that off, and I knew enough to be wary of anyone who seemed too sure about it.

I froze mid-step. The rhythm of the ocean punctuated the silence between us. Pivoting toward him, my gaze cut through the darkness. "You're sure you're ready to do this? I hope you know I won't make his death easy or quick. Reina has made her peace with that."

"The second he put a hit out on my head, he was dead to me." There was something about the way he spoke—rough and raw, a wound left unhealed—that made me trust him to never waiver in his loyalty.

The air stung as it filled my chest. The silence stretched between us. Feeling every bit as though the world was holding its breath. "To be clear, you're implying he knows that it is you leading a rebellion and not Caleb?"

He was still, the space between us thick. "No. Still not sure if he knows about me. I saw him with the group that cornered our caravan near Salem's borders, right before they attacked Monterey. Serenity, Caleb, and I were retreating with some of the others. Our group was separated, and his back was turned to me. He just stood there, watching them terrorize with a smirk on his face. My father was never a gentle man, but this cruelty … seeing it with my own eyes rather than hearing of it was jarring to say the least. My guess is, if he does know I'm out there, then he didn't expect me to hear of Reina or for Reina and I to make contact before you killed me. Your boyfriend's kind of known to keep the habit of killing first, no questions asked before or later. Seth, though, there's no way he'd extend my father's deal if he knew it was my death warrant he was signing."

I took a step closer, the wind pulling at my hair, the salty sting of the ocean air sharp on my skin. "Sounds like your daddy's got a weakness that's ripe for me to exploit."

THE NIGHT HAD PASSED ON FASTER THAN I'D EXPECTED. ALEXIARES and Serenity relieved us from our shift and woke us at the onset of dawn to get moving. We nibbled on what was left of our nuts and dried fruit as Reina worked to refill our canisters of water for the hike back. Instead of the forced small talk we'd imposed on last night, the group sat in uncomfortable silence. There was no use in drawing out the inevitable.

"Enough bullshitting," I said, getting straight to the point. "How many of you are in the area?" I asked.

"None you need to be aware of."

"Okay," I bit back at Serenity, who stared back with a brazen glare filled with distaste. "I'll just leave them outside the walls to either get captured or die. With Ronan on the prowl, probably both."

Hunter held a hand out, pressing Serenity back down, who stupidly had risen to her feet in challenge. "Only about a hundred of us would be comfortable enough to make our way into a space we won't be able to leave at our own will."

"Their demise then," I shrugged, refusing to meet Reina's piercing stare, the silent plea in her eyes burning a hole in my fucking forehead. "Our gates are shut down unless you have proof of identity and others to vouch for your residency from Elko or Sacramento. I can figure it out in small droves, not all hundred at once. Fifteen a day until they all get there."

Alexiares cleared his throat, finishing where I left off. "You'll have to assume an identity from one of the fallen settlements. Avoid the refugees at all costs. If you're pressed, don't volunteer your origins—wait for them to reveal theirs first. If it comes to that."

"My people are curious and skeptical of newcomers," I said, letting the words hang for context.

Caleb shifted uncomfortably. He peered over at Serenity with the slightest of movements. I cut my gaze to follow his, catching the faint, deliberate tap of her fingers brushing toward the ground. Alexiares noticed it too, his body stilling as he gave a single sharp nod to acknowledge the signal.

"We all are," Abel surmised, his heavy stare stopping and landing on essentially three strangers before us. That familiar cocky resolve, a youthful tug of his ego, bringing the rough confidence back to his voice. The same confidence that brought out the warrior in him out on the battlefield.

"Hunter, you come first," Reina insisted as she inched closer to him.

Her brown hair brushed the tips of her shoulders as she tilted her head to take him in. Hunter glanced down at her, caution flickering in his eyes. His gaze shifted from her to Serenity, more focused now, as if he were reasoning with her. Her lips tightened, a silent pull of reluctant defeat.

"Won't people sort of recognize the resemblance between you two?" Abel asked, voicing the concern that had been gnawing at me as I studied the siblings in the unforgiving light of day—no adrenaline to mask the obvious. "Especially if you stand right next to each other."

"Then don't." Caleb's voice cut through the unease, drawing every eye to him. "Look, when this is over, you two can play happy family all you want. But for now, when Hunter arrives, he's nothing more than an emissary from Elko. Their leadership fell, along with most of their top-ranking military officials. No one who matters survived to make a claim against them. Elko wasn't much smaller than Monterey. Faces blur. No one will notice."

"He's right," Serenity added, her tone firm as her gaze pinned Hunter. "For your safety, once we're there, if you're in the same room, you stay on opposite sides. Minimal interactions—at least in public."

Reina flinched under the weight of her words, exchanging a glance with her brother. The tension between them grew thick enough to cut before they finally nodded. It wasn't peace—it was a fragile agreement, hanging in the air with all the tension of a storm not yet broken.

None of us moved. The quiet pressed heavy on my chest. Somewhere, this plan felt destined to break.

"We should move out." Alexiares's voice was low, but it broke through the silence with finality.

CHAPTER
TWENTY-EIGHT

ALEXIARES

We passed through the small, abandoned fishing town on the way back. This was the second time today we'd crossed through the street full of eerily quaint shops at my insistence. After this, we'd pass through a neighborhood next to the highway before the final trek back. My steps slowed, instincts flaring—someone was out there. A glance at the uneasiness in my girl, and without a word, it was evident we were aligned in our thinking. Something was up and it was best to cover our tracks, change up our route for anyone on our trail until it was safe to make a run for home.

"Reina, don't be mad, but I have a question." Abel broke the silence for the first time in a few miles.

Reina slowed her steps to match his and grabbed his hand with the purest of smiles. "Why would I be mad? I love the inquisitive mind."

"It's about Hunter," I stated the obvious, and Amaia jabbed me hard in the gut with eyes of fire. Grabbing her wrist, I pulled her into my side, wrapping my arm across her shoulder with an evil smirk.

"Oh." Reina's soft tone was light as a whisper.

"No offense," Abel said, slow and hesitant. "But how are we supposed to excuse fifteen new faces, let alone one hundred with Bietoletti and the others lurking around every corner?"

Reina's jaw clenched in an attempt to hold back the urge to snap at him. His doubt ate away at her positive facade. This wasn't the time to address this shit. Something pricked at the edge of my senses. Movement? A sound? I couldn't place it, but Amaia noticed it too. Her shoulders tensed, her sharp gaze scanning the distance.

We didn't need words to communicate. *Stay calm, don't react.* Her unspoken command was clear.

Amaia had been on edge ever since the reports of Ronan's men had trickled in from our patrols. Claims of refugees being hunted down along with anyone dumb enough to stray outside enclosed settlements. Quick and brutal. Battered bodies left behind—beaten to death, it wasn't Ronan's usual style.

Riley had his theories of course. Transient Nation cast-offs causing chaos. Mass panic. The oppressive shadow of impending doom swallowed the fear of many. Timing may have fit, but as far as I was concerned, nothing had been confirmed.

"Amaia said she'd figure it out," Reina murmured, her voice barely a whisper, her posture sagging with defeat. "We can trust him, Abel. He's not like Seth."

I glanced at Abel and dared him to argue. He didn't. Instead, he opted to give Reina an awkward pat on the shoulder, his smile uneasy. "Okay then," he muttered, unconvinced.

A flicker of a shadow snapped my attention to the window of a two-story house. I didn't need to think. I turned at the same time Amaia did, shifting Reina and Abel behind us.

"Someone's here," Reina whispered, her voice shaking.

"On the ground!" Amaia barked.

We hit the dirt half a second before the bullets started spraying. Debris kicked up around us. The sting of adrenaline hit me hard. An orgasmic power that sharpened my focus, slowed things down. I crawled, dragging myself toward cover. Amaia and I worked in tandem. A wall of fire went up to shield the others. It was good enough for now, but fire wouldn't stop bullets.

Amaia muttered a curse and rolled onto her back. I felt the rush of air before I saw her plan—a dome of compressed air forming above us, deflecting the next round of shots. Smart. My fucking warrior princess.

We pushed forward, army-crawling until we were behind the nearest house. My back hit the wall, and I exhaled in excitement. The thrill of my next kill had me calculating our next move. Whoever was out there had made a mistake firing on my family. For that, they would pay.

They always did.

"How many?" I called out over the gunfire to Reina.

She pressed her body back against the wall, arms spread out wide as though she'd wished she was stuck to it. "Unsure," she said, eyes closed as she focused on her magic, face red. "A lot."

"Down!" Abel screamed and pulled Reina flat against the earth. A spray of bullets came from another house, closing us in along with the sounds of whoops and shouts from each direction.

We were surrounded. Amaia punched through the glass of the downstairs window behind her. Blood dripped down her shredded fingers, but she hardly blinked as she ushered the others inside.

"In here," Amaia ordered, grabbing Reina and hoisting her inside. I inched closer to her and offered additional support to get Abel through. She stopped for a moment, assessing me, the willingness I'd have to follow her command when in danger.

I'm not going anywhere without you. She stared back at me in protest and rolled her eyes before holstering her gun and making her way inside. I made it approximately one step inside before realizing it was far too quiet for them to be clearing the house. Dust speckled in the sunlight inside the dark kitchenette as my eyes adjusted.

"Well, it was either this house or the one across the way. We laid a bet." Some random guy sat in the chair at a round glass table, flask in hand, owning the damn place without a second thought. He tipped it back and chugged as if it were the only thing keeping him alive. "Like a mouse in a maze."

He licked his lips as he glanced between each of us. His black hair was uneven, longer on the top and stuck out on the sides. Between his stench, the dark bags under his eyes, and the aura of exhaustion around him, it was clear he hadn't slept in days.

A gun was placed at Amaia's back. Two men clutched their arms around Reina and Abel's necks as tears streamed down Reina's cheeks. The sack of shit at the table, their leaders presumably, settled his dark, darting gaze on me. Sizing me up, he turned with a scoff, a faint smirk tugged at his pale face that held no indication of amusement. Nah. There was a confidence there, the kind that said he thought himself to have already won.

I heard the crack of her skull, her yelp of surprise, then watched as Amaia fell to the ground. Her body crumpled lifeless before me and terror struck my heart. Its hammering beat rang in my ears, my vision closing into a tunneled red fury. Reina panicked, her anger swarmed through the room to our disservice. Abel clamped down on the man's arm, the retaliation of the effort came fast with the hard shove into the wall. It stunned him and I leaped to catch his head from splintering into the table. I was tossed back into the window, shards of glass jamming into my back and severing nerves. Pain seared through me. I was fucking stuck. Reina yelled, throwing her head into the now blood gushing nose of her handler. I gathered what strength I had left and lifted myself free.

The sound of the warm, sticky, blood leaking down my back dribbled against the quieting chaos of the room. I reached for my flames but they were quickly doused with ease by the man at the table. With Amaia, Abel, and Reina down, the fight became four on one. Something hard slammed against my skull, and consciousness slipped through my fingers.

CHAPTER

TWENTY-NINE

ALEXIARES

Pressure built behind my eye with such intensity it might've cracked my skull the fuck open. I kept my body still, eyes closed as I lay in wait. The dull, hum of an engine and the subtle sway of the ground beneath me told me I was in a moving vehicle. I was about done with the whole innovative *Tinkerer* gene shit. Life was better a year ago, when I barely saw a car let alone found myself hogtied in the back of one. This was becoming a pattern I wasn't thrilled to repeat.

I needed to get my bearings, figure out where Amaia was. She was my priority. Then the others. My heart pounded against my will—too fast, too loud. I focused on the sounds around me: the shuffling of bodies with each pothole, the steady rhythmic breaths filling the hot, stuffy air. Five … *no, six*. Six other people were here. All a bit too close for my comfort.

"You can stop pretending to be asleep now." The words succeeded by a sharp, deliberate stomp to my stomach.

I fell flat, eyes widening as I gasped for air. White stars filtered my vision. Amaia's beaten, roughed up face fought to center me. Her eyes strained by the tugging of her curls the man clamped on to in order to keep her upright. He held a knife to her throat, a threat that dangled before me at every rough patch in the road. She remained stoic, her eyes darting over to the side. Reina sat next to her. Deep bruising stained under her eyes, blood clumped around Reina's nose, her cheeks flushed and wet with tears and spit from the cloth stuffed into her mouth. She was still and stiff though she was alert and searching in her gaze.

Abel had received the worst of it. He was slumped over, still unconscious.

"Hell of a bounty out on your heads, and lucky, lucky sonofabitch that I am, I found ya," the man said, his free hand forming a pointed finger back at himself. The tease of his tongue shined against the sunlight pouring in from the window at the back of what I now knew to be a van. I couldn't wait to cut it off.

Amaia's glare was sharp enough to cut steel. We were both tied up, but her message was crystal clear: keep him distracted.

I leaned back as much as the ropes allowed and forced a laugh. "Let me guess," I said, the words dripping with disdain. "Ronan."

The guy's brow twitched, face contorted in strained anger. "Malachai. He really wants you dead."

Figured. Malachai had gone behind Ronan's back. I studied the guy, some low-level bounty hunter eager for an easy payday. He wasn't important—what mattered was that Malachai had put a price on our heads without Ronan knowing. That meant one of two things: either Ronan was losing control, or Malachai had decided we weren't Ronan's problem anymore. Both were bad. We weren't just looking over our shoulders for Ronan anymore. Malachai wanted us gone, and he wasn't waiting for permission.

That was going to be a problem.

"Tell us something we don't fucking know," Amaia growled. Her eyes dropped to my wrists then over to the flammable items in the back. Two guards laughed in front of them, their guns strapped around their shoulders and dropped into their laps at the ready.

"Oh that," The man tsked twice in Amaia's ear, the sound too smug for my personal taste. "A little safety measure since we don't have a way to limit your magic."

"I'm going to kill you." The words uttered from my mouth but I found myself completely detached. All I could focus on was picturing slicing him up, piece by piece, limb by limb. Watching as he screamed in agony. Spitting in his face with each cry for mercy. The vision I imagined sent a ripple of cold satisfaction through me. His screams? *Music.*

That was the only thing to get me through having to watch him snatch Amaia's head back with such force I swore it would snap. "Maybe one day, but not today," he teased, the spit flying from his mouth and landing on her ear. "Today, my group earns passage back into Transient Nation. Free rein."

Of all times, my girl, my princess, decided to poke the bear. "Oh please, if Ronan isn't aware, don't think for a second he'll respect it. What deal do you think we made?"

"As far as I'm concerned, I don't care. You lot were the big price, the others are assurance he won't need any of us once we turn you over."

Amaia and I exchanged a glance, both of us frozen on the same question: *What others?*

"Not too bright, are we?" she taunted as her ropes fell to the ground with simmered edges. Amaia didn't move. She never moved too soon.

She was waiting for the right moment—waiting for me.

If my restraints hit the metal bottom of this van, he would see them. I caught the look in her eyes. I needed a distraction and that would cost her. Painfully. I couldn't refuse her. Not without giving away our plan. So I took myself back to my happy place, the one filled with *his* pain. We had to get out. I had no other choice.

"Slick mouth for a dead girl," he sneered.

"Dead girl has a name."

"Dead girls don't talk."

"Sure, but this one bites." Amaia's words were low, savage. Her teeth sank into his leg and he howled. The distraction was enough. She slammed his head into the side of the van with a brutal crunch, the motion swift. Powerful.

I was already in motion. The ropes tight around my wrists simmered with a familiar, blissful heat. They burned away into ash. A stream of my water magic disarmed the guard without gracing him a moment to catch up to what was happening. The second guard panicked. Untrained for the situation unleashing around him. His hand wavered toward his gun, primed to raise it and pull the trigger.

My fist collided with his throat, collapsing his trachea. His last breath didn't reach the air before I tossed him on the floor. I glanced back with a smile. Amaia straddled the man who had initiated this all. He leaned against the wall as she withheld any oxygen from him with a sinister grin. In one swift movement, she pulled her confiscated knives from his holster and jammed them into his temples.

With a sigh of relief, she pulled them free, wiping them against the side of her pants. "I'm getting extremely fucking tired of the misogynistic bullshit running rampant these days. Haven't they ever heard that a woman *is* king?"

She handed them toward me without turning back. Her focus was on something else. Something she'd never expect to have taken. Jax's twin swords. Amaia placed them back into the back harness as the van came to an abrupt stop. Quick on my feet, I holstered the pistols taken from us at the house. I tucked the last one into my waistband and brown, doe eyes met mine, smile lines crinkling the sides of them.

"Ready?" she asked as she moved toward the doors.

"After you, Princess."

She kicked open the doors. They slammed to the sides, taking down two assailants from the front. Amaia unlatched both swords and twirled them in her palms. We were in the middle of nowhere. An open field with no witnesses other than the company en route speeding toward us. I spun around, dropping both knives into the stomach of presumably the driver and pounced. Pulling them free, I drove them back down, over, and over again. His puncture wounds oozed with the metallic scent of blood as it painted my face.

Unfortunately, we were not alone. Four vans had been keeping our tail, all stocked with armed, stupid in the fucking head guards. I watched on as the women in the bunch narrowed in on Amaia, wrongfully taking her as the weaker target. She smirked in acceptance of the challenge and we fell into step. The assailants charged forward, lacking the understanding that we were clearly outnumbered yet unfazed.

They lacked common sense, and I took joy in the offering of a good fight. I pulled free two of my guns. Firing through two of the targets, their bodies fell in tandem. We stepped over them like neglected cobblestone roads and they groaned under our weight. Amaia tossed free some of her fire. The putrid smell of human barbecue clustered at the base of my nostrils. They circled us and we fell back to back. Assaulting us was a group effort—one they still managed to fail.

Though Amaia had lost one of her swords in the fight, she still swung one proudly before her face in dare. She yelled with the heart of a dragon and worked her way through their bodies. I followed suit, dropping the guns when I ran out of ammo. The soft push and pull of stabbing had always felt more therapeutic of a death to bring. I ducked as a metal chain laced baseball bat swished through the air above my head. I grabbed onto it and brought it down. His head splintered, the burst reminiscent to a dropped melon but I kept moving.

I grounded myself and scoped out our current situation. Amaia did the same, reaching her hand out briefly to clasp within mine. Ten down, two to go.

"On your left, *Bloodhound*," she said with the nod of her head.

I smirked, eyes falling to the approaching hulk of a man heading right for her. "On your left, Princess."

My knees were kicked out from under me but I was quick to hop back to the balls of my feet. A wiry yet oddly strong hand gripped at the knives in my hands and pulled them free. It turned into an all-out brawl as he flipped one around and dove for my gut. I tossed out an arm, stopping him with the hard contact of forearm on wrist. Reaching for the side of his neck, I brought him closer, offering a false sense of an opening.

He took it, leaning forward with the momentum I needed to drive a strong push down and flip him to his back. With one stomp to the base of his palm, the knife fell. I picked it up and stabbed it into the side of his neck with a sickly melodic sound of metal entering flesh.

The scent of flames came close behind me but made no move to strike. "You look great," Amaia said and I pulled my gaze up her body.

Red splattered like freckles across her nose and forehead. Her shirt was torn on the side and there were several slash marks on the brown skin of her torso. The rise and fall of her chest was ragged. Tired. But otherwise, she was in mint condition considering the shit we'd just gone through. There was resolve in her posture.

"As do you," I said, tapping her ass with a hard slap as I guided her back toward the van we'd arrived in. She leaned down, swiping up the sword she'd lost.

"Freaking finally," Reina complained the moment Amaia removed her gag. "I coulda helped more than inspire fear you know, not totally useless."

"Pretty sure they were scared because he damn near painted his face in blood," Abel groaned, barely coming to. He was bleeding from the back of his scalp but it had slowed to but a dribble at the first contact of Reina's touch. "Actually, he's scaring me. Please back up."

"My bad," Amaia shrugged. "Thought you could get going on Abel during the wait."

She scooted out the bed of the van and offered Reina a hand. I dragged Abel to the edge then hopped down. Amaia stood next to me, hands on her hips, eyes squinting as she considered our choice of vehicles to make the drive back. "See what we can take and put it in one car. I'm ready to get the fuck home."

Reina offered a polite smile and brushed herself off. With quick reassurance she helped Abel lean against the side of the van before making her way toward the one on the far left. The van I tackled was empty minus the storage of gas stockpiled in the back. At first, I assumed we were riding solar, but with all this gas and ignoring the stench of death, I realized it was a regular engine.

None of it was anything that could be of use for us. We'd drive a vehicle back but all it did was cut the two hours we had left down to thirty minutes. Monterey had chosen not to clear the roads long ago. Now it was a tactical advantage Amaia had no intention of changing anytime soon. I walked back to the center, coming shoulder to shoulder with my girl, who appeared faintly annoyed at finding nothing useful. We got to work on the bodies, collecting their weapons, ammo, and anything else that could take or spare a life.

"It's like a video game," I teased, my heart skipping at Amaia's genuine burst of laughter. I joined in, covering my mouth at the faint snort I'd never heard myself make before. There was a joy only she could bring out of me and I hoped to revel in it for the rest of my life.

Amaia dropped to her knees, clutching her stomach as she mimicked the sounds of a war game. "Ding. Ding."

A gunshot rang out. "Uh, guys? There are people back here," Reina called, her gun trained on a group as a guard slumped to the ground behind her.

Within two seconds I'd realized Abel was no longer at our backs and the sound of gunfire had come from the van Reina had gone to investigate. We rushed over, peering into the back of the van. Ten bodies were crammed inside. I didn't know what the fuck I was looking at or where they'd come from. I couldn't have guessed from their attire alone.

Their expressions ranged from utterly terrified to menacing and likely to try me at first opportunity. Abel stood over another guard with his jaw blown off. I strode off, offering some support and removing his leaning body off the door of the van for stabilization.

Amaia side-eyed me in question. The floor was hers. It wasn't my job to influence her decisions. She was general. I was a soldier under her command. I'd played this role for years, but it was only now that I felt comfortable enough to offer full control with the trust that she would do the right thing. She always did in the end. Even if that meant walking the thin line of being the bad guy to do so.

"No," Reina spoke, either sensing Amaia's emotions through her magic or reading the remorse clearly etched on her face.

Abel straightened, "No, what? What's going on?"

"She wants to leave them."

"Not only would that be extremely reckless of me—they're witnesses," Amaia said, referring to all that they might have heard, addressing Reina and Reina only. At the end of the day, Abel was a soldier too. Reina's objection had no merit on whether he would follow through with orders or not.

"Witnesses to what? Look at them," Reina raised a finger, pointing to the objectively most innocent looking one. "They're terrified. I can *feel* it."

"Which means you can also feel their anger and disgust," Amaia closed the doors to the van though I took Reina's gun and stood guard with Abel half-here and half wherever the hell the pain was taking him to dissociate.

"Our gates are closed," she continued, removing the ammo and weapons off the extra two fallen bodies. A loose curl snagged on the rifle she hitched over her shoulder and she pulled it free with the tilt of her neck. "Closed, as in, I already have to excuse a hundred new faces somehow—"

"What's another ten?" Reina challenged.

Amaia's jaw ticked, "Another ten I don't have time to prove the merit and goodwill of. Get your stuff, Reina, we're leaving."

Reina reached back for her gun and I popped it in her hand. She slipped it into her waistband with a dramatic huff. Her feet dragged as she followed Amaia who was already back at the driver door of 'our' van.

"At least they get to keep their lives," Abel said. It was an attempt to show her the light of the situation but it had the exact opposite effect.

Reina swiveled in place, causing Abel to flinch back in surprise. "Will they though? We can take them back, help them."

"In a few days the gates will be closed for good. Resident of Elko or Sacramento. A random person from within the territory. Doesn't matter, they won't make it in. We have higher priorities than figuring out who these people are and whether they're lying to our fucking faces."

"What reason would they have to lie to us?" Reina popped the question back to me. "We didn't even give them the chance to explain themselves."

Amaia sighed, unmoving from her stance at the van. Her fingers danced on her thighs as she nibbled on her bottom lip. "I cannot account for more mouths to feed than we already have. Things are just now getting back under control, and for the moment, the new additions to Monterey Compound have been peaceful. I'm unsure how many stragglers are out there and I'll have to turn away some soon enough to make the space your brother will be filling. I'm sorry, Reina, but no. They can keep all that's here or we can kill them now to save them the pain of whatever life is left out there. But we have to go. Get your stuff and get in the car."

"Kill? Have you lost your marbles?" Reina screeched at the same time Abel hollered.

"What the hell. I'm not killing anyone without cause."

"Without cause?" Amaia said, striding back over to the van. "Those two," she pointed, "The mean motherfuckers in the back, stripped off their vests, which is the same shit *our* guards have on. They tried to tuck it behind them like we're fucking blind. The *innocent* looking one with the half-baked teenager in front of her like a shield? See the marking on the back of their necks. Covert."

I yanked the teenage boy away from his mother and pressed him flat against the truck bed. A lion was branded on his skin, beneath a small "O." *Outskirts?* Was this a clue at the infamous zone Jessa and our tortured little soldier feared? Amaia wasn't done. She'd already assessed the occupants of this van with zero interest in excuses or explanations. They could be victims. Like us. Or, it could all be a ruse.

Given what we knew about Hunter's connection, Ronan's knowledge of our movements, and the bounty on our heads, anyone we encountered was guilty by default. Survival demanded it. Sparing the wrong person now could cost us later.

I couldn't ignore the irony—our alliance with the rebellion existed only because Amaia had once spared one of theirs.

Abel found his strength and placed himself between Amaia and the van. "Look at me, Amaia!" She took him in with only a flicker of acknowledgment. "We still help people, no matter the potential cost. You understand? That is who we are on a fundamental level. I didn't sign up to lose that."

"No," Amaia said. "You signed up for your freedom from familial ties and to follow orders that fall into the law of our home: Compound first."

Her throat bobbed as she studied the other faces among those she'd already labeled. "If I'm too hopeful, too optimistic, we die. If I'm too negative, too skeptical, we die. If I don't overestimate our opponent—We. Are. Dead. If you can't tell, Ronan is both capable and willing to do whatever till whatever end. So we have to be too. You all wanted me to make decisions, take charge, look! I'm fucking doing it! And now that I am, it's a problem. Everyone wants a leader, someone to make decisions and work through the bullshit, but when I do, no one likes the answer."

Her frustration crackled in the air between us, her expression drawn tight. I'd seen it one too many times when it came to Amaia. She wasn't just mad—she was tired. Tired of having to be the one to weigh every risk, to make choices she could never take back.

Pretty, brown eyes filled with strength commanded my attention. I granted her the look we'd shared now more than a handful of times; the one that said I was ready to do whatever the hell she wanted. Her request was my command. Reina pushed her power into the world, demanding the situation unfold the way she desired. She could not change Amaia's mind, not with words, not with pushing for control by manipulation of emotions—but she *could* tug on that sisterly connection she shared with Amaia. She could let her know exactly how walking away or killing them would make her feel.

Amaia let out a short, humorless laugh, shaking her head before tipping her face toward the blindingly bright, cloudless sky. "Goddamn it," she muttered, dragging a hand down her face. "Fine. Whatever. They come in after dark. *You* and Abel go out to get them. Handle the intake and have their files on my desk at first light—*fully detailed*. I want to know the damn name of the doctor that signed their birth certificates. The Covert two stay behind. Kill the two dipshits in the back or Alexiares will."

"Your way's guaranteed to be more humane than mine." I warned Reina, who muttered something under her breath that sounded similar to a reluctant victory.

"I got it," Abel said, firing two quick shots without hesitation and ignoring the yelp of the others. "Covert out, or I … well, out now before *he* decides what to do with you. Everyone else decides whose driving. We'll see you tonight. Monterey Compound, South Gate."

I stepped away, leaving Reina and Abel to take care of the rest. My gaze lingered as the Covert woman and her son rushed out of the van and made a beeline for the main road. Wherever the hell we were, they had a long way back type of shelter or food.

Wiping the blood from my hands onto my cargo pants, I gripped the door and inhaled deep. The metallic tang still clung to the air. My boots crunched against the ground as I leaned against the frame and peered in.

Amaia sat there, her shoulders squared, head titled enough to catch the light streaming through the windshield and warming her sienna skin. Even now, smeared with grit and guts, she was something no short of divine—untouchable and all-consuming. Persephone, draped in shadows she hadn't asked for but wore better than anyone else.

I climbed in and shut the door behind me. She caught me still staring, her dark eyes narrowed and made my pulse spike. "What?" Amaia asked.

Sinking into my seat, the smirk I could no longer fight took over. "Just admiring how dangerously beautiful you are in *General mode*."

"If I recall correctly, you used to hate that."

"Yeah," I said, letting the silence between us stretch. I watched as Reina and Abel made their way back in the side-mirrors. The car shook as they climbed in and closed the door, slapping the divider in indication they were ready to go. "I was a dumbass. I thought we already established that."

I was stuck, lost in her gaze. It softened, melted in a way she would never admit, before she scoffed and turned away. I reached for her, my fingers cupping underneath her chin as I pulled her close. Her lips met mine. Gentle. Sure. Sweet. She leaned her forehead against me, her eyelashes tickling my cheek. The storm inside me quieted. The monster that tore its way free to guarantee her safety finally fell to a hush.

She pulled back and smacked the side of my head. "You're still a dumbass."

"Yeah," I murmured, a wicked edge to my tone. "But I'm yours."

The engine roared to life and dread filled her features once more. I rested my hand against her thigh and gave it a reassuring squeeze. She wasn't making this decision alone. As long as she was with me, I'd have her back into whatever came next, consequences be damned.

CHAPTER
THIRTY

TOMOE

The sun was out and bright as ever, yet I found myself strolling through the mists of the alleyways and homes nearest The Kitchens. Thin rivulets of water traced along the gutters, vanishing into the stone like veins. The air smelled fresh, damp, carrying the scent of earth and growing things.

It was a great decision on Amaia's end. Helping the sustainability through technology with a touch of magic in order to utilize the hands that would care for the greenery elsewhere in The Compound. That was how things were these days. Focused on maximizing efforts and exhausting what resources we had.

This little cove of apartments was my favorite. The wrought-iron gateway that serves as an entryway to a sliver of Mediterranean architecture calmed my nerves. Something in me unraveled, thread by thread, until I was just hollow. The strain on my magic was unforgivably taxing on my mental state. Yet, I found no rest when I had a moment to sleep. My mind kept pulling, tugging, yearning for me to fall victim to the world it wanted to show me.

Here—as far 'in nature' I could get—was quiet.

There were no kids playing out on the cobblestone, pretending to play Mortals and Zombies. Those days were long gone. Instead, the children of Monterey Compound spent their time preparing for the real thing. Screams of faux terror were a thing of the past. If they were playing, they were working on how to survive, walking through our city as silent as can be. Moving with grace and stealth. It was dystopian as hell.

The windows of the homes that were usually left open for fresh air were shuttered closed. Doors of homes one could freely walk into were now locked. The smiles of the citizens here had the unpleasant resemblance of the forced ones in The Before. With the world around me having changed so much, I yearned for a moment of reprieve where my mind would stop telling me just how bad shit was about to get.

I faltered mid-step. The ground tilted beneath me as my vision smeared like wet paint. The greenery around me blew in the wind around slow and warped. Stretched. My feet refused to move the way I commanded. *Not this shit again.* Bracing myself against the rough stucco, I tried to shake the fog from my mind. Willing the creeping shadows at the edge of my sight to retreat. I refused to fall out in the middle of The Compound.

Pushing my body forward, I staggered toward the closest place I'd feel safe. A place where no one could see me break. Whatever the universe was intent on me seeing, wanting my attention, and it wanted it now. The clarity of what I saw had intensified since power sharing with the others. After Reina, I not only *saw*, but felt. Experienced the emotions of others as I peered through their eyes. Not in the same way. Certainly not on the same level that it was when I shared my magic with hers directly—but the clarity in which I received them took more out of me than I was accustomed to.

Short of breath, the door opened with ease. Alexiares never locked his shit. He didn't have to. No one would dare enter without his permission. And he enjoyed the taunt of giving them the chance. There was excitement when he'd explained his reasoning to Amaia over dinner. The chase that would ensue if someone decided they were dumb enough to cross that barrier would make his fucking year.

Sterile. That was the best way to describe the way he chose to keep his space. There was no sign he'd used it, but I knew he was around whenever he wasn't with Amaia or Riley. Sharp tools hung on the walls, perfectly aligned. The desk? Immaculate. Not a speck of dust. Everything screamed *untouchable*. Except the corner. Dog bowls and a nest of blankets. The only thing messy, real, about Alexiares's study. I slung Wrath off my back and pressed it on the ledge of the desk, supporting my weight and testing the sturdiness of the chair.

"I got it." It was Abel's voice. A brown hand raised in front of his face, pistol cocked, his finger on the trigger. He pulled it twice. Whimpers ensued. Shaky breaths begged him for mercy.

"Covert, out," he said. His voice held no strength. There was hesitation there. Like he was acting against his interests in carrying out this task. "Or I … well, out now before he decides what to do with you. Everyone else, decide who's driving. We'll see you tonight. South Gate."

Abel's head turned slightly, and he watched Alexiares take his retreat away from the van. He glanced back up and held Reina's tearful stare. She looked back inside at the occupants of the van and offered them a sympathetic nod.

I lost my footing. Knees buckling and kissing the hard, cold floor. My mind felt as though it were splintering in half. It wanted me to focus on the vision. On my mission. But I was so fucking tired. It was hard, recovering from emptying my power reserves to near drops of magic in order to stabilize Lilia. She'd fallen dangerously close to losing it all. My tether had saved her, kept her from needing the help of Henry and the other healers. If there was anything that could even be done at that point. When it came to magic, a healer made no difference. Only brought comfort from the pain of running your tank too low.

The deep rumble of an engine cut through the stiff, hot air inside the car. It was low. Angry. Dust kicked up the windows as we tore down the road. The Compound sat shadowed in the distant night. Wild, blue eyes of the teenage boy in the passenger seat sent the thrill of excitement through my stomach. He leaned forward like he could will the car to go faster.

"Do they know the plan?" I asked, my voice high in pitch. A woman.

The answer came quickly. "Yeah. They know."

A fist pounded on the door. Once. Twice. Three times—followed by a chorus of whoops. They were obnoxiously loud. Giddy. Like this shit was some sort of game.

Pain seared through my cheekbone. My face rested against the cold, stone floor in Alexiares's study. The chill of it bit into my skin. Oxygen slipped from my reach, my chest heaving with sharp, frantic pulls. Disjointed flashes of the future flickered inside my mind. My eyelids fluttered erratically. Too heavy. Threatening to never open again.

Time of day did not exist down here. Hunger pains and dehydration sent my nerves and muscles into a frenzy. They clenched, then released. Ate away the fat on my body. Parasitic to my flesh.

Alexiares tilted his head, blood smeared around his mouth from the dripping gore of his hands. He glanced toward Riley who looked on. Watching. His arms crossed tightly over his chest. The kind, brown eyes he stared through each day were hardened. A lump slid down his throat, Adam's apple bobbing. The veins of his forehead were strained.

Guilt washed over me. How could I feel such a thing? *Sobs came from either side of me. Something horrible had happened.*

"We didn't know! We didn't know. They were going to leave us," an older man begged. "He said as long as we kept our mouths shut, they'd take us to

Monterey. We wouldn't have survived out there on our own. Without food or water. Weapons."

"Once you knew you were safe, you should have spoken up," Alexiares said, bored.

Riley shook his head, doing his best to keep it together. "There is no room at Monterey Compound for traitors or Covert sympathizers. I'm sorry, Rolfe, there's nothing I can do. There's nothing I want to do."

The older man held his head in shame. Alexiares caught me staring and pounced. His fist connected with my jaw first. The pain whitening. Radiating. I took two in the temple and could no longer see the hits that followed.

"Enough," Riley said. His command was calm. Quiet. Muted. Alexiares was off all the same.

"Henry's wife is dead because of this fucker and his silence." Alexiares growled, panting from the burst of energy. "Your friend—Margot. Children died."

I laughed, "Weak. All of you."

"He's not worth losing control. We're better than that."

"You're better than that," Alexiares emphasized.

"Please," a smaller voice begged, out of sight. "You have to understand. Our choice was not a simple one. We risked our ability to stay either way."

"There wasn't a guarantee that you wouldn't clump us together anyway, Riley. We fought our way to the gate that night together. If I wanted you dead, I wouldn't have turned back to help you, I could have left you."

"Maybe you should have," Riley said and turned on his heels.

Alexiares's gaze swept the room. Slow and deliberate. His eyes never lingered long on any one person but always flickered back to mine. Assessing. Searching. Like he could peel back every layer, strip you down. His expression went unchanged, but the weight of his judgment was suffocating. He'd already damned us all. Guilty or not. It didn't matter. We were never meant to plead our case. I could only feel sorry for those who had not known the gravity of the chaos we'd been sent to ensue.

Amaia and Reina entered the room. Riley held the door open, but no one moved, no one dared. The storm in Reina's eyes was alive. Her face flushed, crackling with heat as she took us in. No mercy lay in her stare. No pity like there was when she looked at someone who was bad but chose to find the good. Blood seeped into her clothing in the shape of a clinging child. Small hand prints desperate for grip dragged down her skin, her shirt, her pants.

Amaia was different. Her face wasn't blank the way Alexiares's was. It was alive with emotion. Fury radiated from her. Not loud or wild, but silent. The kind that promised death. She moved slowly, pacing before each of us, studying each of our faces in a way that told me she could see every secret, every sin. Then, without a word, she turned and left, Reina in her wake.

"Executions at dawn," Alexiares's voice was casual. A crooked smirk that didn't reach his eyes pulled at his lips. "Sleep tight, fuckers."

Electricity snapped through my nerves. A thunderstorm raged around my skull. I lost control, neurons firing in patterns that didn't belong to me anymore. The world shrank to the size of a pin. Each of my thoughts were scattered. Torn up the way paper would in a hurricane. Heat bloomed behind my eyes. Blinding. Sharp. My muscles betrayed me, pulling taut and slack in uneven ways.

I could not speak. Could not scream. Couldn't even fucking cry. All I could do was drown in the chaos of my own body. I was trapped inside myself. Utterly, hopelessly, alone. Helpless.

"Tomoe," the voice was distant. It didn't sound real. A mere figment of my imagination.

"Tomoe."

Someone was there, shaking me, their urgency cutting through the haze. Their touch was a tight squeeze that forced the sensation back into my body. Light. There it was. That blinding, small sliver of vision returning as my eyelids found the strength to move on their own. The haze cleared.

Tomás's figure came into sharp focus. His shirt was soaked with the sweat of panic—clinging into his lean and annoyingly sturdy body. Instead of panic in his brown eyes, there was a maddening sense of calm. His gaze was fixated on me. Equal parts sharp and soft.

The usual stupid smirk he bore each time I saw him was gone, a tight line replacing it. He cradled me in his lap. I groaned, shaking myself back to reality. *Fuck.* I overdid it. Expelled too much magic too soon. A warm hand cupped my chin, tilting it up as his brows pinched in scrutiny.

Sunlight spilled across a tiny living room filled with books. Laughter curled through the air thicker than smoke, and there he was, standing too close, his hand brushing against mine as I reached for my cup of tea. Tomás had an easy grin. A carefree disposition that was a rarity in my life.

I snapped back, breath sharp in the depths of my chest as Tomás's face blurred into focus. His hand was on my arm, steadying. I wrenched away. He didn't burn me but his touch felt like a punishment of pleasure. "I'm fine. Never seen someone have a vision before?"

"No." He chuckled and helped me sit up. "Though I'm positive that was a seizure, my friend."

"What are you, a doctor?"

"Well, not here no. I worked as a paramedic before though and—"

"So not a doctor," I mumbled. The sun still lit up the room, I hadn't been down for long. "Got it."

Tomás recoiled as though I'd struck him, the warmth behind his golden skin absent. "Did I do something? To offend you, I mean."

I flicked my gaze toward him and took him in. He had a ruggedness to his otherwise put together appearance. A faint trace of a healed scar cut from his neck and under his shirt. He'd certainly been through some shit, that much was clear. And I had no intention of finding out what woes he'd nearly lost to. There was little interest I had in spending time with anyone outside of my family. It wasn't worth the pain. Life had more to offer than romantic love. *Who the hell said anything about romance? Dammit.*

"Other than constantly invading my space … no."

"This is Alexiares's office," Tomás said with hesitation. He pushed himself to his feet and scanned the room, his hand swiping across his low-buzzed hair. "And the first time was in Reina's lab."

That stupid little smirk had returned to his face. I scoffed, pressing my hands into the ground to summon the strength to stand on my own. "Their space *is* my space."

"Understood."

"What are you doing?" I asked, watching him get far too comfortable in the metal chair behind Alexiares's desk.

He shrugged, the tightness of his fucking t-shirt uncomfortably distracting. "Waiting for Alexiares."

"And you have to do that here because …"

"Because it's his office, and it's where he told me to meet him when he gets back this afternoon." Tomás was cocky, and I utterly despised the way I found his cheekiness endearing. "If I'm making you uncomfortable, you always have the option to leave."

I dug my fingers into my sides as a way to hold back and cut him a glare sharp enough to cut glass. Each muscle in my jaw pulled tight, straining to the point of rupture. "I'm not uncomfortable. I'm working. Some of us have jobs to do around here."

"You make the statement as though we aren't all required to serve The Compound in some capacity."

"Yours is …" I asked, arching my embarrassingly over plucked brows. Complimentary to Reina's anxiety and general boredom.

"Originally it was bionics. Engineering nanomechs—tiny machines that adapt and rebuild on the fly. Specialized in war tactics and adaptive weapons. Think the Shadowstep and Plasma blades. Nothing fancy."

"I know what nanomechs are. You don't have to explain it to me." I did not understand nanomechs. Hadn't even ever heard the word.

"No, you don't." His smirk turned into a cheshire grin.

"'Yours is,' is present tense." I ignored his call out. "Let's try that one more time."

"I work for Alexiares."

"Now *that* is something I couldn't see coming. Sounds ominous. Wish I cared enough to ask for more detail."

Tomás chuckled, the sound low and easy. I bit down the urge to join him. Then the air shifted, tension creeping back in.

"Your vision seemed intense," Tomás said finally, his voice careful. Too careful for my taste. I was not a wounded doe.

"Just tired is all."

"Looks it."

I rolled my eyes and took a step back, hair falling in front of my face. "Thanks. I'll go now."

"Wait." His fingers twitched, caught between impulse and restraint, as my hand dropped to Wrath resting against the desk. "I didn't mean it that way. I only meant that you seem like you could use a break."

"Breaks are time wasted. Amaia will be back soon and she'll expect resolution."

"Resolution to what?" Confusion contorted his defined features.

"If I have a vision that is a product of a problem, I present Amaia with options for resolution," I snapped, tone tight with frustration. "She has enough on her plate as is. Going to her and asking her to interpret the shit inside my head so I can go back to try to make an accurate prediction of the future benefits no one. All it does is waste time."

He stared at me. Face blank and void of all emotion with each slow blink in the absolute silence of the room.

"What?"

"Nothing. Your voice … It's nice." He leaned his head to the side, bemused. "I think that's the most I've ever heard you speak."

"Because having you ask more questions wastes time," I shot back with a hint of humor.

Give a man an inch, he'll fucking propose. A bright smile shined back at me. "How can I help?"

"You don't."

"Oh, come on. I have nothing to do until he gets here. Besides, now I'm curious about how the whole vision thing works. Not a lot of you all out there."

I glanced at him out the side of my eyes as I lowered myself back to the floor, back against the wall for support. "Fine. Keep quiet. And stop breathing so hard, it's throwing off my focus."

CHAPTER
THIRTY-ONE

TOMOE

"About time." I settled into an oddly comfortable couch in Amaia's quarters.

She closed the front door with a groan, her head slamming against it two times. Ever dramatic, she turned her back to me, hand pressed to her forehead as if she contemplated walking back out the door. Her bag fell off her arm, and she removed the personal armory from around her body. Amaia wasn't going anywhere. "Next time I'll just let another Moore brother walk through our front door without scoping him out first. We see how great that worked last time. What happened to you? You look like Reina's worst nightmare."

"A little low on magic right now. Thanks for noticing." I jolted upright, and the world tilted—stars pricked at the edges of my vision. "Also, what? Run that back for me one more time."

"Bet you didn't see that one coming. I need a drink." Amaia walked over and tossed my feet off the couch.

She sat down next to me before reaching for the box everyone knew she kept under the couch. It wasn't a secret. More so for Amaia, a challenge, a reminder to be a stronger, better version of herself every day. She wouldn't dare disrespect Prescott's space that way. Not with him gone.

I kicked her hand away with a glint of threatening promise. "If you take a drink, I'll make sure you choke on it."

"Seriously."

"Not sorry," I muttered and slid back onto the couch. "Where's the *Bloodhound?*"

Amaia relaxed against the armrest on the other side and brought her knees to her chest. "Off to meet Tomás."

I hated myself. Had to because, for whatever reason, heat flushed from my neck to my cheeks against my will. Glancing in the other direction, I muttered a curse. Amaia and her ability to read body language was a skill set I appreciated, as long as it wasn't me on the other end of her scrutinizing.

"What was that?" Amaia said. Stray curls fell from her messy bun as she crossed through the boundaries of my personal bubble.

I busied myself, pushing to my feet and wandered near her bookshelves. "What was what?"

"Cute." Amaia's laugh was full of mockery, her face lined with accusations.

A gossip. No matter the rank she achieved or the status she and Reina gained, the two of them would always find time to chat shit.

I kept my back to her. There were more important things to discuss right now, and time was of the essence for at least half of them. "Back to the Moore brother."

"Hunter Moore is alive and well. Raising a rebellion, actually. *The* rebellion. Oh, and Caleb too. Remember him? Go me for not fucking killing him, I guess. So yeah, all of this—everything—

has been for, you guessed it, absolutely nothing." Amaia threw her arms wide, the sharp movement pulling my focus even from the corner of my eye.

The word hit harder than a punch to the gut. "Fuck me." My balance wavered, as though the ground itself had betrayed me.

"Don't beg," Amaia said, and I turned back toward her. She sat on the couch, staring off into the distance. "The world already fights to flick our beans every day."

"Tell me that's not who's headed here in a van."

That caught her attention. Her gaze widened, full of questions. "That's not who's headed here in a van."

"This conversation is giving me whiplash."

"And me a headache," she said dismissively. "How do you know about the van?"

I paced the room, trying to wrap my head around what I saw and what I know now. "I had a vision. How do you plan on harboring another Moore without Ronan's idiots calling you out on your shit?"

"I'm figuring it out as we speak." Her voice was muffled as her face fell into her hands. Amaia's elbows rested on her knees. She sounded deflated. Like she had lost control yet maintained clarity at the same time.

It was hard to imagine the decisions I would have to make if I were in her shoes and, to be honest, I didn't want to. There was no envy in my heart for the choices Amaia was confronted with every day. The consequences of them inevitably followed, and they *always* came with them, a solid decision or not.

"And the van?" I was afraid to ask. At least if it was a Moore, we'd have some sort of insight. Background knowledge to make sense of it.

"Full of people Reina insisted on taking in."

"That tracks," I said. With a sigh, I took my seat back next to her, wanting to offer a way to relieve her from at least one of her burdens—because damn, did she have many. "I'll tell her no dice. Covert has sleepers in the back. You bring them here and you'd have a binder full of problems on your hands. I'll spare you the details since I've seen an out."

She shook her head absentmindedly, brows bunching together. "I already kicked those two out. If they show up, they'll have to come right to the gates."

"It stings a bit that you don't trust I didn't see that far ahead," I messed with the chess pieces on the board of her coffee table. "Obviously, I knew. You didn't realize the whole damn van was crawling with them—not just the two you tossed out the back."

"Awesome," she said, sounding as though she couldn't be any less thrilled. Her tongue rolled across her teeth, pupils dilating. "I'll send Alexiares out after dinner."

I sighed and stood, reaching down to pull her up. She didn't resist. "Time to go break Reina's heart." I steadied her. "Up you go. I need you to tell Riley to shut down our gates, anyway."

She snatched her hand free, shaking her head and clasping her hands behind her back as she paced in front of the stone fireplace. "We can't, not for a few more days."

"Any room for me to argue here?"

There was none. I knew that. Once her mind was made up, whatever followed was inevitable. That meant nothing. Not at this moment. Whoever these people were—the threat they posed—was imminent. I'd spent time trying to discern exactly what I was seeing and when, but in the end, all I gathered from context clues was a few days, at best.

"Depends. Was your vision about why I shouldn't?" Amaia said, reading the fear in my eyes.

"Yes," I mumbled, holding her stare. "Another Moore inside the gates. History repeats."

"Hunter's not with them. He's not a threat, but I won't force you to stand his presence if you're not ready. He … How do I say this with as much respect for the Seth we'd come to love. Hunter is more like Reina than he is Seth. He has a conscience—that much is obvious. Now, we have to see if the weight of it will make a difference."

"What business does he have here, anyway?" I shot back. My heart sped up.

Seth and Hunter were twins. I'd seen the one picture that Reina managed to save before fleeing the ranch. I knew the brothers didn't resemble each other. But what if it was in his laugh? His smile. The way he spoke. "We don't have the means or the privacy to hide an army full of rebels."

"I already told Reina he could stay while we work all that shit out. He has the resources and intel I need. If he's here, and we close our gates, that means he's with us and not his father. Ronan wants him dead, which means *we* want him alive. Got that?"

I tossed my hands up gently, then dropped them in defeat with a sigh. "I can give you twenty-four hours to figure your shit out before we're screwed."

"Let's make it count." She bent down, pulling the box from under the couch and giving it a playful shake, though the longing in her eyes betrayed her. Amaia forced a laugh, set the box back in place, and took my hand, guiding me toward the door.

"We need Riley," she thought out loud as we moved toward the door, her eyes sharp with focus. "And a few of his associates."

"Allow me to catch up on the visions you missed on the way," I said with a grin, but there was no real humor in it—just urgency.

CHAPTER
THIRTY-TWO

AMAIA

There are people the world seems to chew up and spit out. Perpetual victims of the universe. Like it was testing how much they could take before they broke. People who were stubborn in a way that made it impossible for them to lay down arms no matter how many times they hit the ground.

These are the individuals society loves to call heroes. But they're not. They're survivors. And part of me believed everyone left alive in this moment of time had a little bit of that in them. I wasn't quite sure if the idea of that scared me or brought me great joy.

Our gates had closed permanently days ago. We weren't hiding our lack of cooperation anymore. He'd bought our story about the cavalry—for now. At first, our performance in front of Bietoletti and the others had been convincing enough for them to report back exactly as I'd hoped. Ronan would never believe I'd offer up people without a fight.

When the sympathizers showed up at his first camp, the gig would be up. Yet his emissaries remained. Waiting, watching. For what, I had no idea. I could've tossed them out before we locked down, but as with Hunter, I preferred to keep people where I could see them. Let them think they were keeping an eye on us while I did the same. They only saw what I wanted them to see, and I was certain the feeling was mutual.

But with the gates sealed and under close watch, their only way to communicate with the outside world was through monitored messengers. Which meant they'd have to get creative. And fuck, I'd be lying if I said I wasn't daring them to try.

Knowing we'd saved lives didn't sit as cleanly when I knew it'd cost any honest people theirs that now camped outside our walls. Hoping. Praying. Pleading to let them in. Keeping Monterey Compound safe didn't exactly ease the guilt of slipping past weary families to steal a quiet moment by the rocks.

I dove beneath a wave, letting the cold water swallow me as I sank a few feet below. Pulling my knees to my chest, I hung there, suspended in the nothingness of the bay. The weight of the world slipped away for a fleeting moment. Stars danced behind my eyelids, lungs on the verge of collapse, and I surged upward. The sounds of my gasps were swallowed by the quick bark of a greeting from Suckerpunch. I turned back toward the shore. Alexiares stood there, arms crossed as he took me in.

"Come and get me!" I called out over the crashing waves. The current fought me now. It tugged my body further out to sea, making it more of an effort to tread. The strain was welcome—a reminder of where I was. What was real. But even as the water pulled at me, my focus stayed fixed, drawn like a tide to him.

He didn't respond, but he didn't hesitate, either. With practiced ease, he stripped off his boots, cargos, and shirt, leaving them in the sand before stepping into the waves. The water calmed the nearer his presence grew. Moving to the call of his power and slowing to his will.

We didn't speak. For a few minutes, all we heard was the ocean and the quiet rise and fall of our bodies as I wrapped myself around him, resting my head on the cusp of his neck. He treaded water for the both of us. The weight of everything hung there in the silence—unspoken, undeniable. Yet him being here, holding me, us holding each other—it was grounding, in a way the ocean alone could never be.

I raised my head, resting my forehead against his, the world shrinking until it was just us. His eyes sparkled in the falling light of the day. Water traced lazy paths down his face, catching on the ink that curled over his tan, sculpted body. I closed the distance, pressing my lips to his. Alexiares's hands slid around my waist, drawing me closer until every inch of me was pressed against him. The ocean swirled around us. I tasted the salt on his skin, the sensation stealing my thoughts and sending my pulse racing. My lips tingled, my heart thundered. The chaos inside me stilled.

"Come back to the rocks with me?" he asked, falling to his back and pulling me toward the beach.

I closed my eyes, floating, his arm steady beneath my shoulders, guiding me effortlessly through the water. The waves lapped at my sides. When the pebbled, sandy floor tickled my toes, I opened my eyes, blinking against the fading sunlight. Letting go of his hand as we waded to the shoreline wasn't an option I was willing to consider.

Harley pranced toward us, licking the salty water off my arms and legs. I pulled my shirt and shorts back on, leaving my weapons off to the side. I didn't need them right now. Not with him by my side. The fear left my body when we fought together.

Three crows flew above our heads in tight arrow formation. Their caws echoed sharply against the sky. I tracked them until they fluttered out of sight, my gaze settling back on the sand and rock melting into the fiery hues of the setting sun. But Alexiares wasn't watching the sunset. His eyes were on me. Unflinching. It made me feel as though I were the only thing worth noticing. Rare was a moment untouched by chaos with us. Far too rare.

"You've been staring at me nonstop the last few days," I said, shaking my head and hiding a tender smile on my shoulder. "More than usual. I'm starting to feel like prey."

"Amaia …"

"I love you," I interrupted.

The words weren't planned, but they were true—etched into every corner of my being. I'd been a coward to not have said them before now when I'd felt this way for months. From the moment that I woke until the time I closed my eyes at night, I wanted to be by his side. Every meal was incomplete unless we shared it. In those rare moments of relief, I found them best spent with him. But of all the terrors in this broken world, love was the most fool- ish to fear.

Alexiares glanced away, his shoulders stiffening as if bracing for a blow. His throat bobbed with a hard swallow. "No."

"No?"

"You don't say those words."

I was going to throw up and evidently, so was he. Panic carved itself across his face—caught somewhere between the urge to leap off a cliff and the temptation to stand at the edge, pretending the void wasn't calling.

"The world as we know it is probably going to end … again. Is being in love truly such a terrible thing?"

He froze, my words cutting through whatever storm brewed in his head. His eyes darted away, then back to me, guilt flickering in their depths.

"No," he said, his voice soft. Tender in a way I'd never heard from him before. "I don't think it's a terrible thing at all, Princess."

He tilted his head, those eyes of his locking onto mine and I knew, somehow, I was the only thing keeping him tethered. "Especially if that love is coming from you."

Heat rose to my cheeks. "Okay, then say it back," I demanded. "Because I feel really fucking stupid over here."

A slow, lopsided smile tugged at his lips. "How about I say it back for the rest of our lives?"

"You're crazy," I muttered. Was my heart fluttering inside my chest like a butterfly with rabies? Absolutely. I could only hope he couldn't hear it.

"And you're insane," he countered, his face hanging low to capture me in a kiss. Sweet and sobering.

When we broke apart, his hands lingered on my face, his thumb brushing over my cheek. He leaned in close, his breath warm between us. "I don't feel like such a monster when I'm with you. Stuck in that pit of hell Sloan called a home, you made yourself a safe space for me when you didn't have to. Fuck, it would've been easier for you if you hadn't. I didn't deserve the benefit of the doubt—not with you, not with the lies I've told or the past I've hidden. You walked through flames with me, Amaia, several times despite everyone's best wishes. And that … that's just one thing on a list of many that makes you one hell of a woman."

I swallowed hard, his words unraveling me, but I kept quiet.

"There's compassion in your heart, that you refuse to let the world strip away," he continued. The emotion and devotion in which he spoke moved me to tears. "You don't hide it; you wear it on your sleeve and dare anyone to take it from you. It's fascinating, truly. That's not even one of the top five reasons I admire you. You gave me freedom when I didn't think I deserved it. You forgave me without saying the words, even knowing every awful thing I've done. And you love me anyway.

"The way you make me feel … fuck, I don't know what to do with myself. Jump for joy like an idiot? Fall to my knees and thank a God I'm not even sure I believe in for allowing me to breathe the same air as you? When I'm away from you, all I feel is an ache that doesn't stop until you're back in my arms. And that leads me to the most important point of my life: There was a time when I didn't think I'd live past twenty, and then twenty-five. At twenty-eight, I'm still here and for once, I don't hate it. I want to grow old and I want to do that with you."

He grabbed my left hand, dropping to his knee. My heart lurched as he fumbled in his pocket and pulled out a ring. My ring. *The* ring.

"Holy shit," I gasped, snatching my hands away and covering my mouth. "You keep a lot of weird shit in your pockets, *Bloodhound*, but this? This was the last thing I expected. Have you been carrying that around for months?"

"Ever since I realized it will always be you."

I grew anxious and pulled him into another kiss. From hatred, love is born. It had been less than a year since Alexiares had walked into my life, but everything with him felt unarguably right. Like I was in the right place at the right time and though everything else around me fell apart, he was my sun. My North Star. I would always orbit around him. Drawn inescapably by the gravity of who he was. I poured every unspoken promise into that kiss, every shred of hope I dared to hold on to in a world that threatened to strip it away.

His hand found mine when I pulled away, his touch deliberate, certain. The edges of the coffin-shaped ring caught the light, scattering faint prisms in the falling light.

"I understand," he began, his voice thick with emotion, "that you have … fears about love. About spending forever with someone. And I don't blame you for that, Amaia. I don't fear death. If I'm honest, I would take a never-ending amount of painful deaths if only it meant I got to spend another moment with you. The only thing I fear in this world is living a life without Amaia Bennett—soon to be Drakos—in it."

My lips twitched into a smile, a warmth blooming in my chest that I couldn't suppress. "I said you're my infinity, didn't I? Promise me something?" I whispered.

"Anything," he said, his thumb brushing tenderly against my cheek.

"Live," I murmured. "No matter what, *live*."

He nodded, solemn, the smallest hint of a morbid smile. "Cross my heart."

He slipped it onto my finger, the cool metal warming against my skin. My hand trembled as I stared down at it, the reality of it all settling in.

"It's perfect," I whispered. The words a reflection of both the ring and the man standing before me.

"You're perfect," he replied without hesitation. "This is forever, Amaia. Even if the rest of the world falls apart, even if everything burns—I'm with you."

My gaze lifted to meet his, a playful grin slipping past the seriousness of the moment. "That's a lot of confidence. Sure you can keep up with me?"

"I've already been running after you this long. I'm not about to stop now."

The sharp crunch of footsteps in the sand behind us shattered the fragile silence. Instincts took over. We exchanged no words, simply moved in sync as we turned, hands raised, magic crackling to life. My fire burned in my palms. Golden-orange glow illuminated on the dimming beach—a mirror image of the sunset. Water thundered to life behind us, twisting and leaping with the restless energy of a storm bound by threadbare reins.

"Woah, calm down. It's just me." Reina paused a few feet away, her own water bubbling around her in defense. "Crazies," she muttered.

Relief hit me, but it was temporary. The last time she'd come to find me on an afternoon off, my fiancé was assassinated. "What are you doing out here?"

Reina was armed with her bow and arrow, pistol at her hip, knife at her thigh. Slowly but surely, she'd increased her artillery. I'd never so much as seen her shoot a gun five months ago. Now, it was a staple in her everyday apparel. For a moment, she was taking scissors to it every week. But she'd finally stopped, and silly me to think it meant she'd recovered from the misery of betrayal. It bristled over her shoulders and touched the thick army green straps of her crop top.

"Looking for you, *obviously*," she said, hands on her hip as she animatedly spoke. "Hunter's heading to The Kitchens for dinner. It's been a few days of him being out and about. No one's looked at him twice, so it's probably safe to meet. Plus, last night, when Adelaide came for bedtime stories, I was braiding her hair … Jessa made us hot chocolate, which like, where'd she even get the chocolate from? We don't have any ready to harvest, since it's not a priority. Yet another hidden thing about—"

"Fucking Christ, Reina. Focus." Alexiares pinched the bridge of his nose.

Reina gave him a once-over, then shook her head slowly, her smile bright and honest. "Hunter mentioned when he picked her up that he figured out some plan to save the world. God, you know, you and him have a lot in common, Maia. Always scheming. Anyway, I'm headed there now and Riley said I could find you here. So, yeah. Let's go."

She dropped down to greet the dogs. Their tails wagged violently, slobbering her with kisses, reveling in the purity of her joy when she rubbed them. Alexiares shifted, his expression carefully neutral as he met my glance. He shook his head once. I tucked my hands behind my back, walking ahead of him and allowing him to fall in line. One night. We only wanted one night to enjoy what this meant, just us, no one else. Lately, the only time we were alone was at bedtime—too tired to talk, we settled into silence. It wasn't the same.

I barely made it a few paces before realization smacked me. "Damn it," I muttered, spinning on my heel. "The guns."

"You're welcome." Reina waved my weapon belt over her head. I reached out to grab them, remembering all too late of what I'd wanted to hide. "Why are y'all being so—"

Her eyes squinted, focused on the sparkle that even a barely lit sky could not hide. She rushed over, grabbing onto my hand with unexpected strength. "Oh my God. What's that? Did you propose?"

"No," Alexiares's voice was laced with sarcasm. "I just wanted her to feel pretty."

Reina lifted my hand up near her face, stretching my finger in angles and lengths I hadn't thought possible. "That is a terribly gaudy piece of hardware. You couldn't rob a jewelry store or something? Let me guess, you can excuse murder and torture, but robbery is where you draw the line?"

"It's what I wanted, Reina." I snatched my hand back and flexed the fingers in a deliberate twirl. A faint smile played on my lips.

"Oh. I love that … that ring. It's very … you." Reina grimaced, the forced grin truly comical. "I'm really happy for you, Maia. This is good. Good things are happening. Aw man, I love love."

She tugged us into a group hug. Alexiares grumbled but didn't resist. It had taken time for him to get here, to become accustomed to Reina's inability to respect others' space or any sort of affection, to be frank. I'd loved the Alexiares who stood tall with me through the raw beauty and pain of life, the one willing to let his beast take control—but the softness and peace of this version of him … happy looked good on him. Reina sniffled, happy tears falling down her pink tinted cheeks.

"Thanks," I said with the roll of my eyes. "Let's not make it a thing?"

"A thing?" Reina stared at me like I'd told her I saw a pig flying in a pink tutu. "I'm going to make this the biggest event Monterey's ever seen. Ugh, young love. It's so beautiful. Don't make this a thing. Honestly, Maia, I'd ask you if you were drunk, but that would be considered insensitive."

Reina walked ahead of us mumbling to herself as she worked out a to-do list of everything she needed. The dogs ran ahead, scouting out the way and making sure we had a clear path home. Alexiares laced his fingers through mine, tugging for my attention, horror filling his eyes.

"We aren't doing that," he said.

"No." I laughed, covering it with a cough, before Reina turned around. "No, we are not. I have an idea."

"You have a lot of ideas." That slip of his accent with a musical cadence of the vowels made my heart thunder. "Most of which I hate."

"You'll like this one."

His fingers toyed with the ring slightly loose on my finger as we made our way back to The Compound. "I doubt that, Princess. But where you go, I follow."

CHAPTER
THIRTY-THREE

AMAIA

I pushed Reina past Elie working at the coffee counter for her evening shift. Elie lifted a skeptical brow, and I shook my head in dismissal. Brushing it off as typical Reina, overly excited about anything, everything. Alexiares bit down a smile as he carried both our dinner trays, leading the way to a room that embraced us like home away from home.

The lanterns hanging from the ceiling cast shadows against the wall, painting them across Tomoe's angular face as she sat staring at Hunter—who only looked back with curiosity, assessing her. I glanced around the table, only to find Abel and Serenity in a similar stare down. Riley was the only one who noticed our arrival. His dark brown eyes shifted from Reina then over to Alexiares, finally landing on me. There were a thousand questions as he peered at me. He shifted in his seat and pulled out a chair directly next to him. I took it with a rigid posture. Riley wasn't Reina. He could not *feel* how she could, but he could read me just as well, maybe better.

Dinner had the essential adults present only. Before they'd even arrived, we'd talked about what to do with Caleb. He had dyed his hair a sandy brown from some concoction Reina had made with beet juice and walnut husks. With the addition of thin, metal framed glasses that no doubt hurt the shit out of his eyes, he was hardly recognizable—to the untrained eye, that was. Given the spectacle made of exile, dinner in a room full of high-ranking soldiers and council members, Caleb wouldn't stand a chance.

Alexiares took the empty chair next to me, and Reina fell into the one closest to her brother. The only sound for an exhaustive few minutes was the clinking of our spoons against the bowls of stew—still 80 percent broth. Low chatters interrupted the grinding noise, but I found impatience to take control. I traced a finger over the outline of the ring inside my pocket: *my* ring. That ring that I had accepted …

I cleared my throat and let the spoon clatter to the table with a sharp clang. My voice cut through the silence. "Are you going to speak, or is this an excuse for a twisted family dinner?"

The blunt heel of Reina's boot dug into my shin beneath the table. Her lips pulled into a tight, warning smile that screamed *behave*.

"Can't a man enjoy the ambiance?" Hunter slurped his broth with exaggerated relish.

"Don't waste my time, Hunter," I snarled, my patience razor-thin. There were a million better ways to spend my evening, and while I didn't dislike him, he wasn't my first choice for company. "We're big on family dinners around here, so if you're going to sit at my table and disrupt it, you'd better make it worth our time. And before you even think about saying your family—let me be clear. You're Reina's family, not ours. You're an ally. An ally who, so far, has done nothing but leech off my resources and hang around his sister. I don't tolerate people reaping the benefits of my hard work without pulling their weight. I let it slide during the last war. I won't let it slide again. Now tell me, do you have a plan—or not?"

Hunter leaned forward, a lazy smirk playing at the corners of his lips. "All you had to do was ask. I'm an open book."

"Sure you are," Alexiares said, studying Hunter with dark, scrutinizing eyes.

Reina placed a gentle hand on Hunter's shoulder and gave it a squeeze. "Go on, Hunter, tell 'em."

"There's two parts to it," Hunter began, glancing around the table and then the room.

It was prime dinner hours, and the room buzzed with chatter, packed to capacity. Though everyone here held the highest security clearance—save for Hal and a select few connected to trusted families—these weren't the kind of details we wanted out in the world yet. Hunter's eyes mirrored Reina's softness.

"Spit it out for fuck's sake," Moe's voice was even, monotone.

Serenity scoffed and gave her a slow once-over. "Scorned ex?"

Tomoe's eyes didn't leave Hunter for a second. "More like murderous mistress." Her lips twitched, but a slight wobble betrayed her, despite her best efforts.

"I'm sorry," Hunter said, his tone sincere. "I truly wish we'd met under better circumstances." He turned back to me. "I've arranged a rendezvous with the other settlement leaders to assess what we're working with. The meeting is next Sunday at sunset, Royal Oaks. Bring any advisors you trust. No weapons."

"I don't need weapons to kill someone, but I'm not traveling outside these walls unarmed." I folded my arms across my chest, leaned back in my chair, settling into the warmth of Alexiares's arm draped behind me.

Hunter glanced my way, his expression edged with indifference. "Anyway," he said, "Try to keep that kind of talk to a minimum. Before we get to that, we've got a few problems on our hands."

I gestured for him to continue, waiting.

"San Jose and Fresno are sympathizers. They're hosting my father's military but are situated near your border to keep eyes. It's why you were captured the other day."

I froze. We'd chosen not to tell Hunter about our trip back and had specifically instructed Reina to keep her mouth shut. Her eyes darted over to me and she shook her head. She hadn't said shit. "They are our closest allies, they would never betray the treaty."

"You mean the treaty that was made null and void the second he breached Transient Nation? They *surrendered*. It's every man for themselves out there." Serenity said, her eyes narrowing with cold precision.

"*Niklas* would never," Tomoe stated with clarity. "Unfortunately he's dead and the rest of them have been under pressure for months."

"I have it on good authority—"

"I'm sure that you do," I cut Hunter off. The revelation hit like a blow to the gut. Salem's recovery had leaned hard on the strength of what we'd built together. San Jose and Fresno weren't just allies; they were friends. From their leadership to their military, even down to their citizens, we had forged a tight-knit bond.

But, apparently, bigots were everywhere. And desperation—the primal need to survive, the beast within us all—could twist people into embracing beliefs and doing things I never thought them capable of. Silly me. By now, I should've known better. Always expect the worst.

Hunter's expression softened into a measured expression of pity, his eyes briefly flickered, weighing the cost of my response. "If you have the right people in place, should take 'em no longer than a week to get it done. We need to slow my father down, lower his numbers, or we don't stand a chance—especially with them being so close. If you think we can hit them with brute force to win this thing, then you've vastly underestimated Ronan Moore."

"Don't question my intelligence; it's insulting." My hand cut through the air as I raised it, expression twisting into a disgusted frown. "Brute force is for amateurs, but I need more to go on than a hunch. He won't sit quietly after a move like this—he'll retaliate."

"Of course, he will." His tone was calm in a way that told me he'd already thought this through. "But whatever he throws at you will be a fraction of what he'd have unleashed once he got what he wanted from your deal. Better to act now while you still have the upper hand."

"Okay, I'll ask; how does taking out two people solve that problem?" Reina's thick brows pinched together, skepticism written all over her face.

The room was clearing out, our words able to flow freer with the absence of diners in our immediate vicinity. The rich aroma of coffee mingled with the scent of fresh-baked bread and the faint, earthy notes of herbs trailing from the overhead planters. Dinner was winding down, and with it came the shifting of schedules. The navy crew was swapping out, their rotations more seamless now that our forces had nearly doubled. A rare upside to this chaos—our sailors were finally getting the rest on land they'd been denied for too long. Caffeine, as always, was a welcome ally for those heading back into the night beyond these walls.

"It doesn't solve it outright." He leaned forward, resting his elbows on the table. "But it sets the pieces in motion. They'll handle each other for us."

"Explain." My voice cut through the room like a blade.

"Ronan's inner circle runs on ego and self-interest. Do you really think any of them believe half the nonsense they spout? No.

To them, it's all about securing their futures, their comfort—no matter who they crush to get it. Take out the men at the top, and the loyalty holding them together shatters. Get them paranoid, turn them on each other, and they'll be so busy ripping themselves apart, they won't have the strength to lend a helping hand to dear old Dad. The soldiers at the bottom, *that's* who you want. Someone actually fighting for something or someone they want to protect."

My jaw dropped, body freezing at the fucking audacity … if there was one thing men had. Jesus Christ. "You're working on nothing but hypotheticals. Hope. Don't give me that crap."

"Human nature is quite repetitive if you haven't figured that out yet." A sly grin tugged at his lips.

"I can … escalate the issue." Alexiares spoke up, the promise of danger in his tone. "Let me do the dirty work, Princess. You worry about the rest."

"This is to happen before the meeting even begins," I said, ignoring the way that made my heart patter in my chest. There were more important things to focus on, such as saving Salem Territory, *again.* "If we can't get anyone to cooperate—"

"Then we're screwed," Tomoe chimed in, arms crossed, leaning back with a dry chuckle. "But hey, it's a war cry, right?"

Hunter spread his hands out in mock surrender. "I brought the extra bodies and the intel. She's the general of legends, figure something out. Rebellion, at its core, runs on hope and the belief that God—or the universe, if that's your thing—hates your oppressor more than it hates you."

Riley's eyes were daggers. Sharp. Skeptical. "How can we trust the accuracy of this information? That you're not setting us up?"

Hunter's gaze hardened, the water in his bowl vibrating, gently sloshing inside. "I wouldn't do that to my sister." His voice remained steady despite his show of magic.

"Then you admit," Abel shifted in his seat, muscles tensing. "This is all for her?"

"He has more at stake than his sister," Serenity barked back.

"Good," I said, eyes narrowing as I leveled a cold stare down the bridge of my nose at the nuisance of a woman across from me. "Our objective is to promise a better tomorrow for *everyone,* not just Transient Nation or those closest to your heart. You lose sight of that, then we're no longer on the same side in this fight."

"You have your reasons, we have ours. As long as we have the same end goal, I see nothing wrong with that."

"I do," I retorted, a cold edge creeping into my voice. If she couldn't understand that, then we had bigger problems. "If you're here for your own agenda, we might as well call this quits now because the only way that ends is with all of us dead, or worse."

If Ronan got his hands on any of us sitting around this table once we broke the deal, death wouldn't be his answer. Death would be too easy in his eyes. No, he'd have to make us suffer in the way that would hurt us the most: turning into one of them. A weapon for his disposal.

"You'll never get far by focusing on yourself." Reina tempered the emotions flaring in the room. Her hands were instinctively out, motioning for us to calm down.

"Individualism was the downfall of our society the first time," Tomoe added, a reminder of how things had unraveled before.

I trailed my eyes over Hunter, my gaze unwavering, steady as stone. "If we're going to do this, we do it my way."

Hunter's lips twitched, the faintest trace of a frown tugging at the corners. His scoff was low, as if he'd heard it all before. "Sounds familiar."

"Look," I said, voice lowering as the room around us fell to near silence. "If this is going to work, we need to move as *one.* A little gathering to go over rules of engagement won't change the outcome when we hit the battlefield. War is on the horizon, but it's not imminent. Ronan needs time to prepare, as do we. I don't just need to sit down with their leaders, I need to speak to the generals—*and* I need them to bend the knee."

"You're not thinking clearly. A political leader and General, that's a dictatorship. And that's certainly not something I can guarantee others will comply with." Hunter's tone was measured, cautious.

"We don't need a guarantee." Alexiares's honey brown eyes hardened, his sharp jaw ticking. "All we need is acknowledgment that they've been warned."

"Of?" Serenity laughed, dismissing our clear intentions.

"Any form of dissent will be crushed before it can spread," Riley said plainly, his words speaking undeniable truth.

The words that I didn't want to say myself. Hunter was right—this wasn't how I wanted to lead, but it was necessary to keep everyone safe. Sacrifices now for survival later. And then, after it was over, everyone could go back to normal. Start over. Try this all again. With new leadership this time, solid people that understood the importance of balance and the value of the softer side of humanity.

"A threat to The Compound is a threat to all," I added quietly, my voice soft but firm, letting the words settle over the room.

One compound, *one* unit.

Reina was determined to make her brother understand, her hand fell atop his. "That's the mindset we all gotta have, Hunter. Last time, people suffered that didn't need to because others opted out. It's not gonna work that way this go around."

"We won't let it," Abel said with finality— a promise he'd carry through no matter what. I didn't need to hear more. He meant it. We all had come to understand the cost of failure, and Abel had no intentions on letting history repeat itself.

Hunter nodded. "Understood."

"I am merciful within reason," I said. "So don't give me an opportunity to show you my wrath."

Tomoe's gaze lingered on Hunter, distant and unfocused as if caught between thoughts. Then, her eyes shifted, meeting mine. I offered her a slight nod. She straightened in her chair, her voice steady but tinged with the weight of deeper contemplation. "This goes beyond how we handle this war. We have to consider what the world will look like for us after it's over. What victory means."

The room fell silent, every pair of eyes on her now, wavering to me only when I spoke. "I don't know what that means yet. Hopefully that will be clear to me once meeting with the others, after seeing where their heads are at."

CHAPTER
THIRTY-FOUR

RILEY

I was always one to focus on the facts. Use the information before me and respond within reason. Although things were falling into place, things appeared rather bleak for the foreseeable future. Even if everything went according to plan, people would still die, and I could only hope those people weren't the ones I cared for. Amaia would be front and center of it all. I knew better than to try to convince her otherwise.

Pulling her from danger would be like removing food from a reactive dog. You just didn't do that shit unless you were okay with getting bit. The energy was heavy everywhere but home. With Amaia granting us an evening of rest, my feet could not carry me there any faster unless I took off in a full sprint.

There was a source of light awaiting me if only I could get there. I gathered my thoughts, then unlocked the door and stepped inside. Yasmin sat on the couch in front of the window overlooking The Pit. We were still adjusting and moving things around to make this place more ours. A home. Amaia had an … eclectic sense of taste. We needed more plants, more decor, and according to Yasmin, a pop of color. Which was easy to fulfill given I was lucky enough to be in love with an artist. Her paintings were beautiful, full hues and shadows I swore my eyes had never seen before.

I locked the door behind me and she glanced up with a small smile. The most beautiful one. Her long, silky brown hair was tinted red in the candle light from the sconces on the wall. She closed the book she was reading and tucked it in between her body and the cushion to her left. The only thing I could think about was showing her how much I missed her throughout the day. Our relationship didn't have the luxury as some of the others, not that Moe's was an example of what I wanted to be, but even so, Alexiares and Amaia were able to spend time together via work. While I was rather glad Yasmin wasn't mixed up in our mess, I still envied the fact that it was easier for them to steal moments to themselves. I had to wait until I got home. *If* I made it home at a decent time before Yasmin had fallen asleep—something she was doing a lot more of these days.

She was strict about her sleeping schedule. Routine brought her comfort. It was something we struggled to fall into once moving in together. Structure was a part of my everyday life and I always had to be *on* when I was outside these four walls. I had little interest in bringing that home with me. But for her, I would try. Cupping her face, I squeezed her cheeks then offered her a gentle, lingering kiss. Yasmin kissed me back, but it lacked the usual passion. My keys fell from my pocket, she caught it with her magic, using the air to place it on the shelf next to me with a smug grin.

"You okay?" I asked, settling into the couch at her side and pulling her close. "How were the kids today? I know you said Lilia was still having a hard time."

She peered up, her hand brushing with a whisper of softness as she traced my jawline. "Yes, my love. Everything is okay."

"It's not," I said, and tucked her hair behind her ear. I lifted her chin gently and offered her some silent encouragement.

We sat in silence for minutes that dragged on far longer than I'd have preferred. Patience was key with Yasmin. She would talk when she was ready to. Pushing her would get the words out, yes, but it wasn't worth how upset it would make her. And I never wanted to be the reason for her pain.

"I'm pregnant."

"We're…" I trailed off, my brain doing its damn best to catch up to my heart, which was already sprinting ahead. "We're having a baby?" The words felt foreign in my mouth. Too big and too small all at once.

A laugh bubbled up before I could stop it, shaky and raw. "I get to be a dad?" They were words I never thought I'd have the joy of muttering but always hoped to own. I pressed a hand to my face, dragging it down as a grin broke free. "Holy shit, I get to be a dad."

It wasn't just joy; it was everything all at once—fear, hope, love, and the kind of happiness that burned, all tangled up together.

Yasmin's somber expression cracked, then gave way to that brilliant smile of hers. "You get to be the best Baba." Her voice carried a soft certainty, not a mere fact but a promise.

I kissed her. Once. Twice. Three times. She laughed, trying to pull away, but I wasn't letting go. Not yet.

"Man, this might be the best day of my life," I muttered, the weight of it all settling in my chest.

But then she paused, her brow pulling tight, doubt creeping in where happiness had been. "Is this … wrong? In theory, this was a good idea. I mean we talked about the 'what if' for months now. That was just a daydream … I didn't think … What I'm trying to get across is that, now that it's real, it feels a little crazy. Doesn't it?"

"No," I said, dragging the word out. A flicker of doubt flashed in her eyes. My lips twitched, but I didn't fully let the smirk take over. Instead, I tipped my head and shifted on the couch, watching her, needing to lock this moment in place.

I traced my thumb along her lower lip, my voice low. "With a face like that, you really shouldn't say things that make me want to lose control."

I kissed her again, slower this time, daring her to say something back. Her body tensed, and I felt a wave of heat shoot through me. Rolling to my feet, I bent down, running my hands up her waist and finding a good grip. I picked her up, one hand on the curve of her ass. "Do I need to remind you of the very words that kept me from even considering pulling out?" I whispered into her ear.

Throwing the bedroom door open, Yasmin was lost to a flurry of soft giggles. The sound music to my ears.

"You mean, *I love you?*" Yasmin asked, that playful sarcasm I loved coupled with my favorite words made me feral for her.

I set her on the edge of the bed then dropped to my knees. The soft give of her hips beneath my palms was a promise of happiness. I let my thumbs skim the curve of her thighs, savoring every inch. Her breath hitched as I reached for the hem of her shirt, lifting it with deliberate care. The way she fit so perfectly, so fully, against my hands and lips—it was everything.

"Yep," I murmured, now too occupied by desire to speak coherently. "Those are the ones."

"So, we're doing this?" Yasmin said, propping herself up on her elbows.

"Start a life together?" My gaze locked onto hers. "I can think of nothing I've wanted more in this life."

She scoffed dismissively. "We're in the middle of a silent war in a zombie apocalypse, I can't think of a more dangerous situation."

My lips curled into a quiet smile. "I'd cut my way through a thousand Pansies to get to you," I pressed another kiss to her stomach, lingering there. "To get to both of you."

"I love you," Yasmin said, a sultry smirk tugging at her lips. A smile that had a habit of driving me out of my damn mind.

I closed the distance between us and pulled her into a kiss that was anything but gentle. She wrapped her arms around my neck, drawing me closer as the world blurred to nothing but her. The warmth of her skin. The taste of her tongue intertwined with mine. And the best yet, the way Yasmin held me, as if she couldn't fathom ever letting go.

I deepened the kiss, my hands roaming, memorizing. When I pulled away, it was only to dip my head, lips brushing her jaw before trailing lower, teasing the spot where her pulse pounded beneath soft skin. A teasing claim. I trailed to the side and down the valley between her breasts. They fell free at the pinch of my fingers warring with the clasp of her bra. I tossed it off the bed, desperate to see her clearly. She was a work of art. A piece I wanted to take my time studying. I could take a hundred years carving a sculpture of her and it still wouldn't be enough time to showcase her beauty. Her perfection.

Yasmin's body responded, a soft moan escaped her plump lips, the sound sending a rush of blood to my dick. Urging me to lose control. The encouragement drove me to her voluptuous breasts, my mouth desperate to explore. I traced a circle with my tongue and sucked with each arch of her back.

"God, I'm lucky." I mumbled against the spot on her chest directly over her heart. My hands fell to the zipper of her jeans and I held her stare as I tugged them down. "Lift up for me, baby."

Eyes lined with coal darkened at my command. And like the good girl she was, she did as she was told.

Yasmin gasped at the soft touch of my fingers drawing circles over her clit. I grew frustrated at the fabric preventing me from drowning in her wetness. But this wasn't about me, her pleasure would bring me my own, and I wanted to drag every moment of that pleasure out. Lifting her legs, I placed them over my shoulders, using my hands to pull her panties off in the same motion.

"You don't even realize what you do to me," I whispered, gaze lingering on her as though committing her to memory. Kissing down the side of her legs, I lowered myself, settling at her core. I dipped my fingers in her arousal and sucked them into my mouth. "The way you respond to me, it's the most beautiful thing I've ever seen."

I couldn't resist. The whimpers she released made me crave her. I kissed her again, slow and deep, tasting the sweetness of her coconut ChapStick lingering on her lips. My hands moved on their own, tracing every curve and hollow of her body. God, she was everything—my future, my peace, my home.

Trailing back down her body, I made sure to take my time. She shivered beneath me at the sensation of my lips on the soft curve of her stomach. I settled back between her thighs and allowed myself to feast. She bucked against me, her gasps and soft moans filled the room. Pulling back, I nibbled on the skin between her pussy and her inner thigh right before she found release, taunting her, driving her mad with need. I smiled against her skin knowing *I* was the one who could make her fall apart this way.

"Riley," she whined.

Fuck, I loved hearing my name like that.

Yasmin shoved my shoulders back, and I didn't hesitate as I moved, finding her entrance and joining us in one seamless motion. Her eyes rolled heavenward, mouth fixated in a silent scream. For a second, it was just us—no chaos, no danger, no war. Just her. Just this.

She felt like heaven. The way she clenched around me—tight, warm, pulling me in deeper. Yasmin's fingers dug into my back, and her face pressed against my chest, muffling those soft, desperate sounds. Every whimper, every gasp, it fueled me. I couldn't get enough.

I pulled out slow and teasing, finding joy in the way her body trembled at the loss. Flipping her over, my hand slid under her stomach, arching her how I wanted. She let me guide her. Pliant. Eager.

She shivered as I traced a finger down her spine, my lips following until I found her waist. I gripped both sides firmly, grounding myself as her pussy clenched against my dick as I slid back in.

"You're so beautiful," I said, my voice rough with a mix of awe and urgency.

She didn't answer. Yasmin shifted beneath me as I squeezed her again and pulled her back enough for the base of my shaft to press against her wetness.

"Say it," I murmured, leaning forward until my lips brushed her ear. "Make me happy. I want to hear you say it."

Her voice was barely above a whisper. "I'm beautiful."

"Yes," I groaned with pleasure, sliding into her again, the word a promise. "You are."

Her body responded in perfect rhythm with mine, her movements matching my intensity, and I knew I was a goner. "I love you," she gasped, her voice full of everything I ever wanted to hear.

"I love you too," I managed, the words breaking free as I lost myself in her completely.

The bathing room was quiet save for the soft crackle of fire we'd ignited before getting in. Its glow danced along the stone walls and cast shadows that stretched across the wall. Maybe it was Jax's ghost or my own damn haunting thoughts, but this room always seemed to carry a chill despite the warmth throughout these quarters.

Yasmin nestled against my chest. Her breaths were even as she slept, completely at ease, fingers intertwined with mine. I tilted my head, studying her. The peace on her face right now was rare, hard-earned, and I'd fight to keep it for her.

So many lives depended on me now. Not just hers. Not just Amaia and my family. And somehow, it no longer felt impossible. This was the family I'd dreamed of having since I was a kid. Something real. Something to fight for—not just survive.

"I will not fail," I whispered, letting the words settle in the air with promise.

CHAPTER THIRTY-FIVE

ALEXIARES

San Jose, you son of a bitch. I'm coming for you. And for the price of stressing my general the fuck out, I promise not to be gentle.

Suckerpunch lurked at my side as we made our way through the abandoned streets of Los Gatos. It'd been a long fucking day. We'd pushed it on the whole daylight thing, but we needed to find a place to rest. My boy had done great. The two of us, out on the road alone, on a mission for our woman. I laughed to myself; Amaia does always say history repeats itself. At least this time, I was certain that I was irrevocably and unconditionally in love with her, and what we were doing was for a good cause. It was nice to be able to say that with confidence.

Sixty-two miles and a fifteen hour push with minimal stops for hydration, I wish I could make Suckerpunch a damn steak. And here I was thinking he'd turned into a lazy mush living a cushy life in Monterey. This was the first time he had a home to live in. Finley had refused to let him inside the house. Now he was clutching the ridiculous red squid Reina had made, refusing to leave it behind.

We passed by a faded sign: *The Billy Jones Wildcat Railroad*. I raised my hand, palm flat, then pointed two fingers at my eyes before sweeping them out toward him. It was a silent command we hadn't used in far too long, sharp and precise: *watch me*. His massive frame went taut with controlled energy. His ears pitched forward, amber eyes scanning the world around us as I walked up to the ticket booth. In my experience, no one ever thought to hide out in them. In fact, places like this sat pretty much untouched since the fall of the world. But, just in case someone else had the same idea of a hideout, they provided an opportunity for a quick escape. Usually two windows and a door. At the front of all parks, it allowed you to hear and see before they hear or see you.

I kept my steps silent as I approached and my knife clutched tight in my hand. There used to be a peace in doing this shit alone. There was still a peace in a sense, from being away from responsibilities and *always, always,* some group of people. So less than twenty-four hours away from Amaia, going on this mission alone was … boring. Simply put, I'd rather be doing *this* with *her*.

No rush of adrenaline came with that first cautious peek inside a place before clearing the ticket booth. Settling in at night wasn't the same without the soft curls tickling my chin or the sound of her breathing beside me. The absence of a racing heart at night while I pretended that closing my eyes was the same thing as sleep in case someone or something crept up in the darkness was monotonous. And walking the rest of the way to San Jose fending off small herds and stray Pansies gave me no real thrill. None of it mattered when the distance between us meant my eyes weren't on her for the first time in eleven months. I had no way to make sure she was safe.

This mission would be over soon enough. I'd get back to her. And when we finally put all of this behind us, I couldn't wait to make her mine—for good. For infinity.

VEGETATION RECLAIMED THE TWO MILES LEADING UP TO THE GATE OF San Jose. Since I had the best luck in the world, I ran into about fifteen escorts of Coverts army, laughing. Having the grandest of times. I grumbled a curse as I weaved behind abandoned cars on the sides of the street in the remnants of an old suburb. They were crowding around something that moved in front of them. By the giant pile of shit sitting at my feet, a horse led their caravan. The crowd of them broke revealing a group of women hunched over in the back of a cage. It was about six by six. Not large enough for the amount of people inside, as if people ever belonged in them.

I scratched the side of my head, wondering when the fuck I started caring about shit like that. This wasn't my business. It was important to focus on the mission—but Amaia and the others had this whole empathy thing going on that was rubbing off.

Un-fucking-fortunately, this two-mile stretch was the *only* way into San Jose coming from the south. An intentional strategy Amaia had helped them develop that was now working against our interests. Now I was stuck behind them. Forced to move at their pace and not mine. They were in no rush to get back, not with these women in tow. My mind called on a memory from outside Montello a few months back.

Covert was going to auction them.

That's what we'd seen. Watched as they were brought as a reward for soldiers who performed well. There wasn't anything Amaia could do about it then, but damn had she wanted to.

With as many soldiers as there were, masking the sound of my steps wasn't exactly top priority. Their attention was fixed on the girls—smirking, laughing, some leaning closer to the cages in order to get their hands on what they wanted through the iron bars. Getting closer didn't scream out 'risk', not unless one of them turned around.

I crept nearer, straining to catch bits of their conversation. Anything useful. A hint of security changes, new patrol patterns—something Monterey hadn't picked up on yet. But the closer I got, the more the reality of the situation sunk in.

The 'women' in the cages weren't women at all.

The oldest might have been eighteen. And the youngest … My stomach twisted, bile rising at the back of my throat.

Sick bastards. Every single one of them.

"Malachai's confident this batch'll be better than the last. Said they put them in some suite before transport. I bet that made y'all feel real special, huh?" one of the soldiers said with a cruel chuckle. "*Dysentery.* Thought that was some shit of the past. Wasted effort."

"Seem to be prime breeding age too," another chimed in, reaching through the bars to pinch one of the girls. She yelped and jerked away, her sobs growing louder, her shoulders shaking as snot dripped down her face.

"Gross," another muttered, his nose wrinkling in disgust, though it didn't stop him from watching.

My jaw tightened, but I didn't move. Not yet. My fists itched to do something—anything—but I couldn't risk blowing this before I had a chance to get inside. The fate of Salem Territory depended on it.

The oldest girl stepped forward, putting herself between the others and the soldiers. Something shifted in the hot, still, summer air. The wind picked up, tugging at the edges of the soldiers' uniforms.

She wasn't subtle about her focus. The one closest to her grabbed at his throat. His face turned red as he gasped, his lungs seemingly on the verge of collapse.

For a second, I thought she'd done it.

The caravan slowed, the others hesitating. Then, the bastard stopped coughing. He peered up with a grin stretching across his face as he straightened. The others caught on quickly, falling into hysterics as the girl froze, horror etched into her face.

"I keep telling you," one of the soldiers said. "Your magic doesn't work with the suppressant."

The girl cowered slightly then straightened, her lips pressing into a tight line as the soldiers kept laughing.

"Looked like it worked just all right for a few seconds," a smaller brunette said. Still tucked behind the oldest but her words were steady and bold. "Are you blind?"

The soldiers hesitated for a moment before one of them moved—a hulking brute with a sneer deep enough it could have been carved into his face. He didn't bother with words, shoving his arm through the bars as if he had every right to without remorse. The girls screamed, scrambling back in a desperate tangle, but the brunette wasn't fast enough. His hand closed around her arm, yanking her forward until she hit the cage with a sharp clang.

"Defiant one, aren't you, sweetheart?" he sneered, his lips curling into something ugly. "Don't worry, they'll fuck that right out of you."

Her eyes widened, but she didn't cry. She didn't beg. No. Instead, she held her head up high—it pissed him off.

Some of the soldiers shifted uncomfortably, glancing at each other with darting eyes, as though they weren't sure if they should step away or laugh along. Others turned their backs, muttering under their breath. But most of them stayed planted right where they were, letting out low, guttural laughs.

The soldier who'd mentioned the suppressant earlier stepped forward. His tone remained flat, tinged with apathy, as though he couldn't be bothered to give a damn. "Give them another dose and call it a day. We're almost back. You won't have to see her again, so stop wasting our time. Some of us have families to get back to."

The cage rattled softly as the brunette stumbled back, her chest rising and falling unevenly.

"Nah," the brute said, his grip tightening as he leaned closer to the cage. "I'll see her tonight. After she gets cleaned up."

I thought my jaw might crack from how hard I clenched it, but I stayed hidden. Timing was everything.

The other soldier stepped closer, placing a hand on the brute's shoulder, his grip firm. "Victor," he snarled through his teeth, "would never waste her perfect genetics on a brute like you."

The brute froze. They remained locked in a standoff as a flock of crows flew overhead. He let go of the girl. She stumbled back, her arm cradled to her chest, and the soldiers fell into silence. I took a moment to study them all. Memorize every face, every name I could catch, and every word they said.

Their time would come.

Upon closer inspection, a small detail on the uniform of the one who'd spoken up became apparent. Instead of the pouncing lion of Covert, a raven black as night sat on his lapel. Salem. Though his uniform was the same green and tan as Covert's, the divide between allies was clear enough that they made sure to distinguish who was who.

The patch next to the raven was the same as Reina's. A DNA helix. Scientist. It didn't match the rest of the group—most wore the classic shield, their gear dirtied by time in the field. Two others, like him, didn't fit. They were the same ones who were visibly uncomfortable earlier, their unease written across their faces.

The brute sniffed out a laugh, sharp and mocking, slicing through the heavy silence. Like trained dogs, the others followed suit. He held up his hands and backed off with exaggerated ease. "Ahh, I'm just inspiring a little fear. Take it easy," he said, his grin stretching wide, the same sick satisfaction crawling across his face. He turned to the group, voice shifting to something almost friendly. "I could use a warm meal right about now. How 'bout you, brothers?"

A few murmurs of agreement followed. The caravan groaned as it trudged down the dirt road. I kept my distance, the nausea twisting deeper inside me. Every laugh, every careless comment, every smirk—they all lingered, the scent of decay sticking to me, sinking under my skin.

It was too easy to off the idiot in the 'watchtower.' If this was what I was up against, tonight would be a walk on the beach. Or whatever the hell Reina always said. I pulled on his uniform and caught back up on the tail of the others. A reasonable, fair guess? I had maybe fifteen minutes before someone realized he wasn't where he was supposed to be.

The gate, a solid slab of concrete reminiscent of Monterey's defenses, greeted me as I stepped into San Jose. The flow of soldiers and the caravan moved with such precise rhythm, such practiced ease, no one gave me a second glance. I kept my pace steady, moving with the rhythm of their steps, blending in as a shadow among them.

I followed. Watched. Took mental notes on where the caravan ended up. And made a promise to myself—I'd be back for those girls before anyone ever touched them.

MONSTERS LURK IN THE DARK. EVERYONE KNEW THAT. IT'S WHY FEAR trickles up your spine when there's a spot that's a bit *too* dark in your room or at the entrance to an alley. Demons exist and so do their hounds.

I leaned against the harsh stucco of a house as I lay in wait. The small path between houses was pitch black, making it a nice little opportunity to keep cover after the debacle I'd caused. No one had come to get him yet to my dismay. To warn him that the girls were loose. They were timid at first, not wanting to trust someone they deemed another man in a world full of cruelty. But at the opportunity of freedom the brunette and the oldest took the others and ran. I'd given them the option to wait for a few miles outside the gate. From there, I'd escort them a town over before they'd be left on their own. If I had to guess, the ones that successfully made it out, would not be there. I wouldn't if I were them.

Finally, the patchy green door of the house across the street opened, and he walked out. He'd glanced around a few times then turned to lock his door. With a sickening little grin, he swept a hand through his peppered hair and smoothed down his clothes. The little pep in his step as he jogged down the steps made my skin fucking crawl.

I stepped out the alley way, Suckerpunch tucked low at my side. The movement put him on alert and his head went on a swivel. Our eyes met and recognition set in. Terror crept into his gray eyes as I closed the distance between us, the grin falling right off his face.

And as I suspected, Victor ran.

Of course he had. They always fucking did. I followed at a leisurely pace. The frantic shuffle of his boots and the slam of the door sliced through the calm San Jose night as he disappeared into his house.

"Knock, knock." My boot connected with the door, sending it crashing open with enough force to make my entrance memorable. One step in, then another, slow and deliberate. The knife in my hand caught a sliver of moonlight through the window, its edge gleaming. I gave it a little twist, letting the light dance along the blade before pointing it at him. "Victor, right?"

He spat in my direction, a pathetic attempt at defiance as he shuffled backward. His hands fumbled against the table behind him, searching, desperate. For what, a weapon probably. Didn't care. Wasn't planning on letting him live long enough to find out.

"Not going to answer me?" I tilted my head, watching him the way a wolf watched its prey stumble. "That's fine. Odd, though. A lieutenant general wandering around unarmed. Did you have plans tonight, Victor?" My laugh came low, sharp. Cruel. "I'm afraid you won't be making them. None of you will."

"This is how she wants to play, huh? So much for the fight Ronan promised. Send you out to do her dirty work? Pathetic."

"I volunteered," I said, my voice steady, almost conversational. My thoughts strayed from him, landing on the blade in my hand. Slowly, I pressed a fingertip against the tip of the knife, watching as a bead of blood welled up, bright and mesmerizing. "Though I must admit I expected a bit of a fight myself."

The room had grown too quiet, save for his ragged breathing. I finally glanced up, letting the faintest smirk tug at my lips.

"I wouldn't give you the pleasure," he sneered.

"Oh. It's *always* a pleasure."

"You're sick."

"*I'm* sick?" A clipped, harsh laugh broke free from my throat. "Me? The sick one."

I stepped forward, the knife gleaming in my hand, the weight of it familiar and steady. Each step drew me closer until the space between us felt suffocating—for him, not for me.

"I look death in the face and feel nothing. San Jose made the wise choice in choosing Covert. What we're building here will surround them with greatness—from the architecture and inventions, down to the people. I'd say you'll see it, but … you're on the losing side of this war. There will be no bending the knee here, *Blood-hound*. To die standing is to die with honor."

I could no longer resist the urge. Lunging forward, I sliced across the back of his knees. Victor crumbled to the ground. Blood pooled beneath him but he clenched his teeth together, resisting the urge to release a cry. I crouched down to his level and pulled him close by the collar of his shirt.

"You have no honor," I whispered, each word sharp and deliberate. "And I'm going to make this hurt, you sick, sick fuck."

He tilted his head, staring back at me with empty, unflinching eyes. An unapologetic smile cracked across his tawny skin. "I don't know what you're talking about."

Fury swelled in me, a familiar beast awakening within. My knife moved before I thought, cutting a deep line across his chest. Blood welled up, stark against his skin. The bastard didn't even flinch.

"Those are *children*," I hissed.

"I. Don't. Know. What. You're. Talking. About." His tone was flat, his stare unbroken.

My grip on the blade tightened as the heat of my anger warred with an unwelcome flicker of doubt. He didn't deny it outright. His confusion felt too raw. *Damn it.* This was supposed to be simple. Kill him, make an example, move the fuck on.

But his words lingered, carving a small crack in my certainty. What if he wasn't lying? What if there was something I didn't see?

"Are there more?" It was a simple question.

His smile faltered, almost imperceptible, then slid back into place, a faint shadow of something shattered. "Perhaps," Victor said, his voice soft, mocking. "You're mistaken."

His answer—or lack of one—nagged at me, sharp and unwelcome. A feeling I wasn't sure how to explain presented as a crack in the armor I didn't even want to admit existed.

I pressed the knife harder, focusing on the steel's edge to silence it. "I know what I saw. What I heard."

"Do you?" Victor's tone dripped with condescension. "If you came across children, you saw only a sliver of the greater vision. They deserve care. *Structure.* A chance at life within a proper home." The crisp pop of his p on *proper* made my jaw clench. "That's all we're doing—restoring order. Ensuring the right values are instilled in them. But of course, you'd find that wrong. The intelligence required to understand such a concept is clearly beyond your capability."

I scoffed, my voice cutting. "Pardon my lack of subtlety, but, when do the breeding programs start?"

Victor didn't flinch, his expression an infuriating mask of indifference. He stayed silent.

"Continue," I snapped, leaning forward, letting the threat hang in the air.

He stared at me, unblinking, before smirking ever so faintly. "I think I've said enough."

I took a step back, holstering the knife. My fingers twitched, magic simmering beneath my skin. Fire wasn't necessarily as discreet as I was hoping given I still had two other stops to make. Then I made the call—*fuck it.* Closing the distance, I let the heat build.

"Torture won't work on me, Bloodhound," Victor said with a low chuckle. "A lieutenant general doesn't rise in the ranks without surviving a few rounds. Ask your general. Oh, wait. One of those times was at your *other wife's* hand. Remember that? Wrong time to ask your secret? It's just one powerful piece of ass after the other. Though I must say, I prefer blon—"

Before the words fully left his mouth, my knife was already in my hand, a blur of steel that moved with precision and finality. In one clean, deliberate stroke, the blade sliced deep into his throat. His flesh severed with a force that silenced him mid-taunt. I tilted my head back, releasing a low, orgasmic moan. Blood spilled in a hot rush, staining the air with the metallic tang of death.

I didn't bother with the mess. Let it rot. That wasn't my problem. Instead, I crouched by the body, fingers dipping into the still-warm blood pooling around him. They'd wanted everyone to know who had been here, who had done this. Fine. My name would be the first thing they'd see.

With deliberate strokes, I painted it onto the wall: **Bloodreina + Bloodhound**, finishing it off with a sharp, dripping heart. A cruel grin tugged at my lips. Let them choke on the irony.

Monterey would be ready to fight. The other settlements wouldn't stand a chance. Amaia didn't want to catch them off guard, but that wasn't purely kindness. Their survival meant reinforcements down the line. If they fell, it'd just be fewer people left to wipe out Covert—and make no mistake, Covert needed to burn.

When the work was done, I moved to the next names on my list: the top two officers who'd fight to take Victor's place. Amaia hadn't asked for this, but she didn't need to. I knew what had to be done. She could fight me on it later. It wouldn't change the fact that I'd spared her another reason to hate herself. Her conscience didn't have room for this—not in a war like this. Hesitation was a luxury none of us could afford, least of all her. I'd make the hard calls if it meant keeping her from breaking under the guilt.

CHAPTER
THIRTY-SIX

RILEY

"**T**ime for a quick game?" I climbed through Amaia's open window. An old habit I'd hoped made her smile.

She didn't jump. Didn't react other than glance up from her paperwork with a stiffened back. I leaned over her to see what she was working on as I moved from behind her desk. *Evacuation Plan: E.* Plans that, unfortunately, would be coming into play sooner than desired.

"You plan on finishing the alphabet?" I asked, waving up the wooden board I clasped in my hand.

She dropped her pen and reached out in expectation. I smirked, dropping it into her hand, walking toward the door. My back pressed against it and I watched her open it carefully. Her eyes lit up from across the room. "Where'd you get that?"

"I made it for you," I said, pretending it was no big deal, though I was anxious as ever. It'd taken two days to find the perfectly round pebbles along the beach, but I wanted them to mean something. That little cove was her place of peace, and this was more than a simple gift. "Travel sized."

She ran her fingers along the hand-carved, maple colored mancala board. Tears lined her eyes as she inspected it. "Thank you, it's beautiful." Amaia's gaze was intense.

I broke our eye contact, shoving my hands into my pockets, and looked around the room. I'd passed Elie out on her run and Alexiares was still on a mission. Just the two of us. *No better time than now man.*

"Not gonna offer me some coffee?" I bit my tongue at the wrong words finding their way out.

"Offering implies that you're a guest," she scoffed with the roll of her eyes. "Which we both know you are not."

"Okay, how about some pie for celebration?"

"While you're quite the artist, Ril, this is hardly something to celebrate." She laughed a small, quiet chuckle then stood to close the window. I watched as she placed the coffee pot in the fireplace and it ignited without effort.

I moved over to the couch and cleared off the coffee table to make room for the board. Amaia sat across from me on the floor, legs crossed. "Before the game gets going, I have good news and pretty shitty news."

She stopped setting up the game, and the pebbles clattered against the sides. "Hit me with the shit first."

"Ronan's on the move. We have about a day or so before we're surrounded."

"That was fast," she muttered and resumed placing the beads.

"You sent *the Bloodhound*." The heat from the fire warmed the room to an uncomfortable level. Sweat beaded my forehead, and

I tugged at my shirt. "It's hot in here. Don't tell me you expected slow results."

"I expected some temporary plausible deniability. Next time I'll be clearer." Amaia turned the fire down to a low flame and motioned she was ready to play.

I shoved the board toward her. Partially as a way to tell her to go first, partially because she needed to look closer, or I was going to lose my mind. The small contours along the board were intricate. Complex. A real work of art, according to Yasmin. It was a lot to take in, but she'd notice. She always did.

"Hunter's back and while Hollis may be stupid, Bietoletti and Tyler are not. The cavalry never made it to Ronan, and you ... *we* sent suspected traitors in their stead. I'd say he was itching for a reason to come after us and was more than happy we finally made our move."

Amaia sighed, tucking a stray curl behind her ear, then made her play. "Okay. We expected this. It's fine. I thought we'd have until after the meeting, but we can make it work."

I tilted my head to the left with the downward tug of my lips. "Tell me what you need."

"I've been reading—"

"Predictably." I cracked a grin, and she tossed a pillow at me. I caught it, throwing it back with half the effort.

"The Vietnam War is fascinating, you know?"

"To you, yes," I concurred.

She narrowed her eyes and shook her head. "Hunter suggested that brute force won't work, but I'm inclined to disagree." Amaia held a hand up, knowing I was about to question her memory. "I know what I told him. This is what I'm telling *you*. They don't need to know everything. Guerrilla warfare is brute force by nature. In the same vein, it's extremely strategic. Every strike, every movement—intentional. Our defensive location isn't just a shield; it's a weapon. We can turn this place into seven different levels of hell."

God, I never had a clue where she was going with that brilliant mind of hers. It was like chasing smoke—impossible to catch, mesmerizing to watch. One thing I did know? If I kept quiet and listened long enough, the work I needed to do would eventually come into focus. She had a way of making it all click down every avenue of chaos.

I exhaled, already resigned to the inevitable. "Let me guess. I'm in charge."

"This is why we're a great team," she teased, leaning over the table to give my shoulder a shove. "I don't even have to tell you the plan, but yes. With Alexiares still gone, I need you and Abel here on set up."

At times I hated being lieutenant. It meant that there was inherently less room to argue—not that there ever was with her. Every part of me wanted to be out there with her. It would allow me to support her where it mattered the most. Except at her side wasn't where it mattered the most for The Compound, only for me.

Staying back in Monterey was best for everyone. It meant Abel would have more time to adjust and avoid unnecessary risks. Yasmin was here. It made sense. Yet, knowing what was right didn't make me want what I wanted even less. I met her stare with a resigned nod.

Amaia's movements were quick, decisive, like she'd been replaying this moment in her head all day. She unrolled one of the larger maps and smoothed it across the table on top of the board. "You're going to judge the shit out of me for this, but I've been busy."

"Oh?"

Amaia being 'busy' could mean anything from restructuring evacuation plans to whatever this was about to be.

"Elliot has tested it out per my request up in Duluth on a smaller scale with success. So, um, I may or may not have been collecting Pansies," she said casually. "They're, uh, trapped in caves here, here, and here." Amaia jabbed at points on the map without pause. "Oh, also here and here. Possibly a few right here, too, if the tide didn't drag 'em."

I sat unmoving. Wondering when the hell she'd had time to collect dead people along the coastline, let alone without Alexiares or me tracking her movements.

"Not judging. Not at all." I never judged anyone. This … *this* would happily be my first time. After hearing of her antics in Duluth, I thought she was done with the risky side quests. Apparently, we were all wrong to have hope.

"Imagine if—" her eyes lit up with that dangerous spark.

I cut her off, "The lead up to every bad idea you've ever had has started exactly like that."

"Yep. You're gonna hate this. Chain them around the forest."

I stared at her, unblinking. Over the weeks I'd worked on expanding the maze we'd already constructed before our first battle with Ronan. It completely circled The Compound now. Dense and unashamedly chaotic. That didn't make her plan any easier to digest. "You're joking."

"Then have the archers set them on fire," she replied, unbothered.

"If I say this plan can't get any worse," I muttered, "I have an extensive amount of faith that you can—and will—prove me wrong."

"Moving on," Amaia continued, as if I hadn't spoken at all. "We're going to need every earth elemental in our troops on the front line. I know it's a bit of a risk, but if they're quick, they'll finish before Ronan's forces even arrive. I want trenches beginning ten miles out."

"A defensive perimeter around The Compound," I nodded, finally seeing where she was going with this.

"The only way to us is through trees or trenches," she tapped her finger hard against the map. "Neither option is a fun time. Watch towers are for snipers only. No one crosses through our gates again."

"You're diabolical," I broke into a laugh and a smile widened across her face.

"I prefer mastermind, but thank you."

I shook my head and thought it over. "I'll brief the night shift and have the earth elementals get moving. We'll set fire guards to watch over them. Best to conserve ammo for when it's critical. Our last inventory is in line with standard defense, but I'd feel better saving rounds until we can recoup or produce excess. Tomorrow morning, I'll prepare the rest of our troops. Don't worry. I've got it covered."

"I know. I never worry with you." The warmth in Amaia's smile softened the edges of her usual intensity. "I suppose Luna should handle the day-to-day. There's no reason to halt things behind the walls until it's absolutely necessary. We just got some semblance of stability. You two make whatever call necessary once I'm gone."

"Consider it done."

Her breath loosened and her body relaxed. Amaia scooted the game back to the center of the table, discarding the maps onto the floor. I played my turn as she removed the coffee from the fire and poured it into two cups. She crossed the floor and grabbed cubes of sugar, dropping them in, making mine the same as hers. A habit I previously found disgusting. Amaia had found it amusing to add her own twist each time she made me a cup. Eventually, I'd seen the light in her ways. Or so she liked to tease. Her gaze settled on me as I took a sip, softening with the familial love that always caught me off guard. For so long in my life, I had yearned for it, yet she gave it to me freely.

"So," she said, her voice lighter but still carrying the weight of the moment. "The good news, then?"

"Might want to look at the board one more time."

I waited, watching as she leaned forward, eyes narrowing. Her brows pinched together. "Jaxon's godmother? Jax never played until he met me. I thought you made this."

"I did," I said simply.

"Then wh—" Recognition set in. "Oh my … oh my fuck. Oh my fuck. You're joking?"

"You do realize who you're talking to, right?"

The speed with which she got up and leaped over the table to my couch was faster than the amount of time it took me to blink. She jumped onto the cushions in a childlike fashion, her hands clapping in uncharacteristic glee, then fell over her mouth to compress her screams. I rose to my feet, and she forced me into a hug that Reina would kill for the opportunity to give. Her energy lifted, genuine happiness making her glow.

"A baby!" she said after she pulled away. "Riley Sullivan, leave it to you to try to start a family in the middle of a goddamn war."

"No time like anytime." I let my smile free, enjoying this moment, just us. Amaia was my family and this … this is how I imagined moments went in a normal household, the kind I'd dreamed of having in The Before.

"Shit. I'm beyond happy for you, Ril. Wait … Godmother. Me?"

"You." I placed both hands firmly on her shoulders, leaning down slightly to make sure she caught every ounce of sincerity in my gaze.

"That's a big role," she muttered, hopping off the couch as though the weight of it had physically propelled her to move. Her fingers tangled in her curls, a nervous habit that always seemed to surface when she was overwhelmed.

"No bigger than that of a general."

"Jaxon?" A happy tear fell down her cheek. She was quick to wipe it away with a sniffle. "As in Jax?"

I nodded. "Jaxon Abdul Sullivan. After Jax and Mohammed. We cheated a little bit. Had Abel peek into the day of his birth."

"Wow," she shook her head in disbelief, moving to pace in front of the fireplace. "How do you feel?"

"Scared out of my mind," I said. Might as well be honest. If I were going to confess it to anyone, there was no one else who'd make it easier than her. I didn't want to burden Yasmin with such doubts.

"What? You? Scared? Psh."

"Maia, I could really screw this kid up. You have no idea. Look how things with Elie turned out, and I was only responsible for her for 50 percent of the time."

"That's not fair. Don't do that to yourself," she said with a quick wave of her hand. "And, honestly, I'm not sure I'm the one to be dishing out advice. Given that I'm in the same boat. But this? It's different. Some of us aren't meant to be parents. That 'some' does not include you. Come on, what's the worst that could happen? Let me hear it."

I exhaled sharply, dragging a hand over my face. "The worst? That I bring a kid into this world just to bury them. That I can't keep him or Yasmin safe. It's hard enough trying to survive, let alone trying to build something *worth* surviving for. What happens if I screw this up? I'm already stretched thin. The Compound, the war that will last until God knows when. Then the war that comes after that war … it's all balancing on a knife's edge. What if there's no room for a family in all of that? What if he grows up to resent me?"

Amaia's jaw dropped slightly before snapping shut. She crossed her arms, her voice deliberate and firm. "Then fuck The Compound."

"What?"

"You heard me." She took a step closer, eyes burning, that familiar intensity returning to them. "If it ever came down to your family or The Compound, the choice is simple. The choice is the same. But you put them first. You do what you need to in order to make it back to them because you surviving is how they will survive. Jaxon's not gonna grow up resenting you because you made a choice to give him a chance to live. If anything, that's the most honorable damn thing you could do."

Amaia had a way of simplifying the impossible. "Where does that leave you? The others?" I asked, voice thick with guilt. It was hard, but not impossible, to envision a world where she didn't come first—where this family did not.

"Who cares?" Amaia stepped forward and hugged me tightly, her face resting against my chest. "I love you. You're going to be the most amazing dad. You were made for this shit. And I seriously doubt Jaxon will grow up to hate his hero."

"I don't know what the future here looks like, and that's pretty terrifying, but with Yasmin, with you and Abel … it'll all be all right."

For a moment, Amaia's expression shifted—something unspoken flickered in her eyes, distant and strange. But she shook it off quickly, her trademark smirk returning as she gave my shoulder a playful shove. "Yeah, yeah. Whatever. Make sure you name the next one after me."

CHAPTER
THIRTY-SEVEN

ALEXIARES

None of the girls waited.

Without the extra weight, I made my way to Fresno. Three days of pushing it to the max and I was exhausted. Suckerpunch too. He'd even ditched the stupid squid a day and a half back. I kept it in my pack. Would serve as a nice little reward for when this job was done.

I shoved my hands into my pockets, tossing a nod at the man-child manning the gates. He appeared to be about eighteen or nineteen. Fuck if I knew why they put him in charge, but it was to my advantage, so oh well. There was no reason to stop me and that had converged into a pretty simple plan for getting in: walking through the front door. Pretend that I belonged because I did. As far as Fresno was concerned, Monterey Compound remained oblivious to their betrayal. Covert troops weren't wandering about in an obvious way like they did at San Jose.

Caution was my first priority as I hunted down my prey. The stares of the citizens of Fresno were piercing. They knew who I was. Everyone did here. But more importantly, they knew who I belonged to now, and her wrath was far more terrifying than my previous owner.

The secret of switching sides was known to the residents of this compound. And judging by the way they shrank into shadows or quickly looked away, the unspoken rule was clear: don't let the Bloodhound find out.

I moved through the narrow streets, keeping my steps measured and my expression neutral. The last thing I needed was to startle Alaric into running. Not yet.

A child darted out of a side alley, her laughter loud and grating as she chased after a loose ball. She got distracted, the smile dripping with drool at the sight of Suckerpunch at my side. The little girl made a beeline for us. Her mother snatched her arm and pulled her back before her gaze flickered up and landed on me. The blood drained from her face. Something flickered in the beady eyes that hardened in recognition. I stared back at her, eyes trained on her as I stepped around them, not breaking my stride.

Fresno was no stranger to monsters. It just so happened that I wasn't the scariest one here anymore.

Soldiers lingered against the older infrastructure of Fresno—their quadrant of the city. The divide here already existed prior to Covert's presence. Other side of the tracks kind of thing. Soldiers on one side, civilians on the other. Their families often resided somewhere in between—hence the woman and her child, walking close enough to feel the tension. I could sense her eyes on my back still. Then it clicked. It became clear once I fully took in my surroundings.

No women. Fresno's military had female soldiers up until now. I allowed myself one quick check over my shoulder. They were gone. *Shit.*

Ducking into the nearest building, I signaled Suckerpunch to get lost until I emerged. The stench of stale beer and weak moonshine slapped me in the face. A tavern. *Fucking fantastic.*

It was as decent a hideout as any. Anyone here was already plastered beyond belief. All but the bartender, her exhaustion written in every motion as she slid a cup my way.

"One of two options and this ain't the worst of it."

I pulled out one of the coins Salem Territory traded with and pushed it across the table without a word. She took it and made her way down the bar toward the drunkest of the bunch. He rambled on incoherently, and she tossed her dark hair over her shoulder, pretending to be intrigued.

"All I'm sayin', man. Listen, listen." A drunkard seated beside me slapped his buddy on the shoulder, nearly spilling his drink as he gave him a shake. "They're already prisoners. Life could be worse than a little jab in the arm to figure out where they belong." He downed his drink in one long gulp, his face reddening further as he slammed the empty glass onto the counter.

"Yeah, but … you hear what happened to the ones who didn't pass?" his buddy muttered, his voice low but not low enough. "Got processed, sent to … I don't even know where. They say the program's cleaning things up, but …"

The man cut himself off, glancing around as if the walls might be listening.

"From what I hear, Covert Province's got it pretty nice. Electricity, air conditioning, real order—not this make-believe shit we've been playing at for years. 'Purification,' they're callin' it," the first man said with a grim chuckle. "Makes you wonder if they're cleanin' anything or just takin' out the trash."

I dipped my head, hiding my face. The ink lining my body already gave me away, but they were too far gone to notice. Hopefully, they'd chalk the tilt of my head up to me being amused by their drunken rambling.

"Yeah, well. Better hope the people of Fresno's not next," the other muttered. "San Jose was just the start. If they got their eyes on here … lot of us aren't passing a damn purity test."

The bartender returned, her tray of empty glasses clinking faintly. Torture flickered in her eyes when she glanced at me—a soul silently begging for help. She leaned across the counter, twirling her hair in a halfhearted act of flirting as she whispered, "You get what you needed?"

I gave her a curt nod, my mind already spinning with the weight of what had been revealed.

"You don't write, you don't call," Alaric greeted the second I stepped out of the tavern. His voice carried the kind of fake warmth people used to smooth over tension.

"Are there working power lines I'm unaware of?" I replied, not bothering to turn around as he approached.

He chuckled dryly, swaggering to my side and extending a hand for a shake. "If we did, you'd be the first to know."

"Is that right?"

Stark white teeth flashed across his forgettable face. "Found your dog."

"Did you find him, or did Suckerpunch find you because I was ready to talk?" My tone was razor-sharp. We walked and kept his pace. "Anyway, I'm famished. You heading to lunch?"

He waved a hand, the gesture casual, though his eyes flicked to me, gauging my mood. "Funny you should ask. Melissa made some sandwiches back at the house. I'd be grateful if you could join me."

Melissa. His wife. The same woman who'd once begged us for Henry's help to deliver their baby via C-section, back when survival meant setting pride aside. Funny how quickly they used what they needed and turned when it suited them.

I offered a faint smirk but said nothing, following him as we crossed a few streets. He stopped in front of a tidy little house and gestured toward the door.

"You'll have to forgive me. Georgie seems to have an allergy to the fur," he said apologetically.

I turned to Suckerpunch, resting a hand on his neck. "Stay." He huffed, but obeyed.

The house was too perfect. They were trying too hard to pretend everything was fine. Neat furniture, pictures on the walls, even the smell of vinegar and mint lingering in the air—it was almost enough to make me laugh. No one lived like this anymore. Not unless they were holding onto scraps of The Before with a death grip.

"Melissa and Georgie are out for the afternoon. It's just us," Alaric said as he led me to the kitchen, gesturing for me to sit.

I didn't move right away, letting my eyes wander around the place. "Nice setup," I said finally, taking the chair he'd offered. "Real homey."

He ignored the jab, going to the fridge and pulling out a container. Sandwiches. I watched as he set them on a plate, fussing with napkins with trembling hands. There was no telling where his nerves came from. Could be anything, really. Or it was the fact that he was alone in a room with me. I tended to have that effect on people.

"Alaric," I said flatly, watching him pour lemonade into glasses.

He finished with the drinks and set them on the table. One in front of me and one for himself. With a sigh, he sat down across from me, then, head bowed, said a quick prayer.

"I know why you're here," he mumbled, his fingers twitching against the table's edge.

"Okay." I picked up the sandwich, took a bite, and nodded. It was the first non-soupy or dried anything I'd had in who knew how long.

Alaric looked up. Something desperate flickered in his eyes before he straightened up. "It's about the meeting, isn't it? In a few days. We heard about it through the grapevine. When the invite didn't come, I assumed it was an oversight."

I leaned back, forcing a smirk that cut sharper than it should. "Usually, Reina's our go-to for things like this," I said, keeping my tone light. "But given the … current climate, the general thought it might be better to send someone with a different skill set." I tipped my chin, offering him the wink of a criminal.

He gave a weak chuckle. The kind that barely touches the throat. "Understood. Yes, of course. Our council has been …" He paused, tilting his head side to side, weighing his words. "Torn on how to move forward after our defeat."

"Defeat," I repeated, rolling the word off my tongue with a slight shrug.

"Yes," he said quietly. "But we're here. We're alive none-theless."

I took another bite of the sandwich, raising a brow as I watched Alaric pick at his own food in small, timid bites. His hands still trembled, and the corners of his mouth twitched as though he was trying to hold something back. He was unraveling.

Alaric wasn't built for this.

He'd been thrown into a leadership role after the untime-ly death of Fresno's previous mayor—his older brother. They'd worked closely together for years. People here trusted him to run in the interim as they prepared to hold their first election since they'd been established. Then war erupted, and he was stuck, much like Amaia.

It'd taken me approximately two seconds to write him off as a threat the first time we'd met. Stupid move on my behalf. I'd forgotten how dangerous a weak and desperate mind could be when cornered.

"Then you'd better hope your council gets its act together," I said, sipping slowly on the bitter lemonade. "I heard Covert dug their claws into San Jose. Breeding programs."

Alaric stiffened, but quickly waved his hand as if brushing the thought away. "You can't believe every rumor," he said, quick to be defensive.

He shifted uncomfortably in his seat. I leaned forward, my gaze steady, patient, the quiet promise of a predator circling right out of reach.

"Oh, but you know something," I pressed, my voice quiet. Cold.

He hesitated, his fingers twitching against his lap. Alaric released a heavy sigh. Breath hot. "I don't know details, but I've heard … whispers. Something about running more tests on the Pansies. Experimenting on those who they don't think have what it takes to make it in a world like this and keep the human race propelling on a greater path forward. It's … terrifying, what they're capable of. If San Jose were to, I don't know, be threatened with such options, they have no choice but to do what's necessary to survive. That's the name of the game. Right?"

The vein on my forehead pulsed against the skin, a flicker of tension I couldn't suppress. His words were careful. Deliberate on the justification of it all specifically. The cracks in his composure told the truth he couldn't bury. Not from me. I no longer had to wrestle with the unnatural twist of guilt I'd felt since stepping foot in this house. Fresno wasn't turning a blind eye to Covert Province—they were in on it.

Their survival balanced on complicity in the suffering of others.

I took another sip of the lemonade, its sharp bitterness grounding me, masking the bile rising in my throat. "Survival's a funny thing," I said, my tone even, the words deliberate. "Everyone's got their limits. Yours just seem a little … flexible."

He nodded, mistaking my calm for understanding, a flicker of hope easing the desperation in his eyes. "I have to say there's a sense of relief in you saying that. They're reasonable if you know how to bargain. The deal was; provide resources in any way. We offered support in order to protect our own. Food, weapons, records. Whatever they needed, but not our people. It was San Jose or us. I had to choose us. There's still some on The Council who think we have a chance against Ronan. Against Covert. I think it's best if we play it safe. Wait things out, see how it goes."

I shrugged in understanding. "But of course."

His shoulders relaxed slightly, his face an open book of fragile relief. He thought he'd gotten through to me, that his reasoning had earned him a reprieve.

It hadn't.

The blade was out before he saw it coming. I moved without hesitation. The steel pierced his chest, silencing him mid-breath. His eyes widened, shock frozen in them as his body slumped forward.

"Sorry, Alaric," I murmured, standing and wiping the blade on his carefully folded napkin. The irony was not lost on me. Laughter found its way to my lips. I couldn't decide if it made the act more poetic or more bitter. "It was you or us."

Suckerpunch caught my attention in the kitchen window, peeking in with a soft whine. The sound of the front door opened. I had about thirty-seconds before whoever came through that door made their way to my little mess. Swiping my fingers in the blood dribbling out his mouth, I scribbled **Bloodhound** into the maple round table, then sprinted through the back door. The distant shouts reached my ears as I slipped into the shadows of the back alley, Suckerpunch back at my heels. The air was cold, heavy with tension and the faint metallic scent of blood that clung to me like a second skin.

THE ALARM BELLS RANG FAR TOO FAST. WE BARELY MADE IT OUT BEfore the gates went on lock down. Not that we'd used them.

I wasn't an idiot. This was their problem. To find the Bloodhound, you must *think* like one. If they weren't going to seal the manholes into the sewage system, then they should've at least had someone posted at the access points.

It became clear on the reason why the further we went. I had no doubt Suckerpunch could sniff out a threat, but his presence did nothing to ease the gnawing unease in my gut. Something was off.

The air shifted, thick with the scent of decay. I'd been down enough of these passageways to know when something felt wrong, and this was all wrong. The ground seemed to absorb my footsteps as I made my way deeper into the shadows.

And then I saw them.

A mass grave. No real attempt to hide the fact that bodies were piled high. Discarded like trash. Suckerpunch went on alert as I inched closer. The smell was overpowering. The urge to bring the sandwich and stale beer back up was nearly impossible to shove back down.

My eyes narrowed at the condition of the bodies. They weren't just *dead*—they were *wrong*.

Suckerpunch's ears perked up, nose twitching as he sniffed the air. Men. Women. And—*fuck*—children. Elders. They all bore the same mark in the center of their head. The lion of Covert Province. I could think of only one reason to brand a body. To make sure they couldn't go anywhere else without anyone knowing who they belonged to. Any settlement these people could have gone to if given the chance of freedom, would not be able to deny knowing who they were helping. Property of Ronan Moore. But it wasn't their fate alone that stood out. No. It was the way they looked. The way they *all* looked.

I crouched low, inspecting one of the bodies. They were pale, their skin sickly gray, almost … *like a Pansie*. The texture was different—rougher, more brittle—but the gray was unmistakable. I picked up their forearm, studying the one mark of red that appeared on every single one of them. One bite. Their faces were too human, too *normal* otherwise, but the skin, it didn't match the usual waxy cast of death.

Suckerpunch growled low in his throat, a deep warning. I pushed up from the ground, eyes lingering on the bodies a beat longer before signaling him to stay sharp. There were bigger things at play. This war with Ronan was only the beginning.

THE FIRST NIGHT IN SAN JOAQUIN PASSED WITHOUT INCIDENT. SURprising given the increased patrols searching for us in the heat of the night. This was far from my first time dodging law and order, and it wouldn't be my last. People rarely saw past their own blind spots. Everyone had them. For Fresno's military, it was their own outpost. We lingered along the outside of the cluster of buildings until dawn broke.

By morning, the boredom set in. Panoche Road was nothing but dry air and cracked pavement, stretching endlessly into nowhere. Suckerpunch padded along beside me, silent except for the occasional huff of annoyance. At least one of us was used to the monotony.

The next day we should have been home bound. Instead, it brought a storm. Black skies churned angrier than the North Sea. Rain came down in torrents. Mud sucked at my boots with every step, and Suckerpunch kept glaring at me with eyes that screamed *Really? This is the plan?*

"Don't start," I muttered.

We reached Hollister, drenched, cold, and ready for a break. A less than impressive slab of an abandoned house seemed promising enough—a roof, four walls. No immediate signs of a corpse. Suckerpunch whined at the command to wait outside. Without the others here, I needed eyes on the outside while I cleared the inside.

The floor creaked upstairs. Distant. Behind a closed door and faint, but there.

Knives in hand, I moved silently up the staircase. The first blade was ready, drawn and hidden against my forearm. The second rested in my palm for a quick throw.

I stood in the hallway surrounded by three doors. One in front and two on the side. I kept still, waiting, letting the hairs on the back of my neck do the sensing. Where my body didn't want to go, laid fear. That fear was there for a reason. Fear of the unknown that laid behind the door to my left. I threw it open. Two young small, frail bodies were huddled in the corner. They froze the moment they saw me.

"What the hell," I spat, lowering my knives.

The girls from San Jose. My stance was loose but ready. Never underestimate a wounded animal.

The older one met my gaze with defiance. She exhaled slowly and nudged the brunette, "He can help."

The brunette hesitated, glancing between us, then nodded.

"No," I said. "*He* can't. I told you to wait."

"No, you said if we wanted your help, we had to wait. We didn't then. We do now," the brunette replied quietly.

I whistled, and Suckerpunch crashed through the front door, bounding into the room like a wild thing. I holstered my knives, watching as the girls visibly relaxed, softening a bit at the sight of the dog.

"I don't have the time to help you now," I muttered, digging through my bag. There wasn't much left, but I was only a day away from Monterey. I tossed what little food I had left at them. "Here. Stay out of the storm." I turned to leave.

"Wait," the oldest reached out, halting me in my steps with the grab of my wrist. "Please. Our magic still hasn't fully returned and they're going to take them back soon."

I noted the way her hand hovered, then met her eyes without a word. She hesitated. I could tell it took everything in her to touch me, to hold this contact, but there was something in her eyes—a quiet desperation.

"Take who where?" I asked, irritation creeping into my tone.

"The other girls. They're still alive, I think," the brunette added.

"You *think*?" I groaned, running a hand through my over-grown buzz cut. "What happened?"

"They took 'em. Covert did," the oldest said, clearing her throat. "They tracked us here to bring us back to San Jose."

"Yeah, they took the others when we were sleeping. Killed Josephine by accident. Then, when we freaked, they cut our ropes and stuff. Said we weren't worth the effort and that it would be worse for us out here on our own. That this was our real punishment."

I closed the gap between us, the squeak in the floor that gave them away the first time, screamed under the weight of my boot. "If this is a trap, I'm not above killing you."

"If this was a trap, we wouldn't be asking a serial killer to fall in it."

I raised an eyebrow. "You've heard of me?"

"Oh, shit," the youngest murmured, her eyes wide. She backed into the wall, pressing tight against it as if it would help her disappear.

The older one stepped in front of her, voice calm though the tremble in her lip gave her away. "No. It was a guess, considering you took out three guards on your own to free us. Who are you—" She stopped herself, reconsidering. "It doesn't matter. I won't ask questions. Just, please. Help us."

"This is a border town between the settlements. Monterey border patrol could stop through here as easily as San Jose. Why the hell would they risk chasing you an entire day's walk out here?"

"We're… hard to replace," the brunette winced.

"Talk," I said, my tone cutting through the air. "Now."

The oldest introduced herself as Memphis, the other Denver—fake names, but whatever. Apparently they were a part of a caravan in Transient Nation that was attacked. A group known for having extraordinary powers. *Hunter's* group. That connection I kept to myself. No rhyme or reason other than gut.

Memphis paused, her eyes darting nervously to Denver before she spoke again. "We were a part of something bigger. A group of … people like us. Some of us were always more, um, unique than the others. Ronan found it fascinating. We were stuck in his camps for months. Used as experiments. I don't know what he was looking for or if he found it but, one day we were shipped off for the next phase."

"Breeding," Denver added with air quotes and the roll of her eyes.

"Covert …" Memphis spoke, her voice breaking slightly. "Covert is using women as breeding stock. Sterilizing some and selecting others based on a mix of things. DNA. Different tests."

"First, they separated us by the physical stuff. Race, height, body shape. See how smart we are and if we're able to be 'molded.'" Denver met Memphis's eyes, and they grabbed hands. "We're the 'lucky' ones. The ones they deem *worthy*."

"They're being held in the center of town. An old outpost." Memphis continued. "I think they're still alive … but we don't know for sure. If more of them tried to run—"

"Tell me exactly where this facility is," I demanded, my voice low and dangerous.

Memphis's eyes filled with uncertainty. "It's heavily guarded. If you go in there alone without knowing what you're walking into, you won't make it out. We've been trying for days."

"I don't need you to tell me what I can and can't do," I snapped.

"Tomorrow morning," Denver cut in. "After breakfast is a shift change. There is exactly two minutes and forty-three seconds that the back door is left unguarded."

I gritted my teeth, pacing for a moment. The day was closing in fast and the rain had stopped, the minutes slipping away.

"I have somewhere to be tomorrow. My—" I groaned in frustration. "I have someone counting on my presence, and I can't afford to let them down. What you're asking of me, it requires me to risk it all."

Memphis reached out again then thought better of it. "Please," she whispered. "If we don't help them … what's waiting for them is worse than death."

There was raw fear in her eyes. It wasn't simply desperation—it was terror.

I cursed under my breath. "Fine. Get whatever shit you need and let's go. I need to see the layout with my own eyes."

Denver sighed in relief. "Thank you. You have no idea what this means."

I threw a glance toward the darkening horizon. "Don't get your hopes up. If there's any indication this is a suicide mission, I'm taking both of you and leaving. Won't have your death shitting on my consciousness."

I heard them gather their things behind me, but I didn't look back.

THEY KEPT THEM IN THE BAR ACROSS FROM A CHURCH. INNOVATIVE. Nothing says 'we're the bad guys' like holding trafficking victims across from holy grounds.

We spent every scrap of daylight left camped out across the street, eyes trained on the guards. Three out front, three in the back and one at the side. None patrolled the businesses nearby. *Amateurs.* Lazy ones at that.

Darkness fell, and we made our way back to the house. Suckerpunch was lounging on the porch like he owned it, tail thumping once when we appeared. With no mangled bodies left waiting, I assumed it meant things had been rather uneventful for him. Small mercies.

Memphis and Denver were tight-lipped, telling me little of their time away from the caravan. The silence between us was only broken by asking direct questions. Even then, their answers were clipped. Trained silence. Every sentence was drenched in things they wouldn't—or couldn't—say.

I dropped my bag onto the hardwood with a heavy thud and Memphis flinched hard enough that her water spilled across the floor. Denver didn't even react. Just stared at Memphis shaking hands until I tossed her an extra t-shirt to dry off. They'd both avoided eye contact after that.

"Get some rest," I said, deciding leaving them to their own corner of the house would be best. "We move out at first light."

THE SUN BREACHED THE CLOUDS AS WE APPROACHED THE BAR, CASTing long shadows across the empty streets. Two hours crawled by as we waited. Lurking in the shadows out of sight. The tension mounted with the ticking clock. I was going to miss their departure. After everything she'd worked for these last few months, I was going to let her down when she needed me the most.

Riley and Abel were staying back for the sake of The Compound and any retaliation which meant it would be her, Reina, and Tomoe *alone* with Hunter, Serenity, and Caleb. Uneasiness quelled in my throat. No. I wouldn't make her face the other leaders alone. I'd meet them there just in time if I kept a decent pace. Which meant I needed this shit to wrap up.

Fucking finally. The guards scheduled to take over the back door took their time walking up to their shift change. They stood around chatting, not yet heading around the front to grab their morning coffee off the fire as Denver swore they always did. It was a small miscalculation but time was a critical currency.

We were across the street the second they wandered off. Two minutes and forty-three seconds to execute this shit of a plan.

The door creaked slightly as I pushed it open, revealing a guard standing inside. I drove my knife into his neck, not giving him a moment to react, silencing him instantly. His body hit the floor with a thud and I motioned for Memphis and Denver to follow me. Denver bit down hard on a cry, her hand covering her mouth as she stepped over the growing pool of crimson. Suckerpunch held our rear, nudging her forward with his nose and away from the body.

Stale alcohol and the stench of sweet. *This place is fucking disgusting.* I took in the room. Dust clung to every surface as did puke, shit, and every other bodily fluid you could imagine. Three doors lined the back hallway—two marked as bathrooms and one unmarked. Suckerpunch crossed the room, sniffing softly at the bottom of the doors, then stopped in front of the last one.

"Office. One o'clock," I said, raising my hand to cover my nose.

We moved quickly across the bar. I kicked the door in without hesitation. The guard behind lunged for my knife, knocking it from my hand. I was fast. I slammed him into the wall, stunning him. His head hit the corner of a shelf and Suckerpunch dragged him the rest of the way down. When I stomped on his skull, the sound was pleasantly final.

"Behind you!" Memphis yelled, tossing me my knife.

I caught it midair and spun. The blade sliced through the throat of a second guard. Blood sprayed across my face as he crumpled. Suckerpunch ran to the door, standing guard, ears low, neck forward.

The girls had gotten to work on the captives, their fingers fumbling with ropes tied in intricate knots. I reached down, trying to cut through the thick bond of the girl closest to me. They were too dense to slice through quickly and using my flames risked burning her skin. She'd been through enough. Her hands fell free at the same time as the girls Denver and Memphis had worked on. The three of them standing up, wobbling with the awkwardness of newborn deer.

They crowded at the door as Memphis and I worked on the remaining two. Suckerpunch went into a frenzy. His bark pierced the air. Shrill screams rang out. Three more guards stormed the room, guns drawn, magic flaring. Their voices shouting over one another.

Suckerpunch latched thigh of the guard closest to the girls. Granting Denver the opportunity to usher the others toward the door. He tore a chunk of the guard's leg out at his attempt to reach after them. The guard raised his gun, pointing it at Suckerpunch at the same time my view of him was cut out.

"Go, Memphis! Now!" I shouted.

A chair flew across the room and two shots rang out. Denver launched herself at the guard and pulled him back from his neck.

He dropped the gun, and I took a sigh of relief at the blur of Suckerpunch launching at his jugular.

Memphis hesitated. "We can't! Jersey and Dakota are still tied up!" Her voice cracked as she fumbled with the ropes of her friend.

Denver moved to cover the other girls at the door, the swirling air magic in her hands a warning to anyone who dared approach. It wasn't much, but it was raging in the way any air magic I'd ever seen. Almost resembling a storm inside the palm of her hand.

I dodged a blow to the head. The squat down bought me a second to take in the room. Suckerpunch pressed his head against Denver's thigh, forcing the group from the door and out to what I hoped was safety. If we had any luck at all, these three guards were here for the shift change and had come inside from the noise, only after the others had left.

"Everyone stop, or they're dead!" one of the guards yelled. He dragged Jersey and Dakota into view with a gun pressed to each of their heads. Memphis backed away slowly, arms raised.

The rest of the room froze.

His partner, face bloodied from our brawl, stalked across the room. "I'm done chasing after these brats." He muttered, vines growing through the cracked wooden floors. In two seconds, it was over. Jersey and Dakota's necks snapped with a sickening crack.

Memphis's scream was earsplitting—a piercing wail of anguish. Her knees buckled, and she fell to the floor, her face twisted in shock.

Rage surged through me, a wildfire consuming everything in its path. The guards in front of me didn't have time to react before I incinerated them right where they stood. Their bodies crumpled into ash. The room lit with an ominous glow as flames spread, licking at the wooden walls and ceiling. The amount of water it would take to extinguish them would flood the room.

I turned to Memphis, shaking her by the shoulders. "Hey!" I barked. "Get it the fuck together. We have to go. Now."

She stared past me, her eyes glassy and unfocused, still locked on the bodies of her friends. The fire was closing in, smoke thickening the air. I shook her again, harder this time.

"Memphis! Move!"

She blinked and stumbled to her feet. I damn near dragged her out, coughing as the smoke clawed at our throats.

The others waited out the back door. No other guards in sight. Luck had funny fucking timing. Memphis doubled over and vomited onto the pavement, her body racked with sobs. Grief clung to the others just as heavily, hollowing their faces.

"I'm sorry about your friends," I said, though the words tasted like ash in my mouth. They didn't mean anything—not to them, not to me. Apologies wouldn't bring back the dead.

But I couldn't stay. Not with the meeting set for tomorrow. Not with the information I possessed.

"The other group," It came out sharper than I intended, even as my insides churned. "The one I told you about—they need this information. If I leave now, I might still make it."

I glanced at Memphis, then Denver. Both were worn thin, the fight in them more instinct than choice at this point. "You've got two options: Monterey border patrol is west of here. I'll give you a codeword to get them to take you to Monterey. Some of your caravan's already there. Or you come with me to Hunter."

Memphis met my eye, her face etched with lines of exhaustion and pain though recognition of Hunter's name sparked a glimmer of hope. "We don't belong behind walls. I like our chances now that we're all together … most of us. But thank you, for everything."

I nodded, but her gratitude struck hard, a blade sinking into my chest. I hadn't saved them all. As I turned to leave, Denver's voice called after me, quiet but firm.

"We'll be around when you need us."

Suckerpunch bounded off ahead. I didn't answer. Couldn't. The effort it took to leave them there, half-whole and on their own, was almost enough to stop me in my tracks. Almost.

CHAPTER
THIRTY-EIGHT

AMAIA

"**H**e should be back by now," I paced the contoured walkway atop the wall.

It was impossible to tell in the darkness of the night but if he were close, I would have felt it. I knew I shouldn't have let him run off on his own. It was what he did, his job at St. Cloud Compound at least, but here, in today's turmoil, I'd misjudged the weight of this task. *No, you can't think that way.* But it was hard not to.

Doubting myself was dumb. I didn't doubt any of the other calls I made in the field. Everything happens for a reason, and if Alexiares was late, then he had a reason to be. Perhaps him being tardy had saved his life in some other aspect. Who the hell knew? Not me. Worrying would only serve as a distraction.

Hunter came to my side, taking in the sea of fires sprawling the foreseeable distance. Ronan's soldiers had appeared at dawn two days ago. Apparently Alexiares had been *efficient* in San Jose and our consequences had come swift.

"Sunrise is an hour out. Fog's rolling in," Hunter said with no real emotion. Only fact.

Reina shuffled behind me, her floral scent breaking through the dewy morning stench of grass. "We have time."

"No, we don't," I mumbled. It was already a fifty-fifty chance of a fight out and I had to have trust. "He's fine. If he isn't here, then he'll know to meet us there. He'll track us. Ye of little faith, Reina."

Offering her a tap in the shoulder, I carried the false confidence all the way down the ladder, allowing myself only one quiver of the lip now that I was out of sight. This meeting could make or break us, but leaving my people behind with Ronan so close risked everything. I ran the numbers through my head once more. *It is a calculated risk. You cannot defend with your numbers alone.*

Tomoe was the first to hop down after me. Her hazy eyes studied me. "You were right to put Luna in charge. The people trust her and her transparency will help calm their concerns."

I'd spent the night weighing the pros and cons with Riley. Ultimately, we'd decided that trusting our people to revert to their training over hysteria was the way to go. We'd run simulations on how to handle an attack since the last one. Sure, Ronan's emissaries may have tipped him off here and there, but they didn't know *everything*. There were ways to inform our people without them knowing. Secrets Ronan couldn't touch.

This was a matter of survival. One unit, one compound. That would always keep us alive, inspire people to protect each other. I would be back soon. The same way I trusted Alexiares, Riley, and Luna to take care of business, I had to trust the people of Monterey Compound could do the same.

I nodded, the others soon falling in line as we made our way from North Gate, through GLQ and toward the earth slide. It had proven oddly useful. *Ten points for Riley's knack for innovation.* Given the time of day, the pathways and side streets should have been quiet but not today, not when everyone knew who sat outside our gates. Sleep wouldn't find any of them anytime soon.

THE SKY WAS STILL PITCH BLACK, PINK AND ORANGE YET TO CREST over the horizon. TV shows, movies, they never really showed the perspective on exactly how fucking dark it is in the middle of the night. Thankfully, the clear sky lighting our way would serve as enough of a guide until the clouds not too far off rolled in along with the morning fog.

A hand fell upon my shoulder for support. We'd have to guide each other for a while with only the silhouette of the person before you as reference. I led the way, my knowledge of the lay of our land serving to our advantage. Hunter was behind me, Reina next, then Serenity, Caleb, and Moe at the rear. Exactly as we'd practiced. I didn't feel an ounce of guilt disguising my lack of trust as defensive tactics against whatever we ended up facing in the dark. We kept a steady pace, needing to clear the areas Ronan's troops lingered by sunrise or we'd be shit out of luck.

Twenty minutes and one mile. That's as far as we got before the fog rolled in place of the rising sun in the sky before realizing we were fucked. I sensed them before I heard them. That creaky-clicking, throaty sound of Pansies. Then their mildewy, rotten smell filled my nostrils. I couldn't see them through the cloudy, thick white fog, but I sure as hell could smell them, and there were a lot.

With Pansies, a lot ranged from a group of five to over a hundred. There was no way to tell with the way we were trapped in the haze of a Monterey morning. Right now, at this very moment, it sounded like maybe ten. That was only for our immediate vicinity. Only time would tell if they had spread out from a herd with the confusion of the fog or if a few of the plenty was all we were dealing with.

"Nobody. Move. A. Muscle," I said, my voice a harsh whisper.

The inability to identify how many walked among us left us at an extreme disadvantage. With visibility reduced to nothing, I judged that engaging only when necessary was the best bet. Clicking with complex patterns echoed around us. Ronan's experiments.

These weren't OGs.

OGs were predictable—mindless, slow, and easy to dispatch if you stayed alert. But these? These were something else entirely. Faster. Smarter. They communicated, their patterns of movement coordinated in ways that defied what we thought we understood. And if we got caught by one, it wouldn't be alone for long.

I tempered my breathing, hoping, praying, the others were doing the same. No matter how many you killed, the complete terror of confronting them never went away.

Time dragged as we held our position, even though I knew it had been just a few minutes. My legs burned, muscles trembling under the pressure of remaining utterly still. The damp chill of the air clung to my skin, mixing with the sweat that had soaked through my shirt. Then the wind shifted. A faint rustle reached my ears, just enough to send my heart stopped.

"Fuck," I hissed, my hand already closing around the hilt of the blade at my waist. "Make it quiet and make it quick," I commanded the others and chaos erupted.

I couldn't see shit between the dense fog and the early morning sun. The concern wasn't necessarily the Pansies but making sure we avoided each other. Sound became our lifeline, guiding us in the blind field of death. Something moved to my left. I swung on instinct, my blade finding purchase in the throat of a Pansie. The flesh gave way with a wet, sickening sound. I yanked the blade free, driving it upward into its skull before it could lunge again.

Jaws clamped open then shut behind me. Fingers sharp as talons raked at the uncovered skin of my forearm. One at my six, another at one o'clock. I ducked and sheathed the blade back in the holster, falling to a side lunge position. With the same movement, I grabbed one of the twin blades and twirled it forward, the hilt firm in my grip. Rising to my feet, I pivoted sharply, spinning in a full circle. The blade's edge met resistance—twice—slicing clean through two Pansies' necks with force. The strain rippled through my core, each muscle screaming from the effort.

The sharp whistle of an arrow grazed past my ear. "Reina," I snapped.

"To be fair, I threw that," her voice called out, closer than I'd expected.

"There's this thing called a knife," Tomoe shouted from somewhere ahead. "Use it."

"I lost it," Reina admitted, her floral scent cutting through the surrounding stench of death as she moved to my side.

I sighed, yanking the knife from my hip and pressing it into her hand. "Don't lose this one."

"Thank ya kindly," she chirped, and then she was gone again, slipping back into the fray.

The fog loosened, no longer swallowing the sound and movement of our fight. We needed to end this quickly. I swung my blade low, severing a Pansie's leg at the knee before I leaped on top and drove the knife into its skull. Hunter's deep grunt echoed as he grappled with one, punching with pointed brass knuckles into its head with brutal efficiency.

To my right, Serenity's voice cut through the chaos. "Caleb, duck!" A boomerang flew in the direction of her shout and cut through a Pansies gaping mouth as it lunged for Caleb. He rolled to his feet, his saber sword flashing in the muted light. It cleaved through a neck while then slid out in perfect timing to embed in a skull with a sickening crack. Serenity stood, watching Caleb with relief to have not had to witness his death.

"Serenity, move!" Hunter bellowed. His hatchet became a blur, sweeping in an arc that split two Pansies in half.

Serenity sidestepped and raised a hand instead of reaching for her dagger. A Pansie lunged, slamming to a sudden stop midair, its limbs spasming as if caught in an invisible vice. She flicked her fingers, and the creature whipped sideways, crashing into another with a bone-crunching thud. Only then did she draw her dagger, finishing off a smaller one that had slipped past Hunter's range.

I had just enough time to see a shadow surge at my side. Twisting, I raised my blade, catching the Pansie mid-leap. The momentum drove me backward, and my back hit the ground hard. White stars soured my vision but the loss of breath hurt me more. It fell atop me and I pointed the blade up in a defensive motion. Then the weight vanished.

The Pansie shot upward, flung into the air as if a giant hand had yanked it back. It crashed down hard, skull cracking against the hard ground. I sucked in air, my chest heaving, as Serenity lowered her hand. Her silence said it all—*You owe me one.*

The field was a frenzy of snarls and glinting steel, but slowly, the sounds thinned. By the time the last Pansie fell, we were panting, bloodied, but alive.

"Everyone okay?" I asked, forcing my voice to stay steady despite the lingering adrenaline.

"Hands out, let me assess," Reina said, already moving to check on Tomoe.

Hunter moved with his sister, checking her over before moving on to Serenity. "I'll help."

I straightened, my eyes scanning the group. We were all still standing. For now, that was enough.

"Let's get moving," I said, not granting the group more than a few moments to catch their breath. "Fog will clear out soon and the sun's nearly up."

Serenity offered me a sarcastic salute, her face covered in guts and gore. "After you, General."

CHAPTER

THIRTY-NINE

ALEXIARES

"**Y**ou left without me," I said with a smirk from the top of the red bricked roof, feet dangling over the side. "Ouch."

A ball of fire shot past my head as a warning. I ducked, but it was a futile effort. If I still had more than a short buzz of hair on my head, she'd have singed it off. Another one came in quick succession, burning right through the slab of stucco under my feet. *Oh. She's pissed.* Just how I liked her.

I surged to my feet, sprinting across the roof and launching myself onto the tree at the edge. The branches groaned under my weight. Flames licked at the leaves until a blast of water magic that was not mine, put it out. A rush of water crashed down, soaking me and Suckerpunch who waited at the base.

The beast let out a low, impatient whine, his massive body coiled and trembling. He pawed the ground, desperate for release on his hold. He looked up, golden eyes shining with the weight of a moment long anticipated.

"Go ahead," I growled, water dripping down my face, uncomfortably clinging to my ragged clothes from a week out on the road.

Amaia met Suckerpunch halfway, crouching to rub the spot in between his ears. "You poor baby," she cooed, her voice honey-sweet. "Did the mean man make you late for your trip home?"

The little mutt barked, offering her a paw, his tail wagging furiously as he licked her hand—the same hand wearing the ring caused a sparkle to catch my eye.

"Fucking traitor," I muttered, closing the space between us.

I reached for her hand first, fingers grazing over the piece of rock that officially claimed her as mine. She sank into my chest, letting out a sigh that seemed to have been trapped for far too long. I pressed a kiss to her curls, holding on to the feeling of her small body folded into mine.

Behind her, Reina and Tomoe waited. Reina's grin stretched wide, as smug and pleased as ever, while Tomoe's face stayed frozen in its usual visage of disinterest. Something scowl adjacent. I closed my eyes, taking in Amaia's presence and warmth one last time, knowing exactly what was coming my way.

She pulled back too soon, giving me one hard shove. Her dark eyes pinned me in place. "What the hell! Where were you?"

Hunter came up behind his sister, Serenity on his other side and Caleb at their backs. "Do they always make people this uncomfortable?" Serenity muttered.

"Yeah, pretty much," Reina said with a shrug, "Ain't it just darlin'?"

"Not as uncomfortable as you three make the rest of us," Moe muttered at the same time.

"There was some trouble—"

"I thought you were dead."

"Would you prefer me to go back?" I asked, arching a brow and crossing my arms. "There are plenty of people across several territories who'd like another shot at it."

She gave me another shove, this time a grin tugged at her lips. I caught her wrist then tilted her chin up gently.

"Careful," I murmured, brushing my lips against hers. The tension melted between us for a moment, but when I pulled back, I didn't let go. Those fierce brown eyes were the color of home. They locked on mine and I felt the weight of everything I'd done. And everything I hadn't.

"We need to talk before the others arrive," I said quietly.

I stood at the center of our sorry excuse for a meeting spot. Complimentary Hunters planning. The others watched me as I ran through the debrief. San Jose, Fresno, everything I'd uncovered—it all came out clipped and to the point.

Then I got to the girls.

I almost faltered. Almost. But showing cracks in my armor wasn't something I'd grown accustomed to. Not unless it was just her.

"Aw, you're we have our own little superhero," Reina said. She perched cross-legged, elbows on her knees, hands cupping her face.

"Bite me," I said, shooting her a glare.

"Well, guess I can't be mad about that," Amaia said, her voice no-nonsense though her eyes told a different story. She turned toward Hunter, features sliding toward all-business. "I don't know how much this will sway the others, but it's good information to have up front, nonetheless. If they're going to fight on our side, they'll come prepared to do so. Those we have to convince? I'm not sure breeding programs will be the make or break—as much as I hate saying that."

She wasn't wrong. Convincing people to care about their humanity's long-term survival was … complicated. Sucked to say I knew firsthand that you needed something, *someone* you love to flip that switch back on. If they ever had it.

"Oh God," Serenity muttered, and for the first time, she looked shaken up. Vulnerable, even. "But they're okay? What did Memphis look like? Denver?"

I dragged a hand down my face, taking a second before answering. Giving the specifics, the details, was equivalent to pouring salt in an open wound. "Memphis was Amaia's complexion. Shorter hair, tighter curls. Maybe eighteen or nineteen. Denver had long brown hair, tan skin. Maybe seventeen."

Hunter snorted. "A gaze that screamed she was marking you for death?"

I let out a bitter laugh. "Yep."

"It's them," Serenity said, her voice soft with relief. But it didn't last long. Her expression crumpled when she remembered the ones I mentioned didn't make it.

No one asked more questions. I didn't push. Breaking their last thread of hope wasn't on my to-do list. Caleb stared at me, green eyes sharp, not with malice, but with quiet curiosity. He glanced away after a few seconds.

"Millie," Reina blurted out, pushing to her feet.

Amaia reached for her power, magic swirling in her hand. "Who?"

"Great Falls," Moe said, her usual brevity intact.

Everyone stood as Millie and three others emerged from the distance, all armed to the teeth. She removed her tan cowboy hat, letting sun-kissed hair spill down her back in a loose braid.

"Reina," Millie said first, locking eyes on her as they approached. Reina flushed, eyes darting toward the ground.

"General Amaia, pleasure to meet you," Millie continued, her gaze sliding over to Amaia with calculated respect. Amaia shifted, her eyes flicking to the rest of us as Millie's sharp gaze scanned our group. "You, I know." She jabbed a finger at Tomoe. Then her smirk turned on me. "And you, I'm assumin', must be the Blood-hound since you're practically glued to your general's ass."

I bit back the urge to reply, keeping my stance neutral. It wasn't worth it.

Millie's attention shifted briefly to the others, more dismissive now. "New faces. How y'all doin'? Millie," she offered as if they didn't already know.

We went through introductions like it was a damned cocktail party and not a war council. Millie introduced her lieutenant and two soldiers who were clearly high-ranking, though she didn't offer much detail. Their general was apparently holding the fort back in Great Falls. Smart.

One by one, the others trickled into our meeting point. Leaders and their entourages from Salem and The Expanse. Twelve from one. Twenty-nine from the other, not including Lola who had already cast a 'vote' on behalf of all sectors in St. Paul. We'd have two more if my mission proved successful. Nine refused to show up, siding with Covert. Still, we outnumbered them in allies, but it hardly mattered with the odds still stacked against us. We moved inside the dilapidated building behind us, an old dinner, as we prepared to get the discussion going.

The door creaked open, and in she strode.

Finley. Last, of course, making sure she was front and center of attention. All swagger and that infuriating air of superiority.

I glanced away before her eyes could lock on mine. No way in hell was I giving her the satisfaction of acknowledging her presence.

"Oh, how I loved getting this message," she purred, heading straight for Amaia. Her steps were measured. She leaned in, her voice low but loud enough for me to hear. "Begging for my help, I thought you were above that, General."

Amaia didn't flinch. Didn't so much as blink. Instead, she tilted her head slightly, a razor-sharp smile curling her lips. "If you think I'm above tearing you apart when this is done, keep testing me. I'm all for a little fucking around and finding out."

Her hand pressed lightly to Finley's shoulder, a deceptively gentle push to create distance before Amaia turned and stepped to the front of the room.

I followed, falling into step behind her as Hunter joined us. We stood at her side, casual but solid. A shadow at her command.

"Never underestimate a human's desire to survive," she kicked things off as she faced the room, standing tall, arms tucked behind her back. "All of us are proof of that."

CHAPTER FORTY

RILEY

Yasmin blocked the door, tears streaming down her face. "Luna wants you to stay here. Behind the walls put in place to protect us."

Elie and Emma sulked deeper into the study, making themselves busy with checking their weapons. They were supposed to be helping me convince Yasmin to cooperate. But Elie avoided my eye and Emma only ever mirrored Elie. The fact that Yasmin's refusal to head down to the bunker meant the girls and Harley would have the opportunity to stay behind and defend didn't help my case. Elie was all too eager to have the opportunity to rig this place with explosive traps should the enemy try to make their way in.

"I don't answer to Luna," I said as gently as possible. Hoping the desperation to get out there and lead my troops wasn't voiced as irritation with her. The seconds were ticking away. This place needed to stand or all else would fall.

Monterey was a settlement born from a city of ash, and like a phoenix, we would *always* rise.

Yasmin's words came out a swallowed, painful whisper, "She's going to get you killed."

"Then I will die knowing I was following orders, following through with my commitments." I tapped my hands expressively against my chest. "I will die without having failed."

"What about your commitments here?" she demanded, her hand resting against her stomach that had barely begun to form a safe space for my son to grow. "The ones at home."

This had always been a point of contention between us. She fell for a soldier, yet my loyalty was only admirable in her eyes when it came to the people that lived inside these four very specific walls. Us and only us. Never The Compound and most certainly *never* Amaia.

I didn't have time for this. People were counting on me to make sure their loved ones made it back home tonight. Tomorrow. This could last longer than any of our minds could fathom. We'd shown Ronan our hand and underestimated how hard he'd swing the axe—how *soon*. So while Amaia worked to secure our alliances, I needed to do my part. We, as a compound, were only as strong as our loyalty extended. That's what she'd taught me over the years and that was the soldier I would be today.

"My commitment to you and our family is everything, Yasmin. But my commitment out there … to Amaia." Yasmin flinched at my words and I corrected myself, clearing my throat. It was bigger than the two of us. She had to understand. "To The Compound—it's just as important to me. Fulfilling my duty is what lets you make this a home. It's what ensures you, the woman I love endlessly, and our child, can survive. Can thrive. Grow old. *This* is the best way I can show you I am committed to us."

"I told Amaia once not to ask me to choose between you and her, and now I'm asking you the same. Because if you make me choose, I'll lose a part of myself. I'd choose you and our family every time, but it would break my soul to lose her. She's not just my general, Yasmin, she's my family too. This isn't about choosing one over the other. It's about honoring both commitments. Because protecting her and The Compound is what allows me to protect you, too."

"She has her own family now," Yasmin said, her voice quieter than I'd ever heard it. My woman was loud and joyful—radiant with a kind of life that painted my world in color. This muted version of her was almost unbearable. I nearly gave in. Ready to give it all up if only it meant I could see one more glimpse of her smile.

I met her sad charcoal eyes, steady despite the storm raging inside me. "And yet she's never made me feel as though I'm not a part of it."

Her gaze softened. Before I could say anything else, she took a step closer, lips pressing against mine. The weight of the world fell away at the touch of her warm hands caressing the sides of my face.

Yasmin pulled back enough to take me in, fingers brushing the edge of the vest of my uniform. A hesitant brush of skin, voiceless but aching to be understood. I took a step back. The chill air filled the space where her warmth had been. I didn't linger on it. I couldn't—not now.

The battlefield was ready. Every trap, every defense, exactly as my general requested. Right now, it was time to walk into the fire.

I moved toward the door, glancing at the light of my life one last time. "I'll come back, I promise."

The words were for her as much as they were for me. "You'd better," she said. Her voice was steady, but the fear in her eyes betrayed what she wanted me to see.

Glancing toward the girls in the corner, I offered them a small nod. For Yasmin, for Amaia, for all of them—I'd see this through.

CHAPTER
FORTY-ONE

AMAIA

The room was heavy, soaked in silence and barely veiled hostility. Good. Let them sit in it. I stood at the center of the room, gaze sweeping over them. Generals, mayors, opportunists—it didn't matter the title they held. They were all here because they wanted something from me, and I wasn't about to beg for their cooperation. I glanced out the window of the broken hinged door. Suckerpunch sat guard outside, our first alert if this was going to go south from the outside.

Finley leaned forward, a sneer tugging at her lips. "Oh, wonderful, a suicide mission. I thought you at least had a plan. Ego's big enough," she mumbled.

I flashed her a grin. "Oh, I have a plan. But if you're too short-sighted to see past your own death, I won't waste my breath."

Isabella Everhart snorted from her seat, boots kicked up on the table, spinning a dagger like it was an extension of her hand. "Big talk, Amaia. You sure your head's not too heavy for that crown you're trying to wear?"

"Try it on sometime, Isabella," I shot back, my tone sweet with teasing venom. This was the banter that bonded us together during the first war. "But fair warning, it's got a nasty habit of crushing people who don't deserve it."

"Hey, Finley, you should go try it on," Isabella jested, her comrades chuckling in response.

"Don't make me kill you," Finley rolled her eyes, tone light, but the sinister sparkle in her icy eyes made it clear that it was anything but.

"Aw, if only you had the chance. I'm sitting right here." Isabella's voice dripped with amusement.

"Bitch fight," someone chuckled off to the left of me. "Hot."

"This is a waste of time," another called out from across the room. It was barely audible, coming from the back, but it was enough to spark a ripple of doubt around the room.

Pockets of discontent bloomed in every corner of the room. Finley and Isabella's bickering became background noise. My chest clenched as I fought to steady myself. Looking around the dusted, dilapidated old diner, catching the faces that stared back at me—some with clear disdain, some indifferent, others tired. Exhaustion was evident in the lines wearing their faces and the heavy bags beneath their empty eyes. These were supposed to be easy allies, supposed to believe in this cause. But as I stood there, their voices blurred together, and I just felt … small.

You can do this, Elliot's voice tickled my mind. *Stay the course. Half of them only wish to give you a hard time, but intend to follow anyway.*

I found him across the room, his gaze locked on mine, a peppered beard now framing his withered face. A silent nod. A push forward.

How the fuck had any of this become my responsibility? When did the torch pass to me to lead a rebellion that had been doing just fine without me? For someone who thrived off confidence solid as stone, it wavered. It felt like a mirage. Something built off fragile hopes and piss-poor excuses for dreams.

I'd done what I could. Laid it all out for them. Everything we knew about Ronan's forces, the camps, the programs, his desire to squash a rebellion before it could take root—before it had the chance to become a revolution. And still, the doubt swirled. The desire to persevere when the odds were stacked against us was nonexistent.

They were too comfortable being complacent.

"You're telling us there are thousands of soldiers stationed across the territories, and somehow, not a single one of us has noticed?" The accusation came from a man in the middle of the room, his voice sharp, cutting through the chatter.

"Yeah," Hunter replied, his tone maddeningly nonchalant.

"Where they're stationed is none of your concern," I said firmly, meeting the man's glare. What I couldn't tell him is that Hunter's rebellion had grown within the troops of others. Most of his soldiers *were* theirs—fighters who had quietly defected over the years, granting small mercies where they could. The rest were recruits from Transient Nation. "Not until we have confirmation that you intend to fight."

"Are we really listening to this?" someone else shouted. "She's the reason thousands died in the last war!"

"Her strategy won that battle of Yellowstone," Reina said, her excitement pushing her to her feet. "She risked her life to pull it off."

Casper and Cheyenne leadership flinched, two spots over. The repercussions of the violations she committed—what some would consider war crimes—was fresh in their minds. Semantics.

"All of us reaped the benefits of her stupidity." The room went quiet with Finley's words, and she rolled her eyes at the collective shock. "I hate the bitch, but I'm not ignorant. The casualties we would have suffered in St. Cloud would have wiped us off the map."

"Maybe it should have," Aberdeen's general snickered.

The general of Des Moines snarled in agreement. "Wiped a few thanks to the hound."

Finley let out a sharp, humorless laugh that sliced through the room. Then, in Finley fashion, she took two strides toward Isabella, and grabbed her knife without so much as a glance. With uncanny preciseness, she hurled it in between the small space between the Aberdeen general's fingers. It landed with a solidifying thud. His smug expression melted into stunned silence.

"Careful, babe," Finley said casually, back turned as she walked back to her chair. She sank into it and glanced down at her nails as if the entire exchange had been nothing more than a game. "I'm a little sensitive when it comes to the safety of my people."

Chairs scraped against the checkered tile floor. The screeching mingled with the stomp of boots and the rise of voices. The room vibrated with tension as arguments erupted, spreading faster than wildfire. We hadn't even started the real work yet, and we were already so divided. Nevada and Arizona settlements sat motionless, their gazes sharp and assessing. They'd already pledged their loyalty before the meeting began. Now, they were simply wolves watching the herd unravel.

Boise and Twin Falls were the only surprising flips of Salem Territory. Everyone else had either been absorbed by us after the last battle or were determined to be a certain 'yes' once it was time to take a vote. The rest of the room, The Expanse, was as predicted—panicked and ultimately useless.

Finley leaned back in her chair, delight radiating from her. Her fingers drummed idly against the table as if she were orchestrating the chaos herself. I wanted to smack her. The sick little curve of a smirk on her annoyingly perfect lips and dance of mischief in her eyes … The chaos around her was her own private entertainment.

The noise level swelled. Voices crashed into each other in a symphony of outrage. Fists slammed against tables. A man in plain clothes, a mayor presumably, Ogden I believe, hurled his chair at the booth next to him. The sound of splintering wood only amplified the turmoil. A woman in uniform sitting next to him shouted over whatever he was saying, the veins bulging in her neck as she jabbed a finger at him. *Great. In-fighting.*

"Enough!" I barked, but the buzz of the room swallowed it whole.

Finley clapped her hands once, slow and mocking, drawing a few startled glances. "This is *fantastic*." Her tone dripped with mockery. "Keep it up, folks. Real inspiring stuff. Think we have a real chance here."

One of the louder men from Wind River Reservation turned, glaring at her, fists clenched. "You think this is funny?"

Her grin widened. "Oh, *honey*, I think it's hilarious."

The air thickened with the heat of too many bodies and too much anger. That mixed with magic—a recipe for disaster. A ticking bomb waiting to go off. My jaw tightened as I watched their tempers boil over, their unwillingness to stand united blinding them to the stakes.

Alexiares leaned toward me, his voice a low murmur beneath the disarray. "You need to say something."

"What do you expect me to do?" I muttered back.

"They're vultures," he said, gesturing with the tilt of his head. "Pick one off, and the rest fucking disappear."

Hunter balked. His dark brows pinched his sunburned skin. "That's not what we discussed."

The incessant buzz in the room still hadn't died down. Their voices blended into a static hum of discontent. I took a step closer to Hunter, an exhibit worthy of calm. "Did I not say this plan involves Ronan dying?"

"You did," he muttered, jaw set.

"By extension, that means all who align themselves with your father *also* die," I continued, letting the weight of my words settle. "And you are aware that this is war now?" I pressed, my gaze sweeping between Hunter and the room beyond him. I forced more confidence to seep into my voice. In truth, I didn't want to do this anymore than he wanted to watch. "War means taking sides. There is no more *us*, *them*, and *Ronan*. It's us versus Ronan. His side or our side."

Hunter held my gaze, eyes swirling that familiar raging storm. "I'm aware."

"Then you also recall heading a rebellion, then?" Alexiares chimed in, his tone smoother than silk. "You *do* know that by definition, it means people have to die."

"It's in the dictionary," he added with an infuriatingly reassuring smirk.

Hunter held his silence. It said more words than he was capable. Knowing something was the situationally appropriate thing to do was tremendously different from finding the courage to do it.

"Great," I said dryly. "Now that we're all aligned, I'll have a word with the congregation."

I locked eyes with Alexiares for a brief second, wanting to run my fingers over his ever present smirk, before stepping forward, my boots heavy against the floor. "If you're done acting like children, maybe I'll teach you how to survive," I called out. My voice cut clean through the noise this time.

Heads turned, some slow and reluctant, others jerked with open defiance. Finley sat up straight, her elbows propped on the table. "Oh, look. Mom's mad."

Alexiares fumed at my side, his magic palpable in the air between us. His vision was laser sharp, tracking across the room to everyone but the one who last spoke. "You want to act like prey? Then don't be surprised when you're hunted. You want to be predators? Then stop the pathetic amount of whining and start fighting like you aren't a bunch of pussies waiting around for a twenty-eight-year-old *girl* to tell you what the fuck to do and just *do*."

They gawked at him, blinks audible in the tense quiet of the room. I cleared my throat. We had them now, and I wasn't done. "But clearly since the mass of you can't seem to handle doing *anything* on your own, I'm here to save your asses. Again. Lucky you." I paced, walking between the mess of chairs and tables all clustered into one swamp of a mess. "If you think 'surrendering' to a man who rules through a caste of power alone is freedom, then you're a damn fool. There's no freedom in being absorbed by someone who sees you as nothing more than a tool—a stepping stone for more power. To shape society as *he* sees fit, while we've all fought and bled to carve out the lives and communities *we* believe in. Our home. Our people. Our values. And you'd trade all of that to avoid getting your hands dirty? Remain complacent until it happens to you?"

I paused, the weight of my wisdom pressing down on the already quiet room. My eyes caught Elliot's across the crowd, his steady nod giving me the encouragement I didn't want to admit I needed.

I wish Sloan were here.

His sharp eyes were some of the kindest in the room. *Me too, kid, me too.*

"We've all lost a lot," I continued, my voice softer now. "I hate to be the bearer of bad news, but we stand to lose a hell of a lot more if we sit here bent the fuck over for a territory that doesn't respect a damn thing we've built. Hunter's already laid out the main objective—kill Ronan. But right now, looking at you sorry bunch in this room, I don't expect any of you to show up on the battlefield with anything other than hopes and fucking prayers. Not without my help first."

"Get on with it, then. We don't have all day." The mayor from some settlement I didn't care to remember muttered the words, his expression defiant. *And the list of people I want to punch continues to grow.*

"You have all the time she needs," Alexiares snapped before I could reply, his glare pinning the man in his seat.

My fire simmered under my skin at the way Finley's lips curled up in satisfaction as she took him in. His throat bobbed as he swallowed hard, his posture stiff with barely restrained anger. At the attention she was desperate for—*his.* I wanted nothing more than to have my ring on, if only for the comfort he'd find in it. Logic had us agree it was best to keep things under wraps during the meeting. We couldn't afford the distractions, not now.

I stopped right behind her, staring down at the top of her head, still struggling to recover from the haircut I'd beautified her with. I hoped she could hear the grin in my voice. "General Matheson and General Lane were key to our strategy in the first war. And I'm sure word's spread about Prescott by now. But their wisdom isn't lost on me. I've been studying—"

A scoff cut me off. "Studying? A book? You want us to risk our communities because you've been reading fucking books?"

"Yes," I snapped, leveling a glare that could've cut glass. Alexiares moved to step forward, but I met him halfway and stopped him with a hand, keeping my focus on the soldier. "What the fuck do you think West Point was for? Officer school? AIT? You think the United States military—or any military, for that matter—just walked onto the field and winged it? I studied because I believe in learning from the mistakes of the past and absorbing the brilliance of our ancestors' success."

The energy of the room shifted. Some of the settlements who had been fidgeting moments ago sharpened their expressions. Reina grinned out the corner of my eye, only for Moe to elbow her, forcing her to bite it back.

"You're asking for a lot, General," Claes, the leader from Casper, finally said, breaking the silence. "But trust isn't built on insults or forces of magic," he added with a pointed glare in Reina's direction. She sank lower into her seat, but the fire in her eyes didn't dim. "Perhaps you can enlighten us as to how this … gambit of yours is supposed to work?"

Gambit. The polite word for desperation. I straightened, crossing my arms as I met his stare. "Simple. We prepare now— before the choice is ripped from us. Then, when we're ready, we strike before they can. Hit them where it hurts, cripple their supply lines, and force them to their knees before they realize what's happening. Take the fight to them. We don't wait for permission. We make our own rules."

Claes frowned, his lips pursing as if he'd tasted something sour. "And we get past their borders, how?"

"Leave that to us," Tomoe said with confidence—we would not reveal Lilia to any of them.

"If that fails?" a soldier from Ogden questioned. He seemed skeptical, but not quite dismissive.

"Then we regroup and hit them again. And then again. And again. Until they have nothing left." My voice was a blade honed sharply. "You think we can afford to play it safe? To wait for their mercy? If you do, you're in the wrong room. No, fuck that, you're in the wrong reality."

The silence that followed was different than before. It wasn't tense or uncertain. It was the quiet of the realization of inevitability. They were starting to see how the rest of us were already facing the pressures authoritarianism did. The truth they couldn't outrun.

"She's the reason some of us survived," Millie reasoned, calm and collected. I glanced over in approval. Hm. *Reina was right. She does look good in jeans.*

Great Falls may not have been an ally I'd thought as important to keep, but Reina's actions and her relationship with Millie had allowed us to know with certainty that Montana settlements would choose our side. Millie had advocated for Monterey since coming into power—even initiated the first cross-territory trade when she'd learned we were running low on necessities. They didn't have much, but she gave what they could.

"Oh, please. You sat on your ass and reaped the benefits while the rest of us suffered," a soldier from Ogden snapped, his tone venomous.

"We'll train together," I restated firmly, meeting the soldier's glare until he finally broke his glare. "My people have a saying: one unit, one compound. That now extends to all of you. We came here to talk about an alliance, so let's talk about it. The offer I have for you is simple: join us or die."

"What?" The word was shouted louder than the others, and the room erupted into chaos once more. But this time, more people stayed seated. I could see it in their faces. Decisions had been made, even if they weren't ready to voice them yet.

I held my ground. "That's not a threat. Not in this current moment. Not for you. It's a warning. With or without you, we will take on Covert Province. If you choose not to join us in that effort, then Monterey Compound will be forced to deem you the enemy. We're not taking prisoners this go round. Monterey was merciful in the last war. I don't have the energy to extend it again."

The ruffle of shifting seats echoed around the room. The group of imbeciles glanced between each other, uncertainty blatant in their sheepish eyes. Isabella smiled at me, offering a subtle nod of approval. I returned a small, hidden grin before shifting my gaze, desperate for clarity from allies I'd assumed were secure. Millie winked at Reina, who immediately darted her gaze away, and Elliot and Finley exchanged a glance. It was brief and begrudging. The truce flickering between them. Others whispered, their faces neutral. Only three territories—Ogden, Wichita, and Cedar Rapids—sat with deep frowns, their discontent written plain as day. Ogden's defiance was no surprise; Hunter had warned me.

"Now, everyone who doesn't have a vote, out," I commanded.

"We need to speak as a council," the general of Aberdeen protested.

"*We* don't need to," the mayor of Ogden interrupted. He stood abruptly, his entourage following suit. "The answer is no. We came here to hear you out, thought you might have something to offer other than some folly 'it could be you' argument and *practice sessions.*"

"Sit down," I said evenly, doing my best to not close my eyes at the slap in the face. To wince or show an ounce of weakness because none of them would ever respect me enough to lead if I did. As much as I hated it, I was the face, the fallback person to rally around when things were good and blame when things went wrong.

He narrowed his eyes. "You do not make—"

"I said, *sit down.*" The words slipped through clenched teeth.

"To be clear, that was her asking nicely," Alexiares added, walking to my side. Fire raged in his eyes.

The soldier to his right glanced at Hunter still standing in the center of the room, then over to me with the slightest of nods. *Last chance.* "We only agreed to hear you out. That was the agreement."

"Okay. Sure," I replied, motioning with my hand. Like it was all simple. "But now that you've heard me out … It's join us or die."

"That makes you no better than Covert," the second Ogden soldier spat.

I let out a soft chuckle and crossed my arms. "I don't believe in being the bigger person. Never have with no plans to start now. So yeah. Do with that what you will."

"You wouldn't do that. Don't have the balls," Finley said with a laugh. Her eyes flickered with curiosity, testing me. Genuinely intrigued by how far I was willing to take this. I hated that she underestimated me. More importantly, I hated that she was right—under normal circumstances.

"Wouldn't I, though?" I asked, my lips curling into a dangerous smile and I forced my eyes to dance with fire.

"You wouldn't," the mayor said, his confidence brazenly unshaken. "That's not what Monterey stands for, and you know it."

I shrugged. "Okay. Test me. Walk out there and see if I'm the same person I was a few years ago."

The room held its breath. The only sound was the stilted heartbeats around me. He glared at me, undoubtedly weighing his next move. The nervous flicker in his eyes forced a prayer to mutter through my tightly squeezed lips. It felt as though I'd dropped down on my knees and begged him not to move another muscle.

He didn't listen.

Didn't follow that feeling I know he ached in his damn gut that said to stop, that this wasn't the way. His defiance was stubborn. As he moved to clear the entrance, my heart tightened at the draw of my pistol, the guilt clawing at the edges of my resolve.

This wasn't who I wanted to be.

But who I wanted to be wouldn't win this war. Who I was would not help people survive. That was how war worked. You sacrificed, and you sacrificed, until the only thing left to offer was your soul.

"Sorry, but I can't let you leave unless I know you're on our side," I said, keeping my voice cold and detached. Before anyone could argue, I pulled the trigger, and the mayor crumpled to the floor.

Reina's eyes went wide, darting to Hunter, who gave her a reassuring nod. Serenity tilted her head, her gaze narrowing as she examined the body now lying lifeless near the door.

I swallowed hard and forced myself to stay upright. To let them see the person they should fear being on the opposing side. I kept my expression unyielding even as my chest ached. This wasn't the leader I wanted to be. But right now, fear would last longer than love. Alexiares had said so himself. He was right. And maybe, just maybe, the good could come after.

The room froze. I turned to the next in line, the person Tomoe had identified as the soldier likely to attempt to take over next. "He was going to run to Covert. Let them know every single one of you was here. Isn't that right, Hunter?"

Hunter's voice wavered slightly, the kind of slip you'd only catch if you knew him. "I've got a witness willing to testify to that fact."

The Ogden soldier I didn't have at gunpoint nodded, his expression grim. Trustworthy, but shaken. One of Hunter's inside guys, presumably.

"I'm no better than Covert," I said, addressing the rest of them. "Because if we want to hang with the big boys, we have to act like it. This isn't about me or Monterey Compound. Sure as hell isn't about what I would or wouldn't do under normal circumstances. These aren't normal circumstances. Surprise! This is how we live now. This is how we push forward for the people under our protection." I motioned around the room. "This? This is for them. Who we become is all for the people inside our walls. Now, I'll ask you one more time, no time to chat, sorry. Are you with us, or are you against us?"

Finley broke the silence with a yawn, stretching as though none of this fazed her. "There's something else. Another reason to work together or whatever. He's got a new variant. It's a threat to all of us."

Reina snorted. "A little late on that one."

Finley raised a brow. "Your daddy's been cooking up different strains. We're beyond the ones that are faster, the ones that *think*. He's found new interests. Evolving them so that they can spread and infect. Turn us."

I expected an uproar with the news, but we all sat in muted shock. Of all the things I'd brought to the table today, *this* may be the binding force of the alliance.

Reina crossed her arms. "And you've ruled out a pure anomaly?"

"Forty-three of them? I mean, I love a good collector's item as much as the next gal, but that number's a bit ridiculous, don't you think?"

"Sample size?" Reina asked, narrowing her eyes.

"Two hundred," Finley answered, shrugging.

They fell into a rapid-fire discussion on genes, mutations, and whether Finley had the capacity to determine which they were natural, evolved, or … forced into the DNA. I caught snippets of it. Technical terms and probabilities that I trusted Reina to handle and absorb what was important as I tuned out, taking in the details of the room instead.

Their chatter slowly but surely pulled others. The curiosity seemed to break through their fear. That was good. Something that *could* affect them no matter how much they followed Ronan's authority. Especially since they all had a trip to make back.

"Duh." Finley stared blankly at Reina at one point, twirling a strand of her hair and then smirked at Alexiares. "This is the idiot you're stuck with? Don't ya miss home?"

"Not even remotely," Alexiares rolled his eyes.

"And *this* idiot," Reina cut in smugly, pointing toward herself, "is the reason we can give ourselves new power, too. Control what powers we get and limit the effects of infection."

Finley crossed one leg over the other, brow raising, suddenly intrigued. "Please, tell us more."

Reina's face flushed as Tomoe jabbed her in the ribs, hard. "Uh, no thank you," she stammered, her earlier confidence evaporating.

"Doesn't seem like much of an idiot to me," Millie said, her eyes trailed up Reina's body. From the trousers hugging her hips and flickering over the loose buttons of her top that revealed the lace of the bra she sported underneath.

"Consider us curious," a representative announced, cutting through the tension, "if only to know half the secrets Monterey and St. Cloud are harboring."

"Ooh, that's going to be tough. I heard negotiations were closed, right, Mai Mai?" Finley piped up, her tone dripping with mock sweetness.

"Shut up," I snapped, giving her a sharp glare. "I'm not opening negotiations. You'll receive information that is pertinent to our cause at the time that is most beneficial for you to find out."

"And who deems it beneficial? You?" he scoffed.

"Yes," I said, flashing a thin smile.

He tossed his hands up in exasperation and scoffed, "Not that there's much of an option. We're not signing anything without reading the terms," the leader added. "But Grand Forks and the other settlements of North Dakota are willing to have a discussion on what this *partnership* may look like."

Fargo and Lincoln nodded in agreement. A murmur spread through the room as a few other settlements voiced their amiability to take this rebellion and turn it to a revolution. It wasn't a resounding victory, but it was something.

"Good," I said, straightening my posture, arms falling back behind me and I continued pacing the room. Circling them, a shark in the water at the slightest drop of blood. "Simulations will commence here two weeks from today. An hour after dawn. If you're late, well, don't be. It's rude. If you find it beyond your means to return to your compound and mobilize your troops in time, our cavalry will send a rider with a message ahead of your return. Give me your best hundred; they'll need to train the rest by leading on the battlefield."

Two weeks should be enough for most. A new alliance meant no more sneaking along back roads, no more wasted days avoiding patrols. Those who still couldn't make the journey in time would have riders sent ahead to gather their troops and meet them here. No excuses. No delays.

I paused, letting the words resonate before continuing. "I must warn you: Ronan's troops are currently engaged with ours back home. We can keep him occupied for now, but once we mobilize, that's it. He'll draw back, and from there, we take the fight to him."

Fear, doubt, and determination played across their faces in equal measure. Good. They needed to feel it all. They needed to understand exactly what was at stake.

"You have two weeks," I said, my voice firm. "Make it count."

RILEY

F ire crackled in the distance. It was low. Hungry. A growl that wrapped around Monterey Compound with deafening ferocity. Heat rolled in waves, twisting in the air, the trees shimmering in smoke and steam. Our fire fields stretched out for ten miles of carefully laid defense. Pansies writhed against the chains, the muted sound a juxtaposition to the groans of the dying sprawled across the surrounding field. Knowing there was someone in there, trapped beyond reach, now used as a weapon, was as horrific as it was brilliant.

Us versus them. That's what I had to remind myself. And anyone that wasn't *us* was considered *them*.

Pansies, Ronan, Fresno, and anyone else out there who dared tried to take our home, our lives. Our set up was a nightmare for anyone trying to breach us—but it wasn't impossible. Not with time. Not with resources and numbers. All of which Covert Province possessed. And yet, Ronan was pulling back.

"Troops are gone," Abel muttered beside me. His Plasma blade hung loosely in his grip, eyes distant as he stared at the blown up scramble of body parts at our feet. "Snipers confirm they've retreated from North Gate."

I scanned the tree line through my binoculars, but all I saw were the bones of the forest, twisted and blackened from flame. No shadows darting. No troops pressing the perimeter. Pushing my magic out, I searched through the whispers of nature that whispered to me. Nothing.

Covert had not only fled, they'd disappeared before our eyes.

"Why the hell would he pull back?" I growled.

"Emissaries are gone too," Abel added, quieter this time. "They left with the troops."

That stopped me cold. *How?* All gates but one were sealed shut behind layers and layers of concrete. The only way out was through destruction or through the East Gate—easiest to control access through and heavily guarded. And during this battle, twenty-five soldiers had been stationed on both sides. Wired from base to the top, the only way that gate could open is after it'd been disarmed. I turned to him sharply, heart thudding in my chest. "All of them?"

Abel nodded. "Every single one."

Something's wrong. Covert had lost as many soldiers as we had in this battle. A small number in the grand scheme—despite the weight of having to tell their loved ones had on my soul. They were my soldiers, my responsibility. The fire fields, the chained Pansies, the layered tunnels—they were all solid defenses. But Ronan would never retreat out of mercy. If he wasn't attacking, it meant he was recalibrating.

We'd played our entire hand, and Covert Province had only just begun.

I glanced up toward the watchtowers. The snipers were silhouettes against the darkening sky, their scopes glinting faintly as they tracked the nothingness. Beyond them, Finley's shields flickered—shimmering with the fragile sheen of glass. Good for its purpose. Worthless against what I suspected was coming.

"Send a rider out," I said, my heart pounding with fear. "Get word to Amaia. I want her back here. Now."

Abel kept his composure, but I saw his tell. The one the other soldiers would never recognize as anything more than the twitch of a hand that had fired far too many rounds in one given day. "You think they're going after her?"

"I think Ronan doesn't do anything without a reason."

Abel nodded grimly and took off toward the comms tent, shouting for a runner.

I let my gaze drift across the perimeter as the aftermath of battle hummed around me. The nearest trench squad pushed themselves free, hands glowing faintly with magic as they reinforced the ground. A patrol in sleek black moved through the smoke—shadows of death scanning for heat signatures. Tech from our labs. Work of the best *Tinkerers* Salem could find. One of the few advantages we still had.

And yet it still didn't feel like enough.

Turning toward the cliffside, my eyes closed as a wave of calm washed over me. *Everything will work out. They're going to be okay.* My eyes readjusted to the streak of light peeking through a cloud. It was evening, and a storm was brewing. Had rolled in minutes after the battle ended, and the scene was violent. We needed to gather our injured and get back behind the relative safety of our walls.

The horizon darkened as jagged shadows emerged from the mist, drifting into the bay. Ships. Massive ones. Battleships from The Before—reinforced with Covert's magic and tech. Their hulls gleamed in the dim light.

"Tell me I'm seeing shit," Abel said as he reappeared at my side.

"You're not."

Abel swiped his thumb across his brow, removing a speck of dirt. "Can't you please lie for two seconds?"

The crack of cannon fire echoed over the water, deep and rhythmic—tsunami waves breaking on the ground.

Our navy scrambled to intercept. Monterey's Navy was equipped to take on pirates, guard the coastline—we were smaller, faster, but painfully outdated. Outside of the Coast Guard cutters we'd taken, or the previously decommissioned USS Monterey, we were powered entirely by civilian vessels; fishing trawlers, yachts, ferries, and tugboats. We pushed forward and returned fire in quick bursts of smoke and flame. They held the line as best they could, but it was as harrowing as watching sparrows dive at hawks.

"We don't stand a chance against that," Abel watched the carnage unfold before us, other soldiers falling in close behind us looking helplessly on.

He was right. Ronan's ships weren't simply bigger—they were powered with magic. The energy rolling off them was palpable from here. Blue fire churned along their decks. Waves bucked and surged unnaturally, propelling them forward with impossible speed. Running over our smaller vessels as though they were nothing but a buoy in their way.

"Watch the water," I told them. "It's not just ships."

Streaks of white burst from below—jets of high-pressure water that cut through the air with harpoon-force precision. Helpless. We stared on helplessly, forced to watch as they sliced through our weaker vessels. A smaller ship split in half only to be swallowed by a churning wave in seconds.

"Land defense status?" I shouted to the captain sprinting up to us with a comms note in hand.

"Already firing but not slowing," he said breathlessly. "Our rounds are getting redirected. It's like they have shields too."

Jesus. Ronan had planned for this—wore us down, then went for our weakest point while we recovered.

I turned back to The Compound. "Get everyone on the shore-line—rifle squads, fire-binders, whatever we've got. I want trench-es reinforced, bunkers sealed, and snipers positioned. If they make land, they'll enter through The Docks. We are not prepared for that scenario to become a reality, am I clear?"

The captain nodded and bolted, his boots pounding against the dirt.

Abel scanned the scene again, "We can't hold this, Riley."

I didn't argue. In the past fifteen minutes, we'd lost half our ships docked in the bay. Fire bloomed across the water, engulfing our crumbling navy. The roar of cannon fire and magic mixed with the screams of the wounded and drowning.

"I know," I said. "Let's go. We say our prayers as we make our way down to help."

We locked in to start our repel when shouts rang out. Miller's yell cut through the chaos, asking us to hold. A group of soldiers pulled along several girls around Elie's age. *What the hell are they do-ing out on the battlefield?* As we'd set up in preparation, any stragglers outside our gates had headed anywhere but here. Miller jerked her chin at me, her taught bun fried off at the base. They'd obviously been through hell holding their position.

"Sir, we found 'em out on the battlefield. They claim they can help."

One of the girls stepped forward, older than the others. Her warm brown skin and frame swallowed by a shirt that was familiar. Standard issued. *One of ours.* My hand fell to my holster and Abel followed suit, sheathing his sword into a reinforced scabbard with a quick-release mechanism, custom-fitted to his right side. It al-lowed him to draw with ease despite the loss of use in his left hand.

"Alexiares helped us."

"We have a debt to pay," added another, a small brunette.

I stared at them, hand falling at my side. *Alexiares?* Not *the Bloodhound*. The man had one hell of a reputation, yet they spoke his name as though he was a savior.

Ronan's navy was minutes out from shore. We were out-gunned, outmatched, and frankly, desperate. I glanced back at Abel who gave me a nod.

"Fine," I said. What other option did we have? "What do you need?"

The older girl turned toward the brunette, "Denver."

'Denver' strode to the edge of the cliff without hesitation. I frowned, following her movements, "What is she——"

Then she moved her hands.

Wind whipped violently around her, funneling into a tight spiral that rose from the ocean in the fashion of a vengeful spirit. A tornado.

Abel cursed. "What the *hell*."

"A little assistance here please, Austin!" Denver called, her voice strained.

Another girl moved forward—this one with softer features and a determined glare from hell. She raised her hands at Denver's side. The dark clouds above us churned with thunder.

The two girls worked in tandem as we watched on in awe. The tornado became a monstrous lightning fed vortex. Bolts of lightning crackled and twisted through the spiral. Covert's massive battleships buckled and splintered under its wrath. Soldiers flailed in the water with panic, abandoning what remained of their ship and swimming for shore.

But something else shifted in the water. A sick feeling curled its way through my stomach as I saw it. Sharks. Dozens of them. The rocks along the cliffside came alive, seals splashing into the water and darting through the wreckage. They attacked, tearing through Ronan's troops in a frenzy. All of them.

I turned, heart hammering in my ears. The oldest stood completely still, her gaze locked on the carnage. Not watching, *commanding*. Her eyes burned with an intensity I'd only seen in battle-hardened veterans. A lack of mercy issued to enemies who'd thought themselves unstoppable.

She blinked once, breaking out of her trance. "It feels good to use our magic again," she said calmly. When her gaze met mine, her expression softened. "Is our group truly here?"

"Your group?" I repeated.

"Hunter's people," she clarified. "I suppose that's what you'd know them as. Alexiares said they were here. I would like to see them."

"Is he …?" Abel asked, concern etched on the lines of his skin.

The oldest offered a slight nod. "Alive and headed for your general. Our group? Take us to them."

Hunter's people. That explained the power simmering off them. When he'd mentioned he had numbers with extraordinary blessings, he wasn't lying. My gut told me there was more to all of this than any of them let on. I couldn't trust it—not yet. Magic like that didn't come without a price. It couldn't. We'd used spells and science to get even half of what they possessed.

"Of course," I said smoothly, hating the taste of the lie. I valued honesty, but it was earned over time, not given out right. "Help them," I ordered Miller. "On your way in, have Barnes see that the stragglers in the water are finished off. No prisoners. There's only about a hundred left—it should be more than manageable."

"Don't dispose of the bodies."

The quietest of them all spoke in a breath, barely enough to catch. I turned to her, "I'm sorry?"

Memphis edged closer, the discomfort from the proximity of our bodies radiated off her as she winced back. "She needs them. Sedona is a siphon healer."

There was a beat of silence as Miller and I shared a glance—her face twisted with confusion, mine probably not far off. I cleared my throat. I had no interest in giving orders I didn't understand.

"Most healers," Memphis explained, "draw their power from water. Hunter, for example."

I gave her a slow nod, piecing it together best I could. Miller appeared less convinced, muttering something along the lines of *what does that even mean?*

"But *her* power," Memphis continued, with a small tilt of her head toward the girl. "Feeds on the magic of others—preferably the dead before their energy fades completely. It's … more comfortable that way."

Sedona didn't look very comfortable to me. She looked like she spent a lot of time with the dead.

"Oh, Reina would've had a field day with this lot," Miller chided slyly to herself.

Denver's face flashed with interest as she stepped closer. "Reina Moore? I'm shocked."

There was no indication of that being true with the skepticism laced in her tone. I flicked the tip of my nose and sighed, giving Miller the nod of approval to carry out the orders.

Miller nodded sharply, already turning to bark orders at the others. I kept my attention on the oldest girl, but something shifted. Her focus shifted, moving past my shoulder to the others.

I followed her gaze.

This one was far younger than the others—younger than Elie but older than Emma—her face ringed with dark blue circles. Her eyes were hollow, like someone who'd seen too much and didn't have the desire to ever forget the tragedies of life. The oldest turned her body, circling me to put the girl out of sight and tucked behind her. Protective in a way that set something uneasy in my gut.

"What's your name?" I asked.

"Memphis," she replied. "That's Eden," she nodded toward her.

Eden's steel colored eyes were unsettling as they flickered to me, hard, sharp, and unreadable. I turned back to Memphis. "How did you say Alexiares helped you out again?"

"We didn't," she leveled. "We owed him a favor. I had hoped to be able to see my family. He offered us safe harbor. However, is it a correct assumption to say once we cross through those gates we won't be allowed out?"

I sighed, "That is correct. Yes."

Memphis nodded solemnly, her hands trembling as she clenched and unclenched, stuck in a pattern. My gaze drifted to the soldiers who'd accompanied Miller. They were all women.

It sent a pang through my chest.

Memphis straightened again, her voice quieter now. "Eden is thankful for your honesty," she said, nodding back to the one with the hollowed out eyes. "The taste of lies is rather repulsive to her."

Eden blinked at me. The girls gathered around her, nodding in unison before they turned to leave as abruptly as they arrived.

"Thank you. All of you," I called after them. Keeping them out seemed right, but sending young women into this world alone was a neglect of the authority I wielded. "If I were to let you enter, we could not let you leave until this war is over. A security risk. I hope you understand."

Memphis paused then glanced over her shoulder at me with an unreadable expression. Eden stiffened, her head shifting toward Memphis who awaited her confirmation. She offered a small tick of her head.

"At least let us get you some food, weapons. A change of clothes," I said.

Denver and Memphis barely moved, but something passed between them—silent, decided.

"Okay," Denver agreed.

"Abel," I called, the single word clipped and sharp, enough to carry the weight of the order.

"Already on it," he replied, moving swiftly, his boots scuffing against the debris-strewn ground.

Memphis broke from the group, her steps deliberate as she made her way to my side, settling into the spot Abel had vacated seconds ago. She didn't look at me. "You're not ready for what's coming," she said softly.

"We know."

CHAPTER
FORTY-THREE

ALEXIARES

There was always the option to sleep when I was dead, *I guess.* We'd taken approximately two steps into The Compound before Amaia had sent Reina to summon Riley to our quarters and Tomoe to Tomás. It wasn't as though we had time to fuck around. I just wished I could at least wash my ass and use an actual bathroom before getting down to business.

Suckerpunch barreled through the door to our quarters first, sprinting toward the half-full food dish he'd left behind and inhaling it. Pulling Amaia into the room, I sank onto the couch and brought her down to my lap, torturing her with the most tender of kisses. That was something I'd learned to enjoy these last few months. The tenderness of her touch. Knowing that not every kiss, every hug, every touch was given freely and out of love. Without condition.

The knock at the door shattered any illusion of peace. *Predictable.* I should have known Riley wouldn't waste a second after learning we'd returned. Tossing my head back with a groan, I plucked her off my lap and stepped to the side.

"Where are you going?" she asked, disappointment creasing the lines near her eyes. Not at my departure, but at the stolen moment now passed.

"Besides the obvious reunion I'd be forced to endure," I said, giving her a knowing smile. "The two of you are capable of handling a debrief on your own. Give me the spark notes when you're done, I'm off to scrub a week's worth of hell off me, and then, a nap. Don't wake me if the house is burning down."

She chuckled, opening the door with a squeal. Harley barked with excitement, the commotion causing Suckerpunch to stir from the corner, pushing past me for the front of the room. I slipped out before Riley could start talking.

I woke up from my nap in time to catch tonight's entertainment. Riley lounged across the couch, boots kicked up on the armrest. There'd been a lot of good news between the three of us as of late and dare I say, I was excited for the … addition to the family. Amaia sat on the floor in front of him, head propped against the cushion. She seemed completely spent.

Though the hours passed in my nap, time told a different story. Despite spending half a day hiking back through an annoying amount of fucking herds, it wasn't even dinner time yet. She smiled faintly and reached out a hand. I took it, helping her up and giving Riley a clasp on the shoulder as I passed behind him on the couch.

The front door opened, and the room froze.

Elie stepped through, "Oh great. You're back. Do we still have to do that stupid family book club thing tonight?" Her moody hazel eyes scanned the room, landing right on Riley, locking in on him like a target. A repeat fight I'd pay great money to miss.

Amaia moved in front of him, her arms crossing over her chest, my attention stuck on the swelling of her breasts pushed up with the movement. She glared at me and cleared her throat, turning back toward Elie. "Sorry to disappoint, Els, I'm meeting with Tomás in a bit to go over some blueprints. We need every second we can get before we leave in two weeks. You can sit in on it if you want."

"Pass." Elie's frown deepened, but she smoothed it quickly, always trying to play the little soldier. I recognized it because I'd done the same. Extremely different circumstances, same crushing weight. Amaia saw it too.

"It's pretty early still," Amaia added. "Let's do dessert in a few hours and then reschedule for after? What'd ya think?"

"Sure. Whatever," Elie muttered, her gaze flickering to Riley one last time. "I'll be in my room."

She stormed off, dogs trailing her, slamming the door with a reverberating thud that could be heard throughout The Compound. The room went silent. And awkward as hell.

"I should go—" Riley started. The neutral expression he wore day in and day out crumpled to the textbook display of regret. Something else lingered; if I was an idiot, I'd call it hopelessness, but that didn't quite portray the crinkling lines of heartbreak etching along his face.

"No, Ril," Amaia cut him off, reaching for his wrist. "Stay. You're right. We should figure this out sooner rather than later."

A heavy knock rattled the front door. All of us turned, caught off guard for a moment. I stared between them, watching them have their own silent argument. *I got it, don't worry.*

"It's Tomás," I said flatly, crossing the rest of the way across the room to get it myself.

Amaia shot me that irritated headshake she'd perfected since the day we'd met. "It's probably Miller, she was supposed to drop off updated patrol routes thirty minutes ago." She pushed past me, still in her usual cargos, now stained with dirt and guts, and her tucked-in tank top. The only indication she'd even attempted to relax were the curls now framing her face. Amaia opened the door and sighed, frozen in the doorway.

"Told you," I muttered. The knock that came hit four times, not Miller's usual three.

"It hurts, ya know?" Tomás said, stepping inside with the same sly grin of his brother. *Fuck*, even the inflection of their voice when they were making some shitty joke was identical. "Being greeted by beautiful women with such disappointment."

I clasped his hand in a quick, familiar greeting. Thumping and muffled shuffling from Elie's room pulled our attention. The dogs were still with her, quiet, so whatever she was doing in there, she was safe. Tomás's eyes flicked toward the door and Riley shifted, his Adam's apple bobbing as he audibly swallowed. Without a single word, he charged through the front door.

"Riley …" Amaia's voice wavered, her hand reaching for the empty space in front of her but didn't follow. Her posture stiffened, the general snapping back into place, but the crack in her resolve was hard to miss—if you knew where to search for it. And I did.

Tomás glanced at the ceiling like he was trying to disappear into it, his hands shoved in his pockets, shoulders raised. "Should I come back or …?"

"You deal with this," I said, gesturing to Amaia. "I've got Elie."

Her head snapped toward me at the lack of negotiation left in my statement. Something flickered in her eyes. Gratitude. Guilt. She nodded, deciding to trust me on this.

I turned toward Elie's room and paused, shaking my head with a wry smile. "This is going to take a while. Have a good night, man."

"Yeah, you too." Tomás replied, his usual jest nowhere to be found.

Amaia closed the front door behind Tomás. They dipped into hushed tones as their conversation began. I turned away, granting Elie no more than two quick knocks before making my way in. *Fuck, wait, privacy. I'd never gotten any of that, but hey, here's to gentle parenting or whatever.*

I took an awkward step back, "I'm coming in," I said, cracking it open. No protests came, only silence. Suckerpunch and Harley rushed the doorway at my entrance, tails thumping against the only portion of the floor not covered in various rugs. I gave them both a tap on the head then stepped inside, shutting the door quietly.

The room was once Prescott's personal library. His collection was vast, ranging from literary greats, to a weird amount of books about birds. Similar to Amaia, Elie had insisted on keeping Prescott's presence here strong and adding their own touches here and there instead.

Heavy orange curtains hung across the large wall to ceiling window, her twin sized bed shoved right in front. Mix matched patterned pillows were tousled across the bed, resting against the wall and the plants lining the window-pane. They matched the vibrant colored oriental rug that spanned most of the wooden floor. A floor that was now covered in torn pages from Prescott's precious books.

In the center of it all sat Elie, knees to her chest, chin resting on top. Her light blue jeans were darkened with tear stains, streaked through with old coffee splatters from her shift in The Kitchens.

"Love what you've done with the place," I said, leaning against the door.

"Oh, screw you." She didn't look up.

I pushed off the heavy oak and into the room, lowering my-self onto the floor beside her. Harley wandered over and flopped down belly-up. Elie's hand moved instinctively to swipe her fingers through the dark as night fur.

"We gotta talk about this, Elie," I said.

"No, we really, really don't."

I sighed and leaned back on my hands. "I mean, sure. If you want to stay angry at the world and end up like me, be my guest."

"What's so bad about that?" she said, finally glancing my way. *Ah.* There it was. That hint of defiance in her red-rimmed eyes. "You seem relatively well-adjusted."

"Relatively," I admitted with a shrug. "It works when you've got someone like Amaia in your corner. But when you don't? It's a lonely, miserable existence."

"There's no point. She's just going to die too."

The moment they left her lips, my veins ran cold, every ounce of warmth ripped away. "Don't say that."

"It's true," she snapped back. All ferocity and malice, but also, fear. "You think she's invincible? Just wait until she leaves the gates with Riley. The second things go south, she's gone."

I stared at her, forcing myself to see the child that was hurting standing in front of me and not someone purposely antagonizing me. Hitting a spot they knew would hit deep. "What the hell is wrong with you?"

"You came into *my* room and bothered *me.*"

"Yeah, because Amaia and Riley care about you. It's killing them to see you like this. It's killing *all of us.*"

"Drama queen." She rolled her eyes, pressed off the floor and onto her bed, sitting cross-legged against the wall.

I stayed where I was and turned my body to face her. "Your life doesn't suck. Grow up. People die, it's an apocalypse, and we're stuck in some made-up community inside a made-up territory with a piece of paper everyone calls an alliance, which means jack shit when someone like Ronan Moore exists."

Her expression shifted to one of horror as she leaned back against the window. A pillow reached its tipping point, taking a small plant with it as it tumbled into a mess of dirt on her colorful quilt. The dogs perked up, their eyes sweeping the surroundings before settling back down.

"What's wrong?" I asked with bitter sarcasm. "I'm only saying the quiet part out loud. That's what you were thinking, right? I get it."

"Do you?" Her voice cracked but her eyes stayed locked on mine. Angry. Hurt. Sad. Guilt. All of it lingered there, fighting for a brief moment to shine, to allow her to grieve what she had already lost and what she feared could be taken next.

"No." I stood up and took a seat next to her on the edge of the bed. "I gotta be honest, kid… If I had the support that you do, at your age, I wouldn't be the shithead I am now."

She didn't respond. Her fingers worked at the edges of her nails, pulling at the cuticles, her gaze fixed downward. I recognized the habit. The need to do something, anything, to keep from unraveling completely.

"Life sucks, and then you die," I continued. "That's the only guarantee you get. The *only* promise in everyone's life. But how you deal with the bullshit while you're stuck on this floating rock? That's up to you."

Her shoulders sagged, the fight draining from her frame. I waited, watching as she swallowed hard, the tremor in her hands barely visible.

"At first, I was angry. I mean, I'm still angry, just not as much. Now I'm sad. Kind of confused. But mostly, I think … I think I'm mourning the realization that I was never enough," Elie said, her voice broke on a choked sob. "She left us. My mom. She decided

Dad was never coming back and in the same breath took away our mom. And then Rex left too. He checks in on me every few days, but he's not the same. He's … not here. Not really present. *Refuses* to talk about anything of the past. 'Forward thinking only.' I feel like I don't even know who he is anymore. My brother—he doesn't get it. He doesn't see how much I need him, and that … that makes everything so much worse. Last year, I had a mom, I had a dad, and I had a brother. Now? I have none of that. Four months ago, I had Prescott. He was the one who helped things make sense when Amaia wasn't here. Now he's gone too."

I gave her a moment, letting the tremble in her voice settle. She wiped her nose with the back of her hand. I didn't speak. Didn't try to fix it. Because there was no fixing this.

"You know, all I can think sometimes is how selfish they are."

"Who?" I asked. My first word in minutes.

"My mother. Prescott. They gave up in the end."

I could have pushed back, told her she was wrong. But that wasn't my place, and it wasn't what Elie needed.

"My mom gave up in the end too," I admitted. "Except she chose to die long before she physically left this earth."

Elie turned her head toward me, confusion in her tear-filled eyes.

"Pills," I said flatly. "Made it easier to swallow what our father was doing to us. All of us."

"I think it was the bottle for her in The Before. That's what I remember—I'm pretty sure. But once we got here, she was better. I *thought* she was better."

"Amaia—" *Shit.*

"Please don't tell her. I know she says she's better," Elie interrupted. "But … but maybe if she never broke in the first place, things would be different."

"Only people that would know that as fact is a *Seer*."

"Sure, I'll go ask Abel. Be right back," she shot back and rolled her eyes.

I stood, tossing my head toward the door. "Why not? He's only a few streets down. Come on, I'll go with you." I offered her a hand.

She took it reluctantly. "I don't understand."

"If that's what you think. Then go and find out. No one is stopping you."

Elie snatched her hand back and planted her feet. She crossed her arms, brow arching with annoyance.

"Thought so," I said, striding over and giving her a small shake of the shoulders. "Be angry. That's fine. That's normal. I reckon Reina would say it's healthy in moderation. But stop pretending everyone around you is to blame for the actions of others. We aren't in their heads. I didn't know Prescott well, but considering he was basically Amaia's dad, I'm assuming self-sacrificial shit runs in the family.

"They're *soldiers first*, Elie. Riley too. They have a job to do. A job they love because it means they get to protect the people they care about. That includes you. Love the people around you while you can. They could be dead tomorrow."

"Some pep talk," she grumbled with a huffed laugh. "She really sent you in here? You kinda suck at this. I think I actually feel worse."

"I came in here by choice because this isn't a pep talk—it's a reality check. One you needed. Bad." I turned and walked toward the door then paused. "In my experience, shit will always feel worse until, one day, it doesn't suck as bad anymore."

I opened the door. Amaia stood there, her doe eyes snapped to mine immediately. She was drained, the kind of tired that went deeper than purely physical exhaustion.

"Alexiares ... Amaia," Elie said, her voice faint but strong enough to stop us in our tracks. "Please don't die. Not in a few weeks meeting with the others. Not during this stupid war. Not anytime soon."

I swiveled in place to face her. Breath escaped me as I was engulfed in a hug. The force knocked me off balance, her head pressed against my chest. I didn't know what to do with my hands.

Amaia stepped in and I wrapped an arm around her, bringing her into the embrace. Her shoulders loosened, a bit of warmth emanating in her complexion once more. She tugged Elie closer. "We'll do our best."

CHAPTER
FORTY-FOUR

AMAIA

"Did you really pack a book?" Alexiares held up my camo bag, the middle zipper undone.

We were all packed and ready to go. The simulations would take about a month. Milking every spare second it would take for the bulk of Ronan's troops to organize and attack. Three weeks, three phases of training, and one delusional mind that I could make this all work.

I snatched it from his hands. "Give me that." I tossed a small flame his way, catching the edge of his shirt. He doused it immediately with an unimpressed flick of his water magic as he grumbled a series curse words.

"It's my emotional support book." I clutched it tight against my chest. He'd have to pry this from my cold, dead arms, if he thought for even a second I would leave it behind for the sake of saving space for something else.

He swiped through his hair, grown out enough to barely follow the rules of the gel he used to force it back and out of his face. "Weren't you crying over this exact book two nights ago?"

"Is there a point there, *Bloodhound?*" I shot back with a glare, not appreciating the thick mockery in his tone.

Alexiares stepped closer to me, peering down at me with lowered lids. "Got you something for the journey."

It was a drawing—a sketch of the two of us. He was so cynical I expected there to be some semblance of a joke within the gesture. Caught in the pose or funny faces, but no, we looked almost … normal. Alexiares and I stood hand in hand, our gazes caught in each other, the gentle tug of his lips lifelike. I ran my finger along the raised lines, then held it over my heart, meeting his eyes. He watched me for a moment, then leaned forward to grab the book I'd easily discarded upon seeing his gift. Alexiares flipped open the front cover and motioned for me to place the drawing inside.

I shook my head, a quiet ache pressed against my chest. *Hold your composure.* I smoothed my expression before he had a chance to notice the shift. With the toss of my head, I lured him into our bedroom and walked toward the nightstand. It took courage to look at the faces that sat there every night. Carefully, I laid the drawing against a row of photos—faded, worn, but always cherished. Back from when our group had been whole. Back when there had still been film to capture moments, before things had begun to fall apart a year ago in three days.

I traced the edge of the drawing with my thumb. We wouldn't be here to mourn the losses properly, to sit with the grief or reflect on what had been. There wasn't time for that anymore. Which made the drawing all the more precious.

"I want to leave it here," I said quietly. "Have something to come home to."

I turned to face him fully, letting myself look at him. *Really* look at him. God, he was ethereally beautiful. The sharp lines of his face, those piercing eyes, the harsh bridge of his nose. Having forever to stare at him would not nearly be enough.

It always made him squirm when I did this—when I let the silence stretch and refused to fill it with meaningless words. He wasn't used to being seen for more than the stone-cold persona he always tried to be.

"What?" he asked, shifting under the weight of my gaze.

"I never would have guessed you a romantic," I mocked, hanging my jaw in faux shock, covering it with the tips of my fingers and showing off my ring. "It's alarming … yet, oddly endearing."

"Shut up," Alexiares muttered, the faint twitch in his jaw letting me know I'd hit a nerve.

"You like, *love me* love me," I pressed, stepping closer. He instinctively took a step back, which only fed the smirk spreading across my face.

He crossed his arms, unamused. "So."

"You cleaned guts out of my curls last night," I reminded him, shaking my curls out.

"Two hours I got to watch you in the bath. If you're trying to make a point, get there faster."

I backed him into the wall, feeding off the slight flare of his nostrils. "Already did."

He grabbed me by the waist before I could get another word out, flipping us in one fluid motion. My back hit the wall with a soft thud. Alexiares braced an arm over my head, his eyes pinned me, sending a jolt of intensity through me.

"Tell me something," he said, his voice low, head tilted enough to meet my eye.

"Something," I shot back and bit the inside of my cheek in a poor attempt to keep the smug grin slipping into place in check.

A flicker of a smile danced across his lips but it didn't stick. I frowned at the softening in his expression, my hand falling to the base of his neck.

"If we met in The Before," he murmured, only but a breath away. "Would you still find me?"

The Before.

The two words hit harder than a punch to the gut. Before the bombs, before death, before we became who we are now. Before the fucking world demanded everything we had and then pulled, threatened for us to give more. But under all the wreckage, all the pain, all the never-ending loss, I knew who we were at our core—who he was, who I was. And we were the same. Soulmates.

But it was hard to answer his question. Because in this lifetime, there had been love before him—and they were as real as he was, even though the love was not the same.

I held his gaze and stared into his eyes, in a world that wouldn't stop spinning. "I think there is a part of me that would love you in every lifetime."

Of that I was sure.

His lips brushed mine as he whispered, "All of me would love you in every lifetime—but damn, this one's my favorite."

Love. Fucking love. A word that had been poisonous to me for years and now ... all I wanted to do was shout it over and over again. To spend every second I had left with him, every breath until my last. Hate had been strong in my heart when we'd first met and slowly but surely my *Bloodhound* had melted it away. Torn down the wall and destroyed the idea of being satisfied of just surviving until my time ran out. I'd lost so much, but fuck, did I gain a once and a lifetime type of love.

A Sunday kind of love.

His lips found mine, and the world narrowed to the two of us. I opened my mouth, letting him in with a moan. He groaned, nibbling on my bottom lip with a whimper of desperation. I smiled, the power I held over him more than a turn on. The knowledge that I was the only one who could unravel him both here and out there in front of the world was a thrill I didn't bother hiding.

His rough, calloused hands skimmed my lower back, digging beneath the thin fabric of my shirt and ripping it over my head. Alexiares gave me no time to process the movement. Fingers thread through my curls, finding root at my crown as he lowered his mouth back to my lips, the intensity leaving us both gasping for air. For more.

We stumbled back toward the bed and he trailed lingering kisses down my neck. His breath was hot against my skin as he drifted lower. Intoxicating electricity slithered through my body at the warm tracing of his tongue. I let out a low sigh the moment he reached the curve of my hip.

His name was there—carved into me. He paused. The tips of his fingers traced the scar then he pressed a kiss to the mark. Our eyes met, communicating the rest. Our decision to mark each other wasn't about pain or what came before. It was about us, the only language either of us had left to say *I'm still here.*

That gave me pause. Because we *were* still here. But for how long?

The weight of everything rushed back in, drowning out the warmth of the moment. Two days until the simulations. Two days until I had to lead us all into the unknown. And I couldn't stop thinking about what Lola said. Her words had been circling me like vultures, ready to pick apart my resolve.

"What's wrong?" Alexiares asked, picking up on the subtle change of energy.

I pressed against his chest to create the slightest amount of space in order to organize the storm inside me. "Lola was right."

His brow furrowed, and he pushed himself up right moving back to lean against the wall. "Say that three times and you might summon her."

"I'm serious," I said, pulling my shirt back on and tucking it into the waistband of my training cargos. "We need a plan."

He knew *exactly* what I meant, and he wasn't happy about it. His face reddened, eyes darkening in his quiet rage that always burned hotter than him shouting ever could. "That's not our responsibility. We are only obligated to care for the people of Monterey once this is done."

I took a step closer, lifting my chin to meet his gaze head-on, warring with being a general or his … his future wife. "You think I don't know that? You think I don't think about washing my hands of all of this and focusing on the people I love? Focusing on what I *know* I can control? But that's not who I am, Alexiares. I won't look the other way and pretend it's not my problem to solve when I know I can make a difference."

"They do not deserve you," he said with weighted conviction.

"I don't care," my voice broke at the premature visage of loss staring back at me. "What we're doing here—four territories filled with settlements—it's not sustainable. Like, fuck, it hasn't even been a decade and these people, they can't just sit still and relax. Humans are such stupid creatures."

"We are," he agreed, his voice quieter now. "And I don't see that changing anytime soon."

"But it *has* to." I couldn't hide the crack in my demeanor any longer. Tears of hopeless rage welled, threatening to pour down my face to show how weak my resolve had become. The laugh I released was harsh and humorless, *and you can't even have a drink to silence the thoughts.* "God, it's the same story every fucking time. People settle and they get bored and then they fight. We are constantly clawing for something to make ourselves feel bigger, better, more important than the next person, and it's all just *bullshit.*"

I strode across the room toward our dresser and picked up a book off the top, waving it in the air then letting it drop to the floor with a hollow thud. "All of it is right here! Documented. Thousands of years of warnings, lessons, obvious fucking patterns—wasting trees, ink, people's time. And for what? For us to keep repeating the same goddamn mistakes."

The silence in the room was broken only by the harsh rhythm of my breathing. I pulled at my curls, twisting them in large chunks, willing myself to keep it together. "This has to be it. No more. It ends here, with this war. Because if it doesn't, we're going to destroy ourselves all over again. And next time, I can't guarantee there will be anything left worth saving."

"Your desire is to fix something that's broken on purpose."

I nodded, swallowing down a lump in my throat. "When this is over, we need something bigger. A system that doesn't fall apart at the first sign of greed or flat our delusion. If we don't build something better, then we're leaving the fight for the next guy. And I can't—I won't—force someone else to spend the rest of their life cleaning up another person's mess."

Alexiares leaned back against the wall, the lean muscle of his arms folded taut, veins popping as he studied me, his expression unreadable. "Okay."

"That's it?" I asked incredulously, admittedly looking for a bigger fight. "I tell you I'm planning on tossing a treaty we just signed in the trash and betraying the very people we swore we were there to help?"

"*You* swore you were there to help." His tone was dry. Unbothered. "I made no such promise."

"Maybe Moore is right," I muttered, suddenly hit with the urge to second guess myself. "Maybe we have more in common than I thought."

"You are nothing like that man," Alexiares's voice sharpened to a dangerous edge.

"No, I'm worse. Judge, jury, and executioner. That's what I've become."

I paced the room, tripping over a pair of sweatpants and kicking them out the way in frustration and borderline embarrassment. Alexiares stuck his hand out, stopping me from making my third lap.

"Decisions were made that were necessary to push this movement forward. To keep Monterey Compound on its feet. And more will come," he said, as though it were simple as that. It pissed me off that it was, truly that fucking simple. It was inevitable. "You cannot let the consequences of other people's lack of critical thinking fill you with guilt. Actions have consequences, Amaia. They chose wrong."

"Did they actually choose wrong?" I snapped. "Or did they just choose their own path that didn't align with our goals?"

His jaw clenched. I knew he didn't like when people questioned me, I hadn't realized that included myself. "Don't go there. You're a volatile little thing," he added, smirking as he reached out and pinched my hip. "But you aren't evil. We are going to put that motherfucker in the ground and anyone like him if that's what it takes. I told you I'd burn this world for you—so let's burn it. Then I'll watch as you help what remains rise from the ashes."

"Like Monterey."

"Like Monterey," he agreed with zero hesitation.

My little patriot. I sighed, shaking my head. "Well, I don't know what the plan is from here but I do know a lot of them won't be happy with me."

"They don't need to be happy, they just need to survive."

"No," I said softly, peering out through the window that opened toward The Compound. "That's not how I want to lead. I … I don't know, okay? It was a stupid thought that's been bothering me all day. I don't have the authority to do any of that and I don't want to take that from anyone. The best I can do is come up with a plan, ask for their support, and hope for the best of humanity to show up when I do."

He lingered for a moment, his gaze steady and expectant, like he was waiting to see what I'd do next. His eyes warmed as if he could sense the spark of an idea taking hold. *Now or never*. If I was going to do this, then I wanted to make sure there would be zero regrets I left behind.

"What now?" Alexiares asked.

"Wanna do something kind of crazy?"

"With you, I'm always doing something crazy."

"Fair point." I grabbed his hand. "Pack something nice. Let's go find Riley."

CHAPTER FORTY-FIVE

AMAIA

Nerves never suited anyone well. Yet here I was, surrounded by the people I trusted most, and I couldn't stop pacing the length of the home we'd hunkered down in for the duration of simulations. Royal Oaks hummed with anticipation as battle prep loomed, but I only felt the pressure in my chest growing tighter.

A year. That's all it had been since Jax died. A year of clawing my way forward, of fighting to keep the others from meeting the same fate. And now we were here, staring down another stretch of war games that weren't just for show. We had three weeks to get our shit together—three weeks before Ronan could decide to march his ass back to Monterey. The Compound might hold him for a week at best before my units would have to return. And Riley, left to defend it again, wasn't a thought that settled easy.

San Jose had been the first to arrive as a way to show their most sincere apologies for the chaos they'd caused. Others filtered in not too long after and now, most of the town was occupied or in the process of being prepared for what the next few weeks entailed.

"Fresno may take a moment to join us," Hunter announced from his position in front of the window. The blinds snapped back closed as he turned around. "They're, uh, workin' through some things."

"Well played," I tipped my head toward him. He was proving himself useful in every way that he'd promised.

Unease settled over me once more. I needed some air. To move my muscles and feel anything other than the anxiety that was eating me alive. We had three weeks to get our shit together, and that was *if* Ronan didn't march his ass back to Monterey. Monterey would be able to hold him for a week max before the rest of my units would have to return. Which served as a problem considering I needed them here to lead. Riley would send word if shit hit the fan but the idea of him being left there to defend once more did nothing to ease the tightening of my chest.

I crossed the room, stopping at the round kitchen table where Alexiares sat. He was forced into a travel sized game of mancala with Reina, who looked far too smug for someone losing.

Leaning down, I kissed the side of his head right above his temple. "Try not to find and kill Finley while I'm gone."

"Gone?" He peered up at me, one eyebrow raised.

"I'm off for a run," I said, grabbing my sneakers from beside the door.

He stood, his hand catching mine before I could escape. "Careful, Princess. A lot of wolves hiding among the sheep."

I rolled my eyes, smirking. "Worry about yourself, *Bloodhound*. I can handle a little jog."

His thumb brushed my knuckles, warm and grounding before he let go. "I'm not worried," Alexiares said, opening the door and leaning against the doorway, arms crossed, a soft smile tugging at his lips. "Try not to scare the locals while you're at it."

"Only if they deserve it," I quipped, stepping into the cool night air.

The streets were lit with the fire magic of many, creating a dim glow on the cleared town of Royal Oaks. Cracked asphalt crisscrossed with stubborn weeds of the main roads—hard on the ankles but the sidewalks weren't much better. At least the homes that remained standing were in relatively good condition.

It was weird, running through The Compound or down the coast was one thing, in the remnants of what was once a thriving suburban community was another. I couldn't imagine myself here in The Before. We'd never lived in the suburbs per se, always on a base or an apartment complex not too far outside. Xavier and I had settled on being city-dwellers for life, kids or not.

Vegetation crept into the edges of everything—the skeletons of cars abandoned in driveways, the side of houses, up the posts of mailboxes stuffed with paper no one would ever come for. Shadows danced on the walls of soldiers posted outside bonfires in the back of their respective houses. *Good.* If I were lucky, they would wander, mingle a bit.

I picked up my pace as I neared the center of town. Housing became sparser, and thus, any hint of the vibrancy of human life disappeared. The quiet was peaceful … still—too still. My instinct prickled with unease, the hair on the back of my neck damn near giving me whiplash at the speed it raised. The aggressive thud of my heartbeat pounded in my ears and I rounded the corner in a full sprint. Whatever was triggering that tingle of fear, I had no interest in facing it.

A figure stepped out of the shadows the second I rounded the corner. There was no time to slow my steps as I ran into it, slamming against their dense body, knocking the air out of me and putting me on my ass. I rolled and sprang to my feet in a defensive position. There was no one else out here, just me and the general of Des Moines. And an ugly fucker he was.

"Out for a late-night jog, General?" He took a step toward me, hands in his pockets. I refused to cower. "Seems like a good time to discuss your games."

It'd be a fool's thought to underestimate what general disdain could do to someone who was otherwise rational in thinking. Anderson's hatred for me went beyond the professional sense—it was personal. I could see it in the way his lip curled, the barely contained fury in his eyes. He had never believed I deserved my rank. Not when Matheson and Lane took me under their wing, not when I climbed the ladder faster than anyone had expected. To him, I was reckless, untested, and unworthy. And tonight, this wasn't about the simulations. It was about proving me unfit to lead.

I tilted my head, sensing the threat he posed immediately. "Feeling a bit bold tonight, Anderson?"

Honestly, I welcomed the fight. It was about damn time. Putting him in his place would silence the others. He represented everything I was up against—doubt, condescension, and resistance from the older generation of leaders. Anderson was an even match, and I was thirsting for a fight.

"No more than the usual," he said, a smirk tugging on his lips. "Only aim to show everyone you're nothing but a liability."

There it was—his barely concealed obsession with knocking me off my pedestal. "Funny," I said coolly. "You've been trying to prove that for years. How's that working out for you?"

The flick of his wrist was the only warning I got. A jagged rock flew toward my face. It grazed my cheekbone with a sharp sting as I reached for my blade. Anderson was fast. His fire magic crackled in his palms as he closed the distance.

Flames licked at my skin and I countered with a blast of air magic. It sent him back with a skid, granting me one sweet moment to regroup—but not long enough. He lunged again, this time the fire swirling in his fists threatened me with a burning kiss.

I slashed at him with my knife, feigning right before I drove my knee toward his stomach. He swatted me off, the brutal efficiency of his movements catching me by the wrist until my blade fell to the ground. I let out a cry of agony under the pressure of his brute strength. The smirk on his face deepened as flames sparked back to life in his free hand, the only protection I had at the moment were my own, battling to cover me in the safety of its warmth.

"You'll need more than that, General." He sneered, tightening his grip and dragging me around like a rag doll.

I kicked out, desperate to find some hold on the ground or an ounce of momentum. With more effort than I cared to admit, I wrenched my arm free, throwing another burst of wind his way. It sent him stumbling. He recovered quick, hurling a piece of debris at me—a fucking door hinge of all things.

The fight spilled onto the wrap-around front porch of a house. The spot where he'd begun his attack feet away thanks to the precious moments he'd stolen moving me where he pleased. I backed into the door, ducking as his foot slammed into it and falling to the ground. Anderson reached down, dragging me by my feet, attempting to pull me deeper into the house. *No witnesses,* were the only words echoing around my mind.

Like fucking hell.

I latched onto the door frame, teeth gritting as I took in the house, desperate to find anything to work in my advantage. I was panicking. Caught off guard. What had I told my soldiers? The second you panic in a life or death situation, you're fucking dead.

The walls were crumbled around us and furniture scattered. We got the same idea at the same time, both scrambling toward whatever we could use and letting the magic of being an *Umbra*

Mortis guide us. With the newly acquired gift of air magic, I had a momentary advantage. Shards of glass flew through the air and I worked to throw them with deadly precision. He hissed, cupping his stomach, but my victory was short-lived. I glanced down, one had clipped my thigh, slicing deep.

There was no time to focus on the blood seeping into my pants and dripping down my leg. Anderson didn't let up. He refused to. Large hands gripped my shoulders and sent me careening into the wall with immense force. My head slammed hard enough into the exposed brick to blur my vision. He grabbed a fistful of my hair and yanked my head to the side. I heard a crack before I felt the cold whisper down my spine.

No. No. You have to see them again.

Panic distracted me. I couldn't let my family find me this way. What Anderson would do to me. If I died right here, right now, that was it for every territory and settlement. They would turn on each other and Covert would win. My family would never get to live a life of peace.

I wiggled my fingers. It was just the crack, the bursting of gas bubbles within my body, nothing was broken—and I wasn't done fighting. He pulled me further back, arching me at an unnatural angle but enough to grab the knife strapped to my ankle. With a surge of adrenaline, I drove the blade into his side. Quick and vicious, I stabbed him again and again. And again.

Anderson snarled. Pure adrenaline kept him going, his fury controlled but lethal. He disarmed me with terrifying ease and sent the last knife I had clattering to the floor as he pinned me against the wall.

"Is that all you got, *girl?*" he growled, eyes alight with fury.

I ignited, flames erupting across my body. The sudden heat and lack of his own protective layer of flames forced him back, granting me a moment to gasp for air. Like the trained veteran he was, he quickly matched me, his own fire roaring to life and neutralizing my advantage.

He was relentless. Anderson grabbed me by the throat and slammed me against the wall once more. His grip tightened, and I struggled against him, clawing and kicking, but he only clenched harder, cutting off my air. Desperate, I remembered to draw on my air magic, siphoning the breath from his lungs. His grip faltered. We locked in a stalemate, both gasping for air.

You stupid bitch, you really should have tried to master the whole air magic thing. I closed my eyes, digging deep, sifting through my power and searching for the well that fed my air. Anderson stumbled back, coughing and disoriented. I dropped to my knees, vision swimming as I fought against the black tunneling in, struggling to stay conscious.

The motherfucker refused to fall. He surged one final time, hurling debris and shards of glass with ruthless precision. Something caught in my already leaking wound, slashing deeper and nicking an artery. Pain exploded through me as warmth soaked my leg. I staggered, gasping, the coppery tang of blood thick in the air.

He smirked, triumphant. "Still think you belong on top, General?"

Anderson advanced, slower now but no less calculated, still lethal. I met him halfway, drawing on every ounce of strength I had left.

The room blurred into motion as we collided, a flurry of strikes and counters. His fist connected with my ribs, sending a sickening crack through my chest. I barely held back a scream, instead grabbing the nearest weapon—a splintered chair leg. I swung low, sweeping his legs out from under him. He hit the ground hard. Dropping onto his chest, I pinned him with every ounce of weight I had left. My knife was gone, but my hands found his throat, squeezing the life from him, letting my magic take every ounce of air from his body.

"Bleed for me," I hissed through gritted teeth. My vision was red with fury.

His hands clawed at mine, but I squeezed tighter, his struggle weakening. With a savage cry, I slammed his head against the floorboards until blood poured from his scalp.

Anderson thrashed with a burst of defiance. I caught his wrist, twisting, finding sick joy in the snap of bone that echoed, followed by his howl of pain.

Using his own momentum against him, I drove his body into the jagged glass scattered across the floor. Blood spattered. It was warm. Thick. An oddly comforting coating of my hands as he gurgled, his strength ebbing.

His blood stained my lips as I whispered into his ear, "You were never strong enough to stop me. None of you *pathetic little boys* are." I twisted his head sharply, ending it. Anderson crumpled beneath me, lifeless, a puddle of crimson spreading around in a dark halo.

I stumbled back, drenched in his blood, a sick satisfaction settling in my chest. My legs gave out, and I sprawled out next to his corpse. Time passed as I searched for the strength to get up. What seemed like hours later, I forced myself upright, the world spinning around me—blurred by the pounding in my skull and the searing pain in my thigh.

The streets of Royal Oaks blurred around me, dim firelight casting eerie shadows on the ruins. I leaned against a half-collapsed wall, gasping for air, before pushing off and forcing myself forward.

Home wasn't far. One more turn. Or maybe two. My mind fogged over, and for a second, I wasn't sure if I was heading in the right direction. But then I saw it—the old house where we were hunkered down in for the simulations.

Good. You made it.

I crumpled on the front porch with a dramatic thud. The door slammed open and Alexiares was there. He swooped me into his arms, cradling me as we passed under the threshold of the home and I made an ill-timed joke. He swelled, his expression shifting from alarm to fury as he took me in under the light of the living room.

"Amaia." His voice was sharp, snapping me to attention and focusing on his beautifully pissed face. "What the hell happened?"

"Ran into a problem," I managed, resting my head against his chest.

"A problem? Looks like a massacre," I heard Tomoe closing in as Alexiares set me onto the couch.

I made an attempt at a sigh. "He was a gusher."

Reina appeared behind him, her gaze darting from my face to the blood covering me. "Move," she ordered, brushing Alexiares aside as she crouched in front of me. Her magic prickled against my skin faintly as her hands hovered over my thigh.

"Bossy," I muttered, collapsing onto the couch with a heavy groan.

Alexiares crouched beside me, his expression sharp with worry. "You were attacked?"

"Anderson," I nodded. "And that's one way to put it."

"Tell me you got him back." His sharp jaw tightened, a muscle ticking in his cheek.

I huffed a tired laugh, gesturing vaguely at the blood staining my clothes. "Oh, I got him. He's not coming after anyone again."

His gaze dropped to my leg, where Reina hadn't gotten to it yet. "You're lucky you made it here."

"Yeah, well," I said, the corners of my lips twitching into something that wasn't quite a smile, "turns out I'm not easy to kill."

Reina's hands pressed against my thigh, warmth radiating as her magic worked its way through the torn muscle. "Hold still," she muttered, her tone clipped. "You've already lost enough blood."

"Feels like it," I murmured, my head tipping back against the couch. My vision swam, exhaustion pulling at me, but not before I caught Alexiares resident glare.

"Don't look at me like that," I mumbled. "If you've got a lecture, save it. I'm not up for it."

"Good," he snapped. "Because you wouldn't listen, anyway."

Reina shot him a glare without glancing up from my leg. "Enough yapping, dog. You're not helping."

I let their voices blur together. Their argument faded into the background as my body sagged further into the couch—the future that once seemed clear twisted into something darker, my dreams becoming a nightmare of what was to come.

CHAPTER
FORTY-SIX

AMAIA

"I was attacked last night. Won't get into names. Not into glorifying the actions of men," I said as I pushed open the double doors from what was once a kitchen and into the main dining room. "Their absence is loud enough."

One hundred souls stared back at me. I searched the room, waiting for someone, anyone, to react in a way that pissed me off. I was over this shit and it had only just begun. Generals and leaders of settlements alike mumbled at their tables, exchanging glances that ranged from confusion to anger. The angry ones gave me the slightest bit of comfort. Anger meant loyalty. They were the ones that would have my back, no matter what.

"Now, let's get this show on the road, shall we?" I strode to the middle of the room, dragging a wooden chair across the floor with an earsplitting screech before dropping into it. I crossed my legs, hands resting on my knees, and leaned back like I owned the place. Because, for all intents and purposes, I did.

"It's a bit of an understatement to say that the trust between territories at the moment is abysmal. Unfortunately for us, that doesn't bode well. If we cannot trust each other, then we as a unit are effectively useless. Each week will be split into one exercise and one drill—one to learn, one to test. Knowing our strengths is essential to maximizing damage and limiting loss. Week one, we'll assess strengths and weaknesses. Find them, exploit them, and understand how they play into the bigger picture."

"More on that later," Alexiares said, rising from his seat in the corner. He crossed the room, his hand settling on the back of my chair. "Week two, the focus is a personal favorite: defense so terrifying it doubles as offense."

A scoff broke through the tension, drawing my attention to San Jose's table. Bold of them to test me again. I zeroed in on their general, his posture betraying that he'd rather be anywhere else but here.

"No better instructor than the inventor themselves," their general muttered.

"That's right," I said, rising from my chair in one fluid motion, kicking out my leg to punctuate the movement. I clasped my hands behind my back and fixed him in his seat with a glare. "So shut up and listen."

Hunter cleared his throat, appearing at my side. "Y'all best pay attention because week three is where things get interesting. War simulations. You'll get an objective, a map, and be placed into units. And God willing, you'll learn how to keep each other alive. In a few weeks, it won't be a game anymore. We hit the camps before engaging with Covert directly."

"Why?" a voice called from somewhere in the crowd, hidden among the bodies packed into the hot, stuffy room.

"Classified." Alexiares cracked a smirk.

I circled them like sharks. Eyeing those who hadn't shown me nearly enough damn respect. It was getting to the point where I'd have to resort to more extreme measures, something I wasn't exactly keen on doing. Respect was earned. I wholeheartedly believed that, but fuck, what else would it take?

The sun glistened through the cracked and shattered windows of the diner. Nearly noon, give or take an hour or two. Fresh air never seemed more exciting than being stuck in the center of a room filled with 80 percent men. I aimed to change that.

If these sacks of balls thought they could outlast me, they'd learn otherwise soon enough. The diversity needed to accomplish this mission was essential to my plans. We could only rebuild what we stood to lose through open-minded individuals. Simply put, half of the men here were old dogs that refused to learn new tricks.

"It serves to benefit our cause, soldier. Your job is to follow orders, not question them." I hated saying the words. I'd never dream of uttering them to *my own* troops. Which, technically, there were now, whether they were happy about that fact or not.

"With all due respect, ma'am, you haven't earned the trust that entails yet," the general from Casper reasoned.

"Respect noted, request denied." I glared in his direction. They'd been reasonable thus far. There was no reason to take his words at anything other than face value.

He nodded his head in subtle submission. "Ma'am."

"Any more questions?" I said, glancing at the others who'd remained quiet since I'd walked into the must smelling room. "None. Fantastic. Get some food. Hit times at thirteen-hundred. Wear something comfortable and, oh, don't be late. All Generals, stay, we have much to discuss."

The room cleared out with a sense of urgency that immediately brought me a smidgen of joy. *And so it all begins.*

With the room cleared, Alexiares stood front and center, demanding their attention as he circled back to the initial question. The reason the camps were our first priority. "Weapons, that's what's at the camps." He stated, his tone making it clear he thought it was beyond debate.

Serenity stared him down in such a way that even Alexiares could not ignore. One that said his words should be reconsidered and fast.

Hunter's voice boomed across the room, recovering for him. "People who happen to be weapons."

PITIFUL. ABSOLUTELY FUCKING PATHETIC. THE DRILLS I RAN WERE beyond basic. Entry-level shit my soldiers warm up to.

We were going to lose this war, and we were going to lose *badly* if we didn't get our shit together.

Hunter, Alexiares, and I sat at a table, dragged into the center of what was once Royal Oaks City Hall, now our official 'war room.' We sat there, staring at them blankly as they watched us, staring back, picture perfect models of various states of flustered, agitated, bored, and amused.

"Well, that was a sad display of complete incompetence," I declared after a few passing moments of achingly awkward silence.

"General Harper," Alexiares called out. He watched in vulture-like fashion as the general of Aberdeen tensed at the sound of his name caught in the *Bloodhound's* mouth. "Did I hear you right when you said the proposed course of action, training wise, was, and I quote, 'fucking reckless and a waste of time.'"

"I believe the words 'dumb bitch' were uttered about our beloved overlord as well," Finley chimed in, her voice as grating as nails on a chalkboard, icy eyes dancing with mischief. "Oops. Sorry, I made it worse, didn't I?"

The sound of bodies turning toward Finley was audible, the attention she was so desperate for all hers. I rolled my eyes, my gaze still stuck on Harper. "Consider me all ears then—anyone else have any strong feelings about my tactics?"

Radio silence. Music to my fucking ears because, quite frankly, I'd had enough of the bullshit. "Didn't think so. Harper, I'm going to choose to ignore what any other general here would deem insubordinate and give you another opportunity to shut your mouth."

Hunter's chuckle eerily resembled his twin's, a sound that sent a pang twitching through my hardly healed heart. Only the choked laugh of Isabella Everhart brought me back to focus.

"Now, let's address the obvious." I leaned forward, elbows on the table, my hands clasped together. I swept my gaze across the room. "You're not ready. Not for this. Not even close. What I saw out there wasn't just embarrassing, it was dangerous. For you, for your soldiers, for anyone who's counting on us to survive."

Harper's jaw tightened, but he said nothing, his glare fixed on the table in front of him.

"Hunter," I said, gesturing to him without breaking my stare at the others. "What do you think the survival rate would be if this group went into the field right now?"

Hunter rubbed the back of his neck, granting them the courtesy of pretending to think about it. "Fifteen percent. Maybe."

"Fifteen percent," I echoed, letting the number hang in the air, then clucked my tongue. "That's a death sentence for anyone who marches with you. Unacceptable. Harper—you seem to think you're the smartest guy in the room—what exactly would you suggest instead of my 'reckless and wasteful tactics?'"

Harper finally looked up, his gray eyes narrowed. "I'd suggest training them on practical scenarios. Real situations they'll face. Not this abstract crap you're pulling from whatever history book you worship."

I raised an eyebrow. "It's Napoleon's, but I digress. Practical scenarios? Like what? Taking the same three positions over and over again while the enemy picks us off because we're predictable?

Or better yet, splitting into smaller groups like in the last war and let them overwhelm us one by one?"

His silence was answer enough.

"That's what I thought," I said flatly. "What you don't seem to grasp, Harper, is that our enemy isn't playing by any rules. They're unpredictable, and if you can't learn to think on your feet, you're already dead."

Alexiares leaned back in his chair, legs spread and arms crossed, a faint smirk tugging at the corner of his lips. "Let me put it in terms you'll understand, Harper. Amaia's tactics aren't reckless—they're adaptive."

Finley's laugh rang out again, sharp and cutting. "God, this is better than the soap operas my mother used to watch. You should've stayed quiet, Harper."

Hunter shot her a warning glare. She mimed zipping her lips, though the grin never left her face.

"This isn't about you or your shitty little settlement, General," I said, leaning forward again to recapture their attention. "This is about survival. You don't have to like me, or my methods, but you will respect me. That's a nonnegotiable, I'm afraid—or I'll find someone else who can lead your people into battle."

The tension in the room was palpable. Hunter stepped forward, his hands settling on his belt buckle. "You're sitting here with your feathers all ruffled like this is optional. Hate to break it to ya, but it ain't. If you're not ready to adapt, you might as well lay down and quit now. This war won't stop to let you catch your breath. So, saddle the hell up or step aside, 'cause we've got work to do."

"Now," I continued, now that the room had sucked into his little speech. "Lucky for you all, our battle plans are built on hitting with our strong points. We don't hit hard once or twice, we keep applying pressure and we don't let them up for air."

"There will be heavy losses across the board," Hunter said, pushing from his seat and standing at my side, arms crossed. "It's important to prepare ourselves for that."

When he spoke, everyone listened. Their eyes homed in on his mouth, waiting patiently to see what would come out next, like he was their messiah or something. *Whatever.*

As long as they were willing to answer to someone who was wholeheartedly on my side—it wasn't a competition. With Adelaide safely tucked away at Monterey Compound, he would never be a danger to my people, to the cause.

"With our technological advances, the extraordinary gifts we're now aware of and prepared to utilize, plus the support of St. Cloud," I added reluctantly, much to my dismay and Finley's overexaggerated joy. "There is the potential that once we clear Covert's borders and see the other side, that we may have the advantage."

"That's on the account that we have what it takes to make it that far," Hunter stated. Not to me, but to others. He'd been thoroughly unimpressed by what he'd seen.

The three of us had gone through the drills with them. In my opinion, the *proper* way to lead was from the front. If I wasn't capable of performing at the same levels as the soldiers beneath me, then who the hell was I to hold such expectations? No. We had to be stronger, faster, *smarter*. An example for them all, a symbol they aspired to live up to.

"And that only works if we train," I added, now on my feet right next to him, a unified front. "*Together.* As one. One unit, one compound. We can go face Ronan now. That seems to be the response you're all itching to hear, which makes sense to *you*, but I'm telling you now, if we do that, we will lose."

"What happens once we're in?" Millie asked, curiosity lining tan features. "Keep going till we reach the capitol?"

A quiet curse slipped out. The hope was that no one would bring this up, at least not yet. I hadn't had the chance to tell the people I loved about my plans. They wouldn't be happy about them and I wouldn't blame them. If it was them in my shoes, I'd riot.

"We distract Ronan while evacuating as many innocent civilians as we can to The Outskirts," I said, answering Millie's question without saying too much. This would have to be enough for now.

"Evacuate?" Claes, the mayor of Casper, questioned, leaning forward, hands folded in front of him as he rested against the wobbling table. "For what reason?"

I gave a tight-lipped, awkward half-smile, more grimace than grin, "We're hitting the capitol. Hard."

"You're staging a coup," Finley exclaimed, not alarmed, but merely putting the pieces together.

"I am."

"With who to replace his stead? You?" General Harper released a laugh that old me would have lunged across the room and slapped the shit out of him for. Unfortunately, I no longer had the leeway to get away with such actions. But damn, did I wish I could let old me at him.

"Is there something humorous about the statement?" I arched my brow, forcing myself to hold a steady, calm voice.

"The only thing humorous here is the amount of men in the room still questioning your authority while taking orders from you within the same breath." Serenity said, in an odd moment of support. It silenced him, if only temporarily, still felt like a small win.

"We can discuss who is best suited to accommodate the needs of the many when we're closer to winning this thing, yes?" I surmised.

Not so much of a suggestion as an end to the conversation. No one argued, though not a single soul appeared happy about it, including our closer allies. *Lucky me.* At least they'd realized they needed me to even make it that far.

The expressions on Harper and those aligned with Aberdeen hinted a wet day dream on my future assassination. They were vocal, loud, but not stupid. They'd bide their time, use me for all they could, and once I served their purpose … it was clear they had no regards for what happened to me after this was all said and done.

Thank you to the powers that may be. At least no one had questioned the distraction portion of my plan. My family knew the basics, but not the part they'd hate the most.

"You can't do that."

Fucking mother of Jesus himself. These people … I didn't have the energy to replace yet another leader, or in this case, General of San Jose. But if it came to that? Fine. I'd do it. We no longer had the privilege of fighting a war with honor and tact to beat someone like Ronan Moore and his sycophants.

"Try and stop me," I said with a daring tilt of my head.

The scrawny man scoffed, tossing a hand in the air as if my words were nothing but noise. "Yeah, right."

I offered him no more than a simple shrug before crossing the room, weaving through the mess of chairs. The room buzzed with tension as I grabbed him by the arm and yanked him to his feet.

"If only this lesson had been taught already." Moe slid into the room, half-laughing. Alexiares leaned back against the wall, one hand holding the door open for her and Reina to slide in, the other in his pocket, a ghost of a smile playing on his lips.

Their general couldn't have been more than a few years my senior. He stammered, trying to find a way out, but there was none. "I want you to kneel," I said, my voice low, commanding.

"Excuse me?" he managed, continuing on with his bravado even though I could feel him shaking beneath my grip.

Before I could go further, Reina's sharp tone sliced through the room. A wave of calm slammed into me. She could sense the others' reactions. I needed to keep my calm—for now. "Amaia. Enough."

I dropped the collar of his shirt with an animalistic growl, still holding his stare with the promise of more to come. "I won't bash your fucking face in for insubordination if you kneel. We've been through this once—ask my soldiers how many times I've repeated my orders to them."

There were a handful of my top soldiers present, here to set an example for the others, Miller of course, front and center. The room sat in stunned silence as they shifted to attention without need for the command. "None, ma'am," they said in unison.

"Well, would you look at that?" I smoothed out my clothes, regaining my composure with the help of Reina's magic, warming me in an empathetic hug. "You cannot repeat yourself in the heat of battle without risking the life of the person fighting next to you. I won't have that on my head. Now bow."

His expression wavered, caught between hesitation and seething anger. A blip of joy grew into something ravenous as I watched him teeter on the edge of action.

"Allow me to restate myself one final time. This only works if there is one," I stated, weighing the pros and cons of kicking him down to his knees, ultimately deciding the impact of him doing it on his own would be all the more satisfying. "ONE. Not several. Not ten. Certainly not over forty. But one general. One rallying point. One leader. That person is me. So kneel, bow, whatever you want to call it, but bend. Your fucking. Knee."

Alexiares wandered to the other side of him. The threat was subtle, but clear. A glimmer of pride shining in his eyes. "Now."

"Can you please just do it already so we can get this whole war thing over with?" Finley drawled from her side of the stark, sterile room. "I miss my boyfriend. I'm ready to go home."

Alexiares damn near snorted and met my humored stare. "Which one?"

"All of them." Finley snapped, her tone no longer teasing, but reminiscent of the woman who tortured me for days in St. Cloud.

Working with her went against everything I believed in. She was vile and had zero redeeming qualities outside of her intelligence. If I could suck it out of her brain and implant it into Reina's, the world would be better for it. Oddly enough, that invention hadn't been one of her successful endeavors, according to Alexiares.

His knees hit the ground with a pleasant, orgasmic thud. I crossed my arms across my chest, my foot extending to push him down to his ass. "Lieutenant's name?"

He glanced up at me from the floor, eyes narrowed, the snarl on his ugly face menacing. "Rossi."

I caught sight of Caleb at the door. He hovered, waiting, watching, doing his best to notice anyone else in the room who was a bit too shifty for our taste. "Caleb." I tossed my head.

He made his way out, the thud of the door sounding more like thunder than the soft close it was. I sighed. "General Rossi has a nice ring to it, I think." I took my foot off his chest, releasing him from his spot of shame. "Get up, *Lieutenant*. I won't have this discussion with you again."

CHAPTER FORTY-SEVEN

REINA

"Still holding your breath when you aim?"

I glanced up at my brother with a smile, keeping my eyes on him as I fired away. "Still making dumb comments when I'm busy outperforming you?"

He whistled, leaning casually against the post, his hands shoved in his pockets. "Cocky as ever."

I already knew I hit the bullseye. Of course I did. I was Reina Adelaide Moore. Honestly, the shocked mumbles and pangs of fear coming from the surrounding soldiers were a bit unnecessary. What'd they think I was gonna do, miss?

"Real guns?"

The question came from somewhere behind me. No way was I getting in his line. Alexiares was a nightmare when it came to teaching, well, among many other things, that made him scary.

Creaking wooden carts and the rhythmic clatter of shifting metal filled the air as a group rolled in crates brimming with weapons. Through the slats, I caught glimpses of polished steel and intricate carvings—Tomás's unmistakable craftsmanship. He was a dang genius and there was a lot I could learn from him. The way his designs didn't suffer from the beauty he etched along the sides. It all fed into magic enhancements that brought additional lethal components to play. *Those* were for later.

"Would you prefer us to assess you with water guns?" Alexiares's voice cut through the murmurs. "Either set your piece up or get the fuck out of my line."

Hard ass. I laughed quietly, slinging my bow over my shoulder and grabbing Hunter's arm to pull him closer to the action. The distinct tang of iron and the earthy scent of sawdust surrounded us as we weaved through the gathered soldiers. Alexiares came into view, arms crossed as he stood there menacingly, Amaia at his side, face set with boredom.

"Then what?" his buddy asked, his tone teasing, but he kept his stare warily on Alexi. "Paintball style exercises?"

Amaia's grin sharpened. She pushed off the fence of our little makeshift range with the easy grace of someone who had already won the argument before it started. Oh boy, I knew where this was going. Her agitation was evident from here, no magic necessary.

"They don't say we got the best troops for nothing," I stepped in, proud enough for us all. "Don't worry though, the simulations don't use weapons with lethal force but the weight and balance of it al—"

The soldiers gave me a once over and turned toward each other with a burst of laughter. I scoffed, jaw on the ground as they brushed past me, talking like I wasn't right there and couldn't hear.

"Rude." I shook my head. "Do you think it was the outfit?" I muttered to Hunter, re-tucking my tank top into my rolled-up shorts, focused on something that hardly mattered.

"I think it was a lot of things, Sis," Hunter said with a light chuckle.

Amaia's gaze shifted across the crowded field as she approached, sharp yet softened when it met mine. I loved seeing her this way. All in charge and stuff. 'General mode' in all her glory. Soldiers moved quickly when she passed, offering quick salutes or nodding in acknowledgment.

"Doesn't matter what they think—half of them are still too scared to be on a squad with you after whatever the hell you pulled in the north. Besides, I can say with absolute confidence that you could outshoot them all. Speaking of which, still set on being a combat medic?" Amaia said, her voice steady, reassuring as the clattering of weaponry and the crackling magic continued behind us.

I shot a wary glance at Hunter, already bracing for his objection.

"Reina is an adult. She can assist where she pleases," Amaia added before he could intervene over the sounds of magic and metal. The sharp *whoosh* of a magic-infused arrow hit its target behind her, the commotion making me feel small, not helped by the thud of boots stomping on the ground around us.

"She's a healer, not a soldier." Hunter's voice cut through the noise, his tone firm. "Like hell she's seeing any action that's outside of a surgical tent."

"I'll go where I'm needed. Thank you very much," I shot back, heat rising in my chest, though I knew better than to expect anything other than support from him. He may protest the hell out of a situation, but he'd never hold me back from doing something once I had my mind made up. Hunter had been my main advocate for leaving the ranch and going to college.

"She's already seen combat. Why do you think she's here?" Amaia said matter-of-factly.

Hunter snorted. "Emotional support."

"Sexist much?" I shot him a glare.

The thrum of elemental power surged behind us. Air and earth elementals worked together, partnering up and calling on their power as they moved around rocks and earth from the ground, hovering them with trained efficiency.

"I'm your brother," he said dismissively.

"That doesn't make your statement any less shitty," Amaia interjected, her eyes narrowing in amusement. She remained entirely unfazed as a wave of soldiers brushed against us in the process of changing stations.

"All I'm saying is, I mean it in an overprotective brother way not—" Hunter sighed, his shoulders slumped in defeat. "Ya know what? Screw it. What do you need from her, and how can I help her prepare?"

"Music to my ears," I said, grinning as excitement bubbled up in my chest. Aerial drills began, sending gusts of wind swirling above our heads. My hair flew into my eyes, blinding me and catching in my mouth.

"Ramona isn't here to train the cavalry since they're needed on patrol now. That leaves Marco, Hayfield, and Wells to assess the others *and* run the exercises."

"But they're idiots," I mumbled in confusion, still fussing with my hair. *Okay, the Katniss braid was a bad call.*

The three were good at doing their job, but their job was to follow orders, not instruct or call any fundamental shots. Certainly didn't possess the brain power it took to help other riders figure out or overcome any hiccups.

"Exactly." Amaia pursed her lips, a knowing glint in her eye.

It hit me then. My heart thudded against my ribs at the realization of what she was getting at. "You want me to lead an impromptu cavalry?"

"She's not a rider," Hunter protested immediately, his eyes flicking to the mounted units performing maneuvers across the field.

The sound of hooves pounding the earth, the low whine of horses … and half of their riders struggled to stay on while following Hayfield and Wells movements. Marco stood on the side yelling out commands, red with frustration as he tossed his hat onto the ground.

"Sorry, you keep speaking for Reina when I'm talking directly to her." All patience in Amaia's tone had disappeared. She stood tall once more, the relaxed posture no longer present. A flash of blue light from a nearby combat magic duel illuminated her face. "Either stand here as a supportive, proud brother and shut up or get lost."

I bit my lip, doubt creeping in. "He's right. Seth and Hunter were always the better riders. Hunter competed. He can probably help 'em better than I can."

"If I thought that was the best option, I'd have asked him," Amaia said firmly, leveling her stare. A heavy *thud* shook the ground, emphasizing her point as two horses took off … without their riders. "I asked *you*."

"Are you askin' as my friend or my general?"

"As your general. But as your *friend*, I'll have you know I'm asking because I've seen you ride. You may not be your brother, but you're still better than half the riders these ingrates have. And more importantly, you have the heart to get them to commit to believe in themselves. Millie will probably lead the push to Covert."

"Ramona?" I asked, even though we all knew she wasn't here.

"Will receive orders to protect our borders when we move east. She is irrelevant to this conversation both now and in the future."

A warmth spread through me as her words sank in. I straightened, meeting her gaze with a smile wide enough it dang near hurt my cheeks. "I won't let you down."

"You never do." Amaia turned, already walking away. "Skip the combat assessments to run barrel drills with them. But if you want back on my field, I want you training on the mat morning and night. Don't embarrass me."

Excitement fizzed in my chest, and I couldn't help the little hop and clap that escaped.

Hunter groaned. "Does she always scheme on her own and then drop bombs on y'all like that?"

"Yeah, pretty much," I admitted, still grinning ear to ear, the sounds of magic and battle melding into the background like a war symphony.

"And how often does that usually work out for her?"

"Annoyingly," I said, switching the shoulder of my bow. "All the time."

A messenger approached Hunter, his face tense as he relayed the news that his people had finally arrived.

"I need to talk to them before they interact with the others," he said, squeezing my hand before walking off, his footsteps swallowed by the noise around us.

I watched him go, the familiar ache pressing at my chest. Seth should've been here with us. That was all he ever wanted—just to stand side by side with us. If only things had been different. If only Seth had known Hunter was still alive … But he had known. That was the whole point.

DAY ONE OF ASSESSMENTS AND MY LEGS ACHED LIKE NO OTHER, MY back protesting every movement, and my hands were a reddened raw mess from hours of drills. There'd been no time to mend myself in the blur of chaos. Soldiers bustled around me, hauling gear back to where it couldn't be touched by weather conditions, while others sparred, getting in extra sessions or showing off.

I tended to my bow, trying to ignore the noise, lingering far beyond what was expected of me. Going home right now didn't excite the way that it should. Maybe because it wasn't really home at all, just a place to sleep for the next few weeks. Old me would've loved having my family all together under one roof—but I wasn't old me anymore and a lot had changed.

"You've been avoiding me."

I kept my eyes on my bow, forcing my voice to stay even and not give me away. "It's been a busy day, that's all."

Jessa's boots crunched closer. I knew what she would say before she even spoke. "This thing with the cavalry—Amaia shouldn't have put you in that position."

Again with this. Except she wasn't Hunter—Jessa would never support what I was doing, no matter how much I wanted it. "Amaia is my general. She can ask me whatever the heck she wants." I sighed, finally turning to face her.

Her sandy blonde hair was pulled taut in a ponytail, the sun having kissed her cheeks. *God, she's so beautiful.* Almost enough to distract from the fact that she was a healthy reminder that not all light is good.

"Yeah, she can. That doesn't mean you have to say yes. That's the beauty of you being a medic and not a soldier," Jessa snapped.

I moved my hand in a mocking motion, mimicking the words she was saying. "Whatever, Jessa." Her words struck hard, igniting a surge of anger in my chest.

I was beyond done arguing with her. That's all everything was with her now. No such thing as a pleasant conversation between us, even ones that started off tender, with good intent, ended with me walking away. I hated being an angry person, and that's all I was these days. *Especially* in her presence.

"And you know what? I can do both, *actually*," I said, brushing past her then whipping back around, having more to say than I originally intended. "Hello? What do you think a combat medic does in the first place? The only difference now is I'll be doing it from the top of my mare. Amaia trusts me—something you couldn't seem to do in the first place."

Her expression flickered with guilt for a moment before her ocean eyes hardened again. It didn't matter; it lingered beneath the surface, just waiting to break free. "That's not fair."

I scoffed, taking out my braid and ruffling through my hair. "Neither is lying to someone who cares about you. But life's not fair so, cry me a freaking river."

We were attracting attention now. *Great.* Any respect I'd gained these last few hours was officially out the window thanks to my … my what? My girlfriend? We barely functioned as roommates. I'd wanted to fix this—at first. Now I realized it wasn't my thing to fix and trying to 'fix' everything that was out of my control had resulted in a dead brother, so maybe I should stop.

"We aren't doing this again. I'm not going there with you, not right now. This is war, Reina. It's serious." Jessa took a step closer, lowering her voice. We stood eye level with each other, locked in a quarrel only lovers could fight with merely just the eyes. "Now isn't the time to worry about proving yourself to her. Or anyone, for that matter. It's about doing what it takes to make sure you stay alive."

"You think I don't know that?" I gestured to the swirl of energy around us—the sparring soldiers, the endless row of weapons, the hum of magic that never seemed to face. "This is what staying alive looks like, Jessa. Fighting, training, stepping up to do what's right for the group when no one else can or will."

"Even if it kills you?" she asked, her raspy voice cracking slightly, that edge of vulnerability cutting through her frustration.

No faith. She has *never* had any faith in me. And it didn't help that I could feel it—every spike of doubt, every sharp pulse of frustration.

I opened my mouth to argue, hesitating because right now wasn't the time or the place, and in that pause, I caught movement out the corner of my eyes. Millie. She stood across the field near the cavalry's makeshift stables. Her hands rested against her thick, muscular thighs as she buckled over. The sweet song of her laughter carried over the rest of the noise. She leaned back up against a post, talking animatedly with another rider. Her ease in all this mess was a knife twisted in my gut. I didn't want to think about her, about that night. Right now probably wasn't the time to acknowledge any feelings that lingered from a brief dalliance.

Jessa followed my gaze, her eyes narrowing when she saw Millie. "Of course—your new 'captain.'"

"Don't," I whispered, not having the energy to run back through this fight either.

Her laugh was bitter, cutting through my ears like a splintered piece of wood. "Don't what? Say what we're both thinking."

I turned fully to her, "Our problems have nothing to do with Millie. Aren't you tired, Jessa? This isn't what it used to be. When's the last time you can honestly say we got through the day without arguing? It's not *fun* anymore, and it hasn't been in a long time."

Jessa's face fell as she stepped closer, the space between us now limited to a shared bubble of oxygen. "Of course it isn't. How can it be when you're throwing yourself into every role Amaia gives you, pretending like you're fine, pretending like we're fine—"

"Stop," I said, my voice firm, though it wavered under the pressure. "Just stop. I'm exhausted. I'm not doing anything I don't want to do of my own free will. None of this is a job for me. I want to help my friends, *my family*."

Jessa's expression softened, but the tension didn't leave her body. "Reina, you're spreading yourself too thin. And if you're doing it to avoid dealing with us, then I—"

"There *is* no us," I snapped, my voice rising despite the soldiers milling around us. Millie and the rider turned their heads, curiosity flickering in their gazes, but I didn't care. "Not really and you know what? Maybe there never was. You made sure of that the second you decided to spy for my father."

Her face drained of color, lips parting like she might protest. But then her shoulders lowered, quiet acceptance settling in. I knew denial when I saw it. I *was* denial for the last four years. "You don't trust me. I get it. But I'm here because I want to help. I want to make this right between us."

I shook my head, the ache in my chest too heavy to ignore. "Between *us*? No, Jessa, that's the problem. The difference between you and me and why this will *never* work no matter how much I want it to—I'm here for my family, for *me*. You're here for me because it's convenient to the cause and Amaia's conditions on the grounds that it was this or execution. Because Riley's spy network needs the intel and you're mapping borders. You're a useful piece on the chessboard for the others."

The words were callous—cruel, even. Unnatural coming from my mouth. But they were the first honest ones I'd spoken to her in months, and now that they were out, I couldn't bring myself to stop. Kindness was already scarce in this world, and I refused to be the one to spread more venom. Though the urge to say more tugged at me, I chose mercy instead.

I told myself I meant them. That I wanted this to be the end of whatever thread still tethered us together. Maybe, one day, I'd regret it. Maybe, one day, I'd want to make things right. But not now. Not here. Not during the simulations.

Jessa didn't say anything else. She stood there, her gaze flicking between me and Millie one last time before she turned and walked away. The weight in my chest didn't ease as I watched her go. If anything, it settled deeper, a stone sinking into dark water.

I turned back to my bow, my fingers trembling as I gripped the smooth wood. Tomorrow was another day, another fight. But this fight—the one I'd been fighting for a while, maybe it was finally over. At least, that's what I told myself.

CHAPTER
FORTY-EIGHT

REINA

*F*ocus. But it was really hard to do that over the stench of damp earth and decay, the kind that clung to the air after years of neglect, when nature took over for good. Not to mention I was hot, sweaty, and these stupid socks Amaia let me borrow were super itchy. I tossed my head back, staring up at the dull gray sky. To be honest, it matched the mood of this horribly paired group as we trudged through the overgrown streets of Royal Oaks. *Be down for the cause, I said. It'll be fun I said.* It wasn't—and everyone desperately needed a bath. I adjusted the strap of my med pack near the neck of my mare, beyond irritated with the idiots arguing behind me.

"We should be heading east, not wasting time here," a soldier from Lincoln barked; his voice grated against my eardrums rougher than sandpaper.

I exhaled in frustration, whipping Nala around. "Unless you've got a compass hidden in that big poofy hair of yours somewhere, I'd suggest you stop questioning everything Isabella—"

"General Everhart." She cleared her throat with an appreciative smile.

"*General Everhart.* Let her do her job so we can eat something other than the crappy, wilted lettuce you've managed to grow in the last eight hours. I swear on everything I love, if we don't, it's going to be a long, terrible night for you if I go to sleep hungry."

He grumbled in response, shooting a silent plea for help toward Hunter, who walked next to my horse near the reigns. Imagine, thinking *my brother* would—well. Hunter ignored him, his eyes remained on Isabella, effectively the general of our unit.

"Tracks lead this way," she said, pointing toward a maze of dense underbrush and collapsed buildings. "Supplies should be close."

This survival drill had been disastrous, and it wasn't even officially the full twenty-four hours yet. It'd taken approximately all of thirty seconds for everyone to start arguing once we'd been dropped at base. Which was not what I expected by the way—they'd dragged us out of bed at three a.m., told us to get dressed, assigned us a number and told us we had twenty minutes to find our home base before the games commenced. If this was how territory survival drills would go, I didn't want to even think about what war simulations had in store.

When we'd finally decided who was assigned where, every protein supply box in our territory had been stolen, which meant we had to go fight and steal someone else's. At least we'd managed shelter. Apparently part of survival training was training as if your magic was useless. It made sense, I guess. If you were burning dangerously low to your reserve or got drugged some kind of way, you had to know how to take care of yourself. Once every four hours were granted five minutes of free magic—to be used once, in a way that best benefits the group. Sometimes I seriously hated how thorough Amaia was in her planning.

The unit spread out, and I groaned. Our objective was teamwork just as much as it was to survive, yet they all wandered off in their own groups, not a desire to work together in sight.

"Let it be, Sis," Hunter said, patting Nala on the neck and guiding us down our own path.

I shook my head, adjusting my bow over my shoulder. "You'd think she'd at least try to force them to work together."

"Why would you ever think that?" Hunter questioned, like I was silly for optimism. "Her job is to keep them alive and right now, they're more likely to kill each other. When shit hits the fan, they'll learn."

He spoke with such certainty. Then it dawned on me, Hunter had lived a whole life without me at this point. I knew Hunter, my brother, but I didn't know Hunter of Transient Nation. Survival wasn't exactly easy out there for several reasons.

"Hey! They found something!" a Portland soldier called, pointing at the group from Topeka.

And then, the arguing began. Hunter was the first to reach the crowd as Portland and Redding worked to pry the lid open, shoving Topeka's soldiers in the process.

"This is ours," a woman declared, stepping forward. "We found it. If there's any left we'll give you the scraps when we're done."

"Excuse me?" snapped another female soldier from Madison. "We wouldn't have made it here without *my* general."

"Look around, she's not here," the Topeka soldier said.

As if that made a difference. It didn't matter how we got here or who found what, if we couldn't learn to share now when it didn't matter then it'd be a complete and total disaster out on the battlefield.

"You want to fight, Fiona?" the woman from Madison stepped forward. "Cuz I'd love the opportunity to shut you up myself."

"Oh shit. Dude, they're gonna chick fight."

I rolled my eyes at all of them—especially the nuisance from Redding, whose ridiculous, childish statement was the last thing I had patience for. I'd seriously had enough. And I was starving.

Hunter could step in anytime now. But instead, he simply watched me.

Oh. Right.

If Isabella wasn't around, the next highest-ranking officer was supposed to step in. Millie had been assigned to another unit for the exercise, which meant that should be Hunter… except—wait, *crud*. Right now, it was me. Because I was the dunce on the horse, acting as Lead Rider instead of a medic.

"Enough!" My voice cut through the growing tension of the group, others had wandered over, picking sides which had somehow turned into Salem Territory versus The Expanse. "Stop acting like children and figure out how we're carrying this back to base. Because that's where *all* of this is going, back to base to be divided equally. You hear me or do I need to remind y'all that sharing isn't just caring, it's survival. You want to argue? Do it at base."

They all stared at me blankly, blinking in shock. "My goodness, do I need to clap my hands? Let's go, people, load it up!"

The tension diffused with the added thump of Nala's hoof emphasizing our urgency against the pavement. Soldiers removed their packs, filling them to the brim with enough protein to feed our entire unit.

MY EYES SCANNED THE OVERGROWN STREETS, DOING MY BEST TO note every broken window and rusted-out car that made a solid hiding space. Royal Oaks had an eerie way of making one feel watched. Heightened emotions thickened the air, the others suppressing down their angst for now.

Hunter walked in front of Nala, his hand on the reins. He kept the Portland soldier at his side and by proxy, my side. She was the primary antagonist for the last twenty minute trek back. I ignored her as she muttered something under her breath—loud enough for me to hear, quiet enough to not make out exactly *what* was said.

"I see you're still good at bossin' people around," Hunter teased.

"Real easy when you spent your whole life corralling dumb, dumber, and dumbest."

Hunter was quiet for a moment before saying, "I mean it. You're a natural."

"This is nice. I'm glad we somehow ended up on the same team." I winked at him, knowing exactly what Amaia and he had done. "I keep expecting you to disappear again."

His expression tightened, guilt flashing across his face, merely a mirror of my own. "Reina—"

"We don't have to talk about it," I interrupted, suddenly no longer interested in having this conversation. It was too … painful. I averted my eyes, locking onto the road in front of me. "Not now."

"If you really don't want to, then we don't have to. But you should know, even if this war wasn't happening, I would have come to find you the second I heard you were alive."

Movement caught my eye up ahead. "Stick together!" I called over my shoulder. No one bothered to answer me. *Typical.*

Isabella held up a hand, signaling the front of the line to stop. A shout exploded out of nowhere, too fast for my mind to fully grasp.

"Move! It's an ambush!"

Chaos swallowed us whole. Because why bother to hold the line when you could forget all of your training and try to outrun the person next to you. *Jesus Christ*. Figures emerged from the buildings yards away. A bolt flew by, the gust of wind from its passage leaving a sting on my cheek. I yanked Nala to the side with a yelp, trying to find cover in the chaos but there wasn't much to work with.

"They're from Salt Lake and Denver," someone called out behind me.

"Does it matter?" I said, "At least they're working as a team!"

Whipping Nala around, I caught sight of Miss Portland tumbling to the ground. Her hand flew to her ankle as she sprawled out in the open and released a cry of agony. *Ouch. Achilles.* "Stay here," I barked at Hunter who was busy knocking his own arrow and firing into the shadows.

Drills and simulations would use nonlethal force—that meant anything that wouldn't kill you was fair game. Kicking Nala hard, I bolted toward our downed soldier. The mare's hooves pounded against the cracked asphalt as I leaned forward. Every nerve in my body screamed, not accustomed to riding as much as I had all week, but the show had to carry on, right?

"Come on!" I reached the Portland soldier and slid off the saddle, a move that was muscle memory from my childhood. She was pale and cursing like her life depended on it. "You're fine. Get on already."

She blinked up at me. "What—"

"Get on Nala, *now*! In case you haven't noticed, we're being shot at by a lot of people and I can honestly say, not a fan."

"You talk too much."

"I know, now up we go." The soldier groaned as I hooked an arm under hers, practically hauling her upright.

It was a serious effort to get her onto Nala's back, her injured leg dragging uselessly as I shoved her into position. Nala danced nervously under the added weight, tossing her head as though to object.

"Oh, get used to it with this group, girl," I muttered, giving her a firm pat on the neck. "Go!" I slapped her flank, and she bolted.

We didn't make it fifty feet before something struck me hard, a rubber bullet slamming into my ribs and sending me flying off balance. I hit the ground with a sickening crack, the impact reverberating down my spine. For a moment, I couldn't breathe. No air, no control, just painful gasps and garbled noises leaving my lips as I clawed at the asphalt.

"Reina!"

Hunter's voice cut through the haze. A second later, he dropped onto the ground next to me. He kept his cool, face neutral like this was a normal Tuesday as he examined me. I was too scared to move.

"What the hell was that? Huh?" he hissed, running his hands through what were inevitably badly bruised ribs.

"Saving someone," I managed to gasp. "You should try it sometime."

"You mean like right now?" He huffed a laugh and braced me for impact.

His hands moved quickly, and his magic flared—a sharp burst of warmth and pain as he reset my shoulder. I clenched my jaw, swallowing the scream threatening to break free. Relief flooded me seconds later, the pain easing into a dull ache.

Footsteps echoed too close for comfort. My instincts screamed to move. I reached for the knife at my thigh, my arrows stuck at my back and completely useless, but Hunter stayed still, unconcerned.

Isabella's sharp commands rang out. "Form up! Push forward!"

The rest of the group surged ahead in a wave and I searched for Nala and the woman from Portland. They sat behind a dumpster, Portland passed out on top from the pain, about to glide right off. I sat up and pushed Hunter away, ignoring his cries after me. She fell into my grasp and we both crumbled to the ground. Albeit softer than the fate would have faced had I not gotten to her when

I did. With the cover of the dumpster and the rest of the group between us and the other unit attacking, it left me enough time to heal her up.

I'd learned how to treat wounds less gruesome than this during the last war. There was a technique to it—just enough to get them walking, but not enough to heal them completely. Triage and stabilization were the goals. You needed to leave enough work for proper treatment back at the med tent. It was a delicate balance, like putting a patient on bypass in *The Before*.

Her eyes fluttered as she came back to consciousness. She took me in, then groaned, rolling her eyes and pushing herself up. Hands as pale as mine shook as she touched her forehead.

"You can save the thank you for later, we should get out of here while we can." I helped her back onto the horse. "Hold tighter this time," I ordered, swinging up behind her in one fluid motion. My bow was in my hands before we'd even fully settled, the string taut as I knocked an arrow.

The battlefield blurred around us, smoke and dust folding into a singular focus: survival. I leaned into Nala's movements, letting her instincts guide us. The first arrow flew, striking a soldier square in the shoulder and spinning him into the dirt.

Another enemy stepped into our path. Without hesitation, I drew and released, the arrow slicing through the air to embed itself in his thigh. He crumpled, screaming, but we were already gone, Nala surging forward like a tempest.

"Good girl," I whispered, my voice steady even as adrenaline pounded in my ears.

Behind us, Isabella's voice carried louder than a war drum, driving the rest of the group forward. *Finally, a little teamwork makes the dream work, people.*

Nala darted sideways, narrowly avoiding a burst of gunfire. I twisted in the saddle, losing two arrows in quick succession. One struck the ground at the shooter's feet, scattering them, while the other caught a second enemy mid-charge.

As we approached the base, I could feel Nala's heavy, uneven huffs. "Almost there," I murmured, patting her neck. She gave one last burst of energy, carrying us over the threshold before slowing to a trembling stop.

I slid off her back, my boots hitting the ground hard. The soldier slumped after me, and someone from Portland's group rushed to catch her.

Hunter and the others arrived minutes later, their approach heralded by the crunch of boots and labored breaths. I stood waiting, Nala's reins in my hand as I leaned against her for support, every muscle in my body screaming in protest.

Hunter made a beeline for me, his face torn between relief and exasperation. His gaze swept over me—the sweat slicking my brow, the empty quiver dangling at my side, the streaks of dirt and blood painting a grim portrait of the last hour.

For a moment, he said nothing, shaking his head. Then, his lips twitched into a grin. "God, I'm so fucking proud to be your brother right now."

"Aren't ya always proud?" I bit down on my tongue, happy to hear the words.

He laughed too, loud and unrestrained, before pulling me into a hug. I sagged against him, letting the exhaustion hit all at once.

"Come on," he said, his voice softening as he pulled back. "Let's get inside before you collapse on me."

CHAPTER
FORTY-NINE

TOMOE

F*reedom or death.*
  The freedom to roam throughout all the territories if they let Salem take over. If they helped us win this war. No more division, no more limitations. United.

Those were the conditions I'd stated in my note to Laurel—the one Amaia asked me to send in her stead months ago in Duluth. It had been a shot in the dark. An empty pretty promise that told them exactly what they wanted to hear. I hadn't seen it in any vision—until recently. Until Amaia had settled on one of many damning decisions. Somehow that one note had sparked a damn rebellion. Or fueled one. Chicken or egg type of situation, I supposed.

I sat near the fire, cross-legged on a worn blanket, Wrath resting at my side. Finley Thomas's voice grated against the night air. She never stopped talking. Ever.

"You're going to drive someone to murder," I muttered. "Do you ever shut up?"

She flashed me a smile that let me know I'd handed her an invitation to argue. "Do you ever have anything positive to say?"

"No."

"Well, there you go," she said smug as ever, leaning back with satisfaction in her unsettling eyes.

Amaia's head was mine as soon as this stupid game was over. *Training exercise.* What a joke. More like glorified capture the flag. I said nothing, keeping my gaze on the flames. There were eight of us, risking our sanity over a strip of fabric, pretending it was worth something.

Finley wasn't even General of St. Cloud. Yet somehow, someway, here she was—crouched next to me in the dirt, running her mouth. She'd insisted on being on the battlefield. It didn't get any creepier than wanting to see your own inventions take lives firsthand. Her honorary leadership patch meant nothing in the long run, she still ended up here, doing the grunt work with the rest of us.

Not that I had any room to talk. I wasn't exactly a soldier either. My role as the unit's *Seer* meant I was supposed to help anticipate what could happen—to help us outthink the enemy. Not that it always worked. And we had to be careful about when and where to use it without a guarantee of having enough time to recharge in case of an attack. Add in the fact that *seeing* the possibilities didn't mean I could stop them from happening. Amaia Bennett case and point.

The crackling flames almost drowned out Finley's voice, which had been a constant hum of chatter since we'd been assigned this post. She couldn't seem to sit still or stay quiet for more than five minutes. I let her noise wash over me, her bickering with the others filling the gaps in the silence.

And then, she shattered the fragile peace.

"I love a good campfire story. Moe Moe, tell us the story on how the son of the man we're out to kill, left you high and dry," Finley said, her head tilting, smirk growing in the low glow of the fire.

I blinked, caught off guard. "What?"

"You heard me." Her smirk deepened.

I glanced at her, then at Wrath, fingers twitching before the flag behind us centered me on the mission I was here for. "I wouldn't be so smug. Mine left for what he believed in, yours left for another woman."

The surrounding soldiers snickered. Finley's head snapped around, her glare silencing them instantly. "Got something to say?" she snapped.

They quickly busied themselves, rotating positions as we'd previously discussed, throwing off the other *Seers*. Finley's jaw tightened as she turned back toward me, her irritation simmering beneath the surface.

Finley let out an exaggerated gasp, one hand flying to her chest in mock offense. "Oof. I'm offended."

"You should be. He upgraded."

I had little energy to deal with her juvenile antics. It was hard to imagine Alexiares put up with her bullshit for as long as he did.

Her lips twitched in an attempt to fight back a laugh. "Hmm. I feel like I should be upset by that. I mean, you obviously want me to be. Yet oddly—and unsurprisingly—I couldn't care less. Oh well."

"You can pretend all you want." I rolled my eyes and moved to the other side of the fire, dragging Wrath's pointed edge through the dirt.

"Pretend?" She was swift in her movements. Catlike as she leaned in my ear and I swatted her away, not missing the wild flicker of crazy bitch in her expression.

"It's an act," I pushed. "Be the strongest or get left behind kind of thing. I get it. Been there."

Her expression hardened—the answer in the absence of denial. "I care about the people of St. Cloud," she said, her voice quieter, to me only, no longer putting on a show for those around us.

"Fooled me," I muttered.

Finley turned away, her stark blonde hair nearly hiding the clenching of her jaw. A hopeful moment of thinking I'd struck a nerve passed.

"Alexi can spin it however he wants." Her tone was cold now, threatening. "I'm not much different from that bitch—"

"Watch it," I snapped.

"Than Amaia," she corrected, her voice dripping with sarcasm. "I put my people first. Always. Life isn't the same up there. I wouldn't expect you to get it with your cozy rooms and your little cafés."

My patience with her was thinning, "You say that like it's a bad thing."

"Getting too comfortable will *always* be a bad thing," Finley said, meeting my gaze with a fierceness that matched the flames glowing behind her. "The sooner you people understand that, the better."

I ignored her, watching the others around us watch us as if we were entertainment.

"Brother's pretty cute though. Oh, come on, don't pretend you didn't notice. Far better looking than the other." Finley shoved a finger down her throat and gagged. "Not a fan of red-heads."

"I have an idea. How about *you* tell us the story on what could make a daughter kill her father?"

"Subtle." Air passed through her teeth in a huffed scoff. She tossed her chin my direction. "Why don't you see for yourself?"

I kept my tone even, already bored with the conversation. "That would be a waste of energy on someone who would happily brag, if only asked."

My eyes narrowed. *What an odd gap in greenery,* I noted as I stared into the distance. There was a small, face-sized hole about twenty feet out. I shook my head. *Nope,* I was focusing on channeling any direct attacks to our front door. If there was someone out there waiting for the right moment to capture our flag, I would be the first to know.

"I would never brag about killing someone I love." Finley's voice fell to a hush, and I turned to face her.

She seemed … sad? Her shoulders slumped as she brushed her fingers through the dirt, eyes set on the ground.

"You?" I laughed, refusing to waste guilt for the woman who'd spent days torturing, *humiliating* us and treating us no better than neglected animals not long ago. "Love? Please, spare me."

"I loved my father." Her words were clipped—definite.

"I'm sure he'd appreciate the words more if he were alive."

I hated to admit it, but seeing her show even a glimpse of anything other than smug indifference made me extremely uncomfortable.

"I had no choice."

"There is always a choice."

If I had the choice, my parents would be alive, my sisters wouldn't have faced a brutal death. In no scenario could I fathom how much hate one had to hold in their heart, to kill their flesh and blood. Then again, maybe I did. Maybe it was why I'd refused to let Reina fall victim to her brother's sword. Why I'd insisted on being the one to end him myself—because as much hatred that rested within Seth's heart, it would never be enough to protect him from himself once he'd realized what he'd done. I couldn't let myself live with the guilt of what killing Reina would have done to his soul. So I'd offered my own up instead.

"It's what he wanted," Finley said with a sense of certainty, like she had no doubt. "That is what my daddy expected of me."

"Some father," I grumbled. That explained why she acted … like *that*.

"Don't make me kill you." She pulled her blade and waved it in my face. I refused to acknowledge the threat. Her eyes flickered shut in quick succession as she blinked back … tears? "He had cancer. Before all of this started, he'd gone into remission—that obviously didn't last. Without any doctors worth a damn nearby, his pain became unbearable. It was his worst fear to live the way his life was heading. So I took him out before he had the chance to wonder what his final days would look like."

We sat there in elongated silence. There was nothing left to say. I almost felt bad for taunting it out of her—almost. But I was no saint and Finley was one hell of a sinner. Pity was all I could offer her, and because I knew she wouldn't want it, I granted her the kindness of not showing her any at all.

"You would have made a great therapist." Finley cleared her throat, shifting her weight and tossing the awkwardness away. "Can I schedule another appointment? Wednesday at two."

"Shut up," I spat, over the dramatics.

Slap my ass and call me a whore, she actually listened. But the silence that followed was anything but peaceful. I stared into the fire again, waving my hands in the warmth of its flames. Usually, a fire would be bad. A dead giveaway. For all purposes but this drill—because this drill was to test our level of preparedness when things don't go as planned. Sometimes a fire is the only thing that could save your life, save the soldiers around you. How you handled that with the threat of an enemy striking at any moment determined whether you lived or died in the end.

The flickering glow revealed the faces of the soldiers nearby. A few exchanged quiet glances, but no one dared to speak. Finley's presence was too volatile. She was an anomaly. The sharp edges of her personality hid cracks she refused to let anyone see. Finley wanted to be right at all times. Needed to be. Shit, maybe it was the only way she knew how to keep going. To see another day.

A whistle pierced the night. We all snapped to attention as a runner approached. He was breathless and red-faced, apparently out of shape despite the training we'd been forced to do. "Phase two," he panted, words tumbling out in uneven gasps. "Leadership reassignment … squad leaders down … new chain of command."

"Finally," Finley muttered. She shot to her feet, brushing the dirt from her uniform.

I rose slowly, my gaze shifting from the runner to the fire, which flared unnaturally for a moment, its flames licking higher into the air. A trick of the light, maybe. Or maybe not. I caught Finley's eye.

"Down, now." I ducked, hoping she had the sense to do the same.

A ball of fire shot over our bodies, steamrolling right where we had stood. *Lethal force.* She barked orders to the nearby squad then crawled over to my position. "Shit. I think some son of a bitch tried to kill me."

"Go away," I pushed away from her, the obvious target and slid through the dirt toward Wrath.

"Oh, come on, this obviously isn't a drill anymore."

"Yeah, to *you.*" I barked out a laugh. "I bet the rest of us are fine."

"Okay, well, they're still going for the flag and the others went on outer defense which leaves the two of us …"

I groaned, tossing my braid back over my shoulder and wiping the sweat off my nose with my shoulder. "Dammit."

The ground erupted directly behind us, a plume of dirt and smoke filling the air. I scrambled forward, fingers brushing the hilt of Wrath. She felt good in my grip, steady. Adrenaline pounded in my ears as I scanned the tree line.

"Would it piss you off if I said I wish I wasn't in charge now?" Finley snapped, her eyes darting toward the flag. "Two of us against what? An entire squad? An assassin?"

"There is no *two of us*, Finley. Only me and this flag."

"Fine." Her jaw clenched as she pulled free some cylindrical device and twisted it. "Let's make this work."

She rounded to take up the rear as her little creation hummed to life. Putting her and Tomás in the same room was either brilliant or a disaster waiting to happen. Only time and the victims they stacked up would tell. The weapon hummed to life, cracking with energy. She tossed it out in front of us, then shifted to a defensive stance, clasping my hand with a squeeze. "Nonlethal. Come on, Moe Moe."

"I know. Get off me," I bit out and snatched my fingers out of her grasp. Wrath's blade glinted in the low light.

A figure burst from the tree line at full speed, their movements a blur and now lost in the blue hue of whatever emerged from Finley's toy. My instincts screamed, and I barely managed to intercept a blade aimed straight at Finley. Wrath's steel clanged against their weapon—a short curved knife.

"Watch it! It's not just Finley back here," I shouted as the impact sent a jolt through my body.

"Okay, we have about thirty seconds before they realize the mirage of us walking away is literal smoke blowing up their asses," Finley said, pointing to the smoke that engulfed us now. "Get ready."

"Want to tell me why they're trying to kill you?" I asked impatiently.

"Babe, there's about a million reasons someone would want me dead and standing around listing them off won't make a difference."

Electricity crackled and Finley leaped back. The smoke cleared and our initial attacker was nowhere in sight. Nope. His squad was here and unfortunately for me, their focus was on more than Finley.

"Here for the orgy?" she taunted, sliding rings on and sliding her fingers through the air in a calculated pattern. A shield went up, blocking both of us behind it.

One soldier carried a chain, glowing red-hot at the end, another held a compact launcher slung over their shoulder. Nonlethal but incredibly painful were the options now presented to us. The soldier who'd had it out for Finley was gone, disappeared with the approach of the others.

The one with the chain came for me. Her movements were fluid and calculated. I deflected the first strike. Wrath sliced through the air with precision. The chain whipped back and looped for my legs. I jumped over them, spinning to avoid the glowing links, and brought the flat of my blade down on her wrist.

She hissed in pain, but they didn't drop the weapon. Apparently, she was incredibly motivated to capture this damn flag. She pulled back, the chain snapping toward me once more.

"Finley!" I called, my breath coming hard and fast. It was becoming harder to not kill her. I was accustomed to swinging and being done with it. This back and forth was simply frustrating, especially now that I knew I couldn't trust their motives. Even if she hadn't been the one to target Finley, she'd sat back and watched while her squad-mate took their shot.

"Catch!" Finley tossed a staff through the air. I dropped low, letting the chain whip past my face, sheathed Wrath and in one movement caught the weapon. It was heavy in my hands, unnatural. But it would do.

Finley was already in motion. She possessed an artillery of weapons I didn't recognize along her body. I caught a glimpse of one as it lit up the dark like fireflies on steroids. It defied the laws of physics. Bolts of blue energy whirled from her fists with every swing, forcing an attacker to retreat. Her movements were a kind of scrappy elegance. She chose to fight dirty, that was no surprise, but I couldn't deny her efficiency.

"Come back!" she barked, calling after them. "I wasn't done having fun."

"Sociopath," I muttered, rising to meet the Chain-wielder's next attack. My staff cut through the air, intercepting the glowing links with a satisfying clang. With a twist of my wrist, I hooked the chain and yanked, pulling her off balance.

Her momentum carried her forward. I swung the borrowed staff down with ease. It cracked something on her side. *Sounds like I hit something important.* She crumpled with a grunt, but before I could pin her down, the air shifted.

The ground beneath us trembled, and a wave of heat rolled through the camp. A new wave of enemy soldiers thrust their palms forward. Thick walls of flame erupted between us, forcing Finley and me to backpedal.

"Is now a good time to tell you there's someone behind you?" Finley shouted. "Or should I wait till the first swing since this isn't a team effort?"

I spun in time to block another strike from the Chain-wielder, who'd recovered far too quickly for my preference. Her eyes glinted with determination as she pressed the attack. The staff sang in my hands—but it was getting harder to keep up.

Finley faced the fire-wielders head-on. Two on one, just how she liked it. Her rings hummed, discharging a concentrated burst of energy that collided with the flames. The impact sent sparks flying, and the battlefield sparkled in a fireworks display.

"Base camp's compromised!" someone shouted from the perimeter.

That was fast. Finley's respect didn't extend far when shit hit the fan, they'd already decided to replace her in command. With her assumed fallen, they had no choice. That was the entire point of the drill. To think on our feet when things didn't go according to plan, to step up when needed to ensure the success of the mission. Guess I couldn't be too smug about it. Though, it was sickly sweet knowing she'd failed.

"Secure the flag!" I shouted to Finley, stepping between her and the Chain-wielder. "I'll hold them here!"

Another surge of heat roared toward us. This time I didn't have time to find cover. Instinct took over, and I dropped the staff and unsheathed Wrath, rearing her forward, the steel catching the fire midair. They twisted, spiraling around the blade, their movements echoing the slithering of a serpent.

The Chain-wielder hesitated for the first time as she too recovered, not expecting the blast of power. Her confidence cracked.

"I've about had it with the chain shit," I growled, stepping toward her.

Finley didn't waste the opening. She darted past me, a ring of blades cracked through the air as she drove it into the fire-wielder's chest. A rush of air sent them sprawling at the impact. And by design their flames snuffed out like a dying ember.

I swept the chain-wielders legs out from under her, pressing the tip of Wrath against her chest.

"Yield," I ordered.

She glared at me but didn't move.

A cheer rose from the edges of the camp. Our team had managed to push back the attackers. The triumphant shouts of soldiers reclaiming the perimeter was obnoxiously pleasing to my ears.

"Flag's still up," I said, my voice tight as I released the Chain-wielder. She pushed herself up and took off after her squad-mates that were now weaponless and racing back to their own camp for safety.

"No kidding," Finley snapped, brushing herself off and pushing up from the base of the flag. Her hair was a tangled mess, and soot streaked her face, but she tossed her choppy hair with the grace of a runway model.

"This wasn't random," I said, glancing at Finley. "They were targeting you."

She nodded grimly. "Yeah, just another day in The Expanse."

A knot of discomfort twisted inside me, refusing to loosen. Whoever had blocked my Sight was still out there, powerful and dangerous. And if they'd help hide an attempt on Finley, what else were they capable of?

CHAPTER
FIFTY

ALEXIARES

I'd never thought much of the future. Just surviving the day, the week, was enough. One day at a time. If I made it to the next, fantastic, great—if I didn't, oh well.

But now the thoughts of what was to come were destroying me. I tried my best to shove them away—resist. It was impossible when I knew the woman I loved would be leading the fight into a war meant to ruin.

I was a monster. One of the dangerous ones. I knew what was out there, what she would face … what I had no choice but to sit back, and watch as she met the devil head-on.

No one was working together. That hadn't changed over the last few weeks. A week ago someone made an attempt on Finley's life—to absolutely fucking no one's surprise. *Yeah*, no one could even pretend to care about that. I wish I'd been the one to make it—*I* wouldn't have missed.

Instead, Amaia had met it with the promise of an eye for an eye. You attack someone that was meant to be on your team, the rest of the group comes after you. Same manner, same death, same fate. It didn't matter. Not anymore.

This was it, the final simulation. What we were all working toward. Three weeks of what felt like wasted efforts would all be put to the test. At least there had been no word on any movement from Ronan.

A good thing since it allowed us to focus on the here and now. Individual settlements may not be working as a team but at least individually they'd grown stronger, faster, smarter—more adaptable. We had that going for us and maybe that could be enough in the end. *Maybe.* Fucking doubtful, however.

No one wanted to think of the other possibility. That Ronan was making moves against us, silently so no one would be able to know what was happening. Not with him tucked safely behind his damn wards. Nope. He was safe from any *Seer*, no matter how powerful—no matter how many power-shared.

"You ready for this?" I asked, my eyes scanning up Amaia's lean, muscular legs as she slid her black camo cargos on with a little hop.

She snapped her thigh holster into place right after. Quick and efficient in her movements, her weapons were in place before she even mustered a response.

"What did I tell you about asking stupid questions?" Deep brown eyes as beautiful as undisturbed earth met mine, the sides of them wrinkling with the small smirk curling the tail ends of her lips. She pushed to the tips of her toes and leaned in to kiss the corner of my mouth.

I smiled in response, arguably irritated that she had already moved away from me to pull on the thickly padded vest over her dark gray t-shirt. "It's not that I lack faith in you, don't get me wrong."

Opting to distract myself, I moved to get ready, studying the odd metallic barrel of some sonic gun Tomás had spent hours in my living room working on. Amaia and him made one hell of a team. Technically, he was in my service, but the way Amaia's mind worked mixed with Tomás's natural—and magical—genius, they created weapons I knew Finley was salivating for. It'd been fun to play with. Tiago would have loved this. Our interactions. The way his twin had webbed himself into my life. They were nothing alike except in their humor and loyalty.

"But the last few weeks have been a shitshow in some capacity and you think we're doomed?"

"Is it too late to try Canada?" I teased, but I was dead fucking serious. If she wanted to bolt, I wouldn't stop her. No, I'd follow like a lost fucking dog.

She rolled her eyes. "Ha ha."

"You're right, Mexico is closer."

"Luckily, one of us speaks Spanish." Her soft hands pressed against my bicep as she recalled how I'd surprised her with my knack for languages. Compliments to the chef—a.k.a. the dad from hell. Though, I supposed Reina had far worse luck in that department.

I swore quietly, stalling. I didn't want to go there, not yet—but the window was closing. This information was detrimental to her final placements of individual units. "Speaking of *brujas*—Lola's coven has done what they could with the time they had."

Amaia's head fell heavenward, her curls tickling her spine. "Sounds like bad news."

"It's not great news," I said, pulling her hair tie taut and shooting it across the room to her. "Seventy-five percent, give or take."

She caught it, bunching her curls in her fist and tying them out the way in a low bun that made her features sharp—dangerous and lethal. "Why do I have a feeling that it's take? It's almost always take when someone says that."

"It's better than nothing."

"This is supposed to be our *one* advantage." This wasn't the woman who loved me speaking anymore—it was an irritated general who expected results and, instead, was met with failure. "If only 75 percent of our troops can powershare, that still leaves 25 percent of us without enough power to go against Ronan. Expect the worst-case scenario and whatever it is, set that bar to the lowest level of hell and *that's* what we're dealing with when it comes to them."

Them. Us. Us or them. It was all the same. The same game we'd been playing for over half a decade. A game played with such fealty, it nearly led to humanity's destruction at the end of The Before.

Thanks to Reina's work, we'd been able to give each soldier an additional gift. Something Amaia was certain would have consequences in the future but felt a necessary evil to accomplish our goals now. After all, Ronan was likely doing the same. That left us little time to teach them how to properly wield whatever new powers they received. Said complications were exactly why leadership thought it best to pair up as many people as possible with a complimenting partner and power. Hopeful was the word. Because hopefully, the blind would be able to lead the blind, guide each other into control in whatever magic emerged.

"They weren't exactly intrigued by the idea of over-exerting themselves when we could be attacked at any time," I said the words timidly.

My general was now on edge, and telling her an excuse on why her plans couldn't come into fruition never had a happy ending. There was no such thing as a good excuse according to her. An excuse was just that—an excuse. An attempt to justify why you hadn't worked hard enough to accomplish the end goal.

"Sorry." Sarcasm laced her tongue. "I forgot only the foot soldiers were supposed to be comfortable putting our lives on the line."

"Amaia," I warned her not to go there.

It had less to do with the relationship I had with the *brujas*, with Lola, and more about showing her disappointment to them. Her outlook on their efforts would gain her fewer favors than they were already interested in providing.

"What?" she snapped, voice raising an octave to a level she hadn't used with me since Duluth.

Her gaze softened at the realization. This was out of our control—for now. Unless she demanded otherwise.

"Do you want me to hold them for a few days? Make them finish up? Because I will if only you ask it of me." I lifted my chin, tilting it just enough to meet her gaze, putting us on equal footing.

If I acted in any way other than respecting the *brujas* wishes while Lola was not here to give the command, her permission … Ronan would seem but a small threat. I'd have to face Lola and explain myself, plead for my life and hers after, but if it made Amaia's life easier, then I would do it without hesitation.

"No." I saw the sparkle in her eyes. The momentary consideration as she grappled with the decision, ultimately deciding that there were actions that we couldn't take back. Choices that went too far. "Let's see how this goes."

"After you." I moved toward the door, holding it open and watching as she passed through the threshold, praying to whoever the fuck was up there to let a dreaming soul find rest when this was all over. It was what she deserved.

So it wasn't as fucking tragic as we expected. Still, it was pretty rough to witness.

The air was thick with the scent of moss and rust. Royal Oaks was probably an all right place in The Before. By 'all right,' I mean by some old cuck's standards. Now, it was nothing more than streets swallowed by vines and decay. We passed through the skeletal remains of a monotonous suburban sprawl. A forgotten graveyard of the boring, average, American life.

A hum of anticipation vibrated through the chill of the early morning. Our breath was visible in the air, passing through the protection of the shields enveloping my general and myself. They were a precaution. Every motherfucker here knew that if either of us were hit, it'd be a problem. And we all knew how I handled anything I deemed a 'problem.'

At least in this all, the respect for Amaia had gone up—as deserved. She moved smart. Amaia demanded their initial respect— just enough where they were at least willing to try her methods— but had let her work speak for itself in the end. There was no denying her effectiveness as a leader and a general now. The fact that the war simulation thus far wasn't a complete disaster was every bit of proof that she deserved her reputation. Her spot.

After weeks of assessments, re-evaluation of positions, and overall reluctance to move where they were needed most—Amaia had divided our forces with an efficiency that bordered on ruthlessness. If Ronan thought we were a threat before, we had the potential to be an unstoppable force with the right conditions, the right attitudes, and the overall desire to put an end to his reign.

Infantry held the center of the city, dug in behind crumbling barricades at the old Oakwood intersection. Any scouts had long vanished into the overgrown neighborhoods flanking the borders of this operation—their shadows now danced between husks of long forgotten family homes.

General Silas Trevan, now in charge of Alpha Unit—and general of Salt Lake Compound—led a strike team from the strip mall. He'd been loyal to Amaia from the beginning . With their history from the first war, she trusted him with the right amount of caution, conditions of which made the best partnerships. So she placed him where she needed him the most. Leading charge on our offense.

Perhaps the sexiest she'd ever been was the night she didn't flinch when assigning soldiers to the risky positions. There was no room for hesitation when giving these orders, and she'd held none. I'd watched her send Isabella Everhart to guard the south bridge of the city, knowing the true terrain she was auditioning for offered little cover. Her hands did not shake when she'd ordered Reina to ride as the combat medic under the cavalry and into the collapsed underpass, knowing she'd be preparing her for the very real scenario of evacuating civilians. A task that came with the risk of a possible ambush. She was methodical, decisive—every move calculated for victory, even if it came at a cost.

Amaia was destined to lead us into a victorious war. She was a warrior.

A Queen.

A woman who could not, would not, be stopped.

Her heart was made of fire and ice. The flames that burned for the freedom she could bring. Ice consumed the parts of her necessary to freeze the hatred, the malice—the savagery from the war.

Amaia was a war goddess who only promised peace.

The first wave came fast and hard. Pounding the center line with simulated fire and the surge of 'enemy' troops. Our simulation required an offense and a defense. What the best chance would be to run through the possibilities of the offensive technicalities of leading an attack, meeting the enemy head-on. Then there were the defensive measures to ensure we had what it took to protect our homes with minimal defense. Each soldier had been handpicked by Amaia with the consultation of their respective leadership to determine where they would serve us best.

One unit, one damn compound.

Infantry scrambled to hold their positions. The scouts shouted coordinates over comms *Tinkerers* had spent the last few weeks ensuring worked in the most trivial of circumstances. Amaia didn't waver. She watched as her chosen leaders cut orders through the chaos. As heavy hitters moved to intercept a breach on the left flank, the air buzzed with magic. Every soldier moved in unison, their movements guided by Amaia's beautiful mind. Her presence on this battlefield was admirable, unshakable … commanding.

"Not bad," Amaia muttered, turning away and tilting her chin down, the words meant for my ears alone. "I was considering splitting us into two divisions for the sake of operational flexibility."

"Are you asking for an opinion or telling me what's about to happen?"

"Don't act as if you don't enjoy being told what to do." Amaia bit her lip, cheeks flushing as she continued glancing around the provisional battleground.

I smirked, recalling the semantics of our relationship being the reverse. "Other way around, Princess."

"Anyway," she said, moving with such grace—floating through the convoluted maze of bullshit happening around us. "I think it would be best. Having someone who knows *me*. Who can act as me when I am not around. Give the commands, make the suggestions that I would make."

"Ah. But said person is not here and this ain't the crowd to like a new face."

Amaia's lips pulled into a tight line as she stopped us—turning to watch as a scout returned, searching desperately through the disarray for the highest in command. He found a Sergeant, not exactly the better option considering the Captain directly behind him. The Captain who snarled his lip in lieu of simply correcting the mistake.

I took note of Amaia storing the interaction away. No doubt she was considering if this was a proper match up for when reality had a lot more on the line than guns that simply burned you or blades that only swung to grant flesh wounds.

"Riley is not a new face to any of them."

Her words held a bite, like she did not trust what could happen to her brother if left with any of these settlements alone. And they would be right for whatever wrongs they committed—for Riley possessed information. Details of their settlements, trade connections, research efforts. Riley knew it all. That made him a threat.

A unit spread out, heading the scout's warning. We did not have to be within hearing range to know what was said. It was time for the next phase of this simulation: a threat to supply lines. If they remembered their training, they'd redeploy forces to intercept the interruption without weakening our main line of defense. Which is exactly what it appeared they were doing. I heard Amaia take an easy sigh of relief. Of this at least, she knew she could relax. They had learned.

Because they had, she would now push them one step further, see what would happen if faced with yet another challenge. Something we had yet had time to train them on. That was a realistic outcome of this war. There had not been enough time. If they had trained under our command for months, the day would never have enough hours in it to address the unexpected variables of conflict.

We walked in unison. Left foot, then our right. She led, and I followed. It was casual, the way we passed through soldiers holding steady in their positions, how she meddled and created a new mess without *really* being seen. They thought she was observing— she was not. Amaia was orchestrating an opera.

"Park," she stopped short, right at a scouts rear.

He froze at the sound of her voice. "Yes, ma'am."

"Cut all communications on Route Hemingway and ..." She made a show of considering her next words. "Route Golding."

"Right away, ma'am."

Park took off without another word or glance back. I peered down at her, silently questioning her next command. Her gaze flickered around us and she walked toward the overpass.

It would only be a matter of time before all hell broke loose. With communications cut, units and scouts would no longer be able to coordinate and adapt ahead of time. No. Instead, they'd be forced to rely on pre-established plans, and, fuck, did I hate this the most ... their instincts.

The closer we got to the crumbling underpass, the louder the cries of suffering got. Then gunfire rang out. I had no idea how she'd pulled this off. Using the already injured soldiers from each of the settlements to play trapped civilians was diabolical. I loved her for it.

And so did they. Reluctantly, but the admiration was clear as she offered subtle advice and suggested corrections these last few weeks. Amaia was more than a leader. She was the kind of person who could turn soldiers into believers, fear into courage, and chaos into calculated precision.

With the break in communication she'd put into play, reinforcements that were originally planned to be diverted here to help would no longer be coming. With these 'civilians' in harm's way, the cavalry and unit working at their side, would be tested in their ability to make ethical decisions under fire. The scene quickly fell into disarray.

Their 'instincts' were almost as bad as their memory when it came to sticking to the plan. All it took was one rider being tossed off their horse after a controlled explosion. The riderless horse took off down the main road, barreling through the unit assisting the injured.

Then the mix up of orders began. A captain gave strict, non-negotiable commands while the commander of the cavalry, currently auditioning for the role against Millie, gave conflicting ones. Instead of working together while under fire, they were effectively working against each other. *Idiots.*

"What are you going to do, Commander?" Amaia asked as we approached him, still under the protection of our shield. "Time is of the essence."

Reina rode up to the commander's side, waiting on the response, eyes flickering over to Amaia and she held her head up an inch higher. The commander considered his options, then turned, taking off toward the captain to coordinate their plan of attack. Reina followed close behind, the model of focus and competence, as always. She was good at this, I had to admit. Her heart would allow her to be good at anything she cared about. The perfectionist attitude only served to benefit her end result, achievement alone a good enough prize.

I snorted. "The commander and captain don't work well together. Swap him for Millie. He'll work better with the captain out from Beta Unit. Otherwise these two idiots will be halfway through an argument when Ronan cuts them in two."

Amaia stare was a weapon that could've frozen molten steel. "I don't course correct mid-fuckup. They'll figure it out … or they won't and they'll see their egos will get them killed."

For a minute, it seemed as if they might—figure it out that is. Orders flowed back down the line. Almost.

Then, the air changed.

It wasn't subtle. One second, the ruins of Royal Oaks were full of shouting and weapon fire. Next, the world itself had decided to hold its breath. An unholy scream ripped through the silence. It was not the sound of pain. I knew that macabre of beautiful symphony better than the back of my hand. This scream was full of terror.

The battlefield froze.

"What the fuck was that?" someone yelled, their voice shaking.

The tree line exploded. They came at us in a tidal wave of nightmares. Their movements were fast—damn near too fast to be real. But they were. And there were hundreds of them. They weren't Pansies—not the ones we knew. Not anymore. These were something worse. Taller, their limbs stretched too far, as if Ronan had put effort into taking a human and twisting them until the proportions no longer made sense. Their faces were a mess of sharp angles and glowing eyes, and their movements … fuck me, their movements were all wrong. Jerky, but fast. Impossibly fast.

Shields went up across the field, but not quick enough. Pansies hits met our troops head-on with a sickening crunch, mouths full of jagged teeth snapping through the air.

"Hold the line!" Amaia ordered, her voice cut through the rising panic.

Pure shock halted my steps. Soldiers scrambled to regroup, firing into the horde, Amaia's orders already unraveling before our eyes. They fired into the horde and I watched as the scout—Park— went down, dragged into the swarm. Pansies poured through Royal Oaks for as far as the eye could see.

Amaia grabbed my arm, yanking me out of my frozen disbelief. "Fall back. Now."

Her command jolted the soldiers into motion, but the swarm was faster. It surged forward, cutting off escape routes and cornering entire units.

A roar tore through the battlefield.

It wasn't human. Hell, it wasn't Pansie. It was something in between. The humanoid appearance was a grotesque mockery, it struck a chord of fear within me. It was deep, guttural, and loud enough to vibrate in my chest. Every head that could spare a second snapped toward the sound.

"What the actual fuck," I muttered, mouth dry. My stomach twisted as I met Amaia's eyes.

Amaia looked rattled. Not panicked, not defeated—but rattled. And that scared the shit out of me. The ground trembled, and I realized this wasn't the end of the simulation. This was something else entirely.

CHAPTER
FIFTY-ONE

ALEXIARES

"I'm not one to speak on the cruelty of methods," I said, pulling us down to the ground in order to avoid an out of control burst of fire that was bound to weaken our shield. "But releasing Pansies at a time like this is a bit excessive, no?"

"Those aren't mine." Her eyes shifted with trained efficiency. Fear had been replaced by raw fury.

I cleared my throat, shuffling us toward higher ground. "Pardon."

"Where the fuck would I get Covert Uniforms from, Alexiares?"

I glanced toward her with the jerk of my head. The realization of her statement overshadowed her annoying habit of using sarcasm to communicate when all she needed to do was explain what the—*Never mind. Now's not the time.* "Fuck."

"Fuck is right." She dropped our shield with an exaggerated sigh, like this entire nightmare was a personal inconvenience—which, I supposed it was. "Pros and cons … Pro, this is extremely realistic to what we're likely to face. Con, I promised them no one would die unless it was a tragic accident."

I snorted despite the gore-feast happening around us. "Is this an 'act of God' insurance claim type of qualification for an accident or …"

She glared at me, magic simmering in the cusp of one hand, her knife in the other.

I gestured toward the carnage behind her. "I see at least ten dead bodies, and I'm being generous with the math."

The perimeter had collapsed. If the Pansies were swarming us, our units on the edges of Royal Oaks were either dead, incapacitated, or regretting every life choice that got them here.

"They'll have my head for this," she said, already moving.

"I dare them to try." I followed, knife ready, because if this was how the day was going, I wasn't about to let her take all the glory—or the blame.

The Pansies poured in—fast, jagged, monstrous. Their twisted bodies jerked unnaturally. Earsplitting sounds of joints cracking sent a chill down my spine as they moved with a speed that defied logic. They weren't human anymore. Not even fucking close. Which made things worse, because they were *smart*. They organized themselves. The strong lead their attack, breaking through our lines, testing weak points.

Amaia didn't hesitate. Her knife was a blur of movement, her wrathful red-hot fire burned through the swarm with ruthless precision. I kept pace, blades cutting through the closest threats. It was an exhaustive effort with us all spread out. Every one we took down, five more clawed their way forward.

"This isn't a drill! Move your ass or you're all dead!" I shouted over the chaos, slashing through a Pansie's chest. Its ribcage splintered under my blade, its insides spilled out with an oddly satisfying stench of the finality of death.

Amaia echoed the warning. Her voice was sharp, slicing through the panic. Soldiers scrambled to regroup. They rallied around her, using her as their goddamn North Star, but without the lethal weapons they were accustomed to arming themselves with in the face of Pansies, it was a losing effort.

Steamfire. I caught her eye in a brief moment of still between stabbing. The unspoken solution hung between us. Her hesitation mirrored in my own movements. We'd been saving it, building up our power together in order to create a brutally deadly force, conserving every drop for the real war. But this? Fuck it. It wouldn't matter if we never made it out of this. *This*, it was close enough.

"Use it carefully," she said, her voice tight.

"Sparingly."

We joined hands, her calloused thumb brushing over the space where our bodies connected. *I love you too.* The words remained unsaid, but innately, so deeply understood. Flames roared from our hands, cutting a blazing, blinding blue path through the swarm. The Pansies screeched, their bodies bursting into ash, but the relief was temporary. They just kept coming.

Wave.

After wave.

After wave.

We kept at it. *Every single soldier* on the battlefield worked as a unit until the ground was littered with the remnants of Pansies twisted forms. The swarm thinned as the battlefield settled into an uneasy rhythm of stale victory.

The wreckage was staggering. They would hang Amaia for this. It would not be her fault, yet she would still burn. Blood soaked the earth. Human, not Pansie. Bodies heaped in unnatural angles, and the acrid stench of mortality clung to the air. My muscles burned, every gasp of air a struggle. Through the haze of exhaustion, a scream tore through the eerie quiet. Raw. Piercing.

"Reina."

I DIDN'T THINK, JUST RAN. THE GROUND WAS SLICK WITH GORE. I found her in a clearing, pinned beneath a Pansie, its teeth buried deep in her calf. Blood gushed in sickening pulses.

My blade sliced, carving a clean path through its neck up into its brain. Its jaws snapped one final time as it hit the ground.

Reina sat crumpled, pale as death, her hands clamped over her calf as blood seeped through her fingers in rhythmic pulses. "I'm fine," she hissed.

"Right. Because fine usually comes with arterial spray." I crouched down and ripped a strip from my shirt and wrapped it around her leg, yanking it tight.

"Aw," she chuckled weakly, eyes rolling to the back of her head. "Ya actually listen to me when I try to teach you things. How sweet. I'm fine. Just get my healing herbs from my pack. I'm low on magic."

"Shut up, press your hand to stall for a minute. Where's Hunter?"

Before she could respond, I hauled her into my arms. She was dead weight. My gaze swept the battlefield, still a writhing mess. Her fight was not over. Not today.

Reina pointed weakly toward a partially collapsed building at the edge of the chaos. Through the haze of smoke and carnage, I spotted Hunter, dragging the wounded toward the makeshift shelter. Amaia sprinted toward us. Her fury was palpable, her movements sharp and violent as she carved a path through the remnants of the herd.

"What happened?" she snapped.

"What do you think happened?" I bit back, hoisting Reina higher in my arms. Her blood was soaked through my shirt, warm and sticky, and her breathing was shallow. It was an effort to keep myself calm—Reina usually did that for me.

Amaia spared a glance at Reina's mangled calf, her muscles tensing. "Keep behind me."

I followed, staying close as she cleared the path ahead. Hunter was already rushing toward us as we reached the building, his face having aged ten years in the last few minutes.

"Reina …" His voice cracked as he took her from me. "I've got her."

Amaia's eyes flicked to mine, rage bleeding into every movement. I pulled my knife back free, the weight familiar in my hand, and nodded.

"Let's end this."

We didn't fight like a storm—we fought like predators. Every move was calculated to kill. No wasted effort. By the time the last Pansie fell, the battlefield was an open graveyard, thick with ash and blood. Grabbing injured soldiers, we dragged them toward the triage area without a word.

Inside, it was a hellscape of its own. Healers scrambled, their hands slick with blood, trying to hold lives together with spit, grit and magic. Surgeries were happening in dim corners, the screams raw enough to scrape nerves. No anesthetic. No respite—only survival.

Amaia rushed to Reina's side. Tomoe was already there. Her tawny hands shook as she tried to channel. She resembled someone who'd been dragged through a war zone—and she had.

"I … I can't see. I can't *see*," Moe muttered through clenched teeth. "I need time to recharge."

Another *Seer* at the bedside across the aisle shook their head, just as battered. "We barely had enough strength to warn them in time—"

Tomoe shot them a glare. "Doesn't matter. We did all that we could."

Hunter stumbled over, his face lined with exhaustion but holding steady.

"Serenity? Caleb?" Amaia asked, sharp and direct.

"They're fine," he said, his voice ragged but firm. "Out gathering supplies. Painkillers, herbs—whatever's left out there. They'll be back soon."

For half a second, it seemed like the worst had passed.

The soldier across the room convulsed, foam frothing at his lips, his back arching unnaturally.

"Seizing!" a clearly battered combat medic yelled.

Hunter was already moving, but before he reached the first, another soldier stumbled off the table now turned cot. Then another. They fell like dominos.

"If I have to say what the fuck one more time today ..." I growled. My grip tightened on my blade, ready for whatever fresh hell was about to hit us.

My heart pounded in my skull as my eyes locked with Amaia's. The dread in hers mirrored what was clawing at my chest. She glanced at Reina's leg, then up to her face, pale and barely conscious, before flicking her gaze back to me.

"Shit," she hissed.

"If you two could clue me in to what the hell is happening right now, that would be great."

"Pansies," I answered Tomoe.

That single word was enough. Moe's hand instinctively went to Wrath. Time slowed. Across the room, Hunter froze mid-step, his eyes widening in realization.

People around us were already panicking, and they didn't even understand just how fucked we were. The ripple of fear spread faster than the seizures.

Amaia didn't hesitate. "If they're stable and not bit, get them behind closed doors. Barricade yourselves in and don't you dare open them without my command."

The screams from inside that room would haunt any survivors forever. One by one, soldiers fell as they turned—cut down by General Clayton Harper, Hunter, Tomoe, Amaia, and me. Without pause. No hesitation.

Each kill was clean, but that didn't make it any easier. These were our people once—soldiers, comrades, humans. Now they were nothing more than husks driven by the infection, their eyes vacant, their bodies moving on instinct. Finley had warned us all, yet we had remained woefully unprepared.

The silence was suffocating when the last one dropped. Blood soaked the floor, pooling around our boots as the weight of what we'd done pressed down like lead.

Amaia's voice cut through the oppressive quiet. "Have the medics check for anyone else bitten, keep an eye on them all, even the ones that show no sign of turning. As for these two"—She pointed toward a pair of turned soldiers previously strapped down for amputation, one from Monterey and the other from Duluth, their bodies twitching faintly as the infection worked through them—"We need … data, even if they can't give it willingly."

General Bennett didn't flinch, didn't falter. That was her strength.

With all that I'd seen since arriving at their gates, our people wouldn't question the call—they knew it wasn't malice. It was war. Brutal, unrelenting, where hesitation got you killed and mercy was a luxury none of us could afford. They didn't need reminding of that. Didn't need a speech about the weight of their choices. They already knew the score.

I caught movement out of the corner of my eye and I turned toward Reina. She was awake now, her storm blue eyes wide with fear.

"Am I gonna die?" Reina asked, the fear widening her eyes, lips trembling.

I held her stare and reached for her hand. Her fear was palpable. Reina and I had come to understand one another. I'd never let her know, but she was kind of my favorite. An annoying little sister of sorts. I couldn't lie to her, not with the gifts she possessed. I wouldn't even if I could. "I hope not."

Reina searched my face for something she knew was there— from what she understood of my past. All she wanted at this moment was a promise I couldn't make out loud: if she turned, I'd be the one to end it. Not her brother. Not Tomoe. Not ever Amaia. I nodded slowly in agreement.

CHAPTER
FIFTY-TWO

AMAIA

"First person to move toward you is fucking dead," Alexiares growled at my back.

The cold steel in his voice sent a chill down my spine. He meant every word, and I was thankful for the sentiment. Alexiares grounded me in a way that nothing else could. My thumb rubbed over the bare skin of my ring finger. I'd never expected to wear another ring again, but now the absence of his cut deeper than I cared to admit. At least he was here.

I had him—and I had Elliot. That was about the only guarantee as we approached the doors that hung off the hinges of Royal Oaks City Hall.

Moe and Hunter had stayed behind with Reina. Watching over her and tending to the other injured … waiting. We knew the grim odds. Understood they were fifty-fifty. If you were bitten today, it was a coin toss on whether you'd be one of those things by tomorrow. After the first hour, we didn't witness any others turn. But the waiting, unknowing of what could come later—that was its own kind of hell.

"If they make a move, let them," I said quietly. "It's our law. Either I put them down, or they take me down. Each settlement has the right to challenge me individually for their loss. Fair is fair."

"Fuck fair." The anger cracked in Alexiares's voice.

"It's okay," I murmured, even though it wasn't. I didn't feel okay. Not at all. "That's how this works, my little hound. It's okay."

The doors creaked open, and the noise of the hall hit me all at once—murmurs of grief, the quiet weeping of a broken few, and the oppressive silence of others. Every head turned toward me as I stepped inside. I scanned the room, trying to read their expressions, but all I saw were stone-cold faces, their eyes hollowed by loss and exhaustion.

"Welp. Fuck, you want me dead," I said, letting my voice carry through the space. It wasn't a question. "I get it. You want to challenge me? We can get that over with in a minute. But first—" I paused, meeting each of them in the eye, "I'm here to bear more bad news."

"Riddle me shocked," Finley muttered from the side.

My glare snapped to her like a whip. "Funny you should be the one to speak," I shot back, and she flinched.

I moved to the center of the room, Alexiares a step behind me. His mere presence offered a false sense of safety, though I understood it was meaningless. Only my words could. I needed them to remember what we were here for. Despite the loss. No, fuck that, *because* of the loss. Because there would only be more. More death. More hard choices. More fuck ups.

"What we faced out there is *exactly* what we stand to go against in this war," I said, my voice rising above the scattered murmurs. "We all saw it—their speed, their strength, their *intelligence*. And it doesn't stop there. In case you've been under a fucking rock, any-one bit during that interaction has a 50/50 chance of turning into one of *them*. Pansie, zombie, the walking dead, whatever you want to call it, it's a potential in your future."

The gasps and shifting were immediate, a ripple of fear and disbelief washing over the room. I clenched my fists, pushing for-ward before the panic could spiral into something outside my con-trol. Fear was good. We could adjust to fear, work with fear. Panic would destroy us.

"He's playing games with us," I said, pacing now. "Laughing in our faces, daring us to retaliate. Ronan Moore wants us to know he understands war is coming—and he accepts."

The room quieted as curiosity replaced the fear. I saw it in their eyes: anger. Perfect. Now anger, anger I could make war-riors from.

"But what I've seen today," I said, stopping to face them all, "what all of you managed out there? I don't think he knows half of what's coming to him."

The silence stretched. It was thick—suffocating—as my words settled over them. My heart pounded in my ears, louder than the muffled sounds of grief and anger that filled the room moments before.

Then, slowly, someone stood.

It was General Clayton Harper. He stepped forward, his face like granite, and kneeled, lowering his head. Gray hairs falling into wet, sweaty strands across his weathered forehead.

My chest tightened, the weight of the moment crushing me.

General Rossi from San Jose followed. Then the newly ap-pointed Samantha Serviar, leader of Ogden.

The wave swept through the room, a blaze that spread with ruthless speed. Even Finley, her jaw clenched tight, dropped to one knee.

It wasn't relief that hit me. My chest heaved with a vindication that burned hotter than Steamfire. I willed myself to stay composed.

I stared at them. Not as their superior. Not as a notorious general who sought to be feared, but as the young girl who never asked for this but owned the position she'd fought for. The scared girl Prescott had molded, the one he'd instilled confidence in, made her realize that with blood, sweat, and a determination that refused to falter, I could take on the world. I could rule the world. I had the power to dream and make it a reality, if only I dared to try.

Alexiares was the last to kneel. His gaze held mine as he lowered himself down, both knees hitting the floor in a vow.

"None of us asked for this," I said, my voice steady despite the tremor in my chest. "But here you are, anyway. Stepping up. Doing what's right. Fighting for a better world you may not get to enjoy. That doesn't matter to any of us. I know that innately. It is not why we do what we do. So let me promise you this—when the storm comes, when Ronan Moore and every Pansie in his army comes for us, we won't just fight back."

I scanned over them, my voice rising, bouncing off the empty walls in a haunting echo.

"We'll burn them to the fucking ground."

The roar of cheers erupted, filling every crack in the broken space we stood in. For the first time since stepping foot in Royal Oaks, California, I allowed myself a spark of hope.

They weren't just listening.

They believed.

CHAPTER
FIFTY-THREE

AMAIA

I shot up from the couch, pistol in hand, before my brain had time to catch up to the sound. The knock on the door had been unexpected. Then again, so was my little nap.

Exhaustion didn't begin to cover how I felt. Coming back from Royal Oaks should have been like riding a high. Instead, we'd spent the entire trip obsessing over what would happen to Reina.

There were a plethora of questions and no answers for any of them. None we could focus on getting with the time we had left, at least. I relaxed, realizing that I was home. I was safe. Whoever was at my door was not here to hurt me.

The simulations had ended two weeks ago, giving everyone time to return home, check on their people, and prepare for whatever came next.

And for now, the rest of my family was safe. Or they had been before I'd apparently crashed on the couch last night and slept well into the morning—if the sun's creeping position was anything to go by.

Reina was healthy. She was determined to end this war. Her refusal to dwell on what had happened should've comforted me. Instead, it gnawed at the edge of my mind, because it mirrored my own focus. We'd stopped asking *why*. Now it was only about *how*.

How to finish this.

How to make Ronan pay.

How to survive long enough to see it through.

We couldn't make a weapon out of this new development— not without hurting our own. Thus, the only response was to focus on how to kill them all. Knowing the *why* behind *how* the Pansies were now communicating had become irrelevant too. Our focus was demanded elsewhere.

The soft taps on the door persisted, breaking through the quiet of our quarters. I glanced at the clock. Late morning. The sunlight poured through the curtains, making me squint. I'd slept too long. Another mistake. I stretched, my muscles protesting after a night spent on the couch. Pain stabbed my lower back, and I winced. I'd slept in worse conditions. Alexiares and Elie must've been out doing their own thing. Where Alexiares found the energy, I wasn't sure. Lucky him.

"Okay, okay," I grumbled, swinging the door open. "This better be—"

The words died in my throat.

God, she was beautiful, even with the deep, black circles of grief under her eyes. Luna stood there, her peppery hair framed a face carved from stone. The kind of face that pierced through you and found every crack you were trying to hide. Her bronze skin gleamed in the midday sun, and for a moment, I hated her for it—for the life and strength she carried, even under the weight of all the loss.

The pitter-patter of my heart became thunderous with anxiety. "Is everyone okay?"

"Yes," Luna pushed her way into the door as if she owned the place, which, in some way, she used to. She wrinkled her nose. "You smell. When's the last time you bathed? Had a meal that wasn't cornbread."

"I fell asleep on the couch before I had the chance," I grumbled, lowering my nose to my shoulder and embarrassingly agreeing with her assessment. A crumb of cornbread fell off my lip. *Okay, points were made.*

"Oh, sweet girl," Luna turned back in concern. "If there was any time to take care of yourself, it's now."

I closed the door behind me with a dramatic swat and kicked my way back to the couch, collapsing into it. "What's that supposed to mean?"

She didn't answer right away. Her focus lingered on me as she sat down, close enough that I could feel the warmth of her. *When one parent goes down, another's ready to lecture at the ready. Oh. That's a real dark thought, girl.* I cringed, clearing my throat and fixing myself to grant me a good view of her face.

"You set off for war in a matter of days. *War.* Now, I don't have to tell you how ugly that gets. You remember it well enough." Luna waved her hand nonchalantly as she spoke.

Always so … *alive.* Like Prescott had been—just in a different way.

Of course, I remembered what it was like. All too fucking well. But that's why I was here—to end it. One final battle. One that would silence any other opportunists motivated enough to strike. To make Ronan pay for everything he'd taken. For Jax. For Prescott. For Seth. For Reina's soul. For everyone who'd been swallowed up by his ambition and greed disguised as the desire to do *good*.

"I'm fine," I said, knowing it was a lie. Knowing she wouldn't buy that shit. Not for a moment.

Luna's hand rested on my knee and grabbed my attention, forcing me to look her in the eye—to see the sincerity behind her words. Her touch grounded me, though I hated how much I needed it. "The best thing you can do right now is show your body and mind the same love you've poured into this world. You've sacrificed a lot, but you can't fight for anyone if there's nothing left of *you* to give. Before you go out there and risk it all, promise me one thing?"

"You know we don't make promises we can't keep, Luna. Don't do that. Please." I pleaded, already feeling trapped by whatever she was about to ask.

"No, no. This one's simple," she said gently. "Nothing you can't uphold unless you choose not to. I would not be surprised, by the way. You're stubborn, just like Pres—"

The room stilled.

"I'm sorry," she said quickly.

"Don't be, Lu. Seriously, it's fine," I said, though the tremble in my voice betrayed me. "What's the promise?"

"Stay true to yourself. Wars don't just claim lives—they take pieces of you, carve away at your soul, little by little, until you forget who you were fighting for in the first place. I know you, Sweet Girl. Prescott knew you. The woman he was proud to call his, to call his family. *That* woman has something worth protecting, and that's what Ronan fears the most.

"Don't let fire meet fire. All it does is leave behind ash. War is inevitable and it will rage around you, but you don't have to let it consume you. Survive, not by burning brighter, but by refusing to be burned at all."

I stiffened. Her words hit too close to the truth. I'd been lost, focused on vengeance, on proving myself as general, that I hadn't stopped to think about what I was losing in the process. My humanity? Maybe. But it didn't matter. What mattered was winning. What mattered was making Ronan reap what he'd sown.

Luna didn't know. Couldn't know how far I'd already gone, how much of myself I'd already burned away in my obsession to see this through. The only person that knew how far I was willing to go to protect what I loved was me. And by the time they all figured it out, it would simply be too late.

She didn't understand, and she didn't need to. Luna wasn't carrying the weight of a million lives on her shoulders. She hadn't been forced to step into Prescott's shoes when he'd died and left me to clean up the mess. No. She volunteered. She had not been forced or had expectations thrust upon her. She, like most of the people here, had the option of sacrificing their souls within a level of comfortability. No one expected anyone to do *anything*, except me.

But that wasn't fair.

Luna *had* lost everything. She'd lost Prescott—the love of her life. Her grief didn't resemble mine; it was sharper, heavier. Yet she bore it differently. Silently. She possessed the gift of a quiet strength that was almost unbearable to witness.

I hadn't let myself be angry—not at Prescott. But it simmered beneath the surface, threatening to boil over, an ache I'd buried so deep it had grown roots.

He'd left me. Prescott fucking left me. This was *his* place. Jax's place. Not mine. This had never been my fucking dream. It was theirs. This was all fucking *theirs* …

And here I was.

Alive.

Alone.

And left with the weight of making sure this place stood even though they did not.

Then the guilt hit. None of this was their choice, either. If they could be here—they would be. And if either of them had this power, were in my position, then they wouldn't be victimizing their losses, they'd weaponize them. Use it to fuel them to set the world right once more.

The thing was, I didn't know how. I was lost without them. Jax had always seen the good in me, encouraged it, fed that hopeful version of myself. And Prescott … he had been everything I was not. Wise. Strong. A natural born leader—an ambitious one with dreams he refused to limit. He always knew what to do, and I followed with my own judgment in mind. Now it was all up to me.

Amaia Bennett. The twenty-eight-year-old woman who was on the cusp of losing her damn mind. *All without a drink. Ha.*

"I'll try," I said finally, the words heavy in my mouth.

She gave me a small, knowing smile and pulled a red leather book from her pack.

"This is for you."

I blinked, picking it up and flipping it open. Recognition struck like a punch—I knew that handwriting.

"Luna, what is this?" My voice cracked.

"It's Prescott's," she said softly. "This is for you, and you alone."

I flipped through the pages, my vision blurring. He'd written to me every day since we'd decided to make Monterey a home. Every single day.

"There's more." Luna pulled out another stack of journals from her pack.

I searched for the newest one, my hands trembling with such violence that I could barely turn the pages. When I finally found it—his final entry—something inside me broke. Tears blurred my vision, spilling freely down my face as I traced the date with my fingertips.

The day he died.

A choked sob escaped before I could stop it. His love crashing over me like a tidal wave. I pressed the journal to my chest and clutched it tight as though I were offering him one last hug. A redo of the one I'd given him the morning I'd set off for Duluth. If I could go back in time, I'd hold on tighter, for a half a second longer.

The capacity to hold it all together no longer existed. I broke. Not silently. Not loudly. But simple, unrelenting grief that broke me as I clung to the pieces of us that I thought I'd lost forever—though I'd never known to search in the first place.

"Thank you," I whispered, my voice barely audible as I turned toward Luna and leaned into her.

"Now," Luna said softly but firmly, her hand rubbing my arm before she pulled back. "No more tears. Now that I have you, let's talk shop so we're all ready for your *temporary* absence."

"Ma'am, yes, ma'am."

The plans were already set: once we left, Monterey Compound would go into permanent lockdown until the rest of the troops returned. A skeleton crew would stay behind, Ramona and a small cavalry unit on patrol, enough to mount a defense if needed. But if holding the walls became impossible, their orders were clear—fall back and retreat. The bunker is where they'd make their last stand.

"When you return," Luna began, her tone serious as she locked eyes with me, "which you will, you need to decide what the future will look like."

"What do you mean?" I asked, narrowing my eyes.

"You can be general, or you can lead, but you cannot do both. Not effectively, not fairly. One of the two will suffer, and with a war looming over you like a shadow, it will not be easy to convince them all to keep either."

"I can assure you that won't be a problem," I replied evenly, lifting my chin, guilt washing over me as to the reason why.

Luna's gaze lingered on me, heavy with skepticism as if she were trying to figure me out. But it wasn't my place to make her see. As general, it was up to me to do what was necessary, to make the decisions no one else could stomach, for the good of everyone—even if it cost me more than I could admit.

I hoped Luna would understand someday. That they all would.

THE FIRE CRACKLED IN THE HEARTH, ITS WARMTH PROTECTED BY THE air magic I'd practiced since getting back. Sweet, harsh scents of woodsmoke mingled with faint traces of spice from the food spread across the low table. Prescott's quarters had always carried a sense of calm for me. Fire or not, it had a warmth to it even in his absence. *Despite* his absence.

Tonight, the room was alive. Laughter echoed off the wood-paneled walls, the flicker of flames painted the faces of the people I loved the most in hues of gold. I sat curled on the brown leather couch, a steaming cup of coffee clutched in my hands.

The dogs tumbled near the door, tails wagging as their play became more rambunctious and out of control. I shifted my attention elsewhere, forcing myself to appreciate the here and now, because in twenty-four hours, everything would be different. Tomás leaned on the arm of the chair across the coffee table, talking animatedly to Moe. The same Tomoe who dodged his heavy-lidded stare as though we would all buy the reddening of her cheeks was from the fireplace—not the golden-skinned boy granting all his attention to her. Riley sat on the other side of me, Yasmin tucked under his arm. The two of them whispered to each other and blocked out the rest of us. Across the room, Elie and Emma sat in the corner, their laughter occasionally broke out in waves.

It was chaotic. Loud. Awkward at moments, but it was home— this was my family. *Mine.* Even Adelaide had been allowed to make a rare appearance now that Hunter trusted us all. She watched the dogs with wide eyes, stuffing her face with some oat cookie Reina had baked her. Jessa had the worst of it all, unwanted by everyone but here by grace of Reina's lack of boundaries and weakness to lust. Perhaps the awkwardness of their interactions had spared me the complicated situation of the other woman sharing this couch.

I caught Yasmin's glares, pretended not to notice in the same way Jessa did when it came to Hunter shooting daggers at her from a few seats away. The tension between the Moore's and her was almost comical. Almost. Reina and Jessa's 'latest drama'— *complicated my ass*—had cast a shadow on the first half of the night. Explaining why no one was surprised she'd arrived at Reina's side to Alexiares was, in fact, comical. Some things with Reina would never change—her messy love life was one of those things.

"All right, all right," Reina said, standing up dramatically. "Story time!"

Hunter groaned, "Here we go."

Reina ignored him, grinning.

"So there I was, pulling this soldier from the rubble, literally healing him as I was pulling, and BAM!" She clapped her hands together loudly.

Abel jumped back at the noise, causing Emma to squeal. Her brother, Luke, woke up from his nest near our bedroom door and Hal rushed over, scooping him up to rock him back to sleep.

"BAM?" Alexiares's brow raised.

Reina ignored him, her voice dropping in dramatic flair. "I'm yanked off my mare by not one, not two, but *three* Pansies. Mind you, they aren't even what y'all seen before. These babies were nightmares made of flesh … or is it flesh made of nightmares?"

"It was one Pansie," Alexiares deadpanned from beside me, not bothering to look up from his coffee as he kicked it back.

"Let my sister have her moment," Hunter said, giving Alexiares a silent, menacing warning.

"*Yeah,* pup," Reina said, popping both Ps with a smug grin. "Let me have my moment."

Their relationship was one of the few things that could still coax a genuine laugh out of me these days. The way they balanced each other out—it was a kind of healing I wasn't sure either of them had expected. Reina got the brotherly banter she'd always deserved from Seth, while Alexiares, whether he'd admit it or not, found in her the kind of sibling bond he'd been denied with Evander. It worked for them.

The thought tugged a smile to my lips, my hands tightening around the warm cup in my lap. My thigh bounced, a steady rhythm of nerves that hadn't registered until Alexiares shifted closer. His hand settled lightly on my knee, grounding me. I met his eyes and nodded, grateful.

"Anyway," Reina went on, fully in her element. "First one was off me in seconds. I put an arrow through one eye—WHAM!" She mimed the motion. "Then, for fun, the other eye."

"Tell them, babe," Jessa chimed in, her voice sticky sweet. Reina shot her a sharp stare to silence her before recovering with an exaggerated laugh. Hunter's gaze remained fixed with distaste at the blonde.

Abel was eating it all up, nodding along as if he hadn't heard the story a dozen times. "Then what happened?" he asked, leaning forward.

At least Yasmin and Hal seemed somewhat entertained. Elie watched on, bored but laughing on cues. *Better than before.*

Reina basked in the attention, leaning back as though she were holding court. "I had one arrow left, and I knew I had to make it count. So, I channeled my inner Amaia. I used it to get a new weapon. Improv at its finest."

Abel nodded appreciatively and Hal shook his head in a laugh of disbelief. His middle child, Olivia, hung onto his leg, leaning forward, mesmerized by Reina and her story.

"I don't believe it," Hunter muttered.

"Well, ya should." Reina's gaze hardened, a smug challenge flickering in her eyes. "I've been able to outshoot you since I was in a diaper."

"Whatever," Hunter said with a sharp, bemused laugh.

"You know what?" Reina crossed her arms. "Story time's over. Y'all don't deserve the rest."

"Thank God," Riley mumbled.

That earned him a smirk from Tomoe. The two of them shared a slight tap of their hands that did not slip Reina's notice.

"Okay, not nice," she snapped, but the corners of her mouth twitched in amusement.

"At least she didn't stop for a pair of heels this time," I said with a huffed laugh.

Alexiares choked on his refill of coffee. "She did what?"

There was no such thing as too much caffeine for either of us. It was basically foreplay for a good night's rest at this point.

"Oh, you haven't heard?" Riley jumped in, a mischievous grin lighting up his face.

Tomoe jumped at the chance. "Bonnie and Clyde here were out on a run, and Reina—"

"I tracked them the whole time," Reina interrupted with a wild cackle, barely able to contain her energy. "Firing arrows at leaves, bottles, whatever I could find. They both thought the other was messing with them when they weren't looking. Classic."

Riley groaned, shaking his head, locs flying, like he'd relived this moment far too many times. "You almost got us killed."

"Oh, please." Reina waved him off.

"When I realized it wasn't him—"

"*We* realized at the same time," Riley interrupted, a knowing glint flashing in his eyes.

"We changed our route, ducked into a store, and waited for her to round the corner," I added, dryly. "Not exactly rocket science, but it worked."

"Worked too well. We were supposed to—"

"Not sure who wears heeled boots on a scouting mission," I interrupted with a laugh. "But I digress."

"They were Lockette Beatle Valentino's, thank you very much," Reina shot back like we weren't quite grasping her point of view. "And I wasn't wearing them when I left! I found them. What was I supposed to do? Leave them there to rot?"

"You would've saved yourself the joy of having to heal your own wound," Riley said, smirking now.

"Ouch," Hunter muttered, wincing in sympathy. He knew from experience that healing yourself was a great pain.

Reina shrugged, her grin as sharp as ever. "Worth every second of it."

"It's an apocalypse." Serenity cut in full of disbelief.

Reina shot back with a teasing grin, "That doesn't mean I have to be ugly, Serenity," her tone light and full of playful defiance.

The whole room broke into laughter. Only Reina could make vanity sound as important as basic survival.

"We were stuck in Del Monte Shopping Center all night," Riley explained casually, his hand squeezed Yasmin's shoulder with gentle affection and she glanced down, cheeks reddening with her smile. "Surrounded by a herd of at least fifty Pansies."

"Crazy to think I thought I couldn't handle that back then," I mumbled more to myself than to anyone else.

Emma tilted her head, her expression skeptical. "You really think you could now?"

"Obviously," Elie cut in before I could answer. "She's *her*."

"Yeah, right," Serenity shot back. "You're good, but not *that* good."

I glanced at Yasmin, catching the flicker of discomfort that passed through her as Riley spoke, but she bit it down.

"Jax's timing was impeccable, as always," Reina said, cutting through the tension with her usual flair, sending an extra ripple of happiness through the room.

"Yeah, I wonder why," Tomoe muttered with the roll of her eyes. "*Thank you, Moe, for saving our lives*, says no one. Ever."

"Jax and—"

"Jax and Mohammed," Yasmin corrected, her voice soft. "They got you out. I remember."

The mention of Mohammed hung in the air. The room grew quieter, the tension thick enough to choke.

"Fun times, right?" Reina said, flashing a grin that could melt any awkwardness away. "Anywho, Abel, I think this party needs a little music. Shall we?"

Abel's grin was quick to return, and he stood, helping her to her feet with a dramatic flourish. Reina linked her arm with his, and they made their way toward the door.

"Be right back, my little love bugs!" she called over her shoulder, her voice practically singing with excitement as she led the way. Abel followed close behind, shaking his head with a chuckle.

The room was still for only a moment before Hal spoke. "Should we be concerned about that?"

"Yes," Alexiares said without hesitation.

"It's never fun when they scheme together," Tomoe muttered, his brow furrowed. "The boy knows exactly how to block me out."

She drummed her fingers absently on the table, her brow furrowed as though she were trying to work through a problem no one else could see. If there was anyone who could get under her skin, it was those two.

"Not a fan of surprises?" Tomás asked, his lips twitching in amusement.

"A surprise from my sister can go one of two ways: you wish you could disappear into the void, or—"

The door slammed open. Reina and Abel burst back in, lugging what appeared to be a cobbled-together speaker system.

"Woo! Let's party, people!" Reina announced like she was letting us know she'd single-handedly saved the world.

"Don't worry," Abel added with a grin. "I picked the music this time."

Tomoe froze, her inky eyes narrowing with the slight drop of her jaw. "Is that my record player?"

Reina smirked, the picture of innocence. "Yeah. You like it?"

"We made it," Abel said proudly. "I screwed everything together while she micromanaged," he said with a shrug, brushing imaginary dust off his shoulder.

Elie stepped up, curiosity lighting her face. "Cool."

Tomoe's restraint ticked away, about ready to explode but Tomás took advantage of the moment, holding out a hand. "Dance?"

She snatched her hand back with a hiss and an accompanying glare that reminded me some looks could in fact kill. Emma and Elie weren't having it. They pushed her forward and over to the only clear spot in the room by the door, grabbing her arms and forcing her to dance. Tomás followed with a grin.

Reina grabbed Adelaide, spinning her in an exaggerated twirl. "Clean versions only, pinky promise," she called to Hunter, hanging out her pinky finger.

Hunter put a matching one out in front of him and Serenity leaned into his shoulder with a small, but noticeable grin as she watched on, "Pinky."

The night slipped away and I let my gaze drift around the room, taking in the rare moment of peace. Yasmin and Riley were deep in some conversation I wasn't even going to try to understand, while Jessa and Serenity were actually getting along with Hal and Caleb—surprising, to say the least.

Hunter stood off to the side, watching Reina and Adelaide, his face caught somewhere between longing and frustration. Yeah, I knew what he was thinking. *Seth.* I could practically hear it in the silence around him.

"You good?" Alexiares's voice broke through the quiet.

I met his gaze, his expression softer than usual, waiting. I gave a curt nod, something inside me finally letting go. "Yeah. I think I am."

Surprising myself, I added, "Come on. Let's dance. You missed your chance being a dick last time."

The smile he gave me wasn't a smirk—it was something warm, real. His hand slid to my shoulder, his fingers giving me a light squeeze as he pulled me toward the center of the room.

"I do owe you a dance," he whispered into my ear, the tickle of his breath sending a tickle down my spine and twisting my core. "But for a very different night. One I want us to remember forever."

His hand rested against the small of my back and he pulled me closer, staring down at me with an overwhelming amount of love. And for once, I didn't think about anything else. Just this. Just us.

THE NIGHT AIR OF MONTEREY COMPOUND WAS COOL AGAINST MY skin. A rarity for the month of July. I took a slow drag then let the smoke settle deep before I exhaled, watching it curl up into the dark sky. Out here, in the green space between Prescott's quarters and Compound Hall, I could almost feel stillness. *Almost.*

The crunch of footsteps shattered it. There was no need to turn around. I knew who it was.

I groaned, grinding the blunt against the concrete to snuff it out. "Hi," I said flatly, not bothering to mask my irritation.

"This stays between the two of us," she said, voice carrying the same amount of irritation she only saved specifically for me. *How special.*

My eyes flicked to the small bump now visible beneath her shirt. Riley's child. His *son*. My godson … That had to be killing her. I wasn't sure how Riley had managed to convince her, then again, all bets said she spent her free time praying I'd never make it back—save the argument for something that mattered.

I forced a sharp exhale through my nose. "Everything has always stayed between us," I replied. "I have no interest in straining a relationship with Riley over something I should've solved on the mat back when I had the chance."

Yasmin's eyes narrowed, her lips curled into a bitter smile. I was done being the bigger person with her. Riley had asked me to do my best and I had. If she wanted to act like some child unable to experience simple character development, then that was on her.

"When you come back, are you going to bury him like you buried Prescott? Will you abandon Riley's grave the way you left his? Jax's?" She was so smug—so intent on hurting me and for what?

Literally, for fucking what? I was a general, I owed her no sympathy for the outcomes of my job, a post her boyfriend held for *years* without incident. A position he'd been proud to hold— one appointed to him by Riley himself. All I'd done was sign the dotted line.

I'd granted her space when she'd asked for it, apologized when it was due—profusely—shown her respect when none was due, and overall tolerated her. Yasmin had never shown me the same grace. And now, she'd gone too far.

My body went still. That fire I'd been trying to smother erupt- ed. Slowly, deliberately, I turned to face her, my voice dropping to something deadly—yet calm. "Do not," I said, every word carved from stone, "say their names again unless it's to thank them for the fucking walls keeping you alive or to share a memory worth hearing. Do you understand?"

Yasmin scoffed, but I stepped into her space, forcing her to meet my eyes.

"You're pregnant. But you won't always be. I'm going to ask you again: Are. We. Clear?"

She held her ground for a second, her jaw tight, before her gaze dropped to the side like the coward she was. Had always been. She'd had a chance to confront me when there had been a chance to fight. But she hadn't, because as tough as she acted, Yasmin knew that when it came to me, she would always lose.

"Then you'd lose Riley's loyalty for good," she muttered, but the heat in her words had fizzled into something weaker.

My gaze swept over her, letting the silence drag before answering with a smile. "Would I?" I said finally, cool and deliberate.

I stepped back and pulled the blunt from my pocket and lit it again with a flick of my fingers. The flame flared, reflecting in her hooded eyes. I took a slow drag, watching her, savoring the sweet, earthiness of it.

"Riley's a soldier," I said as I exhaled, smoke spilled out with the wind, blowing it away from her face. "He understands the law of The Pit."

I took a few steps away, pausing long enough to tilt my head back toward her, my voice sharp and deliberate. "Besides, I thought I already killed him."

I didn't spare a second glance. Let her choke on whatever words she had left. *How dare she? How fucking dare she dig her claws into wounds that never healed?* Yasmin's words had almost cracked something in me, something fragile buried so, so deep, but I wouldn't let her see it. The smoke curled around me as I walked away, clinging to me like the ghosts of the ones I loved—the ones I'd failed—pressing down on me with every step.

CHAPTER FIFTY-FOUR

TOMOE

Leaving wasn't supposed to be this hard. I'd told myself that it wouldn't be, had made my peace with it. After all, the people I cared about most were coming with me. There wasn't much I was leaving behind—just walls and furniture, a compound that smelled like drying concrete and damp earth. And herbs. And food. And terribly stale tavern beers. Like home.

That wasn't true though. That wasn't all I was leaving behind. Now there was more than material items. Emma. Olivia. Luke. Hal. Elie. Luna … they would all remain, and the future wasn't set. There was no guarantee we'd all see each other again.

We were already behind schedule. The sun had cleared the horizon an hour ago. Goodbyes were hard. The troops didn't mind. It bought them all precious seconds with their loved ones. Elie and Emma worked to draw it all out—the worst offenders by far. They swore to Amaia up and down that they would do what it took to keep The Compound safe. The over-the-top hand gestures and declarations were nothing but a show, a way to keep us here for if only one more moment. I'd miss them. Emma had made this all particularly bearable when everything else was crumbling around me.

Then there was Yasmin. Her goodbye with Riley had been almost painful to watch. They didn't say much; they didn't need to. The way Riley hugged her, how he watched her growing stomach …

I'd been cornered shortly after that, and though I didn't care for her or her shitty attitude, I let it slide.

"You keep him safe," she demanded, leaving me no room to debate. "And Lilia too. No matter what else happens out there, she is top priority, she is only a child."

"I don't need you telling me how to do my job or keep those under my watch safe."

Yasmin didn't flinch—only stared me down as if I could be intimidated. We were even heights, but that was irrelevant given I could face Ronan head-on and not waver.

"Once she gets those wards down, she goes straight to the safest settlement," she reminded me. "No further. A child does not belong at the center of this war."

I didn't bother bringing up that there were in fact hundreds, no, thousands of children at the center of this war—but sure, I'd keep my promise on making sure this one stayed safe.

Riley arched a brow of skepticism at the two of us as he approached, his pack full and bursting at the seams, axe holstered on one leg, Shadowstep blade on the other. "Amaia wants everyone to wrap things up. Time to move out."

I scoffed a laugh then nodded to Yasmin because arguing with her was pointless. "I'll be anywhere but here."

Amaia stood near South Gate, the dawn light spilled over her like molten gold, softening the hard edges of a woman who rarely allowed herself to be seen this way. She was still—unmoving as she stared at The Compound. Her eyes flickered on every small detail as if she might imprint it into her memory. This wasn't just home for her, it was a battlefield of ghosts. A silent witness to every decision she'd ever made—good or bad.

Leaving here felt final in a way.

Her shoulders sagged betraying words she wouldn't dare say out loud. This *could* be the last time. I watched as her fingers twitched at her sides, her usual confidence faltering. It left me uneasy. Amaia did not waste time second-guessing. And yet, here she was, rooted in front of the gate leading into Entertainment Square like she was afraid to move forward—or maybe she couldn't let herself look back.

I wanted to believe she was tired. That this war hadn't carved pieces out of my sister already. But that would be a lie. One I could no longer spout as I stood here watching her. The way she was staring at Monterey Compound was less about leaving a physical place and having everything to do with the pieces of herself she could never get back.

It was not The Compound she was saying goodbye to. It was the person she'd been when this all began as nothing more than a dream.

"Take care of this place," Amaia said quietly to Luna, her voice steady but weighed down by something she wouldn't let show.

Luna didn't respond right away. Instead, she stepped forward and pulled Amaia into a hug. the kind of embrace that resembled a goodbye wrapped in gratitude. The gesture was normal for Luna—she was warm when she felt up to it—but Amaia … She didn't stiffen or step back. She stood there, still and silent, letting herself be held.

It was unsettling.

From the corner of my eye, I noticed Alexiares watching, his brow drawn tight in confusion, maybe even concern. Our gazes met for a split second, the question hanging between us: *what's going on inside her mind?*

Amaia pulled back, offering Luna the faintest nod before turning to Elie and kissing the top of her golden curls. "I love you and I am proud of you."

Elie froze like she'd been struck. Her mouth opened, then closed, no words finding their way out. Tears streamed down her light brown cheeks, her hand drifted almost instinctively to the hilt of the blade Amaia had made for her.

Amaia reached out, ruffling Emma's blonde hair. "Look after each other," she said softly.

"See ya, wouldn't wanna be ya," she quipped, but her voice cracked at the end.

Amaia turned to the shadow that approached from behind. Her gaze sharpened as she sized Caleb up.

"I'd like to stay," he said, his tone firm but cautious. His fingers ran through his now shaved head, the blond that had previously been dyed a sandy brown back to its natural sun-kissed state.

Amaia's eyebrow lifted. "Give me one reason, soldier."

Caleb squared his shoulders. "My brother's still here. And his fiancée—wife now, I suppose. Nephew too from what I saw. If something happens ..." He paused, his jaw tightening. "I want to be here to protect them. There are amends to make, and if it comes to goodbyes, I'd rather say them in person—during our final moments."

She didn't answer immediately. Her eyes flicked over him, and for a moment, her usual impenetrable resolve cracked enough to let something else through—consideration, maybe even trust.

"You report *directly* to Miller and Luna," she said, voice flat.

Caleb exhaled, a quiet relief. "Thank you."

Amaia's lips quirked in a faint, teasing smile. "That's how re-paying favors works, right?"

It was her way of saying he was okay. That she trusted him now.

The shrill cry of a toddler made me jump. Hunter kneeled in front of Adelaide a few feet away, smoothing her curls as she clung to his leg, her tiny arms refusing to let go. "Hey, honey," he said softly, the latter portion of his sentence breaking off. "You're going to stay here with Luna, okay? She's gonna take good care of you. You mind your manners, best behavior. Pinky?"

Adelaide shook her head fiercely, looking every bit a Moore, her grip tightened. "No! Want you!"

Serenity crouched beside them, tears staining her cheeks. "I know, baby. I know it's hard. But remember when mommy and daddy told you the story about the people who saved the world? It's our turn to help." Her voice wavered, she brushed a soft hand over Adelaide's face as she nodded.

Hunter kissed Adelaide's forehead, "Be brave for us," he whispered.

Serenity finally pried Adelaide's hands free, lifting her into her arms one last time. She hugged her daughter close, swaying gently as if she could soothe them both. Then, with trembling hands, she passed Adelaide to Luna. "Please, keep her safe."

Luna's arms wrapped around the little girl and said, "With everything I have."

Hunter and Serenity lingered for a moment longer, their gazes locked on Adelaide as if they could will this parting not to hurt. Then, wordlessly, they turned toward Caleb, offered him a nod that stated they'd all already said their goodbyes and stepped back toward the transport. Hunter's arm wrapped tightly around Se-renity's shoulders as her quiet sobs broke the silence.

One by one, soldiers readied to move. Riley stood near the back, his jaw set as he watched everyone settle. Reina was by his side, her arms crossed tightly over her chest, her usual soft expression sharpened by Jessa at her side. *I really needed to find a way to get rid of her.* Yasmin, I could tolerate. She loved Riley and Riley was clearly beyond smitten with her. But the clingy blonde shadow who didn't know when to leave my sister alone? That was a problem I'd have to solve later.

Amaia hadn't moved. She stood rooted near the gates, staring at The Compound as though it was both her greatest triumph and her deepest regret. For a moment, I thought she might stay. Her shoulders tensed, her hands clenching at her sides as if holding herself together.

"Amaia," Riley called out, his voice steady. "We do our jobs out there and that will make sure we always have a reason to come back."

Amaia turned her head slightly, enough for the corner of her mouth to twitch in acknowledgment. She finally turned, her boots crunching against the hard ground as she stalked down the road. Alexiares and I hesitated, exchanging another glance.

Neither of us followed right away. We both hesitated, watching her. Amaia's movements were measured, but they lacked the fire she usually carried. There was no anger, no defiance. Just silence.

"What is it?" Alexiares asked quietly, his voice barely audible over the wind.

I shook my head. "I don't know."

THE KENTUCKY BORDER WAS A DISTANT DREAM. ONE MEASURED NOT in miles but in the unrelenting crunch of boots on asphalt. The groan of solar vehicles struggled against harsh elements, and the weary plod of horses who, like the rest of us, smelled like shit and appeared to be reconsidering life choices.

Weeks of snaking through the fractured highways had taken us from Arizona's blistering sun to New Mexico's eerie silence and, finally, into Texas, which was still Texas: too big, too bold, and far too stubborn. The wanderers there clung to the land, convinced they'd inherited it from the universe itself, not realizing how far their roots had rotted.

I sat perched on a supply cart near the front of the caravan. Dust clung to every surface, including my teeth. I wiped at my mouth for the tenth time that morning, spitting the grit to the side. The scent of sweat and worn leather mingled with the sharper tang of the horses.

Other settlements had joined us along the way, a serpentine force winding through a fractured country. Albuquerque had been the first real rallying point. Honestly, the city was barely holding itself together. With most of Transient Nation having the wits to flee, *ghost town* wasn't an exaggeration.

Scouts had timed the rendezvous points perfectly. They ran themselves ragged between settlements, ensuring each group arrived like clockwork. A job completed with such precision that by the time we reached Oklahoma City, the force had grown into something resembling an army. As each convoy added to the mass, more than soldiers arrived. Each settlement had arrived with supplies and healers to dole out—to share. The most conflicting arrivals had been loved ones who'd volunteered.

They'd come because they couldn't bear to let their people fight alone. Brave, stupid, or both—I couldn't decide. I wasn't sure which was worse: to lose someone in battle or to lose them while they held your hand.

Kansas was a hard pass. Traitorous bastards—they'd not shown when it came time to move out. That only meant one thing.

"Why isn't he stopping us?" I'd asked Alexiares as healers worked to address the wounds of the last prisoners we'd managed to set free. There were hundreds of them. It went far beyond Hunter's caravan. We'd found residents from Salem and The Expanse whose loved ones had thought long dead … Ronan's own citizens too.

"Because he doesn't have to," he said, sharpening his blade.

I hated how easily he said it. I hated that he was right.

Weather became our greatest threat the second we hit Oklahoma, pelting us with rain that turned the roads into mud traps. Horses slipped, carts got stuck, and food was lost. Still, morale was at a high.

That wasn't to say there wasn't fighting. No. There was plenty of that—just not the kind that left bodies on the roadside. Leadership clashed constantly, and I had half the mind to stick them in a circle and tell them to hash it out with their fists.

Amaia, of course, was the exception. It was unnerving. She kept her focus on the bigger picture, detached from the smaller dramas. She was *the general* now, and though we all felt it as her family, we couldn't name what had changed within her. The plan to split into two forces once we hit Kentucky was brilliant—strategically sound, even poetic in its ambition—but it was also the perfect fuel for arguments.

Two weeks out from Kentucky and the constant tugging within my mind was going to drive me insane. There was something the universe had intended for me to see, but I could not. Not with Ronan safely tucked behind his wards. Still, I listened—and still I tried.

Ronan was still waiting for us—or not. That was the problem. The camps we liberated were eerily unguarded, their soldiers apathetic at best. Hundreds of prisoners stumbled out of those hellholes, their freedom too easy. Salem. The Expanse. Even Covert's own people. It didn't make sense.

It was against that backdrop of unease that the plan to split forces ignited the argument of the century. I'd never seen Riley and her go at it with such intensity, never seen such piercing rage flow through him. No small amounts of Reina's magic had calmed the situation.

Two routes: one safer, one a gamble.

Amaia had insisted on taking the riskier route. Predictably, no one would let her. It wasn't just about strategy; it was about survival. If one group had to make it to Richmond, it was hers. None of them would say it outright, but I would—Amaia *was* the movement. Without her, this whole thing would collapse faster than Riley's patience when he had to repeat an order.

She didn't fight them long. When Alexiares backed Riley, she let the argument die. Her silence cut deeper than any words she could've spoken. I'd seen her command armies, face impossible odds, and hold her ground against the fiercest enemies. But in that moment, surrounded by her family and closest allies, she looked … cornered.

The plan was simple on paper: our forces would encircle Richmond, dividing its defenses. Amaia's group would head northeast. Follow the river into West Virginia then Virginia—flank Richmond from the northwest.

Riley would take a smaller, more skilled force—to include Hunter and Serenity's caravan as a way to accommodate the lack of bodies and overcompensate with magic—down a southeastern path. From there they'd cut through Arkansas into Tennessee and attack from the southwest. This was where the brute of Ronan's forces laid for it was the more direct route in.

About fifteen miles outside the city the two groups would converge. The larger forces would create chaos at the perimeter while a vanguard unit—Amaia, Alexiares, Riley, Reina, Hunter, Serenity, two cavalry units, and a small squad from Alpha Unit—would slip into Richmond.

Lola would portal them in.

It would use up every ounce of magic gifted from the earth that she had. The kind of spell that left a mark on your soul. She would be punished for daring to wield power so recklessly. She might never cast again. If this failed, there wouldn't be a second chance. The irony in plans were they were only as good as the people willing to carry them out.

And a cornered Amaia would always make her own plans.

But plans, no matter how carefully crafted, didn't account for the weight of perception. Amaia to the masses, was no longer a young, reckless leader—they respected her now. Respect wasn't reverence; it didn't silence dissent.

The soldiers weren't afraid to challenge her, treating her more like an equal than an authoritative entity. She wasn't commanding a broken, desperate army anymore. These people had grown stronger, surer of themselves, and they weren't afraid to meet her decisions with resistance.

Right there, in that challenge, was the beauty of the situation. They had finally seen her for what she was, something more than a girl in a general's role. She was more than a rising leader—they had given her the space to prove herself. And now that she had, they secretly hated her for it.

It was funny, in a way. Most of my life, I'd thought being underestimated was the worst thing you could face. That was in The Before.

In The After, it was better to be seen as weak. To not be a threat.

Because threats get taken out.

CHAPTER FIFTY-FIVE

TOMOE

It'd been days since scouts had reported any movement from Covert on our side of the border. To me, it sounded like we were due a visit. Apparently those who had actual knowledge on this kind of thing didn't agree. We needed quality rest anyway. After hauling ass for fifty-one days, we were on the tail end of this journey.

Strength was a requirement for this endeavor, and one could not gain strength without proper time to recover. Still, sleep evaded some. While the rest of our camp slumbered away, those whom sleep evaded sat around the fires lining down the massive camp. It was a risk, but with most of our troops in the area, Ronan would have to mobilize his army—and even he could not hide an entire

A shadowed figure moved on the other side of the fire. I sat as close as I could, staring into the mesmerizing rise and fall of the flames. My gaze flickered up and landed on eyes so blue they could rival the purest of seas. Hunter's attention stayed fixed. I became painfully aware that there was no one here but the two of us. If now was the time he wanted to enact his revenge, I wouldn't stop him.

He cleared his throat, startling me as his voice cut through the still night of this brute filled camp. "I've got your back out there."

I shifted my weight, uncrossing my legs as my eyes narrowed with confusion. I couldn't tell what his endgame was.

Hunter read the uncertainty across my expression. "You don't need to worry … uh … you know, about if I'll defend you in the same capacity I'd defend the others? I can see the way ya look at me. Just wanted to make that clear."

The muscles tensed along every inch of my body. It was hard to swallow. He should not have to worry about me, how I'm *feeling*. There were bigger problems in the world than how I was doing emotionally. The last thing I wanted was for Hunter Moore to comfort me when I was the one that took the life of his twin. To be frank, I felt like shit every time I looked at him.

Every time I looked into his eyes, I saw Seth Moore—the man I had loved. Maybe it was the kindness in them that Seth had only let me see. Or perhaps it was the intensity, much like his brother's, yet softened by something unfamiliar.

Empathy.

That part was different.

I had never seen it in Seth's eyes, not once—not in the years I spent falling for him, not in the nights we spent tangled together, his gaze void of anything but certainty. I hadn't noticed then what was missing. But now, with Hunter right in front of me, I did.

Standing before his brother, everything I hadn't realized was missing, was suddenly there. The good. The love. The compassion that matched the love for the world that existed within Reina's.

He raised to his feet taking one step, two steps over, then sat down. Directly next to me—*touching* me. His presence was an electric current in the air. It unnerved me. Made me want to squirm and flee. He didn't notice. I turned back to the fire, but I could sense his gaze still trained on me.

The closer we got to Covert's border, the colder the air grew. Hunter's warmth accompanied with the fire made me appreciative of the frigid bite. Last days of summer or not, there were some parts of Transient Nation that were simply unforgiving.

I forced myself to meet his stare once more. There was something there, it wasn't pity nor sympathy. Just ... something else. Something I could not define.

He was the first to break this time. Sniffing, he straightened up and took a deep breath. When he found the courage, he wandered back to hold my eye. "Tomoe," he said, his voice quieter now. "I don't blame you for what happened to Seth."

There was a careful, hesitant honesty in his words. They caught me off guard because I didn't deserve them. In the end, I had to make a choice, me or Seth—and I'd only trusted one of us to do what it took to look out for our family.

Seth's name passing through the lips of a twin who sounded nearly identical to him, made my heart twist into a painful ball. A hand squeezing the life out of my ill-beating heart. I'd expected anger or complete silence from Hunter when he'd arrived at The Compound—once Reina had time to explain everything that had happened from the time the two of them had passed through Monterey's gates.

Instead, he'd shown me nothing but quiet acceptance in front of the others. I'd not been brave enough to be alone with him.

And now, that luck would have it, I was. Hunter's face fell, a shadow of his own pain passing through.

"I do miss my brother. Don't get me wrong," he said. "But I miss ten-year-old Seth who'd swing from ropes with me and jump down the stairs. Sixteen-year-old Seth who raced me out in the fields with nothin' but the moonlight as our guide. The brother I had right before the ranch fell … From what I hear, that was no longer the brother that existed. You didn't have a choice."

My throat tightened. No. This was too much. I did not find myself deserving of his mercy. I wanted there to be accusations. Bitterness. The weight of what I'd done was fucking crushing my soul. It pressed on my chest in a way that made breathing every day a chore.

I had expected them all to hold it against me forever—but they hadn't. *He* hadn't. So why did that hurt?

"I didn't want to …" I trailed off. "I didn't want to be the one … the one who ended it." My voice cracked before I could stop it, and I clenched my fists, grounding myself in the sting of my nails digging into my palms.

"I know," he said softly.

The understanding in his voice—no judgment. Just the quiet acceptance I didn't think I deserved.

"He trusted me, Hunter." My voice cracked, and I hated myself for it. "Seth trusted me, and I—"

"No. He underestimated you, and you saved them," Hunter interrupted. "Not just you or Reina. You saved a lot of people that day doing what you did. And you paid the price for it. I won't lie to you or pretend it doesn't hurt. Shit, it clearly haunts you. But you did something some of us wouldn't have the balls to if it had been us. What had to be done."

"I could've found another way," I whispered. I knew it wasn't true. I'd run the possible outcomes through my mind a thousand times.

"You could've," Hunter said, eyes on the fire. "Doesn't really matter—the end of the road is the same, no matter which way you're coming from."

I didn't respond. What was there to say to that? I watched the fire stretch upward in bursts, sparks vanishing into the night. More soldiers had headed to bed. The camp had finally settled into something resembling peace.

"Fascinating," I muttered after a while.

Hunter glanced at me, his tone carrying that effortless curiosity I could never quite match. "What is?"

"How decent you and Reina turned out," I said, regretting the words the second they left my mouth. Small talk wasn't my thing, and I knew better than to tread here. Still, I forced myself to keep going. "I'd think this was a simple case of the apple not falling far from the tree if you two weren't right in front of me."

"Dropped on the head, or kicked in it," Hunters laughed, radiating through the hollow pathways that crossed every which way. A city of tents. "Turns out you lose a brother either way."

I blinked, then laughed—a real laugh. It startled me more than it should have. "Did you just—"

"Make a dead brother joke?" His smirk wasn't sharp, it was … sad. "Yeah. You get to do that when you have two of them. And since you were there …" He bumped my shoulder lightly, and I let it happen. "I guess that means you're allowed too. Plus, I heard you appreciate a well-placed morbid joke. Been awhile since I came across someone who could find a little humor in all this dark."

"You must spend very little time with the *Bloodhound.*"

"As little as possible. Yes, that's correct. Something is … not right inside that mind," he said, grinning.

I shook my head, but my mouth betrayed me again, another laugh slipping out. The fire popped, the kind of sound that filled the space between words, and I let it.

"You're a strange one, Hunter," I said bluntly.

He turned to face me, lips quivering as he did his best to bite back a laugh—he failed. Miserably, as he laughed in my face. "Strange? What an odd statement to come from such a source."

I rolled my eyes but didn't argue. "Fair point."

Hunter tilted his head, studying me in a way that made the space between us uncomfortably small. "You know, I didn't think I'd ever laugh like that again."

Something in his voice made my chest tighten. I didn't like it. Didn't know what to do with it. So I deflected.

"Well, don't get used to it," I said, standing and brushing off my hands. "I'm not exactly known for my sparkling sense of humor. Besides, I didn't even say anything funny."

Hunter leaned back, eyes steady, the smirk lingering a beat too long. "You don't need to say *anything* to bring a smile to someone's face, Tomoe. You just have to exist."

The fire popped again, making me jump as I turned to leave, the hour of night creeping in around the edges of the camp. I headed for the tent I shared with Reina, my steps swallowed by the camp's quiet. Everyone was asleep, or trying to be, but the world around me hummed with anticipation, as if the night itself were holding its breath.

I only needed to figure out why.

The ground beneath me was hard and uneven, the dirt darkened by the flickering light of lanterns hanging from posts or resting on crates. Everything about the camp felt burned by death and suffering. The hum of soldiers settling into their makeshift homes filled the air—low murmurs, the occasional clink of metal or the rustle of worn fabric.

I was halfway to the tent when the faint light from Tomás's flickered in the distance. The man never slept. He was always up to something—either fixing or creating. He was, unfortunately to me, a refreshing entity to spend time around. The weight of the world didn't appear to crush him the way it did with others.

His tent flap was partially open, the light inside dim, reflecting against his honey skin. He muttered to himself as I approached. Somehow, Tomás always settled across from me and Reina. Dark brows furrowed in concentration. I watched him lose himself in a room full of quiet thoughts. The only sound besides grumbles under his breath being the scratch of the pen over the blueprint sprawled across the floor.

"What the hell are you doing?"

He didn't startle at my words. I appreciated the lack of jumpiness in his demeanor when he was in my presence. Most people flinched when I walked into the room. Like I would look at them and point, maybe spout off the day of their death. Instead, he offered the same lazy grin that made his presence impossible to ignore, and went back to work.

"Ouch," I teased, turning away. "Guess I'm the one interrupting something today."

"No. Never that. My apologies, a bit lost in thought." His words stopped me in my tracks.

I pressed my lips together, refusing to fall victim to whatever this smile on my face was trying to do. "You never sleep."

The words slipped out matter of fact, but I kept my eyes on the plans in front of him. Tomás's intelligence knew no bounds. It was a shame it was only taken into consideration until recent months. Of course, his interests had changed when Alexiares had extended the offer to use his knowledge for evil. Or good. It was debatable given most of his work had been done under Alexiares's discretion.

His sketches were intricate, depicting weapons, magic-fused metal, and gear meant for more than the average soldier.

"Who needs sleep when there's work to do?" Tomás muttered, barely glancing up. A half-smile tugged at his lips. "I think I've figured out how to enhance our weapons with our power. Amaia thinks we'll need it when things get tough."

I stepped closer, leaning in. Couldn't help it. The words pulled me in, but it wasn't that simple. It was the way his eyes flicked up, then back to the papers, like he was waiting for me to say something. Eager to win my approval.

"Of course she does," I said, trying to keep it light. It came out sharper than I intended. "I thought you turned these in days ago?"

"I did," Tomás replied, twirling the pen between his fingers. "But there's always room for improvement."

I raised an eyebrow, my gaze flicking to the designs. "So, what's this do?"

"Make us stronger." Tomás's voice dropped low, and this time, he didn't smile. "To keep it simple: If we fuse our magic with the weapons, they'll respond better to the assigned user's touch. More power. We can use it to hit harder. Even if Covert gets their hands on it from a fallen soldier, they won't be able to use it—not in the same capacity."

I dropped to the ground, leaning in to study the finer details of his etchings. Focused. Too focused to notice the shift in his posture, the slight movement toward me.

Fingertips brushed my temple, light as a whisper. A slow, careful touch as he tucked a strand of hair behind my ear—like it was second nature. Like it had always been this easy for him.

But it wasn't. Not for me.

The moment stretched. There was a second, a beat, when everything went quiet. My pulse skipped. Then, his hand dropped away, but the space between us felt too small. And I could no longer face him.

"You okay?" Tomás asked quietly. He was watching me, and I couldn't figure out what he was thinking.

I cleared my throat, steadying myself. "Goodnight, Tomás," I said, my words rushed, taking a step back, my body already turning toward my tent.

"You know where to find me, Tomoe," he called after me, and I knew that he was smiling.

I turned back to him, no longer able to fight the smile tugging at my lips. The same banter we always fell into—it was easier to pretend it was just that. Easier to pretend it wasn't simmering into something more.

The vision hit me harder than a train. There'd been no warning. No sense of control—because I was not the conductor. I was only along for the ride.

Ronan. His smirk was sharp, knowing—like he had already won. Like this was just a formality.

Our routes would lead to nothing but the slow, agonizing collapse of our army. There would be skirmishes, small and relentless, each one a calculated strike meant to drain us further. Not enough to break us all at once. Just enough to keep us bleeding. And Ronan Moore, the architect of it all, would watch as we crumbled, piece by piece.

We were exhausted. Near broken. No magic left. No strength to fight back. No hope.

Because Amaia would be dead.

Ronan was ready. And he wanted us to feel it—to understand, in the marrow of our bones, how thoroughly we'd already lost.

CHAPTER
FIFTY-SIX

REINA

A lot of times, when Moe talked, it scared people. Maia was never included in that. But ever since that night Moe never came back to the tent, and I'd spotted her leaving Amaia's in the early morning, things around here had been weird.

Amaia had changed our plans. Not by much, and I supposed, that's where all the debate that followed had come from. I knew better than to ask Moe what she'd seen, same way she knew dang well it was bad luck to tell someone about their death. It was the only assumption I could come to after their weird behavior. Still, I didn't question. What did I know? War wasn't exactly new to me, but this position was. I was here to follow orders and shut the heck up. Set a good example for the others.

All of which would have been ten times an easier task if I couldn't feel the anxiety seeping off her, Alexiares, Tomoe, and pretty much every leader that cared about what happened to her outside of the war.

I leaned over the cold ground, wringing my hair out and tossing it in a towel. This bathing tent was absolutely disgusting. The less time I spent here, the better. Luckily, I could use my own water and avoid the harsh tap they pulled from the ground for the showers in order to limit exertion.

"Release your inhibitions. Feel the rain on your skin, no one else—"

"Boo."

The voice caught me off guard. It was still an ungodly hour and I'd thought myself to be alone. There were barriers at least, but when I entered, no one had been here. Of course, over my singing, it was hard to hear anything else. Couldn't say I didn't feel safe here, I supposed.

"Oh. Hi, Finley," I said, taking a step back at the small but mighty blonde who'd managed to sneak up on me.

"*Hi, Reina*, pretty voice," she mocked, rolling her eyes. A smirk tugged at her small, round lips, and she tilted her head, sizing me up. "You're up early."

"Yeah. You know what they say; early bird gets the worm and whatnot." I chuckled, reaching for my toiletry bag.

Finley took a feline step forward, "That is what they say. How's the water this morning? Fresh."

I'll be the first to admit, I was not a fan of how she said that last word. Made me think she wanted to drown me in it for fun and *I* was the one who had the power to wield it. Not once had I felt anything other than general contempt come from her. No real emotion. Not love. Not hate. No fear. No sorrow.

Finley replicated those things, but I never *felt* the true emotion come from her myself.

She was either really dang good at keeping her emotions in check in front of others, or she was a sociopath. Both were pretty terrifying if you asked me.

"I wouldn't know," I answered, adjusting the towel sliding off my short hair. "I use my own. Hard water is bad for your skin and hair."

"Right. I bet you purify yours first and everything." She took another step. I flinched as she bent down, reaching past my body. Finley froze. A cruel smile slipped into place and she rose back to stand directly in front of me. "You dropped something."

Her eyes lowered from mine and down to my throat. They flickered back up again and narrowed. "You're not actually scared of me. Are you?"

She laughed, as though it was an insane thought, though she had tortured my entire family only months ago. I didn't respond. Instead, I grabbed my brush from her strong grip and turned toward the flap of the tent.

"It must be nice. To live life so … free."

Her words stopped me in my tracks. Not because they held malice, but because her guard had finally slipped. When I turned to face her, her crystal eyes held nothing but pain. "It became very clear in the early days of all this that showing any ounce of empathy would end up with me and my father dead."

"No one forced you to torture people and be cruel, Finley," I responded with a scoff. I refused to feel bad for her. There were better people in the world to pity.

"No," she agreed. "No one forced me. But I had to make a choice, and I chose to survive. Same as you, same as your precious general, same as every person in this camp. I won't apologize for the fact that survival looks different on everyone."

"No one asked you to."

"When we first arrived in St. Cloud, it was a mess. They were doing … unspeakable things to … vulnerable people."

How bad could it have been if it had been deemed unspeakable by a woman who not only knew where the line was, but crossed it by choice countless times?

"Then why stay?" I couldn't help myself. I was curious. Everyone had a story. Though hers would make no difference in my opinion of her, I was a Nosey Nancy.

"There are worse places to be. I heard you crossed Yellowstone with only your brother at your side. You're aware of what's out there."

"Yeah and look." I gestured to myself. "I didn't come out the other side a villain. And before you start telling me that our circumstances were different, save it. I don't care, Finley. Keep your sob story. What? I bet you're telling me because you think I'm the weak one, the one you can manipulate the easiest? You made your choices and some of them hurt the people I love."

Finley laughed softly, the sound bitter as she turned the shower on. I turned away, giving her a shred of privacy, and then it slapped me across the face. That sadness. It rolled off her like a wave.

"Not at all, actually," she said, her words muffled against the plopping of water puddled at her feet. "I read people. It's what I do. How I managed to stay alive all this time. I don't think you're weak at all, Reina Moore. I think you're pretty fucking badass. But, little Reina, you also possess the amount of empathy that made me consider, for a fool's moment, that you were the one person in this camp I would be able to talk to, and not be bit back."

Dang my stupid heart. Her words softened me against my will. I glanced over my shoulder, sending her a sliver of peace, as much as I could muster with the amount that I cared. Her eyes revealed everything. Thank *you.*

"I tried things her way—Amaia's. My father and I both did."

"So what the heck happened?"

"Didn't work, obviously. I was shown how sick humans can get. You think I'm cruel? I am nothing but a product of terrible surroundings, and the result of what kindness looks like in that town. I could have left. My father wanted to. They had the equipment, the tools—I thought I could help. So, I became what St. Cloud demanded. I chose to be the evil in order for the greater evil to stand down. And turns out, I liked it. *Love* it. The power. The way grown men cower when I walk into a room. But everything has its price."

I opened my mouth, but she cut me off with a sharp, humorless chuckle.

"I doubt I'll survive this. If Covert doesn't kill me, one of the many enemies I've made throughout the years will. And honestly? I don't blame them. In retrospect, the person I am, the person I've become, is someone that needs to be put down. There's been things that I've done in the name of science and innovation … and then there's what I've done out of pure curiosity. I don't take any of them back, but I wish other decisions I've made had better outcomes. Results that excused what it took to get there. It's harder up north. Every day is a fight. Against the weather, the dead, or each other. Every damn day."

"Everyone has to make hard choices," I said. "If you want to be a better person, then start today. It's not hard to not act like a … you know."

She smirked faintly, though her eyes told a different story. Detached. I was pretty sure I was listening to the mumblings of a guilty dead soul.

"You're adorably optimistically naïve." She shut off the water and grabbed my brush, pulling it through her wet choppy hair. "I killed my father. There's no coming back from that. Not in this life or with the Lord. That's what you believe, right?"

"I guess," I said carefully, staring at my now contaminated brush—the last one I had thanks to Tomoe losing the rest. "I think there's a God, and that God loves all Earth's creations because, at their core, there's good in everyone."

"You think your daddy is good? Think he's seeing pearly gates?" A shadow of amusement flickered across her face, and I froze. "Exactly. I spent years working on a cure for my dad. He went into remission right before the bombs dropped. It came back at the same time his magic arrived. All the *Seers* and magic in the world, and still, nothing worked. So I killed him, but only because he asked me to."

"Why are you telling me this?" I asked.

"I had to tell someone. A girl like me? I've got no one. Before I die, I need to confess. Don't you think?"

I stayed silent.

"His condition turned dire and one night, we were going to give it one last shot before giving up." She laughed, dry and hollow—again her pain inched toward me, barely perceptible. "Cael Thomas was a lot of things; a quitter, he was not. Not until the end. He said his body couldn't take anymore. He asked me to do the deed—said he wasn't strong enough to do it himself."

And suddenly, I understood. Her confession hit a nerve I hadn't expected. Because I'd been there, too. I'd tried to do the same. In the end, I couldn't—and she had.

"It wasn't supposed to be that night." Finley handed the brush back, her fingers brushing mine for a brief second, colder than I expected. "But I knew if I left that room, I'd never have the courage. So I did it then. On the spot."

I waited for some kind of emotional response from her—heck, I would've accepted a physical one at this point. A nibble of the lip. Maybe the quiver of a brow. Something. Anything. But none came. She was back to the same old Finley from before this strange little interaction. Finley shrugged when I offered her no response, as if she hadn't just spilled the juiciest confession I'd ever heard.

She peered over my shoulder with a smirk, "This is probably going to get weird," she tugged at leather pants stretched to the limit, the moisture clinging to her skin as she fought to get them on. "Thanks for the therapy session. Tell your *Seer* she's fired."

And with that, she reached behind me, grabbing an equally tight thermal and dragging it over her wet hair. With a smile, she patted me on the shoulder and pushed her way past. My brain hurt, not understanding what had just happened. *I have to stop making myself so approachable.*

A tan, calloused hand waved in front of my face, and I blinked, startled back to reality.

"Oh," I stammered, cheeks flushing as I set my gaze on yet another blonde in front of me, wrapped in nothing more than a waffle robe tied loosely around her athletic frame. "Hey, Millie."

"Morning, sunshine." Millie grinned, her shoulder grazing mine as she slipped into the stall that was apparently popular today. The brief contact between us sent a jolt of warmth through the crisp morning air. Her robe slipped from her shoulders and hit the ground—leaving nothing but sun-kissed skin and confidence behind.

I lowered my gaze to the ground, refusing to linger on her long, tan legs. The muscle in them certainly didn't catch my eye when it hit the dim light perfectly. And her skin certainly did not appear soft as the beads of water dripped down her body.

"Sleep all right?" she asked casually, dropping her head back under the spray of water. The tents were heated making me grateful that at least this place had some kind of luxuries. Steam rose around her, wrapping her in a halo that made it sort of impossible not to steal a glance.

"As well as one can in the middle of all this," I replied, trying and failing to focus on the wall instead of the way the water slipped down her collarbone, tracing lines I shouldn't be thinking about.

"What's wrong, warrior girl?" Millie teased, turning toward me, her voice soft but laced with that familiar playful edge. The water dripped from her lashes and darkened her hair until it clung to her waist. "Nervous about the real fight?"

I let out a slow, amused breath, turning to her with a smirk. "Nervous? I was only wondering if you'd be able to keep up."

"I love a good challenge. Only one way to find out," she said, smirking as she raked a hand through her wet hair, sending droplets flying in my direction with a careless flick of her fingers.

I took a step back, taking my towel in self-defense. "Watch it. You'll ruin my … towel."

Millie laughed, a rich, throaty sound that made the air feel a thousand degrees warmer. "Towel? Is that your armor of choice today, cowgirl?"

"Why not?" I said, crossing my arms. "It's practical. Light. Easy to maneuver in."

"You've got all the tactical advantages," she said, grabbing the soap and lathering it in her hands, her eyes glinting with mischief.

"It's water resistant."

Millie snorted, her freckled nose crinkled as she shook her head. The banter felt good—normal. Like it was okay to laugh. I bit down on my lip, cheeks heating.

Then the shouting erupted.

Distant at first, muffled by the thick walls, but they grew louder, sharper. Voices overlapping, urgency cutting through the air. My stomach dropped.

"What now?" Millie muttered, cutting the water off abruptly.

I didn't have an answer. The noise outside had shifted into chaos—rapid footsteps, orders being barked, the unmistakable sound of equipment being shoved into packs. Millie grabbed her robe, wrapping it around her quickly. We stepped out into the main pathway of the camp. Soldiers moved frantically, faces tense. The amount of fear I felt was overwhelming. I gripped onto Millie's arm for support, her hand wrapped around my waist as she pulled me back and out of the fray.

"We're moving," someone called out, rushing past us with an armful of supplies.

"Ronan?" Millie asked, but the fury in her emerald eyes told me she already knew the answer.

A response never came. The moment pressed in, thick and suffocating. And all I could think was *not enough time*.

"Reina!" someone shouted. I turned to see a Serenity waving me over.

"Let's go," I said, wrapping my free arm around Millie's neck for support. The fear continued to increase, and I hadn't been prepared to block it out before it'd become all-consuming. She nodded, the teasing smile gone, replaced by the hardened determination we all wore in moments like this.

The lull was over. It was time to fight.

CHAPTER
FIFTY-SEVEN

AMAIA

My mercy only extended so far before I was tempted to ask the devil for a favor.

Those motherfuckers from Kansas were dead the second my troops set eyes on them—I only needed to figure out *how*. Scouts had poured in by the many. Kansas was on the move, and it wasn't to join our cause. Nope. I knew exactly what they were going to attempt, as if Ronan had scrawled their plans in bold across the tundra.

He wanted to chase us to the border—not push. There was a difference there. Ronan desired us to be broken by fear and exhaustion. This was not to be *the* battle, but a series of small ones until we couldn't go on a second longer.

So I'd have to break him first.

We had a day, maybe less, if Wichita, Kansas City, and Topeka kept their pace. I glanced up as Reina slipped into the tent, Serenity's jacket covering her towel shrouded body, light and snow flurries streaming in before the flap fell shut. She was followed closely by Millie, who was soaking wet, and Tomoe, her wide, hazed eyes fogged with exhaustion. *Diagnosis fucked, fantastic.* They pushed into the crowded tent that smelled like ass, must, and everything wrong with the world.

Things had been going too well. I was weary in finding hope in the extended bouts of peace. As we closed in on Covert's borders and the desert merged into the beginnings of a cold, unforgiving tundra, the nerves in me only increased.

This barren land was a graveyard, and the only thing it was missing was bodies. Ours or theirs.

No one spoke. They knew me enough by now to keep their mouths shut when I was in this state—calculating, teetering on the edge of brilliance or disaster. I refused to let us be caught running, but staying meant a fight we might not win. I ignored them, flipping through Prescott's journal instead. I needed to think—to pull from the known to prepare for the unknown.

They probably thought I was reviewing battle plans, options—I wasn't. I was searching for something familiar to anchor me. Anything to help think clearly.

I stumbled across a page I hadn't brought myself to read yet. One of his last entries. Ramblings—random thoughts and bits of history that had struck him as useful once. *Austria. Russia. Snow and ice. Higher ground. Cinematic embellishments.*

A reddish-brown hand reached over my shoulder and onto the journal, stopping me from turning the other page and my heart stopped. I froze before glancing up at Riley. His expression was unreadable, but the moment our eyes met, something clicked. This was it—the answer.

"Napoleon," I mumbled, my mind already racing through the memories I'd stored.

"What?" Finley frowned. Up front. Per usual.

"Napoleon," I repeated with confidence, addressing the rest of my audience. "That's how we do this. I know what to do."

"Yeah, you and you only." Finley raised an eyebrow, leaning lazily against the table.

"Another proposal to lean on the past?" Claes asked from the back, his tone dubious.

"If you don't study history, it repeats itself," Alexiares said dryly, his warmth brushing my arm in a way only I noticed.

"And in this case," I continued, snapping the journal shut with a decisive *thunk*. "Repeating it is exactly what I plan to do. Napoleon was an asshole. Brilliant, but an asshole nonetheless."

"Good ideas. Terrible execution," Riley added.

"What is she on about?" Millie asked from their corner of the room. I glanced over, trying to read the intentions of her statement. It wasn't sarcasm. She appeared genuinely interested in where my mind was going.

Reina gave her a sharp elbow to the ribs. "Shut up. Don't interrupt the maestro at work."

I stepped closer to the table and leaned, tilting my head as I glanced over the officers that had no choice but to meet my gaze. "Most of you old shits went to West Point. Half of what you studied came straight out of Napoleon's playbook. Love him or hate him, the man understood how to win."

"He was a masochist," General Harper countered, shaking his head.

Alexiares scoffed. "'*Sadist*' is the term you're looking for. He won wars."

I glanced at him before I could stop myself. He wasn't looking at me—his focus stayed on the map, his brow furrowed, lips barely moving as he spoke. The words weren't spoken with the kind of quiet confidence that always caught me off guard. I hadn't known him to be an admirer of Napoleon. The way his mind worked, the way he pulled something sharp and useful from a name that everyone else dismissed—it wasn't the first time he'd surprised me.

And damn, it wouldn't be the last.

"Lost a lot of souls too," Harper shot back, the room bristling with tension.

I raised an eyebrow, letting my gaze linger on Harper until the weight of it made him shift uncomfortably. "Are we still talking about Napoleon, General? Or is this about my record once ambushed?"

His jaw tightened, but he didn't answer. He didn't have to. The room knew exactly what he was implying—hell, they were all thinking it, too.

They remembered, as I did, the cost of my last gamble. The bodies that had piled high, the names I still carried with me. The price of my ideas when it mattered most, during the battle with the largest casualties of the last war.

But they also knew one other thing: when my plans worked, we won. And I wasn't about to let Harper, or anyone else, forget that.

Harper flinched, but to his credit, he didn't back down. "You say tomato, General, I say tomato."

"I hate tomatoes. They're bitter." I straightened, my tone frosting over. "Do I need to worry about your ability to do as you're told?"

"No, ma'am."

"Good boy." I let the words hang long enough to sting before addressing the room again. "Any other disruptions? No? Fantastic."

I gestured to the map spread across the table. The Mississippi River cut through the heart of our position like a frozen blade. "Napoleon didn't just fight battles—he dismantled his enemies piece by piece. At Austerlitz, he baited the Russians and Austrians into a vulnerable position near frozen water and lower ground. When their forces were in full retreat, French artillery shattered the ice beneath them, turning the water into their graves. They didn't stand a chance."

The room was deathly silent. I had their attention now. My fingers brushed the edge of the map as I marked key points with sharp jabs. "We'll do the same. High ground here, here, and here." I motioned to a ridge overlooking the river's bend, then another set of ridges further downstream. "Goal is to draw them out onto the ice and box them in. And when they're exactly where we want them—"

"*Boom,*" Reina whistled with excitement, her fingers twirling as she mimicked an explosion. She sat on her hands when all eyes in the room turned toward her.

"We break the ice. They drown. Few, if any, survivors. Easy enough, I consider you all relatively capable."

A murmur rippled through the room. Millie shifted uneasily, her gaze flicking to the river on the map. Harper, ever the thorn in my side, opened his mouth, but I cut him off with a raised hand.

"The ice won't hold under the weight of their arrogance," I continued, lacing my voice with steel. "They'll think they've cornered us."

"Ma'am?" A younger officer from Fargo—Kellan, if my memory wasn't shit—raised his hand tentatively, his face pale. "What about our soldiers? If we're that close to the river, won't they—"

"Then stay off the ice, soldier," I snapped, my tone leaving no room for argument. "Hold the ridges, just far enough to lure 'em forward—"

"But safe enough from the trap," Hunter added from his position near the entrance, Abel on the other side.

I jabbed the map again. "Once they're fully committed, we shell the ice."

Kellan swallowed hard, but nodded. "Yes, ma'am."

Releasing a slow, much needed exhale, I let my gaze sweep the room. It was tense, as to be expected. More shoulders sat rigid near their ears than I'd hoped for, but after the gamble I'd laid out—who could blame them?

It was a calculation that required a certain level of brutality—the fierceness in their eyes showed they understood. Still, I hadn't said the best—or worst—part, because when magic was involved in war, humans would always give way to cruelty, no matter your morals.

Our honor had to fall to ashes in order to survive.

"When it's done," I said, forcing my voice to relay a deadly calm, "we extract any of our people who fell in, then freeze any Covert sympathizers. Fall back and regroup *here*. Fast and clean."

No one moved. No one spoke.

"Brief your units and prepare to move out in fifteen," I barked, the crack of my voice jolting every last one of them into action. Chairs scraped, orders were shouted, and the air buzzed with the frenetic energy of doom.

Alexiares stayed by my side as the others spilled out into the frozen wasteland beyond the tent, Riley the last to leave, his weakening demeanor portraying the words he would not burden me with. Not now. I turned to follow when Alexiares's fingers brushed mine. A fleeting touch that sent a flicker of comfort through me—damn the rest of the world. He didn't speak. He stared down at me, dark eyes saying enough.

We were fighting for many things—our people, our survival, our future—but at that moment, I knew we were fighting for each other more than anything else.

And that was enough to remind me why I was willing to risk all that I did—why I would win in the end.

Only the dead have seen the end of war. Plato.

The air reeked of blood and burning magic. Screams intertwined with the thunder of cannon fire, the sharp hiss of arrows, and the sickening, unforgettable crunch of bodies meeting steel. This shit belonged in a museum. The way the snow fell in a lazy, hyperbolic drift. A shroud settling over the chaos.

From the trenches on the high ground, I could see everything. The frozen, snow-covered Mississippi—now a battleground of desperation and death.

A cannon roared beside me. The blast punched through my ears and sent me tumbling toward the ground. It put me in the perfect position to watch as shrapnel ripped through a soldier's leg down below. He collapsed, blood pouring into the snow like ink in water, sparing him no time to react. His last seconds on this earth, not understood until he was on the other side. Maybe.

"Focus!" I barked, forcing myself upright as another soldier's body fell lifeless at my feet. My voice was hoarse, raw. "Keep firing! Don't let them regroup!"

We had them where we wanted them. It was almost time. If we could keep the pressure for a few more minutes, our losses would remain minimal.

Riley surged forward on my left, his ax cleaving through a Kansas soldier who had somehow made it past the trenches. Blood sprayed across his face. He didn't blink as he turned, the earth rippling at his feet as he threw up a wall of rock to shield our gunners as they reloaded.

Right at the edge of my view, Alexiares shifted, a presence as elusive as smoke. His knives flashed as he weaved through the trenches, carving down attackers. A blade found its mark in our enemy's chest. Alexiares spun before the body hit the ground, firing off a headshot that dropped another from his quick draw.

Flames erupted in his free palm from his quick decision to ditch the metal. Three more Covert sympathizers smoldered in an inferno that lit up the trench around him.

His control was terrifying—and beautiful. Alexiares had mastered his mage, his fire slivering in snake-like fashion in order to avoid our troops.

"Where the hell are Serenity and Hunter?" I shouted over the fray, searching the battlefield for any sign of them.

"Hopefully not dead." Riley ducked an arrow, driving his ax into the neck of the attacker.

Shit. We were losing our footing. Gaps had formed out on the battlefield, leaving more vulnerabilities than I cared to admit.

"Not funny," I snapped, scanning the chaos below.

The cavalry was in trouble. Reina weaved through the enemy lines, her black mare moving with the wind over the ice-crusted river. She leaned to the side, her body lifting off at a near 90-degree angle to avoid a volley of arrows, her medkit bouncing against her back.

Tomoe wasn't far. She issued warnings, keeping the riders around her alive by inches. My heart fumbled when I landed my sights on Abel. He struggled. His Plasma blade clumsy in his hand. No amount of training would make up for the loss of balance caused by an injury we were not ever sure would heal.

In his stubbornness came weakness—not by injury, but ego. Now I was forced to watch as he suffered the consequences of denying Reina's help.

The ice beneath him cracked, a hole forming and slipping two soldiers beneath the ice.

"No."

Abel slid, his foot plunging through the fragile surface. He caught himself on the edge, abandoning his weapon, arm trembling as the freezing water surged around him. With great effort, he pulled himself back up. *Fuck. Fuck. Fuck.*

"Shit." Alexiares appeared at my side as the fractures spread, the weight of too many bodies forcing the river's hand. The bulk of their army was now spread along the Mississippi for as far as the eye could see, but the ice was failing faster than I'd planned. It wouldn't hold.

"Reina!" I shouted, the desperation tearing at my throat. She needed to get to Abel. Yet she could not hear me.

I grabbed the nearest officer, pulling him close. "Get a runner down there. Pull the cavalry back! *Now!*"

He nodded, wide-eyed, and sprinted off, but I knew it was too late. I had a choice to make.

An explosion tore through the river's edge. The ice fractured violently, the sound like thunder splintering the sky. Soldiers screamed as they plunged into the freezing water, the surface collapsing beneath them. Archers fired blindly, and one arrow found its mark.

Reina fell. Her horse went down with her.

"No!" I strangled in my throat. Alexiares grip was the only thing keeping me standing.

Tomoe turned, her face pale, but her warning came too late. Abel, bleeding heavily, staggered as the ice gave way beneath him. He vanished beneath the water, the current swallowing him whole.

My mind split—one part calculating, the other shattering. I was a leader. I knew what had to be done. I knew what I had to sacrifice. The war didn't care that Abel was my family. That Reina was my sister. That losing them would rip me apart.

I needed them alive. I needed them breathing.

Hesitation meant losing everything.

"Break the ice."

"What?" Alexiares whipped his head around, eyes wide as he took in the scene where our friends had previously been, their absence now noted.

"Break it! Now!" I roared, panic lacing my voice.

"Ma'am?" General Trevan protested, his voice tight with concern as he stepped closer. "You want us to break the ice? Our soldiers—"

"Shouldn't be on it. They were warned. Now, *break the damn ice*," I snapped, the words cutting through his hesitation.

Trevan didn't argue. He signaled his unit, holding Alexiares's stare as they flung out their hands. Fire erupted along the river's surface. The heat melted through the ice, the cracks spreading faster, consuming everything in their path.

"Freeze it!" I commanded as soon as the explosions stopped. This had to work ... *needed* to work. But if my timing was off for even half a second ...

Magic surged. Ice crawled over the water, jagged and unyielding, trapping soldiers where they fell. Screams rose again, this time choked and desperate as men drowned or froze in place.

"Fetch anyone still breathing." I barked at the remaining soldiers. "Ours—not theirs. Be quick about it."

Holy shit, it worked. Kansas forces had been decimated. The only survivors were trapped in the trenches, their screams a cruel harmony to the roar of the river swallowing its own.

I tried to feel relief. Tried to tell myself this was necessary. That their deaths weren't in vain. But guilt bled through the cracks like water through fractured stone, soaking me to the core. I hadn't done it to limit our losses—I'd issued my orders to limit *mine*. I turned away as the cries of the dying faded into the bitter wind. No pity, no hesitation. Not until I reached them. My family.

I sprinted toward the river, my legs moving on instinct. Riley caught up, steam curling from his mouth in the cold, ax dragging a crooked line in the mud.

"War is brutal," I replied, voice flat. I ignored the urge to turn around.

A deafening scream cut through my spiraling thoughts. My eyes locked on a cluster of Pansies tearing through the crowd.

Kansas soldiers now turned into weapons of experiment. They moved with terrifying precision, eyes glowing with intelligence, their voices sharp as they barked commands to each other. Communicating. Coordinating.

The herd parted as Hunter's people emerged from the fray and formed a ring of defense—reminiscent of their training. Their hollow stares pierced through the battlefield, eyes spectators from an unspeakable abyss. Magic writhed around them, thick and unnatural, twisting the air as though reality itself recoiled in their presence. It wasn't fire or ice, not any of the tangible elements I knew.

A wiry man with gaunt cheeks and sunken eyes raised a trembling hand. The motion seemed almost hesitant until a ripple came—a force that shattered a line of Pansies, their bodies crumpling as easily as paper. Their bodies collapsed, final croaked out groans ear splitting even in the thunderous roar of warfare.

Lola appeared at his side. Thick tendrils of darkness surged from the ground, coiling around a handful of Pansies at a time, dragging them down, eating away at their decaying flesh. The void of her power consumed them—old and dark.

General, incom—

Elliot's voice seared through my mind, sharp with urgency. I spun, my fire flaring in response, but I wasn't the target.

Right flank—now!

I whipped around before I even processed why. The split-second reaction saved me—a bolt of steel sliced through the space where I'd been standing, embedding deep into the snow. The explosion of impact sent a shockwave rattling through my ribs. I staggered back, catching my balance just as Elliot's breath hitched.

The guttural cry of an unforgiving death made me pause.

I wasn't sure where to look. At the Pansies making their way through my soldiers or the arrow that struck through Elliot's throat.

He fell to his knees, blood pouring between his fingers as he clutched at the wound. Then the blade came. It slashed across his chest, his skin flaying, ribcage now exposed.

He crumpled, lifeless, his wide eyes locking with mine for one agonizing second.

"Elliot!" The scream tore from me. Primal.

Flames erupted from my hands, incinerating his killer, my fury turning on the others nearby. They focused on me with carnal delight.

"Amaia!" Alexiares grabbed my arm, yanking me back as an arrow hissed past my ear. "We can't stand here!"

My legs moved but my mind was stuck on Elliot's broken body. Blood spread beneath him, ink spilling into a glass of water. The sight blurred. I couldn't afford to cry. Not here. Not now.

For Morgan. For Sloan. This was a wound that couldn't be stitched. I stumbled. Alexiares's grip on me tightened, his voice came sharp in my ear. "Focus, baby, please. We can't afford to lose you too."

I had to keep going. To find my family. Elliot's death. The screams of the drowning. The faces of soldiers who trusted me to lead them, now frozen in twisted agony beneath jagged shards of ice.

They'd been damned because of me.

But … It had worked.

Searching the decimated remains of battle, my eyes landed on a glimmer of hope.

"Reina!" My voice cracked as I spotted her, a dark shape barely visible against the icy chaos. Her horse thrashed in the freezing water, dragging her under with every desperate movement. She clung to its saddle, her strength waning as hypothermia took hold. Even from here, I could see the ice clinging to her lashes. Her lips, once flushed with exertion, were turning a sickly shade of blue.

"Someone get her!" I barked, but my order was lost in the cacophony of battle. I whipped my head around, searching for anyone, *anything*.

Tomoe was already moving. Her hand shot out, gripping the reins of Millie's horse. "Take me closer!" she shouted.

"No!" I called out, not wanting to lose her too. I could do it. I would go. I removed my layers to jump in. Cold air sliced through me as Riley and Alexiares grabbed at my arms, fighting me every step of the way.

Millie was covered in decayed flesh and browning blood, her stark green eyes met mine before focusing on rescuing Reina. Determination silencing any additional pleads.

Reina's head disappeared under the surface.

"No, no, no …"

"Let them do their job," Alexiares hissed.

Seconds stretched into eternity. Then, a figure broke the surface of the water. Reina, sputtered, water rushing from her lungs. She shivered uncontrollably in Millie's arms, barely conscious. Tomoe clutched the reins tightly, her eyes scanning for the fastest route to safety.

Millie's horse was near exhaustion. She wouldn't make it much further, but all she needed was a few extra feet and safety was theirs.

But Abel—he wasn't out.

"Where is he?" Riley screamed, his voice hoarse from the cold and panic.

My eyes darted frantically over the battlefield, over the bodies frozen in the jagged expanse of ice.

"I've got him!" A soldier's voice rang out, a flicker of hope amid the carnage. Abel dangled from the man's grip, his arm limp, his face a gray-ish hue. He was barely holding on, his breath visible in shallow bursts.

"Get him to the medics!" I commanded, my voice shaky as I watched them haul him onto solid ground. My heart pounded in my ears, and I felt the weight of every decision leading up to now—every failure.

If I hadn't broken the ice, they both would have slipped away. Drowned. But breaking the ice had hardly saved them and likely made us lose many others. I'd fucked up. I'd exchanged their lives for others.

Reina coughed violently as Millie gently laid her beside Abel, her frostbitten hands clutched his sleeve as if to reassure herself he was real. Her voice was weak, but her spunk was still there. "Can I give you the … arm thingamabob now?"

Abel managed the faintest of smiles, his lips blue, stubborn as the day he'd entered our family. "No."

My boots crunched against the frost, each step heavier than the last. The weight of what I had done coiled around my ribs, squeezing until my lungs seized in uneven bursts. Alexiares's hand gripped my arm, his touch grounding yet infuriating all at once. Riley stood rigid, his jaw locked tight. Blood streaked across his temple, his eyes stayed on me.

"What you did saved lives," Alexiares said quietly, breaking through the war that raged in my head.

"Did it?" I snapped, my voice brittle. "I killed our soldiers too. People who trusted me. I broke the ice early, Alexiares. I sent them to their graves."

Riley's hand clamped down on my shoulder, pulling me toward him. "You didn't damn them. You gave the rest of us a chance. The ice was already breaking, and we were losing control." His tone was sharp, almost scolding, but his eyes were soft.

And yet, this was the truth of war, wasn't it? Victory wasn't clean—it was carved from sacrifice. Some were chosen, others stolen. And in the end, you didn't get to feel good about it.

"War doesn't care what it takes," I muttered to myself. "Only that you're willing to pay the price."

Air scraped down my throat as my gaze locked on the battlefield. Bodies littered the frozen ground, some of them ours, others barely recognizable as human.

Guilt fought against the relief threatening to spill over. "I didn't just do it to save them," I murmured, the admission tearing at me.

Alexiares leaned closer. "No. You did it to win."

The words cut through me. They were only painful because they were true. I swallowed hard and walked off without my family at my side. The battlefield was quieting, but I couldn't let myself revel in the silence. Not yet. Maybe not ever. My eyes drifted over the river, now frozen over with jagged ice, and frozen bodies. The snow had stopped, and in its wake was the light of a sun that didn't deserve to shine today.

THE FIRE PIT CRACKLED WEAKLY, BARELY ENOUGH TO PUSH BACK THE biting cold as the allied leaders faced each other in a tense circle. I stood at the center, my arms crossed, watching their frustrations boil over.

"You're saying this was *our* fault?" Kellan, the young officer from Fargo spat, his voice cutting through the night. "We lost half a unit because of *her* damned plan!" He jabbed a finger at me.

"No," Isabella reasoned, her expression carved from stone. "You lost them because your soldiers broke rank. Orders were clear—stay off the ice."

"You think this is about the ice?" General Mason Wilder— failed commander of our cavalry snapped, stepping forward. The outburst was unexpected; Rochester Compound had been easy going up until now. "It's about leadership, Everhart. Leadership that sacrifices us while keeping her own people safe."

I blinked slowly at him, letting his words hang in the air. Then, with an eerie calm, I spoke. "Leadership is what got you through that battle alive, Wilder. The same leadership that told you how to keep your soldiers breathing. Ensuring they follow orders? That's *your* job."

He sneered but didn't respond, his chest heaving as he tried to find something to throw back at me.

I tilted my head, studying him with a smile that didn't reach my eyes. "Keeping your soldiers in check, making sure they don't step where they shouldn't, holding your own damn line—also your job. My job is to make sure you have no problem doing your job well. Make sure you aren't too fucking incompetent to keep people alive. If I have to do your job *and* mine—if I have to hold your company's hand every time the situation gets hard—then I don't need you. But I do need you, don't I?"

He didn't answer.

"This is where you nod," I whispered, leaning in close enough to make my point clear.

Wilder gritted his teeth with enough force to crack them, then gave a short, jerky nod.

"Great." My voice brightened. "Glad we're on the same page."

"That was her polite way of saying, 'Get the fuck out,'" Alexiares drawled from behind me, his tone as dry as the wind cutting through the camp.

A ripple of uneasy chuckles moved through the circle of gathered soldiers, but they quickly died under Wilder's glare. He stalked off, his shoulders rigid.

Silence fell over the camp, broken only by the crackling fire and the distant cries of the wounded. I looked around at the faces watching me—some weary, others wary.

The plan had worked. It had saved lives, turned the tide of battle. But the cracks in their confidence were visible. They weren't just mourning their dead; they were mourning their belief that this fight could be won without great loss.

I exhaled slowly, the weight of my choices pressing into my chest. "If anyone else has a problem, say it now," I said, my voice low and steady. "Otherwise, get some rest. We'll need it."

No one spoke.

The fire crackled on, indifferent to the weight of the silence. One by one, they drifted away, their faces shadowed with exhaustion and doubt. The battlefield was behind us, but its echoes lingered, carved into every strained step, every hollow stare.

Alexiares didn't move from his spot behind me. A quiet presence that didn't dare encroach on the weight pressing against my chest that was mine—and only mine—to bear.

This wasn't guilt. It was something colder. Something that dug deeper, whispering truths I didn't want to hear. Today was what the history books would claim a victory.

But victory wasn't supposed to feel like this. It wasn't supposed to taste like ash.

Thousands of soldiers were hoping I was strong enough to patch those cracks, to hold them together. But how long could I do that when the person I was trying to hold together was breaking apart? I forced my shoulders back.

There was no time for doubt.

"Go to bed," I murmured. "I'll be there soon."

Alexiares finally stepped closer, his hand brushing against mine. I flicked it away—his comfort was something I did not deserve.

If this was what winning looked like, I didn't want to think about what losing would cost.

CHAPTER
FIFTY-EIGHT

AMAIA

So this was it, I guess. The beginning to the end.

We'd followed the Mississippi south, keeping to the safe side of the river until we found ourselves across from what was once small town Kentucky. Hickman to be exact. According to the child who was leading the way, *this* was the weakest point—where we had our best shot at breaching Covert's borders. Lilia's family had crossed here, and if we had any luck left in the universe, it would remain an easy post to access.

Tomoe and Lola were opposite sides of the same *Seer* coin. Their eyes flickered, one with pupils hazed with white, the other with nothing but black coal filling their sockets. It was never a comfortable feeling being in Lola's presence when you knew what she was capable of—that didn't mean I didn't admire the hell out of her. She was powerful and ruthless, but kind when it mattered.

Kind, not gentle. There was importance in the distinction.

They joined hands with Lilia, essentially astral projecting by power sharing—channeling Lilia's gifts. It wasn't something they did often during this journey. It was draining and dangerous. Lilia's presence was their only anchor—without her, they would not be able to navigate breaking through the wards.

The room stood still as soldiers watched in fascination, the two women and small child at the center of it all. Power hummed beneath the surface of Lilia's pale skin. She was the only one who could truly see Covert's machinations for what they were. The wards didn't touch her memory the way it had others. She held the knowledge—the places and paths—she was not replaceable though it made it no easier to involve someone her age.

"The wards are still intact," Lilia murmured after a moment, her raven colored hair falling across her face, voice flat. "But it's clear for now."

Tomoe's hands trembled from her power being absorbed. "The border hasn't changed. We're comparing it to them, and the connection of the mind of a young boy she met that resides nearby. It's the same entry point as before—there are civilians within the vicinity."

"Dios mío," Lola murmured, her face neutral, though the uncertainty and shock hid beneath the surface. "My coven … I believe we can carve a path. We'll need to channel through Lilia. Her gift gives us a clear way forward. With Sage's assistance—"

She paused, collecting her thoughts. "Sage's power is intricate, delicate, not suited for brute force. She can see the structure of the wards—threads of memory and intent woven into the air itself. Her ability allows her to unravel a small part, just enough to carve a temporary safe passage. But only if we move carefully."

Hunter went mute, nodding and though Lola could not *see* him, she carried on, expression grave. "If no one strays from the set path, we can move through without triggering the memory wipe. It's a tight window, Amaia. We'll need to move quickly. Large groups."

I clenched my jaw as I glanced at Lilia. She was only a kid. Kneeling before her, I caught her blank stare. "You don't have to do this."

The words felt sour. Could I truly offer her an out? It would damn a hell of a lot of people all for the sake of one. Lola and Tomoe released their grip on her, coming out of whatever dream-like world they'd walked.

Lilia shook her head fiercely, eyes coming back into focus. "I'm the only one who can. If I don't, you'll all forget. You'll—" She swallowed at the sharp look from Lola. Slowly, she forced herself to meet my gaze. "I can do it."

I studied her for a long moment, before nodding. It was her choice. Her decision. *But she's just a child*, that small voice screamed at me from the back of my head. I couldn't help but think it sounded a hell of a lot like Jax.

"All right." I scanned the faces around the room. "You heard her. No straying, no hesitation. We stay on Lilia's path, or we don't make it. Understood?"

Riley's fingers twitched against his thigh. They traced that same faint, erratic pattern I'd come to recognize as nerves. A habit he did not realize he had, but I noticed it every damn time.

"Okay," I said, as I moved toward the table a few steps away— deciding to take their silence as an indication to keep talking before they all threw up their nerves.

The war tent was dim, shadows pooling in the corners, the single lamp swaying faintly as if it, too, could sense the unease. Generals and senior officers crowded around the table. The map spread across glared up at me, every line and marking a taunt. My voice was steady as I laid out the plan—splitting into two groups, fighting our way in.

My team would head northeast, skirting the river through West Virginia into Virginia, while Riley's would go southeast. His team would draw the bulk of Ronan's forces—hopefully … if all went to plan. As long as Ronan thought I was with him, which we were banking on.

It wasn't a new plan—I'd walked through it so many times that the words felt hollow now, like repeating a prayer I no longer believed in. But the next part wasn't about strategy; it was about risk. My risk.

The air in the tent thickened as I said it. "I'll cross the wards first and a smaller unit can follow my tail."

Riley's expression hardened, and Alexiares muttered a slew of vulgar language. Their eyes locked on me, then flicked to each other, silent protests etched across their faces. I pushed forward, pretending not to notice.

"The wards are too unpredictable to send everyone at once. If we trip them, the memories of every soldier will be fucked and so will anyone that follows. If I go first, I can test them. Lilia's power can anchor me enough to pull back if something goes wrong."

The generals exchanged concerned glances, but none of them challenged me. Slowly, they filtered out, only my family remained. Their stares pinned me in place, heavy with something worse than doubt—expectation. Like they were already bracing for the inevitable. No one said it out loud, but it was clear the way Riley's hands curled into fists, in the tight set of Alexiares's shoulders. Waiting for me to break. Waiting for me to give in.

I refused to give them that.

This was happening. Whether they could accept it or not.

"Can you all please stop looking at me like I'm about to die," I grumbled, reviewing the map one last time.

"Since no one else here wants to hear you bark back if this is said, I'll say it for them," Serenity snapped, cutting through the tension. Her arms crossed over her chest. "The route you've chosen to take puts you—and the rest of us by default—in a vulnerable position."

"Someone has to go first," I said even as my chest tightened. "We can't afford to lose numbers to the wards. If it works, we move the others in waves. If it doesn't—"

"You lose it all," Alexiares said bluntly, his eyes dark and unflinching. "And the rest of us are left leaderless, stranded in hostile territory."

Tomoe's gaze burned into mine. "It places you into a direct line of fire. Repeatedly."

"I'm not sitting this one out." I snapped, though the weight of their stares was unbearable. I traced the map with my fingertips, finding the routes I'd already memorized. "It would be in poor taste to ask my soldiers to do something their general would not. They've risked enough, I won't force them to lose that last part of their humanity if it goes wrong."

"I don't know much about this military stuff and all, but I'm almost positive the person at the top isn't supposed to be, you know," Reina shifted, her brows furrowing as she glanced at the others and made a vague gesture. "Out there and actually doing stuff."

"Out there and actually doing stuff," I muttered with a dry laugh, shaking my head.

Alexiares stepped closer, his hand brushing my lower back—a steadying touch that should've calmed me. It didn't. Instead, it felt off. Disingenuous. My chest burned hotter when I met his eyes. They were filled with something I couldn't ignore. Concern in the rawest of states. His mask had dropped, no filter or resemblance of *the Bloodhound*. The only person staring back at me, was a man weakened by love.

I hated it. Because it made me weak too. Made my stone-hardened mold I'd been forming over my heart for months, melt away.

The sting hit deep, and I jerked back, my pulse racing with frustration. "I started this war, and I'm going to be the one to stare Ronan in the eyes when it ends."

"That's a perfectly reasonable request," Riley said, and for a second, hope flickered. Then he crushed it. "You can do that when Lola portals us into the city center. It would be irresponsible to allow you to engage beforehand."

"So what? You wanna take my place? Put yourself in the line of fire?" My voice rose an octave and Riley arched a dismissive brow.

"We are not having this conversation again," he said, dismissing me with a pointed glance at the others.

"You're right," I snapped. "We aren't because my decision is final."

The walls closed in with each breath I took. Their eyes trailed me in the suffocating cramped space of this stupid fucking war tent. My skin buzzed. Too hot. Too tight—like the magic inside me was about to free itself whether I was a willing participant or not. I couldn't breathe. Couldn't think. Couldn't stay still.

I needed to move, to do something, anything to release the pressure. I lost control. I spun, grabbing the edge of a chair, throwing it across the space.

"Fuck!" The word ripped out of me as the chair clattered to the ground. "I'm doing my best here. Okay? You're all already so … involved."

My voice cracked, and I yanked at the braids framing my face. "I didn't ask any of you not to serve your purpose in this war for the sake of my heart. Don't ask me to sacrifice mine."

The silence in the tent was suffocating. The faint creak of the lamp swinging above us was the only sound.

Reina shattered the stillness, her voice low but fierce. "Tell her, Alexiares."

"Reina …" There was a warning in Abel's tone—one that said Reina was about to do everything but mind her own fucking business.

She didn't flinch. Instead, she stepped forward, her eyes burning with a mix of fury and sorrow. "Hear what your fiancé thinks of you putting your life on the line every time we turn around. Tell her how I've had to use my magic 24/7 because the anxiety has eaten away at you so much you can barely function. The man eats and breathes fear for breakfast, lunch, and dinner. Fear for *you.* Your safety."

Alexiares's jaw clenched, his gaze hard as steel as he stared her down. But then his eyes shifted to mine, and I wished he hadn't because I knew it would never change. As much as it broke my heart, my duties outweighed the life I desperately wanted the two of us to share. I had warned him that I could not give him what he deserved and now the reality of it was shattering the heart that I swore we shared.

"Uh … congratulations?" Serenity muttered awkwardly.

I hadn't exactly walked around flaunting my ring. Screaming from the rooftops that I was his in the most precious way possible. There were people out there that would hold such a permanence of a title against me—use *him* against me.

"Not really the time," Hunter said, pulling his rifle over his shoulder and nudging her toward the exit.

"Why?" she shot back, but she followed him anyway. "Show's just getting started."

Hunter squeezed Reina on the shoulder on the way out, her head briefly resting against his shoulder before she kissed it, wishing him a good rest of his night.

She turned back to me, voice wavering, but the storm in her eyes never faltered. "We're trying to save you, Amaia. If you'd just let us have an opinion …" Her eyes filled with tears she refused to let fall, but the fury still burned hot in them. "I can't do this anymore—watching you throw yourself into the center of every risk or battle. Please, let us help."

"Save me?" I laughed—bitter, cruel. It felt wrong in my heart and my mind but came out on reflex. "Sorry for being a burden. I'm trying to save you and the whole damn world, apparently, at the same time. I didn't ask for you to save me. I'm doing my *job*. I'm protecting our family. But I can't do that if you keep questioning every damn move and try to make me feel guilty for doing what I'm oathbound to. Seth is dead! Seth is dead, and Abel's arm—" I choked on the words, my voice cracking. "In the middle of an apocalypse, I'm still fighting for you all, and you want to pull me back? To not take risks. You think that's saving me?"

"We never asked for you to save us either." Abel paused, his gaze the only soft one in the room. "I get it, man, it's what family does, we save each other. All I'm seeing here are people who love each other and want the best. And it's not easy watching you march into danger every damn time, knowing what it costs. Tomoe and I are … sensitive to those things, Reina can feel it whether we express it or not, and Alexiares is forced to watch it all play out in real time. I think … I think you can find it in you to see what it's like for the rest of us too. What it's like to live with that fear, not knowing if you'll come back from the next fight."

The room was impossibly still. I could hear my own heart pounding, a beat that echoed in my ears.

I swallowed the lump in my throat. "You didn't ask," I said quietly, the words burning as they left my mouth, "but it was implied the day I met you. The day I called you my brothers and sisters."

Alexiares hadn't spoken a word. Didn't offer anything. His eyes were locked on mine, but I couldn't read him—not this time. It was a wall of concern, one I couldn't tear down.

We needed to talk, but it was a conversation to be had later. In the privacy of our tent. A fight between lovers that did not need the audience of the world.

The silence stretched between us, and the weight of his stillness gnawed at my gut. It was deafening, louder than anything anyone had said. The others seemed to sense it, their reactions as volatile as the air around us.

Tomoe shifted her weight, crossing one leg over the other from her seat. "We're not going anywhere until we've said what needs to be said, Amaia." Her eyes flickered briefly to Alexiares, who remained unmoving, then back to me. "You can't brush this off. Not this time."

Reina's anger matched Tomoe's, layered with something else—a desperation. "You're pushing us all to the edge. Can't you see how much we're bleeding for you? For your decisions?" She stepped forward, hands shaking. "We're not asking you to stop fighting. Only begging you to stop shutting us out."

I flinched, opening my mouth, ready to argue, but the words died before they could escape. They were right. Didn't mean I was ready to admit it. It was easier this way. In hindsight, my family would understand—they were better off not knowing all the facts. Not all promises were meant to be kept.

The tension in the room ebbed, but it didn't disappear. Not entirely.

Then I turned to Riley, needing something—anything to break the silence. "No goodbyes?"

He met my eyes without hesitation. No judgment. No pity. Just that steady, unwavering strength I relied on. "Never goodbye."

The others moved toward the tent, the weight of exhaustion settling over them. No lingering animosity. No unfinished business. They were too tired to hold on to anything more.

I stayed behind, frozen in place. The silence pressed down, a heavy hand louder than the war raging in my head, louder than everything I hadn't said.

Alexiares still hadn't said a damn thing. When I made it to the tent that night, he pretended to be asleep.

THE MISSISSIPPI RIVER CHURNED STEEL-GRAY WATER AS WATER ELE-mentals merged with the forces of nature to freeze our rather—but understandably—hesitant troops a safe crossing. Sky and water matched each other, the murky gray matching the overcast mood of every soul moving in this army. It was late afternoon, the ash-tainted clouds sprinkled soft, persistent snowflakes down from above.

I swiped my hand over my soaked eyelids, the snow not giving me a chance to clearly see what we were working with. The Dorena-Hickman Ferry lay frozen in time. Its hull rested half-submerged against the Missouri shore.

There was an uneasy silence between the puffs of breaths as the troops awaited my command. We'd been prepared for the change of weather but with only half of the men and women here accustomed to cold climates, this would present us with a new test of adaptability. No more fires. No more chances for additional warmth from this point on.

Across the river, the outline of Hickman, Kentucky, rose as a faint image against the swirling snow. From what I could tell it was nothing more than a skeletal silhouette of crumbling stone.

I waved us on and we began our slow approach across. It took every ounce of self-control not to turn back. From here, our group would officially split into two—Riley and Hunter's hanging back a day. With their force being the smaller of the two and taking the brunt of Ronan's forces down the line, it was essential they avoided any initial skirmishes. But without Elliot, there was no longer a way to stay connected, to know what was happening with Riley and Abel. The only thing I could do was hope that my plans continued to work out.

I had to admit—there were some nerves leading up to approaching the wards. Yes, I'd thought things through when I'd volunteered myself. No, I had not considered how heavy the decision would drain me when the time came.

I didn't want to forget. The beautifully painful life I had lived. The love I had found in every form, carved from sorrow and grief.

Memory loss was only part of the risk. For months, I had conserved my magic, waging my flames carefully. They simmered beneath my skin, desperate for release, the pressure of restraint pressing in from all sides. I was lucky I hadn't gone mad.

Once I crossed this border, it was air magic and weapons only. Restraint and control—my only allies now.

Each soldier had orders to conserve their magic. If we came across any Covert troops with numbers that put us at a disadvantage, we'd toss our shields up. Thing was, there was a 100 percent chance Ronan had similar technology—which meant both sides would spend time breaking through them.

Wasting magic unnecessarily could mean running out under less than desirable circumstances. And as much as I hated to say it, not everyone here had magic to spare. They all fought honorably, but when it came to a number on the power scale, some would run out before others.

Our shields would have as many layers as responsibly possible for the fight at hand. With the uncertainty on all things Covert and Ronan, our best chance was for our troops to catch them off guard—something that would be incredibly hard to do the second they realized we'd successfully breached their wards. If I had to guess, Ronan knew we were close, but had confidence that once we crossed, we'd have no recollection on who we were, let alone our mission. The second our presence was sensed, the territory would go on alert and scouts would be everywhere. That meant trouble.

Static pulsed through the air, the electric warning to back the fuck up getting stronger the nearer we drew. From where we stood, it was a vast nothingness stretching ahead.

Fingers brushed against mine—the only indication of intimacy Alexiares had dared to provide since Reina had made a confession on his behalf. I paused when the pushback from the invisible wall of wards became overwhelming. *Here.* Curtains and layers of black hung off Lola's wiry frame as she made her way to my side, Lilia in hand.

I ran through the plan internally once more. Me first, testing the wards, then a small strike team under my command would follow, securing the path before Reina's cavalry unit moved in to escort the civilians. Once they were clear, the main force would advance in staggered formations, maintaining steady intervals to avoid bottlenecks or conflict with civilians.

"Ready for another one of your stupid plans?" Tomoe asked, appearing next to Alexiares, her focus torn between me and the world beyond the wards.

"Always," I said with as much enthusiasm as I could force. She rolled her eyes, muttering something barely audible, but a twitch at the corner of her lips hinted at a smile she was trying to hide.

The weather outside might have been frightening but so was the temperature building underneath my weatherproof coat. Sage approached with the *brujas* in tow.

I had an audience now. Thousands of soldiers spanned into the distance, a sea of bodies flanking both sides of the river.

The coven joined hands with Tomoe and Sage, forming a loose circle with Lilia at the cusp of the wards. Their magic was raw and wild, gifted by a world broken and reforged in chaos. Sparks of energy crackled at their feet.

Low murmurs filled the air, building into a chant. The cadence was sharp. Rhythmic. Laced with Latin that commanded the wards to obey.

Lola tilted her head, her midnight eyes locking onto mine with an unnerving stillness. "It is time."

Sniffling, I nodded in response, fingers clenching and unclenching as I carefully placed well practiced bravado into my features. When I felt steady enough to get on with the show, I approached Lilia, wanting to express more gratitude than words could find me at the moment. Instead, I kept it as simple as I could, "Thank you."

"Free my people, Amaia." The connotation of her tone was from someone wiser beyond the years they had lived. "Make the suffering stop."

A brave little girl who had seen far too much. What a sad reality it was for more than I was comfortable thinking of in a time like this—now was the time to make sure the suffering of many, ended here.

Her lips curved in a faint smile, and she pressed a hand to her chest in acknowledgment. Around us, the wards let out a deep groan, the sound of something ancient and impenetrable beginning to fracture.

Alexiares loomed over me, his expression carved from stone, every ounce of vulnerability locked away. But there it was—the smallest crack. A flicker in his hazelnut eyes as he leaned in, close enough to draw in my scent, his breath brushing against my cheek. His hands moved with deliberate care, tightening the holster on my thigh. Without a word, he slid one of his knives into the narrow gap, the cool steel a quiet reassurance.

"Right behind you, Princess," he murmured.

The wards crackled as I stepped through, the sharp static slicing through the roaring thunder of my heartbeat. One moment, I could hear the muffled rustle of troops behind me; the next, silence pressed against my ears. The world on the other side wasn't just different—it was unnervingly wrong. The air was heavier, the light dimmer, and the town stretched out in eerie stillness.

My pulse quickened as I scanned my surroundings. Hickman, Kentucky—or what was left of it—lay in eerie silence. A ghost town. Buildings leaned under the weight of decay, their windows empty sockets staring back at me. The streets, littered with debris, looked untouched by human hands for years. But it was a lie.

Fresh footprints were everywhere. Overlapping paths of criss-crossed steps that went all the way down the dust-covered streets. They went deep, as though someone had been running. My skin prickled, every nerve screaming the same warning: we were being watched.

I reached for the knife Alexiares had given me, my fingers brushing its hilt. A small amount of comfort after willingly thrusting myself into the unknown. *You're a fucking genius, Amaia. Dumbass,* I scolded myself.

A flash of movement caught the corner of my eye. I pivoted, knife at the ready, but it was only a piece of cloth swaying in the breeze, caught on a bent street sign. The unease didn't lift.

On the bright side, my memory was still intact. The wards hadn't taken them from me, which meant at least one piece of this plan was holding together. For now.

"Come on," I whispered, the words meant as much for myself as for the invisible enemy I knew was out there. "Let's play."

The ground vibrated faintly behind me, a presence I knew without turning. Alexiares.

He stepped through the wards, the tension in his frame snapping into sharp focus the moment he crossed the boundary. *"Fuck this,"* he muttered, his eyes scanning the eerie surroundings. Alexiares sensed it too.

His shadow stretched alongside mine as he moved closer. "I couldn't see you," his voice was rough, low—feral.

I turned slightly, catching that raw vulnerability glinting in his honey eyes. "*They* could, but not me. It still wasn't enough until I set eyes on you myself."

His words stole mine. *Rip my fucking heart out why don't you?* The wards rippled behind us, and the cavalry unit poured through. Millie and Reina came first, their weapons ready, scanning the shadows with that synchronized precision they'd easily slipped into. Tomoe and Finley followed close behind, their movements quiet—equally deliberate. The two of them had been assigned into Isabella's support ground unit for the cavalry. One by one, our first wave of troops fanned out into defensive positions. They sensed it too. The wrongness. The weight of a thousand unseen eyes pressing in on us.

I clenched my fists, forcing a steadiness into my voice as I moved to each of the unit leaders. "We stick to the plan. This isn't the time to fall apart."

They nodded, the same unspoken understanding passing through them. No one argued, no one hesitated.

We moved out, pushing to secure the perimeter. Troops filed through the wards in waves. The bulk of our soldiers were still trapped behind the border—we needed to make space.

The more ground we cleared, the easier it would be for Riley's troops to get through tomorrow. I clung to that thought. Ground myself to it. Riley *would* make it home. To Yasmin. To his child. He had the most to lose yet he risked so much in honor of a promise he'd made, that I no longer held him to. He could not fail me. He never would.

It took nearly an hour to secure the area. There were signs of life—footprints too fresh to ignore, scattered supplies abandoned mid-use, faint wisps of smoke still curling from extinguished fires.

People had been here. Moments from meeting us in the flesh.

But there was no one. Not a single fucking face nor a whisper of movement beyond our own.

Every step tightened the knot in my stomach. We weren't alone.

We were being watched.

CHAPTER
FIFTY-NINE

AMAIA

Low flames danced across the red and black tent. I toyed with the lantern, using my toes to adjust the level of lighting provided as a way of distraction. Alexiares kept his back to me, but the irritated sigh from the constant bright to low light confirmed that he was in fact awake and choosing to ignore me. Again.

"This is oddly reminiscent of our first night camped together," I said, breaking the silence. With my flames brewing beneath my skin, I was burning up despite the cold of the night. Stripping down to my final layers hadn't helped in the slightest.

"This tent is bigger."

"Seriously," I snapped, pushing up to my elbows and glaring at the back of his head. His hair had grown out completely, gone was the buzzed hair, even the sides were not tickling the back of his neck. "We could *die* tonight, and you're not even going to look at me."

That caught his attention and the death glare he directed at me stole my breath. "Satisfied?"

No. Not really. Actually, when the initial shock wore off, it pissed me off. *Someone has to do the hard shit,* I reminded myself. I loved him—so much in fact, that constantly putting myself at risk was gradually becoming harder of a task. Not for his sake, but for mine. Because his love made me selfish, and there were too many condemned souls counting on me to fall back on my selfish ways.

I gathered myself, focusing on finding peace amid the swirling conflict of ego and uncertainty. "I'm trying so hard to be a reasonable individual right now."

"Reasonable individuals don't volunteer to die every fucking day," He spat, his anger bringing forth that slip of an accent. "I don't understand your complete urgency to rush to your grave. You are a *leader*, those soldiers out there are supposed to die for you."

There it was again. That crack in his voice that shattered my heart into a million pieces. I know my family thought I couldn't care less about how they felt regarding my actions. That wasn't true. I did care. In fact, seeing how much my actions hurt them was a heartbreak comparable to no other. But duty was duty. I had an oath to keep and a promise to Prescott to hold true to. They could never know all I had planned for the future because it would destroy them.

"If only it were that easy, my love," I relented. "You want to talk about it? Then come on, let's talk, I'm right here. Give me a chance to listen, just because I may not be able to—"

His laugh was of *the Bloodhound*, not Alexiares. "Give you a chance. Amaia, you wouldn't take my … my feelings into consideration months ago in Duluth and you won't take them now." He paused, carefully considering his choice of words. "I fell in love with you because of your fire—it would be unwise of me to ask you to dim your flame."

Something fragile in my chest broke. That fire, the very thing that drove me, suddenly felt too hot. Too destructive. I reached for his arm, fingers brushing against the bare skin of his chest. "I never meant to burn you."

Dim lighting from within the tent made his eyes glow. He stared into mine, searching—promising. "You didn't. You could never. I suppose we'll have to find balance."

"If only we had the time," I said, swallowing hard. I inched closer, my hand sliding down his arm, stopping to intertwine my fingers with his. Pressing a kiss to his nose, I whispered against his skin. "I am sorry. At times, it's hard to separate the duty I have as your General and the one I have as your lover."

"My lover?" Alexiares let out a cough of a laugh, the sound rough. "I was under the impression the name you now held was a bit more permanent than that."

A ghost of a smile touched my lips as I met his gaze, searching for permission. "Only if you still want me to have it."

For a moment, he didn't move. He just studied me, his face unreadable, and it felt like being stabbed through the gut, the pain sharper than anything I'd felt on the battlefield. Then, his hand slid to my waist, fingers curling as if he were anchoring himself to me. I crawled toward him, sliding into his lap, my knees framing his legs as I straddled him.

"What I want," he said, kissing the crown of my head, "is to grow old with you. To have the chance to love you for as long as possible." He shifted enough to meet my gaze. "Living at The Compound, seeing all that normal shit—the stuff I didn't think I'd ever have—it made me comfortable enough to start dreaming. I didn't dream before … before *you*. Only nightmares."

I swallowed the lump rising in my throat as his voice broke again.

"But at The Compound," he continued, his hands coming up to cup my face with a gaze so intense, it was as if he were studying me for the moment I inevitably disappeared. "Sleeping next to you, I began to dream. I don't think I would ever dream again if I lost you and that scares the hell out of me, because the dreams—they're more vivid than our reality."

Just like that, it was all out in the open. Laid bare between us. Every jagged piece of his soul.

He shifted his weight, sitting up and fumbling for the lantern that illuminated his olive-hued skin. His hands moved to his face, fingers tracing his jaw, then pressing into his temples as though searching for a release. They lingered for a beat, trembling slightly before falling away. I grabbed them, pressing one against my heart while I traced the lines of his ink with my fingers.

I let my head fall against his chest, listening to the steady rhythm of his heartbeat. Neither of us moved, caught in a fragile moment where breathing—just existing in the same space as each other was the only thing that mattered.

There was nothing to say. No grand declarations could change the reality of what we faced. Perhaps that was why we hadn't spoken about this until now. We both knew there was no point. All we had was now, and we would love each other like there was no tomorrow. Because there very well might not be.

I pressed a soft kiss to the corner of his mouth, my voice wavering as I whispered, "In every lifetime, Alexiares. But I hope the next one is peaceful."

He stilled, his forehead coming to rest against mine, his body tense. The hesitation between us was fleeting, days without my mouth meeting his lips made me desperate for his affection—his attention. He kissed me. It was tentative—soft, coaxing, almost afraid to demand too much.

I couldn't take it anymore. I needed him, needed this. The armor we both wore cracked.

His hands tightened at my waist, grounding against me as I clung to him, my fingers threading through his loose hair, tugging lightly. I grinned as Alexiares shuddered under my touch, biting down on his bottom lip gently, then kissing it lightly to encourage it to heal.

The world blurred at the edges; nothing existed in this moment but this—us.

Our breaths, our hearts, our tangled limbs trying to hold on as though we'd never let go. His hands guided me, sliding up to the curve of my spine and pulling me flush against him. His lips found the base of my neck. I gasped, already mourning the loss when he moved away.

But he returned, his mouth claiming mine with a new intensity—deeper. There was no rush, no frantic urgency. We were close enough that I swore our hearts beat to the same rhythm.

"If this is all we have," I whispered, tracing over the scar placed right over his heart: A M A I A. Reluctantly I broke our connection, the words catching in my throat, "it's enough."

Alexiares rested his forehead against mine. My fingers shook as I cupped his face, brushing the stubble along his jaw, memorizing every detail I already knew by heart.

His hands stayed at my waist, his touch feather-light now, like he didn't want to let go. The corner of his mouth lifted, a smile—so small, yet so devastatingly tender. "It'll never be enough, but I'll take it, anyway."

The Outskirts of Covert Province were about the most deplorable thing I'd ever seen in my life—and I considered Before me well-traveled. The further we moved into the territory, the more unsettling it all became. This stretch of land was so barren and broken that it made the emptiness we stumbled upon in Hickman seem like a welcome party. Air felt heavier here. Of course the blistering cold and acrid scent of decay didn't help.

It had been days since we'd seen another living soul. Houses, barns, entire communities stood hollowed out. Laundry lines hung limp against aluminum rooms and wood panels tacked over crumbling brick—the fabric stiff with dirt, time, and ice. Meals were left uneaten on tables. By meals, I meant stale, molded pieces of bread with maggot infested scraps of animal fat.

Every step through these remnants of lives made me want Ronan's head all much more.

Still, the gnawing sensation of being watched clung to me, sharpening my instincts, reverting me back to that primal state humans never evolved from—not truly. There was more than one instance when I turned, catching glimpses of absolutely jack shit but shadows cast by bare trees or the occasional movement of tarp flapping in the wind. The realization doing nothing to ease the nerves my gut told me was validated.

If Ronan knew we were here, why let us get this far?

Why allow us to creep closer to the capitol without a direct challenge?

What the *hell* was happening back home? On the other side of these wards?

The questions were splinters beneath my skin, the answer hidden in the empty silence.

Isabella approached quietly, note in hand. "Scout reports came back," she said. "There's movement to the east. A small unit, but it looks like they're camped out for now."

I paused for a second, catching Alexiares's gaze before turning to face Isabella. "Small doesn't mean harmless."

Here we go. I considered my options, ran through the pages and pages of plans I'd spent years working on and compared them against what our troops were ready for now. "Get Millie," I ordered. "I want a detachment of the cavalry and a squad of your ground support to escort any civilians you find to safety. Move quickly and get them as far away from the area as possible. We'll regroup at Rendezvous Point L."

Part of me knew we weren't finding civilians because we weren't searching for them. We were securing our perimeter and ensuring our safety as we moved through Kentucky, but we were not actively seeking out anyone but soldiers on the other side. There was no reason to put them at the center of a war that had nothing to do with them and everything to do with their leader. They were already casualties of an oppressor, I had no intention of making them casualties of war.

Isabella exchanged a quick glance with Reina, who nodded, her expression determined but tinged with reluctance. We'd known this was the plan for months, separating—this part of war had never been easy for her.

"Keep an eye out for Tomoe, she'll need your help," I teased, trying to figure out what to say that wouldn't end with her or me in tears.

"I heard that," Tomoe grumbled, securing Wrath as she passed by, flipping me off as a way of goodbye. "Until fate decides to intervene, asshole."

"Whenever destiny chooses to meddle once more," I shot back, unable to hide my smirk.

Reina pulled me into a smothering hug, sending one last wave of peace and happiness my way. I hugged her back, taking in her lavender scent she'd somehow managed to maintain without access to a proper bath in God knows how long. "See you soon, lovebug?"

"You better," I replied, smiling as she stepped back and joined her unit. Within minutes, the cavalry mobilized with a practiced, quiet efficiency. Their hoofbeats faded into the distance as I lingered, staring down the road ahead.

The troops left with me adjusted their formations, a ripple of readiness coursing through their ranks as they prepared for the worst. I rested my hand on the hilt of my blade, my grip firm. The silence wasn't empty anymore—it felt alive, as though the land itself held its breath.

"Stay sharp," I murmured, more to myself than to anyone else.

CHAPTER
SIXTY

REINA

I was most certainly terrified. Not sure how great I hid it but it was true. When I'd signed on to this whole thing, being on the front-lines wasn't exactly what I'd meant. But *no*, my entire family wanted to be front and center, now here I was—adjusting the reins of a borrowed horse. A stubborn bay gelding that never felt quite right. He just wasn't my Nala, the beautiful mare that she was. I shivered, the memory of the river—cold, rushing, and merciless against my magic.

It was freezing—catching me off guard. My body locked up as did my mind. Using my gifts to free myself from the unforgiving void of moving water hadn't occurred to me until it was beyond too late to help myself. Nala was so heavy. She'd done her best to keep me afloat but she couldn't … I choked at the taste of loss.

The Outskirts stretched around us in the dead, foggy light. Every inch of this place was wrong. I'd never been to the East Coast in The Before but from my understanding, it was like, really pretty. Wherever we were crawling through right now was the complete opposite. Skeletal remains of buildings leaned against each other, ready to collapse. Burned-out vehicles were rusted in the first, the paint of them stripped away from both time and the elements.

Faded out posters were torn into pieces, my father's stern face staring back through the bits. The message underneath it made me want to throw up: *A safer world. A better future.* Ironic considering the backdrop to such art was the starved bodies left to rot in doorways—like they were crawling out to find a scrap of anything to keep them alive.

Isabella rode up alongside me. "It's worse than we thought."

I nodded, gently easing the tension of the group. Some of the territories certainly had it harder than others, but it was never *this*. There were still snippets of empathy among us. That was not the case here—their leader, my father, did not care if they suffered. They weren't worth his time.

"We should keep our eyes sharp," Millie spoke up, filling the unintentional silence to spare me the spiral I was about to go down. She adjusted her hat as she trotted past me, leading the way.

The swings on the playground to our right creaked in the wind. A child's toy—a headless doll lay crumpled in the mud. The creepy thing had a vacant, mocking smile.

I saw him first. A boy no older than eight, clutching a jagged piece of metal from underneath the slide. His clothes hung in tatters, cheeks hollow enough to break my already aching heart. Focusing on him before alerting the others, I pushed an overwhelming sense of calm to disarm him. We were not a threat, and I had no intention of traumatizing the poor thing.

He didn't run in our approach—just stood there, wide-eyed, and despite my best efforts, he still possessed the overwhelming fear that something terrible was about to happen to his sweet little face.

I dismounted slowly, raising my hands. "It's okay, honey. We're here to help. I'm Reina, what's your name?"

"A-Asher," he stammered, his small voice trembling as he pointed toward the hills. "My baby sister is up there, she's hungry. Can you help us?"

Tomoe appeared beside me, slipping from the shadows with a sharp focus in her eyes. "We are not alone. Let's move."

The rest of the group hadn't noticed, but Tomoe's instincts never failed.

I turned back to Asher. "Where's your sister?"

He pointed toward the hills. "Up there … She's hungry."

"Stay close," Millie ordered. "Isabella, rear."

Isabella fell back as we moved toward the hills. I noticed movement in the distance—shadows that didn't belong.

Ah. So this is what a fallout shelter looked like. Apparently, ours was on the bougie side. Who knew the Appalachians were full of them? Not me. It loomed not too far ahead. Asher nestled into me, stroking the neck of my horse as if it were the best moment of his life.

My nostrils rose in disgust. There was a stale, metallic sharpness that clung to the air. I gathered my composure and dismounted at a safe distance. Millie followed suit, two others at our backs that were deemed least threatening for initial interactions. Naturally that meant Tomoe had to stay parked outside.

Asher moved silently at my side, his small hand gripping the hem of my jacket, our boots crunching on gravel and grass. I let calm trickle continuously through the tether between us, softening the jagged edges of his fear. It wasn't much, but it was a small comfort that I could provide. One that made me happy I was here—the experience he may have had if I had not been … I didn't want to think about it.

"I know you're scared," I said gently.

His gaunt, reddened face tilted up toward mine with the kind of maturity no child of any age should have. "No, not of you. Everyone wants you to win."

My steps faltered. "Then what are they scared of?"

"Ronan." He tightened his grip on my jacket. "If he thinks someone helped you … he'll send them again. Like he did with my parents."

"Who?" Millie said with a bit too much aggression. Her hand flew over her mouth, covering those adorable freckles out of embarrassment. She hadn't meant to scare him, Millie was simply curious.

Asher flinched, and I brushed a calming hand over his head. "Zombies. They made my parents one after they got bitten."

I clenched my jaw, shoving down the rush of fury that threatened to rise. My father—*Ronan's*—experiments. First, he'd turned people into *those things* against their will, and now he was escalating. This wasn't survival of the fittest anymore; it was calculated cruelty.

"Oh, you sweet—" I kneeled to meet Asher's gaze. "You don't have to fear that either. Whatever happens, I promise—we'll protect you. All of you."

His nod was faint, hesitant, but it was trust.

The shelter was nearly worse than outside. Asher guided me through narrow corridors littered with mismatched blankets, expired food, and debris pushed into corners. Faces watched from the shadows—pale, hollow-eyed, clutching loved ones tightly. Whispers followed us, low and fearful.

"It's been a few days, we're pretty sleepy," Asher murmured. "He's been sending them in waves since the wards glitched to let you through. My sister is in our room, come on."

These people weren't running—they were hiding, waiting, and hoping they wouldn't be next. The air turned thick with the smell of damp earth and unwashed bodies. Makeshift beds were crammed into corners and I was pretty sure that was feces on the other wall.

"It's been days, you said?" I asked, voice low.

Asher nodded, "The smell helps keep them away as long as we're quiet and they don't already know we're here. They haven't found this spot yet."

"We need to remain focused on the mission," Millie reminded me and I offered her a nod. And we would do that—find an adult to warn—but first, I was going to give these kids some food and heal what I could.

Thirty minutes had passed, and I'd done my darndest. If I could take the two of them home with me, I would. Sad as it was, that wasn't my objective today and now we needed to do our job. Isabella was getting impatient anyway.

"War is coming this way. If you can, warn others in the area and stay hidden. I can promise you safety from our troops, but there's no telling what will happen if you're caught in the crossfire."

The middle-aged woman nodded, her hair thin strands of gray that didn't match her voice or her face. *God,* all I wanted to do was help. Not warn people and move on. That was the trade off of no longer simply being a medic, I supposed. Healing and helping in the sense I was accustomed to was only a small portion of this job.

A murmur rippled through the crowd, but their response was cut short by a scream.

"We got company!" Isabella's shout snapped Millie and me to attention. "Defensive positions!"

Her command pushed us into action. I couldn't remember much on our way out—only the call over my shoulder wishing Asher and the woman the best of luck and to lock the door behind us.

The sky had opened up in the half hour we were inside. Blinding sun disorienting me as horror unfolded. Pansies swarmed up the hill—feral, rotting creatures moving with unnatural speed. Their hollow eyes gleamed with bloodlust, teeth snapping as they homed in on us.

A mare shrieked and reared, throwing her rider directly into their path. He barely hit the ground before they descended, tearing into him with a sickening crunch that turned my stomach. I notched an arrow and fired. One fell, but more surged forward.

We charged into the fray. Horses surged forward, hooves striking the rotting creatures, sending them crumpling to the ground.

"Keep them back!" Millie shouted, still at my side, refusing to mount her horse when mine was too far to get to without a fight.

"We trained for this, silly, we got it!" I called out, the wild grin on my face causing her to frown.

She replaced it with a matching one as she pulled her spear free. "Your positivity is inspiring," Millie mocked—something about it gave me butterflies despite the chaos around us.

We fought as if our lives depended on every strike—cavalry and ground units syncing in brutal harmony, the rhythm of our movements a life-saving dance. Each blow we landed pushed the tide back, but for every one we cut down, another took its place. Dark, viscous blood sprayed across the dirt. The Pansies were relentless, unfazed by our resistance, but we pressed on. We couldn't afford to slow down.

I scanned the battlefield, my mind working through our dwindling options. We were overwhelmed. The ground was slick with blood, and the cavalry's charge was slowing. I needed to buy us more space to pick them off one by one at our own pace—something big.

My eyes locked on a crumbling structure to our left, barely standing but still large enough to block the Pansies' advance. If I could take it down, we'd have a chance.

I turned to Millie, giving her a quick nod. "Cover me," I said, already pulling my bow. She flashed me a sharp grin and dove into the fray, drawing attention away from me.

Setting my sights on the support beams, every muscle coiled with focus.

"Please don't miss," Isabella shouted over the slashing of metal against flesh.

Millie laughed from her position on the field, "She doesn't miss."

"What she said." My lips curved in a cocky grin.

I drew my bow, aiming for the heart of the support beam. Every muscle in my body tensed, and then I released. The arrow flew, slicing through the air, striking true. The structure cracked and splintered, collapsing with a deafening roar, and the Pansies were forced to halt, snarling as they collided with the debris.

We had a moment—a small one—but we'd used it at a cost. Time was slipping away, and we had to move fast.

"Take 'em out, boys!" I shouted, rallying the team. "Oh, girls too, obviously."

IT WAS A SLOW EFFORT, AND OF THE FIFTY OF US ASSIGNED ON THIS mission, we were only down five. Not that loss wasn't still a loss and all, but I supposed this was something I'd need to get used to. I could only hope the few I'd chosen to get close to would survive till the end. *What a selfish thought.*

We'd loaded up our dead—strapped them down to a few riderless horses to bring to the rendezvous point—checked on Asher and the shelter, then saw our way back through their fallen town. I could only pray that little boy lived to see how great the future could be.

"You good?" Moe asked, her handsome stallion paced alongside me.

I nodded, still lost in thought. "Just thinkin' is all."

She didn't bother with a response. If I wanted to talk, I would; Moe understood that about me and I quite appreciated it. It was odd, I knew for nearly a year now that things were going to go from bad to worse—that we were gradually preparing for some final showdown. But we never had a clue what it was truly like beyond Covert's borders. The way Jessa spoke of The Outskirts, how she'd done what she had out of desperation, under the threat of becoming an *Outsider*. I knew it was bad, but what I had seen was simply unfathomable to me until a few hours ago.

What made it worse, was that I was the daughter of the man who was responsible for it all. He had the ability to help them, to keep children from dying from hunger. Lives he claimed to care so much about sure didn't matter unless he found the potential of their magic worth keeping alive. Stopping there wasn't good enough for him, so terrorizing them to test out his experiments was obviously the natural next step.

Sharing his blood made me sick.

Millie's horse shifted nervously, its ears flattening as if it senses something we could not. I glanced at Millie, making sure she was steady—her shoulders had gone stiff, her grip on the reins far too tight.

"Hey—" I yelled, but before I could get the rest out, she tensed, her body locking up as she toppled from the saddle and onto the ground like a rag doll.

I was off my horse in an instant, "Millie!"

Moe hit the ground running not far behind me, we reached her at the same time. She was convulsing.

"Millie, hey! Listen to me, you're okay—breathe," I said, my hands hovering over her, unsure of what I could do to help. Physically, she was fine, no injuries, no sense of disease at a quick scan. Moe crouched at her other side, keeping Millie's frantic horse from bolting.

Her green eyes hazed over, then rolled to the back of her head. I'd seen this before. Heart pounding, I scooted under her and cradled her head in my lap. My fingers trembled as I adjusted her neck, ensuring she wouldn't hurt herself.

Millie's lips moved, her honeyed voice barely audible at first. "He knows … how can he … Jessa …"

A bolt of ice struck through my body, stomach churning. Jessa was with Riley's group—helping them navigate through the unfamiliar territory.

My blood turned into ice.

"Riley and Abel," I whispered though I knew she could not hear me. "Please—Are they okay?"

"*Oh God*," Millie whimpered, her voice climbing higher in pitch. "He's going to torture her. No. No. Ronan is watching."

Her muttering continued, nonsensical fragments spilling from her lips, but my mind fixated on one thing: Jessa and Riley's group were in danger.

The soldiers edged closer, boots and hooves crunching against the dirt as they tightened their formation. Weapons were raised, not in aggression but in a defensive readiness, their gazes darting between Millie and the horizon.

"Stay back!" I barked without thinking. They shifted uneasily, their readiness palpable.

Isabella strode into the circle, her sharp gaze snapped from Millie to the gathered soldiers. Before I could explain myself, Moe glanced at her and subtly shook her head, the message clear in her hardened expression: *This is confidential.*

Isabella's mouth tightened with displeasure. "Keep moving. Slow your pace." Her glare swept over the soldiers, cutting off any objections. "If you're not caught up in fifteen, I'll send a squad for you," she added, softer as the latter was meant for only our ears.

The unit peeled away, leaving Moe and me with Millie. Not the best position to be in given what we just went through, but hey, choice becomes a mere request when you're traveling miles and miles away from—

I worked to soothe myself. *Calm. You gotta be calm if you wanna be safe.*

Millie's murmurs quieted as her body stilled. Her head lolled as she came out of the vision. I brushed her damp hair out of her face, gently tilting her chin to meet her emerald eyes. They were wild and unfocused.

"Hey, take a breath," I said soothingly. "You're safe."

"For how long?" she rasped, attempting to push herself up instinctively, but her arms buckled. I caught her before she could fall again, her limbs twitching as her nervous system struggled to regain control.

"Relax," Moe said, still crouched beside her. "What did you see?"

Millie swallowed hard, her eyes darting around, searching for something solid to focus on. Her voice trembled as she began.

"I knew that bitch was bitter from the moment I met her but this … this goes too far. It's Jessa, she's going to Ronan."

"What?" I yelped, rearing back. "My father? Ronan Moore?"

Millie's face softened with pity as she met my tearful stare. "She's furious—furious with Reina. About the breakup, sure, but more than that. She feels abandoned … humiliated. Like you used her for information and tossed her aside." There was nothing but ice in her tone.

A lump formed in my throat. Jessa had always been intense— passionate in everything she did—but this?

"Shit," Moe mumbled, backing away and running her hand through her silky hair. "She knows the plan. Where we're going to portal in, the contingency routes—everything. She had to in order for Amaia to know how to coordinate our routes."

"A spy is a spy, no matter how pretty," Millie scolded, and I couldn't explain it, but the sting of her words felt as sharp as a slap. As though she thought I should have known better from the jump.

My blood ran cold. The plan to portal directly into the capitol was risky enough without this. If Ronan knew the entry point, he'd have every advantage to trap Amaia, the cavalry and the squad going with her. He'd know that the battles waged miles away from Richmond were just a distraction for our final attack.

Moe's knuckles whitened as her hands curled into fists. She remained silent, mentally unraveling every thread of what this meant.

"Ugh, what a *fool*," Millie ranted. "He's going to kill her."

My ribs constricted, the pressure suffocating. Jessa. Her name alone was enough to stir the ache I'd been trying to bury. I hadn't ended things because I stopped caring for her. I ended things because her choices—her lies—made it impossible to stay. But *this*? Was my sense of judgment so warped that I couldn't see who she was at her core? She had never cared about doing what was right, had only cared how doing what was wrong made her look in my eyes.

"He'll smile at her, nod along to every damn word, like he's actually listening. But the second she gives him what he wants—"

"We get it," Moe snapped, her eyes flicking toward me, assessing. She'd caught the crack in my composure before I could patch it. The picture was as vivid as if I'd been there. The chill in Millie's voice made my stomach twist. "What else?"

Millie's eyes glazed over as she recalled the rest. "He's watching us. Watching Amaia's forces. Waiting. It's like … he's biding his time for the perfect strike. He wants her to come. To lead the charge herself. Your father is betting everything on her walking into this. He has every intention of breaking her, meeting her in the streets and making an example. And whatever's left of us after that, will crumble."

The silence was stifling. We all knew Amaia's mind. Bold. Fearless. Always ten steps ahead. But my father wasn't just her opposite; he was her equal. For years, he'd studied her every move, countered her strategies, and laid traps to exploit the vulnerabilities she didn't even realize she had.

Moe's voice shattered the quiet. "We can't tell her outright."

Millie's head snapped up, alarm flashing in her eyes. "She has a right to know. If she's walking into a trap—"

"She has already decided this is worth the risk," Moe interrupted. "He's counting on her to adjust if she finds out. We guide her. Quietly. Shift the plan in ways he won't see coming."

Millie swallowed hard, clearly unconvinced, but she didn't argue.

A kiss of light against the darkening horizon snapped us all to attention.

"That's not Amaia," Moe murmured.

"No," I agreed, still shaken to the core. "Based on what Asher told us, it's not the locals either."

"If we can see them," Moe said with warning. "They can see us."

Millie grimaced, clutching her pistol as she pushed herself unsteadily to her feet. "I'm good, you can trust me. I'll stay quiet. You earned my loyalty a long time ago," she said, this time, directly to me. "We can head out. We've lingered too long already."

CHAPTER
SIXTY-ONE

ALEXIARES

Cutting the bullshit, the night didn't sit right.

The nightly briefing broke and I couldn't shake that aggressive feeling of being watched. Our scouts had little information. They'd gotten as close as they could risk in order to ensure their ability to make it back to relay the message. All it was were murmurs of Covert troop movements in our general area—but I'd lived the kind of life that never allowed me to mistake whispers for 'nothing.'

Amaia was the first to sense it. Her posture shifted the moment we stepped into the open air. She didn't say a thing. Doe brown eyes scanned the camp, her fingers brushing the hilt of her blade. Her breathing hitched just slightly—something I found myself overly sensitive to. I breathed when she did. My breath hitched when hers caught.

Even if she had shown no signs of awareness, I felt it in my bones.

Something was wrong. Off. She glanced back at me as if reassuring herself I was still there.

"You good, Princess?" I said, trying to sound casual though I was on high alert, same as her.

She shook her head and turned back toward camp. "Yeah. Just … stay close tonight."

A plea wrapped in steel.

"Don't have to tell me twice," I teased, reaching for her instinctively, then remembering where we were.

It was no secret we were together. It had been a rumor throughout territories for months and confirmed at the first meeting. Where she went, I went. And if I wasn't with her, then I was somewhere carrying out her orders—but out here, she was their general, not the woman who owned my heart.

That earned me a short, uneasy laugh. "Eyes forward, soldier." Her eyes didn't match her smile.

I followed her without another word. There was this crushing certainty that she wouldn't survive this war. It went beyond my chest tightening and my stomach dropping. Every organ in my upper body was under the foot of an elephant while someone kicked at the sides.

The first explosion came as we reached the camp's edge for our night shift check in.

A concussive wave knocked the air out of my lungs, the blast disorienting. I wheezed, searching for Amaia, hands flailing, but I couldn't see, couldn't breathe, couldn't hear. My senses were knocked from me, then returned with a slamming force. The second explosion followed in quick succession and the wards around the camp flickered. Then died.

Magic suppression.

Fog rolled in, creeping through our camp in serpentine fashion. It hissed as it ate away at tents and equipment. The first screams pierced the air as it found flesh. Soldiers scrambled. Their orders were forgotten from shock and fear.

"Remember your training! Hold the line!" Amaia's voice cut through and relief flowed through me, unfreezing me and pushing me into action. "Fall back to the inner perimeter!"

The panic in the camp was a living thing, surging and pulling soldiers apart, swallowing Amaia in the fray. I pushed through it, my focus narrowing to one goal—reaching her. My boots slid in the mud as the fog thickened around me. Choked sobs filled the air, and guttural cries of pain came from every direction.

The wall was there—my power was out of reach. I didn't waste effort calling on it. I knew better. Only time could bring it back.

"Cover your mouths, you fucking *idiots*."

I recognized the grating voice despite the chorus of wails and gags. Finley.

Her stark blonde hair was a blur in the fog, but her blade flashed as she cut down a Covert soldier, fully masked. She moved with trained grace, carving through him as though the man had never been a threat at all.

Another soldier broke from the fog, charging her blindly, and I was already moving. My blade caught him mid-lunge, slicing through his ribcage and silencing him before his weapon could swing.

Finley didn't flinch. "I had him," she said, her tone flat.

"I don't care."

My focus shifted back to the surrounding chaos. The fog was closing in, eating at the camp, and I could hear more soldiers dying—ours and theirs.

"Where's Amaia?" I demanded.

Finley's gaze darted to me, keen and assessing. "Holding the line, obviously. Probably better than you are."

I turned away from her, having no interest in dying by her side if this was the night I was going to have a final dance with death.

"This, unfortunately, is one of mine," she called out, stopping me in my tracks and gesturing to the fog with her blade. "Cover your mouth, *Hound*. You're not vaccinated against this one."

"What the hell did you do?" I demanded.

She shot me an impatient stare that said I was wasting her time. "What I felt like doing, obviously. Developed it after you left. Suppose I should have mentioned this was one of those pesky design documents he stole."

Her attention shifted back to the soldiers pressing through the fog—blade moving fast, precise, mowing them down before they could regroup.

She was good, I'd give her that. But I wasn't relying on her to keep me alive.

A soldier charged from my left, and I spun, driving my dagger through his throat and kicking him to the ground. I kept my movements efficient. Without magic, there was no energy to waste.

I saw Finley glance at me from the corner of my eye, her lips twitching in what could have been amusement. "I missed this, you and me," she said, skewing another attacker and driving her blade into his gut.

"Do you ever shut the fuck up and just focus on surviving?" I said, twisting my blade free from the neck of a meaty motherfucker.

"Nope." She wiped blood from her face with the back of her hand, her expression shifting to something of a menace. "But you better hope Amaia is."

I paid her no mind. Of course, Amaia was focused on surviving—she hadn't made it to Ronan yet. She'd keep fighting until he was dead.

Finley froze. As much as I hated to admit it, the years spent fighting at her side made me … familiar with her style. She never froze, never hesitated. Finley Thomas was all impulse.

I pulled my pistol, dropping the two soldiers closest to us. In the brief pause of the fight, I caught it—that flicker in her eyes. Fear. Something I'd long thought she was incapable of.

"Oh, *shit*," she whispered, grabbing onto my wrist.

I snatched myself away and turned to follow her line of sight. It was hard to see through the swirling fog—but there was a rhythm underfoot … one that didn't belong in battle. The ground shifted.

"What the fuck?"

She dragged me back by the arm, fingers digging into my skin. "Someone should really talk to her about tightening her leash. Did you get hit in the head? Stop standing out in the open."

"The ground—"

"Yeah, I have all five senses too," she snapped, interrupting me, her pupils dilated even in the late night. "Geokinetic trackers."

As if answering the call of their name, the ground where I'd been standing fractured. A narrow fissure opened, and gradually, it gave way to a pit. Soldiers fell, screaming—from both sides.

The healers' tent erupted in flames. I could see the faint outlines of figures trapped inside, shadows scrambling against the firelight. There was nothing to put it out.

Fuck that. I backed away, Finley having the same idea. We moved fast, cutting through the mayhem as the fog thickened. We fell into a routine—old habits took over. Duck. Jump. Left. Right. It was muscle memory, a rhythm beaten into us by too many battles fought side by side. I hated it. But I wasn't stupid enough to fight it. Not if it doubled my chances of making it to Amaia.

"You're going the wrong way," I snapped, shoving a Covert soldier aside with brutal force.

The ground opened with fascinating speed where he dropped. Fissures were sprouting everywhere, jagged wounds tearing through the battlefield. Step wrong, and it was game over.

"I know where I'm going," Finley shot back, her voice sharp. "And if you don't want to end up in a fucking pit of Pansies, you'll follow me."

"Amaia—"

"Won't see you again if you don't shut up and come on."

Pansies. But of course. How original, Ronan.

The massacre thickened around us—healers cut down mid-motion, their bodies crumpling into heaps. This wasn't chaos. It was a purge. We burst through the fog into a clearing near the edges of camp, the ground ahead now sloped downward into a pit crawling with them. A trap.

I yanked Finley back as she stepped near the edge, her foot pushing crumbling dirt into the open earth.

"Relax sweetheart. I've got it." She winked as she pulled a small device from her belt, a sphere that spun every which way, a million cylindrical pieces forming it.

"*Finley*—"

"Oh my God, stop flapping your damn mouth," she interrupted, bringing a finger to her lips. "Trust me, will ya?"

The device hummed in her hand. A pulse shivered through the air, tickling the edges of my brain. It went deep into my chest, rattling against my ribcage. The Pansies froze in place, their jerking limbs now still—stuck in invisible flames.

Finley glanced at me, that cocky smirk tugging at the corner of her mouth as she watched the monsters below, perfectly still now, their guttural growls gone. "You think this is impressive? Stick around and wait to see what happens when it wears off."

I gritted my teeth. "How long have you been able to do this?"

She winked, smirk growing wider. "Not long."

I shot her a cold stare that made her pause for a second. Her expression tempered, but she didn't flinch. "Can we do this later, babe? We're in the middle of a beautiful escape plan, and I've never tested the thing. Don't know how much time we've got."

"Fine." I made my choice before she could say another word. I grabbed her arm, yanking her toward the edge.

"Move slow. It's still a prototype—can't handle too much jostling," she said, taking even, steady steps. One foot in front of the other.

I didn't answer. Didn't trust myself to speak without telling her exactly what I thought—about this plan, about *her*, about the years she'd spent tearing me down every time I attempted to build myself up after Tiago's death. My focus stayed on the ground in front of us, avoiding the twitching Pansies mere inches away. Looking at her would only make me volatile.

"So," Finley murmured, like this was small talk over coffee instead of us surrounded by Pansies. "How's life in Monterey?"

I kept my head forward. "I'm not doing this with you."

Her chuckle was odd—soft. Full of amused curiosity. "Really, I always wondered how you and Little Miss Perfect live."

Jealousy was one of her stronger traits. *She* could do as she pleased. At least that's how she'd always seen things. But me? Never. Another woman even looking my way ended up in punishment for us both. My punishments, however, lasted longer than whatever strike Finley offered them. I lived with her. There was no limit to where the cruelty born from jealousy could touch.

I tightened my grip on my weapon. Every word she said pulled memories to the surface, ones I'd spent years trying to bury. The disorder she reveled in, the pain she'd left behind, the way she'd torn me down simply to see if she could.

"That place would eat you alive," I said, and it was true. Monterey wasn't built for people like Finley. It wasn't about being ruthless; it was about knowing when to change, when to bend.

Finley didn't bend—she broke things. It was why she thrived in war and why she'd never survive peace.

"Oh, come on," she pressed, her tone mocking. "Let me guess. Marriage? House? Kid on the way?"

My jaw tightened. She wasn't far off, and she knew it. If I gave her anything, she'd twist it, use it. That was her nature.

"You know what I miss about you the most?" I asked, enthralled by the way she perked up—still expecting the lost dog to come home.

She spared a glance at me, a small glimpse of faint hope as we weaved between the entranced reeking dead. "Let me guess—fucking?"

"Nope." I didn't spare her a second thought as I answered, nostrils flaring in disgust. Letting the suspense build, I paused, waiting until the other side of the pit was in clear view. "I miss the look on your face when you realized I was leaving and had no plans to come back."

The silence that followed was louder than the animalistic groans of the Pansies around us. I'd wounded her. This was her routine. She expected me to care, to apologize, but I refused. I wasn't here to indulge her. Whether she helped us in this war or not, the day she died would be a day that couldn't come soon enough.

We were so close to freedom, the end within reach, when the world erupted behind us. The frantic pounding of boots on the ground, the sharp, ragged breaths of men running for their lives. They barreled into the clearing, their shouts dissolving into a pandemonium of panic. By the time they realized the trap, it was too late. Bodies hit the earth with a sickening thud as they fell into the pit below.

The impact caused the earth to slide, the pit resettling to adjust to the disturbance. It knocked Finley off-kilter, the device falling from her hand. She retrieved it before it could roll away, but the sound warped, flickered, and then died entirely. The pulse in my head had stopped, and the air was still.

"Fix it!" I snapped.

Finley held up the device, shaking it as though it might somehow wake up. "It's missing a piece. I can't."

"Then run."

The pit's edge loomed a few feet ahead—close enough to see, yet impossibly far. Pansies stirred behind us, the sound a sickening symphony of grinding bone and wet, rasping growls. It would be a fight to get out, not to mention the nearly twelve feet we'd have to climb to pull ourselves free. With the way the earth had given out on the other side, climbing wasn't the most stable choice.

"You need the running start," Finley said, halting abruptly. Her voice was tight, trembling beneath the forced calm. "Pull me up."

I stopped, my chest heaving. My eyes darted ahead, the jagged drop, and then to the mass of death clawing closer behind us. Every instinct screamed the same thing: *Leave her.*

But then she turned, and for the briefest, most torturous second, I saw her. Not the schemer, not the liar, not the cheater—the manipulator. Not the person who had burned bridges just to see the ashes. I saw Finley—the girl I thought I had once loved so fiercely it left scars.

Scars that had been healed by a woman who would never leave another soldier behind.

"Don't make me regret this," I growled, racing to the top.

I made it out and stumbled onto solid ground, only to be met with two originals at the top. They were easy to tear through. It took no extra thought. Likely had come from all the noise in the area. I turned as Finley reached up, her fingers catching the edge. She'd taken her own running leap toward freedom—unsure if I would come back for her. I grabbed her wrist, my other hand gripping her belt to pull her up. The weight of her was in my hands, pulling me down.

No. That didn't make sense. I fought against it.

I thought we'd make it.

Her scream ripped through me. She kicked hard, but it didn't matter. Finley's thigh was within the clamped jaws of what appeared to be a *Supra* mutated into a Pansie—its jaws buried so deep I could see bone glinting through the torn flesh. A second one latched onto her other leg. Blood poured from the wounds, her body jerking violently as they tore into her. The mess of her attack pulled in a third. I tugged harder. This wouldn't be how she died. Her crimes were great, but with her death, more people would suffer.

"I'm sorry," she choked, blood pooling in her mouth. Her eyes locked on mine, wide and desperate. "For everything."

Claws sliced through her torso easier than paper. I pulled harder, my grip slipping against the slickness of her blood. My muscles burned. I refused to let go. This wasn't supposed to happen. Not now. Not to her—not like this. Memories of my mother's face surfaced unbidden, her hand torn from mine in a moment of sheer helplessness. I hadn't been strong enough then.

A sharp, brutal crack rang out as her leg wrenched from its socket. The pressure shifted, and then they were on her—ripping her apart in front of me. I heard the tearing of flesh, the crack of bones.

Her upper body slipped from my grasp, falling into the pit as the Pansies tore into what was left. The scream that tore from her mouth was cut short. I stumbled back, dazed, numb. The noise around me faded, drowned out by the image seared into my mind.

Finley was gone—torn apart. Piece by piece. And I couldn't move. Couldn't speak. Couldn't stop the blood from dripping from my hands.

All I could do was let her go.

"Finley?" The voice was a hollow, confused whisper. "No. Finley?"

It was mine. The Pansies overwhelmed her, their bodies piling on top of hers. Something already broken inside me splintered.

Their snarls shifted, their dead eyes swiveling toward me. I braced myself, my muscles tensing for the inevitable, when Finley's device let out one last, desperate pulse. A deep, resonant hum shook the air, freezing the Pansies mid-motion. Their heads twitched unnaturally, their limbs spasming as if caught in a glitch.

She'd fixed it. In her last moments, she'd found the piece.

I ran. Away from the horror, away from *her*. The woods swallowed me whole, branches clawing at my arms, roots threatening to trip me. My lungs burned, my thoughts a storm of panic, guilt, and something I didn't dare name. All I could think of was finding Amaia. Getting to her before she met a similar fate.

Branches lashed at my face, the taste of bile still sharp on my tongue. Finley's scream echoed in my skull. Trembles coursed through me, my body exhausted.

Pain hit me with the brutality of a tidal wave. I hit the ground hard.

Instinct took over, and I lashed out, shoving the weight off me. My knife was in my hand before I even registered who or what it was.

"Stand down!" a sharp voice barked.

I froze. I knew that voice.

Amaia.

But the haze of panic and lust for blood wouldn't let me trust it. My grip on the blade tightened as I lunged, slamming her back against a tree.

"Alexiares, stop! It's me!" She gasped, her hands coming up in surrender. "Baby, it's me."

"You're lying," I hissed, my voice trembling. My mind raced, twisting her face into an enemy's mask.

She didn't flinch, didn't fight back. "It's *me*. Amaia. Here." She grabbed my hand, guiding it to her face, though I could see but a shadow of it in the moonlight.

For a moment, I couldn't breathe. My heart thundered in my ears as her words sank in. My grip loosened, and the knife slipped from my hand.

"Amaia?" I whispered. Honestly, I wasn't sure if I was begging for confirmation or forgiveness.

She exhaled. "I'm here. Shit, you're okay. Are you hurt?"

"Are *you* okay?" I asked, my voice cracking with a laugh.

She nodded quickly. Her hands gripped my arms. "I thought—I thought you were dead." For a split second, the same fear existed in her that had been suffocating me.

"Finley," My stomach twisted. Her name was poison in my throat.

Amaia's weight shifted, snapping sticks beneath her boots. "She's gone?"

I tried to hold myself together. Didn't want to appear weak or as if I gave a shit. My legs betrayed me—they buckled. The ground came up too fast, and I hit it hard, the nausea rising before the rest of me could catch up. The bile burned in my throat, but I couldn't swallow it down.

Amaia kneeled beside me. "Breathe." Her hand circled the center of my back and I rested my head against her shoulder.

The contorted memories of a life with Finley sliced through me, jagged and unrelenting. Then, the image of her death. Finley's blood, her screams, the snap of her body as the Pansies tore her apart—it was all still there, imprinted behind my eyes.

Amaia cleared her throat. "We can celebrate later, if that's what you want to do. Or we can grieve. Together. Feel what you need to feel. I love you, I'm with you, but right now, we need to get back to the troops. We've regrouped two miles south. They're clearing out anyone and anything left at camp right now and gathering the supplies that survived. A lot of people were bit … we don't know who will make it through the night."

I didn't answer. I pushed myself up and started walking. Her words didn't make sense yet. Finley's face was still too vivid. Because in her final moments, she'd shown me something I hadn't thought possible.

She'd chosen to save me.

I PULLED MYSELF TOGETHER, SHAKING THE WORST OF IT OFF. NOT enough to be fine, but enough to function.

I surveyed the camp, taking in the wreckage, the bodies. One hundred soldiers had been bit and half had already turned. It wasn't looking great for the others. But it wasn't the loss that hit hardest. It was her. Amaia stood at the edge of the clearing, bloodied but still standing tall. Unbroken. She met my gaze long enough for something in her eyes to soften, then turned back to the soldiers.

This—this was a loss, but not like Ronan's. Not by a long shot.

The light from the early morning revealed the damage she'd caused. Every single Covert soldier who'd breached our perimeter was dead. Every last one. And that wasn't all. She'd had a cavalry unit track down healers—Covert healers who'd traveled with the attacking force—and drag them back here, right into the mess they'd made.

Then she did what she did best. She gathered them, every one except the last, into the pit in the center of camp. Let her soldiers have their way with them when their magic returned. Watched. Made the last healer watch, too. Then sent them off with a message:

You play dirty, I'll play in the mud.

CHAPTER SIXTY-TWO

AMAIA

I'd been nudged every which way by Reina and Tomoe—and completely avoided by Millie. Which inevitably meant shit hit the fan. In some theoretical future, there was something they *really* didn't want me to do—and I was pretty sure what it was.

We were a day out from Richmond. The weather hadn't let up, and neither had Ronan. He'd given us a run for our money—but not his best. No, he was saving those soldiers. Those troops would come when we were tired out, starving, and absent of all hope.

Ideas not too far off from our reality, except Ronan hadn't accounted for one thing—he was fighting for possession of something he wanted. We were fighting to keep what we *needed*, what we *loved*.

Feral beasts had formed through the past week. We'd been through hell. Most of our supplies had been destroyed, our healers killed, clothes soaked from the constantly falling snow—now stacked knee high. All odds were against us, and still, our soldiers had hope.

A great thing when their leader did not.

Right now, we had him where we wanted him. On high alert and under pressure to respond. At dawn, the beginning to the end would start, and only one army would walk away.

"I told you it wasn't goodbye."

Every nerve and muscle in my body went rigid. I didn't want to turn around in fear that I was hallucinating. He was here. Riley had made it.

Dropping the plans I'd been reviewing, I whirled around, my brother standing behind me. Relief took my ability to stand—my knees giving out. Riley chuckled, pulling me in for a hug.

"Never goodbye," I whispered, a choked sob.

Putting some distance between us, I turned him in a circle, examining him for any injuries. He spread his arms out and played into the charade with as much of a smile as I'd ever get at a time like this. He was good, in one piece. That's all I'd hoped for at the end of the day. If my family was good, then so was I.

"Cut the tears. We can have our moment later," he teased, pulling me toward the flap of the war tent entrance. "The others are waiting around the fire. Reina said you refused to eat."

Others. That was reassuring, and my chest loosened as far as I was willing to unwind. We'd all made it—every single one of us—to the last stand. Tomorrow, we'd be portaled into the city, and the chances we'd all make it out of that alive were slim to none. Impossible. But still, we had tonight. So tonight, I would be happy to see them all, to share a meal one last time.

"Food is sparse, and I sent all support systems away. Ronan has no respect," I spat, not at him, but at the mention of a monster. "They weren't safe here. With the orders of resting our magic for the morning, no extra food to spare. They need it more than I do."

"Too late," Riley said, offering me what I assumed was the final remains of his trail mix. It was a miracle he still had any at all.

Miracle or planned effort? Likely the latter. He knew me. Knew it was a treat I found hard to resist. He'd saved it for this last night.

I smiled at him, resting my head on his arm, nibbling on the trial mix as we walked through worn and torn tents. Weaving through soldiers sleeping on their packs out in the open, laying as close to the fires as possible.

There was no point in freezing for the night. We wanted Ronan to know we were here. He was essentially surrounded, blocked on two sides. His troops couldn't move without us getting the heads up first.

We rounded the bend. The glow of a dozen campfires came into view and warmth crept throughout my body—not from the fire, but from seeing the rare glimpse of joy on the faces of the people I cared for. Reina was locked in a hug with Hunter and Serenity, relief etched into every line of her face. That spark in her eyes was back now, and I found myself envying her. She still had the ability to feel.

These days, everything just… *was* for me. Another day to keep living, breathing, pushing. Monotonous. A chore, except when I was with him. In the last few weeks, I'd put distance there too. Not intentional—not exactly.

Alexiares stood nearby, arms crossed, mid-conversation with Tomás and Tomoe. I caught the way she leaned toward Tomás, her face softer than I'd seen it in months. They may have included Alexiares into the conversation out of politeness, but it was clear the only words being listened to were from each other. Tomás looked at her the way people watched the sunrise after a long, dark, and stormy night. Longing for the light.

I caught the shift in energy off to the side. Hunter wasn't part of their circle, yet his attention was on them. His jaw tightened, hands fidgeting. Something ugly flickered across his face before he forced himself to turn away.

The moment shattered as Abel barreled into me, throwing his arm around my shoulders and squeezing tight. "Did you miss me?" His juvenile grin was impossible to resist.

It worked, if only for a heartbeat. I let myself succumb to the moment, let it dull the edges of everything else. But the reprieve was fleeting. A gasp of air before the weight returned, heavier than before.

That spark of warmth in the campfire's glow dimmed, swallowed by the tension I hadn't noticed until now. We were down a person.

"Where's Jessa?" I asked, eyes landing on Reina.

Reina, Riley, and Tomoe exchanged a glance that let me know I'd been a topic of discussion long before Riley had announced his arrival.

Riley cleared his throat. "Gone," he answered cautiously.

I reined in my emotions, listening to his words and watching as everyone but Alexiares and Tomoe glanced away from my glare. "*Gone*," I said slowly. "Not dead?"

"Correct," Riley confirmed.

The tension in Reina's tight-lipped expression betrayed her, despite her best effort to hold steady. Her gaze darted, almost imperceptibly, and that split second was all I needed. *That traitorous fucking bitch.*

"I'm going to kill her."

"Well, don't say it out loud," Tomoe deadpanned. Alexiares glared in response and she mumbled an apology.

I dug my nails into my palms. I was one more betrayal away from letting the entire world burn. Reina flinched at the venom in my tone but didn't cower, only nodded slightly in resignation. As though she'd come to that understanding days before.

Ah. Fuck. I pounded my palms to the side of my head—thoughts racing. Everything fucked up, all in the blink of an eye. Plans without plans, steps within steps. I couldn't let my mind go too far—not here, not now. Ronan would be waiting for me to overthink, to walk straight into his trap. He had me figured out, and I hated it.

Commotion broke through what was inevitably a situation meant to test my self-control, pulling every gaze toward the outskirts of camp. Two scouts dragged in a battered soldier, his face swollen, blood dripping from the matching cuts above each brow.

"He demanded to speak with you," one of the scouts said, shoving the soldier to his knees in front of me. Nothing but complete disgust shone back in his beady eyes when he looked at me.

"I wasn't aware we took demands from the barbarians?" I straightened my stance, putting the face of the general back on.

Alexiares scoffed, now closed in behind me. "Don't insult the barbarians."

The man spat blood onto the ground, then peered up, his lips curling into something too smug for someone in his position. I aimed to change that.

"Ronan has an ultimatum. Hand yourself over by dawn, or he'll start with *the Bloodhound*." His gaze went over my shoulder. "Then Riley—Malachai says welcome, by the way." He stared Riley down then trickled his line of sight over to me. "He'll go down the line. One by one."

The camp erupted—protests, shouts, the harsh ring of steel as weapons cleared their sheaths. I raised a hand, and the noise died, swallowed by a tense, crackling silence. I was done with his threats. Done with all the death. I feared for Ronan this was becoming less about the territories he desired to own, the bodies he wanted to control, and more about punishing me. For putting up a fight, daring not to submit or admit defeat, challenging him and meeting him on a level playing field.

I was the greatest opponent he would ever face and even though I thought I was losing—it was clear by his desperation to single me out that I had already won. *He'd seen it*. Which only meant one thing, the only plan I had allowed my brain to settle on, the one no one else knew.

"I'm sure he will. How long did it take you to get here?" I asked, devoid of emotion.

His confidence faltered, "If you're asking how long it will take them to realize I'm not making it back, forty-five minutes."

"Forty-five minutes from the time you left?" I asked a necessary, clarifying question, my fingers tapping against my jaw.

"Does it matter, Amaia?" Serenity asked, and I could immediately tell the trip Riley's group had made, had been haunted by the tales of our own. They hadn't fared much better in the face of Ronan's brutality.

The soldier's teeth ground together, his snarl nasty as he said nothing.

I reached down, palms landing on what were now my last two blades—the rest had been given to my family, to my soldiers, they needed the protection more than myself.

"If you kill me," he sneered, but the panic was there, "they'll still storm this camp come dawn."

"Kill you?" I crouched down to meet his eyes. "Why would I do that? No. I'm just going to make every last second of the next forty-five minutes, the most *excruciating* crawl of your life. My soldiers will meet you there to finish the job. Have fun."

My boot connected with his chest, slamming him to the ground. Alexiares was on him before he could recover, flipping him over as my blades sliced deep into the back of his knees. The scream of a banshee tore through camp.

The jeers and chants of my soldiers were white noise as I stood over him, watching the blood pool beneath his leg. "Tell Ronan to give it his best shot. By the time he gets here, we'll be gone."

Without another glance, I sheathed my knives and walked away. The others fell in line behind me, their protests dying on their lips.

This wasn't a warning. It was a reckoning.

TIME HAD RUN OUT—AND SO HAD MY MERCY.

"It's been an honor, General Bennett." Hell had frozen over as General Clayton Harper extended such a pleasantry as he turned on his heels with pity in his eyes, headed to lead the charge of my troops.

I offered him and Trevan a tense nod at their departure. It was up to them now. We would not all face each other again. The alliance had been tense, a disastrous effort that resulted in a powerful, brutal force when it mattered most.

"One unit!" I called out, head held high as I watched the backs of every single soldier stiffen as they came to a halt, and swiveled into a salute.

"One compound!"

The roar of unity was thunderous. Swallowing became difficult in the attempt of choking down tears. They could do this. *They will make it.* I believed in them—each and every soldier. We hadn't come this far to lose it all.

We would engage Ronan from north and south of the capital and push our way in. This he expected. This he knew. It was a distraction but also ensured we would be able to hold the city in the outcome of a victory. With the cavalry units focused on dividing and conquering, citizens on the outskirts of the capital would be evacuated.

Unfortunately I couldn't say the same for the ones that resided within. Reina and Millie's unit would prioritize getting anyone under sixteen to safety. I held no remorse for what happened to anyone else. The accounts from *Outsiders* in The Outskirts painted the picture of the mentality those within the capital held with such vividness, I found myself personally insulted by the atrocities that went on.

I refused to let their way of thinking survive. We would break this cycle in history—for good.

Ronan being aware of our initial plan had required some adjustments. I wanted him to see them—every recalibration, every pivot. I wanted him to react, to flail. Which now meant Lola and her coven would be left near destitute from the sheer amount of individuals that needed to be portaled in.

I needed an extra ground unit to accompany the cavalry and a tactical team with … specialized weaponry—complimentary collaboration of Tomás and the late and great Finley Thomas.

Hours. That's how long it would take for us to lockdown the city from the outside. Hours we didn't have unless the inside held until I could make it to Ronan. That was the goal: bait him, humiliate him, shatter his ego until his focus narrowed to finding me. By then it'd be too late.

"Ready for this?" I asked.

"Not particularly, no, but here we are I guess." Reina covered her nervous chuckle with her hand. Her horse shifted, and Hunter placed a calming palm on its flank. He glanced at his sister with quiet reassurance. There was every bit a chance they'd have to face their father though neither had the desire.

I had made the right call trusting him. As much as Serenity grated my nerves, they were good people to have in our corner. She worked effortlessly with all of them—Alexiares, Riley, Tomoe, Abel. Add in Tomás's mind, the weapons he'd armed them with, and Isabella's unit—maybe, just fucking maybe, we stood a chance.

Lola appeared with her coven, shadows shrouded in ghostly black.

She drifted toward us, her coven moving ahead without pause, but Lola's focus stayed solely on Alexiares. Her hands framed his face, her touch awkward yet deliberate, like a mother unsure how to comfort her son. The embrace that followed was stiff, neither warm nor cold, heavy with unexpressed remorse. When she stepped away, she didn't look back—and she wouldn't.

I'd asked her to betray him after all.

"Anyone want to exchange goodbyes?" Tomoe quipped, her humor as morbid as ever. Tomás was the only one who laughed. I couldn't bring myself to—she had hope. It was the only reason she'd make such a joke.

"Someone besides Tomoe say the last word before we dive headfirst into a creepy black hole," Abel said, strapping the stabilizer Reina had crafted firmly to his arm. She watched him, a glimmer of pride in her eyes but also the loosening of breath. The device fit perfectly around his forearm, its matte black plating sleek and snug, with thin lines of blue circuitry tracing its edges, faintly glowing like veins of light beneath his skin. One less fear she had to worry herself with—knowing he had that one extra way to protect himself on a battlefield that was not even under the best of circumstances.

Alexiares clapped him on the back and Abel cringed under his touch. "Sure. Don't die. Let's go."

"Don't die," Abel muttered. "Right. Got it. I've only almost done that like three times since meeting you."

"Okay, enough. Focus." I willed myself to command their attention, but in all honesty, I could have lived in the moment of familiar banter forever. Wanted to replay it in my mind, to stay here. But I could not. We could not. And no moment, happy nor sad, could last forever. "Whatever happens once we enter the city … stick to the plan. *Always* stick to the plan, no matter what." I caught the crack in my voice, nearly slipping through—my only hope being that they remembered these words, carrying them with them forever. Through the highs and lows of life. They'd been said to me after all, and Prescott had molded the general that would bring peace.

"Be fierce. Be brave. Stay alive. You are strong." I met each of their gazes, imprinting their faces in my mind. "You are capable, and we are finishing this today, together—always together even if we are fighting apart. It's still the same fight. If you can still breathe, you damn sure can still fight. Remember that. Keep your eyes sharp and your wits about, and yeah, don't die. Or I'll kill you myself."

Abel was the first to react—he snorted nervously as if he hadn't expected me to crack a joke in a time like this. And I supposed he may not have. We hadn't had the gift of time to find out how we fit together as a family in a time outside of complete despair.

"Very inspiring," Tomás broke the ice, garnering a reluctant grin from Reina through her eyes betrayed the anxiety I knew rolled through my chest.

"You all talk too much." Serenity shook her head. "Let's move."

They moved to join Isabella and Millie, now engaged in what appeared to be an incredibly one sided conversation with Lola. Most of her coven had accompanied her here, the others choosing to stay behind to protect their home. Many had answered what I teased to be a recruitment call, coming to St. Paul at her request when she promised to assist us, not yet signing up for war. Her coven had grown in size tenfold.

I truly hope they made it back to them after they guided us through. This was a sacrifice I hoped history would never forget.

Tomoe walked between Tomás and Hunter, glancing over her shoulder at me with knowing eyes.

"No goodbyes," Riley said.

"Never goodbye."

He walked away, his hand brushing mine in a fleeting, almost unconscious goodbye, and then it was just Alexiares and me. The others faded into the periphery, their movements blurring into shadow. We didn't speak—not at first. Those honey brown eyes that I'd despised made me melt. So sharp, so piercing as they held mine unguarded, letting me see the quiet storm that lay beneath.

My chest ached. I wanted to say everything—that I loved him, that I hated that it took twenty-seven wasted years to find him, that he was everything to me, the sun, the moon, the fucking galaxy and beyond. He was beautiful to me and I meant that purely in regard to the complexity of his soul. I wanted to scream to him that he needed to come back, to survive this because I could only imagine the world a bleaker place without him. Even if I wasn't here, even if I didn't have the luck in life to live out those days with him. But all the words that could come to mind felt small. Hollow. I did the only thing I could.

I reached for him.

Alexiares's hand slid into mine, and we stood there, frozen, as the world around us receded into nothingness.

"Alexiares," I whispered, my voice barely carrying over the distance that didn't really exist between us.

"Princess," he said, his tone soft and edged with something close to reverence.

I squeezed his hand. "Use it all," I said, my meaning heavy, pointed. He would understand when the time was right.

An arch of his brow was his only response, but it was enough. The portal ignited before us, a vast, black void, and without another word, we stepped forward together.

The portal flickered closed behind us. Alexiares and I released hands instinctively, both reaching for our weapons. Jax's twin swords glinted in the morning light, their weight as familiar as the other blades lining my body.

A pristine city center stretched before our troops. Between the gleaming structures, freshly painted buildings, and pristine streets, I didn't know what to focus on first—what disgusted me the most.

Maybe it was the cars, perfectly parked, their chrome unblemished. Or the streetlights still glowing faintly, not yet dimmed by the crisp light of a fall morning. No. I knew where to look—the people.

The healthy, well-fed civilians, their magic glowing faintly at their fingertips, dressed in starched suits and impeccable grooming. The women crouched low, their manicured nails clutching their children, those round-bellied toddlers in perfect shoes, staring at us with wide, fearful eyes.

They gaped at us like we were monsters. Yeah, I'd start there.

Not even fifty miles from here, there were children crawling through dust and rubble, begging for scraps of food while their parents broke their backs mining coal or being exploited as human power sources to keep Richmond alight. All so *this place* could live a cushy life. Because they deserved it, right? *The blessed and the favored,* as Ronan's propaganda taunted. *Fuck that.*

This wasn't just a city—it was a symbol of everything we'd been fighting against. And this revolution was where symbols must die.

Reina's unit surged forward first, their movements swift and calculated as they ushered civilians out of the streets. Shouts of confusion mingled with the distant crack of gunfire, shaking the ground beneath us.

"Move quickly, move together!" Millie's voice carried above the noise, the cavalry forming a protective barrier around the civilians while the tactical team worked to secure the city center. Children cried as they clung to their mothers.

I watched it all unfold and felt the weight of the choice ahead, a question that had haunted leaders throughout history. A choice that would define the type of leader I had been years into the future:

Do I let the children live and grow with the hatred in their hearts for who they would now deem their oppressor? Allow them to simmer at the hopes of rebelling in the name of their fathers and mothers that we had slain?

Or kill the weeds before they have the chance to grow.

I wanted to believe in the former, because hatred was taught— that did not mean it couldn't be nurtured away. It was a choice I trusted those around me to make in my stead.

"Ready?" Lola's voice pulled me from my thoughts.

I gave her a curt nod, my heart pounding. "They'll follow the plan." My words were steady, even though they weighed heavily on my chest.

I felt him before I saw him. The air shifted with electricity and I knew Alexiares had found me. He turned, his head snapping toward me with the precision of *the Bloodhound* he was. His eyes locked onto mine, reading every intention I had as though I'd laid it all out.

Shock. Betrayal. The question I couldn't bear to hear, *Why?*, etched itself across his face. His steps faltered, only for a heartbeat. I could see it—the fight in him, the relentless drive that wouldn't let me go without an answer, without a reason.

I tore my gaze away before he could close the distance, before he could speak, before *I* could break. If I let him reach me, if I let him ask, I knew I'd stay. For him. For us. For the selfishness of one more moment.

But war didn't wait for goodbyes. And love couldn't save what I had to do.

Soldiers poured from alleys and rooftops and we were forced to prepare for a fight, their armor gleaming in the dim light of the burning horizon. They came like a wave, relentless and unyielding, their shouts ringing out in unison.

"Hold them back!" Lola's magic crackling to life. A shield of shimmering dark energy rippled around us, deflecting the first volley of attacks.

I twirled the twin swords. "Keep pushing!"

Lola's magic-carved a path through the chaos, and I followed, slashing and weaving through the fray. The soldiers were skilled, but they lacked our desperation.

We broke through the line, though not without cost. One of Lola's coven stumbled, blood streaming from a wound at her side. Lola caught her, her face set with grim determination.

"Go," she urged me, her voice taut with urgency.

I hesitated, my gaze flickering to Alexiares, stuck in a fight where he was outnumbered but still in control. His vines wrapped around the necks of three soldiers. He snapped them without remorse, their bodies crumpling to the ground in broken heaps.

"Lola—"

"I've got this, I have enough energy for another to get out," she said firmly, her eyes locking with mine. "You know what you need to do."

The second portal ignited.

"Where are you sending me?" I asked, though I already knew she wouldn't answer.

"You'll know when you get there," she said softly. "And he won't follow you until it's done."

I clenched my fists, forcing myself to let go of everything tethering me to this moment. The others would fight. They would survive.

Alexiares would hate me for this, but it was the only way.

The portal's hum faded, leaving a sharp stillness in its wake. My boots echoed against the empty asphalt as I stepped forward, the silence almost deafening after the roar of battle.

I slammed myself into the side of the old city hall, taking cover before I had the chance to be seen. *Lola, you fucking genius.* I could kiss her if it didn't mean getting vaporized.

Its dome crowned the symmetrical colonnades that framed its central hall. The columns were thick, carved with intricate patterns that whispered of both artistic desires and dominance.

Wide marble steps led to the grand entrance, where polished steel doors reflected the morning light, their surface unmarred by the grit of war. Golden accents adorned the building's edges.

The surrounding grounds were manicured to perfection—lush green lawns bordered by symmetrical flower beds, each bloom vivid and precise, as though the very soil obeyed its masters. Not a blade of grass dared to stray out of line.

It was beautiful, and it was a lie.

I sheathed the swords. I wouldn't need them from this point on. This was it. The end of the path I had chosen.

I took a step forward, leaving behind everything I couldn't carry.

CHAPTER
SIXTY-THREE

REINA

We had to keep going, had to trust that whatever Amaia's plan was, would work. Who knows what went on in that girl's mind. All I knew was that it usually worked out. That made maintaining the mission goal a priority, to ensure it all worked out.

The devastation was immediate. A brutal kind of chaos that left one little room to think. Building buckled under relentless fire, brought not of magic, but innovation. Tomás was terrifyingly brilliant. I wanted to see his work at play, sit and view it in fascination. There was no time for that, however, and as wondrous his mind was—it was deadly. Debris rained down around us in choking clouds.

It was a muted crumble in comparison to the screams filling the air. The only other sound to cut through was the pounding hooves as Millie's horse surged past me, her spear a blur. Beside her, Tomoe rode with precision, scanning the urban battlefield we'd thrust ourselves upon with calculating calm. If she was gonna be calm, then I would too.

Alexiares tore through anyone he deemed an enemy with the ferocity of a Bloodhound. *The Bloodhound.* His blade was a streak of silver in the haze of magic suppressing gas. He moved with feral intensity, his growls cutting through the buzz of battle. A shadow slipped through the openings of the battlefield—Riley's strikes were swift and silent.

On the flanks, Hunter's voice sliced through the bedlam. His team weaved through the melee as they shielded terrified civilians, guiding them toward the fallback point. Shields raised in an unbreakable line—Isabella Everhart's soldiers. Flames burst to life along the perimeter, their heat distorting the air and forcing Covert soldiers to recoil. Civilians followed Hunter's commands, moving along the sidewalks with wide eyes and stumbling, clinging to each other as they passed through. Was it wrong? That it brought me joy to see them shocked that war came to them.

The suppressant gas was thick now, a suffocating blanket that dulled the edge of magic in the air. Although *we* were immune to such a concoction, the souring smell hit me hard. "Focus on the children," I told Moe as I pushed toward Moe, my hand out ready to join forces.

We extended our power, brushing against their minds with a soothing wave. They did not have to become the seed of which they were sewn. There was hope and happiness in their futures. *You're okay. Stay calm.* Moe's magic amplified mine, together, we opened the door to the vision—a new world.

They saw themselves running through the streets playing Mortals and Zombies, drenched in sunlight, laughing without fear. They experienced the cool breeze of a summer day, heard the hum of a community that valued them not for their power but for who they were at their core.

My magic wrapped around their emotions, letting them feel what had the potential to be real—joy so vivid it melted away all spite. Killed all ego. Tomoe guided their focus, weaving the details of a life that could be: dinners shared at long tables, safety that wasn't earned through the power in their blood, love that was not conditional.

"What are you doing?"

"Stop it!"

"Please, don't hurt them. They're children."

It was all background noise to me. The protests of people who honestly had no business parenting anyone. I silenced them—extending my power to send them a sense of calm they did not deserve. We were doing our best to limit the trauma if they would just give us a second.

"Reina!" Millie's shout snapped me back. "You're overextending!"

She was right. The strain was brutal. My brain hurt, but there were adults clawing at each other to reach their children, panicked and desperate. I stretched my power further, sedating one, then another, until my vision swam.

"We need you in one piece," Moe said, her voice sharp. "Save it for the ones you care don't suffer."

Unfortunately, thanks to daddy dearest, that was true. I was the only healer here and responsible for the care of nearly a hundred. Holding a city this size was supposed to come with resources—but there was no one else to help, not here, not now. We had a healer shortage thanks to his literal war crime.

Luckily, the ones traveling with Riley, hadn't suffered the same fate. There were no reinforcements coming. Not here, not now. The others were spread thin across the actual battlefield where the blood flowed thicker than here.

"Roger that," I bit out, pulling my magic back with an effort.

From the corner of my eye, I caught Moe glancing toward the battle spilling further down the street. Her jaw clenched, her hand tightening on her reins. "We need to move them," she murmured.

A sudden gust of wind slammed into us, cold and razor edged, scattering debris. It wasn't natural. It was too controlled to come from mother nature. Dust and broken glass tore at my skin, and my horse reared, hooves striking the air as a panicked whinny escaped its throat. This wasn't nature's fury; it was too controlled.

"The air elementals Jessa warned us about," I muttered, scanning the air around us. "They're trying to disorient us."

Alexiares's voice carried across the street with desperation that nearly put me on my knees. "Amaia!"

It was not a question—it was a plea. A command to empty air, as though he expected the world itself to present her to him.

He called for her again, the words coming faster now, "Amaia, damn it, where are you?"

Alexiares knew she wasn't here. We all knew.

I couldn't see him through the smoke but he was close. I could feel the tension in the space between us, the primal need in his voice—a thread pulling tight, on the verge of snapping. He wasn't asking for help. He searched, frantic, as though the idea of her being unreachable was unbearable. The panic was clear, the kind of emotion I was all too familiar with having the family I chose, but I never thought I'd hear it from him.

"Get a fucking grip right now." I turned in time to see her press Wrath against Alexiares's throat, her expression deadly calm. Riley hovered right beside them, pacing like a caged animal, his fists clenching and unclenching as though he might bolt after Amaia the moment Tomoe took her eyes off them.

The *Bloodhound* was unleashed, and the sheer ferocity of his fury sent a cold spike through my chest. He was a storm made flesh, eyes blazing with murderous intent. Even from here, his rage was suffocating.

"Don't," Tomoe growled, her eyes fixed on Alexiares. "She didn't tell anyone what she was going to do, because she *couldn't*. Ronan is watching for one of us—just fucking one—to slip up. That's all it takes for this plan to fall apart."

"She shouldn't have to do this alone!" Alexiares snarled, his voice cracking under the weight of his fury.

"She's not alone," I snapped, cutting in before the argument spiraled further. "But if you go storming in like this, she *will* be. We stick to the plan, or we might as well hand my father the victory now."

Riley stood rigid beside him, jaw clenched, hands balled at his sides, watching Tomoe with narrowed eyes, his body trembling with each strained exhale. He was barely holding it together. *Ugh, boys.* You'd think they knew something the rest of us didn't. Amaia was fine and she would continue to be that way if they could stop being so dang emotional. We had a job to do and a specific amount of time to do it.

"It's done, Tomoe," Millie said, her voice cutting through the tension as she joined us. She knew when to push and when to hold back, and this moment was a family one she was best not to interrupt—but she did anyway. Boldly and fiercely.

Moe ground her teeth, Wrath still dangerously close to Alexiares's carotid. She yanked it away, frustration curling in her posture as Alexiares snarled at her. He pushed himself free and found his composure—lethally scary composure, but he was calm now, nonetheless.

He swatted her hand away. "I'm fine."

"We're on the move," Isabella called out over the disarray. They needed to clear out the adults now that we'd rounded up the kids. It wouldn't be long before my father called reinforcements back to the city. We'd been left with the JV squad thus far. "See you at the rendezvous, good luck. It's been fun, but let's make sure this war is the last of it, yeah?"

Without hesitation, Moe swung up onto her horse, steadying herself on the reins. She moved to ride alongside me and I kicked my horse into motion. The pounding hooves on cobblestones echoed as we pushed through the streets, guiding the children through our established evacuation route—the battle behind us still creeping in. Lurking, following us with the promise of violence. Our tactical team was doing a dang good job engaging them. Hunter and his crew had kept them distracted, but that would only last for so long.

"Reina, don't look," Abel called out from up ahead, near the entrance of the park.

I narrowed my eyes, squinting in confusion, not sure what I wasn't supposed to be looking at. Then I saw it.

My blood froze. The wind shifted, carrying with it a faint creak of rope swaying on the breeze, and my gaze locked onto the twisted oak tree standing sentinel over the horror. There, hanging akin to a broken doll, was Jessa.

Her lifeless body dangled from the rope, eyes wide and empty, staring at nothing. A sickeningly jagged sign swung beneath her, the words etched in cruel letters: *Welcome, daughter.*

I couldn't breathe. I couldn't move. The sight of her, twisted and broken in such a careless, despicable manner … I had to swallow against the bile rising in my throat, but the words wouldn't leave my mouth. Nothing would. All I could do was stare at her.

Millie held steady with my pace, reaching for my hand with her free one. "Don't," she said softly, her voice firm but not unkind. "He wants you to break. Don't give him the satisfaction."

I swallowed hard, tearing my eyes away from the scene. We had to keep moving, keep evacuating what children we could before the city went up in flames.

CHAPTER

SIXTY-FOUR

AMAIA

For the first time in a long time, I did not want to die. And that was how I knew my circle of life was complete.

Hadn't that always been the joke of what we called living? When one turmoil ends, another begins—and the second you think it couldn't get any worse, you realize how good you had it. Whatever Millie had seen had changed nothing and everything all at once. But most of all, it'd killed my hope. That last sliver, that final tendril of juvenile thirst for a future.

Dreams weren't for generals.

Dreams were for revolutionaries to form and generals to bring about. The good ones, the greats—they were both.

I did not desire greatness for myself, only others. With that came the necessity of being too comfortable with sacrifice. I was going to blow this motherfucker to the ground.

Reaching into my pocket, my fingers grazed the smooth, cool surface of the most precious thing I owned. With shaky fingers, I slid the ring gifted from the other half of my soul, and placed it where it belonged. That slight narrowing in honey brown eyes and contortion of confusion on Alexiares's face echoed in my mind. I shoved it aside. No distractions. No second-guessing.

This was my choice, my mess to clean up. *You will end this today.* The magic churned beneath my skin. It was hungry—starving, volatile.

There was no creak of the massive doors as I slipped inside the capitol. Suddenly, I felt small as fuck. *What are you doing?* Clutching onto my blades, I stepped down the cavernous halls. They stretched in eerie stillness, light filtered through the large windows.

I moved through the mansion with unexpected ease. It was all wrong. There should be guards, or at least staff—people moving about. They were under attack and *this* was their base—their capitol.

The faintest scuff of footsteps echoed in the stillness around the corner. My pulse spiked as I scanned the shadows, fingers twitching at my sides. I was really about to test my luck here. Pushing into an uncleared room, I stepped behind the door. *Thank fucking God.* It was empty. And beautiful. Focus … *focus.* It was an effort. Danger or not, I loved touring stuff like this.

My awe burned away as the doorknob turned behind me.

The door swung open.

Without thinking through the repercussions, I grabbed them by the arm and dragged them inside, accidentally slamming the door in the process. Before they could so much as yelp, I pressed them against the wall, my forearm pinning them in place.

A girl.

"Talk," I demanded. "Now."

Wide eyes stared back at me. She was somewhere between Elie and Abel's age, her face ghostly and gaunt. She didn't shake or cry. Instead, she tilted her chin up, that recognizable defiance sparking in her expression.

"I'm here to help," her voice was light as the wind—small, but certain.

Oh my God. Were kids everywhere just intent on putting themselves in the middle of a war? "I don't need any help." I scoffed, leaning in closer. She may be but a teenager, but I knew from the one under my care they were not to be underestimated. "I have somewhere to be. Who the hell are you and what makes you think you're capable of providing any help?"

Her lips twitched in a dare. "My name is Miranda," she said. "And I can get you to Ronan. I know this place like the back of my hand. My mother is … *was* on the cleaning staff, I grew up here. You won't find him in any of these rooms."

"What do you have to gain?" I said, easing my hold on her, if only by a fraction.

"I knew Seth—"

"Not a good start," I interrupted, my arm promptly going back to her neck.

"He was the only person in the capital to treat me like a person. You're General Bennett, right?"

I scanned her over, she was maybe a hundred pounds soaking wet—still great condition for someone who obviously lived in The Outskirts. Which meant there was a high chance she was desperate to get out of that place, and desperate people were capable of great things. I pushed harder, cutting off her air supply.

"I never … said … he was kind," she gasped, her lips pursing to the side in an attempt to bring oxygen to her lungs. "He was just … true."

Given the fact that I'd already wasted precious minutes searching through this maze of a place without coming across a single soul, Miranda was the only lead I had at the moment. "Ugh," I groaned, releasing her for good and pacing across the room.

Drawing one of the twin blades, I swung it, pointing it at her. "You have two minutes. Talk fast."

"He loved his sister, Tomoe too. Seth didn't say much most days, but when he did, it would always be about something the two of them liked. I want to help them. He cared about them and now he's not here to protect them. Let me help."

"You want to help because someone was nice to you in passing and talked to you about the people they betrayed?"

Miranda shrugged, "The last time someone was nice to me just for the heck of it, I was a little girl. I want what Seth wanted— what my family wanted—our worlds to blend. There seems to be … freedom in that, I think."

Freedom. It had been a long time since the word had been uttered in any real sense. In one that had zero relation to war. Yellow seeped into the whites of her eyes but the stare in them was sincere. Prescott's words echoed in my mind. *The best thing a person can have in life is the honor of returning a favor. When money no longer has a use, when loyalty can't be bought, your word and life debts are the only currency left.*

"What power do you have?"

"Air. Not much—"

"And you can get me to Ronan?" I asked, narrowing my gaze. Coincidental, how it was all working out.

She nodded, the dry strands of her midnight hair fell over her shoulder as she glanced down, calculating. "There are tunnels beneath the building. They run to other stuff nearby, Governor's Mansion and the Pocahontas Building specifically. Some of it was open to the public at some point. But if I had to guess, they're underground in one of the hidden rooms in between."

"Secret rooms, that you know about?" I asked, a slight edge to my words as I sheathed the blade.

"I found them by accident. A lot of the staff kids would play hide and seek here … before Ronan."

Good enough, I suppose. No time better than the present to have a little faith in someone's morality. "Show me," I said, gesturing for her to lead the way.

We crept from the dusty sitting room and I kept her pace through the winding hallways. The stale cool air wrapped around us once we hit the passageways. Shadows drifted unnaturally, darting in and out of view, always at the edge of my vision. The first sign of life since I'd stepped through the second portal. Despite the shadows, the tunnels were engulfed in silence.

The walls were narrow, tight enough for the damp stone press on every side. Somewhere in the distance, water dripped in a slow, tortuous rhythm. It made me miss my hound. I rubbed the small diamonds on the band against the two surrounding fingers, needing proof of it existing on my body in the present, as a grounding force.

"You came down here as a child?" I asked in a hushed tone.

Miranda nodded, her focus still ahead. "It's … easier when you don't know what's actually around you."

"What's around us?"

As if the universe was suddenly thrilled to answer the questions I had in life, an ear-shattering scream came from beyond the other side of the wall. It muffled out by the next time I blinked.

The tunnels grew narrower as we went and the magic in my chest swirled in unease—as though it could sense something I could not.

We reached a dead end, and for a moment, I thought she'd gotten us lost. But Miranda pressed her hand against the wall, her fingers searching until they found an almost invisible seam. She pushed, and the wall groaned as it shifted, revealing a narrow passage.

"Through here?" Yeah, fuck that. Inside, I was screaming. It was pitch black, save for a single, half-dead torch flickering down the hallway.

"No one comes this way except for the staff. Some of the doors are another exit from rooms facing the main hallway."

"Perfect," I muttered, squaring my shoulders. *Okay. I was really doing this. Everything is fine. You are fine. You are still breathing which means you still have to fight.* I wiggled my fingers, forcing that false bravado I wore for others front and center in hopes that maybe, just maybe, I could fool myself.

"There's light streaming from under three doors in the center. What are those?" I asked, nodding toward the glowing lines.

Miranda hesitated, shifting on her feet. "Never made it that far. The storage for cleaning material is in this one ... for, um, harder clean ups. Mass clean ups." She pointed to the door right next to us.

"Here?" I stopped and turned to her.

"Yeah."

"Okay. Miranda?"

"Mhm?"

"If I tell you this is where your portion of the mission ends, you wouldn't listen, would you?"

Her expression shifted from defiance to resolve in her eyes, the same fire I'd seen in Elie's and Abel's. She was brave, too brave for her own good.

And I couldn't let her die for me.

"Um ..."

"Didn't think so. You don't seem like the type."

"I can help," she insisted, taking a small step closer.

"I know," I whispered, regret curling around the words. "I don't doubt that you could. I'm sorry. When you wake up, press the button in the middle, it will keep you safe. Just ... trust me, which will be hard considering."

Miranda's sparse brows knitted together, confusion flashing across her face. I let my magic unfurl, pulling the oxygen from her lungs. Her eyes went wide, panic flickering there for the briefest moment before her body went slack and her lungs emptied.

I caught her before she hit the ground and pulled her gently into the storage closet. "You'll have a place in Monterey," I murmured, brushing her hair out of her face as I lowered her to the stone floor. "Find Reina."

It was a gamble. The device, clunky and slightly heavier than it appeared, had found its place in my hand. I slid it over Miranda's wrist, positioning it the way Finley had instructed. Leave it to her to give me one last *Fuck you*, even in death. She'd brought it to me a few days before she died, yet another one of her prototypes— except this one she was interested in offering for a trade *after* the war. The button in the middle felt too small against my trembling fingers. When she woke up, she'd need to press it, trust that it would work. Just like I was trusting it now, even as the weight of the choice sat on my chest.

I turned back to the passage, releasing a long, controlled exhale. The doors with the lights on dared me with a devilish glow, to find out what was on the other side. A dare in which I'd have no joy in taking because I knew, without a doubt, that Ronan Moore awaited me on the other side.

I chose the middle door. No particular reason. The path that lay in between seemed as good an option as the other two. I rolled my shoulders, flexing my fingers again as my magic coiled tighter and pushed it open.

The room was too clean, too bright. Screens covered the wall, lit up with cameras on one side, photos of my family and I on the other. Prescott and Jax had one simple phrase noted in red ink over theirs—TERMINATED. Strange. How in such a moment, I knew I should have been filled with rage. My eyes wandered to the picture at the very end of the line-up ... Seth's. And the same message was displayed over his. Ronan's own son, who had lost his head trying to make his father proud, had still been deemed an enemy in the end.

"So you've met my son," Ronan smiled, leaning back in his chair, his desk at the center of the room.

I refused to look at him. Willed myself not to respond immediately. It shouldn't have been painful—seeing Seth on the wall like … *that*. The pain should have come from seeing Prescott's stern military photo from his time in the Marines, pulled from God knows where or Jax's grinning face, a picture that had once been displayed in Compound Hall. But that wasn't where the ache came from. They had family and loved ones to mourn them.

Seth in the end, had no one, only people who'd deemed him a traitor. I hated him, but the complexity of his betrayal had become clear in the passing months. He was nothing more than a boy who had been driven mad by the fact that he knew in his gut that his brother was alive. Yet, he had no resources to find him. Instead, he resorted to the closest source, a man who happened to be a spitting fucking image of him.

"Hunter's more pleasant than the last. I'll give you that," I said finally, glancing around the rest of the room, keeping my voice strong. "Bietoletti, Malachai, as ugly as ever, how are you two doing? Riley says, *Go fuck yourself.*"

I waved to Malachai, decided to hold his grotesque stare instead of his master's. He said nothing, his beady eyes only stared through me, like he couldn't be bothered to see me as a clear, evenly matched opponent. *Fine. Let him think that.*

The door groaned shut behind me, sealing me in. The sound of it latched deep into my chest in a steel trap. The scrape of my boots against the cold floor echoed in the silence, the rhythm of breathing around me adding weight to the air. The room itself seemed to amplify the truth—*you're not getting out of here.* Every step I took sealed my fate.

"He takes after his mother," Ronan said, his voice dripping with casual malice. "You know how genetics are."

"Oh, I'd say you're one to two on the *apple doesn't fall far from the tree*, thing."

He leaned forward in the blurred lines of my vision. "You're outnumbered, why don't you take a seat."

"Please don't insult me, Ronan." I scoffed, eyes glaring daggers into his soul. "I'll get mad. You don't like me when I'm mad."

Ronan didn't move. Didn't blink. The silence between us stretched on, suffocating, unbearable. His eyes were locked on mine, watching for any sign of weakness. I held my ground, refusing to be the one to turn away first. His lips twisted like he wanted to smile, the freckles speckling his face making the harsh wrinkles around his eyes and on his forehead more pronounced. The faint tension rippling through his jaw betrayed him.

It was a small tell, hardly decipherable to the eye of a person unwilling to take risks, but it was enough for me to stay on my feet. That small hesitation to engage, a sliver of uncertainty on which of us would leave the room … It gave me all the confidence in the world to keep going.

I *was* outnumbered, and though I was armed, I should be the scared one. But I wasn't, I was numb. Ronan—the man who had built his empire on corpses and greed—was the scared one. And that made it so much worse. After the glimmer of hope settled, it disappeared. Fear made my situation fatal. A scared dog would always bite.

Malachai moved behind him with methodical ease, dragging a black tripod from the corner. His olive-hued hands adjusted it methodically, as if this was all rehearsed. Bietoletti moved from the door and stepped aside for the camera's line of sight, his frame tilting toward me with renewed interest.

The setup wasn't for show. I knew what this was. He wanted to make an example of me but he had yet to realize this was my stage, not his.

Ronan stood slowly, his steps deliberate on the polished floor. His hands remained behind. He didn't need a weapon. His sheer size as a *Supra* was a threat, every move designed to remind me how much smaller I was. Ronan Moore came to a stop directly in front of me then leaned down, hoping to make me cower in fear. I did no such thing.

I stayed focused, holding a quiet, deliberate calm as I watched him. Where he moved, my eyes followed. Submission wasn't an option. The only thing I had to offer him was the sour taste of absolute disgust of knowing I had to exist and breathe the same air as a murderous sack of shit. One who had zero regard for human life that was unable to serve his benefit.

"Tell me, General Bennett," he said, his venomous breath warm against my skin. Peppermint was now on my *no smell* list. "What's the end goal here?"

His laugh was low and maniacal as he reached out, brushing a curl from my temple, the outside of his hand tracing down the side of my face. I did not back down. The glare aimed at him was meant to mark.

"Funny." I shrugged. "I was just about to ask you the same thing before I realized, I don't really care."

"Tsk." He was amused. Enjoying this. "Now, I don't believe that for a second."

His fingers tangled into the mess of my bun. The sharp pull yanked me off balance and forced me to my knees. The cold stone bit into my skin, but I didn't flinch, didn't cry out.

I glared up at him, the heat of defiance searing through the numbness. He wanted to make me cower. I'd make sure he'd regret it.

Today, he would dance with death—we both would.

CHAPTER
SIXTY-FIVE

RILEY

Main Street Station loomed ahead—its broken clock barely visible through the haze of smoke. I kept my eyes focused and forward, refusing to look at the kids trailing beside me, their small hands clutching at whatever they could carry. Didn't let my eyes linger on the adults, their faces blank with shock. It didn't matter. None of it mattered right now.

Evacuate the civilians, reach the station, and stay alive. That was the plan. Those were my orders.

Stay alive.

For Yasmin, for our son, for her.

For her.

A crackle of electricity made me pause and a sharp blue light flickered against the side of a high-rise. The holographic screen flickered to life against the cracked wall, and a cold stream of panic settled in my veins.

Amaia.

She was on her knees, hair matted with ash colored sweat streaked down her face. I would not panic. Not yet. Her eyes—they still burned. That fire in her was still alive. *Good.* That was good.

"A villain speech, how original," she said, the force in her voice present despite Ronan lingering over her, fingers wrapped in her hair.

"No. Not a villain—a victor." Ronan's smile was cold, lacking emotion—it reminded me of Seth's. It was mechanical, more machine than man. Like they practiced it every morning, to make sure they fit in. "I think you'd appreciate understanding what you're up against, learning all the facts, making sure that the people you care for won't suffer." The word *suffer* slithered out, mocking.

Amaia straightened, shoulders squared against the weight of his grip. I gritted my teeth, the instinct to run to her screaming in my bones. It wasn't simple. It never was. I had to stay alive—she'd want me to stay alive.

My mind raced. Pieces clicked together. *Name the next one after me.* She knew. Fury bubbled in my veins. Hot. Suffocating.

"Let us give them all a show. Say hi to the camera, it's important they understand exactly what happens when you stand against progress. Evolution." He held out his hand, and Malachai stepped forward, placing a knife in his palm. The camera zoomed in as Ronan dragged the blade lightly across her throat. A thin line of blood appeared, and my chest clenched so tight I thought I'd stop breathing.

Amaia didn't flinch. Didn't blink. She just stared up at him with that defiant tilt to her head, offering him more real-estate, daring him to do his worst.

Reina made a small, strangled sound as she moved her horse to block the view from some of the younger children. "What's happening?" she whispered. "What is he—"

"Don't you know, this is all history in the making?" Ronan circled her like prey. "The onset of the new beginning. Future generations will thank us for setting them up for success. You said it yourself, one unit, right? With Covert having hold in the other territories, we eliminate what I like to call, inefficiencies. No more fractured leadership, no more squabbles over resources. Everything is structured, centralized. Controlled. Covert Province becomes the heart of it all—a beacon of progress, of strength. The weak don't get a say in that. Survival belongs to those who take it, who can lead, adapt. You and I understand each other. Both willing to die for what we believe in. It's the reason I refused to doubt you. It would have been dangerous to do so."

"He's making an example of her. Showing what happens if you dare dissent," I said, the words coming out in a growl.

I felt Alexiares stare and refused to face it—that undercurrent of panic, of rage he barely held in check. He would break, and if he broke, I feared I would too. For her, it was so easy to.

Amaia's eyes trailed every inch of Ronan's face, studied every line, every freckle—then burst out laughing. "Wow. All this time, I thought you were just preaching bullshit, saying what you thought people wanted to hear. But you actually believe in what you're doing, don't you? You think this is for the greater good? Hurting people, killing people, *that's* your legacy. You don't get to rewrite history just because you don't like how it'll make you look."

The screen flickered as Malachai stepped into frame. His arm lashed out, the crack of his strike louder than a whip through the air. Her head snapped to the side, hair flying, but she didn't fall.

She didn't even stagger.

Amaia smiled, blood staining her teeth, her lip bulging to a painful swell. "I truly pity the fool. I'm not sure what's worse, preaching harmful rhetoric to climb an ego boosting social ladder or believing the whack job shit that comes out of your mouth?"

She held all the bite in the world with her tone, but I caught it—the slip in her speech pattern, the glimmer of sorrow in her eyes, the faint snarl of her bruised and battered lip. She was afraid. More than afraid, Amaia was terrified. Her right hand fell to her waist, tracing over where she'd been stabbed in the last war—I hadn't been able to help her then either.

"I mean," she continued, her jaw moving at an awkward angle. "All this science and focus on having the greatest minds, and you wouldn't comprehend the data if it slapped you in the fucking face and grabbed you by the balls. Let me guess, anything you don't agree with is a falsity, right? A biased fact? Facts can't be biased, Ronan. They're just facts. And at the end of the day, we are, genetically speaking, 99.9 percent identical. Our roots, magic or not, are tangled together in the same evolutionary soil. That is not an opinion, Ronan, that is molecular truth. We are all the same. What you're doing out here is playing God, disrupting nature's patterns. *Destroying* order, not restoring it."

Malachai struck her again. "Shut your mouth."

"No," Ronan said with a smirk. "Let her continue."

This was a public service announcement. He wanted the world to watch. To see how untouchable he was and how unattainable freedom from his reach would be. The great Amaia Bennett. I had no doubt this was being displayed throughout Covert Province as a whole.

"What you've done with your power *disgusts* me."

Ronan glanced at with more than subtle intrigue—amusement. "You would do it differently? Better?"

"I have done it better." Amaia spit into his face, bloodied saliva dripped down his chin. She locked eyes with the camera. "If you're watching this, the people you call *Outsiders*, they'll be welcome in Salem Territory, Transient Nation, and The Expanse.

Granted immediate citizenship. Wherever they want. One unit, one compound. But the rest of you fuckers,"—a laugh. A stale one at that. "I hope you burn in hell."

"Reina? Are you watching dear?" Ronan's voice was calm as he pressed the knife deeper into her throat, the line forming no longer thin, now threatening to bleed her dry.

Soft whimpers spilled out between Reina's sobs. She sat frozen atop her horse, tears streaking down her face. Her mouth opened and then closed, like she wanted to shout but couldn't. All the words she'd wanted to say but the horror of it all muting her.

"My greatest disappointment," Ronan said, his tone cruel and cutting. *How dare he. How dare he guilt her with this!* "Oh, how I'd ached for a better reunion. I wished better for you. For you both, *Hunter.* Do you see what happens when you're too loud? More particularly, when you're wrong."

Amaia closed her eyes.

No.

Get up. Don't you dare—don't you dare give up!

I was on autopilot, body stepping forward out of instinct. Alexiares's hand caught me, holding me with the understanding of what was about to happen. "Don't," he mumbled.

Not to me. To her.

The fire flickered. It started in her eyes. In an instant, she erupted.

Flames encased her, pouring from her as its own living, breathing thing. The image seared itself into my mind. With each blink, she was there. Her scream thundered from building to building, echoing the agonizing, haunting sound of self-destruction.

It mingled with Ronan's startled shout, his confidence crumbling to the panic of no longer having the control. That flicker of terror when he realized she was more than he bargained for, more than he was equipped to beat, would've been honeysuckle sweet under different circumstances. The knife at her throat was useless now, hovered there, stuck.

Her screams stopped as she fell to her knees, the light in her eyes dimming, body bowing. A marionette puppet whose strings had been severed. She wasn't gone. Not yet—not entirely.

I knew what she was doing. Understood it all too clearly. She wasn't giving up. She was slipping into that *other* place, that hollow space in her mind, so she could let go. Because she had to. She had to release her power, had to let it consume her, and she couldn't do that—not if she still held on to the love she had for us.

There was no goodbye. Not in this family. Not between us.

Four eternal seconds passed between the moment Ronan's blade kissed her throat and the moment she gave herself to the flames. Four seconds, and everything had changed.

"She's burning out," Alexiares said, panic bleeding into every word. "We have to help her."

The words snapped me into action. I didn't think. I just moved, shoving past him, leaving the civilians behind. They'd have to make it on their own now. She needed me.

Amaia needed me.

The first explosion was small. A burst of her flames that struck the ground a few feet away. The next was closer, more violent. I grabbed Alexiares as a blast nearly took him out, hauling him back with me, the earth turning soft underneath us to cushion the fall.

He dragged me up, but it didn't matter. The old gas lines were already erupting, one after another, bursting in flashes of heat and light around us. It was too late. I knew it. My heart screamed otherwise, clinging to denial with a ferocity that left my chest aching. Denial was sweet, so damn sweet. It whispered that she might make it. That if I kept watching the screen, I wouldn't see her die.

"I. Can. Not. Fail. Not again," I muttered, accepting my new mission, the one I could control. The one she'd always held me to. If I could not protect her, then I had to protect them. One last mission, a final one signed off in her blood. "We won't … we can't. The gas lines … It's her. We have to … we have to stay here. Because if she kills one of us before she goes down, she won't survive it. She'd never forgive herself."

"She has to *survive* for me to give a shit what she wants first!" Alexiares roared back, his voice raw with anguish.

I couldn't look at him. Couldn't face the grief mirrored in his eyes. My focus stayed locked on the screen. Amaia stood there, still burning. The fire moved like it was alive, licking at her skin, weaving through her hair, but it didn't consume her. Her movements were slow, deliberate, as she dragged herself to a chair in the center of the room, pulled herself up, then turned toward Ronan.

He scrambled back, his body trembling with an unnatural frailty, yet his eyes burned with unrelenting hatred. The guards around him were lifeless, their weapons scattered and useless. Malachai had vanished. A cockroach scurrying from the light. I knew he was out there somewhere, saving his own skin.

The camera caught the moment she stepped forward—staggered forward. Even through the haze of fire and smoke, I swear I heard her voice.

"I'm sorry," she cried.

The camera fell, clattering to the ground. The angle shifted, capturing Ronan on his back, his face upturned, the reflection of her flames filling his wide, horrified eyes.

"Run! The street … It's gonna blow!" Voices rang out behind me, panicked and desperate as they came running, searching for us.

I spun, spotting Tomás, Hunter, and Serenity racing toward us. The others trailing behind them. Tomoe, Reina, Millie. They'd followed us, their horses weaving through the wreckage.

A door creaked open somewhere—offscreen. Amaia's fire whooshing to chase after oxygen. There was the shuffle of movement. Panic in the room.

I turned back just as the ground beneath us erupted.

The blast tore through the world, a wave of searing heat and thunder that ripped me off my feet. I hit the ground hard, my ears ringing, the air knocked from my lungs.

The screen went black.

Our shield shattered.

And with it, everything fell apart.

Soldiers poured through the breach, their shouts mixing with the chaos. Grenades soared, each burst of magic erupting in flashes of blinding light. The civilians we'd been evacuating—the children—they were caught in the storm, their cries lost in the relentless crossfire.

But I couldn't process it. Couldn't move.

Amaia was everywhere. Her flames, her scream, her face burned into the inside of my skull.

CHAPTER

SIXTY-SIX

REINA

The world was noise and silence all at once. The explosion swallowed everything, all concepts of sound, touch, *taste*. The ringing … the ringing in my ears wouldn't stop. *Stop. Please. Make it stop.* My hands flew to my ears, covering them for protection. The deafening roar tuning with a sharpness that might carve through my skull.

I hit the ground hard, the air stolen from me, my vision splintering into shards. Pain erupted in my shoulder, my ribs, my hands scraped raw against the asphalt. My horse was gone. Bolted—or dead. Who the heck knew? I couldn't think.

What happened?

I couldn't seem to remember what led up to this moment in time. *Oh, my God.*

The ground shook beneath me, rippling as though it might split apart. Distant screams muffled under the weight of the ringing. The capitol building was gone. Blown apart. Shattered into dust and fire.

Amaia.

My stomach twisted. The image of her kneeling, fire pouring from her like a living thing, burned behind my eyelids. Her scream. His face.

"Reina? Are you watching, dear?"

My father's voice echoed in my skull, cutting deeper than the explosion ever could.

"My greatest disappointment. Oh, how I'd ached for a better reunion. I wished better for you. For you both, Hunter. Do you see what happens when you're too loud?"

I clawed at the ground, dirt and glass biting into my palms, trying to chase the words from my mind. He was dead too.

"Reina!"

The sound of my name came from somewhere far away, muffled and warped like it was underwater. Someone grabbed my arm, yanking me to my feet. Hunter. I raised my chin, his face streaked with soot and blood. Tears brimmed in his eyes, sliding down his face and carving through the ash. His lips moved, frantic, but I couldn't hear him.

Devastation blurred in the background. Soldiers darted in and out of the smoke, shadows against a backdrop of flame. People screamed. From fear. From pain. From rage. I felt it all. But none shattered me the way the loss of my sister did.

Amaia was gone. And it was his fault.

Ronan. My father.

The ground beneath me felt funny. Squishy. I glanced down.

Tomás lay sprawled out across the asphalt, his bionic leg shattered into debris. He wheezed in pain, mumbling something indecipherable. A hard shove came from behind, and I whirled around.

Moe hovered over Tomás, trying to stanch the blood pooling beneath him. She whimpered, looking up at me with empty, sobbing eyes. "Help—help him."

I stumbled back, bile rising in my throat. My vision swam. I turned, gagging, and bent over. My father. *Everything* always came back to him. His greed. His cruelty. His bigotry.

"Reina, focus!" Hunter's voice broke through the haze, his grip tightening on my arm as he pulled me away. It was then that I realized Serenity was attached to the other side of him, her eyes locked onto mine, desperate. "We can't stay here."

"Hunter," I choked out. "I—"

"We can hate him later." His voice cracked. "Right now, you have to get away from the area. You're fueling him. Feeding his anger and rage. He's a bomb waiting to explode with you here."

Another scream shattered the air, raw and feral. Alexiares.

"I'm not … that's not me. I—"

It wasn't me. I wasn't angry anymore. Right now, I was numb.

"She's not gone!" His words tore through the chaos, ragged and wild. "Let me go! Get off me or I swear to God I'll fucking kill you too!"

Millie was there, her arms wrapped around him, trying to hold him back. "Alexi, stop! She's—"

"She's not dead!" He broke, strength returning as he turned on her, a knife to her throat. Millie stood tall. Her body was beaten, battered, and bruised, hair tangled, lip busted—but she stood there, meeting his eye as he held her life in her hands, because she understood.

"My *wife* is not fucking dead," he growled.

I couldn't move. Alexiares's pain crashed into me, a tidal wave of splintered emotion that left me drowning. "I can't—" I whispered, my knees buckling.

"I know," he said. "I know, Reina. But you have to keep going. We *have* to keep going."

How? was what I wanted to ask him. Ronan had won. Amaia had secured our freedom, but my father had still won. Amaia was gone. There was no happy ending for her. The life she wanted, the dreams she had, none of it mattered.

"I wish he died a more painful death," I said, the words tumbling out unbidden. They tasted tangier than blood. "I hope he and Seth burn in hell forever."

Hunter's grip tightened. "I do too."

CHAPTER
SIXTY-SEVEN

ALEXIARES

The world crumbled beneath my feet. Literally, figuratively—it was all the same damn thing. Ash and charred flesh rained down around me, the sky an angry haze of smoke and flame. Fire seared along my arms, water seeped into the fractured asphalt, and the earth itself shuddered beneath me. The tremors echoed through my bones, unstable, fractured. Like me.

Yes. They would all suffer like me.

"No," the word tore from my throat as a broken whisper. "She's still in there …" I reached toward the end of the street, where the capitol building no longer rose in the distance.

Hands grabbed at me. Riley and Abel shouted words I did not care to hear over the roaring promise of death to them all roaring in my ears. I twisted violently, throwing Abel off first, then Riley.

"Get off me!" I howled, my voice cracking at the disgusting pitying stare on Millie's face as she watched from steps away. "My wife!" I pointed at nothing, because she existed nowhere. "My … my fucking wife."

I'd never said it out loud before—those words. *My wife.* The memory of our wedding day. The way she looked at me, soft and knowing, as we stood together on the same beach where I had first let her in. The warmth in those beautiful eyes as she whispered, *"I want to be yours in every way that matters before we go."*

I hadn't understood then. The glimpse of happiness that would be taken away. How I wouldn't have the chance to put up a fight.

"She planned this," I choked out as I stumbled to my knees. "She knew. She fucking knew, and she didn't tell me. Didn't warn me."

"Alexi—" Riley's voice was tight.

"She's *not* gone!" I screamed, slamming my fists into the ground. The street cracked beneath me, fire erupting in jagged lines as an injured Covert soldier slipped into the pit I'd raised from hell. "She is not."

The ground heaved from a secondary blast, a thunderous rumble tearing through the air as old gas lines exploded in the distance. My head whipped up at the sound. "No," I breathed, my chest tightening as panic surged.

I was running before I realized it, my body acting on instinct, desperation driving me forward.

"Alexiares!" Riley's voice rang out behind me. His footsteps pounded against the fractured pavement.

I didn't stop. I couldn't. I didn't stop. I couldn't. The world narrowed to a single thought, a single hope. My surroundings were a blur, the screams, the fire, the choking haze of ash. I vaulted over wreckage, my boots skidding on loose debris, ducking under twisted beams and through jagged gaps in the rubble. Pain clawed at my side, the metallic taste of blood sharp on my tongue, but I shoved it down.

We reached the crater where the capitol used to stand. The area was scorched black, smoke curling upward from the ruins. A hole gaped in the earth. It was wide. Endless—as if the world had swallowed her whole.

Riley stopped beside me, his chest heaving. Barely able to utter a whisper. "She's gone."

"No." I choked on tears and the memories we would never share.

Abel stepped closer. "I can't feel her anymore."

The bond between us—that magic string that tethered my family together—was not broken. It was strained. *Yes*. It could be fixed. They could not feel her, but I could.

"I can."

"Alexi—" Abel began.

"I said I can!" I snapped, the words tearing from my throat. "Get away from me."

Abel froze, his face contorting as if he couldn't piece together what I'd said. His confusion was an insult. Riley stood there staring into the crater—hollow-eyed and useless, like his mind had snapped and he was leaving me to drown in this hell alone.

He stepped back, their faces painted with the sorrow of great loss, and I hated them for it. How could they give up on her so easily? So early? Amaia would never give up on us. Not even for a second. She would crawl through fire, tear the world apart if it meant there was even a fraction of a chance to save us.

"She's gone." Millie's voice cut through the silence. Her gaze flicked to Abel and something passed between them. Something I wanted to ignore. "And she's not coming back."

CHAPTER
SIXTY-EIGHT

TOMOE

No matter where I looked, her path was set. Final.

CHAPTER
SIXTY-NINE

RILEY

I failed. I failed. I failed. I failed. I failed. I failed. I failed. I failed. I failed. I failed. I failed. The words pounded in my skull, each repetition louder, harder, angrier. Screaming, shaking, demanded my attention until it wasn't just a thought—it was a roar.

I failed. I failed. I failed.

My fists were clenched so tight, I could no longer feel my fingers. I tasted nothing but iron. My chest heaved, breath short but useless. No amount of air could make up for the loss of the person who'd kept me breathing for years.

I failed. I failed.

I failed.

I failed.

Amaia was dead.

Dead. I couldn't stop hearing it, couldn't stop seeing her—the way she'd fallen to her knees, the light in her eyes dimming as she let go, slipped into another mind space in order to let go. To make it easier to release her power when she did not want to say goodbye. Because there were no goodbyes. Not in this family. Not between *us*.

Together. That's what I'd said. What I'd promised.

Always together.

I was supposed to have her six. At all times. That was my role. That was my job.

And I failed.

I failed her. I failed her when it mattered most.

My knees hit the asphalt with a crack, but I didn't feel it. Pain didn't register—nothing did. Not Alexiares losing control. Not Millie dragging a tearful Reina back, preventing her from further fueling Alexiares's rage and fire. Not Tomoe as she gave way to Wrath, swinging it down, cutting through any and every adult she could find as she made her way to Reina, calling desperately for Millie to get her over here, to help before Tomás died. Not Abel shaking me. Begging me to get up. The snot dripping down his face made him appear every bit the sixteen-year-old I'd found hiding in what had become our home and not the twenty-year-old he was now.

There was no reality except the gaping hole in my heart, my chest, where she used to be.

My hands buried themselves in my locs, yanking hard, as though I could pull myself out of this God forsaken nightmare. But the images flashing through my mind would not stop. Her face, her voice, the feeling of her hand in mine when we'd said goodbye without uttering such words. I wish I could go back, to tell her everything I hadn't. To tell her I loved her and I would take care of our home if she could not. That she could trust me to not fail her this one last and final time.

"I was supposed to protect her," I whispered.

She's gone.

Gone.

I doubled over, forehead pressing against the crumbling, battle-stricken ground, trying to find some anchor—anything to hold on to in this spiraling darkness.

Nothing.

Amaia was my anchor. My tether. One of the few nonnegotiable things I could not lose and still keep my sanity.

But she's gone.

A broken sound escaped my throat, raw and uncontrollable. My shoulders shook and instead of fighting it the way I had for years, I let it happen. I let myself break. Because without Amaia, I didn't know how to stay whole.

CHAPTER
SEVENTY

ELIE

The world shook when she was gone. I felt it from 2,847.5 miles away.

I'd run through Amaia's route every day for the last three months, committing every turn, landmark, and detour to memory. I could make the journey myself with my eyes closed, hands tied behind my back. But now … now, it didn't matter.

Time stood still inside the bunker. It was as they all knew it too. Forty-thousand people underground, and you could hear a pin drop—but I was the only one with the bond to feel the loss. Harley and Suckerpunch could only whimper at my feet in supportive despair.

This place was a tomb carved into the earth. It'd been our entire world for months. The harsh hum of the air filtration system never ceased, and the low, constant buzz of chatter filled the background. It wasn't a home, it was a fortress. Every corridor was the same—gray, harsh, and functional. No amount of repurposing of spaces and makeshift homes from abandoned storage bays could create a pocket of warmth.

My seventeenth birthday came and went inside this steel, cold cage. Three months since I'd seen consistent sunlight aside from what trickled through the cracks of the door during weekly rotations of soldiers swapping from inside to out.

Rex was out there somewhere along the coast—stationed with the remnants of our navy. I hadn't seen him since the bunker doors shut the day the troops left. The only trace of him came during shift changes—letters slipped into my hand from Caleb like contraband.

No letters had ever come from Amaia. Not that it was possible. I didn't need them, not when I could feel her in *here*. In my soul. Guilt ate at me day in and day out for the time I'd wasted on punishing her for things outside of her control. Every choice she made was calculated, every step deliberate. I wanted to be like that— strong enough to carry the weight of the world without breaking.

The thought of her gone didn't just feel wrong; it felt *impossible*. Amaia didn't lose. She couldn't.

Still, I couldn't stop watching the door, willing it to open and prove me wrong.

A gentle hand rested on my shoulder, pulling me out of my thoughts. Luna.

"What's wrong?" Yasmin's voice followed, her hands absently rubbing her rounded belly.

I glanced between them, words catching in my throat. How could I explain something I didn't fully understand? And yet, deep down, I knew. There had been a release from within my chest, an untying of a small fishers knot, that offered a sense of permanent absence. "The world just got a whole lot darker."

Caleb rounded the corner, his floppy blond hair bounced as he walked. His poker face was terrible. Something was happening, and it had nothing to do with Amaia—or maybe it did.

"Ronan's dead," he said, voice heavy with disbelief.

Luna's posture faltered beside me. "She did it …" she whispered.

"How can you be sure?" Yasmin's voice cracked as she spoke, her arms wrapping protectively around her stomach. "Is Riley …"

"I don't have that detailed of a report." Caleb hesitated as to not upset the pregnant woman. "I'm sorry. I'm sorry. Our walls are under siege again—his troops are retaliating."

"Amaia is dead too." The words left my mouth before I could stop them. I turned to face them, my stomach twisting into a knot I couldn't untangle.

"What?" Yasmin's voice sliced through the air, trembling. But her worry wasn't for Amaia. It was for Riley. It was always Riley.

"Oh, please," I snapped, unable to hold it in. "Don't pretend you care."

"Don't say that," Luna said, her hands motioning to settle down.

"There's no word on Amaia," Caleb tried to reason, his voice almost pleading. But I didn't want to hear it. "I'm sure she's fine."

"She's gone." My hand pressed against my chest, to the spot where something had unraveled, slipping beyond my grasp. The room sank into an oppressive stillness, the kind that constricted around my lungs.

Emma sprinted down the hall, caked in dirt, her heavy footsteps echoed. I groaned—there goes our cover.

Hal emerged from the shadows, his hand snapping out to grab her with a force that made her stumble. "What did I tell you about sneaking out?"

"Ow," Emma yelped, feigning pain. "Stop, that hurts. Hey!"

Hal dragged her toward us, his face hard as stone. "This has to stop." His eyes locked onto mine, fueled with accusation. "Sending her out there like this. It's reckless. She could die."

"Emma can take care of herself," I muttered, crossing my arms. "You did a good job teaching her." *Not to mention, she was the one who could fit through the—*

"What did you do?" Luna's voice was ice, her usual warmth gone. "Eleanor."

Emma grinned, completely unfazed. "We took care of it."

"Took care of *what?*" Caleb asked, his voice rising.

"They want to act like animals," I said before Emma could answer. "If they try to breach these walls, they'll be slaughtered like them."

The bunker shook, the deep rumble of an explosion reverberating through the walls. Dust rained down from the ceiling, and I felt a grim satisfaction settle in my chest.

"Eleanor," Luna's voice cracked, desperate for a response. "What did you do?"

"What they taught me to," I smiled—a sharp, cold thing— and walked deeper into the heart of the bunker.

CHAPTER

SEVENTY-ONE

ALEXIARES

I killed them all. Every man. Every woman. Every child that looked to be over the age of eighteen. Luck had me find them and that same luck had me offer their last breaths. If I couldn't have a happy ending, then no one could.

They say grief comes with a strange sense of relief, a loosening of the breath you never realized you were holding. A fleeting peace in knowing the person you love the most can no longer come in harm's way.

That would never come for me.

There was no peace for a widower with nothing but rage for being left behind.

I told my wife I would burn this world for her. And so I would. All of it. Every last brick, every sliver of glass, every vein of life this city had to offer—I had razed it to the ground.

There was no comfort in the fact that Amaia had not died in vain. She won. *We* won. All her hopes and dreams, everything else she lived and died for, were not without reason. Because for now, the world would know peace.

Just not this side of it.

I would lurk in the shadows. Thrive in the darkness. I would not rest until every person responsible for putting Ronan into power begged for death at my hands.

No matter how many jaws cracked under my palm, or bones shattered by the force of my vines—no matter how much blood spilled—it would never be enough.

I could slice a thousand throats and watch them drown in their misery, yet none of it could drown the sound.

The sound.

One. Two. Three. Four. Four eternal seconds had eclipsed between the time Ronan's blade kissed the throat of my Amaia. Four seconds before she gave herself to her flames. It was a whimper, the smallest, most immutable of sounds, but I heard it—felt it as if it had been said through my lips and reverberated around the ribs that held my numb, ever beating heart. It wasn't fear. Amaia wasn't afraid to die.

It was the sound of *knowing*. Knowing she would leave me behind. Knowing that her victory would cost her everything. Knowing that I'd be alone in a world she fought to save. It wasn't fair. It wasn't fucking *fair*.

Every ounce of honor left my body. The desire to preserve the mirage of morality, a sense of honor; it was nothing but ash. Without Amaia, that tinge of guilt that comes with keeping your humanity intact was worthless to me. *No value. No value. No fucking value.*

Not until I found a way to get her back. Reina was smart. She had the *Scholar* gene. With Tomoe's ability to *see*, we could make this work. *Yeah, we could get her back. We could turn back time.*

She had to be out there. I refused to believe her death was a finality. I didn't care what it took—what it cost. Heaven, hell, or whatever was in between. My soul was hers to take. *Always hers.*

I'd pull her back from the light, drag her from the gates of paradise if it meant she could rule this burning hell by my side.

The city burned. I lit it all. Every street. Every sign. Every lamp post or poster. Blew up every car and crumbled every sidewalk. I used every tendril of flame that had been simmering beneath my skin in preparation to powershare *Steamfire* with Amaia. Let the people of this cursed fucking city choke on the smoke of what they'd built. Let them suffocate on the dream they ripped from me—from her.

I couldn't tell who followed at first. Couldn't hear their footsteps over the roar in my chest. The smoke stung my eyes, and my vision blurred, but I didn't wipe it away. Didn't care if they saw it.

Reina limped behind me, her horse gone and yet to return. Her face was streaked with blood. Tomás leaned against her, barely upright, his body shuddering with each step. His wounds were bad, even after Reina had poured her magic into him. She closed her eyes, lips trembling as she forced herself to swallow down the pain of it all. I knew what she saw when she closed them, every time she blinked—Jessa, Amaia, her father.

The urge to unleash more destruction clawed at me, my vines writhing under my skin. *I can still breathe, I can still fight.* I wanted to force the world to its knees just as it had done to me. To Amaia.

Amaia. My Amaia. General Bennett. Amaia Drakos. She was gone. And I was still here.

Metal against asphalt drilled into the screams, pleads for help. Wrath trailed behind Tomoe, her eyes fixed on the smoke-streaked sky, scanning for something—someone—none of us could see.

Hunter walked with the weight of a thousand shattered lives on his shoulders. He didn't cry, didn't speak. He just moved, Serenity at his side, angry for him having to leave behind the ruins of the father he never wanted and the family he'd lost long before this war began.

"This is not how it ends," Riley said, his tone so even, so certain it felt wrong. Abel and Millie flanked his side like shadows, both of them covered in blood—theirs and the fallen.

I froze, his boots crunching against the scorched ground as he stepped closer. Riley wasn't supposed to sound like that—like me. When I turned to him, I didn't see the calm, steady brother Amaia could always count on.

I saw a man ready to burn with me.

The others stopped walking. All of them looked toward him, but he only brushed past me, his gaze fixed on the road ahead. Determined. Dangerous.

Taking in the rest of their faces, I saw the same thing I felt: emptiness. Fury.

Not one of them looked back.

Let it burn. Let it all fucking burn.

EPILOGUE

AMAIA

F^{uck.}

BONUS CHAPTER

RILEY

A slow evening—there was really nothing better. These rooms finally felt like home. I missed the space I had shared with the others before. It had been home for years and held many memories, but now was time for growth. Change.

I sat behind the desk, stealing glances at Yasmin as she sprawled on the couch, sketchbook in hand. Her brow furrowed in concentration, her pencil gliding in quick, precise strokes. The high chair I was carving needed to be perfect. Safe enough so Yasmin wouldn't have to worry every second Jaxon was in it. Comfortable enough for him to nod off without fussing, and fly enough to catch a million eyes. I didn't know much about being a good father—not yet—but I figured small efforts such as this were a good place to start.

Two brief knocks came to the door and Yasmin leaned back to swipe the sheer curtain from the window. She dropped her head with a groan, standing to make her way to the door. I set my tools on top of the desk, watching and waiting to see who it was.

By the agitated toss of Yasmin's silky black hair, I had a feeling who it was. "Let me guess, here for Riley," she said, holding the door open but blocking the path in.

"Well, it's not for you," Amaia said, breezing past Yasmin with the confidence of someone who did not care that she was not welcome by half the people in the room. She dropped a heavy bag to the floor, and Harley and Suckerpunch bolted through after her, tails wagging furiously. "Knocking was a courtesy, by the way."

And I'm up. Crossing the room, I greeted my sister with a curious smile. The last thing I needed were the two of them to go at it … again. Once was enough, twice was an inconvenience, three times was a headache, now—it was simply exhausting.

My grin wavered, there was something off about her and the way her hands were stuffed into her back pockets. Her stance was tense. Uneasy. "What's up?"

Amaia glanced at Alexiares, their eyes locked, simmering from an ember to a glowing flame that refused to dim. I caught Yasmin's gaze from across the room as she plopped back on to the couch and shrugged, silently asking if she was as nauseated as I was. She grinned, her tongue squeezed between her teeth.

"I'm uncomfortable," I muttered, loud enough for her to hear.

"There's no other way to put this so I'm just going to say it." Amaia hesitated, shifting in place and fumbling with her fingers. Oh, she was nervous. That was new. "Uh, we're kind of engaged and now we'd like to get married before you know, one, or both, of us die in Ronan's war."

I offered no response other than a slow, deliberate blink. *Old news.* Harley came to a stop in front of my feet and stared up at me, tongue hanging out of her mouth as she barked one, quick, clip of demand.

Yasmin clipped a sarcastic laugh from the other side of the room, not bothering to glance up from her sketch. "Congratulations," she said dryly. "*Psychopaths*." The latter was muttered under her breath—yet still clear enough to be heard by the one person who couldn't control the urge to bite back.

"Yeah, just wait till the little psycho babies are running around your classroom Titi Yas. The more the merrier, right?" Amaia snapped, the happy, carefree smile on her face replaced by one crafted of spite.

Alexiares placed a calming hand on Amaia's back as Yasmin froze, her face caught somewhere between horror and shock of such a creative threat. "Not to worry. We don't believe that the whole end of the world meets screaming, crying, child thing."

"Child thing—" Yasmin raised her brows, her round, plump lips pulled to the side. The comment was sure to set her off once she processed what he was saying.

She was … passionate about the little's of the apocalypse. It was why she remained a teacher even in The After. She believed kids were the hope we couldn't afford to lose. To Yasmin, there was no circumstance in which not having children running around was a curse and not a blessing. She'd wanted to be a mom since she was a girl, a dream only halted at the onset of all, well, *this*.

"About time you finally spoke up," I said, finding control over the conversation.

Amaia's had whipped toward me, her jaw dropping ever so slightly, eyes narrowed.

I shrugged with a smirk. "I was starting to get offended."

"How did—"

"Reina," Amaia and I said in unison, cutting off Alexiares's questioning.

Amaia's fists clenched, jaw now tight, but it was all a facade. Reina would only tell family, never someone outside of it. "I'm going to kill her."

"Glad you're getting it out the way," I said, enjoying the rare moment of being the group instigator, "because what she and Abel have planned for when we get back is made of your worst nightmare."

"Abel knows too?" Amaia groaned, taking a step back. Suckerpunch was already curled up on her boots, snoring softly.

"Everyone knows," I stated the obvious. "It's Reina."

Amaia exhaled. "Can this be a secret, please?"

Ah. There it was. *The look.* I hated when she did that. The one that screamed *'please Riley the best big brother ever.'* It won me over every time.

"Why are you—" Realization set in. Now this, I had not expected. My mouth fell open. "You want me to marry you?"

"Fuck," Alexiares scoffed lacking all patience. "Took *you* long enough to get there."

I swallowed hard, trying to find steady ground. This was no light favor. This was *us*—what we'd lost, all that we still carried. Jax, who was basically my brother and her everything. Prescott, the steady hand who'd held us both together. They were gone, but their voices lived in the cracks between every memory.

Amaia stood there, the last piece of the life we once knew, staring at me as though she was holding on by a thread. This was it. Just us. The last one's standing and our lives no longer looked as they did when our favorite people were still alive. We'd changed, grown, stepped into ourselves out of necessity in their absence. Alexiares held her hand, his thumb brushing over her shaking fingers.

I pulled her into a hug, squeezing the air out of her as I closed my eyes against the tears threatening to spill over. Yasmin had gone quiet, her usual sharp edges softened. The sketchbook lay forgotten in her lap, and her lips quivered as though she was swallowing her own grief.

"What an honor," I whispered.

RAGING WAVES CRASHED AGAINST THE ROCKS NEAR THE DROP OFF. I leaned against a giant mound of hard earth, holding up a cracked mirror as Amaia fussed over the most trivial aspects of herself.

"So there's nothing in my teeth?" she asked for the third time, her brows furrowed as she checked her reflection.

"No, Amaia. Nothing. You're fine," I replied, biting back a laugh.

"The liner? Is it too much?"

"It's perfect."

"What about my hair?" She pulled it up, then let it fall.

I'd been around enough women in my life to know to say the exact *opposite* of what I think and carefully—so no, the liner around her eyes wasn't too much and yes, she should definitely wear her hair up. It was humorous seeing her this way, but she looked beyond words. From the girl who'd cornered me in a cave not too far from here, with fire in her eyes, to the beautiful woman who was confident in her power … I only wished the others could be here to see it. She caught me smiling and scowled.

"Don't start," she muttered, smoothing the lace of her dress.

"Not saying a word." *Shit, don't cry.* But it was hard not to, she made me so proud.

The orange and pink hues of the sky reflected off her billowing, cream dress. Intricate lace with delicate, pastel flowers hung off her sculpted frame, sweeping down and across the toe of her shoes. A green slithering snake went up the side of the sleeve. It was far from the traditional dress—exactly like her. Down to the Dr. Martens planted on her feet. She smacked her lips together, dotting some reddish powder across them and patting it onto her cheeks.

"You look beautiful."

Amaia paused, her eyes glancing up at the sky as she blinked in quick succession. "If I start crying, I swear I'm going to smack you."

"I didn't think you owned anything that wasn't black," I teased.

"Yeah." She sighed, tugging at the fabric. "I found it years ago. Haven't had a reason to wear it. It was too … I don't know. I left it behind the first time but I kept having weird dreams about it … felt like it was calling to me, so I went back. It's been shoved into the corner of my closet ever since."

Pressing off the rock, pulling out the delicate chain from my pocket. It was London's. I'd been saving it for … well, I wasn't quite sure. "Some would call that a sign," I said, unclasping the lock and placing it around her neck. "Something old."

"Some would," Amaia's fingers brushed over the Medusa pendant as she whispered, "Yes."

"There's more," I said.

It wasn't an awkward moment between us. Those didn't exist. But it was vulnerable, and that was something we saved for the rarest of occasions. Understanding silence had suited our relationship best over the years—there were no secrets between us, and thus, talking about the emotions that went behind them had felt pointless. A self-pitying act.

"Oh?"

"Something new," I said, pulling a small wooden bracelet from my pocket. The carving was simple but careful—woven branches circling together. I'd shaped it from the heartwood of a tree miles outside of Monterey Compound, the kind Prescott always said would outlive us all.

Amaia turned it over in her hands, tracing the grooves with her thumb. "You made this?"

I nodded. "And something blue." I pulled the item I was most nervous about, having grabbed it in the few seconds Amaia had allowed me the space to gather my belongings before making the trek out here. Prescott collected many things. I'd called him out on his hoarding habits. It just so happened collecting hundreds of stones and shells from along the coast had served a better purpose. I'd been saving the earrings I'd made for Prescott's birthday, a way to cheer her up, but given we would be spending that at war, now seemed about the right time as ever.

Her breath hitched as she reached out a trembling hand. I placed them in her palm, watching her put them in, her posture slowly turning rigid. Her shoulders tensed, the shift almost imperceptible—until I saw it in her eyes. The panic. A quiet, creeping thing. She turned toward the ocean as though she might allow herself to fall in.

"You can still run away," I said, placing a hand on her shoulder and guiding her back to face me.

"I know," she whispered, her gaze fixed on the ground.

"I'm proud of you, kid."

"I changed my mind." Her head whipped up with that wicked smile back in place. "I should run."

"You should," I agreed with a shrug. "Anyone with sense would run from *the Bloodhound* waiting for you down the beach."

She shoved me hard enough to send me stumbling back a step in the sand. "Riley!"

"What?" I laughed with the ease only two people could pull out of me. "I'm being a supportive brother. Come on, talk me through it. Why are we here right now?"

Her expression sobered again. "Because ... because I love him," she murmured.

"Right," I nodded, letting her work through this herself. It was her decision, I couldn't decide what was right for her life. Not that

I didn't approve, but commitment in this sense was a fragile topic for her—one she'd never been truly comfortable discussing.

"And he loves me."

"Yeah," I chuckled in agreement. "That's an understatement."

She fluffed up the curls atop her head, eyes darting to the world around us. "That doesn't mean I should marry him though, like that's a really big thing that people do."

"Some of them," I reasoned. "Sure."

"But me?" Amaia's laugh was maniacal even for the crazed.

"Why *not* you?"

That silenced her. I kept pushing, "You deserve a life that includes happiness, Amaia. *Why not you?*"

She chewed her lip, her gaze finally locking on mine.

I gave her a moment, then pressed on. "There was a time where I didn't think you'd ever let anyone in. You know, there are people in your life that you are bonded to, close with, myself included—but to let someone truly know the depths of your soul …" a shaky laugh escaped me. "I'm happy you've found someone that makes you feel so safe, that no matter what, you'll always have a home. And my hope for you is that you'll see this as the blessing it is, and let yourself feel it all. The good, the bad, the ugly, highs and the lows. I had my questions and my doubts, please, don't believe for a second that I did not—but I could not picture a better match."

Tears streamed down her cheeks as she whispered, "Dammit, Riley," and wiped them away.

I pulled her in, tucking her head against my shoulder. "I'll be waiting for you on the other side."

ALEXIARES

"You could have at least dressed for the occasion," Riley grumbled, clapping a hand on my back.

I barely felt it, my attention fixed on the slow, endless pull of the ocean. I was trying to find my calm, but it wasn't coming. Not today.

Never in a million fucking years had I pictured myself getting married—let alone twice. But Amaia made loving her so easy that this dream called to me every night. In the middle of this hell, the idea of marriage ironically meant more than in The Before. It wasn't about tradition. This bond was made with the knowledge that there may not be a tomorrow, let alone a few hours. All you had was now. Showing the greatest commitment that you could while daring death to take it from you. *Take me if you can, but you'll never take this.*

Love made you want to fight like hell.

"I'm wearing nice boots and a starched shirt," I muttered, shaking him off with a smirk. "I even moisturized."

Riley let out a sharp chuckle, shaking his head. Harley and Suckerpunch bounded up to him, tails wagging like they were in on the joke. Then, just as quick, they circled back to my side.

Harley nudged my leg, and I ran a hand absently over her fur, pausing when I felt the twist of vines wound loosely around her neck. Flowers bloomed along the green, bright against her dark coat.

Riley's gaze flicked down, then back to me, amusement clear in his eyes. He didn't say anything, only smirked like he knew exactly what had gone through my head when I'd grown them. I ignored him, movement catching my eyes from down the beach.

Amaia stepped into view, walking down the sand with curls hanging, falling into her face. Her eyes, dark as night with the coal around them, locked onto mine, and I couldn't breathe.

She was perfect.

My knees nearly buckled.

By the time she reached me, I wasn't thinking anymore. I grabbed her hand, pulled it to my lips, and kissed it, my thumb brushing over her fingers, her knuckles, the pulse point at her wrist.

"I love you," I murmured.

Amaia bit the inside of her cheek and her blush deepened. She pulled her hand back only to tap her own cheeks trying to push the heat away.

Fuck. I think I finally believe in luck.

"You ready?" Riley asked, adjusting the buttons on his shirt with a quick glance at us.

Amaia nodded, her voice soft. "Yeah."

I swallowed hard, my fingers twitching at my sides. She was mesmerizing, I could not help the flow of words. "You are astonishing." But even that felt small for what she was.

Amaia let out a raspy laugh—acknowledging that the words weren't meant to have stumbled out loud.

"Well," Riley cleared his throat. "Given I had zero time to prepare for this and I've never been to a wedding … Here goes the TV script."

An uneasy chuckle exchanged between the three of us, the tension in the air electric.

"You two are—" He exhaled, shaking his head as he tried to find the right words. "Balance. That's what you are. And if anyone deserves this … it's you." He turned to Amaia, his gaze softening. "Seeing you happy in a world like this? It's a damn miracle. You've had your share of dark days, and you still manage to hold on to light. You're more than deserving of this." He nodded toward me, a quiet challenge in his eyes. "And you, Bloodhound—you make her happy. That's the most important thing. So don't fuck it up."

It wasn't just a remark; it was his approval. His way of giving us his blessing in a world that didn't often allow for it.

"And I hope," he continued, his voice a little quieter but full of sincerity, "you both have a long, healthy marriage. In a place like this, that's a rare thing to wish for. But I see it in your eyes, both of you. So, here's to it. To you, to her—everything you've got."

Amaia sniffled, a tear slipping down her cheek. I reached for her, brushing the tear away with my thumb though I was damn near right there with her.

"Okay. Vows then?" Riley said.

Amaia and I both opened our mouths at the same time, then hesitated. She let out a small laugh. "Can I go first?"

I nodded, heart thundering damn near out my chest, pounding over the waves in my ears.

Her eyes locked onto mine, and everything else faded. "Alexiares … I love you. Fiercely. Completely. Till the end of my days and beyond them. I thank the stars every day for you. For loving me with as much ferocity as you do—no hesitations, no fears. God, I'm crazy about you, how unapologetically yourself you are, no masks, no pretenses. What you see is what you get, I love it. You have the mind of a warrior, but the heart of a lover—a heart that belongs to me and only me. You make me feel safe, in a way I never thought I'd be. Known in a deeper capacity than I previously thought possible, but most of all, you make me feel seen. And I swear, I'll love you with everything I have. Always."

I grounded myself, gripping her hands harder, as though losing her was a real possibility. "Princess," I smirked, squeezing her hands with slight teasing. "You love every part of me—the good, the bad, the ugly. And that's more than I ever thought I deserved. You've taught me what love is. Love without conditions. And because of you, I'm learning to love the same way. You're not just love to me. You're family. You're peace. You're home. Annoyingly so, you also happen to be the bravest, and most reckless, person I've ever met. The strongest too. You throw yourself into the fire for the people you love without a second thought. You are confidence and compassion and sheer fucking ferocity all in one. And I admire every part of you." I swallowed, my chest tight, my pulse unsteady. "We've fought. We've bled. We've lost a hell of a lot. But if I had to live every second of my life—every moment of pain and suffering—all over again just to be here, standing with you? I'd do it. Every damn time."

Silence stretched between us.

Riley let out a breath, running a hand through his hair. "Damn," he muttered, almost to himself. He glanced between us, something akin to awe in his expression.

I know what he saw. I thought about it every time I caught our reflection in the mirror when we shared the bathing chambers every morning—getting ready for the day. In the passing windows as we walked through The Compound. In the ocean that slammed so violently around us. Two people who had been torn apart by life in ways most would call unrepairable, somehow finding their way to each other. Breaking down walls they swore they'd keep up forever.

He cleared his throat. "Right. Rings. Alexiares, do you take Amaia to have and to hold, or yeah, pretty sure that's how it goes."

I took her hand, sliding the coffin-shaped diamond ring onto her finger slowly, savoring the way it caught the light shimmering against her brown skin. "Fucking of course I do." I leaned in, Amaia giggled, our lips brushing—

"Aht!" Riley stuck a hand between our faces. "Didn't say *kiss the bride* yet. Patience."

"—is a virtue I don't have," I growled, pulling her in again. She giggled, hiding her face against my chest.

"Wait." Amaia reached her hand out and Riley complied, reaching into his pocket. She lifted a ring, flipping it over so I could see the inside. *Til Death.* "I do, too."

I blinked. "Where the hell did you get that?"

She smirked. "*I know people*," she mocked.

"Of course you do." I let out a breathless laugh before pulling her close, our lips meeting in a kiss that made me not only believe in luck—but accept the idea of fate.

Riley huffed. "Okay, *kiss the bride*, I guess," he mumbled, rolling his eyes, but there was warmth in it. A small, knowing smile.

The sun was dropping, casting a warm glow over the beach, the waves crashing softly at our feet. Riley made his way down the shore, giving us the space to enjoy the moment, *each other*, when in a few hours, that would no longer be the case. The water lapped at our ankles, moving like we'd done it a thousand times before as we walked down the beach.

My mind wandered back to that day I'd found her out here. There'd been such hatred, such malice in our words—yet it had been a foundation in our very relationship. It was the first time we'd come to understand each other, the pain we both held.

Amaia and I stayed close, the quiet stretching between us. I drew her close again, comforted by that hint of fire and coffee always lingering in her hair, our fingers intertwining.

I stopped, turned to face her, and tugged her a little closer. "I'm serious about this," I said, my voice low. "This—us—it's forever. No question. Even beyond this life."

Her eyes lingered on me, searching, before the intensity faded and a slow, knowing smile curled on her lips. "You are my infinity."

ACKNOWLEDGMENTS

Well my lovely little misfit, here we are again. I cannot thank you enough for setting out on this journey with me. Where we started, and where we ended up was such a wild ride—one that would have been *impossible* without your support and encouragement. Often times when I start to doubt myself, I remember *you* and what I'm doing it for—who I'm doing it for. So thank you from the bottom of my heart. We have one last ride before the series concludes, and I hope I continue to make you proud.

To my alpha team, Mckenzie, Jaz, and Laura, thank you a million times for the laughs, corrections, and teases along the way. Your feedback has helped me from as a writer and as a person, so thank you for just being you.

Benny, my husband, I love you so much and thank you for always encouraging me to follow my dreams. Another book finished in the middle of a layoff, and when I wanted to quit, you never let me put the keyboard down. I wouldn't be here without you undying support, you are, forever my MMC muse.

Mikayla D. Hornedo, my bestie for the restie. Literally nothing I've done within the last few years would have been possible without you by my side, lol. I love you! Amber Nicole, you are every authors wet dream for a cheerleader and support system. The world would be better with more *you* out there.

Shout out to Emma at EJLEditing, thank you for being you. Giving me feedback on my stressors and still encouraging me when I decide to be hard-headed and do my own thing. We've tackled this series together and I can't wait to close it out that way. To Phil at Editing by Phi, you've saved the day more ways than I can count. Thank you for sharing your genius with me!

As always, this series is dedicated to Drew and my Papa. Without grief, this story would have never happened. In my grief, I found *me*. The version of me you both always encouraged me to live. Mistey is with you now, and I can't wait to see y'all on the other side.

See a glimpse at my new series, *Kuxtal Academy: The Beginning* on the next page.

ABOUT THE AUTHOR

Nelle Nikole was born in Corona, California, spent time in the battlefields of Virginia, and now lives in Atlanta with her soon to be husband, Ben, and their furkid, Sophie. A lifelong reader, she began writing thrilling stories to share with her classmates as early as elementary school.

Having lived a little bit of everywhere, Nelle took her studies internationally and completed her anthropology degree by researching abroad in Rio de Janeiro and throughout Cuba. Driven by an insatiable appetite for knowledge, Nelle pursued a Master of Arts in Public Policy, specializing in Global Affairs. Often stuck within the realms of daydreams and her imagination, Nelle is inspired by all things fantasy, apocalyptic and anything in between.